CRY
WOLF

TAMI
HOAG

BANTAM BOOKS
New York   Toronto   London   Sydney   Auckland

CRY WOLF

A Bantam Book / August 1993
Bantam reissue edition / September 1996

ISBN 0-553-56160-X

Published simultaneously in the United States and Canada

Bantam Books are published by Bantam Books, a division of Bantam
Doubleday Dell Publishing Group, Inc. Its trademark, consisting of
the words "Bantam Books" and the portrayal of a rooster, is Regis-
tered in U.S. Patent and Trademark Office and in other countries.
Marca Registrada. Bantam Books, 1540 Broadway, New York, New
York 10036.

Author's Note

Anyone familiar with my work knows I have a special affection for that part of Louisiana known as Acadiana. My interest has roots in family, even though it was the music that first drew my attention, and branches into history, linguistics, and a love for unique and fragile environments. In *Cry Wolf*, as in my previous books set in south Louisiana, I have done my best to bring to you the feel and flavor of bayou country. I have made a special effort to portray some of the cultural diversity of the area through the use of local dialects—in particular, through the use of a number of Cajun French words and phrases. A glossary of these words and phrases can be found at the back of the book.

Cajun French is a distinct language born in France and raised in Louisiana. About sixty percent of the words in the Cajun vocabulary can be found in a standard French dictionary. The rest are unique to the patois, words and phrases that evolved out of necessity to fit the environment and the people living in it.

My sources for the Cajun French used in *Cry Wolf* include *Conversational Cajun French* by Harry Jannise and Randall P. Whatley, and *A Dictionary of the Cajun Language* by the Reverend Monsignor Jules O. Daigle, M.A., S.T.L., a complete source and especially wonderful defense of a language that deserves to live on and flourish.

In a world where we are increasingly pressured to conform and homogenize, ethnic diversity is a precious gift. My sincere thanks to the people who strive to preserve and nourish such endangered species as the Cajun language. *Merci boucoup.*

Tami Hoag

All things are taken from us, and become
Portions and parcels of the dreadful Past.

Alfred, Lord Tennyson
The Lotus-Eaters

CRY
WOLF

Prologue

The bâteau *slides through the still waters of the bayou. Still, black waters as dark as the night sky. As dark as the heart of a killer. In the water stand the cypress, rank upon rank, tall sentinels as motionless and silent as death. Behind them, on the banks, the weeping willows, boughs bowed as if by grief, and the live oak with their twisted trunks and gnarled branches, looking like enchanted things eternally frozen in a moment of agony. And from their contorted limbs hangs the moss, gray and dusty and tattered, like old feather boas left to rot in the attic of some long-forgotten, long-ruined mansion.*

All is gray and black in the night in the swamp. The absence of light, the reflection of light. A sliver of moon is wedged between high clouds, then disappears. Stillness descends all around as the boat passes. Eyes peer out from the reeds, from the trees, from just above the surface of the water. Night is the time of the hunter and the hunted. But all the creatures wait as the bâteau *slips past them, its motor purring, low and throaty, like a panther's growl. The air of expectation thickens like the mist that hovers between the trunks of the tupelo and sweet gum trees.*

One predator has struck this night, cunning and vicious, with no motivation but the thrill of holding another's life and savoring the power to snuff it out. The creatures of the swamp watch as the predator passes, as the scent of fresh blood mingles with the rank, metallic aroma of the bayou and the sweet perfume of wild honeysuckle, jasmine, and verbena.

The motor dies. The boat skirts a raft of water hyacinth, noses through the cattails and lily pads, and sidles up to the muddy bank, where ferns and creepers grow in a tangled skein. Somewhere in the distance a scream tears through the fabric of the night. Like an echo. Like a memory. The predator smiles, fondly, slyly, thinking not of the nutria that issued the sound, but of the woman lying dead on the floor of the bâteau.

Another kill. Another rush. Another dizzying high. Power, more seductive than sex, more addictive than cocaine. Blood, warm and silky, sweet as wine. The pulse of life rushing with fear, pounding, frantic . . . ebbing, dying . . .

The body is dragged to the bank, left near the end of a crushed clamshell path that glows powdery white as the moon flashes down once again like a searchlight—there and gone, there and gone. Its beam illuminates a dark head of hair, damp and disheveled with no trace of the style that had been so painstakingly sculpted and sprayed hours ago; a face, ghostly pale, cheeks rouged clownishly, lipstick smeared, mouth slack, eyes open and staring, unseeing, up at the heavens. Looking for mercy, looking for deliverance. Too late for either.

She will be found. In a day, maybe two. Fishermen will come to fill their creels with bream, bluegill, sac-a-lait. They will find her. But none will find her killer.

Too cunning, too clever, beyond the laws of man, outside the realm of suspicion this predator stalks. . . .

Chapter One

"I'll kill him."

The hound sat in a pile of freshly dug earth, azalea bushes and rosebushes scattered all around like so many tumbleweeds, a streamer of wisteria draped around his shoulders like a priest's amice. Looking up at the people on the veranda with a quizzical expression, he tilted his head to one side, black ears perked like a pair of flags on the sides of his head. A narrow strip of white ran down between his eyes—one pale blue, one green—widening over his muzzle. His coat was a wild blend of blue and black, trimmed in white and mottled with leopard spots, as if Mother Nature hadn't been able to make up her mind as to just what this creature would be. As people spilled out the French doors of the elegant brick house known as Belle Rivière, he let out a mournful howl.

"I swear, I'll kill him," Laurel Chandler snarled, her gaze fixed on the dog.

Rage and fury burned through her in a flash fire that threatened to sear through all slim threads of control. Two days she had been working on that garden. Two days. Needing desperately to do something and see an immediate, positive result, she had thrown herself into the task with the kind of awesome, single-minded determination that had taken her so far so fast as a prosecuting attorney. She had set herself to the towering task of reclaiming Aunt Caroline's courtyard garden in time to surprise her.

Well, Caroline Chandler had returned to Bayou Breaux from her buying trip, and she was surprised all right. She stood to Laurel's left, a tiny woman with the presence of a Titan. Her black hair was artfully coiffed in a soft cloud of loose curls, makeup applied deftly and sparingly, accenting her dark eyes and feminine mouth. She seemed barely forty, let alone fifty, her heart-shaped face smooth and creamy. She folded the fingers of her right hand gently over Laurel's clenched fist and said calmly, "I'm sure it was looking lovely, darlin'."

Laurel attempted to draw in a slow, calming breath, the way Dr. Pritchard had taught her in relaxation therapy, but it hissed in through her clenched teeth and served only to add to the pressure building in her head and chest.

"I'll kill him," she said again, jerking away from her aunt's hold. Her anger trembled through her body like an earthquake.

"I hep you, Miz Laurel," Mama Pearl said, patting her stubby fingers against her enormous belly.

The old woman sniffed and shifted her ponderous weight back and forth from one tiny foot to the other, the skirt of her red flowered dress swirling around legs as thick and sturdy as small tree trunks. She had been with the Chandler family since Caroline and Jeff Chandler were children. She lived with Caroline not as an employee but as a member of the family, running Belle Rivière like a general and settling comfortably if testily into old age.

"Dat hound make nothin' but trouble, him," she declared. "All the time rootin' in my trash like a pig, stealin' off the clothesline. Nothin' but trouble. Talk about!"

Laurel barely heard the woman's chatter. Her focus

was completely on the Catahoula hound that had destroyed the first constructive thing she had accomplished since leaving Georgia and her career behind. She had come back to Louisiana, to Bayou Breaux, to heal, to start over. Now the first tangible symbol of her fresh start had been uprooted by a rampaging mutt. Someone was going to pay for this. Someone was going to pay dearly.

Letting out a loud primal scream, she grabbed her brand-new Garden Weasel and ran across the courtyard swinging it over her head like a mace. The hound bayed once in startled surprise, wheeled, and bounded for the back wall, toenails scratching on the brick, dirt and debris flying out behind him. He made a beeline for the iron gate that had rusted off its hinges during the time Belle Rivière had been without a gardener, and was through the opening and galloping for the woods at the bayou's edge before Laurel made it as far as the old stone fountain. By the time she reached the gate, the culprit was nothing more than a flash of blue and white diving into the cover of the underbrush, sending up a flock of frightened warblers to mark his passing.

Laurel dropped the Garden Weasel and stood with her hands braced against the gate that was wedged into the opening at a cockeyed angle. Her breath came in ragged gasps, and her heart was pounding as if she had run a mile, reminding her that she was still physically weak. A reminder she didn't appreciate. Weakness was not something she accepted well, in herself or anyone else.

She twisted her hands on the rusting iron spikes of the gate, the oxidizing metal flaking off against her palms as she forced the wheels of her mind to start turning. She needed a plan. She needed justice. Two months had passed since the end of her last quest for justice, a quest that had ended in defeat and in the ruination of her career and very nearly her life. Two months had passed since she had last used her mind to formulate a strategy, map out a campaign, stock up verbal ammunition for a cause, and the mental mechanisms seemed as rusty as the gate she was hanging on to with white-knuckled fists.

But the old wheels caught and turned, and the momentary panic that she had forgotten what to do passed, a tremor that was there, then gone.

"Come along, Laurel. We'll go in to supper." Caroline's voice sounded directly behind her, and Laurel flinched from nerves that were still strung too tight.

She turned toward her aunt, one of the few people in the world who actually made her feel tall at five foot five. "I've got to find out who owns that dog."

"After you've had something to eat."

Caroline reached out to take hold of her niece's hand, heedless of the rust coating her palms, heedless of the fact that Laurel was thirty years old. To Caroline's way of thinking, there were times when a person needed to be led, regardless of age. She didn't care for the obsessive light glazing over Laurel's dark blue eyes. Obsession had landed the girl in a quagmire of trouble already. Caroline was determined to do all she could to pull her out.

"You need to eat something, darlin'. You're down to skin and bones as it is."

Laurel didn't bother to glance down at herself for verification. She was aware that the blue cotton sundress she wore hung on her like a gunny sack. It wasn't important. She had a closet full of prim suits and expensive dresses back in Georgia, but the person who had worn them had ceased to exist, and so had the need to care about appearances. Not that she'd ever been overly concerned with her looks; that was her sister Savannah's department.

"I need to find out who owns that dog," she said with more determination than she'd shown in weeks. "Someone's got to make restitution for this mess."

She stepped over the handle of the Garden Weasel and around her aunt, pulling her hand free of the older woman's grasp and heading back down the brick path toward the house. Caroline heaved a sigh and shook her head, torn between disgust and admiration. Laurel had inherited the Chandler determination, also known in moments such as this as the Chandler pigheadedness. If only Jeff had lived to see it. But then, Caroline admitted bitterly, if her brother had lived, they may well not have been in this mess. If Laurel's father hadn't been killed, then the terrible course of events that had followed his death would never have been set in motion, and Laurel and Savannah would in all likelihood have become very different from the women they were today.

"Laurel," she said firmly, the heels of her beige pumps clicking purposefully against the worn brick of the path as she hurried to catch up. "It's more important that you eat something."

"Not to me."

"Oh, for—" Caroline bit off the remark, struggling to rein in her temper. She had more than a little of the Chandler determination herself. She had to fight herself to keep from wielding it like a club.

Laurel stepped up on the veranda, scooping a towel off the white wrought-iron table to wipe her hands. Mama Pearl huffed and puffed beside the French doors, wringing her plump hands, her light eyes bright with worry.

"Miz Caroline right," she said. "You needs to eat, chile. Come in, sit down, you. We got gumbo for supper."

"I'm not hungry. Thanks anyway, Mama Pearl." She settled her glasses in place and combed her dark hair back with her fingers, then sent the old woman a winning smile as adrenaline rushed through her. The anticipated thrill of battle. "I've got to go find the hound dog that owns that hound dog and get us some justice."

"Dat Jack Boudreaux's dog, him," Mama Pearl said, her fleshy face creasing into folds of disapproval. "He's mebbe anyplace, but he's most likely down to Frenchie's Landing, and you don' need dat kinda trouble, I'm tellin' you, *chère*."

Laurel ignored the warning and turned to kiss her aunt's cheek. "Sorry to miss supper your first night back, Aunt Caroline, but I should be back in time for coffee."

With that she skipped around Mama Pearl and through the French doors, leaving the older women standing on the veranda shaking their heads.

Mama Pearl tugged a handkerchief out of the valley of her bosom to blot the beads of perspiration dotting her forehead and triple chins. "Me, I don' know what gonna come a' dat girl."

Caroline stared after her niece, a grim look in her large dark eyes and a frown pulling at her mouth. She crossed her arms and hugged herself against an inner chill of foreboding. "She's going to get justice, Pearl. No matter what the cost."

Chapter
Two

Things were hopping at Frenchie's. Friday night at
Frenchie's Landing was a tradition among a certain class
of people around Bayou Breaux. Not the planter class,
the gentlemen farmers and their ladies in pumps and
pearls who dined on white damask tablecloths with silver
as old as the country. Frenchie's catered to a more earthy
crowd. The worst of Partout Parish riffraff—poachers and
smugglers and people looking for big trouble—gravitated
over to Bayou Noir and a place called Mouton's.
Frenchie's caught everyone in between. Farmhands, fac-
tory workers, blue collars, rednecks all homed in on
Frenchie's on Friday night for boiled crawfish and cold
beer, loud music and dancing, and the occasional brawl.

The building stood fifty feet back from the levee and
sat up off the ground on stilts that protected it from
flooding. It faced the bayou, inviting patrons in from fishing and hunting expeditions with a red neon sign that
promised cold beer, fresh food, and live music. Whole
sections of the building's siding were hung on hinges and

propped up with wooden poles, revealing a long row of screens and creating a gallery of sorts along the sides.

Even though the sun had yet to go down, the crushed shell parking lot was overflowing with cars and pickups. The bar was overflowing with noise. The sounds of laughter, shouting, glass on glass underscored a steady stream of loud Cajun music that tumbled out through the screens into the warm spring night. Joyous and wild, a tangle of fiddle, guitar, and accordion, it invited even the rhythmically challenged to move with the beat.

Laurel stood at the bottom of the steps, looking up at the front door. She had never set foot in the place, though she knew it was a regular haunt of Savannah's. Savannah, who made a career of flouting family convention. She may even have been sitting in Frenchie's at that moment. She had slipped out of Aunt Caroline's house around five, dressed like a woman who was looking for trouble and fairly glowing at the prospect of finding it. All she had told Laurel was that she had a date, and if all went well, no one would see her before noon Saturday.

Suddenly the hound skidded around the corner of the gallery and came to a halt, looking wide-eyed straight at Laurel. If she'd had any misgivings about coming to Frenchie's Landing—and she'd had a few—sight of the marauder dispelled them. She was on a mission.

A trio of men in their twenties, dressed and groomed for a night on the town, walked around her and started up the steps, laughing and talking, telling ribald jokes in Cajun French. Laurel didn't wait for the punch line. She rushed after them and snatched at the sleeve of the biggest one, a bull of a man with a close-cropped black beard and a head of hair as thick as a beaver pelt that grew down over his forehead in a deep V.

"Excuse me," Laurel said. "But could you tell me who that hound belongs to?"

He cast a glance at the dog on the gallery, as did his companions.

"Hey, dat's Jack's dog, ain't it, Taureau?"

"Jack Boudreaux."

"*Mais* yeah, dat one's Jack's," Taureau said. His look

softened, and a grin tugged across his wide mouth as he gave Laurel a once-over. "What, you lookin' for Jack, sugar?"

"Yes, I guess I am." She was looking for justice. If she had to find this Jack Boudreaux to get it, then so be it.

"Dat Jack, he's like a damn magnet, him!" one of the others said.

Taureau snorted. "*Son pine!*"

They all shared a good male belly laugh over that.

Laurel gave them her best Cool Professional Woman look, hoping it wasn't completely ruined by her baggy dress and lack of makeup. "I didn't come here to see his penis," she said flatly. "I need to discuss a business matter with him."

The men exchanged the kind of sheepish looks boys learn in kindergarten and spend the next thirty years honing to perfection, their faces flushing under their tans. Taureau ducked his big head down between his shoulders.

"Am I likely to find him in there?" Laurel nodded toward the bar's front door as it screeched back on its hinges to let out an elderly couple and a wave of noise.

"Yeah, you'll find him here," Taureau said. "Center stage."

"Thank you."

The smoking reform movement had yet to make inroads in south Louisiana. The instant Laurel stepped into the bar, she had to blink to keep her eyes from stinging. A blue haze hung over the crowd. The scent of burning tobacco mingled with sweat and cheap perfume, barley and boiled crawfish. The lighting was dim, and the place was crowded. Waitresses wound their way through the mob with trays of beers and platters of food. Patrons sat shoulder to shoulder at round tables and overflowing booths, laughing, talking, stuffing themselves.

Laurel instantly felt alone, isolated, as if she were surrounded by an invisible force field. She had been brought up in a socially sterile environment, with proper teas and soirees and cotillions. The Leightons didn't lower themselves to having good common 'fun, and after her father had died and Vivian had remarried, Laurel and Savannah had become Leightons—never mind that Ross Leighton had never bothered to formally adopt them.

Caught off guard for an instant, she felt the old bitterness hit her by surprise and dig its teeth in deep. But it was shoved aside by newer unpleasant feelings as her strongest misgivings about coming here surfaced and threatened to swamp her—not the fear of no one's knowing her, but the fear of *everyone's* knowing her. The fear of everyone's recognizing her and knowing why she had come back to Bayou Breaux, knowing she had failed horribly and utterly . . . Her breath froze in her lungs as she waited for heads to start turning.

A waitress on her way back to the bar bumped into her, flashing a smile of apology and reaching a hand out to pat her arm. "Sorry, miss."

"I'm looking for Jack Boudreaux," Laurel shouted, lifting her eyebrows in question.

The waitress, a curvy young thing with a mop of dark curls and an infectious grin, swung her empty serving tray toward the stage and the man who sat at the keyboard of an old upright piano that looked as though someone had gone after it with a length of chain.

"There he is, in the flesh, honey. The devil himself," she said, her voice rising and falling in a distinctly Cajun rhythm. "You wanna join the fan club or somethin'?"

"No, I want restitution," Laurel said, but the waitress was already gone, answering a call of "Hey, Annie" from Taureau and his cohorts, who had commandeered a table across the room.

Homing in on the man she had come to confront, Laurel moved toward the small stage. The band had slowed things down with a waltz that was being sung by a small, wiry man with a Vandyke and a Panama hat. A vicious scar slashed across his face, from his right eyebrow across his cheek, misshaping the end of his hooked nose and disappearing into the cover of his mustache. But if his face wasn't beautiful, his voice certainly was.

He clutched his hands to his heart and wailed out the lyrics in Cajun French as dancers young and old moved gracefully around the small dance floor.

To his right Jack Boudreaux stood with one knee on the piano bench, head bent in concentration as he pumped a small Evangeline accordion between his hands.

From this vantage point Boudreaux looked tall and rangy, with strong shoulders and slim hips. The expression on his lean, tanned face was stern, almost brooding. His eyes were squeezed shut as if sight might somehow hinder his interpretation of the music. Straight black hair tumbled down over his forehead, looking damp and silky under the stage lights.

Laurel skirted the dancers and wedged herself up against the front of the stage. She thought she could feel the inner pain he drew on as he played. Silly. Easily half of Cajun music was about some man losing his girl. This particular waltz—"Valse de Grand Mèche"—was an old one, a song about an unlucky woman lost in the marsh, her lover singing of how they will be together again after death. It wasn't Jack Boudreaux's personal life story, and it wouldn't have concerned her if it had been. She had come to see the man about his dog.

Jack let his fingers slow on the keys of the accordion as he played the final set of triplets and hit the last chord. Leonce belted out the final note with gusto, and the dancers' feet slowed to a shuffle. As the music faded away and the crowd clapped, he sank down on the piano bench, feeling drained. The song brought too many memories. That he was feeling anything at all told him one thing—he needed another drink.

He reached for the glass on the piano without looking and tossed back the last of a long, tall whiskey, sucking in a breath as the liquid fire hit his belly. It seared through him in a single wave of heat, leaving a pleasant numbness in its wake.

Slowly his lashes drifted open and his surroundings came once more into focus. His gaze hit on a huge pair of midnight blue eyes staring up at him from behind the lenses of man-size horn-rimmed glasses. The face of an angel hid behind those ridiculous glasses—heart-shaped, delicate, with a slim retroussé nose and a mouth that begged to be kissed. Jack felt his spirits pull out of their nosedive and wing upward as she spoke his name.

She wasn't the usual type of woman who pressed herself up against the stage and tried to snag his attention. For one thing, there was no show of cleavage. It was difficult to tell if she was capable of producing cleavage at all. The blue cotton sundress she wore hung on her like a sack. But imagination was one thing Jack Boudreaux had never been short on. Scruples, yes; morals, yes; imagination he had in abundance, and he used it now to make a quick mental picture of the woman standing below him. Petite, slim, sleek, like a little cat. He preferred his women to have a little more curve to them, but there was always something to be said for variety.

He leaned down toward her as he set the accordion on the floor and unfurled the grin that had knocked more than a few ladies off their feet. "Hey, sugar, where you been all my life?"

Laurel felt as if he had turned a thousand watts of pure electricity on her.

He looked wicked. He looked wild. He looked as though he could see right through her clothes, and she had the wildest urge to cross her arms over her chest, just in case. Annoyed with herself, she snapped her jaw shut and cleared her throat.

"I've been off learning to avoid Lotharios who use trite come-on lines," she said, her arms folding over her chest in spite of her resolve to keep them at her sides.

Jack's smile never wavered. He liked a girl with sass. "What, are you a nun or somethin', angel?"

"No, I'm an attorney. I need to speak to you about your dog."

Someone in the crowd raised a voice in protest against the absence of music. "Hey, Jack, can you quit makin' love long enough to sing somethin'?"

Jack raised his head and laughed, leaning toward the microphone that was attached to the piano. "This ain't love, Dede, it's a lawyer!" As the first wave of laughter died down, he said, "Y'all know what lawyers use for birth control, doncha?" He waited a beat, then his voice dropped a husky notch as he delivered the punch line. "Their personalities."

Laurel felt a flush of anger rise up her neck and creep up her cheeks as the crowd hooted and laughed. "I wouldn't make jokes if I were you, Mr. Boudreaux," she said, trying to keep her voice at a pitch only he could hear. "Your hound managed to do a considerable amount of damage to my aunt's garden today."

Jack shot her a look of practiced innocence. "What hound?"

"*Your* hound."

He shrugged eloquently. "I don't have a hound."

"Mr. Boudreaux—"

"Call me Jack, angel," he drawled as he leaned down toward her again, bracing his forearm on his thigh.

They were nearly at eye level, and Laurel felt herself leaning toward him, as if he were drawing her toward him by some personal magnetic force. His gaze slid down to her mouth and lingered there, shockingly frank in its appraisal.

"Mr. Boudreaux," she said in exasperation. "Is there somewhere we can discuss this more privately?"

He bobbed his eyebrows above dark, sparkling devil's eyes. "Is my place private enough for you?"

"Mr. Boudreaux . . ."

"Here's another trite line for you, angel," Jack whispered, bending a little closer, holding her gaze with his as he lifted a finger and pushed her glasses up on her nose. "You're pretty when you're pissed off."

His voice was low and smoky, Cajun-spiced and tainted with the aroma of whiskey.

Drawing in a slow, deep breath to steady herself, she tilted her chin up and tried again. "Mr. Boudreaux—"

He shot her a look as he moved toward the microphone once again. "Lighten up, angel. *Laissez les bon temps rouler.*"

The mike picked up his last sentence, and the crowd

cheered. Jack gave a smoky laugh. "Are we havin' fun yet?"

A chorus of hoots and hollers rose to the rafters. He fixed a long, hot look on the petite tigress glaring up at him from the edge of the stage and murmured, "This one's for you, angel."

His fingers stretched over the keys of the battered old piano, and he pounded out the opening notes of "Great Balls of Fire." The crowd went wild. Before the first line was out of his mouth, there were fifty people on the dance floor. They twirled and bounced around Laurel like a scene from *American Bandstand*, doing the jitterbug as if it had never gone out of style. But her attention was riveted on the singer. Not so much by choice as by compulsion. She was caught in the beam of that intense, dark gaze, held captive by it, mesmerized. He leaned over the keyboard, his hands moving across it, his mouth nearly kissing the microphone as his smoky voice sang out the lyrics with enthusiasm, but all the time his eyes were locked on her. The experience was strangely seductive, strangely intimate. Wholly unnerving.

She stared right back at him, refusing to be seduced or intimidated. Refusing to admit to either, at any rate. He grinned, as if amused by her spunk, and broke off the eye contact as he hit the bridge of the song and turned his full attention to the piano and the frantic pace of the music.

He pounded out the notes, his fingers flying up and down the keyboard expertly. All the intensity he had leveled at her in his gaze was channeled into his playing. The shock of black hair bounced over his forehead, shining almost blue under the lights. Sweat gleamed on his skin, streamed down the side of his face. His faded blue chambray shirt stuck to him in dark, damp patches. The sleeves were rolled back, revealing strong forearms dusted with black hair, muscles bunching and flexing as he slammed out the boogie-woogie piece with a skill and wild physical energy rivaling that of Jerry Lee Lewis himself.

Making music this way looked to be hard work physically and emotionally. As if he were in the throes of exorcism, the notes tore out of him, elemental, rough, sexy, almost frightening in intensity. He dragged his thumb up and down the keyboard, stroking out the final long, frenzied glissando, and fell forward, panting, exhausted as the crowd whistled and howled and screamed for more.

"Whoa—" Jack gulped a breath and forced a grin. "*Bon Dieu.* It's Miller time, folks. Y'all go sit down while I recuperate."

As a jukebox kicked in, the rest of the band instantly dispersed, abandoning the stage in favor of a table that was holding up gamely under the weight of more than a dozen long-necked beer bottles and an assortment of glasses.

Leonce clapped Jack's shoulder as he passed. "You're gettin' old, Jack," he teased. "*Sa c'est honteu, mon ami.*"

Jack sucked another lungful of hot, smoky air and swatted at his friend. "Fuck you, '*tit boule.*"

"No need." Leonce grinned, hooking a thumb in the direction of the dance floor. "You got one waitin' on you."

Jack raised his head and shot a sideways look at the edge of the stage. She was still standing there, his little lawyer pest, looking expectant and unimpressed with him. Trouble—that's what she looked like. And not the kind he usually dove into headfirst, either. A lawyer. *Bon Dieu,* he thought he'd seen the last of that lot.

"You want a drink, sugar?" he asked as he hopped down off the stage.

"No," Laurel said, automatically taking a half step back and chastising herself for it. This man was the kind who would sense a weakness and exploit it. She could feel it, could see it in the way his dark gaze seemed to catch everything despite the fact that he had been drinking. She drew deep of the stale, hot air and squared her shoulders. "What I want is to speak with you privately about the damage done by your dog."

His mouth curved. "I don't have a dog."

He turned and sauntered away from her, his walk

naturally cocky. Laurel watched him, astounded by his
lack of manners, infuriated by his dismissal of her.

He didn't glance back at her, but continued on his
merry way, winding gracefully through the throng, stealing a bottle of beer off Annie's serving tray as he went.
The waitress gave an indignant shout, saw it was Jack,
and melted as he treated her to a wicked grin. Laurel
shook her head in a combination of amazement and disbelief and wondered how many times he had gotten
away with raiding the cookie jar as a boy. Probably more
times than his poor mother could count. He stepped
through a side door, and she followed him out.

Night had fallen completely, bringing on the mercury
vapor lights that loomed over the parking lot and cloak-
ing the bayou beyond in shades of black. The noise of the
bar faded, competing out here with a chorus of frog song
and the hum of traffic rolling past out on the street. The
air was fresh with the scents of spring in bloom—jasmine
and wisteria and honeysuckle and the ripe, vaguely rank
aroma of the bayou. Somewhere down the way, where
shabby little houses with thin lawns lined the bank, a
woman called for Paulie to come in. A screen door
slammed. A dog barked.

The hound leaped out at Laurel from between a pair
of parked pickup trucks and howled at her, startling her
to a skidding halt on the crushed shell of the parking lot.
She slammed a hand to her heart and bit back a curse as
the big dog bounded away, tail wagging.

"That dog is an absolute menace," she complained.

"Don' look at me, sugar."

He was leaning back against the fender of a disrepu-
table-looking Jeep, elbows on the hood, bottle of Dixie
dangling from the fingers of his left hand.

Laurel planted herself in front of him and crossed her
arms, holding her silence as if it might force a confession
out of him. He simply stared back, his eyes glittering in
the eerie silvery light that fell down on him from above.
It cast his features in stark relief—a high, wide forehead,
sardonically arched brows, an aquiline nose that looked

as if it might have been broken once or twice in his thirty-some years.

His mouth was set in sterner lines again above a strong, stubborn-looking chin that sported an inch-long diagonal scar. He looked tough and dangerous suddenly, and the transformation from the laughing, affable, wicked-grinned devil he'd been inside sent a shiver of apprehension down Laurel's back. He looked like a streetwise, predatory male, and she couldn't help second-guessing her judgment in following him out here. Then he smiled, teeth flashing bright in the gloom, dimples cutting into his cheeks, and the world tilted yet again beneath her feet.

"I have it on good authority that hound belongs to you, Mr. Boudreaux." She dove into the argument, eager for the familiar ground of a good fight. She didn't like being caught off balance, and Jack Boudreaux seemed to be a master at throwing her.

He wagged a finger at her, tilting his head, a grin still teasing the corners of his mouth. "Jack. Call me Jack."

"Mr.—"

"Jack." His gaze held hers fast. He looked lazy and apathetic leaning back against the Jeep, but a thread of insistence had woven its way into the hoarse, smoky texture of his voice.

He was distracting her, but more than that, he was trying to do something she didn't want—put the conversation on a more personal level.

He shifted his weight forward, suddenly invading her personal space, and she had to fight to keep from jumping back as her tension level rose into the red zone. She gulped down her instinctive fear and tilted her chin up to look him in the eye.

"I don't even know your name, *'tite ange*," he murmured.

"Laurel Chandler," she answered, breathless and hating it. Her nerves gave a warning tremor as control of the situation seemed to slip a little further out of her grasp.

"Laurel," he said softly, trying out the sound of it, the

feel of it on his tongue. "Pretty name. Pretty lady." He grinned as something like apprehension flashed in her wide eyes. "Did you think I wouldn't notice?"

She swallowed hard, leaning all her weight back on her heels. "I—I'm sure I don't know what you mean."

"Liar," he charged mildly.

With his free hand he reached up and slid her glasses off, dragging them down her nose an inch at a time. When they were free, he turned them over and nibbled on the earpiece absently as he studied her in the pale white light.

Her bone structure was lovely, delicate, feminine, her features equally so, her skin as flawless as fresh cream. But she wore no makeup, no jewelry, nothing to enhance or draw the eye. Her thick, dark hair had been shorn just above her shoulders and looked as though she gave no thought to it at all, tucking it behind her ears, sweeping it carelessly back from her face.

Laurel Chandler. The name stirred around through the soft haze of liquor in his brain, sparking recognition. Chandler. Lawyer. The light bulb clicked on. Local deb. Daughter of a good family. Had been a prosecuting attorney up in Georgia someplace until her career went ballistic. Rumors had abounded around Bayou Breaux. She'd blown a case. There'd been a scandal. Jack had listened with one ear, automatically eavesdropping the way every writer did, always on the alert for a snatch of dialogue or a juicy tidbit that could work itself into a plot.

"What are you wearing these for?" he asked, lifting the glasses.

"To see with," Laurel snapped, snatching them out of his hand. She really needed them only to read, but he didn't have to know that.

"So you can see, or so the rest of us can't see you?"

She gave a half laugh of impatience, shifting position in a way that put another inch of space between them. "This conversation is pointless," she declared as her nerves stretched a little tighter.

He had struck far too close to the truth with his

seemingly offhand remark. He appeared to be half drunk and completely self-absorbed, but Laurel had the sudden uncomfortable feeling that there might be more to Jack Boudreaux than met the eye. A cunning intelligence beneath the lazy facade. A sharp mind behind the satyr's grin.

"Oh, I agree. Absolutely," he drawled, shuffling his feet, inching his way into her space again. His voice dropped a husky, seductive note as he leaned down close enough so his breath caressed her cheek. "So let's go to my place and do something more . . . satisfying."

"What about the band?" Laurel asked inanely, trembling slightly as the heat from his body drifted over her skin. She held her ground and caught a breath in her throat as he lifted a hand to tuck a strand of hair behind her ear.

He chuckled low in his throat. "I'm not into sharing."

"That's not what I meant."

"They can play just fine without me."

"I hope the same can be said for you," Laurel said dryly. She crossed her arms again, drawing her composure around her like a queen's cloak. "I'm not going anywhere with you, and the only satisfaction I intend to get is restitution for the damage your dog caused."

He dropped back against the Jeep in a negligent pose once more and took a long pull on his beer, his eyes never leaving hers. He wiped his mouth with the back of his hand. "I don't have a dog."

As if on cue, the hound jumped up into the driver's seat of the open Jeep and looked at them both, ears perked with interest as he listened to them argue culpability for his crimes.

"A number of people have identified this as your hound," Laurel said, swinging an arm in the direction of the culprit.

"That don' make him mine, sugar," Jack countered.

"No less than four people have named you as the owner."

He arched a brow. "Do I have a license for this dog? Can you produce ownership papers?"

"Of course not—"

"Then all you have are unsubstantiated rumors, Miz Chandler. Hearsay. You and I both know that'll stand up in a court of law about as good as a dead man's dick."

Laurel drew in a deep breath through her nostrils, trying in vain to stem the rising tide of frustration. She should have been able to cut this man off at the knees and send him crawling to Aunt Caroline's house to apologize. He was nothing but a liquored-up piano player at Frenchie's Landing, for Christ's sake, and she couldn't manage to best him. The anger she had been directing at Jack started turning back her way.

"What'd ol' Huey do, anyhow, that's got you so worked up, angel?"

"Huey?" She pounced on the opening with the ferocity of a starving cat on a mouse. "You called him by name!" she charged, pointing an accusatory finger at Jack, taking an aggressive step forward. "You named him!"

He scowled. "It's short for Hey You."

"But the fact remains—"

"Fact my ass," Jack returned. "I can call you by name too, *'tite chatte.* That don' make you mine." Grinning again, he leaned ahead and caught her chin in his right hand, boldly stroking the pad of his thumb across the lush swell of her lower lip. "Does it, Laurel?" he murmured suggestively, dipping his head down, his mouth homing in on hers.

Laurel jerked back from him, batting his hand away. Her hold on her control, slippery and tenuous at best these days, slipped a little further. She felt as if she were hanging on to it by the ragged, bitten-down remains of her fingernails and it was still pulling away. She had come here for justice, but she wasn't getting any. Jack Boudreaux was jerking her around effortlessly. Playing with her, mocking her, propositioning her. God, was she so ineffectual, such a failure—

You didn't do your job, Ms. Chandler. . . . You blew it. . . . Charges will be dismissed. . . .

"Come on, sugar, prove your case," Jack challenged.

He took another pull on his beer. *Dieu,* he was actually enjoying this little sparring match. He was rusty, out of practice. How long had it been since he had argued a case? Two years? Three? His time away from corporate law ran together in a blur of months. It seemed like a lifetime. He would have thought he had lost his taste for it, but the old skills were still there.

Sharks don't lose their instincts, he reminded himself, bitterness creeping in to taint his enjoyment of the fight.

"It—it's common knowledge that's your dog, Mr. Boudreaux," Laurel stammered, fighting to talk around the knot hardening in her throat. She didn't hold eye contact with him, but tried to focus instead on the hound, which was tilting his head and staring at her quizzically with his mismatched eyes. "Y-You should be man enough to t-take responsibility for it."

"Ah, me," Jack said, chuckling cynically. "I don' take responsibility, angel. Ask anyone."

Laurel barely heard him, her attention focusing almost completely inward, everything else becoming vague and peripheral. A shudder of tension rattled through her, stronger than its precursor. She tried to steel herself against it and failed.

Failed.

"You didn't do your job, Ms. Chandler. . . . Charges will be dismissed. . . ."

She hadn't proven her case. Couldn't make the charges stick on something so simple and stupid as a case of canine vandalism. Failed. Again. *Worthless, weak . . .* She spat the words at herself as a wave of helplessness surged through her.

Her lungs seemed suddenly incapable of taking in air. She tried to swallow a mouthful of oxygen and then another as her legs began to shake. Panic clawed its way up the back of her throat. She pressed a hand to her mouth and blinked furiously at the tears that pooled and swirled in her eyes, blurring her view of the hound.

Jack started to say something, but cut himself off, beer bottle halfway to his lips. He stared at Laurel as she transformed before his eyes. The bright-eyed tigress on a mission was gone as abruptly as if she had never existed, leaving instead a woman on the verge of tears, on the brink of some horrible inner precipice.

"Hey, sugar," he said gently, straightening away from the Jeep. "Hey, don' cry," he murmured, shifting uncomfortably from foot to foot, casting anxious glances around the parking lot.

Rumor had it she'd been in some posh clinic in North Carolina. The word "breakdown" had been bandied all over town. Jesus, he didn't need this, didn't want this. He'd already proven once in his life that he couldn't handle it, was the last person anyone should count on to handle it. *I don' take responsibility. . . .* That truth hung on him like chain mail. He leaned toward Frenchie's, wanting to bolt, but his feet stayed rooted to the spot, nailed down by guilt.

The side door slammed, and Leonce's voice came across the dark expanse of parking lot in staccato French. "Hey, Jack, *viens ici! Dépêche-toi! Allons jouer la musique, pas les femmes!*"

Jack cast a longing glance at his friend up on the gallery, then back at Laurel Chandler. "In a minute!" he called, his gaze lingering on the woman, turmoil twisting in his belly like a snake. He didn't credit himself with having much of a conscience, but what there was made him take a step toward Laurel. "Look, sugar—"

Laurel twisted back and away from the hand he held out to her, mortified that this man she knew little and respected less was witnessing this—this weakness. God, she wanted to have at least some small scrap of pride to cling to, but that, too, was tearing out of her grasp.

"I never should have come here," she mumbled, not entirely sure whether she meant Frenchie's specifically or Bayou Breaux in general. She stumbled back another step as Jack Boudreaux reached for her arm again, his face set in lines of concern and apprehension, then she whirled and ran out of the parking lot and into the night.

Jack stood flat-footed, watching in astonishment as she disappeared in the heavy shadows beneath a stand of moss-draped live oak at the bayou's edge. Panic, he thought. That was what he had seen in her eyes. Panic and despair and a strong aversion to having him see either. What a little bundle of contradictions she was, he thought as he dug a cigarette out of his shirt pocket and dangled it from his lip. Strength and fire and fragility.

"What'd you do, *mon ami?*" Leonce shuffled up, tugging off his Panama hat and wiping the sweat from his balding pate with his forearm. "You scare her off with that big horse cock of yours?"

Jack scowled, his gaze still on the dark bank, his mind still puzzling over Laurel Chandler. "Shut up, *tcheue poule.*"

"Don' let it get you down," Leonce said, chuckling at his own little pun. He settled his hat back in place, and his fingers drifted down to rub absently at the scar that ravaged his cheek. "Women are easy to come by."

And hard to shake—that was their usual line. Not Laurel Chandler. She had cut and run. Even as his brain turned the puzzle over and around trying to shake loose an answer, Jack shrugged it off. His instincts told him Laurel Chandler would be nothing but trouble when all he really wanted from life was to pass a good time.

"Yeah," he drawled, turning back toward Frenchie's with his buddy. "Let's go inside. I need to find me a cold beer and hot date."

Chapter Three

"Laurel, help us! Laurel, please! Please! Please . . . please . . ."

She'd had the dream a hundred times. It played through her mind like a videotape over and over, wearing on her, tearing at her conscience, ripping at her heart. Always the voices were the worst part of it. The voices of the children, frantic, begging, pleading. The qualities in those voices touched nerves, set off automatic physiological reactions. Her pulse jumped, her breath came in short, shallow, unsatisfying gasps. Adrenaline and frustration pumped through her in equal amounts.

Dr. Pritchard had attempted to teach her to recognize those signals and defuse them. Theoretically, she should have been able to stop the dream and all the horrible feelings it unleashed, but she never could. She just lay there feeling enraged and panic-stricken and helpless, watching the drama unfold in her subconscious to play out to its inevitable end, unable to awaken, unable to stop it, unable to change the course of events that caused it. Weak, impotent, inadequate, incapable.

"The charges are being dropped, Ms. Chandler, for lack of sufficient evidence."

Here she always tried to swallow and couldn't. A Freudian thing, she supposed. She couldn't choke down the attorney general's decision any more than she could have chewed up and swallowed the *Congressional Record.* Or perhaps it was the burden of guilt that tightened around her throat, threatening to choke her. She had failed to prove her case. She had failed, and the children would pay the consequences.

"Help us, Laurel! Please! Please . . . please . . ."

She thrashed against the bed, against the imagined bonds of her own incompetence. She could see the three key children behind the attorney general, their faces pale ovals dominated by dark eyes filled with torment and dying hope. They had depended on her, trusted her. She had promised help, guaranteed justice.

". . . lack of sufficient evidence, Ms. Chandler . . ."

Quentin Parker loomed larger in her mind's eye, turning dark and menacing, metamorphosing into a hideous monster as the children's faces drifted further and further away. Paler and paler they grew as they floated back, their eyes growing wider and wider with fear.

"Help us, Laurel! Please . . . please . . . please . . ."

". . . will be returned to their parents . . ."

"No," she whimpered, tossing, turning, kicking at the bedclothes.

"Help us, Laurel!"

". . . returned to the custody of . . ."

"No!" She thumped her fists against the mattress over and over, pounding in time with her denial. "No! No!"

". . . a formal apology will be issued . . ."

"NO!!"

Laurel pitched herself upright as the door slammed shut on her subconscious. The air heaved in and out of her lungs in tremendous hot, ragged gasps. Her nightgown was plastered to her skin with cold sweat. She opened her eyes wide and forced herself to take in her surroundings, busying her brain by cataloging every item she saw—the foot of the half-tester bed, the enormous French Colonial armoire looming darkly against the wall, the marble-topped walnut commode with porcelain pitcher and bowl displaying an arrangement of spring blooms. Normal things, familiar things illuminated by the pale, now-you-see-it-now-you-don't moon shining in through the French doors. She wasn't in Georgia any longer. This wasn't Scott County. This was Belle Rivière, Aunt Caroline's house in Bayou Breaux. The place she had run to.

Coward.

She ground her teeth against the word and rubbed her hands hard over her face, then plowed her fingers back through her disheveled mess of sweat-damp hair.

"Laurel?"

The bedroom door opened, and Savannah stuck her head in. Just like old times, Laurel thought, when they were girls and Savannah had assumed the role of mother Vivian Chandler had been loath to play unless she had an audience. They were thirty and thirty-two now, she and Savannah, but they had fallen back into that pattern as easily as slipping on comfortable old shoes.

It seemed odd, considering it was Laurel who had grown up to take charge of her life, she who had struck out and made a career and a name for herself. Savannah had stayed behind, never quite breaking away from the past or the place, never able to rise above the events that had shaped them.

"Hey, Baby," Savannah murmured as she crossed the room. The moon ducked behind a cloud, casting her in shadow, giving Laurel only impressions of a rumpled cloud of long dark hair, a pale silk robe carelessly belted, long shapely legs and bare feet. "You okay?"

Laurel wrapped her arms around her knees, sniffed, and forced a smile as her sister settled on the edge of the bed. "I'm fine."

Savannah flipped on the bedside lamp, and they both blinked against the light. "Liar," she grumbled, frowning

as she looked her over. "I heard you tossing and turning.
Another nightmare?"

"I didn't think you were coming home tonight," Laurel said, railroading the conversation onto other tracks.
She tossed and turned every night, had nightmares every
night. That had become the norm for her, nothing worth
talking about.

Savannah's lush mouth settled into a pout. "Never
mind about that," she said flatly. "Things got over
quicker than I thought."

"Where were you?" Somewhere with smoke and liquor. Laurel could smell the combination over and above
a generous application of Obsession. Smoke and liquor
and something wilder, earthier, like sex or the swamp.

"It doesn't matter." Savannah shook off the topic with
a toss of her head. "Lord Almighty, look at you. You've
sweat that gown clean through. I'll get you another."

Laurel stayed where she was as her sister went to the
cherry highboy and began pulling open drawers in
search of lingerie. She probably should have insisted on
taking care of herself, but the truth of the matter was she
didn't feel up to it. She was exhausted from lack of sleep
and from her encounter with Jack Boudreaux. Besides,
wasn't this part of what she had come home for? To be
comforted and cared for by familiar faces?

Much as she hated to admit it, she was still feeling
physically weak, as well as emotionally battered. Coming
unhinged was hard on a person, she reflected with a grimace. But as Dr. Pritchard had been so fond of pointing
out, her physical decline had begun long before her
breakdown. All during what the press had labeled simply
"The Scott County Case" she had been too focused, too
obsessed to think of trivial things like food, sleep, exercise. Her mind had been consumed with charges of sexual abuse, the pursuit of evidence, the protection of
children, the upholding of justice.

Savannah's disgruntled voice pulled her back from
the edge of the memory. "Crimeny, Baby, don't you own
a nightgown that doesn't look like something Mama Pearl
made for the poor out of flour sacks?"

She came back to the bed holding an oversize white cotton T-shirt at arm's length, as if she were afraid its plainness might rub off on her. Savannah's taste in sleepwear ran to Frederick's of Hollywood. Beneath the gaping front of her short, champagne silk robe, Laurel caught a glimpse of full breasts straining the confines of a scrap of coffee-colored lace. With a body that was all lush curves, a body that fairly shouted its sexuality, Savannah was made for silk and lace. Laurel's femininity was subtle, understated—a fact she had no desire to change.

"Nobody sees it but me," she said. She stripped her damp gown off over her head and slipped the new one on, enjoying the feel of the cool, dry fabric as it settled against her sticky skin.

An indignant sniff was Savannah's reply. She settled herself on the edge of the bed once again, legs crossed, her expression fierce. "If I ever cross paths with Wesley Brooks, I swear I'll kill him. Imagine him leaving you—"

"Don't." Laurel softened the order with a tentative smile and reached out to touch the hand Savannah had knotted into a tight fist on the white coverlet. "I don't want to imagine it; I lived it. Besides, it wasn't Wes's fault our marriage didn't work out."

"Wasn't his—!"

Laurel cut off what was sure to be another tirade defaming her ex-husband. Wesley claimed he hadn't left her, but that she had driven him away, that she had crushed their young marriage with the weight of her obsession for The Case. That was probably true. Laurel didn't try to deny it. Savannah automatically took her side, ever ready to battle for her baby sister, but Laurel knew she wasn't deserving of support in this argument. She didn't have a case against Wes, despite Savannah's vehemence. All she had was a solid chunk of remorse and guilt, but that can of worms didn't need to be opened tonight.

"Hush," she said, squeezing Savannah's fingers. "I appreciate the support, Sister. Really, I do. But don't let's fight about it tonight. It's late."

Savannah's expression softened, and she opened her

hand and twined her fingers with Laurel's. "You need to get some sleep." She reached up with her other hand and with a forefinger traced one of the dark crescents stress and extreme fatigue had painted beneath Laurel's eyes.

"What about you?" Laurel asked. "Don't you need sleep, too?"

"Me?" She made an attempt at a wry smile, but it came nowhere near her eyes, where old ghosts haunted the cool blue depths. "I'm a creature of the night. Didn't you know that?"

Laurel said nothing as old pain surfaced like oil inside her to mingle with the new.

With a sigh Savannah rose, tugged down the hem of her robe with one hand and with the other pushed a lock of wild long hair behind her ear.

"I mean it, you know," she murmured. "If Wesley Brooks showed up here now, I'd cut his fucking balls off and stuff 'em in his ears." She cocked her fingers like pistols and pointed them at Laurel. "And *then* I'd get mean."

Laurel managed a weak chuckle. God, how Vivian would blanche to hear language like that from one of her daughters. Daughters she had raised to be debutantes. Sparkling, soft-spoken belles who never cursed and nearly swooned in the face of vulgarity. Vivian had expected sorority princesses, but God knew Savannah would eat dirt and die before she pledged to Chi-O, and she doubtless lay awake nights dreaming up ways to shock the Junior League. Laurel had been too busy to pledge, consumed by her need to get her law degree and throw herself into the task of seeing justice done.

"Would you prosecute me?" Savannah asked as she reached for the lamp switch.

"Be kind of hard to do, seeing how I don't have a job anymore."

"I'm sorry, Baby." Savannah clicked off the lamp, plunging the room into moonlight and shadows once again. "I wasn't thinking. You shouldn't be thinking about it, either. You're home now. Get some sleep."

Laurel sighed and pushed her overgrown bangs back off her forehead, watching as Savannah made her way to the door with her lazy, naturally seductive gait, her robe shimmering like quicksilver. " 'Night, Sister."

"Sweet dreams."

She would have settled for no dreams, Laurel thought as she listened to the door latch and her sister's footsteps retreat down the hall. But no dreams meant no sleep. She checked the glowing dial of the old alarm clock on the stand. Three-thirty. She wouldn't sleep again tonight no matter how badly her body needed to. Her mind wouldn't allow the possibility of another rerun of the dream. The knowledge brought a sheen of tears to her eyes. She was so tired—physically tired, emotionally exhausted, tired of feeling out of control.

With that thought came the memory of Jack Boudreaux, and a wave of shame washed over her, leaving goose bumps in its wake. She'd made an ass of herself. If she was lucky, he was too drunk to remember by now, and the next time she saw him she could pretend it never happened.

There wouldn't be a next time if she could help it. She knew instinctively she would never be able to handle a man like Jack Boudreaux. His raw sexuality would overwhelm her. She would never be in control—of him or the relationship or herself.

Not that she was interested in him.

Tossing the coverlet and sheet aside, she swung her legs over the edge of the bed, went to the French doors, and pulled them open. The night was comfortably warm, fragrant with the scents of spring, hinting at the humidity that would descend like a wet woolen blanket in another few weeks. The magnolia tree near the corner of the house still had a few blossoms, creamy waxy white and as big as dinner plates set among the broad, leathery, dark green leaves.

She had climbed that tree as a child, determined to find out what the experience was all about. Tree climbing was forbidden at Beauvoir, the Chandler family plantation that lay just a few miles down the road from Belle

Rivière. Tree climbing was not something "nice girls" did—or so said Vivian. Laurel shook her head at that as she wandered out onto the balcony. *Nice girls. Good families.*

"Things like that don't happen in good families. . . ."

"Help us, Laurel! Help us. . . ."

The past and the present twined in her mind like vines, twisting, clinging vines attaching their sharp tendrils to her brain. She brought her hands up to clamp over her ears, as if that might shut out the voices that existed only in her head. She bit her lip until she tasted blood, fighting furiously to hold back the tears that gathered in her eyes and congealed into a solid lump in her throat.

"Dammit, dammit, dammit . . ."

She chanted the word like a mantra as she paced the balcony outside her room. Back and forth, back and forth, her small bare feet slapping softly on the old wood. Weakness surged through her like a tide, and she fought the urge to sink down against the wall and sob. The tears choked her. The weakness sapped the stability from her knees and made her curl in on herself like a stooped old woman or a child with a bellyache. The memories bombarded her in a ferocious, relentless cannonade—the children in Scott County, Savannah and their past. *"Nice girls." "Good families." "Be a good girl, Laurel." "Don't say anything, Laurel." "Make us all proud, Laurel." "Help us, Laurel. . . ."*

No longer able to fight it, she turned and pressed herself against the side of the old house, pressed her face against it, not even caring that the edges of the weathered old bricks bit into her cheek. She clung there like a jumper who had suddenly remembered her terror of heights.

"Oh, God," she whimpered as the despair cracked through her armor and the tears squeezed past the tightly closed barriers of her eyelids. "Oh, God, please, please . . ."

"Help us, Laurel! Please, please, please . . ."

Her fingertips, then her knuckles scraped the brick

as her fingers folded into fists. She sobbed silently for a moment, releasing a small measure of the inner tension, then swallowed it back, gagging on the need to cry even as she ruthlessly denied herself the privilege. She pushed herself away from the building and turned toward the balcony, swiping the tears from her face with the heels of her hands.

Dammit, she wouldn't do this. She was stronger than this. She had come here to take control of her life again, not to fall apart twice in one night.

Using anger to burn away the other emotions, she turned and slammed her fist against one of the many smooth white columns that supported the roof of the balcony, welcoming the stinging pain that sang up her arm.

"Weak—stupid—coward—"

She spat out the insults, her fury turning inward. She kicked herself mentally for her failures as she kicked the column with her bare foot. The pain burst through her like a jolt of electricity, shorting out everything else, breaking the thread of tension that had been thickening and tightening inside her.

Gulping air, she bent over the balustrade, her fingers wrapping tightly around the black wrought-iron rail. In the wake of the pain flowed calm. Her muscles trembled, relaxing as the calm shimmered through her. Her heartbeat slowed to a steady bass-drum thump, thump, thump.

"Sweet heaven, I have to *do* something," she muttered. "I can't go on like this."

That truth had precipitated her leaving the Ashland Heights Clinic. Her stay there had been peaceful, but not productive. Dr. Pritchard had been more interested in digging up the past than in helping her fix her miserable present. She didn't see the point. What was done was done. She couldn't go back and fix it no matter how badly she wanted to. What she needed to do was push it behind her, rise above it. Move forward. Do something. Do what?

Her job was gone. The fallout from The Case had fallen directly on her. She had been stripped of power,

profession, credibility. She had no idea what would become of her, what she would ultimately do or be. Her
job had been her identity. Without it she was lost.

"I've got to do something," she said again, looking
around, as if an answer might appear to her somewhere
down the dark corridor of the balcony or in the trees or
the garden below.

Belle Rivière had been built in the 1830s by a local
merchant to placate his homesick young wife who had
grown up in the Vieux Carré in New Orleans. The house
was designed to emulate the elegant splendor of the
French Quarter, right down to the beautiful courtyard
garden with its fountain, and brick walls trimmed with
lacy black wrought-iron filigree. The garden Laurel had
spent two days trying to put to rights only to have Jack
Boudreaux's dog—*allegedly* his dog—uproot her efforts.
Damn hound.

Damn man.

The garden had been maintained sporadically over
the years. Laurel remembered it as a place of marvelous
beauty during her childhood when old Antoine Thibo-
deaux had tended it for Aunt Caroline. As lush and green
as Eden, spray billowing from the fountain, elegant statues of Greek women carrying urns of exotic plants. Antoine had long since gone to his eternal rest, and
Caroline's latest gardener had long since gone to New
Orleans to be a female impersonator on Bourbon Street.
Caroline, absorbed in her latest business venture, an antiques shop, hadn't bothered to hire anyone new.

Laurel had seen it as the perfect project for her,
physically, psychologically, metaphorically. Clear away
the old debris, prune off the dead branches, rejuvenate
the soil, plant new with a hopeful eye to the future. Res-
urrection, rebirth, a fresh start.

She stared down at the mess Huey the Hound had
left and heaved a sigh. Young plants torn up by the roots.
She knew the feeling. . . .

.   .   .

"Where are you taking Daddy's things, Mama?"

"To the Goodwill in Lafayette," Vivian Chandler said, not sparing a glance at her ten-year-old daughter.

She stood beside the bed that had been her husband's, smartly dressed in a spring green shift with a strand of pearls at her throat. She looked cool and sophisticated, as always, like a model from out of a fashion magazine, her ash blond hair combed just so, pale pink lipstick on. She propped her perfectly manicured hands on her hips and tapped the toe of one white pump against the rug impatiently as she supervised the proceedings. Tansy Jonas, the latest in a string of flighty young maids, hauled load after load of suits and shirts and slacks out of the closet to be sorted into piles.

"Of course, we'll have to take some of it to the church," Vivian said absently as she considered the armload of dress shirts weighing down poor Tansy. Tansy wasn't more than fifteen, Laurel reckoned, and thin as a willow sapling. The girl seemed to weave beneath the burden of silk and fine cotton cloth, her black eyes going wider and wider in her round dark face.

"It's expected," Vivian went on, inspecting the state of collars and cuffs, oblivious to Tansy's discomfort. "The Chandlers having always been the leading family hereabouts, it's our duty to contribute to the less fortunate in the community. Why, just the other day, Ridilia Montrose was asking me if I hadn't donated Jefferson's things," she said, frowning prettily. "As if she thought I wasn't going to. She's got a lot of nerve, and I would have told her so if I weren't a lady. Imagine her looking down on me when everybody in town knows they nearly went bankrupt! And what a shame that would have been, because that daughter of hers has teeth like a mule, and it's going to cost a fortune to fix them."

She selected a pair of striped shirts, impervious to the pleading look on the maid's face, and tossed them into one of several piles on the bed. "I told her I just hadn't been up to sorting through Jefferson's things. Why, the mere thought of it had me on the verge of one of my spells. I can see, though, that I can't put it off a

second longer, or there'll be tongues wagging all over
town. I swear, that Ridilia isn't any better than she has to
be."

Continuing in the same breath, she said, "Tansy, put
the rest of those on the chair."

"Yas'm," Tansy murmured with relief, staggering
away under the weight of the load.

"I'll sort through your father's things," Vivian said to
Laurel. "Never mind that it could send me into a tail-
spin. I'll donate to the church, but I'll die before I see
no-account trash walking around Bayou Breaux in Jefferson's silk suits. They're going to Lafayette, and Ridilia
Montrose can go to blazes."

Laurel scooted off the seat of the blue velvet armchair before the maid could bury her alive. She didn't
like this at all. Seeing all of Daddy's things pulled out of
his neat closet and strewn around his room caused a hollow, churning feeling in her tummy. She had played in
his closet more times than she could count, sneaking in
there with her Barbie dolls, pretending his big shoes
were cars or boats or space ships. It had been her secret
place for when she wanted to be all alone. It smelled of
leather and cedar and Daddy. She had sat cross-legged
on the floor and felt the legs of his neatly hung pants
brush across the top of her head, and pretended they
were vines and that she was inside a secret cave in the
jungle and that his belts were snakes. Now it was all
being torn apart to be given to strangers in another town.

Chewing on a thumbnail, she sidled along the big
mahogany bureau, her eyes on her mother. Vivian didn't
look bothered at all by what she was doing, unless being
cross counted. Laurel didn't think it did. It only meant
that her mother would rather have been doing something
else, not that this job made her sad. She said it might
give her a spell, though, and that was a million times
worse than just plain sad. It scared Laurel something
terrible when her mother went into one of her blue
spells—crying all the time, hardly ever getting out of her
nightclothes, shutting herself up in her rooms—the way
she had done when Daddy died.

Laurel secretly feared she was going to have the same kind of spells. She had felt that bad when Daddy died. She hadn't wanted to see anybody. And she had cried and cried. She had cried so hard, she thought she might just turn herself inside out the way Daddy had always teased her she would. She and Savannah had cried together. She had slipped into her sister's room through the door in the closet because Mama had told her more than once that she was a big girl now and had to sleep alone. She and Savannah had hid under the covers and cried in their pillows until they almost choked.

Ties came out of the closet next, a whole long rack of them that had hung on the clothes pole. The ties drooped down off the rack, nearly to Tansy's feet. The maid struggled to hold it up high, skinny arms over her head so as to give her employer a good look at the strips of silk. Laurel spotted the blue one with the big bug-eyed bass painted on it and almost giggled as she remembered her father wearing it. His lucky poker playing tie, he had always said with a wink and a grin. Vivian snatched it off the rack and threw it on the Lafayette pile.

"But Mama," Laurel said, her heart sinking abruptly, "that was Daddy's favorite!"

"I've always hated the sight of that tie," Vivian grumbled, talking more to herself than to Laurel. "I thought I'd die of embarrassment every time Jefferson put it on. To think of a man in his position going around in a necktie the likes of that!"

Laurel stepped alongside the bed and reached a hand out to brush her fingertips over the painted bass. "But Mama—"

"Laurel, leave that be," she snapped. "Don't you have schoolwork?"

"No, Mama," she murmured, inching back from the bed, staring longingly after the bass tie as her mother tossed three more on top of it.

"Can't you see I'm busy here?"

"Yes, Mama."

She backed into the corner by the dresser again and

pretended to be invisible for a while. She didn't want to
be sent to her room. She wanted to be in here with
Daddy's things—only she didn't want Mama and dumb
old moony-eyed Tansy here rooting through everything.

She wiggled one foot over on its side and back, over
and back, over and back, the way Mama always scolded
her for on account of it would scuff up her shoes. Laurel
didn't care. Mama was too busy throwing out Daddy's
things to notice. Laurel wouldn't have cared anyway, because tears were filling up her eyes and she needed
something to concentrate on so she wouldn't start to cry
and get scolded for that. So she twisted her foot over and
back, over and back, and chewed on her thumbnail even
though there wasn't much left to chew on.

The fingers of her left hand moved along the top of
the bureau, brushing against the edge of Daddy's jewelry
case. Because it made her tummy hurt to watch Mama
and Tansy, she turned and looked at the heavy wooden
box with its fancy inlaid top and shiny brass latch. She
stroked her small hand over its smooth surface and
thought of Daddy, so big, so strong, always with a smile
for her and a stick of Juicy Fruit gum in his pocket.

One big, fat tear teetered over the edge of her eye-
lashes and rolled down her cheek to splash on the polished bureau. Another followed. She couldn't think of
Daddy's being gone forever. She missed him so much
already. He was strength and safety and love. He didn't
care if she scuffed up her shoes, and he always hugged
her when she cried. Laurel couldn't bear the idea of losing him. She didn't want him gone to heaven with the
angels the way Reverend Monroe had told her. Maybe
that was selfish, and she felt bad about that, but not bad
enough to give up her daddy.

Her small fingers fumbled with the latch, and she
lifted the lid on the jewelry box. The box was lined with
red velvet and filled with man things. Daddy's money
clip, the two big chunky rings he never wore, his tie
tacks and cuff links and some Indian-head pennies.

Laurel reached in and lifted out the red crawfish tie
pin she had given him for Father's Day when she was

seven. It wasn't worth much. Savannah had helped her buy it for three dollars at the crawfish festival in Breaux Bridge. But Daddy had smiled when he opened the box, and told her it would be one of his favorites. He had worn it to the father-daughter dinner at school that year, and Laurel had been so happy and proud, she could have burst.

"Laurel," Vivian snapped, "what are you into now? Oh, that jewelry box. I'd nearly forgotten."

She shooed Laurel aside and made a hasty pass through the box, setting aside a pair of diamond cuff links, a signet ring, a diamond tie pin. Then she ordered Tansy to bring a shoe box and dumped the rest of the contents into it. Laurel watched in horror, tears streaming down her cheeks, the crawfish pin sticking her hand as she tightened her fist around it.

Vivian shot her a suspicious look. "What have you got there?"

Laurel sniffed and tightened her fingers. "Nothin'."

"Don't you lie to me, missy," Vivian said sharply. "Good little girls don't tell lies. Open your hand."

Be a good girl, Laurel thought, always be a good girl, or Mama gets cross. She bit her lip to keep from crying as she held out her hand and opened her fist.

Vivian rolled her eyes as she picked up the tie pin, pinching it between thumb and forefinger and holding it up as if it were a live bug. "Oh, for pity's sake! What do you want with this piece of trash?"

Laurel flinched as if the word had struck her. Daddy hadn't called it trash, even if it was. "But Mama—"

Her mother turned away from her, dropping the pin in the shoe box Tansy held.

"B-but Mama," Laurel said, her breath hitching in her throat around a huge lump. "C-couldn't I keep it j-just 'cause it was D-Daddy's?"

Vivian wheeled on her, her face pinched, eyes narrowed like a snake's. "Your father is dead and buried," she said harshly. "There's no use being sentimental about his things. Do you hear me?"

Laurel backed away from her, feeling sick and hurt

and dizzy. Tears spilled down her cheeks, and a hollow ache throbbed inside her heart.

"You're just being a nuisance in here," Vivian went on, working herself into a fine lather. "Here I am, doing my best to finish an awful job, a migraine bearing down on me, and pressures like no one knows. We have guests coming for dinner, and you're underfoot . . ."

The rest of what she had to say sounded like nothing to Laurel but blah blah blah. Her ears were pounding, and her head felt as though it might explode if she couldn't start crying hard real soon. Then Savannah was behind her, putting her hands on Laurel's shoulders.

"Come on, Baby," she whispered, drawing her out the bedroom door. "We'll go in my room and look at pictures."

They went to Savannah's room and sat on the rug next to the bed, looking at a photo album full of pictures of Daddy Savannah had stolen from the parlor the day of Daddy's funeral. She kept it under her mattress and had told Tansy if she ever tried to take it out or tell Vivian about it, she would have a voodoo woman put a curse on her that would give her warts all over her face and hands. Tansy left it be and had taken to wearing a dime on a string around her neck to protect her from *gris-gris*.

They sat on the rug and looked at their father in the only way they would ever be able to see him again, and felt alone in all the world, like two little flowers pulled up by the roots.

That night Ross Leighton came to dinner.

Savannah sat with her back to her dressing table, one foot pulled up on the seat of the chair, one arm wrapped around her leg, the other hand toying with the pendant she never took off. Lost in thought, she ran the gold heart back and forth on its fine chain. Through the French doors that led onto the balcony she could just see Laurel leaning against a column down the way. Poor Baby. The Case had taken everything out of her—her pride, her fight, her self-confidence, her independence.

Everything that had taken her away from here had been taken away from her, and now she was back. Poor lost lamb, weak and sorely in need of comfort and love. Just like old times. Just like after Daddy died and Vivian had offered as much solace as a jagged piece of granite.

Funny how time had run in a circle. All during their growing-up years Savannah had mothered and nurtured and protected, and Laurel had grown stronger and brighter and burned with ambition, reaching higher and going further, eventually leaving Savannah in the dust. But now she was back, in need of mothering and nurturing again.

She turned and looked at herself in the beveled mirror above her dressing table, taking in the tousled hair, the bee-stung lips she pumped with collagen at regular intervals. Her robe had slipped off one shoulder, baring creamy skin and the thin strap of her chemise. Her breasts were barely contained by the lacy cups, their natural shape augmented by silicone implants she'd had put in years ago in New Orleans. She traced a fingertip across her lower lip, then along the scalloped edge of lace, her nipple twitching at the slight contact, a response that triggered a quick, automatic fluttering between her legs.

Laurel had gone off to Georgia to gain fame and fight for justice. To do the family proud. And Savannah had stayed behind, carving out her reputation as a slut.

Shedding her robe, she crossed the room and lay down on the bed with the elegantly carved, curved headboard. Leaning back against a mountain of satin pillows, she lit a cigarette and blew a lazy stream of smoke up toward the ceiling. Life had come full circle. Laurel was home, and Savannah was being given the chance to be important again, to do something worthwhile. Her baby sister needed her. Life could be turning around for her at last. Now all she needed was for Astor Cooper to die.

Chapter Four

Jack jerked awake, bolting against the cluttered mahogany desk, throwing his head back away from the black Underwood manual typewriter that had served as pillow for the last—what? hour? two? three? He looked around, blinking against the buttery light that filtered down through the canopy of live oak and through the sheer lace curtains at the window. He rubbed his hands over his lean face and cleared his throat, grimacing at the taste of stale beer coating his mouth. With his fingers he combed back his straight black hair, which was too thick and too long for south Louisiana this time of year.

The old ormolu clock on the bedroom mantel ticked loudly and relentlessly, drawing a narrow glare. Eleven-thirty. The respectable folk of Bayou Breaux had been up and industrious for hours. Jack had no memory of coming home. It might have been midnight. It might have been dawn when he had stumbled across the threshold of the old house the locals called L'Amour. He cast a speculative look at the heavy four-poster bed with its drape of *baire* carelessly stuffed behind the carved head-

board. There might have been a woman dozing among
the rumpled sheets. He had a vague memory of a woman
. . . big blue eyes and an angel's face . . . fire and fragility . . .

There wasn't a woman in his bed, which was just as
well. He was in no mood for morning-after rhetoric. His
head felt as though someone had smashed it with a mallet.

The last thing he remembered was Leonce's leading
him away from Frenchie's. He might have gone anywhere, done anything after that. Pain jabbed his temples
like twin ice picks as he tried to remember. Funny, he
thought, his mouth twisting at the irony, he drank to forget. Why couldn't he just leave it at that?

"Because you're perverse, Jack," he mumbled, his
voice a smoky rumble, made more hoarse than usual by a
night of loud singing in a room where ninety percent of
the people were chain smokers.

He pushed himself up out of the creaking old desk
chair, his body doing some creaking and groaning of its
own after God knew how many hours in a sitting position. He stretched with all the grace of a big lean cat,
scratched his flat bare belly, noted that the top button on
his faded jeans was undone but left it that way.

The page in the typewriter caught his eye, and he
pulled it out and studied it, frowning darkly at the words
that must have seemed like gems at the time he had
pounded them out.

*She tries to scream as she runs, but her lungs are on
fire and working like a bellows. Only pathetic yipping
sounds issue from her throat, and they are a waste of
precious energy. Tears blur her vision, and she tries to
blink them back, to swipe them back with her hand, to
swallow the knot of them clogging her throat as she runs
on through the dense growth.*

*Moonlight barely filters down through the canopy of
trees. The light is surreal, nightmarish. Branches lash at
her, cutting her face, her arms. Her toes stub and catch
on the roots of the oak and hackberry trees that grow
along the soft, damp earth, and she stumbles headlong,*

twisting her head around to see how near death is behind her.

Too near. Too calm. Too deliberate. Her heart pounds hard enough to burst.

She scrambles backward, trying to get her legs under her. Her hands clutch at roots and dead leaves. Her fingers close on the thick, muscular body of a snake, and she screams as she tries to escape the triangular head and flashing fangs that strike at her. The stench of the swamp fills her head as the copper taste of fear coats her mouth. And death looms nearer. Relentless. Ruthless. Evil. Smiling . . .

Crap. Nothing but crap. With a sound of disgust Jack crumpled the page and hurled it in the general direction of the wastebasket—an old Chinese urn that may well have been worth a small fortune. He didn't know, didn't care. He had stumbled across it in the attic, buried under a decade's worth of discarded, moth-eaten clothing. Apparently it had been there some time, as it was a third full of the dead, decaying, and skeletal remains of mice that had fallen into it over the years and been unable to get out.

Jack owned antiques because the old decrepit house had come with them, not because he was culturally sophisticated or a conspicuous consumer or particularly appreciative of fine things. Material things had become irrelevant to him since Evie's death. His perspective of the world had shifted radically downhill. Another irony. For most of his thirty-five years he had fought tooth and nail to achieve a status where he could own "things." Now he was there and no longer gave a damn.

"Dieu," he whispered, shaking his head and wincing at the pain, "old Blackie must be sittin' in Hell laughin' at that."

Bon à rien, tu, 'tit souris. Good for nothin', pas de bétises!

The voice came to him out of the past, out of his childhood. A voice from beyond the grave. He flinched at the memory of that voice. A conditioned response, even after all this time. Often enough a slurred line from

Blackie Boudreaux had been followed up with a back-hand across the mouth.

Jack pulled open the French doors and leaned against the frame, the smooth white paint cool against the bare skin of his shoulder. His eyes drifted shut as he breathed in the sweet green scent of boxwood, the fragrant perfume of magnolia and wisteria and a dozen other blooming plants. And beneath that heady incense lay the dark, insidious aroma of the bayou—a mixture of fertility and decay and fish. The scents, the caress of the hot breeze against his face, the chorus of bird song instantly transported him back in time.

He saw himself at nine, small and skinny, barefoot and dirty-faced, running like a thief from the tarpaper shack that was home. Running from his father, running to escape into the swamp, his bare feet slapping on the worn dirt path.

In the swamp he could be anyone, do anything. There were no boundaries, no standards to fall short of. He could conquer an island, become king of the alligators, be a notorious criminal on the run. On the run for killing his father, which he would have done if he had been bigger and stronger . . .

"Shit," he muttered, stepping back into the bedroom.

He left the doors open and shuffled toward the bathroom some previous forward-thinking owner of L'Amour had converted from a dressing room back in the twenties. It still "boasted" the original white porcelain fixtures and tile. Not much of a boast, considering all were dingy with age, cracked, and chipped. Fortunately, Jack's only prerequisite was that they work.

With the flick of a switch the boom box sitting on the back of the old toilet came to life, belting out the bluesy, bouncy Zydeco sound of Zachary Richard—"Ma Petite Fille Est Gone." Despite the fact that it jarred his aching head, Jack automatically moved with the beat as he filled the sink with cold water. The music defied stillness with its relentless bass rhythm and hot accordion and guitar licks.

Gulping a big breath, he bent over at the waist and

stuck his head in the basin, coming up a minute later cursing in French and shaking himself like a wet dog. He gave himself a long, critical look in the mirror, debating the merits of shaving as water dripped off the end of his aquiline nose. He looked tough and mean in his current state, a look he didn't let many people see. The gang down at Frenchie's knew Jack the Party Animal. Jack with the ready grin. Jack the lady's man. They didn't know this Jack except through his books, and it amazed them that the Jack Boudreaux who was touted by the publishing world as the "New Master of the Macabre" was *their* Jack.

He sniffed and tipped his head to one side, a wry half smile curving his mouth. *"Pas du tout, mon ami,"* he murmured. *"Pas du tout."*

As he reached for his toothbrush, the music on the radio was cut short in midchorus.

"This just in," the deejay said, his usually jovial tone stretched taut and flat by the gravity of the news. "KJUN news has just learned of another apparent victim of the Bayou Strangler. This morning, at approximately seven o'clock, two fishermen in the Bayou Chene area in St. Martin Parish discovered the body of an unidentified young woman. Though authorities have yet to release a statement, reliable sources on the scene have confirmed the similarities between this death and three others that have occurred in south Louisiana in the past eighteen months. The body of the last victim, Sheryl Lynn Car-mouche, of Loreauville, was discovered—"

Jack reached over and hit the tape button. Instantly the frantic fiddle music of Michael Doucet whined through the speakers, snapping the tension, drowning out the grim news. He'd had enough grimness to last him. He had a stock stored up, ready to be called upon and brought down on his head like a ton of bricks any time he wanted. He didn't care to bring in more from outside sources.

Don't get involved. That was his motto. That and the traditional Cajun war cry—*laissez le bon temps rouler.* He didn't want to hear about dead girls from Loreauville.

He couldn't give Sheryl Lynn Carmouche her life back. He could only live his own, and he intended to do just that, starting with a big shrimp po'boy and a bottle of something cold down at the Landing.

Sweat trickled between Laurel's breasts as she knelt in the freshly turned earth. It beaded on her forehead, and one drop rolled down toward her nose. She reached up with a dirty gloved hand and wiped it away, leaving a smear of mud.

No one would have spotted her for a once-aggressive attorney—a fact that suited her just fine. She wanted to lose herself in mindless manual labor, thinking of nothing but simple physical tasks like turning soil and planting flowers. She suspected she would appear to have bathed in dirt by the time she finished her work in the courtyard. There were worse things to become immersed in.

She poked at the root of a new azalea bush with a small hand spade, mixing in the special compost Bud Landry at the nursery had sent home with her—his own secret blend of God-knew-what that would grow anything, "guar-un-teed."

She spent most of the morning sweeping up yesterday's carnage and supervising the hanging of a new gate at the back of the courtyard. Not pausing for more than a sip of the iced tea Mama Pearl brought out for her, she swept and raked and piled. She then hauled the mess, one load at a time, to the edge of the small open field that lay to the east of Aunt Caroline's property, where she piled all the debris of her first two days' work, and would burn it all before it could become a haven to snakes and rodents.

She made a mental note to call city hall and check to see if she would need a permit. No one in Bayou Breaux had ever been much on that kind of formality, but times changed. She hadn't lived here in a lot of years. For all she knew the place could have been taken over by yuppies on the run from suburban life. Or the Junior League might have decided environmentalism was in vogue—so long as it didn't interfere with their husbands' businesses. Laurel could well imagine her mother leading the crusade against common folk burning brush while Ross Leighton polluted the bayou with chemicals intended to keep his cane crop money-green and safe from insects.

Thoughts of Vivian erased what was left of Laurel's smile. She had been in Bayou Breaux four days now without making a call to Beauvoir. That wouldn't be tolerated much longer. She had no desire to visit her childhood home or the people who resided there, but there was such a thing as family duty, and Vivian was bound to bring it down on Laurel's head like a club if she didn't make the expected pilgrimage soon.

The idea hardly overjoyed her. The fact that she would have to deal with Vivian and Ross, if only to sit at the same table with them for dinner, had been enough to make her reconsider the wisdom of coming back. But the instinctive need for a place that was familiar had overridden her aversion to seeing her mother and stepfather.

The thought of going off someplace on her own, someplace where her anonymity would be absolute, had been too daunting. Go someplace where the only company she would have would be herself? That was company she didn't want to keep just now. She had longed for the reassurance of Caroline Chandler's formidable personality and unconditional love. She had felt a need to see Savannah. She had missed Mama Pearl's fussing and truculence. The occasional encounter with Vivian and Ross seemed small enough penance to pay for the privilege of coming home.

With considerable force of will she shut the door on the topic and focused on other things. Her hands packed the soil around the roots of the azalea bush. The scents of ripe compost and green growth filled her nostrils. Across the courtyard bees were buzzing lazily over a wild tangle of rambling roses and wisteria that clung to the brick wall. A Mozart quintet drifted from the boom box she had left on the gallery of the house.

The heat grew a little thicker. She sweated a little harder. Overhead wispy clouds writhed and curled their way across the blue sky, scudding northward on a balmy Gulf breeze. The quintet ended, and the news began, signaling the start of the lunch hour.

"Topping the news this hour: the discovery of another apparent victim—"

Laurel jerked her head around as the announcement was cut short. Savannah stood on the gallery, hands on her hips, a pair of square black Ray-Bans shading her eyes. She had pulled her wild hair up into a messy topknot that trailed tendrils along her neck and jawline, and had dressed with her usual flare in a periwinkle spandex miniskirt that hugged the curves of her hips and backside, and a loose white silk tank that managed to show more than it covered. A diamond the size of a pea hung just above the deep shadow of her cleavage, just below the necklace Daddy had given her years ago, and gold bangles rattled at her wrists as she shifted her weight impatiently from one spike heel to the other.

"Baby, what in the world do you think you're doing?"

Laurel pushed her bangs out of her eyes and flashed a smile. "Gardening! What's it look like?"

She abandoned her tools and straightened up, dusting the loose dirt off the knees of her baggy jeans before heading for the gallery. Mama Pearl would cluck at her like a fat old hen if she tracked it into the house.

"You've spent the entire last two days gardening," Savannah said, frowning. "You're going to wear yourself out. Didn't your doctor tell you to relax?"

"Gardening is relaxing, psychologically. I've needed to do something physical," she said, toeing off her canvas sneakers and stepping up beside her sister. In her heels Savannah towered over her. Laurel had always felt small and mousy in Savannah's presence. Today she felt like a grubby urchin, and the feeling pleased her enormously.

Savannah sniffed and made a comical face of utter disgust. "Mercy, you smell like a hog pen at high noon! If you needed to do something physical, we could have gone shopping. Your wardrobe is begging for a trip to New Orleans."

"I have plenty of clothes."

"Then why don't you wear them?" Savannah asked archly.

Laurel glanced down at the shapeless cotton T-shirt and baggy jeans that camouflaged all details of her body. Most of what she had brought with her was designed for comfort rather than style.

"It wouldn't be very practical for me to do gardening in stiletto heels," she said dryly, eyeing her sister's outfit. "And if I had to bend over in that skirt, I'd probably get arrested for mooning the neighbors."

Savannah looked out across the courtyard to L'Amour, the once-elegant brick house that stood some distance behind Belle Rivière on the bank of the bayou. The corners of her lush mouth flicked upward in wry amusement. "Baby, you couldn't scandalize that neighbor if you tried."

"Who's living there? I didn't think anyone would ever buy it, considering the history of the place and the state it was in the last time I saw it."

L'Amour had been built in the mid-nineteenth century for a notorious paramour by her wealthy, married lover. By all accounts—and there were many versions of the tale—she died by his hand when he discovered she was also involved with a no-account Cajun trapper. Laurel had grown up hearing stories about the place's being haunted. No one had lived there in years.

"Jack Boudreaux," Savannah answered, her smile turning sexy at the thought of him. "Writer, rake, rascal, rogue. And when he gets to be old enough, I imagine he'll be a reprobate too. Come along, urchin," she said, turning for the house. "Go hose yourself down. I'm taking you out to lunch."

Jack Boudreaux. Laurel stood on the veranda, staring at L'Amour.

"Baby, you coming?"

Laurel snapped her head around, a blush creeping up her cheeks like a guilty schoolgirl's. Concern tugged at

Savannah's brows, and she pushed her sunglasses on top
of her head.

"I think you've been out in the sun too long. You
should have worn a hat."

"I'm fine." Laurel shook her head and dodged her
sister's gaze. "I'll just take a nice cool shower before we
go."

Cold shower indeed, she thought, shaken by her response to the mere mention of a man's name. Lord, it
wasn't as though she had enjoyed their encounter. It had
unnerved her, and in the end she'd made a fool of herself. Mortification should have been her reaction to the
words "Jack Boudreaux."

She showered quickly and dressed in a pair of baggy
blue checked shorts and a sleeveless blue cotton blouse.
Barely ten minutes had passed by the time she trotted
down the stairs and turned into the parlor, a room with
soft pink walls and the kind of elegant details that put
Belle Rivière on a par with the finest old homes in the
South.

". . . poor girl over in St. Martin Parish," Caroline
was saying in a low voice.

She sat in her "throne," a beautifully carved Louis
XVI man's armchair upholstered in rose damask. Home
from her regular Saturday morning at the antiques shop,
she had settled in place, kicking off her black-and-white
spectator pumps on the burgundy Brussels carpet and
propping her tiny feet on a gout stool some woman in the
eighteenth century had doubtless gone blind needle-
pointing the cover for by lamplight. A tall, sweating glass
of iced tea sat on a sterling coaster on a delicate, oval
Sheraton table to her left.

"I turned the radio off before she could hear," Savannah said, her voice also pitched to the level of conspiracy. She sat sideways on the camelback sofa, leaning
toward her aunt, her long bare legs crossed.

"Before I could hear what?" Laurel asked carefully.

The two women jerked around, their eyes wide with
guilty surprise. Savannah's expression changed to irritation in the blink of an eye.

"It should have taken you at least another twenty minutes to get ready," she said crossly. "It would have, if you'd bothered to put on makeup and do something with your hair."

"It's too hot to bother with makeup," Laurel said shortly, her temper rising. "And I don't give a damn about my hair," she said, though she automatically reached up a hand to tuck a few damp strands behind her ear. "What is it you didn't want me to hear?"

Aunt and sister exchanged a look that sent her ire up another ten points.

"Just something in the news, darlin'," Caroline said, shifting in her chair. She arranged the full skirt of her black-and-white dotted dress slowly, casually, as if there were nothing more pressing on her mind. "We didn't see the need to upset you with it, that's all."

Laurel crossed her arms and planted herself in front of the white marble fireplace. "I'm not so fragile that I need to be shielded from news reports," she said, tension quivering in her voice. "I don't need to be cosseted from the world. I'm not in such a precarious mental state that I'm liable to fly apart at the least little thing."

Even as she spoke the words, her mouth went dry at the taste of the lie. She *had* come here to be cosseted. Only just last night she had gone to pieces arguing with a no-account drunk about a no-account hound. *Weak.* She shivered, tensing her muscles against the word, the thought.

"Of course we don't think that, Laurel," Caroline said, rising with the grace and bearing of a queen. Her dark eyes were steady, her expression practical, straightforward with not a hint of pity. "You came here to rest and relax. We simply thought those objectives would be more easily attained if you weren't dragged into the torrent of speculation about these murders."

"Murders?"

"Four now in the last eighteen months. Young women of . . . questionable reputation . . . found strangled out in the swamp in four different parishes—not Partout, thank God." She gave the information flatly and with as

little detail as possible. Now that the cat was out of the
bag, she saw no point in dancing around the issue with
dainty euphemisms. Certainly her niece had dealt with
cases as bad or worse in her tenure as a prosecuting attorney. But neither did she see the need to paint a lurid
picture of torture and mutilation, as the newspapers had
done. She only hoped the case wouldn't snag Laurel's
attention. Coming away from the situation in Scott
County, she didn't need to become immersed in another
potboiler case of sex and violence.

"All in Acadiana?" Laurel asked, narrowing the possibilities to the parishes that made up Louisiana's French
Triangle.

"Yes."

"Are there any suspects?" The question was as second-nature to her as inquiring after someone's health.

"No."

"Do they—"

"This doesn't concern you, Baby," Savannah said
sharply. She rose from the sofa and came forward, her
pique doing nothing to minimize the sway of her hips.
"You're not a cop, and you're not a prosecutor, and these
girls aren't even dying in this jurisdiction, so you can just
tune it out. You hear?"

It was on the tip of Laurel's tongue to tell Savannah
she wasn't her mother, but she bit the words back. What
a ludicrous statement that would have been. Savannah
was in many ways more of a mother to her than Vivian
had ever been. Besides, Savannah was only trying to protect her.

Hands on her hips, she tamped down her temper,
sighing slowly to release some of the steam, feeling
drained from what little fury she had shown. "I don't
have any intention of trying to solve a string of murders,"
she assured them. "Y'all know I have my hands full just
managing myself these days."

"Nonsense." Caroline sniffed, tossing her head.
"You're doing just fine. We want you to concentrate on
getting your strength back, that's all. You're a Chandler,"
she said, seating herself once more on her throne, ar-

ranging her skirt just so. "You'll be fine if your stubbornness doesn't get the better of you."

Laurel smiled. This was what she had come to Belle Rivière for—Caroline's unflagging fortitude and ferocious determination. There were those around Bayou Breaux who compared Laurel's aunt to a pit bull—a comparison that pleased Caroline no end. Caroline Chandler was either loved or hated by everyone she knew, and she was enormously proud to inspire such strong reactions, whatever they were.

"We're going to lunch, Aunt Caroline," Savannah said, slinging the strap of her oversize pocketbook up on her shoulder. The Ray-Bans slid back into place, perched on the bridge of her nose. "Come along? Mama Pearl's gone to a church meeting."

"Thank you, no, darlin'." Caroline sipped her tea and smiled enigmatically. "I have a luncheon appointment with a friend in Lafayette this afternoon."

Savannah tipped her glasses down and arched a brow at Laurel, who just shrugged. Caroline's friends in other towns never had names—or genders, for that matter. Because she'd never been married, or even seriously involved with any of the local men, Caroline's sexual preferences had long been a source of speculation among the gossips of Bayou Breaux. And she had always staunchly, stubbornly refused to answer the question one way or the other, saying it was no one's damn business whether she *was* or *wasn't*.

"What do you think?" Savannah asked as they slid into the deep bucket seats of her red Corvette convertible.

"I don't," Laurel said, automatically buckling her seat belt. Savannah drove the way she lived her life.

Savannah chuckled wickedly as she put the key in the ignition and fired the sports car's engine. "Oh, come on, Baby. You're telling me you've never tried to picture Aunt Caroline going at it with one of her mysterious friends?"

"Of course not!"

"You're such a prude." She backed out of the driveway and onto the quiet, tree-lined street that led directly downtown. Belle Rivière was the last house before the road stretched out into farmland and wetlands. But even up the street, where houses stood side by side, the only activity seemed to be the swaying of the Spanish moss that hung from the trees like tattered banners.

"Not wanting to picture my relatives engaging in sex doesn't make me a prude," Laurel grumbled.

"No," Savannah said. "But it sure as hell makes you the odd one in the family, doesn't it?"

She let out the clutch and sent the Corvette flying down the street, engine screaming. Laurel fixed her eyes on the road and fought the urge to bring her hand up to her mouth so she could gnaw at her thumbnail.

Sex was the last thing she wanted to talk about. She would have preferred there were no such thing. It seemed to her the world would have been a much better place without it. It certainly would have been a better world for the children she'd fought for in Scott County, and for countless others. She tried to imagine what Savannah might have achieved with her life had she not become such a sexual creature.

Those thoughts brought a host of others bubbling to the surface and set her stomach churning. She tried to turn her attention to the familiar scenes they were passing at the speed of sound—a block of small, ranch-style houses, each with a shrine to the Virgin Mary in the front yard. Shrine after shrine made from old clawfoot bathtubs that had been cut in half and planted in the ground. Flowers blooming riotously around the feet of white totems of the Holy Mother. A block of brick town houses that had been restored in recent years. Downtown, with its mix of old and tacky "modernized" storefronts.

She didn't turn to look at the courthouse as they passed it, concentrating instead on the congregation of gnarled, weathered old men who seemed to have been sitting in front of the hardware store for the past three decades, gossiping and watching diligently for strangers.

The scenes were familiar, but not comforting, not the way she wanted them to be. She felt somehow apart from all she was seeing, as if she were looking at it through a window, unable to touch, to feel the warmth of the people or the solace of long acquaintance with the place. Tears pressed at the backs of her eyes, and she shook her head a little, reflecting bitterly on the defense of her mental state she had made to Caroline and Savannah in the parlor. What a crock of shit. She was as fragile as old glass, as weak as a kitten.

"I'm really not very hungry," she murmured, digging her fingers into the beige leather upholstery of the car seat to keep her hands from shaking as the tension built inside her, the forces of strength and weakness shifting within, pushing against one another.

Not bothering with the blinker, Savannah wheeled into the parking lot beside Madame Collette's, one of half a dozen restaurants in town. She took up two parking spots, sliding the 'Vette in at an angle between a Mercedes sedan and a rusted-out Pinto. She cut the engine and palmed the keys, sending Laurel a look that combined apology and sympathy in equal amounts.

"I'm sorry I brought it up. The last thing I want is to upset you, Baby. I should have known better." She reached over and brushed at a lock of Laurel's hair that had dried at a funny angle, pushing it back behind her ear in a gesture that was unmistakably motherly. "Come on, sweetie, we'll go have us a piece of Madame Collette's rhubarb pie. Just like old times."

Laurel tried to smile and looked up at the weathered gray building that stood on the corner of Jackson and Dumas. Madame Collette's faced the street and backed onto the bayou with a screened-in dining area that overlooked the water. The restaurant didn't look like much with its rusted tin roof and old blue screen door hanging on the front, but it had been in continuous operation long enough that only the true old-timers in Bayou Breaux remembered the original Collette Guilbeau—a tiny woman who had reportedly chewed tobacco, carried a six-gun, and dressed out alligators with a knife given to her by Teddy Roosevelt, who had once stopped for a bite while on a hunting expedition in the Atchafalaya.

Rhubarb pie at Madame Collette's. A tradition. Memories as bittersweet as the pie. Laurel thought she would have preferred sitting on the veranda at Belle Rivière in the seclusion of the courtyard, but she took a deep breath and unbuckled her seat belt.

Savannah led the way inside, promenading down the aisle along the row of red vinyl booths, hips swaying lazily and drawing the eyes of every male in the place. Laurel tagged after her, hands in the pockets of her baggy shorts, head down, oversize glasses slipping down her nose, seeking no attention, garnering curious looks just the same.

The scents of hot spices and frying fish permeated the air. Overhead fans hung down from the embossed tin ceiling, as they had for nearly eighty years. The same red-on-chrome stools Laurel remembered from her childhood squatted in front of the same long counter with its enormous old dinosaur of a cash register and glass case for displaying pies. The same old patrons sat at the same tables on the same bentwood chairs.

Ruby Jeffcoat was stationed behind the counter, as she always had been, checking the lunch hour receipts, wearing what looked to be the same black-and-white uniform she had always worn. She was still skinny and ornery-looking, hair net neatly smoothing her marcel hairdo, lips painted a shade of red that rivaled the checks in the tablecloths.

Marvella Whatley, looking a little plumper and older than Laurel remembered, was setting tables. There was a fine sprinkling of gray throughout the black frizz of her close-cropped hair. A bright grin lit her dark face as she glanced up from her task.

"Hey, Marvella," Savannah called, wiggling her fingers at the waitress.

"Hey, Savannah. Hey, Miz Laurel. Where y'at?"

"We've come for rhubarb pie," Savannah announced, smiling like a cat at the prospect of fresh cream. "Rhubarb pie and Co-Cola."

At the counter Ruby eyed Savannah's short skirt and long bare legs, and sniffed indignantly, frowning so hard, her mouth bent into the shape of a horseshoe. Marvella just nodded. Nothing much ever bothered Marvella. "Dat's comin' right up, then, ladies. Right out the oven, dat pie. You gonna want some mo' for sho.' M'am Collete, she outdo herself, dat pie."

The table Savannah finally settled at was in the back, in the screened room, where abandoned plates and glasses indicated they had missed the lunch rush. Out on the bayou, an aluminum bass boat was motoring past with a pair of fishermen coming in from a morning in the swamp. In the reeds along the far bank a heron stood, watching them pass, still as a statue against a backdrop of orange Virginia creeper and coffee weed.

Laurel drew a deep breath that was redolent with the aromas of Madame Collette's cooking and the subtler wild scent of the bottle brown water beyond the screened room, and allowed herself to relax. The day was picture perfect—hot and sunny, the sky now a vibrant bowl of pure blue above the dense growth of trees on the far bank. Oak and willow and hackberry. Palmettos, fronds fanning like long-fingered hands. She had nowhere to go, nothing to do but pass the day looking at the bayou. There were people who would have paid dearly for that privilege.

"We-ell," Savannah purred as she surveyed the room through the lenses of her Ray-Bans, "if it isn't Bayou Breaux's favorite son, himself."

Laurel glanced across the room. At the far corner table sat the only other customer—a big, rugged-looking man, his blond hair disheveled in a manner that suggested finger-combing. He might have been fifty. He might have been older. It was difficult to tell. He had the look of an athlete about him—broad shoulders, large hands, a handsome vitality that defied age. He sat hunched over a spiral notebook, glaring down through a pair of old-fashioned round, gold-rimmed spectacles. His expression was fierce in concentration as he scribbled. A tall pitcher of iced tea sat to his left within easy reach, as if he planned on sitting there all day, filling and refilling his glass as he worked. Laurel didn't recognize him, and she turned back to Savannah with a look that said so.

"Conroy Cooper," Savannah said coolly.

The name she recognized instantly. Conroy Cooper, son of a prominent local family, Pulitzer Prize–winning author. He had grown up in Bayou Breaux, then moved to New York to write critically acclaimed stories about life in the South. Laurel had never seen him in person, nor had she ever read his books. She figured she knew all she needed to about growing up in the South. She had listened to him tell stories on public radio once or twice and remembered not the tales he had told, but his voice. Low and rich and smooth, the voice of old Southern culture. Slow and comforting, it had the power to lull and woo and reassure all at once.

"He moved back here a few months ago," Savannah explained in a hushed tone of conspiracy.

Her gaze was still directed at Cooper, her expression masked by her sunglasses. She trailed a fingertip up and down the side of the sweating glass of Coke Marvella had brought, a movement that reminded Laurel of a cat twitching its tail in pique.

"His wife has Alzheimer's. He brought her back here from New York and put her in St. Joseph's Rest Home. I hear she doesn't know her head from a hole in the ground."

"Poor woman," Laurel murmured.

Savannah made a noise that sounded more like indigestion than agreement.

The pie arrived, steaming hot with vanilla ice cream melting down over the sides to puddle on the plate. Laurel ate hers with relish. Savannah picked and fiddled until the ice cream had completely returned to its liquid state and the pie was a mess of pinkish lumps and crust that resembled wet cardboard.

"Is something wrong?"

She started at the sound of Laurel's voice, dragging her gaze away from Cooper, who had yet to acknowledge her presence. "What?"

"You're not eating your pie. Is something wrong?"

She flashed a brittle smile and fluttered her hands. "Not a bit. My appetite just isn't what I thought it was, that's all."

"Oh, well . . ." Laurel shot a considering glance at Cooper, huddled over his writing. "I was thinking I would just run up the street to the hardware store. Aunt Caroline needs a new garden hose. You wanna come?"

"No, no, no," she said hastily. "You go on. I'll meet you at the car. I'm going to have Madame Collette box up one of these pies and take it home for supper."

Savannah forked up a soggy bite of pie and watched as Laurel ducked through the doorway, leaving her alone with the man who had effortlessly snared her heart and seemed determined to break it.

Anger shimmered through her in a wave of heat, pushing her toward recklessness. She wanted him to look at her. She wanted to see the same kind of hunger in him that she felt every time she saw him, every time she thought of him. She wanted to see the same raw longing burning in his eyes. But he just sat there, writing, oblivious of her, as if she weren't any more important than a table or a chair.

She rose slowly, smoothing her short skirt, her every movement sensuous, sinuous. For all the good it did her. Cooper went on scribbling, head bent, brows drawn, square jaw set.

Slowly she sauntered across the room, stiletto heels clicking on the linoleum floor. She tossed her sunglasses down beside his notebook, and slowly raised the hem of her skirt, inch by inch, revealing smooth, creamy thighs and a thicket of neatly trimmed dark curls at the juncture of those thighs.

Cooper bolted in his chair, dropping his pen and nearly overturning the pitcher of tea at his elbow. "Jesus H. Christ, Savannah!" The words tore from his throat in a rough whisper. He glanced automatically toward the door for witnesses.

"Don't worry, honey," Savannah purred, sliding the fabric back and forth across her groin. "There's nobody here but us adulterers."

He reached across the table with the intent of pulling the skirt down to cover her, but she inched away from him and slowly moved around the end of the table, her back to the door.

"Like what you see, Mr. Cooper?" she murmured in a voice like honey, wicked mischief flashing in her pale blue eyes. "It's not on the menu, but I'd give you a taste if you asked me real nice."

Blowing out a sigh, Cooper sat back and watched as she lowered one knee onto the chair beside his. The initial shock had subsided, and his usual air of calm settled over him as comfortably as the old tattersall shirt he wore. It was Savannah's nature to shock. Overreacting only pushed her to be more outrageous, like a naughty child seeking attention. So he settled himself and looked his fill, knowing he would see anyone intruding on the moment quickly enough to act before they could be caught.

"Maybe later," he drawled. "Tonight, perhaps."

She pouted, staring at him from under her lashes. "I don't want to wait that long."

"But you will. That'll only make it better."

He reached out again, slowly, casually, and drew his fingertips up a few smooth inches of leg, meaning to tug the skirt down out of her grasp, but she caught his hand and guided it between her thighs.

"Touch me, Coop," she whispered, leaning against him, pressing her cheek down on top of his head. She wound her right arm around the back of his neck, anchoring his face against her breasts as her hips began to move automatically, rhythmically against his hand. "Please, Coop . . ."

She was hot and silky, her body instantly ready for sex. She moved against him wantonly. Cooper had no doubt that she would have straddled him on the spot if he would have allowed it, without a care as to who might walk in on them. The idea held a strong fantasy appeal, he thought, grimacing, as desire pooled and throbbed. But he wouldn't follow through.

He thought that might be the only thing that set him apart from the sundry other men Savannah had cast her spell over—that he somehow managed to maintain the voice of reason in the face of her overwhelming sexuality, instead of losing himself in it.

"Please, Coop," Savannah breathed. She traced the tip of her tongue along the rim of his ear, panting slightly as need gathered in a knot in the pit of her belly.

The need swirled around her like a desert wind, heating her skin. She wanted to tear her blouse open and feel his mouth, wet and avid, on her breasts. She wanted to impale herself on his shaft and go wild with the pleasure of it. She wanted . . . wanted . . . wanted . . .

Then he pulled his hand away and stood, disentangling himself from her, and the want congealed into a hard ache of frustration.

"You're such a bastard," she spat, jerking her skirt down, straightening her top. A strand of hair fell across her face and stuck to her sweat-damp cheek. She tucked it behind her ear.

Cooper pulled his glasses off and began cleaning the steam from them, methodically rubbing the lenses with a clean white handkerchief. He looked at her from under his brows, his gaze as blue as sapphire, as steady as a rock. "I'm a bastard because I won't have sex with you in a public place?"

Savannah sniffed back the threat of tears, furious that he had the power to make her feel shame. "You wouldn't even look at me across the goddamn room! You wouldn't even give me a civil 'Good afternoon, Miz Chandler.' "

"I was concentrating," he said calmly.

He settled his spectacles back in place, folded the handkerchief, and returned it to the hip pocket of his khaki pants. That task accomplished, he gave her a tender look, the corners of his mouth tilting up in a way that was, despite his fifty-eight years, boyish and unbelievably charming. "I'm a sorry excuse for a man if my work can so involve me that I miss one of your entrances, Savannah."

He reached out a hand and touched her cheek with infinite gentleness. "Forgive me?"

Damn him, she would. That low, cultured drawl wrapped around her like silk. She could have curled up beside him and listened to him talk for a hundred years, glad just to be near him. She sniffed again and looked at him sideways.

"What are you working on? A short story?"

Coop picked up the notebook as she reached for it and closed it, forcing a grin. "Now, darlin', you know how I am about letting anyone read my work. Hell, I don't even let my agent read it until it's done."

"Is it about me?" The storm clouds gathered and rumbled inside her again. "Or is it about Lady Astor?" she asked petulantly, giving her head a toss as she moved restlessly away from the table.

She paced along the screened wall, oblivious to the shabby pontoon tour boat that was ferrying a load of unsuspecting tourists up the bayou and into the sauna that was the swamp at midafternoon.

"Lady Astor Cooper," she sneered, planting her hands on her hips. "Patron saint of martyred husbands."

"Better I martyr myself to my marriage than to my cock."

"Are you implying that's what I do?" she demanded. "Martyr myself to sex?"

Cooper hissed a breath in through his teeth and made no comment. They were treading on dangerous ground. He had his own theories about Savannah's sexual motives, but it would do no good to share them with her. He could too easily envision her in a rage of hurt and hysteria, wildly lashing out. And he had no desire to hurt her. For all her faults, he had fallen in love with her. Hopeless love in the truest sense.

"Well, I've got news for you, Mr. Cooper," she said, leaning up into his face, her lovely mouth twisted with bitterness. "I get fucked because I like getting fucked, and if you don't want to do it, then I'll go find someone who will."

He caught her arms and held her there for a moment as she breathed fury into his face, steaming his glasses all over again. A deep, profound sadness swelled inside him and he frowned. "You make yourself miserable, Savannah," he murmured.

She shivered inside, trying to shake off the chill of the truth. Coop saw it, damn him. He caught her eyes with that worldly-wise, world-weary, worn blue gaze, and saw he'd struck a nerve. She jerked away from him and grabbed her sunglasses off the table.

"Save your insights for your work, Coop," she said waspishly. "It's the only place you really let yourself live." She jammed the Ray-Bans in place and flashed him a mocking smile. "Have a nice day, Mr. Cooper."

She whirled out of Madame Collette's in a huff and a cloud of Obsession, not bothering to pay the bill. Ruby Jeffcoat knew who she was, the dried-up old bitch. She'd just add it to the tab and tell every third person she saw what a slut Savannah Chandler was, prancing around town in a skirt cut up to her crotch and no bra on.

Laurel pushed herself away from the side of the Corvette as Savannah stormed across the parking lot, all pique and no pie in sight. She looked furious, and Laurel had a strong hunch it wasn't anything to do with the restaurant, but one of its patrons. Conroy Cooper. Old enough to be their father Conroy Cooper. Married Conroy Cooper.

Oh, Savannah . . .

"Let's get the hell out of here," Savannah snarled. Tossing her purse behind the seat, she jerked open the driver's door and slid in behind the wheel.

Laurel barely had time to get in the car before the 'Vette was revved and rolling. They hit Dumas, and Savannah put her foot to the floor, sending the sports car squealing away from Madame Collette's, leaving a trail of rubber.

"Where are we going?" Laurel asked as casually as she could, considering she had to shout to be heard above the roar of the wind and the engine.

"Frenchie's," Savannah yelled, pulling the pins from her hair and letting them fly. "I need a drink."

Laurel buckled her seat belt and held on, not bothering to comment on the fact that it didn't look as though they'd be having rhubarb pie for supper, and trying her damnedest not to think about Jack Boudreaux.

Chapter
Five

"Jesus saves!"

"Jesus lives!"

"Jesus Christ," Savannah snarled as she stopped in her tracks, propped a hand on one hip, and took a look at the scene outside Frenchie's.

Patrons crowded the gallery, staring down, bemused at a dozen protestors who were toting signs bearing such intelligent slogans as "Close Frenchie's. End Sin." The picketers were gathered in a knot at the bottom of the steps, putting on a show for the camera of a Lafayette television station, chanting their slogans in a vain attempt to drown out the swamp pop music that spilled through the screens.

In the center of the righteous stood the ringleader of their band, Reverend Jimmy Lee Baldwin, resplendent in a white summer suit, fresh out of the JC Penney catalog. Two thousand dollars' worth of too-white caps shone as he spoke to a reporter who looked as though he used enough hair spray to put his own personal hole in the ozone.

Jimmy Lee was good-looking, standing an inch or two past six feet tall, and had once been lean and athletic, though in the years since high school basketball, firm muscle had softened. He wore his tawny hair slicked straight back from his face, drawing attention to his eyes, which were the color of good scotch, and to the dazzling dental wonders that lined his smile like big white Chiclets.

Though he was barely thirty-eight, lines of dissipation were etched deeply beside those tawny eyes and around a mouth that had a certain weakness about it. Between the teeth and the tan that looked as though he'd gotten it down at the Suds 'n' Sun Laundromat/Tanning Parlor, Jimmy Lee looked just a little too tacky to be truly handsome. Not that anyone could ever have convinced him of that.

"Who is it?" Laurel asked, shoving her glasses up on her nose. The sight of the white news van automatically made her nervous. The irrational fear that they had come here to track her down flashed through her mind, but she resolutely crushed it out with the gavel of practicality. She wasn't news any longer.

"The Reverend Jimmy Lee Baldwin. Saver of lost souls, purveyor of heavenly blessings, leader of the Church of the True Path."

"I've never heard of it."

"No. I reckon Georgia had its own religious screwballs. The Revver showed up here about six months back and started to gather himself a flock. He's got his own show now on local cable up in Lafayette. Fixin' to be a big star in the televangelist ranks, he is."

Savannah dug a cigarette out of her pocketbook and lit it, taking a long, considering drag as she stared at Jimmy Lee through her sunglasses. He was on a roll, gesturing like a wild man as he began ranting about the dens of iniquity.

"Come on, Baby," she said on a breath of smoke. "I need to get me that drink."

Laurel started for the side door, having no desire to call attention to herself by crashing a picket line. But

Savannah made a beeline for the action, miniskirt twitching across her thighs, hips swaying alluringly. She gave her head a toss, fluffing her long, wild mane with her free hand as she went. She looked like a walking ad for wanton sex and decadent living. Laurel bit back a groan and followed her. Trouble had always been a magnet to Savannah, and she was headed toward this mess with a sly smile teasing the corners of her mouth.

Her approach did not go unnoticed. Almost immediately a chorus of wild cheers and wolf whistles rose from the men on the gallery. Of the group involved in the protest, the reporter saw her first, his head snapping around in a classic double take as he held the microphone in front of Reverend Baldwin. He elbowed the cameraman, who swung his lens in her direction. Reverend Baldwin broke off in midtirade, clearly annoyed to have his moment in the spotlight cut short. He recovered quickly, though, and moved to turn the situation to his advantage.

"Sister, sister, be redeemed!" he called dramatically. "Let Christ Jesus quench your thirst."

Savannah stopped a scant six inches from the minister, cocked a hip, and blew a stream of smoke in his face. "Honey, if He shows up in the next five minutes with a Jax long-neck, I'll be glad to let Him quench my thirst. In the meantime Frenchie can serve that need just fine."

She blew a kiss to the camera while the crowd on the gallery howled laughing, and sauntered on, the picketers-turned-gawkers parting like the Red Sea to let her pass on up the steps. Laurel tried to hurry after her before the faithful closed ranks on their leader again, but Baldwin caught her by the arm.

"Turn to God, young woman. Find the True Path! Let the Lord quench the thirst in your soul with conviction and righteousness!"

Laurel looked up at him, her brows pulling together in annoyance. She had no patience for the likes of Jimmy Lee Baldwin. Televangelists ranked a notch lower than disreputable used-car salesmen in her book, bilking the poor and the elderly out of what limited funds they had, selling them the kind of salvation God offered free of charge in the Bible. She hadn't come here looking for a fight. In fact, she would have given anything to have passed unnoticed through the throng. But she wasn't about to be used as a pawn. She pulled in a deep breath and felt the fire that had been turned low leap inside her.

"I have convictions of my own, Mr. Baldwin," she said, smiling inwardly as he jerked his head around and looked at her as if she were a mute suddenly healed. He hadn't expected her to stand up to him. "All of them more important than the sale of perfectly legal alcoholic beverages in a licensed establishment."

Jimmy Lee recovered admirably from his shock. "You condone the sin of drink, lost sister? May the Lord have mercy—"

"If I'm not mistaken, it was Christ who changed the water into wine at the wedding at Cana. John, chapter two, verses one to eleven. Liquor itself isn't bad, Reverend, just the foolish acts committed by those who overindulge. And alcoholism is an illness, not a sin. Perhaps God should have mercy on *your* soul for suggesting otherwise."

He bared his snowy-white teeth at her in what would pass for a smile on videotape, she supposed, and his fingers tightened on her upper arm, telegraphing his anger. "I come only as God's soldier in the war to save men's souls. Our battlegrounds are the dens of iniquity where men's weaknesses are exploited for monetary gain."

"If you're only interested in saving *men's* souls, then perhaps you could take your hand off me," she said dryly, pulling free of his grasp. "As to exploiting people's weaknesses for monetary gain, my interests run more in the direction of the disposition of monies solicited by television preachers. I wonder what the Lord would have to say about that."

As the audience on the gallery cheered, Baldwin flushed red. His mouth tightened, and the whiskey-brown eyes, which had moments ago glowed with the bright lights of glory, hardened like amber. He took a step back from her, admitting defeat as far as Laurel was concerned. She gave him one last hard look and started to turn for the steps, but the reporter outflanked her, and she flinched away from the light of the hand-held strobe an assistant shot up behind the cameraman.

"Miss, Doug Matthews, KFET-TV, can we please get your name?"

Memories of other times and other cameras flashed through Laurel's mind. Reporters pressing in on her, yapping and jumping at her like a pack of hounds. Questions, accusations, snide remarks, hurled at her from all sides like darts.

"No," she murmured, fighting the tightness that suddenly squeezed her chest. "No, please just leave me alone."

Savannah stepped down off the gallery and pushed the cameraman's lens down. "Leave my sister alone, sweetheart," she said, her gaze leveled on the reporter, "else I'll take that cute little microphone and shove it up your tight little ass."

Hoots and shouts issued from Frenchie's patrons. Gasps rippled through the crowd of believers as the Chandler sisters went up the steps and into the bar.

Jimmy Lee stepped away from them, dragging Doug Matthews with him. "You'll take that shit out, or I'll beat her to that goddamn microphone," he growled, looming over Matthews, who was jockey-short and coward-yellow.

Doug Matthews sent him a contentious look, making a token show of journalistic integrity as he smoothed a hand carefully over his blond hair. "It's news, Jimmy Lee."

"So is your penchant for pretty young men." His eyes darted to his throng of disgruntled followers who were milling around the parking lot looking as though their parade had been hailed on. "Fuck news. This is supposed to be the launch of my big campaign against sin. I'm not gettin' shown up by some little skirt in horn-rimmed glasses. You take that tape and cut and paste until I look like Christ himself forgiving Mary Magdalene." He

cuffed Matthews on the chest, scowling ferociously. "You
got that, Dougie?"

Matthews pouted and rubbed at the sore spot, carefully straightening his turquoise tie. "Yeah, yeah. I got it.
I wonder who she was, anyway. She sure as hell cleaned
your clock."

Jimmy Lee rubbed his knuckles against his chin, his
gaze on the screen door the two women had gone
through. "Sister," he murmured, the oily wheels of his
mind whirring like windmills. "Savannah Chandler's sister." Awareness dawned, and he brightened considerably
as the seeds of a plan took root. "Laurel Chandler."

"Poor Jimmy Lee," Savannah said without sympathy as
they stepped into the cool, dark interior of Frenchie's.
"He's only trying to rid the town of impurities, immorali-
ties, and prurient behavior. He's a firsthand expert on
prurient behavior." Sliding her sunglasses down her
nose, she looked at Laurel and smiled wickedly. "And I
ought to know, 'cause I've gone to bed with him."

"Savannah!"

"Oh, Baby, don't look so scandalized." She chuckled
as she glanced around the room for a choice place to
roost. "Preachers get the itch too. And let me tell you,
Jimmy Lee likes his scratched in some of the most inven-
tive ways. . . ."

She sauntered toward a table, feeling a little bit mean
and a little bit vindicated. Coop had rattled her, something she didn't like at all. Making a fool out of Jimmy
Lee went a long way toward making up for the scene at
Madame Collette's. And truth to tell, shocking Laurel
made up the rest. Laurel, such a good girl. Laurel the
upstanding citizen. Laurel the golden child. It did her
good to get thrown for a loop every once in a while. Let
her see how the other half lived. Let her think *There but
for the grace of God and Savannah. . . .*

The crowd in the bar greeted her like the conquering
heroine, calling to her, raising their glasses. A sense of
warmth and importance flowed through her. This was

her turf. These were her people, much to the dismay of
Vivian and Ross. Here she was appreciated. She smiled
and waved, the kind of all-encompassing, regal gesture of
a beauty queen.

"Hey, Savannah!" Ronnie Peltier called from over by
the pool table, where he stood leaning on the butt of his
cue. "Dat's some tongue you got on you, girl."

"So I've been told, honey," she drawled.

He grinned and shifted his weight. "Oh, yeah? Well,
why you don' come on over here, *jolie fille*, and show
me?"

Savannah tossed her head and laughed, assessing his
charms all the while. Ronnie was big where it counted
and cute as could be. Conroy Cooper could go to hell.
She had just found herself a fun-loving Cajun boy to play
with.

Leonce Comeau swiveled around on his barstool and
slid his hand down her back as she passed. "Hey, Savannah, when you gonna marry me? Me, I can't live without
you!"

She slid him a sly look over her shoulder, mentally
shuddering at the grotesque scar that bisected his face,
the long, shiny-smooth pink line that began and ended in
strange knots of flesh. "If you can't live without me, Leonce, then how come you ain't dead yet?"

"I yi yiee!" He clutched his hands to his heart as if
she'd shot him, a big grin splitting across his bearded
face. "You heartless bitch!"

Laurel watched the proceedings with a sinking heart
and a churning stomach. It tore her up to see this side of
her sister—the seductress, the slut. Savannah had so
much more to offer the world than her sexual prowess.
Or she once had. Once she had been full of promise, full
of hope, bright-eyed at the possibilities life had to offer.
Once upon a time . . .

"You want a toothpick, *'tite chatte?*"

The voice was unmistakable. Whiskey and smoke and
a vision of black satin sheets. His breath was warm
against her cheek, and she jerked around, cursing herself
for bolting.

"Why would I want a toothpick?" she demanded indignantly.

Jack grinned at the flash of temper in her dark blue eyes. It was a hell of an improvement over the sadness and guilt he'd glimpsed there a moment before. For a moment she had looked like a lost child, and the impact of that impression had slammed into him like a truck. Not that he really cared about her, he assured himself. Miss Laurel Chandler was hardly his type. Too serious by half. Too driven. He liked a girl who liked her fun. A few good laughs, a nice healthy round of mattress thumping, no strings attached. Laurel Chandler was a whole different breed of cat—as evidenced by the mincemeat she'd made of Jimmy Lee Baldwin.

"Why, to pick all those pieces of Jimmy Lee out your teeth, sugar," he said. "You sure chewed him up and spit him out. Remind me not to get on your bad side."

She scowled. "You're already on my bad side, Mr. Boudreaux."

"Then why I don't just buy you a drink, angel, and we can make up?" he suggested, smiling, leaning down just a little closer than he should have. Her frown tightened, but she held her ground.

"I'd rather be left alone, thank you very much," Laurel said primly, avoiding those dark eyes that had managed to see past her carefully erected defenses once already. She fixed her gaze on one deep dimple and did her best to ignore its blatant sex appeal.

"Oh, well, then you came to the wrong place, sugar."

He draped an arm casually around her shoulders and steered her toward the bar, completely ignoring her wishes. She held herself stiffly, resisting his herding. She looked up at him sideways. He wore a battered black baseball cap that had "100% Coonass" machine embroidered on the front in glossy blue thread. A blood red ruby studded the lobe of his left ear. The wild Hawaiian print shirt he wore hung completely open, revealing a broad wedge of tan chest, well-defined muscle lightly dusted with black hair, a belly that looked as hard and ridged as a washboard. A line of silky-looking hair curled around his belly button like a question mark and disappeared into the low-riding waist of his faded jeans, as if beckoning curious female eyes to wonder about the territory that lay beyond.

She jerked her gaze away, pushing her glasses up on her nose in an attempt to hide the blush that bloomed instantly on her cheeks.

He wasn't her type at all, she reminded herself. He wasn't the kind of man she usually allowed to touch her. He wasn't the kind of man she would ordinarily have known at all. And he wasn't charming her. She was only letting him shepherd her toward the bar because she didn't want to watch Savannah seducing the pool players.

"Talk about chewing ass," he said, an unholy light in his eyes. "What's black and brown and looks good on a lawyer?" Laurel shot him a scowl, which he fielded with an incorrigible grin. "A doberman."

The laugh that rolled out of him may as well have been a pair of hands that skimmed boldly over her. Laurel ground her teeth at her unwanted reaction, berating her body for its inability to judge character.

"Hey, Ovide!" Jack called. "How 'bout a drink here for our little tigress?"

Laurel blushed again at the name and climbed up on a barstool, figuring she would at least be rid of Jack Boudreaux's touch now. She was wrong. He merely stood beside her, arm hooked around her loosely but possessively. Worse than standing beside him, she was now at eye level with him, and he didn't hesitate to lean close and murmur in her ear.

"That's Ovide," he said, his voice as low and intimate as if he were whispering words of seduction. He fished a cigarette out of his shirt pocket and dangled it from his lip. " 'Frenchie' Delahoussaye. The man you were stickin' up for out there."

The man behind the bar was in his late sixties, short and stout with sloping shoulders and no neck. He was bald as a cue ball on top, with shaggy steel gray hair ringing the sides of his head and sprouting in fantastic tufts from his ears. A cloud of curly gray hair spilled out of the V of his plaid shirt, and a thick mustache draped across his upper lip and trailed down past the corners of his mouth. His eyebrows were so bushy, they could have been pads of steel wool glued to his forehead. He looked like a nutria that had taken human form by enchantment. He moved purposefully if slowly, filling tall mugs with beer from a tap.

In contrast, the woman behind the bar with him moved at the speed of light, dashing to fill glasses, grab a pack of cigarettes, call an order for a po'boy back through the window to the kitchen. She was younger than Ovide, though not by a lot, and her face showed every day of her years, with lines etched beside her eyes and thin mouth that was painted poppy orange to match her tower of hair. Her skin had the leathery look of a lifelong smoker. It was stretched taut and shiny against the bones of her skull, giving added emphasis to the large dark eyes that bulged out of her head as if she were perpetually startled. Despite her obvious age, she was still petite, with a hard, sinewy body beneath tight designer jeans from the seventies and an electric blue satin western shirt.

She snatched the two mugs from Ovide and plunked one down on the bar in front of Laurel, scolding Frenchie nonstop.

"What'sa matter wit' you, Ovide? Jack, he don' wan' no damn glass, him!"

She snatched a long-neck bottle of Pearl from the cooler and popped the top off while she grabbed a rag with the other hand and wiped a trail of water off the bar, her mouth going a mile a minute.

"Ovide, he don' know which way is up, *cher*, what wit' all this preacher and ever'ting all the time carryin' on outside our door." She sucked in a breath and cast a glance heavenward that looked more like annoyance than supplication. *"Bon Dieu*, what dis world comin' to wit' the like of dat Jimmy Lee callin' himself a man of the cloth? *Mais, sa c'est fou!* It pains me to see."

She cocked a thickly penciled brow at Jack and chastised him for being remiss in his manners, as if he could have gotten a word in edgewise. "So, *cher*, you gonna introduce me to *une belle femme* or what?"

Jack threw back his head and laughed, his arm automatically tightening around Laurel. She stopped breathing as her breast came into contact with his side.

"T-Grace," he announced, "meet Miss Laurel Chandler. Laurel, T-Grace Delahoussaye, Frenchie's right hand, left hand, and mouthpiece."

T-Grace slapped at him with her wet towel, even as her attention held fast on Laurel. "You say some pretty smart things to dat horse's ass Jimmy Lee, *chère*."

"Miz Chandler is a lawyer, T-Grace," Jack offered, a comment that made T-Grace lean back and eye Laurel as dubiously as if he had announced she was from outer space.

Laurel shifted uncomfortably on her stool and tried in vain to discreetly tug some of the wrinkles out of her blouse. "I'm not practicing at the moment. I'm just in town to visit relatives."

T-Grace eyed Laurel critically, then said, "Ovide, he's jus' beside himself over dis 'End Sin' thing with dat preacher and all," as she accepted a tray of empty glasses from a waitress and whirled to set them next to the bar sink.

Laurel glanced at the impassive Ovide, who stood beside his wife, silently pouring drinks and lining them up on the bar for distribution. Either T-Grace was psychic or the man's moods were too subtle for normal human eyes to detect.

"You say some pretty hard things to make a man think, *oui*"? She gave a snort and swiped a fly off the bar with her rag. "If dat Jimmy Lee can think. He's all the time so busy talkin', him, can't be nothin' much left in his head to think about. So you gonna be *our* lawyer, *chère*, or what?" she asked baldly, crossing her arms beneath her bosom impatiently while she waited for an answer.

Laurel gaped, stunned by the question, left speechless by T-Grace herself. The proposition was ludicrous. She wasn't a lawyer here in Bayou Breaux; she was just

Laurel Chandler. The idea that she could be both was the furthest thing from her mind right now. She had come here to rest, to heal, not to take up the fight.

"Oh, no," she said, shaking her head, nervously stroking a finger through the condensation on her beer mug. "I'm sorry, Mrs. Delahoussaye. I'm only in town for vacation. All you really need to do is file a complaint for trespassing. If you feel you need help, I'm sure there are any number of local attorneys who would be glad to represent you."

T-Grace sniffed and shot a look at Jack. "Some less than there oughta be."

He scowled at her, picking the unlit cigarette from between his lips to gesture with it. "I told you, T-Grace, I couldn't if I wanted to. Besides, you don' need no lawyer. Jimmy Lee's just a pest. Ignore him, and he'll go away."

The older woman stared hard at him, all pretense of teasing gone from her bulging dark eyes, leaving her looking old and tough as boot leather. "Trouble don' jus go away, *cher*. You know dat good as me, *c'est vrai.*"

Laurel watched the exchange with interest. Jack's bad-boy grin had vanished into that hard, intense look she had glimpsed the night before. A look that clearly told T-Grace to back off, a look that most grown men would have heeded. T-Grace pretended to shrug it off and turned away from him. She glanced sideways at Laurel as she pulled a pair of bottles from the cooler and popped the tops off.

"Why for you wearin' dem big glasses, *chère*? You in disguise or what?"

She moved off to do a dozen tasks at once before Laurel could formulate any kind of answer. Laurel pushed the glasses up on her nose and frowned.

"It's not much of a disguise, angel," Jack said.

"Not compared to yours," Laurel returned. The best defense was a good offense. She didn't like being so easily read, and she had no intention of talking to Jack Boudreaux about her motives for doing anything. She certainly wasn't about to let him escape being questioned himself.

"Mine?" he scoffed. He shook his head, took a long drink of his beer, and wiped his mouth with the back of his hand. "No disguises here. What you see is what you get, sugar."

The wickedness returned, sparkling in his eyes, curling the corners of his mouth, digging those breath-stealing dimples into his cheeks. He leaned close, sliding his hand around to the small of her back. His fingers teased her through the thin cotton of her blouse, rubbing lazy circles.

"You like that promise, no?" he breathed, leaning closer still, his lips just brushing the shell of her ear. Laurel shivered, then gasped as his hand slipped beneath the hem of the loose-fitting blouse.

"No," she said emphatically, batting his hand away. She gave him a look that had made better men back off and ground her teeth when he only smiled at her. "Don't try to change the subject."

"I'm not. The subject is us. I'm just tryin' to get past the talkin' stage, angel."

"When hell freezes over."

"Well, that devil, he's gonna feel a chill one of these days real soon."

She arched a brow at him, thwarting the temptation to be either flattered or amused. "Is that a fact?"

"Oh, absolutely," he drawled, dark eyes shining.

His intent was clear. For reasons Laurel couldn't begin to fathom, he'd set his sights on her. Probably because she was the only female in his territory he had yet to notch his bedpost for. His arrogance was astonishing. But more astonishing was the vague sensation of arousal his words, his touch, his nearness conjured inside her.

It was a simple matter of physical needs, she rationalized, needs too long ignored and a handsome man all too willing to rectify the situation.

"You think too much, angel," Jack said, replacing his cigarette. She was as transparent as glass, working out in her mind a logical excuse for the physical attraction that arced between them like electric sparks. He bumped her glass closer. "Have a drink. Have a good time. Lighten up."

His philosophy in a nutshell, Laurel thought. She was about to give him her opinion on the subject when Savannah appeared to her right, draped all over the Cro-Magnon pool player like a vine.

"Baby," she drawled, her gaze fastened hungrily on Mr. Cuestick as she rubbed the flat of her hand over his chest. "Me and Ronnie got plans for the evening."

She sounded drunk, though they hadn't been in the bar long enough for that to have been the case. Drunk on arousal. Drunk on the need for sex. Laurel sighed and glanced down, finding no relief as Savannah's bare knee came into view—sliding up and down Ronnie's muscular thigh.

"What about supper?" she asked shortly.

"Oh . . . we'll eat later." The pair of would-be lovers shared a laugh over that, ending the joke with a kiss, open mouths meeting briefly, tongues teasing. Ronnie's hand slid down from the small of Savannah's back to grope her ass, and she groaned deep in her throat.

"Fine," Laurel murmured, turning to stare at her untouched beer. "Just how am I supposed to get home?"

"Here. You can take the 'Vette." The keys landed on the bar with a rattle. "I'll get my own ride."

Another round of salacious laughter. Laurel shook her head.

Savannah caught the action from the corner of her eye. Putting her enjoyment of Ronnie on hold for an instant, she turned her head, taking in the total package of sisterly disapproval.

"Don't knock it till you've tried it," she said peevishly, forgetting about love, forgetting about Laurel's current state of frailty and her own vow to help her baby sister through it all. Right now *her* needs were all that mattered, and what she needed most was to get naked with Ronnie Peltier and forget all about her good girl sister and Conroy Cooper and wanting to be something she wasn't. "Loosen up, Laurel. Have a little fun of your own for a change.

"Come on, Ronnie, sweetie," she said, disentangling herself from him and taking him by the hand to lead him away like a prized stallion. "Let's go."

Laurel didn't turn to watch her leave. She sat staring at her drink, staring at Savannah's key ring with the little rubber alligator hanging from it by his tail. The gator looked up at her, jaws open, with a tiny boot lying on its red tongue. It was supposed to be a joke, but she didn't feel like laughing. There wasn't anything funny about people being swallowed up—by alligators or by their own demons.

The noise level in the bar suddenly seemed to increase in volume, the clank of glasses, the noise of the jukebox, the sounds of voices all becoming too loud for her ears. She grabbed the keys and pushed herself away from the bar.

Outside, the protesters had gone, and the news van with them. There was no sign of Savannah and Ronnie Beefcake. Out on the bayou someone was fishing among the spider lilies and water lettuce along the far bank. The sky that had been a fine clear blue earlier was now striped with clouds tumbling up from the Gulf. The wind had come up as well and shook the heart-shaped leaves of a redbud tree that grew at the edge of the parking lot, flipping them inside out.

Laurel stood for a long moment beside the door of the Corvette, just staring across the bayou, wondering if she'd made a mistake in coming back here. Time away had somehow softened memories of Savannah's penchant for self-destruction. The lure of familiar faces had outweighed the potential for resurrecting old pains, old guilt.

"It's not your fault, Baby."

"But he doesn't hurt me."

"You're lucky and I'm not, that's all. Besides, I'd never let him hurt you. I'd kill him first."

"Killing's wrong."

"Lots of things are wrong. That doesn't stop people from doing them."

She raked a hand through her hair and rubbed at the tension in the back of her neck. She should have stayed home, stayed in the quiet seclusion of the courtyard at Belle Rivière. Maybe she could have talked Savannah into it, and they would still be there now as afternoon edged toward evening, sipping iced tea and lounging on the chaises, talking of nothing important. Or she could have taken her sister up on the idea of shopping. Anything would have been better than this outcome.

The *if onlys* piled up one atop the other, adding to the pile she'd started as a child, like live coral settling on dead to form a reef. The layers below were thick with remorse, hard with guilt. *If only she had stopped Daddy from going out in the field that day . . . If only she could make Mama see the truth . . . If only she could make the attorney general believe . . .*

If only she weren't so powerless, so weak . . .

She hung her head and closed her eyes for a moment. When she opened them again, she was staring at the foot pedals of the Corvette—all three of them—and yet another wave of impotence crashed through her. She had never learned to drive a standard transmission.

"Come on, angel," Jack said as he materialized beside her. She shied away from him, but not before he slipped the keys from her limp fingers. He tossed them up in the air, catching them with one hand, and grinned like a pirate. "Let's go for a spin."

Chapter Six

He hopped over the door and settled easily into the driver's seat, his graceful hands smoothing over the leather-wrapped steering wheel. Huey bounded over the passenger door and sat in the bucket seat, head up, mismatched eyes bright, ears perked, alert, and eager for adventure.

Laurel rushed around the hood of the car. "Get that mangy hound out of my sister's car!" she demanded, yanking the door open. She tried to shoo the dog, but he only thought it was a game and yipped at her and wagged his tail in Jack's face as he play-bowed and batted a big paw at the hand she was waving.

"Get out, you flea-bitten, garden-digging, contrary mutt!" She leaned into the car and tried to haul him out bodily, straining and swearing as the dog wriggled and twisted and got his head up in her face and started to lick her.

"Uck!" Laurel jumped back, wiping slime off her face, shooting a glare at Jack. "You could be a little more helpful."

He shrugged and grinned. "He's not my dog."

A growl rumbled between Laurel's teeth. Huey gave her an incredulous look, whined a little, and jumped out of the 'Vette. Jack laughed, amused by her pique and glad to see something in her expression other than the bleakness that had been there a moment ago as she'd stood looking out at the bayou.

He had followed her out of the bar, intrigued by her reaction to Savannah's sudden "date." After the way she'd torn into Jimmy Lee Baldwin, he fully expected to see her chasing her sister down to give her what-for. He hadn't expected to see her standing by the car looking lost and in pain.

Not that that was the reason he had stepped forward and taken the keys from her hand. He wanted to put the Corvette through its paces, that was all. He had given up his Porsche when Evie died. It was too much a symbol of the attitude that had led to her death. He didn't miss the car, but he sometimes missed the raw power, the feel of a sleek machine jumping beneath him, hugging the curves, roaring down the highway. His Jeep got him where he was going, but there was nothing quite like a hot sports car for unleashing something wild in a man.

That was the reason he had snatched the keys from Laurel's hand. It wasn't because he wanted to offer her any kind of comfort. Hell, he wasn't even sure what her problem was. And he didn't want to know. He didn't get involved. If she had a beef with Savannah's taste in men—which encompassed almost the whole of the gender—then she would just have to take it up with Savannah. All he wanted from her was a little fun and the chance to study an intriguing character.

She stood looking at him with stern expectation, her small hand extended. "The keys, Mr. Boudreaux."

He had already put the key in the ignition and looked down now, flicking the little alligator into motion. "But you can't drive this car, can you, sugar?"

"What makes you say that?"

"'Cause you would'a left already. Hop in. I'll drive you home."

"I have no intention of going anywhere with you. Give me the keys. I'll walk home."

"Then I'll walk with you," Jack said stubbornly. He pulled the keys back out and stuffed them into the pocket of his jeans as he climbed out. "Pretty ladies shouldn't go walking 'round these parts alone just now," he said, giving her a look of concern he would never admit to. "But I'll warn you, sugar, Savannah's gonna be none too pleased to hear you left her pet 'Vette in the parking lot at Frenchie's. There ain't liable to be nothin' left come morning."

Laurel heaved a sigh and weighed her options. She could ride home with Jack Boudreaux, or she could walk home with Jack Boudreaux. There was no reliable taxi service in Bayou Breaux; a town where people were seldom in a hurry to get anywhere didn't warrant it. She didn't know anyone else at Frenchie's to ask for a ride home, and Aunt Caroline wasn't likely to be back from Lafayette to come and get her.

"Women shouldn't accept rides from men they barely know, either," she said, easing herself down in the bucket seat, her gaze fixed on Jack.

"What?" he asked, splaying a hand across his bare chest, the picture of hurt innocence. "You think *I'm* the Bayou Strangler? Oh, man . . ."

"You could be the man."

"What makes you think it's a man? Could be a woman."

"Could be, but not likely. Serial killers tend to be white males in their thirties."

He grinned wickedly, eyes dancing. "Well, I fit that bill, I guess, but I don' have to kill ladies to get what I want, angel."

He leaned into her space, one hand sliding across the back of her seat, the other edging along the dash, corralling her.

That strange sense of desire and anticipation crept along her nerves. If she leaned forward, he would kiss her. She could see the promise in his eyes and felt something wild and reckless and completely foreign to her raise up in answer, pushing her to close the distance, to take the chance. His eyes dared her, his mouth lured— masculine, sexy, lips slightly parted in invitation. What fear she felt was of herself, of this attraction she didn't want.

"It's power, not passion," she whispered, barely able to find her voice at all.

Jack blinked. The spell was broken. "What?"

"They kill for power. Exerting power over other human beings gives them a sense of omnipotence . . . among other things."

He sat back and fired the 'Vette's engine, his brows drawn pensively as he contemplated what she'd said. "So, why are you going with me?"

"Because there are a dozen witnesses standing on the gallery who saw me get in the car with you. You'd be the last person seen with me alive, which would automatically make you a suspect. Patrons in the bar will testify that I spurned your advances. That's motive. If you were the killer, you'd be pretty stupid to take me away from here and kill me, and if this killer was stupid, someone would have caught him by now."

He scowled as he put the car in gear. "And here I thought you'd say it was my charm and good looks."

"Charming men don't impress me," she said flatly, buckling her seat belt.

Then what does? Jack wondered as he guided the car slowly out of the parking lot. A sharp mind, a man of principles? He had one, but wasn't the other. Not that it mattered. He wasn't interested in Laurel Chandler. She would be too much trouble. And she was too uptight to go for a man who spent most of his waking hours at Frenchie's—unlike her sister, who went for any man who could get it up. Night and day, those two. He couldn't help wondering why.

The Chandler sisters had been raised to be belles. Too good for the like of him, ol' Blackie would have said. Too good for a no-good coonass piece of trash. He glanced across at Laurel, who sat with her hands folded and her glasses perched on her slim little nose and thought the old man would have been right. She was prim and proper, Miss Law and Order, full of morals and high ideals and upstanding qualities . . . and fire . . . and pain . . . and secrets in her eyes. . . .

"Was I to gather from that conversation with T-Grace that you used to be an attorney?" she asked as they turned onto Dumas and headed back toward downtown.

He smiled, though it held no real amusement, only cynicism. "Sugar, 'attorney' is too polite a word for what I used to be. I was a corporate shark for Tristar Chemical."

Laurel tried to reconcile the traditional three-piece-suit corporate image with the man who sat across from her, a baseball cap jammed down backward on his head, his Hawaiian shirt hanging open to reveal the hard, tanned body of a light heavyweight boxer. "What happened?"

What happened? A simple question as loaded as a shotgun that had been primed and pumped. What happened? He had succeeded. He had set out to prove to his old man that he could do something, be something, make big money. It hadn't mattered that Blackie was long dead and gone to hell. The old man's ghost had driven him. He had succeeded, and in the end he had lost everything.

"I turned on 'em," he said, skipping the heart of the story. The pain he endured still on Evie's behalf was his own private hell. He didn't share it with anyone. "*Rogue Lawyer.* I think they're gonna make it into a TV movie one of these days."

"What do you mean, you turned on them?"

"I mean, I unraveled the knots I'd tied for them in the paper trail that divorced them from the highly illegal activities of shipping and dumping hazardous waste," he explained, not entirely sure why he was telling her. Most of the time when people asked, he just blew it off, made a joke and changed the subject. "The Feds took a dim view of the company. The company gave me the ax, and the Bar Association kicked my ass out."

"You were disbarred for revealing illegal, potentially

dangerous activities to the federal government?" Laurel said, incredulous. "But that's—"

"The way it is, sweetheart," he growled, slowing the 'Vette as the one and only stop light in Bayou Breaux turned red. He rested his hand on the stick shift and gave Laurel a hard look. "Don' make me out to be a hero, sugar. I'm nobody's saint. I lost it," he said bitterly. "I crashed and burned. I went down in a ball of flame, and I took the company with me. I had my reasons, and none of them had anything to do with such noble causes as the protection of the environment."

"But—"

" 'But,' you're thinking now, 'mebbe this Jack, he isn't such a bad guy after all,' yes?" His look turned sly, speculative. He chuckled as she frowned. She didn't want to think he could read her so easily. If they'd been playing poker, he would have cleaned her pockets for her.

"Well, you're wrong, angel," he murmured darkly, his mouth twisting with bitter amusement as her blue eyes widened. "I'm as bad as they come." Then he flashed his famous grin, dimples biting into his cheeks. "But I'm a helluva good time."

The light had not yet turned green, but he floored the accelerator, sending the Corvette lunging forward like a thoroughbred bolting from the starting gate. A pickup coming down Jackson had to skid sideways to avoid hitting them. Its driver stuck his head out the window and shouted obscenities after them. Laurel grabbed the armrest and gaped at Jack. He laughed as he shifted the car, feeling wicked, feeling reckless. Miz Laurel Chandler needed some shaking up, and he was just the guy to do it.

They barreled down Dumas, the business district a blur. Laurel cut a glance toward the courthouse, fully expecting to see beacons flash on one of the parish cruisers in the parking lot, but they shot past without incident and headed toward the edge of town. Past the brick townhouses, past the shrines to Mary, past the cutoff to L'Amour, past Belle Rivière, and into the country, where planters warred with the Atchafalaya for control of the land.

Apprehension clutched Laurel's stomach. She had taken a calculated risk getting in the car with Jack Boudreaux, but she thought her logic had been sound. Now other possibilities flashed in her mind. Maybe the killer hadn't been smart, just lucky. Maybe Jack was just plain crazy. Nothing he'd said or done so far in their short acquaintance could have convinced her otherwise.

God, wouldn't that be just the way? She would have survived every rotten thing that had happened in her life to date, fought her way through a breakdown, only to be done in by a disbarred lunatic.

She pushed the fear aside and let anger take hold.

"What the hell are you doing?" she yelled, twisting toward him on her seat. The needle on the speedometer had gone out of her range of vision.

"Taking you for a ride, angel!"

He pushed a cassette into the tape player, then settled back in his seat, right hand resting lightly on the steering wheel, left arm propped on the door frame. Harry Connick, Jr., blared out of the speakers—"Just Kiss Me." The road stretched out before them like a ribbon, flat and snaking around canebrakes and copses of trees, skipping over fingers of Bayou Breaux. Driveways to plantations blinked past, and the countryside grew wilder with every second.

Laurel looked behind her, toward rapidly retreating civilization, and kicked herself mentally for taking such a ridiculous chance.

"I don't want to go for a ride! I want to go home!" she shouted, smacking Jack hard on the shoulder with a fist. "Turn this car around right now!"

"Can't!" he called back to her.

"The hell you can't!"

Jack started to shoot her another grin, but swallowed it as she reached into her purse and pulled out a gun.

"Jesus!"

"Stop the damn car!"

She looked mad enough to shoot him. Her dark

brows were drawn together in a furious scowl, her mouth
pressed into a thin white line. Her glasses were slipping
down her nose, and the wind was tearing at her hair and
making her blink, but none of that negated the fact that
she had a stainless steel Lady Smith clutched between
her dainty little hands.

He jerked his attention back to the road. They were
coming up too fast on a sharp lefthand curve. He let off
the gas and touched the brake, shifting down into fourth.
The engine roared in protest, but the 'Vette came under
control, rocking only slightly as it bent around the curve.
They might have made it if it hadn't been for the alligator taking up half the road.

"Shit!"

"Aaaahhh!"

He swerved to miss the gator, but they missed the
end of the curve, as well, right-side wheels hitting the
shoulder and yanking the 'Vette off the road. Jack fought
with the steering wheel to keep the car upright, swearing
a blue streak through clenched teeth. Their momentum
sent them crashing through the dense undergrowth, the
'Vette bucking and rocking like a spooked horse, brush
and grass and cattails whipping at the windshield. They
finally came to rest at the base of a sweetgum tree, just
inches from smashing into the trunk. Just beyond the
tree the land became water.

"Oh, my God. Oh, my God," Laurel muttered over
and over. She was shaking like a palsy victim. The gun
lay at her feet, and she stared at it, grateful she hadn't
taken the safety off.

Jack leaned over and caught her chin in his hand,
turning her face toward him. "Are you okay? Are you all
right?" he demanded, his voice harsh and low. He was
breathing as hard as if he'd carried the car out here on
his back.

Laurel looked at him, stunned, shaken. "You're
bleeding."

"What?"

"You're bleeding."

Lifting a hand, she brushed at a line of red above his

left eye, smearing it with her thumb. He caught her by
the wrist and drew back to see the blood on her hand,
then looked in the cockeyed rearview mirror to check
out the wound himself.

"Must'a hit the windshield."

"You should have worn your seat belt," Laurel mumbled, still too shaken to be coherent. "You might have
been killed."

"No one would'a missed me, sugar," he said darkly as
he fought to get his door open. Swearing in French, he
gave up and climbed over it to survey the damage to the
car.

An ominous hiss sounded beneath the long, sleek
hood; steam billowed out from under it. The paint job
was shot, scratched all to hell by the bushes and saplings
they had crashed through. The wheels would be out of
alignment, and it would be a pure damn miracle if the
undercarriage wasn't twisted.

"Oh, man, Savannah's gonna have my ass."

"Not if I have it first," Laurel said, stepping across
the console to crawl over Jack's door. Hers was opera-
tional, but too near the trunk of a willow to get open.
With both feet planted on the squishy, oozy ground, she
faced Jack, her hands jammed on her hips and fury lighting a fire in her eyes. "Of all the stupid, irresponsible—"

"Me?" He slapped his hands against his chest, incredulous. "You were the one pointing the gun!"

"—moronic, sophomoric, juvenile things to do. I
can't believe anyone would—" She broke off as he
started laughing. "What?"

He only laughed harder, wiping at his eyes, holding
his stomach.

Laurel frowned. "I don't see the least little thing
funny about this."

"Oh—yeah—you got a lawyer's sense of humor all
right." Jack straightened and tried to compose himself.
"The whole thing's ridiculous. Doncha see it? You, you
prim little angel, pull a gun on me. We almost hit an
alligator—" He broke off and started laughing again.

Laurel watched him, feeling her temper let go by de-

grees. They were safe. Savannah's car was worse for
wear, but no one had been hurt. As anger and fear subsided, she began to see the lunacy of the situation. How
would they ever explain it? She put a hand to her mouth
and giggled.

Jack caught the motion and the stifled sound. He
looked at her, at the sparkle in her eyes and the shaking
of her shoulders as laughter tried to escape, and he felt
as though he'd been hit in the head all over again. On
impulse he reached out and pulled her hand down, grinning like an idiot at the bright smile that lit up her face.
Dieu, she was pretty. . . .

"I don't know what I'm laughing about," she said,
embarrassed.

"I don't care." He shook his head, stepping closer.
"But you oughta do it more often, angel."

Her glasses were askew, and he took them off as he
moved closer still. Laurel stopped laughing . . .
stopped breathing. Her gaze was locked on his face. Her
body was very aware of his nearness, responding to it in
ways that were instinctive and fundamentally feminine—
warming, melting. She was backed up against the side of
the car, caught between an immovable object and an irresistible force. He lifted a hand to stroke her hair, low-
ering his mouth toward hers inch by inch.

She should have moved. She should have stopped
him. She didn't know much about this man, and what
she did know was hardly good. He was—what had Savannah called him?—a writer, a rake, a rogue. He was a
man with a reputation for seduction and a past that was
probably shady, to say the very least. He had no business
touching her, and she had no business wanting him to.
She should have stopped him. But she didn't.

She shivered at the first touch of his lips, blinking as
if the contact had given her a shock. He held her gaze,
his eyes dark and intense, mesmerizing. Then he settled
his mouth over hers, and thought ceased. Her eyes
drifted shut. Her hands wound into the fabric of his
shirt. Jack pulled her close, slanting his mouth across
hers, taking possession of it. At the first intrusion of his

tongue, she gasped a little, and he took full advantage,
thrusting slowly, deeply, into the honeyed warmth of her
mouth.

She tasted sweet, and she felt like heaven against
him. Jack groaned deep in his chest and pressed closer.
The scent of her filled his head. Not expensive perfume,
but soap and baby powder. He spread his legs and
inched closer, fire shooting through him as his thighs
brushed the outside of hers and his groin nudged her
belly.

The need was instantaneous and stronger than anything he'd known in a long time. Strong enough to make
him think, something he generally avoided doing when
he was enjoying a lady's charms. It was crazy to want like
this.

Crazy . . . She'd had a breakdown. She was vulnerable, fragile. Like Evie had been.

Desire died like a flame that had been suddenly
doused. Jesus, what kind of jerk was he? He didn't
bother to answer that question. It was a matter of record.
He was the kind of man who took what he wanted and
never gave a thought to anyone else. Selfish, self-absorbed. He had no business touching her.

Laurel opened her eyes as Jack stepped away. She
felt dizzy, weak, as shaken as she had been when the car
had finally rolled to a halt. Like a woman in a daze, she
lifted a hand and touched her fingers to her lips, lips that
felt hot and swollen and thoroughly kissed. Her skin
seemed to be melting—warm, wet—then she blinked
and realized with no small amount of surprise that it had
started to rain.

The sky that had shone in various shades of blue all
day like a lovely sapphire had gone suddenly leaden.
Weather in the Atchafalaya was always capricious. A perfect afternoon could yield to a hurricane by evening, or a
tornado, or a shower. Showers could become torrential
downpours in the blink of an eye.

"We should get the top up on the car," she said
blankly, her body not receiving any of her brain's com-
mands to move.

Jack didn't move, either. He stood there in the rain looking tough and sexy. His cap was gone. His tousled black hair glittered with moisture. It ran down off his nose, dripped from his scarred chin. The bleeding on his forehead had stopped, leaving an angry red line. His eyes were dark and unreadable, and Laurel shifted nervously against the side of the car.

"I . . . I don't ordinarily just let men kiss me," she felt compelled to explain. She didn't even kiss on the first date. It had taken Wesley months to coax her into bed, months before she had trusted him enough.

He grinned suddenly, once again transforming himself. "Hey, I'm no ordinary guy," he said, shrugging, arms wide, palms up.

They worked together to get the top up and secured on the 'Vette.

"We'll have to walk for help," Jack said, raising his voice as the rain began to fall harder. "This car, she's not gonna go nowhere, and the rain could keep up all night."

Laurel said nothing, but followed him along the path they had mowed back out to the road, glad there was no sign of the alligator. She took a good look at her surroundings, getting her bearings from familiar landmarks. If you followed the dirt path into the woods to the north, you eventually came to the place where Clarence Gauthier kept his fighting dogs. A sign made from a jagged piece of cypress siding was posted on the stump of a swamp oak that had been struck by lightning and killed twenty years ago: "Keep Out—Trespasser Will Be Ate."

"Come on, sweetheart," Jack said, nodding toward town.

"No." Laurel shook her head and swiped at the rain drizzling down across her face. "This way." She turned and headed east.

"Sugar, there's nothin' that way but snakes and gators," he protested.

A ghost of a smile turned the corners of her mouth. Snakes and alligators. And Beauvoir, her home.

• • •

Beauvoir made Tara look like low-rent housing. It stood at the end of the traditional *allée* of ancient, moss-draped live oak, a jewel of the old South, immaculately preserved and painted pristine white. A graceful horseshoe-shaped double stairway led from the ground level to the upper gallery of the house. Six twenty-four-foot-tall Doric columns stood straight and white along each of the four sides of the building, supporting the overhang of the Caribbean-style roof. Entrance doors, centered on both the upper and the lower levels of the house, boasted fan lights and sidelights and were flanked by two sets of French doors, which were themselves set off by louvered shutters painted a rich, money green. Three dormers with Palladian windows called attention to the broad-hipped slate roof. A glassed-in cupola crowned the architectural work of art.

Beauvoir was a sight to take the breath away from preservationists. Laurel thought it might have inspired something like awe or love in her, as well, if her father had lived. But the plantation had gone into her mother's control at his death, and Vivian had seen fit to bring Ross Leighton to it. Laurel doubted she would ever feel anything but regret and loss when standing before the facade of Beauvoir—regret for her father's untimely death, for the childhood she had endured instead of enjoyed, loss for the generations of tradition that would die with Vivian. Neither Laurel nor Savannah would ever live here again. The memories were too unhappy.

It was a pity. There were few houses of its ilk left. Fire and flood had claimed many over the years. Neglect had taken its share. The cost of keeping up a house of that size was an enormous financial burden in an area that had suffered too many lean years in the decades since the fall of the Confederacy. In modern times greed had claimed most of the rest. Many a fine old home had survived all else only to fall to the wrecking ball, making way for oil derricks and chemical factories.

Laurel walked up the drive, lost in thought, almost

forgetting the man who walked beside her. She jumped a little when he spoke.

"If this is your home, how come you're not stayin' here?"

"That's none of your business, Mr. Boudreaux."

Mr. Boudreaux again. The bright-eyed angel who had taken him halfway to heaven with a kiss was in full retreat. "Just like it's none of my business why you're carryin' a gun around in your pocketbook?"

Laurel let silence be her answer. She had no intention of telling him the gun had been a necessary fashion accessory back in Georgia, when death threats had come in the mail as often as sweepstakes offers. Wesley had been appalled at the thought of her carrying a handgun. Jack Boudreaux had laughed. She herself saw the gun as a sign of weakness, but she carried it still, unable to part with the security it represented.

"You don' live here. Savannah don' live here. Who's left?"

She walked on for a moment. "Vivian. Our mother. And her husband, Ross Leighton."

Vivian. Jack arched a brow at the flat tone of voice. Not *our mother, Vivian,* but *Vivian.* A name spoken like that of an acquaintance—and one she was not overly fond of at that. There was a story there. Jack had never in his life called his mother anything but Maman right up to the day she died. A matter of respect and love. He heard neither in Laurel's voice, saw neither in her face. Her expression was tightly closed, giving away nothing, and her eyes weren't quite visible to him behind the rain-streaked lenses of her glasses.

She had grown quieter and quieter on the hike, not even rising to the bait of one of his lawyer jokes, but pulling in on herself and drawing a curtain of silence around her. Coming home wasn't eliciting the traditional joyous response. Her step didn't lighten, the closer they got. She marched along like a prisoner being escorted to the penitentiary.

And you would do the same, Jack, if you were walking down the path to that tarpaper shack on Bayou Noir.

It wasn't the dwelling that mattered. It was the memories.

That revelation made him glance once again at the woman who walked beside him. A grand house didn't guarantee happiness. She might have had as bleak a childhood as his own. The possibility stirred the threads that might have formed a bond between them if he hadn't known enough to snap them off. He didn't want bonds.

A white Mercedes sedan was parked in front of the house, looking like an ad layout for the car company, waiting for some elegant couple to emerge from the grand house so they could be whisked away in Bavarian-made opulence to some nearby exclusive restaurant for dinner. It was Saturday night, Laurel reminded herself. Dinner and dancing at the country club. Socializing with peers. As queen bee of Partout Parish society, Vivian had the night to lord it over the less wealthy. She wasn't going to care for an interruption to her plans.

Laurel tried to tamp down the automatic rise of anxiety as she pressed the lighted button beside the door. She could feel Jack's eyes on her, knew he was wondering why she would feel compelled to ring the bell at the house she had grown up in, but she offered nothing in the way of explanation. It was too complicated. She had ceased to feel welcome in this house the night her father died. Beauvoir was not a home; it was a house. The people in it were people she would sooner have considered strangers than family. And those were feelings that brought on an even more complicated mix of emotions—resentment and guilt warring within her for supremacy over her soul.

The servant who answered the door was no one Laurel had ever seen before. Vivian and Ross were not the kind of people who inspired great loyalty in their employees. Vivian fired maids and cooks with regularity, and those she didn't fire were usually driven away by her personality. This maid, a whey-faced zombie in a sober gray uniform, looked at her blankly when she announced herself and left the cool white entry hall without a word, presumably to go find her mistress.

"Fun girl," Jack muttered, making a face.

Laurel said nothing. She stood where she had stopped just inside the door, dripping rainwater on the black-and-white marble floor. While Jack inspected the portrait of Colonel Beau Chandler that hung in a huge gilt frame over a polished Chippendale hall table, she caught a glimpse of herself in the beveled mirror that hung on the opposite wall above another priceless antique table. There was also a mirror at floor level, where antebellum belles had checked their hems and made certain their ankles weren't showing. Laurel wasn't concerned about her ankles. She winced inwardly as she took in her drenched hair and soggy blouse. A fist of anxiety tightened in her stomach. The same one she had felt as a child coming in from play with a grass stain on her dress.

". . . *what's the matter with you, Laurel? Shame on you! Nice girls don't get stains on their clothing. You're a Chandler, not some common little piece of trash. It's your duty to conduct yourself accordingly. Now go to your room and get changed, and don't come down until I call for you. Mr. Leighton is coming to dinner. . . .*"

"Hey, sugar, you okay?"

She jerked her head around and looked up at Jack, who was eyeing her warily.

"You look like you saw a ghost," he said. "You're whiter than that big boat of a car sittin' outside."

Laurel didn't answer him. The sound of a sharp, angry voice caught her ear, and she looked toward the door that led to the parlor, her blood pressure jumping higher with every word.

". . . told you never to disturb me when I'm getting ready for a dinner engagement."

"Yes, ma'am, but—"

"Don't you talk back to me, Olive."

Silence reigned for several moments, expectation swelling in the air. Laurel pulled her glasses off and slicked a hand back through her hair, hating herself for giving in to the impulse.

"*. . . be a good girl, Laurel. Always look your best, Laurel. . . .*"

Vivian stepped out of the parlor. She was fifty-three now, but still looked like Lauren Hutton—cool, elegant, alabaster skin, and eyes the color of aquamarines. What outward beauty God had given her, plastic surgery was preserving well. Only a hint of lines beside her eyes, none near the sharply cut mouth that was painted a rich, enticing red. Her body looked as slender and hard as a marble wand, and was draped to perfection in emerald green silk. The simple sheath masterfully accented the sleek lines of her body.

The heels of her pumps snapped against the tile floor as she came toward them, her attention on the clasp of the diamond bracelet she was fastening. Then her head came up, and she touched a hand to her neatly coiffed ash blond hair, a gesture Laurel remembered from infancy.

Vivian's eyes went wide with shock. "Laurel, what in God's name have you been doing?" she demanded, her gaze sliding down Laurel from the top of her wet head to the tips of her ruined canvas sneakers.

"We had a little accident."

"Well, for heaven's sake!"

Vivian's gaze flicked to Jack and held hard and fast on him, disapproval beaming from her like sonic waves. Jack met her look with insolence and a slow, sardonic smile. His shirt still hung open. He stood with his hands jammed at the waist of his jeans and one leg cocked. Finally he gave a mocking half bow.

"Jack Boudreaux, at your service."

Vivian stared at him for a second longer, obviously debating the wisdom of snubbing him. Jack would have laughed if it hadn't been for Laurel. He knew exactly what was going through Vivian Chandler Leighton's mind. He didn't quite fit into any of the neat little pigeon holes she usually assigned people to. He was notorious, disreputable; he wrote gruesome pulp fiction for a living;

and he had a past as shady as the backwaters of the Atchafalaya. Women like Vivian would ordinarily have written him off as trash, but he was stinking rich. The Junior League didn't have an official category for riffraff with money.

"Mr. Boudreaux," she said at last, nodding to him but not offering her hand. The smile was the one she had been trained to give Yankees and liberal democrats. "I've heard so much about you."

He grinned his wicked grin. "None of it good, I'm sure."

Ross Leighton chose that moment to make his appearance. He stepped out of his study down the hall, a glass of scotch in his hand, looking dapper and distinguished in a tan linen suit. He was of medium height and sturdy frame, with a ruddy face and a full head of steel gray hair he wore swept back in a style that suggested vanity.

"We have company, Vivian?" he asked, ambling down the hall, lord of the manor, usurper to the throne of Jefferson Chandler. He wore a big smile that tended to fool too many people. It didn't fool Laurel. It never had. It widened as he recognized her, and he came toward her, chuckling. "Laurel! My God, look at you! You look like a drowned mouse."

He bent to kiss her cheek, and she stepped away from him, sliding her glasses back on and tilting her chin up to a truculent angle.

Jack watched the exchange with interest. There had been no words of greeting or concern from any of them, and if looks could have killed, Ross Leighton would have been dead on the floor. Charming family.

"We had us a li'l car trouble," Jack said, drawing Leighton's attention away from Laurel. "You got a tractor I could borrow? If we don' get that car out'a where it is quick, the swamp she's gonna swallow it right up tonight."

"It's a poor night to be out on a tractor," Ross said, chuckling, bubbling over with condescending bonhomie.

Jack slicked a hand over his damp hair, then clamped it on Ross Leighton's shoulder, flashing a grin as phony as the older man's laugh. "Ah, well, me, I don' mind gettin' a li'l wet," he said, thickening his accent to the consistency of gumbo. "It's not like I'm wearin' no five-hun'erd-dollar suit, no?"

Ross cast a pained look at the hand print on the shoulder of his jacket as he led the way back down the hall to his study so he could call the plantation manager and order him to go out in the rain with Jack.

Laurel watched them go, wishing she could have been anywhere but here. She wasn't ready to deal with Vivian yet. She would have liked another day, maybe two, just to settle herself and gather her strength. She would at least have liked to look presentable instead of like a drowned mouse. Damn Ross Leighton—with that one offhand remark he had managed to make her feel like a ten-year-old all over again.

"Laurel, what on earth are you doing out with that man?" Vivian asked, her voice hushed and shocked. She pressed a bejeweled hand to her throat as if to make certain Jack hadn't somehow managed to steal the diamond-and-emerald pendant from around her neck.

Laurel sighed and shook her head. "It's nice to see you, too, Mama," she said with the faintest hint of sarcasm. "Don't worry about our well-being. Jack hit his head, but other than that we're fine."

"I can see that you're fine," Vivian snapped.

She turned and went back into the parlor, expecting Laurel to follow, which she did, reluctantly. Vivian lowered herself gracefully onto one of a pair of elegant wing chairs done in cream moiré silk. Laurel ignored the implied dictate to occupy the other. That was a trap. She was wet and presumably dirty. She knew better than to touch the furniture while she was in such an appalling state of dishabille. She stationed herself on the other side of the gold Queen Anne settee, instead, and waited for the show to begin.

"You've been in town for days without so much as

calling your mother!" Vivian declared. "How do you
think that makes me feel?" She sniffed delicately and
shook her head, pretending to blink away tears of hurt.
"Why, just this morning, Deanna Corbin Hunt was asking me how you were doing, and what could I say to
her? You remember Deanna, don't you? My dear good
friend from school? The one who would have written you
a letter of recommendation to Chi-O if you hadn't broken
my heart and decided not to pledge?"

"Yes, Mama," Laurel said dutifully and with resignation. "I remember Mrs. Hunt."

"I can only imagine what they all think," Vivian went
on, eyes downcast, one hand fussing with a loose thread
on the arm of the chair. "My daughter home for the first
time in how long, and she isn't staying in my home,
hasn't even bothered to call me."

Laurel refrained from pointing out that telephones
worked two ways. Vivian was determined to play the
tragically ignored mother. She had never been one to see
ironies, at any rate. "I'm sorry, Mama."

"You should be," Vivian murmured, casting big blue
eyes full of hurt up at her daughter. "I've been feeling
just ragged with worry, not knowing what to think. I
swear, it'd like to have given me one of my spells."

Guilt nipped at Laurel's conscience at the same time
the cynic in her called her a sucker. She'd spent her
entire childhood tiptoeing around the danger of causing
one of her mother's "spells" of depression, and her feelings had engaged in a constant tug-of-war between pity
and resentment. On the one hand, she felt Vivian
couldn't help being the way she was; on the other, she
felt her mother used her supposed fragility to control and
manipulate. Even now, Laurel couldn't reconcile the po-
larized feelings inside her.

"How do you think it looks to my friends to have my
daughter staying in town with her lesbian aunt, instead
of with me?"

"You don't know that Aunt Caroline is a lesbian,"
Laurel snapped. "And what difference would it make if

she were?" she asked, pacing away from the settee, away from her mother, and toward the mahogany sideboard, where half a dozen decanters stood on a silver tray. She wished fleetingly that her stomach could have handled a drink, because her nerves sure as hell could have used one about now. But she turned away from it and went to the French doors to look out at the rain and the gathering gloom of night.

"It's nobody's business who Aunt Caroline sees," she said. "Besides, I don't hear you complaining about the fact that your other daughter *lives* with Caroline."

Vivian's perfectly painted mouth pressed into a tight line. "I quit concerning myself with Savannah's actions long ago."

"Yes, you certainly did," Laurel mumbled bitterly.

"What was that?"

She bit her lip and checked her temper. No purpose would be served by pursuing this line of conversation now. Vivian was the queen of denial. She would never accept blame for her daughters' not turning out the way she had planned.

She pulled in a calming breath and turned away from the window, her arms folded tightly against herself, despite the fact that her clothes were soaking wet. "I said, what's so wrong with Jack Boudreaux?"

Vivian gave her a truly scandalized look. "What *isn't* wrong with him? For heaven's sake, Laurel! The man barely speaks the same language we do. I have it on good authority that he comes from trash, and that's no great surprise to me now that I've met him."

"If he were wearing a linen suit, would he be respectable then?"

"If he were wearing any less of a shirt, I would ask him to leave the house," she stated unequivocally. "I don't care how famous he may be. He writes trash, and he is trash. Blood will tell, after all."

"Will it?"

"My, you're snippy tonight," Vivian observed primly. "That's hardly the way I raised you."

She rose and went to the sideboard to prepare herself a drink. For medicinal purposes, of course. Very deliberately she selected ice cubes from the sterling ice bucket with a sterling ice tongs and dropped them into a chunky crystal glass. "I'm simply trying to guide you, the way any good mother would. You don't always seem to know what's best, but I would have thought you had better sense than to get involved with a man like Jack Boudreaux. God knows, your sister wouldn't hesitate, but you . . . Coming away from your little trouble and all, especially . . ."

"Little trouble." Laurel watched her mother splash gin over the ice and dilute it with tonic water. The aroma of the liquor, cool and piney, drifted to her nostrils. Cool and smooth and dry, like gin, that was Vivian. Never mar the surface of things with anything so ugly as the truth.

"I had a breakdown, Mama," she said baldly. "My husband left me, my career blew up in my face, and I had a nervous breakdown. That's more than a 'little trouble.' "

True to form, Vivian sifted out the things she didn't want to discuss and discarded them. She settled on her chair once again, crossed her legs, took a sip of her drink. "You married down, Laurel. Wesley Brooks was spineless, besides. You can't expect a man like that to weather much of a storm."

"Wesley was kind and sweet," Laurel said in her ex-husband's defense, not impressing her mother in the least.

"A woman should marry strength, not softness," Vivian preached. "If you had chosen a man of your own station, he would have insisted you give up law and raise his children, and none of this other unpleasantness would have happened."

Laurel shook her head, stunned at the rationalization. If she had married her social equal, a well-bred chauvinist ass, then she could have avoided dealing with The Scott County Case. She could have given up the pursuit of justice and concentrated on more important things, like picking out a silver pattern and planning garden parties.

"We're having guests for dinner tomorrow." Checking the slim gold watch she wore, Vivian set her drink aside and rose, delicately smoothing the wrinkles from her dress. "The guest list will provide more suitable company than what you've been keeping lately."

"I'm really not feeling up to it, Mama."

"But, Laurel, I've already told people you would be here!" she exclaimed, sounding for all the world like a spoiled, petulant teenager. "I was going to call you today and tell you all about it! You wouldn't deny me the chance to save face with my friends, would you?"

"Yes" hovered on her tongue, but Laurel swallowed it back. *Be a good girl, Laurel. Do the proper thing, Laurel. Don't upset Mama, Laurel.* She stared down at her squishy sneakers and sighed in defeat. "Of course not, Mama. I'll come."

Vivian ignored the dolorous tone, satisfied with the answer. A smile blossomed like a rose on her lips. "Wonderful!" she exclaimed, suddenly fluttering with bright energy. She moved from table to mirror and back, smoothing her skirt, checking her earrings, gathering up her evening bag. "We'll sit down at one—after Sunday services, as always. And do wear something nice, Laurel," she added, casting a sidelong look at her wilted, rumpled daughter. "Now, Ross and I are already late for our dinner reservations, so we've got to rush."

"Yes, Mama," Laurel murmured, gritting her teeth as her mother bussed her cheek. "Have a nice evening."

Vivian swept out of the room, regal, imperious, victorious. Laurel watched her go, feeling impotent and beaten. If she hadn't been such a coward, she would have told her mother years ago to go to hell, as Savannah had. But she hadn't. And she wouldn't. Poor, pathetic little Laurel, still waiting for her mother to love her.

She snatched a glass off the sideboard, intending to hurl it across the room at the fireplace, but she couldn't manage to let herself go even that much.

Don't break anything, Laurel. Mama won't love you.

*Don't say the wrong thing, Laurel. Mama won't love you.
Do as you're told, Laurel, or Mama won't love you.*

The front door closed, and she listened to the engine
of the Mercedes fire and the car's tires crunch over the
crushed shell of the drive. Then she set the glass down,
put her hands over her face, and cried.

Chapter Seven

Jack stood in the doorway to the parlor, in the shadows of the now-darkened entry hall. The sound of Laurel's tears tore at him, raked across his heart, and drew not blood, but compassion. He knew nothing of this house, these people, but he knew what it was to be part of a dysfunctional family. He could remember only too well the bitter words, the angry fights, the air of tension that had made him and his sister tiptoe around the house, afraid that any sound they might make would spark an explosion from their father and bring the wrath of Blackie Boudreaux down on one or all of them.

He knew, and that was all the more reason he should have just left. Beauvoir was a nest of snakes. Only a fool would poke at it. He was no fool. He was many things, few of them admirable, but he was no fool.

Still, he didn't move. He stood there and watched as Laurel scrubbed the tears from her face and fought off the next wave of them. She fought to school her breathing into a regular rhythm, blinked furiously at the moisture gathering in her eyes, busied herself cleaning her glasses off with the tail of her shirt. *Dieu*, she was a tough little thing. She thought she was alone. There was no reason she shouldn't have just flung herself down on the fancy gold settee and bawled her eyes out if she wanted to. But she struggled to rein her emotions in, fought for control.

Before sympathy could take root too deeply, Jack pushed himself into motion.

"You ready to go, sugar?"

Laurel jumped at the sound of his voice. Fumbling, she put her glasses back on and smoothed a hand over her hair, which had begun to dry. "I . . . I thought you went to pull the car out."

Jack grinned. "I lied."

Too aware of being alone with him, she stared at him for several moments while the grandfather clock across the room ticktocked, ticktocked. "Why?"

He was prowling around the room, carelessly picking up knickknacks that had been in the family for generations, absently looking them over, setting them aside. He glanced up at her as he picked up a lead crystal paperweight and hefted it in his hand like a baseball.

"'Cause I didn' like your *beau-père*. And I can't say I was all too fond of your *maman*, either."

"They'll be crushed."

"Naw . . ." He grinned that wicked grin again, tossed the paperweight up, and caught it with one hand. Laurel's heart jumped with it. "They'll be pissed. Late for dinner."

They *would* be pissed. Vivian especially so. Laurel fought the urge to smile, her mouth quirking like the Mona Lisa's. "Well, you're easily amused."

"So should we all be, angel. Life's too short."

He was right beside her now, facing the opposite direction. His arm nearly brushed her shoulder as he reached out to touch something on the sideboard. She told herself to move, but before she could he turned and was behind her, his arms slipping around her, head bending down so he could whisper in her ear.

"So why don' we go find your old bedroom and

spend some time amusin' each other, *catin*? Me, I'd like
to get out'a these wet clothes and into somethin' . . .
warm. . . ."

A shiver feathered over her skin as his breath trailed
down the side of her neck and right on down the front of
her blouse, stirring those strange embers of desire inside
her. She tried to step away from him, but he held her
easily, pressing his hands flat against her stomach. He
nibbled his way down the side of her neck, nuzzling
aside the collar of her blouse to sample the curve of her
shoulder, and her pulse jumped.

Jack gave a low, throaty chuckle. She sure as hell
wasn't thinking about Lady Vivian now. "Come on,
sugar," he murmured. "There's gotta be a whole lotta
empty beds in this big ol' barn."

"And they're going to stay that way," Laurel said.
This time when she tried to escape his hold, he let her
go. She shied away and turned to face him. "How do you
propose we get back to town?" she asked, trying to tram-
ple down all her tingling nerve endings with pragmatism.

Jack stuck his hands in his pockets and cocked a hip.
"I called Alphonse Meyette. Him and Nipper's gonna
come tow the 'Vette back to the station. I told him to
stop down to the Landing and have Nipper drive my
Jeep out. I'll give you a ride home, darlin'."

Laurel scowled at the devilish grin. "Where have I
heard that before?"

He leaned toward her, daring her to hold her ground,
dark eyes snapping with mischief. "I'd rather give you a
ride upstairs," he said, his voice dropping to a smoky
rumble.

She couldn't help laughing at his audacity. Crossing
her arms, she shook her head. "I know all about your
reputation with women, Mr. Boudreaux."

He moved closer still, no more than inches from
touching her, and she realized too late that he had her
neatly trapped against the back of the settee. He planted
a hand on either side of her and tilted his head as he
lowered it, his gaze holding hers like a magnet. "Then
how come we're not in bed yet?"

"God, the size of your ego is astonishing," she said dryly.

The dark eyes sparkled, the smile widened, the dimples cut into his cheeks. He bobbed his eyebrows. "You oughta see the rest of me."

The humor did her in. If his statement had indeed been ego, she might have slapped him, she certainly would have singed his ears with a scathing commentary regarding her opinion of Neanderthals who thought a man's worth and a woman's willingness all came down to a few inches of penis. But it was humor in those dark eyes, inviting her to share the joke, not be the butt of it. She tried to give him a stern look and failed, giving over helplessly to giggles instead.

"If I didn't have such healthy self-esteem," Jack said as he leaned a hip against the settee and crossed his arms, "I might be offended."

Laurel sniffed and pushed her glasses up on her nose, feeling better, feeling stronger. Vivian had knocked her badly off balance. Coming to Beauvoir had shaken loose too many feelings she wasn't ready to deal with. But Jack had distracted her from the dark emotional whirlpool that had threatened to suck her in, letting her get her legs back under her. She shot him a sideways glance, wondering if he had any idea she hadn't laughed in this house in twenty years.

The Corvette was extricated from the edge of the swamp with minimal fuss and towed away to Meyette's garage. Laurel watched the proceedings from the passenger's seat of Jack's Jeep with Huey the Hound sitting in Jack's spot behind the wheel. The rain had stopped, leaving everything dripping and glistening. The clouds had cleared a path for a melted bronze sunset that cast the swamp in silhouette. The air was fresh and cool, but the dark underlayment of the bayou lingered as always. Laurel shivered in her damp clothes as her attention drifted from the tow truck to the dense wilderness that lay around them. Without thinking, she raised a hand to nibble at her thumbnail.

She had grown up here on the edge of the Atchafalaya, but she had never felt a party to its secrets. The swamp was a world unto itself, ancient, mysterious, primal. She had always thought of it as an entity, not just an ecosystem. Something with a mind and eyes and a dark, shadowed soul. That impression closed in on her as Alphonse Meyette's tow truck rumbled off toward Bayou Breaux and quiet descended. The expectant, hushed silence of the swamp.

Thoughts of murder came, seeping into her like cold, and she shivered again and rubbed her hands over her arms as an image flashed through her head. A young woman lying out here, alone, dead, the swamp watching, knowing, keeping its secrets . . .

"Hey, ugly, outta my seat."

Jack's voice snapped the terrible vision, and she jumped. Huey grumbled a protest and clambered between the seats to the back, where he curled up in a ball with his back to them.

"Not your dog." Laurel rolled her eyes.

Jack grinned as he climbed behind the wheel, teeth flashing bright in the gloom. "I can't help it if he finds my personality irresistible." He tossed a dirty denim jacket across her lap. "Put that on. I charmed Nipper out of it on your behalf."

Laurel wasn't sure whether she should thank him or not. The jacket reeked of male sweat, cigarette smoke, and gasoline, but the Jeep was open, and the ride back was likely to be a chilly one, considering her damp state. She wrinkled her nose and shrugged into the coat. The sleeves hung past her fingertips.

"You okay?"

She glanced up from rolling the cuffs back.

"You looked a little peaked there a minute ago."

"I was just thinking . . . about that girl they found . . ." And what it would be like to die out here with no one to see, no one to hear but the swamp. She kept that part of her thoughts to herself. She had too vivid an imagination, put herself too easily in the place of others. Not a good trait for someone who had to deal with the victims of violent crimes. It was that inability to draw the line between sympathy and empathy that made her vulnerable.

"Bad business, that," Jack said softly, his hand on the key, his eyes scanning the darkening swamp.

A barred owl called four round notes, then lifted off from the branches of a nearby cypress tree, its wide wings beating the air, barely making a sound. Laurel pulled the smelly jacket tighter around her.

"Did you know any of them?"

He shot her a hard glance. "Are you questioning me, counselor? Should I have a lawyer present?"

Laurel pushed past the question of whether his tone held sarcasm or defensiveness, not sure she wanted to know the answer. "I'm asking an innocent question. Self-professed lady's man that you are, it wouldn't seem too unreasonable that you would have known one of the victims."

"I didn't. None of them were from here."

Four bodies. Four parishes in Acadiana, but not Partout. No victims from Partout Parish, no victims found here. Laurel couldn't help wondering if that was by chance or by design. If Partout Parish might be next on the killer's list. She looked at the wilderness around them and thought again about the terrible loneliness of dying out here.

The swamp was an unforgiving place. Beautiful, brutal bitch. Steamy and seductive and secretive. Death here was commonplace, a part of the cycle. Trees died, fell, decayed, became a part of the fertile ground so more trees could grow from it. Mayflies were eaten by frogs, frogs by snakes, snakes by alligators. No death would find sympathy here. It was a place of predators.

She glanced at Jack. Jack, who had teased her out of her mood at Beauvoir. Jack, with his devil's grin. He wasn't grinning now. That mask had fallen away to reveal the intensity that she suspected was the core of him. Hard. Hot. Shadowed.

"The only place I kill people is on paper, sugar," he said. He pulled a cigarette from his shirt pocket, dangled it from his lip.

The word "liar" rang in his head as he swung the Jeep around in a U-turn and headed for town.

Savannah stood outside the French doors of Coop's study, hiding among the overgrown lilac bushes beside the comfortable old house, watching as he worked. He sat at his desk, hunched over his notebook, a cigar smoldering in the ashtray, a snifter of brandy sitting beside it. The desk lamp was the only light on in the house, creating an oasis of soft, buttery light around him. Through the glass he seemed like a dream, a warm, golden dream she would never be able to grasp and hold on to. Always held at bay by an invisible barrier. Her past. His devotion to his wife.

Damn Astor Cooper. Why couldn't she just die and be done with it? What a cruel bitch she was, hanging on to him with her invisible threads when she was nothing more than a shell. She may have been a lovely woman in her time. Savannah imagined her as being sweet and demure and gracious. Everything *she* wasn't. Respectable, the perfect wife, the perfect hostess. But Coop's wife was nothing now, and she could give him nothing but heartache. Her mind was gone. Only her body lived on, functioning automatically, tended by nurses.

I could give him something. I could give him everything, Savannah thought, absently smoothing her hands down her wrinkled silk tank.

Like she had given Ronnie Peltier everything?

She tightened her jaw at the bitter inner voice, tightened her hold on the lilac branch. She'd had sex with Ronnie because she had wanted to, needed to. There was nothing to feel guilty about. Not the way she had offered herself, not the way she had given herself, not the greedy, insatiable way she had taken him.

"It's what you were made for, Savannah. . . . You always want it, Savannah. . . ."

That was the truth. The truth that had been burned into her brain night after night. She was a born seductress, built for sin. There was no use fighting her true nature.

She hadn't fought it tonight. The scents of sex and Ronnie's Aqua Velva after-shave lingered on her in testimony to the fact. They hadn't even made it to his trailer house before succumbing to their passions. Savannah had made him pull his truck in around back of the old lumber yard and climbed on him right there on the bench seat of his Ford Ranger. Ronnie made no protest, asked for no explanations. That was what she liked about young men—they were uncomplicated. There were no moral millstones weighing down Ronnie Peltier. He was perfectly willing to drop his Levi's and just go at it for the sheer fun of it.

Arousal and shame grappled for control within her, twisting, struggling against each other, and tears rose in her eyes, blurring her vision of Coop as he sat writing.

"Damn you, Conroy Cooper," she mumbled, hating the feelings writhing inside her, and directing that hate at Coop. It was his fault. If she hadn't fallen in love with him, if he weren't so damn noble . . . He was the one who made her feel like a whore.

No. She *was* a whore. She had been born a whore and trained to perfection. Cooper made her ashamed of it.

Crying silently, she pushed herself away from the lilac bush and sidled along the house like a thief. She pressed herself against the clapboard siding and crept along to the edge of the French doors, where she pressed her face against the glass.

Cooper straightened his back slowly, wincing as he set his pen aside. His brain felt numb and empty, like a sponge that had been wrung out by merciless hands. The analogy struck him as one last drop of inspiration, and he started to reach for his pen again to scribble it down when a movement at the French doors caught his peripheral vision.

"Savannah?" He mumbled her name to himself,

straining his eyes against the darkness that cloaked her features. Of course it was. She would come to him now in contrition, as she always did after one of her little blowups. And he would take her back and comfort her. They had gone through this cycle before. Savannah was a creature of habit. He frowned at the thought that her habits included self-inflicted torment and degradation.

She fell into his arms the second he opened the doors, sobbing like a child. Cooper folded his arms around her and rocked her and murmured to her, his lips brushing softly against her wild mane.

"I'm sorry!" she cried, grabbing handfuls of his shirt in her fists. "I'm so, so sorry!"

"Hush," he whispered, his voice low and smooth and soothing. "Don't cry so, darlin', you're breaking my heart."

"You break my heart," Savannah said, aching so, she felt completely raw inside. "All the time."

"No," he murmured. "I love you."

"Love me." She drew a shuddering breath and whispered the words again and again as scalding tears squeezed through the barrier of her tightly closed eyelids. "Love me. Love me."

Wasn't that all she had ever wanted? To be loved. To be cherished. And yet she gave herself away time and again to men who would never love her. Confusion boiled and swelled inside her, and she cried it out against Cooper's solid chest, wrapping herself in his warmth, anchoring herself against his strength. She felt so lost. She wanted to be strong, but she wasn't. She wanted to be good, but she couldn't. The only thing she was good at was sex, and that wasn't enough to make Coop forsake his vows.

"Hush, hush," he whispered, rocking her.

She smelled of sex and cheap cologne. She'd been with another man. He was neither surprised nor dismayed for his own sake. He didn't expect fidelity from Savannah. She was, by her own definition, a harlot. It saddened him, though, in a deeply fundamental way. Savannah was in many ways the embodiment of the South, he thought. Beautiful, wanton, stubborn, victimized . . .

". . . Cooper?"

Savannah leaned back and looked up into his face, her fists still wound into the fabric of his shirt. He blinked at her, his thick blond lashes sweeping down behind his spectacles, clearing the glaze from his too-blue eyes.

"Damn you," she snarled, pushing herself away. "You're not even listening to me! You're off with *her* in your mind, aren't you? Off with Lady Astor. Pure, chaste Lady Astor."

"I wasn't," he said calmly. He went to the desk, dismissing her, and went about the business of putting his notebook and pen away, tamping out the last of a good cigar that had gone to waste.

"You'd rather she were here," Savannah said bitterly. "She wasn't off fucking Ronnie Peltier eight ways from Sunday tonight. No, she's sitting over at St. Joseph's, pretty as an orchid, dumb as a post—"

"Stop it!" Cooper's voice tore like thunder through the air. He wheeled and grabbed her by the arms and gave her a rough shake. He caught himself before he could shake her again and reined his temper in with an effort that made him tremble.

"Damn you, Savannah, why do you do this?" he demanded, his voice harsh, his fingers biting into the flesh of her arms. "You beg for my love, then you make me want to hate you. Why can't you just take what I can give you and be happy with that?"

"Happy?" she whispered bleakly, looking up at him, her heart in her eyes. "I don't know what that is."

Cooper closed his eyes against a hot wave of emotion and pulled her against him, holding her tight.

"Don't hate me, Coop," she said softly, sliding her arms around his waist. "I do enough of that for both of us."

"Shhh . . . Hush . . . " He brushed her hair back from her cheek and pressed a kiss to her temple, then to her mouth. "I love you," he said, the words barely more than a breath as his lips brushed against hers. "I love you."

"Show me."

The hall clock ticked away the seconds of the night. Savannah listened to it in the stillness as she lay curled against Cooper's side. He was asleep, breathing deeply, one arm still holding her close. He looked older sleeping. With his vitality turned off, his athletic energy refueling, there was nothing left but the face that had weathered fifty-eight years of life.

For just a moment she imagined he was her father lying there, alive, holding her next to him. Jeff Chandler would have been fifty-eight if he had lived. And for a moment she allowed herself to wonder what her life would have been like. How different she might have been. She might have been the famous one of the Chandler sisters. She might have been an actress or a fashion designer. And Laurel . . . Laurel might not have needed to fight so hard for justice.

Poor Baby. Guilt nipped her as she thought of the way she'd left Laurel at Frenchie's. She really should have been home now, seeing to it that Laurel was getting some rest. Seeing to her sister's recuperation was her job now. But she had needed this time with Coop. Time without fighting, without words, with nothing but love between them.

There was never anything less than gentleness in his lovemaking. He was always so careful with her. No hurry. No frantic grappling. No rough urgency. Tenderness. Reverence. As if every time was her first time.

No, she thought, her mouth twisting into a parody of a smile. Her first time had been nothing like that.

"You want me, Savannah. I've seen the way you look at me."

"I don't know what you mean—"

"Liar. You're a little tease, that's what you are."

"I'm not—"

*"Well, I'm going to give you what you're asking for,
little girl."*

"No! I don't want you to touch me. I don't like that."

*"Yes, you do. Don't lie to me. Don't lie to yourself.
This is what you were made for, Savannah. . . ."*

And she had closed her eyes against the first burning
pain and damned Ross Leighton to eternal hell.

*Lady-killer . . . Killer . . . "The only place I kill peo-
ple is on paper." . . . Liar . . . You're a liar, Jack. . . .*

He paced the halls of L'Amour, oblivious of the wallpaper that was peeling off the walls, oblivious of the
dust, the dank odor of mildew and neglect, oblivious of
everything but his own inner torment. It snarled and
snaked inside him like a caged beast, and there was
nothing he could do about it but stalk the dark halls of
the house. He couldn't set the beast loose because it terrified him to think what he might do—go mad, kill himself.

Kill himself. The idea had crossed his mind more
than once. But he dismissed it. He didn't deserve the
freedom death would offer. It was his punishment to
live, knowing he was worthless, knowing he had killed
the one person who had seen good in him.

Evie. Her face floated before his mind's eye, soft,
pretty, her dark eyes wide and trusting. Trust—that cut
at him like a razor. She had trusted him. She was as
fragile as fine blown glass, and she had trusted him not
to break her. In the end he had destroyed her, shattered
her. Killed her.

A wild, indistinguishable cry tore up from the depths
of him, and he turned and slammed his fist against the
wall, the sounds of agony and impact echoing through
the empty house. Empty, like his heart, like his soul, like
the bottle of Wild Turkey dangling from the fingers of his
left hand. The beast lunged at its barriers, and he
whirled and flung the bottle and listened to it smash
against a door down the hall.

"Worthless, useless, rotten . . ."

The image of Blackie Boudreaux rose up from one of the dark corners of his mind to taunt, and he stumbled from the hall, through a dark room, and out onto the upper gallery to escape it.

"Bon à rien, tu, bon à rien . . ."

The memory came after him like a demon, painfully sharp and so bright, he squeezed his eyes closed against it. He pressed his back against the brick wall, braced himself, held himself rigid until every muscle quivered with the effort, but nothing stopped the memory from coming.

His mother stood doubled over by the kitchen sink, blood running from her nose and lip. Tears swam in her eyes and streamed down her cheeks, but she didn't cry aloud. She knew better. Blackie didn't want to hear caterwauling; it made him meaner. *Le bon Dieu* knew he was mean enough in the best of times.

Jack clutched at her skirt, frightened, angry, ten years old. Too small to do anything. Worthless, useless, good for nothing. Good for hating. He figured he was an expert at that. He hated his father with every cell of his body, and that hate launched him away from his mother's trembling legs and into Blackie's path as he advanced, arm drawn back for another blow.

A high-pitched scream pierced the air as Marie came running in. Jack didn't glance at his little sister, but yelled for her to get out as he flung himself at their father. He wished he were bigger, stronger, big enough to hit Blackie as hard as Blackie hit Maman, but he wasn't. He was just a puny runt kid, just like Papa always told him.

That didn't mean he wouldn't try.

He balled his fists, meaning to pound his old man as best he could, but Blackie had other ideas. He swung the arm he had pulled back to strike his wife with, instead backhanding Jack across the face, knocking him aside like a doll.

Jack hit the floor, his head spinning and throbbing, tears clouding his vision, hate burning through him like acid.

Then suddenly he wasn't ten anymore. He was a teenager, and he got to his feet and grabbed the iron skillet off the stove and swung it with both hands as hard as he could. . . .

He jerked as his mind slammed the door on the memory.

"The only place I kill people is on paper, sugar. . . ."

From where he stood in the deep shadows of the gallery he could see Belle Rivière. He could see across the darkened courtyard to the back door, where the outside light was still burning. All the windows were dark. Sane people were in bed at this hour. Laurel was in bed.

"And I sit in the still of the night and howl at the moon," he mumbled, sliding down to sit on the weathered floor of the gallery. Huey materialized from the shadows and sat down beside him, a grave look on his face, pendulous lips hanging down.

"You don' know enough to stay away from the like of me, do you, stupid hound?"

Laurel knew enough. She was wary of him.

"And well you should be, *mon ange*," he murmured, staring across at the black windows of Belle Rivière.

She had let him kiss her, had let him get close, but in the end she had shied away. Just as well for her sake. He was a user and a cad. *Lady-killer . . . killer.*

The word simmered in his brain as he pushed himself to his feet and went inside to work.

Chapter Eight

Savannah took the demise of her Corvette with remarkable good grace. It was news of who had been driving she took exception to.

"Jack?" She arched a brow, stiffening slowly but visibly, her back straightening. She sat on Laurel's bed, wearing her champagne silk robe open over a black lace teddy, looking like an ad for Victoria's Secret with her hair mussed and her lips kiss-swollen. "What the hell were you doing out on the bayou road with Jack Boudreaux?"

"A question I asked myself as we hurtled along like some kind of rocket test car on the salt flats," Laurel grumbled as she studied herself with a critical eye in the cheval glass.

The skirt she wore was soft and flowing with a pattern of mauve cabbage roses and deep green leaves on an ivory background. The waist was riding at the top of her hips, and the hem hung nearly to her ankles. Weight loss was hell on the wardrobe. It would have to do. She hadn't brought many good outfits with her. At any rate,

the petal pink cotton summer sweater was baggy enough
to hide the sagging waist. She heaved a sigh of resignation and looked at her sister via the glass.

"I can't drive a stick. He offered—no, he *commandeered,*" she corrected, irritated all over again with his
highhandedness. If he hadn't been so pushy, she never
would have ended up kissing him, never would have
ended up staring at the ceiling half the night.

Savannah frowned, hit unaware by a jolt of jealousy.
Frenchie's was her territory, her little kingdom of men.
Jack Boudreaux was a member of her court. She didn't
like the idea of his sniffing around her baby sister, especially when he had yet to come sniffing around *her.* And
she didn't like the idea of sharing Laurel, either. Laurel
had come home to her big sister for love and comfort,
not to Jack Boudreaux.

"He's trouble," she said, rising to come and stand
behind Laurel. "Stay away from him."

Laurel shot a curious look over her shoulder as Savannah fussed with the lace collar of her sweater. "Yesterday you seemed charmed enough by him."

"It's one thing for me to be charmed by him. I don't
want him charming you, Baby. The man's a cad."

Savannah the great protector. Always watching out
for her while no one watched out for Savannah. A cad
was good enough for Savannah, or a pool shark ten years
her junior, or a married Pulitzer Prize–winner old
enough to be her father. Laurel chewed back the urge to
say something she knew she would regret. She loved her
sister, wanted something better for her than the life Savannah had chosen for herself, but now was not the time
to say so. She had enough on her mind thinking of the
dinner she had no appetite for.

"You said he was a writer. What does he write?"

"Oooh," Savannah cooed, a wicked smile curling the
corners of her mouth and sparkling in her eyes. "Deli-
ciously gruesome horror novels. The kind of stuff that
makes you wonder how the man sleeps nights. Don't you
ever go to the bookstores, Baby? Jack's practically always
on the best-seller lists."

Laurel couldn't remember the last time she'd read anything that wasn't written in legalese. The Case had consumed all her time, pushing all else out of her life— her hobbies, her friends, her husband, her perspective . . . at any rate, she wasn't given to reading the kinds of books that kept people up wide-eyed with fear of everything that went bump in the night. She didn't need to pay money to be horrified and get depressed. She dealt with enough real-life horrors. Depression was something she could get for free.

She tried to reconcile her image of Jack, the piano-playing, car-stealing, kiss-stealing rogue, with her mental image of what a horror novelist would be like, and couldn't. But there was another Jack, the man she had caught glimpses of at odd moments. A harder, darker man with an inner intensity that unnerved her. Just the memory of that man brought out a strange skittishness in her, and so she dismissed all thoughts of him and concentrated instead on the matter at hand.

She looked at herself in the mirror again, deciding she looked like a little girl playing dress-up in her mother's clothes. Not that Vivian had ever allowed them to do such a thing. Savannah rummaged through a drawer in the walnut commode and came back with two safety pins. She made a pair of pleats in the front waist of the skirt and secured them, hiding the pins with the hem of the sweater.

"Instant fit. Old fashion-model's trick," she said absently, studying Laurel with sharp scrutiny.

"Why didn't you stick with it?" Laurel asked.

"You'll wear my new gold earrings," she muttered, then snapped her head up. "What? Modeling?"

"You had a good thing going with that agency in New Orleans."

Savannah sniffed, lifting one shoulder in a casual shrug while she picked up a makeup brush and a pat of blusher and expertly dusted soft mauve along Laurel's cheekbones. "Andre loved me for my blow jobs, not my portfolio. I wasn't good enough—at modeling, that is. I happen to give the world's greatest blow job."

Laurel didn't comment, but Savannah caught the tightening of her jaw, the thinning of her mouth. Disapproval. It stung, and she resented it. "Do what you do best, Baby," she said, a fine razor edge to her voice. "Your thing is justice. My talents lie elsewhere.

"Now, let's take a look at you," she said briskly, setting the makeup aside. "I can't imagine why you're going to this. I would have told Vivian to go to hell."

"You have," Laurel said flatly. "On numerous occasions."

"So it's your turn. She jerks you around like a dog on a leash—"

"Sister, please." She closed her eyes briefly. Lord, if she wasn't up to this fight, what in hell would she do at Beauvoir? A tremor of nerves rattled through her. Dinner with Vivian and company was like dancing through a mine field. God, she thought derisively, how had she ever survived in the courtroom when she was such a coward?

"I could have said no," she said wearily, "but I don't need the trouble. One meal, and I'm off the hook. I might as well get it over with."

Savannah made a noncommittal sound. "Well, please borrow my new gold earrings, and for chrissakes, don't wear those awful Buddy Holly glasses. They make you look like that little chicken in the Foghorn Leghorn cartoons."

Laurel arched a brow. "You don't want me to go, but you want me to look good?"

Her pale eyes turned hard and cold, and a bitter smile cut across her lush mouth. "I want Vivian to look at you and feel like the dried up old hag she is."

Laurel frowned as Savannah went to fetch the earrings from her room. They had always been adversaries—Savannah and their mother. Vivian was too selfish, too self-absorbed to have a daughter as beautiful, as attractive to men as Savannah was. Their rivalry was yet another unhealthy facet in an unhealthy relationship. That rivalry was one reason Laurel had always downplayed her own looks. Always the little diplomat, she hadn't wanted to rock an already listing boat by attracting attention to herself. Her other reason wasn't so noble, she admitted, scowling at herself in the mirror.

If I'm not as pretty as Savannah, then Ross will leave me alone. He picked Savannah, not me. Lucky me.

There wasn't a word for the kind of guilt those memories brought, Laurel thought as Savannah returned. Her robe had slipped off one shoulder as she fiddled with the earrings, revealing a hickey the size of a silver dollar marring her porcelain skin. Laurel's stomach knotted, and she wondered how she was ever going to choke down pot roast.

Sunday dinner at Beauvoir was a tradition as old as the South. The Chandlers had always attended Sunday services—as much out of a sense of duty and obligation to the community as out of reverence for the commandments—then a chosen few would be invited to dine at Beauvoir and pass the day away in genteel pursuits. There were no Chandlers left at Beauvoir, but the tradition endured, a part of Vivian's twisted sense of social responsibility.

If only she had possessed a fraction of that sense of responsibility for her own family, Laurel thought as she stood on the veranda and rang the bell. It had begun to rain again, and she listened to it as she waited, hoping in vain that the soft sound would soothe her ragged nerves. She thumbed a Maalox tablet free of the roll in her skirt pocket and popped it in her mouth.

The downtrodden Olive answered the door, as gray and gloomy as the afternoon, looking at Laurel with dull eyes, as though she had never seen her before. Laurel tried to give her a sympathetic smile as she stepped past the woman and headed toward the main parlor, visions of old zombie movies flickering in the back of her mind.

This would be the perfect setting for a horror movie or a horror novel. The old plantation on the edge of the swamp, a place of secrets, old hatreds, twisted minds. A place where tradition was warped into something gro-

tesque, and family love curdled like spoiled cream. She
tried to imagine Jack writing it, but could picture him
only in a Hawaiian shirt with his baseball cap on backward and that cat-that-got-the-canary grin on his face.
The image brought a ghost of a smile to her lips as she
pictured him here, in the main parlor of Beauvoir, observing the assembled guests.

That he wouldn't exactly fit in was the understate-
ment of the year. Ross stood near the sideboard looking
freshly pressed and perfectly groomed in a silver-gray
suit. He was the model of the well-bred, distinguished
Southern gentleman, right down to his neatly manicured
fingernails. The easy, patronizing smile. The aura of authority.

Laurel dragged her gaze away from him, sure the
hate she felt for him was strong enough, magnetic
enough to draw the attention of everyone in the room.
She focused instead, briefly, on the other guests, quickly
sizing them up in a way that was automatic to her. As a
prosecuting attorney she'd had to draw swift and accu-
rate impressions of victims, perpetrators, prospective
witnesses, defense attorneys. She did so now for many of
the same reasons—to give herself an edge, to formulate a
strategy.

The man Ross was speaking with wore a clergyman's
collar. He was small and thin and balding, and nodded so
often in agreement with Ross's pontificating that he
looked as if he had some kind of nervous condition. She
labeled him as weak and obsequious and moved on.

A middle-aged couple stood behind the settee where
Jack had corralled her the night before. A pair of plump,
pleasant faces—the man's slightly sunburned, the
woman's pale and perfectly made up. The woman wore a
pale pink suit with a flared jacket that looked too crisp
not to be brand-new, and her black hair had that wash-
and-set roundness achieved by an hour of teasing and
back-combing in a chair at Yvette's House of Style. Her
gaze strayed continually, covetously to the obvious signs
of wealth in the room. They would be neighbors, Laurel
guessed. Planters, but not on a par with the massive

Chandler-Leighton holdings. People who would be suitably humbled and impressed with an invitation to Beauvoir.

She moved on to Vivian, enthroned in her wing chair, looking cool and sophisticated in a royal blue linen dress. The other wing chair was occupied by a tall, dark-haired man who sat slightly turned, so that Laurel couldn't see his face. Before she could shift positions to get a quick look at him, Vivian caught sight of her and rose from her chair, the corners of her mouth curling upward in her version of a motherly smile.

"Laurel, darlin'."

She came forward, hands extended. Dutifully, Laurel took hold of her mother's fingers and suffered through the ritual peck on the cheek as they became the focal point in the room.

"Mama."

"We missed you at services this morning."

"I'm sorry. I wasn't feeling up to it."

"Yes, well . . ." Vivian kept the thin smile in place. Only Laurel caught the censure in her gaze. "We know you need your rest, dear. Come meet everyone. Ross, look, Laurel is here."

Ross came forward, his smile like a banner across his face. "Laurel, darlin', aren't you looking pretty today!"

He put a hand on her shoulder, and she moved deftly away, not willing to suffer his touch for anyone's sake. "Ross," she murmured, tipping her head to avoid making eye contact with him.

The clergyman was introduced as Reverend Stipple. His handshake was as soft as a grandmother's. The couple, Don and Glory Trahern, had recently taken over the plantation of Glory's uncle, Wilson Kincaid, whom Laurel remembered vaguely as a friend of her father's. Don Trahern seemed a nice mild-mannered sort. Glory was obviously courting Vivian's favor, smiling too hard and gushing too many pleasantries. Laurel murmured the requisite greeting, then found her gaze straying to the last of the group to be introduced.

The little circle of guests opened to make way for

him, everyone looking up at him as if he were the crown prince of some foreign place come to grace poor little Bayou Breaux with his presence.

". . . and our guest of honor today," Vivian said. "Stephen Danjermond, our district attorney. Stephen, my daughter Laurel."

A setup. Laurel felt as though she'd been blindsided. She had expected Vivian's usual assemblage of minor local royalty. She hadn't expected her mother to play this game. She and Danjermond were the only people in the room younger than forty-five. The only two people conspicuously unattached. She felt like a fool, and she felt like leaving. But she gritted her teeth and held her hand out, tilting what she hoped was a blandly pleasant look up at the district attorney.

"It's a pleasure to meet you, Mr. Danjermond."

"The pleasure is mine," he said smoothly.

His gaze caught hers like a tractor beam and held it, steady, unblinking, calm. Flat calm, like the sea on a windless day. His eyes were a clear, odd shade of green. The color of peridot, fringed by thick, short lashes and set deep beneath a strong, straight brow. He was strikingly handsome, his face a long rectangle with a strong jaw and a slim, straight nose. His mouth was wide and mobile, curving up on the ends in a sensual, almost feline way.

He would be a formidable opponent in the courtroom. Laurel knew it instinctively, could feel the power of his personality in his gaze even while she could read nothing of his thoughts. She started to draw her hand back, but he held on to her—lightly but firmly, closing both his long, elegant hands over her much smaller one.

"I've heard so much about you," he said. "I've been looking forward to meeting you, Laurel."

There was something almost intimate in his tone. His voice was a warm, well-schooled, well-modulated baritone that vibrated with the ring of old Southern money.

"Stephen is from New Orleans," Vivian said brightly, raising her voice a fraction as thunder rumbled overhead. "I met his mother years ago—though no one will get me to confess how many years," she added coyly, lashes fluttering. "Back when I spent summers with my cousin, Tallant Jordan Hill. You remember Cousin Talli, don't you Laurel? Her father was in oil, and his brother was the one who made such a fortune in the silver market and then lost it all on the New York Stock Exchange? It was such a scandal!

"Laurel was a junior bridesmaid in Cousin Talli's second wedding," she explained. Glory Trahern hung on every word. Everyone else's eyes had begun to glaze over. "Her first husband was crushed to death, you know. Lord, it was a horrible thing! But Talli bounced back and remarried well.

"A remarkable woman, Talli. She introduced me to Stephen's mother at a soiree. A lovely woman, just a precious, lovely woman! As it turns out, we had both attended Sacred Heart, but she was several years older than I, and we ran in different circles.

"The Danjermonds have been in shipping for years," she said in conclusion, mention of business making the men tune in once again.

"Shipping and politics," Danjermond said. To his credit, he had managed to smile all the way through Vivian's monologue. "My elder brother, Simon, went into the shipping business. That left politics for me."

The rest of the cast cooed and bobbed their heads approvingly. Laurel bristled. He still held her hand, and she couldn't pull it loose without creating a scene. She brought her chin up a notch and looked him hard in the eye.

"I've always been of the belief that a prosecuting attorney's first loyalty is the pursuit of justice, not public office."

Glory Trahern sucked in a little gasp and put a hand to the bow at her throat as if it were choking her. The rest of the party stood staring at Laurel with owl eyes, except Vivian, whose stare more resembled a she-wolf's. Only Danjermond himself seemed unoffended. His smile curled a little deeper at the corners of his mouth.

"I'd heard you were quite the champion for Lady Justice."

"That was my job," she said flatly, refusing to be charmed. "And yours."

He tipped his head, conceding the point. "So it is, and my record speaks for itself. The good people of Partout Parish can attest to that."

"We certainly can, Stephen," Vivian chirped.

Beaming a smile at him, she stepped to his side and slipped her arm through his, as if she had decided Laurel wasn't worthy of him so she was taking him back. Laurel pulled her hand free and crossed her arms, thinking she might have been amused if she hadn't been so damn angry with her mother to begin with.

"Your record is impeccable," Vivian went on, glowing proudly at him, as if she were somehow responsible for this paragon of manhood. "I declare, I don't know how we'd get along without you. While all around us crime is running rampant throughout Acadiana, Partout Parish has become a virtual haven for the law-abiding."

"I swear," Glory Trahern gushed, leaning over to touch Danjermond's arm as if he were a lucky charm. "I hardly dare to set foot across the parish line, what with all these murders going on around us."

Danjermond's green eyes glowed with amusement as he met Laurel's skeptical stare. "You see, Laurel, the advantage of having a politically ambitious district attorney? I have to do my job well, or no one will vote for me when I run for office."

The comment drew chuckles all around. Vivian patted his sleeve, pleased with his benevolent good humor. Laurel managed a smile. Stephen Danjermond was hardly the first politician to train for the job in the district attorney's office. She was hardly up to arguing philosophy with him at any rate. She had come here to put in her required appearance, that was all. By the looks Vivian was sliding her, she figured she would do well to stick to that plan.

Be a good girl, Laurel. Don't rock the boat, Laurel. Always say the right thing, Laurel.

Olive slunk into the room, looking almost apologetic, and announced in a meek monotone that dinner was ready, flinching like a whipped dog as lightning flashed outside the tall French doors.

"Well, I certainly have an appetite!" Ross announced with a blazing smile. He slapped Reverend Stipple on the shoulder. "How about you, Reverend?"

The minister bobbed his head like a window ornament in the back of a hopped-up Chevy. "I surely do."

Everyone moved on toward the dining room, Vivian leading Danjermond ahead, then returning without him to herd the rest of her guests out of the parlor. She snagged Laurel by the arm and held her back as the others continued down the hall, chatting amicably.

Laurel closed her eyes briefly and bit down on a sigh.

"Laurel Leanne! How dare you be rude to a guest in this house!" Vivian snapped, her voice a harsh whisper, her bony fingers biting into Laurel's arm. "Stephen Danjermond is an extremely important man. There's no telling how far he will go in politics."

"That doesn't mean I have to agree with him, Mama," Laurel pointed out, knowing it wouldn't do her any good. Her mother's code demanded that ladies be agreeable regardless. It wouldn't have mattered if Stephen Danjermond's politics had rivaled Adolf Hitler's for extremism.

Vivian pinched her lips together and narrowed her eyes. "Be civil to him, Laurel. I raised you to be a lady and won't tolerate less in this house. Stephen is educated, powerful, from a very good family."

Translation: Stephen Danjermond was a prize catch. No doubt every debutante in the parish had her sights set on him. Laurel wanted to tell her mother that she wasn't fishing, but she kept the comment to herself. Somehow it had never occurred to Vivian that she might need time to heal in the wake of all that had happened to her.

"I'm sorry, Mama," she murmured, not wanting to prolong the argument.

"Oh, well," Vivian said with a sigh, her temper cool-

ing as abruptly as it had flared up. "You've always had
your headstrong moments. You're just like your father
that way."

She reached up to brush lightly at Laurel's bangs, her
expression softening into one of her rare, truly motherly
looks. "You do look pretty today, darlin'. This shade of
pink becomes you."

Laurel said thank you, hating herself for letting the
compliment mean anything to her. She never seemed
able to escape that childish need for her mother's approval.

A weakness. One of many.

She glanced at her watch as Vivian took her by the
arm and led her out of the room, wondering how soon
she could leave. This emotional tug-of-war wasn't what
she needed to get herself back on track.

*It's just a dinner, just a couple of hours. Get through
it and go home.*

The dining room was as elegant as the parlor, as filled
with heirlooms and oil portraits of Chandlers dead and
gone. The Hepplewhite table and shield-back chairs
shone from two centuries of hand-polishing. Footfalls
sounded against the cypress floor and bounded up to the
twelve-foot ceiling. Glory Trahern stared up as if she
were trying to see them rather than calculating the worth
of the blown glass chandelier. Her husband snatched her
arm and herded her toward a chair.

Not surprisingly, Laurel found herself seated directly
across from Stephen Danjermond, who had the place of
honor—at the right hand of Vivian, who sat at one end of
the table, opposite Ross. Laurel slid into her chair and
focused on her Wedgwood plate, uncomfortably aware of
the handsome, elegant, articulate man across from her,
wishing she had worn her glasses. She didn't want to
attract his attention any more than she had wanted to
attract the attention of her stepfather two decades ago.
There was no room in her life for a man right now.

The image of Jack's mocking smile appeared before
her mind's eye, and she frowned and speared a stalk of
baby asparagus.

The topic of law and order had survived the trip down the hall, and the participants discussed the dynamic duo of Partout Parish—Sheriff Duwayne Kenner and District Attorney Danjermond—pleased and proud of the fact that crime here was being kept to a minimum.

"People can say what they will about Kenner's personality," Ross said with his usual air of supreme authority, "but the man does his job. I dare say if those killings had taken place in our parish, Kenner would have had the man responsible by now."

"Perhaps," Danjermond murmured as Olive collected his salad plate and slunk away. "He would certainly do his utmost. He's a very capable man, and tenacious as they come. However, we have to remember that killers of this sort are notoriously clever. Brilliant even."

"Sick," Glory Trahern said, fussing with her bow as she shivered. "Crazy and sick, that's what he is."

He tipped his head, conceding the possibility. "Or cold. Emotionless. Soulless." He turned his intense, mesmerizing gaze on Laurel. "What do you think, Laurel? Is our Bayou Strangler crazy or evil?"

Laurel twisted her napkin in her lap, wishing herself away from this conversation, afraid that it would gradually turn her way and the Traherns and Reverend Stipple and Stephen Danjermond would want to hear all about her life as "the prosecutor who cried wolf." "I . . . I couldn't say," she murmured. "I don't have enough knowledge about the cases to form an educated guess."

"There is a difference, though, don't you agree?" he prodded, the insistence in his voice subtle, smooth, strong. "While society deems all murderers insane to one degree or another, the courts have a different criterion. In the eyes of the law, there is a distinct difference.

"You believe in evil, don't you, Laurel?"

Laurel met his steady gaze, uneasiness drifting through her. She didn't want to be drawn into this conversation, but Danjermond held her attention, and the other diners waited expectantly. She could feel their eyes, sense the pressure of their held breath. Thunder rolled through the leaden skies outside. The rain came a little harder.

"Yes," she said softly. "Yes, I do."

"And good must triumph over evil. That is the foundation of our judicial system."

Yes, but it didn't always. She knew that better than most, and so she held her tongue and glanced away, and Danjermond's cool green eyes held fast on her, speculating.

"Speaking of good and evil," Laurel said, catching the eye of Reverend Stipple, "what do you make of Jimmy Lee Baldwin, Reverend?"

"As much as I hate to speak ill of anyone, my own opinion of him is less than complimentary," the minister said as he served himself a portion of beef. "He's a bit too fancy for my tastes. However, his television ministry does reach out to the homebound and calls back those who may have left the fold of Christ on the wayward paths of life."

One opinion was canceled out by the other, but Laurel bit her tongue on the urge to point that out. *Just do your time and get the hell out of here.*

"And he *is* campaigning against sin in the community," Reverend Stipple went on, looking as though he might just convince himself to like Baldwin after all.

Laurel thought of Savannah's comment about Jimmy Lee Baldwin's twisted sexual preferences and held her tongue as the potatoes came her way.

"I hear he's going to try to close down Frenchie's Landing," Glory Trahern said, her eyes lighting up at the chance to pass on gossip.

"Yes," Laurel said, "and the owners are very upset about it." At least T-Grace Delahoussaye was upset. She had to take T-Grace's word for it that Ovide was upset.

"You've been there?"

Laurel winced inwardly at Vivian's tone, but pushed the fear of her mother's reaction aside. She was a grown woman, able to go where she chose. "I had to see a man about a dog," she said, cutting the one thin slice of roast she had taken. "While Frenchie's doesn't compare with the country club, it hardly seemed the den of sin Mr. Baldwin is trying to make it out to be."

"It's nowhere for respectable people to go," Vivian commented, her face tight with disapproval.

"I see your point, though, Laurel, darlin'," Ross announced. "Skeeter Mouton's is by far the most notorious place in the parish. If Baldwin were serious about this war against sin, Mouton's would be the likely target. I suspect, however, that Mr. Baldwin knows too well the kind of trouble he'd be asking for poking at that hornets' nest. He'd get himself killed."

"Instead, he's harassing a legitimate business."

"Are you taking up the Delahoussayes' cause, Laurel?" Danjermond asked mildly.

Laurel met his steady gaze once again. "I'm not practicing at the moment, but someone should take up their cause."

He shrugged slightly. "I can't act on their behalf unless they make a formal complaint. You might pass that information along. It isn't against the law to preach; trespassing is another matter."

"Yes, I already have made that suggestion to them."

He smiled slowly, as if to tell her he knew her far better than she knew herself. "So you *are* taking up their cause, aren't you, Laurel?"

The truth of his statement stopped her short for a second, but she shook it off. "I merely made a suggestion."

"Stephen has more important causes to take up. Don't you, Stephen, dear?" Vivian said, reaching out to pat his hand approvingly. "Why don't you tell us about the state attorney general's appointing you head of the Acadiana drug task force?"

The meal progressed at a snail's pace. Laurel picked at her food and glanced at her watch every thirty seconds. Finally, they left the table and went back to the parlor for coffee. While Vivian bossed Olive around and the Traherns settled on the gold settee, Laurel roamed to the French doors and stood with her cup in her hand, staring out wistfully at the rain-washed garden. The thundershower had passed. When she escaped, she would go back to Belle Rivière and take a book out to the courtyard and sit in a corner reading and absorbing the quiet, the scent of rain, roses, and wisteria.

"Is the company really all that unpleasant?"

She started and glanced up, surprised to find Danjermond standing so close beside her. He had abandoned his coffee and stood with his hands tucked into the pockets of his fashionable pleated trousers.

"No, not at all," Laurel said quickly.

Danjermond smiled like a cat. "You're not a terribly good liar, Laurel. Tell the truth now. You'd rather be elsewhere."

"I admit I didn't come back to Bayou Breaux to socialize."

"Then it's my good fortune you made an exception in this case. Unless I'm the reason you're staring so longingly out that window, wishing yourself away."

"Of course not."

"Good, because I was about to suggest we get together in a more intimate setting one evening soon. A candlelit dinner, perhaps."

"I hardly know you, Mr. Danjermond."

"That's the whole point of intimate dinners, isn't it? To get to know each other. I'd like to find out more about your views, your plans, yourself."

"I have no plans for the moment. And I don't care to discuss my views. I'm not trying to be rude," she said, lifting her free hand in a gesture of peace. "The fact of the matter is I was recently divorced and have been through a great deal in the past year. I'm simply not up to a date at this point."

"Or a job offer?" he queried, lifting a brow, seeming not the least affected by her rejection of him personally.

Laurel tucked her chin back and eyed him with more than a hint of suspicion. "Why would you offer me a job? We've only just met."

"Because I can always use another good prosecutor in my office. The Scott County case notwithstanding, you have an excellent record. Your work on the Valdez migrant worker case was outstanding, and you went far above and beyond the call of duty investigating the rape of that blind woman back when you were little more than a clerk for the DA's office in Fulton County."

She had been barely out of law school. It was ancient history. The fact that he had for some reason dug that deeply into her past brought a return of the uneasiness she had felt earlier. She crossed her arms in front of her, careful not to dump coffee down the front of her sweater. "You seem to have an inordinate knowledge of my career, Mr. Danjermond."

"I'm a very thorough man, Laurel." He smiled again, that even, handsome smile. "You might say attention to detail has gotten me where I am today."

To the DA's office in backwater Louisiana? It seemed an odd thing to say, considering Stephen Danjermond had Bigger Things written all over him. With his pedigree and family connections, Laurel would have expected him to be firmly entrenched in Baton Rouge or New Orleans.

"There is a method to my madness, I assure you," he said, reading her silence with amazing accuracy. "Ambitious prosecutors are a dime a dozen in New Orleans. Acadiana offers me the chance to shine on my own. And there are unique problems here, problems I feel I can help control—drug smuggling, gun running. There is a certain element in the bayou country that remains largely uncivilized. Bringing that faction to heel and making them realize the days of Jean Lafitte are long past is a worthy goal."

"And one that will attract the attention of the powers that be."

His broad shoulders rose and fell. "*C'est la vie. C'est la guerre.* To the victor go the spoils."

"I know how the game is played, Mr. Danjermond," Laurel said in a cool tone. "I'm not naive."

"No, you're an idealist. A much more difficult lot in life. Better to be a cynic."

"Is that what you are? A cynic?"

"I'm a pragmatist." He held her gaze and let the silence build between them until Laurel had to fight herself to keep from stepping back. "Will you consider my offer?"

She shook her head. "I'm sorry. I'm flattered, but I can't think about work yet."

"But it's not just work to you, is it, Laurel? The pursuit of justice is a calling for you, an obsession," he said. "Isn't it, Laurel?"

The question was too personal. She was feeling too sensitive. He stood a little too close, watched her too intently. He looked relaxed, and yet she had the impression of leashed power beneath his calm facade. He was too . . . everything. Too tall, too handsome, too charming. Too still.

She glanced at the platinum Rolex strapped to his wrist, and relief flooded through her. "I'm afraid I have to be leaving now, Mr. Danjermond. I promised my aunt I'd help her with some things this afternoon. It was a pleasure meeting you."

"Until we meet again, Laurel."

When donkeys fly, she thought. She hadn't come home for challenges or entanglements or trouble. She backed away another step, some primal instinct keeping her from turning her back too quickly on Stephen Danjermond. He watched her, calm amusement lighting his green eyes, and she turned then, simply to escape looking at his too-handsome face, turned just as Savannah walked in the door.

Chapter Nine

Tension, like electricity, filled the room instantly, tightening skin, raising short hairs, freezing breath. The initial shock held everyone motionless, speechless, then Olive rushed into the room, chalk-faced, eyes brimming with tears.

"I didn't let her in, Mrs. Leighton!" she wailed. "I didn't! She shoved me!"

Vivian grabbed the maid by the arm and hustled her out into the hall. Savannah watched them go, a smirk tugging at the corners of her lush mouth. The initial responses to her appearance made it worth the trouble she had taken to get out here. She could have turned right around and left, only she wasn't satisfied. She wanted to tear through this little civilized, socially correct affair like a tornado and carry her baby sister off with her when she went. Damned if she was going to let Vivian dig her claws into Laurel or let Ross get within two feet of her.

She looked past the shocked faces of Glory and Don Trahern and Reverend Stipple, to her dear old step-daddy. Ross's expression was guarded, like that of a

poker player bluffing on a busted hand. He still wanted
her. She was sure of that, and she smiled at him to let
him know she knew. To remind herself he had chosen
her over his wife, over her mother. To reinforce the truth
in her own mind—that she was a born whore and would
never be anything else. And she reveled in the moment,
in making him wonder, making him squirm.

Feeling smug, she strolled into the room, her gait
loose, hips swinging. She had dressed for the occasion in
a scandalously short, sleeveless dress that was white with
large red amaryllis blossoms splashed across it, and fit
her like skin on a sausage. Aside from her red stiletto
heels, it was the only article of clothing she wore. She
had looped a long strand of pearls carelessly around her
neck to accompany her ever-present pendant, and
brushed her hair upside down so that it was now like a
cloud around her shoulders, wild and sexy. Her Ray-
Bans completed the outfit, hiding her eyes, giving her an
air of mystery.

"Savannah," Laurel said, finding her tongue at last.
She studied her sister and chose her words carefully.
"We didn't expect to see you."

"I had a change in plans," Savannah said evenly. "I
need to borrow your car, Baby. Seeing how mine is temporarily out of commission."

"Of course." Laurel took a step toward the door. "You
can give me a ride back to Belle Rivière. I was just leaving."

"So soon?" Savannah cooed, disappointment plump-
ing out her lower lip as she slid her sunglasses down her
nose and stroked a gaze down Stephen Danjermond. "I
haven't even been properly introduced."

Laurel bit her tongue and held her temper, saying a
quick prayer that her sister wouldn't do anything more
outrageous than she already had. She slipped an arm
through Savannah's, intent on controlling her in some
way.

"Stephen Danjermond, my sister, Savannah. Savannah—"

"District Attorney Danjermond," Savannah murmured, preening like a cat, offering her free hand to the man Vivian had obviously marked for Laurel. "Such a pleasure, Mr. Danjermond. Savannah Chandler Leighton at your . . ." Her gaze slid down the long, lean, elegant length of him, lingering suggestively. ". . . service."

"Miss Leighton?" One dark brow rose a fraction. "You go by your stepfather's name?"

"Oh, yes," Savannah purred, stroking the palm of his hand with her fingertip. She shot a look at Ross across the room. "I owe my stepdaddy *so* much after all." She lifted one shoulder in a casual shrug. "Ross made me what I am today, you know."

"Savannah." Vivian's voice cut across the parlor like a scimitar. She stood rigid and queenly beside her chair, hands clasped tightly in front of her. "What a surprise to see you here."

"Yes, I expect it is," Savannah drawled sweetly, cocking a hip and planting her hand on it in a belligerent stance that perfectly mirrored her attitude. "Seeing how you told me once to get the hell out of this house and never come back."

Laurel flinched inwardly as her stomach knotted with tension. She moved toward her sister, reaching out to put a hand on Savannah's arm. "Savannah, please, let's just go."

"Yes," Vivian snapped, her alabaster complexion mottling red with anger. "Please do go. If you can't keep a civil tongue in your head and behave as a lady, you are *not* welcome here."

Savannah shrugged off Laurel's hand and sauntered toward the door, stopping within a yard of their mother. All the old bitterness seethed up inside her like acid, boiling and churning, eating away at her. Her face twisted into a sour mask. "I've never been a lady in this house, and I used to be *welcome* day and night."

"Sister, *please*," Laurel whispered, taking hold of Savannah's wrist. Her gaze darted between the raw fury and sheen of tears in Vivian's eyes to Ross, who stood across the room, suddenly fascinated by the pattern in the Aubusson rug. "*Please*, let's go."

The tremor in Laurel's voice was the only thing that kept Savannah from lighting into her mother and shouting to the very proper guests that she was what she was because Ross Leighton had mounted her four times a week from the day she turned thirteen. And her very proper, perfect belle mother had never even suspected—because Vivian saw only what she wanted to see.

Vivian and Ross deserved whatever humiliation she brought them. But now was not the time. Poor Baby, always the peacemaker; she didn't need the tension. Savannah had, after all, come here to rescue her. Besides, she preferred to torture her mother and stepfather in little, never-ending ways.

"Come on, Baby," she murmured, sliding an arm around Laurel.

They walked out of the parlor in no particular hurry, down the hall past Olive, who stood red-eyed, her flat face pale and wet, her stringy red hair clinging to her cheeks. The maid glared at Savannah. Savannah just laughed.

Laurel wanted to run and fling the door open and sprint for her car, but she was stuck beside Savannah, moving with nightmarish deliberation, their shoes clicking against the marble floor. She didn't dare try to rush. When Savannah was in one of her moods, there was no telling what she might do, what might set her off. Outside, the sun was breaking through. The low clouds that had brought the shower were already tearing apart into thin, gauzy strips and floating away. Humidity hung in the air like steam, thick and hard to breathe, intensifying the rich green scents of boxwood and bougainvillea. Savannah paused on the veranda as if she had all day and surveyed what might have been her kingdom if their father had lived.

Laurel saw it too. The broad sweeping emerald lawn, the lush semitropical growth of the cypress swamp beyond, the broad money green leaves of the sugarcane that stretched off in the other direction beyond the pecan grove. Home to generations of Chandlers. Generations that would end with them.

"Why did you have to do that?" she asked.

Savannah slid her sunglasses off and arched a brow. "Why? Because they deserved it. I came here to save you."

"Save me?" Laurel shook her head. "I was doing just fine. It was only a dinner. I was about to leave."

"Well, isn't that gratitude?" Savannah said sarcastically, cocking her hip. "I did what you've never had the nerve to do—I stood up to them—"

"I don't see the point in making a big public scene—"

"You wouldn't, would you?"

The remark cut Laurel to the bone. She sucked in a breath and looked away, guilt and anger twining inside her like vines. It wasn't fair of Savannah to blame her for not having been abused by Ross, but it was unpardonable that Laurel felt lucky for the same reason. The cycle of feelings never ended.

"Let's just go home and start the afternoon over, okay?" Start over. That was what she had come to Bayou Breaux to do. Why had she thought she would be able to start over in a place where the past never went away? She wanted to think they could all rise above it and move on, but with every moment she spent here, she felt it pulling at her more and more, like quicksand, like the thick mud of the swamp, sucking her down, draining her strength.

Savannah climbed in on the driver's side of Laurel's black Acura, her dress riding up her bare thighs. Laurel went around the hood and slid into the passenger's seat, her eyes on the veranda of Beauvoir. Olive stood at the main door, glaring at them. There was no sign of Vivian, who was doubtless in the parlor, trying to smooth things over as best she could with her guests.

Poor Mama, always so afraid of what people would think.

"How did you get out here?" she asked absently.

Savannah started the car and swung it around the circular drive, flinging a wave of crushed shell across the yard. She eased off the accelerator as they headed down beneath the canopy of the live oak.

"Ronnie Peltier gave me a ride." She laughed at that and draped her left arm casually along the open window. "I gave him three rides last night. I figured he owed me."

Laurel blew out a sigh and speared a hand back through her hair. "I wish you wouldn't do that."

"What? Have sex with Ronnie Peltier?"

"Tell me about it. I don't want to hear it, Sister."

"Christ, Baby," Savannah snapped. "You're such a prude. Maybe if you *had* sex once in a while, you wouldn't be so uptight about it." She barely slowed for the turn onto the bayou road, wheeling out in front of a four-by-four truck and squealing away from it as a horn blasted indignantly. "Maybe you ought to take that long, tall district attorney for a ride. He had a look about him." She smiled slowly, savoring the idea of going a round or two with Stephen Danjermond herself. "I'll bet he's got a ten-inch cock and screws with his eyes open."

"I'm sure I don't care," Laurel grumbled.

"Yeah? Well, I'll bet Vivian cares. A fine, upstanding, well-bred man like Mr. Danjermond. She'd hand you over to him on a platter if she could. Think about it. She could marry you off to a man with money, power, prestige, a big future in politics, and snuff out the last embers of your big scandal all at once. How perfectly neat and tidy and cold—just the way Vivian likes things."

There was nothing for Laurel to say. She had seen Vivian's game for what it was, too, and it didn't bear comment as far as she was concerned. She had no intention of letting her mother manipulate her—except that she already had. The thought struck her like a hammer to the chest. She had gone to Beauvoir to placate Vivian. Nothing that had happened during the course of that visit could be undone. Because of Vivian, Danjermond was interested in her personally and professionally. Because of Vivian, Savannah had caused a scene, and now there was this tension between them, calling to mind the

wedge that would forever both bind them together and
hold them apart—Ross's abuse.

"I never should have come back," she whispered.

"Baby, don't say that!" Savannah exclaimed, stricken
by the thought. She shoved her Ray-Bans on top of her
head and stared at her sister, taking her eyes off the road
for a full ten seconds. "Don't say that. You needed to
come home. I'm going to take care of you, I promise."
She changed hands on the steering wheel and reached
across to brush her fingers over Laurel's hair. "That's all
I was doing at Beauvoir—taking care of you, protecting
you from Vivian. We'll start all over, starting now. It'll
just be you and me and Aunt Caroline and Mama Pearl.
We won't do anything but have fun. It'll be just like old
times."

Laurel caught her sister's hand and kissed it and
hung on tight while Savannah's attention cut back to the
road. *Just like old times. Old times here are not forgotten.*
. . . But they should be . . .

"I-I d-didn't mean for Mama to c-catch me! I-I thought
she was g-gone to her m-meeting!" Laurel clutched at
her sister, crying, miserable, desperate, her cheek still
stinging and burning from the slap of Vivian's hand.

She'd done wrong. Mama was furious with her.
Heaven only knew but that she might end up having a
spell. And it would be all my fault, Laurel thought. She
knew she wasn't supposed to have the pictures of Daddy
out in the parlor, 'cause if Mr. Leighton saw them, he
wouldn't like it. She winced again as the memory
swooped down on her like a hawk. . . .

Vivian stepped into the room with a smile on her
face, a smile that vanished as she saw what Laurel was
playing with. The photo album, the crawfish tie pin, the
bass tie Savannah had stolen out of the boxes for the
Lafayette Goodwill. All their little bits of Daddy. They
kept them up in Savannah's room, but just once Laurel
had wanted to take them down to the parlor and sit by
the window where Daddy had held her on his lap on

rainy days and told her funny stories that he made up off
the top of his head.

"Laurel, what are you doing?" Vivian asked, drifting
across the room. She'd been to her hospital auxiliary
meeting. She always wore her double pearls to the hospital auxiliary. They clicked together like teeth chattering
as she came toward Laurel, her face turning red beneath
her perfect makeup as her gaze settled on the collection
of mementos. "Where did you get these things?"

"Um . . . um . . . " Laurel's fingers curled around
the edge of the photo album, and she pulled it protec-
tively against her, but it was too late. Vivian jerked the
book away from her and gasped.

"Where did you get this? What is it doing out here?
Shame on you for dragging this out!" She slammed the
album closed and tossed it onto the seat of the old red
leather wing chair that had been Daddy's favorite.

She pressed her hands to her cheeks and paced in a
short line back and forth, back and forth, as nervous as a
racehorse, her eyes flashing with something like panic.
"Shame on you for bringing that out! Mr. Leighton is
new to this house, and you're dragging out all this! What
would he think if he saw this?"

Laurel didn't really care what Mr. Leighton thought.
She didn't like him. Didn't like his staying in Daddy's
room. Didn't like the way he patted her head. Didn't like
the way he looked at Savannah. She didn't want him at
Beauvoir.

"I don't like him!" she blurted, popping up from her
seat on the floor, anger making her feel like she could
grow to be ten feet tall and mean as an alligator. "I don't
like him and don't care what he thinks!"

The slap came hard and fast and turned her head.
Tears rushed up from deep inside and poured down her
face, her cheek stinging and half numb. Vivian grabbed
her by the shoulders and gave her a shake.

"Don't you *ever* say that!" she said fiercely, her eyes
bright with temper and tears. "Your father is dead. Mr.
Leighton is head of this house now, and you will be a

good girl and mind him and show respect. Do you understand me, Laurel Leanne?"

Laurel stared at her, wishing she didn't have to say yes. Wishing she could dare say no and still have Mama love her. But she couldn't, and she knew it. Mama already didn't love Savannah most of the time.

"Do you understand me?" she repeated, her voice trembling, on the verge of the kind of hysteria that always came before one of her spells.

"Y-yes, Mama," Laurel stammered, anger and sorrow tumbling together inside her like a pair of fighting cats. "I-I'm sorry, Mama."

That quickly, Vivian's temper cooled visibly. Her hold on Laurel's arms eased. She bent down awkwardly, so as not to wrinkle her new hot pink dress, and stroked Laurel's hair back from her forehead again and again, wiping tears into it. A trembling smile wobbled across her perfectly painted mouth. "That's my girl. I know you'll be a good girl. You know what's important, don't you, Laurel? You're always such a good girl," she whispered, sniffling. "Mama's little pet. You run along now and play elsewhere."

And Laurel had run. She had run out to find Savannah in the rickety old boathouse down on the bank of the bayou. They sat in the old wooden *bâteau* Daddy had let them use, and Savannah hugged her and wiped her tears. Laurel desperately wanted her to say everything would be all right, but Savannah had stopped saying that after Vivian and Ross had come back from their honeymoon.

So many things had changed so fast. Daddy gone. Ross Leighton taking his place. Some nights it just scared her so to think of it that she couldn't sleep, and she tried to sneak into Savannah's room as she always had, but Savannah kept the secret door locked now and wouldn't tell her why.

"I wish we could take the boat and float all the way to New Orleans," she mumbled against her sister's shoulder. "I wish we could run away."

"We can't," Savannah murmured, stroking her hair.

"We could go and live with Aunt Caroline."

"No," she whispered, staring out at the water. "Don't you see, Baby? There's no getting away."

The way she said it made Laurel scared all over again, and she shivered and looked up at her sister, feeling all hollow and achy inside at the sadness in Savannah's eyes. Then Savannah smiled suddenly and tickled her.

"But we can go out on the bayou and pretend we're shipwrecked on a jungle island," she said, twisting around to untie the *bâteau* from its mooring.

And they let the boat drift out of the old cypress shed that looked like a junk heap and smelled like fish, and headed up the bayou to a place where they could pretend the world was perfect and Ross Leighton didn't exist.

"Dat Armentine Prejean, she kin cook, her," Mama Pearl declared, shaking her wooly head as she snapped beans into a plastic bucket wedged between her tiny feet. "She don' cook nothin' good for Vivian, but she kin cook, I tell you. If she wasn' cookin' for Vivian, you would'a ate her dinner, *chère*."

Laurel glanced up from the shrimp salad she was picking at. She had changed out of her skirt into a pair of faded denim shorts and a loose purple cotton blouse, and was feeling comfortably inconspicuous again with her glasses perched on her nose. Everyone had trailed out onto the back gallery of Belle Rivière and settled in, cocooned in the quiet of the courtyard and the warmth of the afternoon. "The meal was fine, Mama Pearl. I just didn't have much of an appetite, that's all."

Pearl snorted, her fleshy face folding into creases of supreme disapproval. "Nothin' but bones, you. You gonna dry up an' blow away if you don' get some fat on you."

Savannah stretched back on the cushioned lounge and set her book aside. "Aw, you know what they say, Mama Pearl, a girl can't be too rich or too thin."

Pearl snorted again. *"Sa c'est de la couyonade."*

Caroline twirled the ice in her glass of tea, her dark eyes carefully fixed on Laurel. "We saw you on the news last night, darlin'. Standing toe to toe with that televangelist."

Pearl cackled and slapped her knees. "You give him good, talk about! Even knowed your Bible verse! *Ma bon fille!* I tell ever'body at church dis mornin', dat's *my* girl!"

Laurel made a face that was a cross between a smile and a frown and said nothing. What little appetite she had managed to work up for the shrimp salad fled, and she laid her fork across the plate.

"The Delahoussayes are good people," Caroline said evenly. She let that hang in the air while she recrossed her legs and arranged the hem of her slim pale yellow skirt. "Would it be difficult to stop Baldwin from harassing them?"

Laurel shrugged. "Maybe not. They could talk to Judge Monahan. But that doesn't stop Baldwin from waging his war against sin in other ways."

"A little action is better than a whole lot of talk," Caroline said. She took a sip of her tea and set it back down, tracing a fingertip down the side of the sweating glass.

"Lord knows, *action* is right up the Revver's alley," Savannah said dryly, winning herself a frown from Laurel. "If Jimmy Lee is a man of God, then the Marquis de Sade is right up there in heaven, tying the lady angels to the pearly gates and licking his lips."

Mama Pearl flung a bean down and scolded Savannah in a rapid stream of Cajun French that rolled off Savannah like water off a duck. Inside the house the telephone rang. Savannah unfolded herself from the chaise in no particular hurry and went to answer it. Pearl collected her bucket and waddled in after her, muttering under her breath.

Laurel quelled the urge to go after them. She could feel Caroline's gaze weighing on her.

"You still belong to the Louisiana Bar Association, don't you?" her aunt asked innocently.

"Yes, but I'm not ready to take anything on," Laurel argued, her fingers curling into fists on the glass table-top. "I don't need the trouble."

Caroline rose, brushing an imaginary crumb from her loose-fitting chocolate silk tunic. She moved a step toward the house, glancing at Laurel as if in after-thought. "Neither do the Delahoussayes."

Laurel ground her teeth as her aunt sauntered through the French doors that led directly into her study. "I came here to rest," she muttered, crossing her arms and sitting back in her chair. "I came here for peace and quiet."

No one answered her. Mama Pearl had gone off to the realm that was her kitchen. Even as Laurel thought of seeking out Savannah so she could vent her spleen, she heard the Acura start and squeal away from the front of the house. Aunt Caroline had given her words of wis-dom and retreated.

Suddenly restless, Laurel stood and paced along the gallery for a moment. The afternoon breeze caught at the hem of her blouse, stirred the trailing fronds of a hanging fern, fluttered the pages of Savannah's abandoned book. Sorely in need of a distraction, Laurel bent and snatched up the paperback.

Evil Illusions by Jack Boudreaux.

The cover depicted the swamp at night, misty and dark, the water shining like black glass under a pale moon. Among the dense growth along the bank, a pair of eyes peered out, glowing red. The artwork was enough to make Laurel shiver. She turned the book over and read the back copy as she stepped down off the gallery and wandered along a brick path toward the back of the courtyard.

Master of suspense, New York Times *best-selling author Jack Boudreaux creates another spine-tingling read guar-anteed to keep the bravest cynic awake nights.*

. . .

Something is stalking the town of Perdue, Louisiana, preying on children and spreading a terror that threatens to tear the town apart. By day Perdue maintains the facade of a picture-perfect small town, but appearances are illusion, and evil lurks in the woods beyond, waiting for the sun to set.

Beautiful young widow Claire Fontaine has come to Perdue with her daughter to claim an inheritance the locals say is cursed. Haunted by a violent past, she hopes to make a fresh start. But even as she begins a new career as a nurse practitioner in the local clinic, a shadow is falling across her path to happiness. A shadow of menace . . . and death.

As terror tightens its grip on the town, Claire must decide whom she can trust. Is the dashing Dr. Verret a worthy candidate . . . or a killer? Is resident magician Jalen Pierce a harmless huckster, or is his innocent guise . . . an Evil Illusion . . .

Intrigued, Laurel settled back on a stone bench in a corner of the courtyard and opened the book at random.

Night clutches the swamp in a grip as cold and black as death. Fingers of mist slither among the trunks of the cypress like ghostly snakes. From somewhere in the distance comes a roar that calls to mind prehistoric times, primeval swamps, ancient monsters.

Fear runs in rivulets down Paula's back. As she sits in the bâteau, *waiting, watching, a sense of evil presses in on her. It is thick and heavy in the air. As thick as the mist. As suffocating as a blanket. She claws at the collar of her blouse and tries to swallow, swings around at a rustle in the underbrush behind her.*

A nutria screams as it meets its death. A cottonmouth breaks the surface of the bayou, its long, lithe body wrapped around the thrashing body of a bullfrog. Over-

*head a winged black shape swoops down from the
branches of a tree. Another night predator. An owl . . .
a bat . . . something hideous . . . something terrify-
ing . . . And a scream rips from Paula's throat. Hot,
wild, raw. A scream like the nutria's. The scream of prey.
Heard by no one. Swallowed up by the night.*

"I'm flattered."

Laurel jumped, her heart leapfrogging into her
throat. Jack stood not two feet away, leaning indolently
against one of Aunt Caroline's Grecian lady statues, his
hands in the pockets of his worn jeans, one leg cocked.
He looked tough and sexy in a faded black T-shirt de-
picting a dancing alligator and the slogan "Gator Bait
Bar. *Restaurant et Salle de Danse.*" The cut above his left
eye only added to his aura of dangerous mystery, and
somehow complemented the tiny ruby that winked blood
red on his earlobe.

Laurel gathered her indignation and hopped to her
feet, slapping the book shut. "You scared the life out of
me!"

Jack grinned at her outrage. "My editor will be glad
to hear it. She pays me bags full of money to scare people."

"That's not what I meant, and you know it. What do
you think you're doing, sneaking up on me?"

He pressed his hands to his heart and looked too innocent to be believed. "Me, I was just walking along,
thinking to myself I oughta do the neighborly thing and
stop by for a visit."

She crossed her arms and tapped her toe, eyeing him
with open suspicion. Jack stepped closer, lifted the book
from her fingers, and tossed it onto the bench.

"You know what your problem is, sugar?" he murmured, sliding his arms around her. She jumped, eyes
wide at his nerve, and tried to bolt back, but he locked
his hands behind her at the small of her back and held
her easily. His wicked smile cut across his face. "You're
too tense. You gotta loosen up, angel."

"Let go of me," Laurel demanded, holding herself as

rigid as a post as her nerve endings snapped like whips in response to his nearness.

"Why? I like holding you."

"I don't want to be held. I don't like to be held."

He studied her expression for a long while, reading something like fear. Fear of him? Or was it something deeper, more fundamental? Fear of intimacy, maybe. Fear that she might actually enjoy it.

"Liar," he said softly, but set her free just the same. She should have been afraid of him. He was a user and a bastard. If he'd had a shred of decency, he would have left her alone. But she intrigued him, little bundle of contradictions that she was. And he wanted her. He couldn't escape that fact, and he didn't want to deny it.

He pulled his cigarette out from behind his ear and dangled it from his lip as he bent to retrieve the book. *Evil Illusions,* his latest best-seller, for all it meant to him. He wrote to kill time, to give himself some outlet, some way to vent what was inside him. He had never set out to become a success, an attitude that drove his editor insane. She wanted him to go on tour, to play the celebrity. He refused. She wanted him to court booksellers and distributors. He stayed home. His attitude exasperated her, but Jack just laughed it off and told Tina Steinberg she had enough energy, enthusiasm, and ambition for both of them.

"Are you ever going to smoke that cigarette?" Laurel snapped.

Jack glanced at her from under his brows and grinned, cigarette bobbing. "Nope. I quit two years ago."

"Then why do you keep sticking that cigarette in your mouth?" she asked peevishly.

His gaze held hers and all but caressed it, devilish lights dancing. "I've got an . . . oral fixation. You wanna help me out with that, sugar?"

Laurel scowled at him and at the wave of liquid heat that washed through her as her gaze strayed to the sexy curve of his lower lip and she remembered the feel and taste of his mouth on hers.

"Why horror?" she asked suddenly, reaching out to tap a finger against the book cover.

A wry smile pulled at one corner of Jack's mouth. *Because it's my life. Because it's what lives inside me. Dieu,* she'd run like a rabbit if he told the truth. Lucky he'd never had any particular aversion to lying.

"Because it sells," he said, tossing the paperback down on the bench.

Better she think of him as a mercenary than a lunatic. A mercenary probably still stood a chance of getting her into bed. And a mercenary he was, after all. Hadn't he spent half the afternoon rummaging through old newspapers, studying Miss Laurel Chandler's life as a prosecuting attorney? Not because he wanted to know more about her as a person, he told himself, but because he found her intriguing as a character. He had even jotted down a few notes about her for future reference, thinking she would make a fascinating heroine with her mix of fragility and strength.

"Come on, *'tite chatte,*" he said, nodding toward the back gate. He caught her small hand in his and started walking.

Laurel dug her heels in and scowled at him. "Come on where?"

"Crawfishin'."

She tried in vain to tug her hand away even as her feet took a step in his direction. "I'm not going crawfishing with you. I'm not going anywhere with you!"

"Sure you are, sugar." He grinned like the devil and drew her another step toward the gate. "You can't stay holed up in this garden forever. You gotta get out and live with the common folk."

She gave a sniff. "I don't see much of anything common about you."

"*Merci!*"

"It wasn't a compliment."

"Come on, angel," he cajoled, changing tacks without warning. He sprang toward her, landing as graceful as a cat, and swung her into a slow dance to music only he could hear. "Me, I'm jus' a poor Cajun boy all alone in this world," he murmured, his voice warm and rough like velvet, his accent thickening like a fine brown roux. He captured her gaze with his and held it, his head bent so that they were nearly nose to nose. "Woncha come crawfishin' with me, *mon coeur*?"

Temptation curled around her and drew her toward him. It seemed insane, this attraction between them. She didn't want a man in her life right now. She had all she could do to manage herself. And Jack would not be managed. He had a wildness about him, an unpredictability. He could tell her he had suddenly decided to fly off to Brazil for the day, and she wouldn't have been a bit surprised. No, he was no man for her.

But his offer was tempting. She could almost feel the mud between her toes, smell the bayou, feel the excitement of lifting a net full of clicking, hissing little red crawfish out of the water. It had been years since she'd gone. Her father had taken her and Savannah—against Vivian's strident objections. And she and Savannah had snuck away on their own a time or two after he had died, but those times were so distant in the past, they no longer seemed real. Now Jack was offering. Good-time Jack with his devil's grin and his air of *joie de vie*.

She looked up at him, and her mouth moved before she could even give it permission. "All right. Let's go."

Chapter
Ten

They rode in Jack's Jeep down the bayou road, turning off on a narrow, overgrown path a short distance before the site of their accident. Lined with trees, rough and rutted, it had Jack slowing the Jeep to a crawl, and Huey jumped out of the back, eager to begin his exploration of this new territory. Laurel hung on to the door as the Jeep bounced along, her attention on the scenery. She knew the area. Pony Bayou. So named for a prized pony owned by a local Anglo planter back in the late seventeen hundreds. The pony was "borrowed" by a Cajun man who planned to use the stallion for breeding purposes. A feud ensued, with considerable bloodshed, and all for nought as the pony got himself mired in the mud of the bayou and was devoured by alligators.

Despite its gruesome history, Pony Bayou was a pretty spot. The stream itself was narrow and shallow with low, muddy banks and a thick growth of water weeds and flowers. A perfect haven for crawfish, as was evidenced by the presence of two beat-up cars parked along the shoulder of the road. Two families were trying their luck in the shallows, their submerged nets marked by floating strips of colored plastic. Half a dozen children chased each other along the bank, shrieking and laughing. Their mothers were perched on the long trunk of an ancient brown Cadillac, swapping gossip. Their fathers leaned back against the side of the car, drinking beer and smoking nonchalantly. Everyone waved as Laurel and Jack rumbled past in search of a spot of their own. Laurel smiled and waved back, glad she had come, feeling lighter of heart away from the aura of her family.

They parked the Jeep and gathered their equipment as if this were an old routine. Laurel pulled on a pair of rubber knee-boots to wade in, grabbed several cotton mesh dip nets, and clomped after Jack, who had nets tucked under his arm and carried a cooler full of bait. Huey bounded ahead, nose scenting the air for adventure. Jack scolded him as the hound splashed into the bayou, and Huey wheeled and slunk away with his tail tucked between his legs, casting doleful looks over his shoulder at Jack.

Jack scowled at the dog, not appreciating the fact that he felt like an ogre for spoiling Huey's fun. Laurel was giving him a look as well.

"There won' be a crawfish between here and New Iberia with him around," he muttered.

"Depends on how good a fisherman you are, doesn't it?" She lifted a brow in challenge.

"When you grow up fishin' to keep your belly full, you get pretty damn good at it."

Laurel said nothing as she watched him bait the nets with gizzard shad and chicken necks. He had grown up poor. Lots of people had—and did—in South Louisiana. But the hint of defensiveness and bitterness in his tone somehow managed to touch her more than she would have expected it to.

There was such a thing as being poor and happy. After her father had died, Laurel had often offered God every toy she possessed, every party dress, for the chance to have parents who cared more about her and Savannah than they did about wealth. She had known a

number of families whose parents worked on Beauvoir,
who had little and still smiled and hugged their children.
The Cajuns were famously *un*materialistic and strongly
family-oriented. But she had a feeling this had not been
the case with Jack's family.

Curiosity itched inside her, but she didn't ask. Personal questions didn't seem wise.

They each took a net out into the water, spacing
them a good distance apart. Jack worked quickly and methodically, the ritual as second-nature to him as tying his
shoes. Laurel kept stumbling over tangles of alligator
weed that was entwined with delicate yellow bladder-
wort and water primrose. The spot she had chosen to
drop her net was choked with lavender water hyacinth
that fought her for control of the net.

"Uh-huh," Jack muttered dryly, suddenly beside her,
reaching around her, enveloping her in his warm male
scent. "I can see you grew up eating store-bought crawfish."

Laurel shot him an offended look. "I did not. I'll have
you know, I've done this lots of times. Just not in the last
fifteen years, that's all."

Jack set the net and helped her wade back to shore,
balancing her when the roots and reeds caught at her
boots. When they were back on solid ground, he gave
her a dubious look.

"I saw where you grew up, sugar. I can't picture any
daughter of that house wading for mudbugs."

"That just shows what a reverse snob you are," Laurel said as she stepped out of the hot boots and let her
bare feet sink into the soft ground of the bank. "Daddy
used to take Savannah and me."

She leaned back against the side of the Jeep and
stared across the bayou, thinking of happier times. On
the far bank lush ferns and purple wild iris grew in the
shade of hardwood trees dripping moss and willows waving their pendulous ribbons of green. In brighter spots
black-eyed Susans and white-topped daisy fleabane
dotted the bank like dollops of sunshine. Somewhere
along the stream a pileated woodpecker began drum-

ming against a tree trunk in search of an insect snack and the racket startled a pair of prothonotary warblers from their roost in a nearby hackberry sapling. The little birds fluttered past, flashes of slate blue and bright yellow.

"What happened to him?" Jack asked softly.

Emotion solidified in Laurel's throat like a chunk of amber. "He died," she whispered, the beautiful growth along the far bank blurring as unexpected tears glazed across her eyes. "He was killed . . . an accident . . . in the cane fields . . ."

One swift, terrible moment, and all their lives had been changed irrevocably.

Jack watched the sadness cloud her face like a veil. Automatically, he reached for her, curled his arm around her shoulder, pulled her gently against his side. "Hey, sugar," he murmured, his lips brushing her temple. "Don' cry. I didn' mean to make you cry. I brought you out here to make you happy."

Laurel stifled the urge to lean against him, straightening away instead, scrubbing at the embarrassment that reddened her cheeks. "I'm okay." She sniffed and shook her head, smiling against the desire to cry. "That just kind of snuck up on me. I'm okay." She nodded succinctly, as if she had managed to convince herself at least, if not Jack.

He watched her out of the corner of his eye. Tough little cookie, bucking up when she wanted to crumble. She was a fighter, all right. He had learned that not only by experience, but through his reading. According to the papers he had culled out of his collection of a year's worth, she had been as tenacious as a pit bull going after the alleged perpetrators in the Scott County case. She had driven her staff mercilessly, but worked none harder than she worked herself in the relentless—and, as it had turned out, futile—pursuit of justice. He couldn't help wondering where that hunger for truth and fairness had come from. Reporters had described it as an obsession. Obsessions grew out of seeds sown deep inside. He knew all about obsessions.

"How old were you?" he asked.

Laurel pulled up a black-eyed Susan and began plucking off the petals methodically. "Ten."

He wanted to offer some words of sympathy, tell her he knew how tough it was. But the fact of the matter was, he had hated his father and hadn't mourned his passing for even a fraction of a second.

"What about you?" Laurel asked, giving in to her curiosity on the grounds of good manners. He had asked her first. It would have been rude not to ask in return. "Do your parents live around here?"

"They're dead," Jack said flatly. "Did he want you to be a lawyer, your daddy?"

Laurel looked down at the mutilated flower in her hand, thinking of it as a representation of her life. The petals were like the years her father had been alive, all of them stripped away, leaving her with nothing but ugliness. "He wanted me to be happy."

"And the law made you happy?"

She shook her head a little, almost imperceptibly. "I went into law to see justice done. Why did you go into it?"

To show my old man. "To get rich."

"And did you?"

"Oh, yeah, absolutely. Me, I had it all." *And then I killed it, crushed it, threw it all away.*

Jack shifted his weight restlessly from one squishy wet sneaker to the other. She was turning the tables on him, neatly, easily, subtly. He shot her a glance askance. "You're good, counselor."

Laurel blinked at him in innocence. "I don't know what you mean."

"I mean, *I'm* the one asking the questions, so how come I'm all of a sudden giving answers?"

Her mouth turned down in a frown. "I thought this was a conversation, not an interrogation. Why can't I ask questions?"

"Because you won' like my answers, sugar," he said darkly.

"How will I know until I hear them?"

"Trust me."

Laurel took advantage of the silence to study him for a moment as he stared out at the brown water, that intense, brooding look on his face. The feeling that he was two very different men struck her once again. One minute he was the wild-eyed devil who wanted nothing more than to get into trouble and have a good time; the next he was this closed, dark man who kept the door shut on the part of himself he didn't want anyone to see. She found herself wanting to know what was on the other side of that door. A dangerous curiosity, she thought, pulling herself back from asking more questions.

Down the bank Huey suddenly bounded out of a stand of cattails and coffee weed, baying excitedly. The children who had been chasing around their parents' cars farther downstream came running, squealing with excitement to see what the hound had discovered, shrieking delightedly when they found the dog's quarry was a painted turtle with a spotted salamander riding on its back.

The turtle lumbered along, ignoring the sniffing hound, its lethargic gait seeming out of sync with its gaudy coloring. Its ebony-green shell shone like a bowling ball and was crisscrossed with a network of reddish-yellow lines. A broad red stripe stroked down the center of it from head to tail. The salamander flicked its long tongue out at the dog, sending Huey into another gale of howls that in turn set the children off again.

Poor Huey couldn't seem to figure out why the turtle didn't spring away from him so he could give chase. He batted a paw at it and yipped in surprise as the salamander shot off its hard-shelled taxi and skittered into the tall weeds. The hound wheeled and ran, bowling over a toddler in his haste to escape.

Being the closest adult, Laurel automatically went to the little girl's aid. She hefted up twenty pounds of squalling baby fat and perched the child on her hip as if it were the most natural thing in the world.

"Don't cry, sweetie, you're okay," she cooed, stroking a mop of black curls that were as soft as a cloud.

The little girl let out a last long wail, just to let the

world know she had been sorely mistreated, then subsided into hiccups, her attention suddenly riveted on her rescuer. Laurel smiled at the swift change of mood, at the innocence in the chubby face and the wonder in the round, liquid dark eyes. A muddy little hand reached up and touched her face experimentally.

"Jeanne-Marie, are you okay, *bébé*?" The child's mother rushed up, her brows knit with worry, arms reaching out.

"I think she was just startled," Laurel said, handing the baby over.

After a quick inspection satisfied her parental concern, the young woman turned back to Laurel with a sheepish look. "Oh, look! Jeanne-Marie, she got you all dirty! I'm so sorry!"

"It's nothing. Don't worry about it," Laurel said absently, reaching out to tickle Jeanne-Marie's plump chin. "What a pretty little girl."

The mother smiled, pride and shyness warring for control of her expression. She was herself very pretty in a curvy, Cajun way. "Thank you," she murmured. "Thank you for picking her up."

"Well, I'm sure the dog's owner would apologize to you," Laurel said dryly, shooting Jack a glance over her shoulder. "If he would ever admit the dog is his."

The woman was understandably baffled, but nodded and smiled and backed away toward the rest of her group, telling Jeanne-Marie to wave as they went.

Laurel waved back, then turned toward Jack, a smart remark on the tip of her tongue. But he had a strange, stricken look on his face, as if he had seen something he hadn't been at all prepared for.

"What's the matter with you?" she said instead. "Do you have a phobia of children or something?"

Jack shook himself free of the emotion that had gripped him as he had watched Laurel with little Jeanne-Marie. *Dieu*, he felt as though he'd taken an unexpected boot to the solar plexus. She had looked so natural, so loving. The thought had crossed his mind instantly, automatically, that she would make a wonderful mother—as

Evie would have if she had ever gotten the chance. If their child had ever been born. Thoughts he didn't usually allow himself during daylight hours. Those were for the night, when he could dwell on them and beat himself with them and cut his soul to ribbons with their razor-sharp edges.

"A—no," he stammered, blinking hard, scrambling for a mental toehold. He shrugged and flashed her a smile that was pale in comparison to his usual. "Me, I just don' know much about babies, that's all."

Laurel gave him a look. "I'll bet you know all about making them, though, don't you?"

"Ah, *c'est vrai*. I'm a regular expert on that subject." His grin took hold, cutting his dimples deep into his cheeks. He looped his arms around her, catching her by surprise, and shuffled closer and closer, until they were belly to belly. "You want for me to give you a demonstration, sugar?" he drawled, his voice stroking over her like long, sensitive fingers.

Laurel swallowed hard as raw, sexual heat swept through her.

"You certainly have a high opinion of your own abilities," she said, grabbing frantically for sass to ward off the other, more dangerous feelings.

He lowered his head a fraction, his dark eyes shining as he homed in on her mouth. "It ain't bragging if you can back it up."

Laurel's pulse jumped. "I'll back *you* up," she threatened with a look of mock consternation. She planted both hands against his chest and shoved.

He didn't budge. Just grinned at her, laughing. Fuming, she pushed again. He abruptly unlocked his hands at the small of her back and she let out a little whoop of surprise as she stumbled backward. Momentum carried her faster than her feet could catch up, and she landed on her fanny in a patch of orange-blossomed trumpet creeper. Peals of high-pitched laughter assured her that the children had witnessed her fall from dignity. Before she could even contemplate resurrecting herself, Huey bounded out of a tangle of buttonbush and pounced on her, knocking her flat and licking her face enthusiastically.

"Ugh!" Laurel snapped her head from side to side, in a futile attempt to dodge the slurping dog tongue, swatting blindly at the hound with her hands.

"*Arrête sa! C'est assez! Va-t'en!*" Jack was laughing as he shooed Huey out of the way. The hound jumped and danced and wiggled around their legs as Jack stretched out a hand to Laurel and helped her up. "You can't get the better of me, *catin.*"

Laurel shot him a disgruntled look. "There is no 'better' of you," she complained, struggling to keep from bursting into giggles. She never allowed herself to be amused by rascals. She was a level-headed, practical sort of person, after all. But there was just something about this side of Jack Boudreaux, something tempting, something conspiratorial. The gleam in his dark eyes pulled at her like a magnet.

"You only say that 'cause we haven't made love yet," he growled, that clever, sexy mouth curling up at the corners.

"You say that like there's a chance in hell it might actually happen."

The smile deepening, the magnetism pulling harder, he leaned a little closer. "Oh, it'll happen, angel," he murmured. "Absolutely. Guar-un-teed."

Laurel gave up her hold on her sense of humor and chuckled, shaking her head. "Lord, you're impossible!"

"Oh, no, sugar," he teased, slipping his arms around her once again. "Not impossible. Hard, mebbe," he said, waggling his brows.

The innuendo was unmistakable and outrageous. Their laughter drifted away on the sultry air, and awareness thickened the humidity around them. Laurel felt her heart thump a little harder as she watched the rogue's mask fall away from Jack's face. He looked intense, but it was a softer look than she had seen there before, and when he smiled, it was a softer smile, a smile that made her breath catch in her throat.

"I like to see you laugh, *'tite ange,*" he said, lifting a

hand to straighten her glasses. He brushed gently at the smudge of mud Jeanne-Marie had left on her cheek. His fingertips grazed the corner of her mouth and stilled. Slowly, deliberately, he hooked his thumb beneath her chin and tilted her face up as he lowered his mouth to hers.

Not smart, Laurel told herself, even as she felt her lips soften beneath his. She wasn't strong enough for a relationship, wasn't looking for a relationship. She couldn't have found a more unlikely candidate in any event. Jack Boudreaux was wild and irreverent and unpredictable and mocked the profession and system she held such respect for. But none of those arguments dispelled the fire that sparked to life as he tightened his hold on her and eased his tongue into her mouth.

Jack groaned deep in his throat as she melted against him. His little tigress who hissed and scratched at him more often than not. She didn't want him getting close, but once the barrier had been crossed, she responded to him with a sweetness that took his breath away. He wanted her. He meant to have her. To hell with consequences. To hell with what she would think of him after. She wouldn't think anything that wasn't the truth—that he was a bastard, that he was a user. All true. None of it changed a damn thing.

He tangled one hand in her short, silky hair and started the other on a quest for buttons. But his hand stilled as a high-pitched, staccato burst of sound cut through the haze in his mind. Laughter. Children's laughter. Jack raised his head reluctantly, just in time to see round eyes and a button nose disappear behind the trunk of a willow tree.

Laurel blinked up at him. Stunned. Dazed. Disoriented. Her glasses steamed. "What?" she mumbled, breathless, her lips stinging and burning, her mouth feeling hot and wet and ultrasensitive—sensations that were echoed in a more intimate area of her body.

"Much as I like an audience for some things," Jack said dryly, "this ain't one of those things."

Another burst of giggles sounded behind the tree,

and Laurel felt her cheeks heat. She shot him a look of disgust and gave him an ineffectual shove. "Go soak your head in the bayou, Boudreaux."

He grinned like a pirate. "It ain't my head that's the problem, *ma douce amie.*"

She rolled her eyes and sidled around him, lest he try anything funny, heading back to the Jeep and her boots. "Come on, Casanova. Let's see if you can catch anything besides hell from me."

They went back into the water, and Jack lifted the first of the nets, revealing a good catch of fifteen to twenty crawfish. The little creatures scrambled over one another, hissing and snapping their claws. They looked like diminutive lobsters, bronze red with black bead eyes and long feelers. Laurel held an onion sack open while Jack poured their catch in. They moved down their row of nets, having similar luck with each. When they were through, they had three bags full.

By then the sun had turned orange and begun sliding down in the sky. Dusk was coming. With it would come the mosquitoes. Ever present in the bayou country, they lifted off the water in squadrons at sunset to fly off on their mission for blood.

Laurel arranged things neatly and efficiently on her side in the back of the Jeep. Jack tossed junk helter-skelter. The bags of crawfish were stowed with the rest of the gear, an arrangement Huey was extremely skeptical of. The hound jumped into his usual spot and sat with his ears perked, head on one side, humming a worried note as he poked at the wriggling onion sacks with his paw.

On their way back out to the main road Jack stopped by the old Cadillac and gave one bulging bag to the families, who probably relied on their catch for a few free meals. The gift was offered without ceremony and accepted graciously. Then the Jeep moved on, with several children chasing after it, flinging wildflowers at Huey, who had garnered a daisy chain necklace in the deal.

The whole process was as natural as a handshake. Reciprocity, a tradition that dated back to the Acadian's arrival in Louisiana, a time when life had been unrelentingly harsh, the land unforgiving. People shared with friends, neighbors, relatives, in good times and bad. Laurel took in the proceedings, thinking that since her father's death, no one at Beauvoir had ever offered anyone anything that didn't have strings attached.

"That was nice," she said, sitting sideways on the seat so she could study his response.

He shrugged off the compliment, slowed the Jeep for the turn onto the main road, pulled his cigarette out from behind his ear, and dangled it from his lip. "We caught more than we need. They got a lotta mouths to feed. Besides," he said, cutting her a wry look, "I don' want 'em gettin' any ideas about suing me for Huey traumatizing their *bébé*."

"How could they sue if he's not your dog?" Laurel asked sweetly.

"Tell it to the judge, angel."

"I may just do that," she said, crossing her arms and fighting a smile. "There's still the little matter of my aunt's flower garden. . . ."

"Only through God may you be set free, brothers and sisters!" Jimmy Lee let the line echo a bit, loving the sound of his own voice over loudspeakers. Never mind that they were cheap, tinny-sounding loudspeakers. Once the money started rolling in for his campaign against sin, he would go out and buy himself new ones. And a new white suit or two. And a fancy French Quarter whore for a weekend. . . . Yes, indeed, life was sure as hell going to be sweet once the money came rolling in.

He had no doubt he would be rich and famous. Despite the betrayal of that little faggot Matthews, who had run the "news" version of Saturday's debacle instead of the version Jimmy Lee had envisioned on the ten o'clock report. Jimmy Lee was too good-looking not to make it, too charismatic, too good at pretending sincerity. He had it all over the other televangelists. Jim Bakker was a fool and had gotten his ass thrown in prison to prove it.

Swaggart was careless, picking up prostitutes on the street. They had both fallen by the wayside, opening the road to fame and fortune for Jimmy Lee Baldwin. In another five years he'd have himself a church that would make the Crystal Cathedral look like an outhouse.

The followers of the True Path cheered him, looking up at him as though he were Christ himself. Some wore looks of near-rapture. Some had tears in their eyes. All of them were saps. In another era he would have made a fortune selling snake oil or the empty promise of rain to drought-plagued farmers. He was a born con man. But in this the age of self-awareness and the search for inner peace, religion was the ticket. As L. Ron Hubbard had once said, if a man wanted to get rich, the best way was to form his own religion. Jimmy Lee looked out on the pathetic, avid faces of his followers and smiled.

"That's right, my friends in Christ," he said, walking to the other end of the rented flatbed truck that was serving as his stage for the afternoon. "Only through faith. Not through liquor or drugs or sins of the flesh!"

He loved the way he could build a sentence to a thundering crescendo. So did his faithful. There were women in the crowd who looked positively orgasmic over the magic of his voice.

"That's why, my beloved brothers and sisters," he said softly.

He raised his crumpled handkerchief to his face and blotted away the sweat that was running down his forehead. The day had turned into a damn steambath. His white shirt was soaked through. His cheap linen-look jacket hung on him like damp wallpaper. He wanted desperately to take a cool shower and lie naked on his bed with a lovely young thing reviving his energies with her sweet hot mouth. But for the moment he was stuck on the back of this flatbed truck with the sun beating down on him, boiling the sweat on his skin. The first thing he was going to do when he was rich and famous was move his ministry the hell away from Louisiana.

"That's why we have to do this battle. That's why we have to vanquish our wicked foe who would lead us all into temptation and deliver us into the hands of evil. That's why we must smite down the dens of iniquity!"

He swung his arm in the direction of Frenchie's, which was across the parking lot behind him, and his small gathering of devout cheered like the mob at Dr. Frankenstein's door. Such eager little sheep. Jimmy Lee grinned inwardly.

Laurel climbed out of the Jeep, took several swift, angry steps toward the gathered crowd, then stopped in her tracks, the soles of her sneakers crunching on the fine white shell. Her every muscle tensed as her conscience warred with the part of herself that was preaching self-protection. This wasn't her fight. She wasn't up to handling a fight. But it made her so damn mad. . . .

"You fixin' to whup him onstage this time, *'tite chatte*?" Jack asked, curling a hand around her fist and lifting it experimentally.

She shot him a look of pure pique and jerked away. "I'm going to have the Delahoussayes call the sheriff. If no one else is going to help them, that's the least I can do."

Jack shrugged. "Go ahead, darlin'. For all the good it'll do."

"It most certainly will do good."

He rolled his eyes and trailed after her as she marched onward. "You haven't met Sheriff Kenner, have you, sugar?"

Laurel considered the question rhetorical. She couldn't see that it would make any difference. Baldwin and his congregation were trespassing. Trespassing was against the law. The sheriff's job was to uphold the law. It was as simple as that.

They had to pass Baldwin's makeshift stage on the way to the bar. Laurel held her head high and fixed the self-styled preacher with a baleful glare.

Jimmy Lee had caught sight of her the second she had wheeled into the lot with Jack Boudreaux. Laurel Chandler. God was smiling down on him today, indeed.

He waited until she was almost even with the truck

before calling out to her. "Miss Chandler! Miss Laurel Chandler, please don't pass us by!"

She shouldn't have slowed down. She should have kept right on marching for the bar. She didn't want to go any deeper into this than she was already. But her feet hesitated automatically at the sound of her name, and something pulled her toward Jimmy Lee Baldwin. Not his charisma, as he would probably have preferred to believe. Not his air of authority. But something that had been with her since childhood. The need to stand up to a bully. The need to try to make people see a charlatan for what he was. The need to fight for justice.

She turned and marched right up to the front of his stage and glared up at him.

"Join us, sister," Jimmy Lee said, holding his hand out toward her. "I don't know what hold this vile place has over you, but I know, *I know* you are a good person at heart."

"Which is more than I can say for someone bent on harassing law-abiding citizens," Laurel snapped.

"The law." Jimmy Lee bobbed his head, a grave expression pulling down his handsome features. "The law protects the innocent. And the guilty would hide like wolves in sheep's clothing, hide behind the law. Isn't that true, Miss Chandler?"

Laurel went still. His eyes met hers, and a chill of foreboding swept over her skin despite the heat of the day. He knew. He knew, and the bastard was going to use it to his own end. Without looking, she could feel the curious eyes of his fifty or so followers falling on her. He knew. They would know. That she had failed. That justice had slipped from her grasp like a bar of wet soap.

"My friends . . ." Baldwin's voice came to her as if from a great distance down a long tin tunnel. "Miss Chandler has herself been a soldier in the fight against the most heinous of crimes, crimes against innocent children. Crimes perpetrated by depraved souls who would masquerade among us, showing us righteous faces by day and by night subjecting our children to unspeakable acts of sex! Miss Chandler knows of our fight, don't you Miss Chandler?"

Laurel barely heard him. She could feel the weight of their gazes press in on her, the weight of their judgment. She had failed. ". . . *unspeakable acts of sex.* . . ." She shivered as she felt herself drawing inward, pulling in to protect herself. ". . . *unspeakable acts of sex.* . . ." "*Help us, Laurel! Help us . . .*"

Jack watched her go pale, and he damned Jimmy Lee to eternal hell. His own personal philosophy of life was live and let live. If Jimmy Lee wanted to make a buck off God, that was his business. If people were stupid enough to follow him, that wasn't Jack's problem. He would have gone right on ignoring Baldwin and his band of lunatics. He wasn't out to fight anyone's fight. But the bastard had gone too far. He had somehow, some way managed to hurt Laurel.

Before he could even fathom what lay beneath his response, Jack hopped onto the hood of Baldwin's borrowed truck and proceeded to climb over the cab. He jumped down onto the flatbed, landing right smack behind Jimmy Lee, who bolted like a startled horse, but didn't move quickly enough to get away.

Jack caught hold of Baldwin's arm and deftly twisted it behind the preacher's back in a hold he had learned the hard way—from his old man. He grinned at the man like a long lost brother and spoke through his teeth at a pitch only Jimmy Lee could hear. "You got two choices here, Jimmy Lee. Either you can suddenly succumb to the heat of the day, or I'll break all the fine, small bones in your wrist."

Baldwin stared into those cold dark eyes, and a chill ran down him from head to toe. He'd heard rumors about Jack Boudreaux . . . that he was wild, unpredictable, affable one minute and mean as sin the next. Boudreaux was, by all accounts of the people who read his books, seriously unbalanced. The hold tightened on his wrist, and Jimmy Lee thought he could feel those small bones straining under the pressure.

"That's right, Jimmy Lee"—the smile chilled another degree—"I'd sooner break your arm."

Restless murmurs began rumbling through the crowd like distant thunder. The preacher ground his teeth. He was losing his momentum, losing his hold on them. Damn Jack Boudreaux. Jimmy Lee had had them on the brink of a frenzy, champing at the bit to launch him on the road to televangelist greatness. He cast a glance at his followers and back at the man beside him.

"Sin," he said, and the pressure tightened. "I-I can feel the heat of it!" He rolled his eyes and swayed dramatically on his feet. "Oh, Lord have mercy! The heat of it! The fires from hell!"

Jack let him go and watched with a mixture of cynicism and satisfaction as Baldwin staggered away across the flatbed. Obviously a disciple of the William Shatner/Captain Kirk school of acting, Baldwin stumbled and swayed, contorting his face, wrenching his back, calling out in staccato bursts as his audience gasped in alarm. Several women screamed as he finally collapsed onto the bed of the truck and writhed for another thirty seconds.

People rushed for the stage. Jack strolled across to the prostrate form of the preacher and calmly snatched up the microphone.

"Hey ever-body! Come on inside and douse those fires of hell!" he called, grinning like the devil. "Drinks are on me! *Laissez le bon temps rouler!* And tell 'em Jack sent you!"

The contingent of Frenchie's patrons who had been standing at the back of the crowd or lounging on the gallery sent up a wild chorus of hoots and cheers and made a mad dash for the bar. Jack hopped down off the truck. Laurel didn't even look up at him, but turned and started back for the Jeep.

"Hey, sugar, where you goin'?"

"Home. Please," Laurel said, emotion tightening around her throat like a vise. There was a pressure in her chest, in her head. She wanted—needed—to escape.

Jack caught her by the arm and shuffle-stepped

alongside her. "Hey, hey, you can't run off, spitfire. T-Grace is gonna have the place of honor all set for you."

"What for?" She stopped and wheeled on him, her body vibrating with tension, her face set in lines of anger and something like shame tinting the blue of her eyes. "I failed. I lost."

Jack's brows pulled together in confusion. "What the hell are you talkin' about? Failed? Failed what?"

She'd choked. She'd lost it. If it hadn't been for his coming to the rescue, there was no telling what humiliation she might have suffered. She felt as if Baldwin had reached right into her and pulled out that part of her past to hold it up to his followers like a science experiment gone wrong.

"You stood up to him, Laurel," Jack said softly. "That was more than anyone else was willing to do. So you didn't deliver the knockout punch. So what? Lighten up, sugar. You're not in charge of the whole damn world."

His last line struck a chord, brought back a memory from her stay at the Ashland Heights Clinic, brought back Dr. Pritchard's voice. How egotistical of her to think that she was the center of all, the savior of all, that the outcome of the future of the world rested squarely on her shoulders.

She was overreacting.

She had come here to heal, hadn't she? To take control of her life again. If she ran now, from this, she would be giving in to the past when she had vowed to rise above it.

She looked up at Jack, at the concern in his eyes, and wondered if he even knew it was there.

"Thank you," she murmured. She wanted to reach up and touch his cheek, but it seemed a dangerously intimate thing to do, and so curled her fingers into a loose fist instead.

Jack eyed her suspiciously. "For what?"

"For rescuing me."

"Oh, no." He shook his head and backed away from her a step, raising his hands as if to ward off her gratitude. "Don' make me out to be hero, sugar. I had a chance to make a fool outa Jimmy Lee, that's all. Me, I'm nobody's hero."

But he had saved her—several times—from her own thoughts, her own fears, from the dark mire of depression that pulled at her. Laurel studied him for a moment, wondering why he preferred the image of bad boy to champion.

"Come on, *'tite ange*," he said, jerking his head toward the bar. "I'll buy you a drink. Besides, I've got a lawyer joke I just remembered I wanted to tell you."

"What makes you think I want to hear it?"

Jack slid an arm around her shoulders and steered her toward Frenchie's. "No, no. I know you *don't* wanna hear it. That's half the fun of tellin' it."

Laurel laughed, the tension going out of her by slow degrees.

"What's the difference between a porcupine and two lawyers in a Porsche?" he asked as they skirted around Baldwin's truck. "With a porcupine, the pricks are on the outside."

They crossed the parking lot, Jack laughing, Laurel shaking her head, neither one aware that they were being very carefully watched.

Chapter Eleven

Savannah sat in a far corner of the bar, an aura of silence enveloping her like a force field, while all around her the air was filled with raucous sound. Filé was blasting out of the jukebox—"Two Left Feet." Billiard balls smacked together, people shouted to be heard above the general din. Savannah blocked it all out. Anger simmered inside her, hot and bitter and acidic.

The call from St. Joseph's had broken in on her time with Cooper like an unwelcome news bulletin. Mrs. Cooper was suddenly having a bad spell, and couldn't Mr. Cooper please come? He had been there all morning and half the afternoon as it was. Selfish, greedy bitch. It wasn't enough that she had to hold on to him mentally, she had to drag him away physically, as well.

"I hate her," Savannah snarled, the feeling too strong to keep bottled up inside.

No one noticed she'd spoken at all. No one was paying any attention to her.

She took a gulp of her vodka tonic and did a slow reconnaissance of the room through the dark lenses of her sunglasses. The place was crowded for a Sunday evening. Thanks to Laurel. Laurel. Everybody's little heroine. Everybody's little savior.

The anger burned a little hotter, flared up as she tossed another splash of alcohol on the flames. The irony was just too bitter. Laurel was what she was because of Savannah. She was the chaste and pure one because Savannah had been her savior, her protector.

She stared hard toward the bar, where her Baby was being toasted and cheered by T-Grace and the regulars. And Jack Boudreaux stood by her side, the least likely white knight she'd ever seen. Baby was supposed to be home, brooding, hiding, weak, and in need of her big sister for comfort and support. Damn her. She was getting stronger by the day, by the minute, snatching away Savannah's chance to be the stronger one, to play the role of protector again, to rise above her station of town tramp and be somebody important.

She picked a matchbook up off the table and mutilated it while she watched the way Jack hovered over Laurel, touching her shoulder, the small of her back, leaning close to whisper something in her ear then throwing his head back and laughing as she slugged him on the shoulder.

He had never whispered anything in Savannah's ear, damn his miserable Cajun hide. She would have given him the ride of his life, but he'd never shown any interest in her beyond the casual flirting he did with every female on the planet. He was sure as hell showing an interest in Baby, and Savannah didn't like it one damn bit.

"Damn you, Baby," she muttered, polishing off the last of her drink.

"You talkin' to me, *ma belle*?" Leonce bent over her from behind, sliding one bony hand down over her shoulder to fondle her breast.

"Damn right, you jerk," she complained. "You're not paying any attention to me at all."

His scar repulsed her. It constantly drew her eyes to the grotesque lumps at either end of it and the misshapen end of his nose in between. She'd heard a story once that a woman had given him the mark with the business end of a broken bottle, but Leonce seemed to bear no ill will toward the gender. He came on to anything in panties.

"I'll pay anything you want if you get naked with me, *chère.*"

Whore. You're nothing but a whore, Savannah. . . .

Her anger spiked, breaking through her facade of boredom. She wasn't for sale. She did what she wanted when she wanted with whomever she wanted because she *wanted* to. Which made her a slut, not a whore. The bitter distinction burned in her stomach like an ulcer, and confusing, conflicting emotions twisted and writhed in her chest, the pressure building like steam in a radiator.

Needing to take it out on somebody, she grabbed a chunk of Leonce's beard and gave it a vicious twist, wringing a howl out of him. He staggered back the instant she let go and crashed into a pool player getting ready to take a shot, earning himself a jab with a cue stick and an earful of four-letter words.

Leonce ignored the other man, his glare fixed on Savannah as he rubbed his cheek. "What the hell you do dat for?"

Savannah stood up, kicking her chair back. "Go fuck yourself, Scarface. Save your money to buy yourself a brain, you asshole."

She snatched up her glass and threw it at him, bouncing it off his shoulder as he ducked away.

"Crazy bitch!" he yelled as sneers and chuckles rumbled behind him. "You goddamn crazy bitch!"

Savannah ignored him, snatched up her pocketbook, and went on the prowl. She didn't need to settle for Leonce Comeau; there were plenty of younger, good-looking bucks who would appreciate her company and her expertise. Her gaze caught on Taureau Hebert across the room, regaling his buddies with the tale of his latest run-in with the game warden.

She'd had her eye on him for a while now. He hadn't

been nicknamed Bull for nothing. He was all of twenty-three and built for service from his mile-wide shoulders on down. It seemed like the perfect time to put him to the test.

But as she set off, hips swaying, tossing her wild mane back over her shoulder, concentrating all her considerable energy into the total package of allure, Annie Delahoussaye-Gerrard bounced into the picture, and the men at Taureau's table snapped their heads around to ogle her cleavage as she served their drinks and flirted with them.

Savannah fought off the wild urge to scream. This was *her* territory. Who the hell did this cheap little waitress think she was, anyway?

Young and pretty, that's who she was. And she had a sunny smile and a sweet laugh. Like her mother, T-Grace, Annie favored her clothes a size too small, pouring her ample curves into tight jeans and tank tops that left nothing to the imagination. A tangle of fake gold chains hung around her throat, and she wore a cheap ring on nearly every finger. No style at all, Savannah thought bitterly as she fingered the long strand of real pearls she wore and briefly contemplated wrapping them around Annie Gerrard's pretty young throat.

The little bitch had no business sniffing around the men here. She had a man of her own, a husband. Savannah very conveniently forgot the fact that Tony Gerrard—Annie's husband—had only just been released from a stay in the parish jail for knocking her around, and rumors of a divorce were in the air.

She strolled around behind the table, slipping in between Taureau and the waitress, sliding an arm around Taureau's thick, sunburned neck as if they were longtime lovers. She ignored his startled expression and fixed a hard-eyed look on Annie. "Why don't you run along and get me a fresh vodka tonic, sweetheart? That *is* your job here, isn't it?"

Annie narrowed her dark eyes and propped her empty tray on her well-rounded hip. "*Mais yeah,* that's my job," Annie sassed, looking her adversary up and down with undisguised contempt. "What's yours, *grand-mère*? Molesting young men?"

Savannah didn't hear the obscenities that spewed from her own mouth. With a blood red haze clouding her vision, she launched herself at the waitress, grabbing a handful of overpermed dark hair. She swung her other arm in a wild, roundhouse punch that connected solidly with Annie's ear.

Taureau and his buddies shot up out of their chairs, eyes round with astonishment. Someone yelled "Cat fight!" above the blare of the jukebox. There was another call of "*Grand rond!*" and instantly a circle of spectators formed around the two women as they crashed into a table, sending bottles and glasses flying. Beer spilled in a foaming river across the wood floor, making the footing treacherous and giving an advantage to Annie, who was in sneakers.

Savannah didn't notice herself slipping. Her perceptions had become strangely distorted, her vision zooming close up on her adversary, hearing nothing but a loud, chaotic babble of sounds—screeches and screams and crashing. She felt nothing—not the other woman's hand yanking on her hair or fingernails biting into her flesh or toe connecting with her shin—nothing but the white-hot rage that roared within. She swung and clawed and shouted, holding on tight to whatever part of Annie Ge-rard she could grab, and they spun, stumbling around the circle of spectators like wind-up dolls run amok.

T-Grace let out a sound that was something between fury and a war cry as she barreled out from behind the bar, elbows flying into the ribs of anyone who didn't get immediately out of her way. She plunged through the crowd, shouting at the top of her lungs, her eyes bulging wildly as she rushed to save not her daughter but her glassware and furniture. Annie could take care of herself.

Laurel jerked around on her barstool to see what the commotion was all about, and her heart clutched in her chest as a red-on-white dress caught her eye. "Oh, my God, Savannah!"

Without a thought to her own safety, she launched

herself off the stool and dove into the crowd. Jack swore
under his breath as he grabbed her from behind and
swung her out of his way. He made it to the melee about
the same instant as T-Grace, and they danced around the
combatants, angling to get a hold on one or the other of
them to pull them apart.

An old hand at brawls, T-Grace was less than diplo-
matic. She didn't hesitate to land a few blows of her own
or grab a handful of Savannah's hair as she struggled to
get her youngest child extricated from the fight that was
smashing up the bar and putting a hold on drink orders.

Jack jumped in behind Savannah and wedged an arm
between the two women, getting bitten for his efforts. An
elbow caught him above the left eye as they lurched
around the circle like rugby players in a scrum, reopen-
ing the cut he'd gotten crashing Savannah's 'Vette. He
gritted his teeth and cursed a blue streak through them,
wondering what the hell had compelled him to get involved in this mess in the first place. He wasn't a fighter;
he was an observer. If two women wanted to tear each
other's hair out, he usually just stood back and took
mental notes. He winced and swore in French as a spike
heel dug into his instep. He wouldn't have to take mental
notes this time; his body was going to be a pictorial essay
on the intricacies of a barroom cat fight. An elbow dug
into his ribs, and he grunted and angled for a better hold
while his feet slipped precariously in the spilled beer.

Laurel hovered on the edge of the action, her stomach twisting, her breath like two hard fists in her lungs,
disjointed thoughts shooting through her mind like
shrapnel. She hadn't even been aware of Savannah's
presence in the bar. Seeing her like this, locked in combat with another woman, was too surreal to be believed.
She brought a hand up to her mouth and bit down hard
on her thumbnail.

Suddenly an explosion rent the air, followed by a
chorus of screams, and everyone went absolutely still for
a split second. Laurel was sure her heart stopped, sure
one of the women had fired and someone had been
killed. But the fighters broke apart, Savannah with Jack

dragging her backward, T-Grace with her daughter in a choke hold. Heads turned toward the bar.

Ovide held a smoking .38 in one meaty fist. The gun was pointed toward the ceiling, and a telltale plume of plaster dust was floating down. The bartender's face was as impassive as ever. He looked like a ridiculous cartoon character standing there, his walrus mustache drooping down, tufts of white hair sprouting out of his ears. He didn't say a word as his patrons stared at him, but set the gun down behind the counter, calmly picked up a glass, and went on drying it with the rag he had never bothered to put down.

T-Grace gave her daughter a rough shake. "Fightin' with the customers. Talk about!"

Annie wiped a drizzle of blood from her nose with the back of her hand, her gaze, still hot and angry, locked on Savannah Chandler. "*She* started it, Maman—"

T-Grace cut her daughter off with a wild-eyed look. "I don' wanna hear no more. Get on with you! Go fix yourself up." She gave her daughter a shove in the direction of the ladies' room and clapped her hands over her head as she turned back toward the rest of the crowd. "*Allons danser!*" she ordered as Roddie Romero and the Rockin' Cajuns wailed out of the jukebox.

The bar patrons drifted back to their prefight activities, several couples taking T-Grace's command to heart and swinging out onto the dance floor to work off the excitement by working themselves into a sweat.

Adrenaline was still scalding the pathways of Savannah's blood vessels. She felt wild and irrational and didn't give a damn who saw it or what anybody thought. She shot Jack a pointed look over her shoulder. "If you wanted to put your hands on me, Jack, all you had to do was say so."

He let go of her abruptly. His face was set in stern lines. He pulled a handkerchief out of his hip pocket and offered it to her. "Your lip is bleeding."

Savannah just stared at him, recklessness rolling through her in big waves. Very slowly, very deliberately, she ran her tongue along her bottom lip, licking the blood away.

"You want to do that for me, Jack?" she murmured seductively, swaying toward him. "I'll bet you go for that sort of thing, don't you? Writing all those bloody, gruesome books gives you a taste for it, doesn't it, Jack?"

Jack said nothing. He had thought more than once of succumbing to Savannah Chandler's charms, but always something made him steer clear at the last second. Some instinctive wariness made him keep his distance. He hadn't understood until that second it was fear. Not of the woman, but of what they might become together. She would pull him over the edge with her, then only *le bon Dieu* knew what would happen as they tumbled together into madness. A cold chill trickled down his back at the thought.

"We're two of a kind, you and me, Jack," she whispered, holding his gaze.

Laurel arrived at her sister's side, pale as chalk, frightened and furious, trembling as she reached out to touch Savannah's arm. "My God, are you all right? You're bleeding! Jesus, Savannah, what were you thinking?"

Savannah shrugged off the touch and glared at her. "I wasn't," she snapped. "That's your department, Baby. You think, I act. Maybe if someone could put us together, we'd be a whole person."

She spun away and bent to snatch up her red calfskin pocketbook from the floor, not in the least bit concerned that the hem of her dress rode all the way up to her bare ass as she did so. Laurel's breath caught in her throat, and she took a step toward her sister meaning to pull the skirt down to her knees if she could.

"Savannah, for God's sake!"

Savannah gave a derisive sniff as she dug a cigarette and slim gold lighter out of her bag. "God's got nothing to do with it, Baby," she said as she lit up. She took a deep, calming drag and blew the smoke toward the ceiling, never taking her eyes off Laurel. "He's a sadist, anyway. Haven't you realized that by now?" She smiled bitterly, a smile made gruesome by the bright red blood staining her lush lower lip. "The joke's on us."

Satisfied with having the last word, she turned on her red stiletto heel and strolled out the front door as calmly as if nothing had happened at all.

"She gonna come to grief, dat one," T-Grace said, her voice vibrating with anger. She stood beside Laurel with her hands jammed on her hips, electric blue cowboy boots planted apart. Her tower of red hair was listing perilously to the left. Her leathery face was suffused with color, and her dark eyes bugged way out, making her look as if some invisible hand had her by the throat.

Laurel didn't bother to argue the point. Her heart sank at the thought that it was quite probably true. Savannah seemed bent on destroying herself one way or another, and Laurel had no idea what to do to prevent it. She wanted to believe she could stop it. She wanted to believe they could control their own destinies, but she didn't seem to have control of anything. She felt as if she were trying to stop a crazily spinning carousel by simply reaching out and grabbing it. Every time she caught hold, it flung her to the ground.

"I'm sorry, Mrs. Delahoussaye," she murmured. "Please be sure to send the bill for damages to my aunt's house."

T-Grace wrapped an arm around her and patted her shoulder, instantly the surrogate mother. "Don' you be sorry, *chère*. You don' got nothin' be sorry 'bout, helpin' us out like what you did with dat damn Jimmy Lee. You come an' eat some crawfish, you. You so little, I could pick up over my head."

"T-Grace," Jack said, resurrecting his smile with an effort, "who you tryin' to fool? You could pick *me* up over your head and dance the two-step."

She shook a bony finger at him, fighting the smile that pulled at her thin ruby lips. "Don' you tempt me, *cher*. You so full of sass, I jus' might show you who's boss, me. You come on sit down 'fore dat bump on your head make you more crazy than you already is."

As they wound their way through the throng,

T-Grace snatched hold of Leonce and ordered him to mind the bar. Leonce swept off his Panama hat and made a courtly bow, the tails of his Hawaiian shirt drooping low. He came up with a big grin that split his Vandyke and gave Jack a punch on the shoulder.

"Jumpin' into cat fights, talk about! What you gonna do next, Jack? Mud wrasslin' with women and alligators?"

Jack scowled at his friend, reached out with a quick hand, and flipped Leonce's hat off Leonce and onto his own head, leaving Leonce blushing back across his balding pate. "You're just jealous 'cause you were only the warm-up act."

Comeau's face darkened at the reminder, his scar glowing an angry red like a barometer of his temper. He tried to snatch the hat back, grabbing air as Jack ducked away. "Fuck you, Boudreaux."

"In your dreams," Jack taunted, laughing. "Go water the liquor, *tcheue poule.*"

T-Grace whirled around and boxed his ear, knocking the hat askew. "We don' water nothin' here, smart mouth."

She hardly broke her stride, continuing toward a little-used side door, barking orders at a waitress along the way and signaling to her husband to join them. Jack rubbed his ear and shot her a disgruntled look from under the brim of the straw hat—a look that was tempered by a twinkle in his eye.

They went outside and across a stretch of parking lot to the bank of the bayou, where a picnic table and assorted lawn chairs sat, divided from the yard of a tidy little forest green house by the requisite flower shrine to Mary. The area was partially illuminated by cheap plastic Chinese lanterns alternated with yellow bug lights strung up between two poles. The sun had sunk, but night had yet to creep across the sky. The bayou was striped with bars of soft gold light and translucent shadow.

Ovide planted his bulk in a lawn chair and said nothing while T-Grace supervised the layout of food on the picnic table. Laurel hung back, uncertain, wary of why she was being treated as a guest. She glanced at her watch and started to back away.

"I appreciate the offer, Mrs. Delahoussaye, but I think I should probably go. I ought to find Savannah—"

"Leave her be," T-Grace ordered. "Trouble, dat's all what she'll get you, *chère,* sister or no." Satisfied with the spread, she turned toward Laurel with her hands on her hips and a sympathetic look in her eyes. "*Mais yeah,* you gotta love her, but she'll do what she will, dat one. Sit."

Jack put his hands on Laurel's shoulders and steered to the picnic table. "Sit down, sugar. We worked hard catchin' these mudbugs."

She obeyed, not because she was hungry or eager to please, but because she didn't want to think what she would do if she could find Savannah. She wanted to talk, but the talk would invariably turn into an argument. When Savannah was in one of her moods, there was no reasoning with her. A headache took hold, and she closed her eyes briefly against the pain.

"Eat," T-Grace said, sliding a plate in front of her. It held a pile of boiled crawfish, boiled red potatoes, and *maquechou*—corn with chunks of tomato and peppers. The rich, spicy scents wafted up to tease Laurel's nostrils, and her stomach growled in spite of the poor appetite she'd had two seconds ago.

Jack tossed the Panama hat on the end of the table, straddled the bench, and sat down beside her, too close, his thigh brushing hers, his groin pressing against her hip. The air seeped out of her lungs in a tight hiss.

"She's a debutante, T-Grace," he said. "Probably don' know how to eat a crawfish without nine kinds of silver forks."

"I do so," Laurel retorted, shooting him a look over her shoulder.

Defiantly, she snapped off a crawfish tail, dug her thumbs into the seam, and split it open to reveal the rich white meat, which she pulled out and ate with her fingers. The flavor was wonderful, making her mouth water, evoking memories. In her mind's eye she could see her father wolfing down crawfish at the festival in Breaux Bridge, his eyes closed with reverent appreciation and a big smile on his face.

"You gonna be a real Cajun and suck the fat out'a the head?"

She jerked free of the bittersweet memory and scowled at Jack, who was slipping his arms around her to steal food off her plate. "Go suck the fat out of your own head, Boudreaux. That ought to occupy you for a while."

Ovide's mustache twitched. T-Grace slapped the arm of her lawn chair and cackled. "I like this girl of yours, Jack. She got enough sass to handle you."

Laurel tried unsuccessfully to scoot away from him. "I'm afraid you've got the wrong idea, Mrs. Delahoussaye. Jack and I aren't involved. We're just . . ." She trailed off, at a loss for an appropriate word. Friends seemed too intimate, acquaintances too distant.

"You could say lovers, and we'll make good on it later," he murmured in a dark, seductive voice, nuzzling her ear as he reached for another crawfish.

T-Grace went on, unconcerned with Laurel's definition of the relationship. "A girl's gotta have some sass. Like our Annick—Annie, you know? She gets herself in a scrap or two, but she takes care of herself, *oui*? She's a good girl, our Annie, she jus' can't pick a good man is all. Not like her *maman*."

She reached over to pat Ovide's sloping shoulder lovingly, her hard face aglow with affection. Ovide gave a snort that might have been approval or sinus trouble and tossed a crawfish shell into the bayou. A crack sounded from the dark water as a fish snapped up the shell.

"We raise seven babies in this house," T-Grace announced proudly. "Ovide and me, we work every day to make a good home, to make a good business. Now we got this damn Jimmy Lee making trouble for us, sayin' Frenchie's is the place where sin come from. Me, I'd like to send him to the place where sin come from. Ovide, he's gonna get the ulcer from worryin' 'bout what dat Jimmy Lee gonna do next."

She patted her husband's shoulder again, brushed at

the wild gray hair that fringed his head and poured out
of his ear. She shot a shrewd, sideways look at Laurel.
"So, you gonna help us wit' dat or what, *chère*?"

The other shoe fell. Laurel felt trapped with Jack on
one side and T-Grace staring her down on the other. She
shifted uncomfortably on the bench, wanting nothing
more than to escape. She shook her head as she abandoned her supper and extricated herself from the bench.
"I believe we've already had this conversation, Mrs.
Delahoussaye. I'm not practicing law—"

"You don' gotta practice," T-Grace said dryly. "Jus'
do it."

Laurel heaved a sigh of frustration. "Really, all you
have to do is call the sheriff the next time Reverend
Baldwin comes on your property—"

"Ha! Like dat pigheaded jackass would bother with
the like of us!"

"He's the sheriff—"

"You don' understand, sugar," Jack drawled. He
swung his right leg over the bench and stretched his feet
out in front of him, leaning his elbows back against the
table. "Duwayne Kenner only comes runnin' if your
name is Leighton or Stephen Danjermond. He's got too
many important meetings to bother with the common
folk. He isn't gonna get mixed up with Jimmy Lee and
his Church of the Lunatic Fringe unless a judge tells him
to."

"That's absurd!" Laurel exclaimed, rounding on Jack.
"That's—"

He raised his brows. "The way it is, sweetheart."

"He's sworn to uphold justice," she argued.

"Not everybody has the same conviction about that
you do."

She said nothing, just stood there for a long moment.
He had no such conviction. Jack made his own rules and
probably broke them with impunity. He joked about the
system, derided the people who tried to make it work.
But he knew she didn't.

He watched her, his eyes a dark, bottomless brown,
his expression intense. He was trying to read her. She

felt as if those eyes were reaching right into her soul.
Abruptly, she turned back toward T-Grace.

"There are several attorneys here in town—"

"Who don' give a rat's behind," T-Grace said. She
abandoned her plate on the ground, forfeiting her dinner
to Huey, who crawled out from under the picnic table
and laid claim to the crawfish. T-Grace ignored the dog,
her hard gaze homing in on Jack. She walked up to him
with her hands on her hips, her chin tipped in challenge.
"Jack here, he could help us, but here he sits on his cute
little—"

"Jesus Christ, T-Grace!" Jack exploded. He got up
from the bench so quickly, it tipped over backward with
a crash that sent the hound scurrying for safe cover. "I'm
disbarred! What the hell am I supposed to do?"

"Oh, nothin', Jack," she said softly, mockingly, not
giving up an inch of ground. "We all know you jus'
wanna have a good time." Daring more than any man
would have, she reached up and patted his lean cheek.
"You go on and have a good time, Jack. Don' bother with
us. We'll make out."

Jack wheeled around in a circle, looking for some
way to vent the anger roaring inside him. He wanted to
yell at the top of his lungs, bellow like a wounded animal. He snatched a beer bottle off the table and hurled
it, narrowly missing the bathtub shrine to the mother of
God, and still the fury built inside him.

"Shit!"

T-Grace watched him with wise old eyes. "That's all
right, Jack. We all know you don' get involved. You don'
take responsibility for nothin'."

He glared at her, wanting to grab her and shake her
until her bug eyes popped right out of her head. Damn
her, damn her for making him feel . . . what? Like a
cad, like a heel? Like a good for nothing, no-account
piece of trash?

Bon à rien, T-Jack . . . bon à rien.

That's what he was. No good. He'd had that truth
drilled into him since he was old enough to comprehend

language. He had proven it true time and again. He had no business howling at the truth.

His gaze caught on Laurel, who stood quietly, her arms folded against her, her big eyes round behind her glasses. The champion for justice. Willing to sacrifice her reputation, her private life, her career, all for the cause. *Dieu, what she must think of me . . . and all of it true.*

That was the irony—and he had a finely honed appreciation for irony—that he was everything T-Grace accused him of and less, that he was exactly what he aspired to be, and now the image he had settled into was turning on him—or he was turning against it.

"I don' need this," he snarled. "I'm outta here."

Laurel watched him stalk away, a little shaken by his outburst. A part of her wanted to go after him, to offer comfort, to ask why. *Not smart, Laurel.* She had enough trouble of her own without taking on the burden of Jack Boudreaux's darker side . . . or the plight of Frenchie's Landing. . . .

But as she turned back toward T-Grace, she couldn't bring herself to say no. It was no big deal, she told herself. Just a visit to the courthouse, a phone call or two. She wasn't taking on the world. Just a pair of honest, hardworking people who needed a little justice. Surely she was strong enough for that.

"All right," she said on a sigh. "I'll see what I can do."

For once, T-Grace was speechless, managing only a smile and a nod. Ovide hefted himself out of his chair and dusted remnants of crawfish shells off his belly. Laying a broad hand on Laurel's shoulder, he looked her in the eye and growled, *"Merci, chère."*

Chapter Twelve

Jimmy Lee sat on the window sill, feeling sorry for himself, wearing nothing but his dirty white trousers and a frown. Sweat trickled in little streams down his chest to pool on his belly. He sipped at a glass of brandy, brooding, reliving his humiliation in his mind, tormenting himself with it. He had had that crowd in the palm of his hand, he thought, curling his fingers into a fist. Then that damn Chandler bitch had ruined everything. Of course, he had managed to salvage the situation with his quick thinking, but the moment of glory had been spoiled, just the same.

Women were the bane of his existence. Sluts and whores, all of them. Some came in more respectable packages than others, but they were all alike underneath the wrapping. Wicked as Eve, every last one of them.

He laughed a little at the biblical reference and tossed back a gulp of brandy. Shit, he was even starting to *think* like a preacher.

The night was still and hot as hell, the air electric with something like expectation. A dark restlessness shifted inside him and he lifted his glass and tried to douse the feeling with the last of his drink. The quiet pressed in on him, irritating raw nerve endings like fingernails on a chalkboard. He longed for the noise of New Orleans, the sounds and smells of Bourbon Street, the dirt and dark alleys of the Quarter, the places the tourists never saw.

A man could get anything he wanted in New Orleans, any way he wanted it.

But he was out here, stuck on the edge of the godforsaken swamp. He had an apartment up in Lafayette, but he had chosen Bayou Breaux as the spot to launch his campaign, and so had rented this one-room bungalow at the edge of nowhere in order to have some privacy.

Bayou Breaux had seemed the perfect choice for his "War on Satan"—the heart of Acadiana, where good Christian people were as thick as ants on a watermelon rind, where times were a little lean these days because of the perilous state of the oil industry and the agricultural economy, where crime was pressing in and people needed something to grab onto and believe in. There were too many Catholics to suit him, but there were also busloads of fundamentalists fervent enough and gullible enough to believe anything. They were the core of his ministry. They would bankroll him into stardom and carry him there on their shoulders.

If Laurel Chandler didn't get in the way.

The screen door swung open with a creak and Savannah Chandler walked in, a seductive vision in her short flowered dress and red high heels. Her gaze scanned the shabby little room, taking in the dingy yellow walls, the cheap, mismatched furniture, the bottle of E & J on the battered coffee table, assessing the surroundings the same way she might judge a new boutique.

Finally she turned toward him, not saying a word, acting as if she had more right to be there than he did. She had eyes like a she-wolf—pale, translucent blue—and something in them sent a shiver of awareness down his spine. A white-hot flame that burned. A hunger that called to his own. A recognition of a common need.

"All dressed up and nowhere to go, Jimmy Lee?" she drawled.

"I could say the same to you."

She shot him a sly look from the corner of her eye. "No, you couldn't. I came here."

"What for?"

"For a while."

He said nothing as she skirted around the old iron bed, trailing a forefinger along the foot rail. She stared at him from under her lashes. He could feel the heat of her gaze on his face, on his bare chest, and he couldn't quite resist the urge to suck in his stomach. She came toward him, head down, her long wild hair tumbling over one shoulder, twining with the long strand of pearls she wore. Her hips rolled sensuously from side to side. The only sounds in the room were the click of spike heels against linoleum, the creak of the old ceiling fan as it turned, and the soft, seductive swish of fabric as it rubbed against skin.

Jimmy Lee held himself still as lust rose up inside him like a demon. She stopped a scant inch away. Her perfume mingled with the faint scent of brandy and the damp, earthy aroma of the swamp that drifted in through the window, and beneath it all lay the unmistakable musk of arousal—hers, his. . . .

"Your sister made a fool of me today," he said, his voice low and whiskey-hoarse.

One corner of her mouth curled into a subtle sneer. "You oughta be used to that, Jimmy Lee."

He moved so quickly, she couldn't help gasping as his hand closed, tight and punishing, on her upper arm. "I'm gonna be a star," he said softly.

She didn't ignore the pain of his fingers biting into her flesh. Instead she drank it in, fed on it, smiled a little deeper. "You're nothing but a two-bit hustler."

"And you're nothing but a cheap piece of snatch," he said. "A whore without a price tag."

She slapped him so hard that the blow sang up her arm and her palm burned like live ash. In one explosive move, Jimmy Lee was on his feet, his hand thundering down to return the slap. It snapped her head back and the split that had knitted together along her bottom lip cracked open, instantly filling her mouth with the sharp, thick taste of her own blood.

As if a door had been suddenly thrown open inside her, all the restlessness, the recklessness, the wildness rushed out on a wave of hate. Hate for him, hate for herself, an all-encompassing, drenching, drowning hate that washed away control, compunction, restraint. And all of it—the need, the hate, everything—glowed in her eyes as she turned her head and looked up at Jimmy Lee Baldwin.

He stared down at her for a long while, feeling again that strange kinship between them. Something dark, something evil. And it stirred arousal like nothing else he'd ever known. Desire rose up like a beast inside him, wild, rabid, unchained. A sound of animal need rose up the back of his throat as he pulled Savannah roughly against him and crushed her mouth with his.

She fought his embrace—not to escape, just to fight—but all her hands could grasp was the fever-hot, sweat-slick skin of his chest and upper arms, and she groped and clawed and pinched as the ripe male scent of him filled her head and his tongue filled her mouth.

Behind her back, his fingers worked frantically at the zipper of her dress. He pulled the tab down a few inches, then curled his fingers into the opening and tore it the rest of the way. He worked it past her shoulders and lower as he dragged his mouth from her lips to her throat. He grasped the neckline of the dress in both hands and jerked it down, hunger snarling inside him like a wild dog as her breasts sprang free, full and firm. He bent over and caught one turgid peak in his hot, avid mouth, sucking hard, wringing a frantic sound from her . . . and another and another. Winding his hand into her pearl necklace, he rubbed the cool, satiny beads across her other aching point.

Unsure of whether she wanted to hold him to her or push him away, Savannah shoved at his shoulders, tangled her hands in his slicked-back hair and pulled. This was a battle for her mind, for her soul, and desperation gripped her throat at the idea that she stood no chance of winning. *This is what you were born for, Savannah. Don't try to deny it. . . .*

For an instant she was back in her room at Beauvoir, and the man sucking greedily at her breast was her step-father. She cried out, not at the assault of her body, but at the conflicting feelings that assaulted her. Her body responded to his touch, tingled and burned and ached. In the beginning she hadn't liked it, but over time she had come to see that Ross was right—this was what she was made for, this was what she was good at. But the pleasure that ribboned through her body brought with it a wrenching shame. She was a whore. That was all she would ever be. That was all any man would love her for—sex.

She sobbed a little, feeling trapped, but she cast aside the sensation and let Ross's words balm her rav-aged heart. *"You're so beautiful, Savannah. You're so much more woman than your mother. I want you all the time. Sometimes I think I'll go mad with need of you. . . ."*

Need of her. He needed her. He wanted her. The words gave her a sense of power, and she grasped it and hung on.

"You're wicked, Savannah," Baldwin muttered, trail-ing his mouth down the slope of her breast, over the quivering muscles of her stomach. "You're a witch the way you make a man want you."

A wild, bitter laugh tore from her. She braced her hands against the window frame as Jimmy Lee went down on her. He caught the hem of her dress and shoved it up past her hips, so that it bunched around her waist. The strand of pearls hanging down between her breasts, she teetered on her red high heels, feet braced apart, head swimming dizzily, drunk on a mix of need and hate and self-pity and self-loathing and rapacious, insatiable arousal.

Jimmy Lee devoured her, as greedy and ravenous as a glutton at a feast. His tongue teased and flicked and probed, bringing her to the edge of orgasm but never beyond, never granting her satisfaction, only pushing the pain of unfulfilled arousal to its outer limits.

"I hate you, Jimmy Lee!" Her voice was little more than a rasp, as tormented as the rest of her body, as seized by desire and frustration. "You're a son of a bitch."

He tumbled her back across the creaking, sagging mattress of the old bed, falling across her, pinning her arms above her head with one hand. She struggled beneath him as he reached down with his free hand and stripped his belt from his trousers.

"You're nothing but a pervert, Jimmy Lee," she taunted, her heart racing as he bound her hands to a rail on the iron headboard.

"It takes one to know one," he growled.

She laughed, a throaty, seductive laugh, her cool, she-wolf eyes glowing with hunger and anticipation as he sat back, straddling her thighs, and unfastened his trousers. He didn't bother to take them off, but he did bother to protect himself, pulling a condom out of his pocket and slipping it on with practiced efficiency.

"Can't be too careful these days," he said. He braced himself above her on his elbows and stared down at her, his breath coming in hard pants. "My adoring public wouldn't take it too kindly if I caught something nasty from some alley cat who spreads her legs for every man in town."

Savannah glared at him. "I'll be sure to tell them you said that."

"Who'd believe you?" he asked, contempt for her festering inside him like a boil. "I'm their savior. You're just a bitch in heat."

"Don't bother telling anyone, Savannah. No one will ever believe you. . . . They'll see you for what you are— little slut, little prick teaser. . . . You're a bad girl, Savannah, and everyone knows it. . . . There's no use telling. We both know you seduced me. . . ."

She closed her eyes as the voice played in her head. She raised her hips as Jimmy Lee thrust into her . . . and hated herself.

. . .

The midnight moon cast a silvery sheen down on the trees, and the mist crept, soft and white, across the surface of the black water.

A lot of women were afraid of the swamp. A lot of *men* were afraid of the swamp. It didn't frighten Savannah. She felt something other than fear out here. Something ancient. Something that called to her and stirred her blood.

This place had always been her escape. This was where she and Baby had run to get away from home and the unhappiness there. Out here she felt free. She felt like a part of the swamp, like an animal—a deer or a bobcat or a copperhead snake. She wanted to take her clothes off and be naked here, be a part of it, a creature of the Atchafalaya.

Giving in to that primal desire, she slipped off the dress the Revver had ruined for her, tossed it on the hood of the car, and slicked her hands down over the curves of her naked body.

For a moment she closed her eyes and imagined what it would be like to lie down here on the mat of dead leaves and welcome her lover into her body beneath the light of the bayou moon. They would mate as all animals mated, without guilt, without inhibition, glorying in the pure excitement of it. She would scream out in ecstasy, her cries mingling with the eerie cacophony that carried across the swamp at night.

The mental image wrung a low moan from her, made her ache with need, a need Jimmy Lee hadn't been able to assuage no matter how many ways he used her—and he had used her in every way a man could use a woman. This was a need no man could quench, a need that was rooted deep in the core of her.

She threw her head back, lifting her face to the moon, tumbling her wild hair down her back. The restlessness stirred harder, hotter. The wildness pulled at her, drew on something deep within. She needed . . . needed . . . needed . . .

.   .   .

*Need drives the predator. Not the need for food, but for
sustenance of another kind. A need for blood, a taste for
death. A need to punish, a desire to inflict pain. To watch
pain grow like a cancer, from a simple response into
something all-consuming. A need to control. To play God.*

*To play. A game. The thought brings a smile. The
smile brings a chill to the prey. For every game there is a
loser. The one bound and held captive knows the outcome
before the game begins. For the victim there is no game,
only anticipation, pain, terror, and, she prays, death.
Please, death. Soon . . .*

*No one hears her screams. No one comes to her aid.
There are no saviors in the swamp. Cruelty here is a way
of life. Death as commonplace as snakes. Danger hidden
in beauty. No salvation. No justice. Life. Death. The
hunter and the hunted.*

*The knife gleams silver in the moonlight. The blade
cuts delicately, with skill, slicing like a bow across the
strings of a violin. The song it plays high-pitched and
eerie. Human. A prelude to death.*

*And in the end, the instrument will fall silent, the prey
will succumb. She will die as the predator believes she
deserves to die—naked and defiled. Another dead whore
left to rot in the swamp. A fitting end, a fitting place. And
the predator will glide away in the bâteau, silent, safe, the
secret shared with only the trees and the creatures of the
night. . . .*

Laurel sat up suddenly, shaking, cold, her skin slick with
sweat, her heart pounding. The nightmare faded as she
grounded herself in reality, but the sounds of the children's cries still echoed in her mind, driving her from
bed. She crossed to the highboy and pulled out another
oversize T-shirt, trying to crowd the last of the dream
from her brain. She was trembling violently, her stomach
knotting with residual anxiety, and she cursed a blue
streak under her breath, battling the weakness.

Her hand brushed across the bottle of tranquilizers tucked in among her underwear, left over from her stay at Ashland Heights. Dr. Pritchard had told her to take them when she needed help sleeping, but she wouldn't. No matter how badly she wanted to, she wouldn't take any. They were a crutch, another weakness, and she was so damn tired of being weak.

She changed quickly and went out onto the balcony, hoping to rejuvenate herself with fresh night air, but the air was heavy and warm, without a breath of a breeze. Folding her arms against herself to keep from shaking, she padded down to the French doors of Savannah's room and peeked in. The bed was unmade, the rich gold-and-ruby spread a tangled drift across the mattress, lace-edged satin pillows mounded along the ornate French headboard and tossed carelessly onto the floor. The rest of the room had Savannah's stamp of housekeeping draped everywhere in the form of discarded lingerie and articles of clothing that had been dragged out of the closet and abandoned in favor of something brighter, skimpier, sexier, trashier.

Fear cracked through the other emotions that were thick in Laurel's throat as a medley of lines played through her head. *"Murders?"* . . . *"Four now in the last eighteen months . . . Young women of questionable reputation"* . . . *"She gonna come to grief, dat one."* . . .

She chewed hard on her thumbnail as she wrestled with the urge to call the police. She was being silly, jumping to conclusions. There was nothing unusual in Savannah's staying out past two—or all night, for that matter. She could have been anywhere, with anyone.

With a killer?

"Stop it," she ordered, her voice a harsh whisper as she reined in the irrational urge to panic. Dammit, she wasn't an irrational person. She was logical and sensible and practical. Wasn't that what had saved her when she was growing up in the poisonous atmosphere of Beauvoir?

That and Savannah.

Her gaze fell again on the bed, and she jerked herself away and headed for the stairs that led down to the courtyard, her stride brisk and purposeful.

She was feeling unsettled, skittish. The evening at Frenchie's had rattled her, from her encounter with Baldwin to Savannah's fight to Jack's tirade to the role she had agreed to play for the Delahoussayes. Truth to tell, that probably had her the most on edge. Tomorrow she would have to go down to the courthouse and see about solving the problem of Jimmy Lee Baldwin. She would have to go to work as if she had never stopped, as if she hadn't left her last job in disgrace. She would go into the halls of justice and face the secretaries, the clerk of court, the judge, other attorneys, Stephen Danjermond.

She had been mulling over that prospect as she walked home from Frenchie's. With Jack nowhere to be found, and the last rays of day still seeping through the gloom of evening, she had set off for Belle Rivière on foot, hoping to walk off some of the anxiety and self-doubt. But after only two blocks, a bottle green Jaguar pulled alongside the curb, its passenger window sliding down with a hiss.

"Might I offer you a ride, Laurel?" Stephen Danjermond leaned across the soft gray leather seats of the car and stared up at her, his green eyes glowing like jewels in the waning light. He smiled, that handsome, perfectly symmetrical smile, tinting it with apology. "As much as I enjoy bragging about our diminished crime rate in Partout Parish, I hate to see a lady take chances."

"I could be taking a chance with you, for all I know," Laurel said evenly, keeping her fists tucked in the deep pockets of her baggy shorts.

Danjermond regarded her with a touch of disappointment, a touch of amusement. "I think you know me better than that, Laurel."

She looked at him blankly, trying to cover her confusion. They had only just met, but somehow she knew if she pointed that out to him, he would only be more amused. She felt as if he were a step ahead of her in time, that she was coming into a play already in progress and missing her cue. If he could rattle her this much with a simple conversation, he had to be hell on wheels in a cross-examination. A man destined for great things, Stephen Danjermond.

She pulled open the door of the Jag and sank down into the butter-soft seat. "I don't know you at all, Mr. Danjermond," she murmured, her tone as cryptic as his expression.

"I intend to remedy that situation."

He let the car ease along the deserted street, silent for a moment, the Jag as quiet as a soundproof booth. He had shed his tailored suit for a knit shirt the color of jade and a pair of tan chinos, but he still looked immaculate, perfectly pressed.

"Dinner with your parents was an interesting occasion," he said.

"They're not my parents," Laurel blurted automatically, a hot flush stinging her cheeks as he looked at her with one dark brow raised in question. "What I mean to say is, Ross Leighton isn't my father. My father passed away when I was small."

"Yes, I know. Killed, wasn't he?"

"An accident in the cane fields."

"You were close to him." He stated it as a fact, not a question. Laurel said nothing, wondering how he knew, wondering what Vivian might have told him. Wondering if he was privy to Vivian's plans for the two of them.

He shot her another steady look. "Your aversion to Ross," he explained. "I suspect you never accepted his taking your father's place. A child loses a beloved parent, resentment toward the usurper is natural. Though I should think you would have gotten over it by now. Perhaps there's something more to it?"

The answer was none of his business, but Laurel refrained from saying so. Her skills were rusty, but the instincts were still there. Danjermond's were honed to perfection. He didn't have conversations, he had verbal chess matches. He was never off duty. Every exchange was an opportunity to exercise his mind, sharpen his battle skills. She knew; she had been there. She had been that sharp, that focused. She knew an answer to this question would put her in check.

"I'm sorry about the scene my sister caused," she said casually. "Savannah does love to be dramatic."

"Why are you sorry?" He stopped the Jag for the red light at Jackson and pinned her with a look. "You aren't the one who caused the commotion. You have no control over your sister's actions, do you, Laurel?"

No. But she wanted to have. She wanted control. She wanted the components of her world to fit neatly into place. No messes, no unpleasant surprises.

Danjermond's gaze held fast on her. "Are you your sister's keeper?"

She shook off the thoughts and kicked herself mentally for not seeing the potential hazards of this subject she had diverted them onto. "Of course not. Savannah does as she pleases. I know she won't apologize for disrupting Vivian's gathering, so I will. I was merely taking up the gauntlet for etiquette."

"Ah," he smiled, looking out over the hood of the car, "the gauntlet. You might have been a knight of the Round Table in a past life, Laurel. Galahad the Good, adhering to your strict code of honor."

He seemed amused, and it irritated her. Did he think he was too urbane, too sophisticated for the quaint, provincial ways of Bayou Breaux—he the privileged son of old New Orleans money?

"Hospitality is the Southern way. I'm sure you were raised to have better manners than to, say, interrogate a guest," she said sweetly, shifting to the offensive.

He looked surprised and pleased at her parry. "Was I interrogating you? I thought we were getting acquainted."

"Getting acquainted is generally a reciprocal process. You haven't told me anything about yourself."

"I'm sorry." He sent her a dazzling smile that had doubtless knocked more than one simple belle off her feet. Laurel reminded herself she was no simple belle,

had never been. "I'm afraid I find you such an interesting and enchanting creature, I lost my head."

The sincerity in his voice was too smooth, too polished to be real. Laurel had the unnerving feeling that
nothing on this earth could rattle Stephen Danjermond.
There was that sense of calm around him, in his eyes, in
the core of him. She wondered if anything could ever
penetrate it.

"False flattery will get you nowhere, Mr.
Danjermond," she said, glancing away from him to her
reflection in the mirror on the visor. "I hardly look enchanting tonight."

"Fishing for a compliment, Laurel?"

"Stating a fact. I have no use for compliments."

He turned in at the drive to the carriage house that
served as Belle Rivière's garage and let the Jag idle in
park. "Practicality and idealism," he said, turning toward
her, sliding his arm casually along the back of the seat.
"An intriguing mix. Fascinating."

Laurel's fingers curled over the door handle as he
studied her with those steady, peridot eyes. "I'm so glad
I could amuse you," she said, her tone as dry as a good
martini.

Danjermond shook his head. "Not amuse, Laurel.
Challenge. You're a challenge."

"You make me feel like a Rubik's Cube."

He laughed at that, but his enjoyment of her spunk
was cut short as his pager went off. "Ah, well, duty calls,"
he said with a sigh of regret, punching a button on the
small black box that lay on the seat between them.
"Might I beg the use of a telephone?"

He made his call in the privacy of Caroline's study
and left immediately after, leaving Laurel feeling a mix of
relief and residual tension. She had dreaded the prospect
of introducing him to Aunt Caroline and Mama Pearl and
having to sit through coffee and conversation. She had
escaped that fate, but the tension lingered.

It lingered, still, as she wandered the cobbled paths
of the garden in her bare feet. What a nightmare that
Vivian saw them as a match.

Even if she had been in top form, Laurel wouldn't have wanted anything to do with him personally. He made her uneasy with those cool green eyes and that smooth drawl that never altered pitch or tempo. He was too composed when she felt as if she were scrambling on the side of a steep hill, scratching for a handhold. He was too intensely male, she supposed.

An image of Jack came to her, unbidden, dark, brooding, intense. Intensely male in a more basic, primal way than Stephen Danjermond . . . and desire stirred when she thought of him.

It made no sense. She had never been attracted to bad boys, no matter how seductive the gleam in their eyes, no matter how wicked their grins. She was a person who lived by the rules, stuck to them no matter what. There hadn't been a rule made Jack Boudreaux wouldn't go over, under, or around. She had always been one of the world's doers, tackling problems head-on. Jack's credo was to avoid as much responsibility as he could, to lay back and have a good time. *Laissez le bon temps rouler.*

It made no sense that she should feel anything toward him except contempt, but she did. The attraction was there, pulling at her every time he looked at her. Strong, magnetic, beyond her control. And that made her uneasy all over again. He was trouble on the hoof. A man with secrets in his eyes and a dark side he took great pains to camouflage. A man whose baser instincts ran just beneath the surface. Dangerous. She'd thought so more than once.

"Dreamin' about me, sugar?"

Laurel started, clutching at her heart as she whirled around. Jack stood just inside the back gate, leaning indolently against the brick gatepost. Shadows fell across his face, but she could feel him watching her reaction, and willed herself to relax and stand calm.

"You don't give a fig how much it sells," she said, dryly. "You write horror because you love to scare people. I'll bet you were the kind of little boy who hid in the closet and jumped out at his mother every time she walked past."

"Oh, I hid often enough." His voice came so softly, Laurel thought she was imagining it. Low and smoky and laced with old bitterness. "My old man locked me in a closet for a couple of days once. I never tried to scare anybody, though. *Mais non.* My sister, Maman, and me—we were pretty much scared all the time as it was."

His words, so casually delivered, hit Laurel with the force of a hammer. In just those few sentences he had painted a vivid and terrible picture of his childhood. With just those few words he had stirred within her compassion for a small, frightened boy.

He stepped out of the shadows, into the silvery light, his hands in his pockets, his shoulders sagging. He looked beat, drained. She had no idea what he had been doing in the time since he had stormed away from Frenchie's, but it had sapped his energy and etched lines of fatigue across his face.

"Oh, Jack . . ."

"Don't," he said sharply, shaking off her sympathy. "I'm not a little boy anymore."

"I'm sorry," she whispered.

"Why? You were Blackie Boudreaux in another life?" He shook his head again, took a step closer. "*Non, 'tite ange.* You weren't there."

No. She had been busy surviving her own nightmare, but she wouldn't say that, wouldn't share it . . . had never shared it with anyone.

"What are you doing here?" she asked. "What are you doing out at this hour?"

"Prowling." He smiled slowly, his gaze roaming deliberately down from the top of her head to her tiny bare toes. "On the lookout for ladies in their nightclothes."

Laurel had forgotten her state of undress. Now that Jack had so graciously pointed it out to her, she was acutely conscious of the fact that beneath a thin T-shirt that fell shorter than a miniskirt, she wore nothing but a pair of lavender panties. His grin deepened and he bobbed his eyebrows, an expression that clearly said "Gotcha."

She crossed her arms and scowled at him. "People can get shot creeping around backyards in the dead of night."

Jack let his gaze melt down over her again, lingering on the plump curves of her breasts. "Mmmm . . . you don' look armed, sugar, but you could be dangerous—to my sanity," he growled.

Laurel tried to scoot away from him and found he had backed her around into a position that trapped her between an armless statue of a Greek goddess and the bench where he had caught her reading his book.

"I wasn't aware your sanity was in question," she said sarcastically. "The general consensus seems to be that you're crazy."

He chuckled and inched a little closer to her. "You got a lotta sass, *'tite chatte*. Come here and give me a taste."

He didn't give her a chance to say no, but closed the distance between them and stole a kiss, slipping his arms quickly around her. Laurel reacted with an unfamiliar mix of desire and pique. Temper overruled temptation, and she started to bring her knee up to teach him the wisdom of asking for permission. Jack reacted instantly, twisting out of harm's way, throwing Laurel off balance. Before she could realize what he was doing, she was sprawled on top of him on the stone bench, her chin on his chest, eyes round with astonishment.

He sat with his back propped against the wall, one foot planted on the bench, one on the ground. He grinned at her. "All right, sugar, have your way with me."

"I'll thank you to let me up," Laurel said primly, shoving against his chest.

"No," Jack murmured, holding her, pulling her back down when she would have shot to her feet and stormed away. He wanted to hold her, needed to feel her softness against him. He pulled her close and nuzzled her ear while he rubbed a hand gently over her back. "Stay," he whispered. "Don't go, angel. It's late, and I don' wanna be alone with myself."

His strength wouldn't have kept her there, but the need in his voice was another matter altogether. It was subtle, couched in threads of humor, but there nevertheless. Laurel stilled against him, her eyes finding his in the moonlight, searching, wondering, a little wary.

"I never know who you are, Jack," she said softly.

She wouldn't want to know who he really was, he thought. If she knew everything about him, she wouldn't stay. If she knew anything about him, she would steer clear, and he would never have the chance to hold her, to take some solace in the feel of her against him—never have the chance to lose himself, however briefly, in the sweet bliss of kissing her.

He couldn't run that risk tonight. He had spent too much time tearing up what was left of his conscience and flogging what was left of his soul. He felt too beaten, too battered, and she was too pretty and too good.

Too good for the like of you, Jack . . .

She stared at him, her eyes as dark as midnight, as uncertain as a child's. In spite of all she'd been through, an aura of innocence still clung about her like a fading perfume. Like Evie. God, what pain that thought brought with it! If he touched her, he would sully her innocence, destroy it as he had destroyed Evie. But he wasn't strong enough to be noble, wasn't good enough to do the right thing. He was a bastard and a user and worse, a man caught between what he was and what he wanted. And he was so damn tired of being alone. . . .

"You don' trust me," he whispered, tenderly brushing her hair from her eyes. He grazed his fingertips along the delicate line of her cheekbone. "You shouldn't. I'm bad for you."

The warning was diluted to nothing by the sadness in his face. His mouth twisted into a half smile that was cynical and weary. His dark eyes looked a hundred years old. Bad Jack Boudreaux. The devil in blue jeans. Self-professed cad. Warning her away. He didn't see the paradox, but Laurel did. He was nobody's hero, but he would save her from himself.

She had spent too much of her life with people who claimed to be good and weren't. Jack claimed to be bad, but if he were truly bad, she would have known, would have sensed, wouldn't have wanted him to kiss her, to touch her, to hold her while the night lay warm and fragrant around them.

He's dangerous. . . .

Yes, she had thought that. And if Jack himself wasn't dangerous, then what she felt when he was this near surely was. She couldn't fall for him, not for his body or his tarnished soul or his allure of the forbidden. There was no room in her life for a rogue. She couldn't have her heart broken again; she was still trying to glue the pieces back together from the last time she had come apart.

She could feel it beating, thumping against Jack's chest through the thin fabric of her white T-shirt and his black one. She held her breath and counted the beats, her eyes on his, wondering why she didn't take her own advice and walk away.

"Well, hell," he muttered, pulling her closer, "you don' wanna believe me, I might as well prove it."

The kiss was carnal from the first. Burning hot. Frankly sexual. He traced his tongue slowly around the inner edge of her lips, then slipped deeper, probing, exploring. Laurel tried to catch her breath and caught his instead, hot and flavored with the taste of whiskey.

He ran his hands over her back, chasing shivers, setting off new ones, sliding lower. Desire swelled inside her, pushing aside sanity, blazing a trail for more instinctive responses. She arched against him, losing herself in the kiss, in the moment. She tangled her hands in his hair. His hands slid over her buttocks, kneading, stroking. He caught the hem of her T-shirt and dragged it up, his knuckles skimming over the taut muscles of her back, skating along the sides of her rib cage.

Laurel felt as if she were tumbling through space, dizzy, hanging on tight to her only anchor. Then sud-

denly she was on her back with no roof but a sky full of
diamond lights and branches strung with lacy moss, and
Jack was at her breast, his tongue rasping against her
nipple, his lips tugging gently. The sensation was incredible, setting off a flutter of something wild inside her,
tearing away her self-control—

Control. Panic rose inside her. She never lost control.
Couldn't lose control. She was no creature of passion like
Savannah.

"No." The word came out as a puff of nothing. She
swallowed hard and tried again, pushing at Jack's broad
shoulders as guilt and fear and a dozen other emotions
twisted in her chest and tightened like vines around her
lungs and throat. "Jack, no."

His hand stilled as his fingertips were sneaking under
the waistband of her panties. He raised his dark, glittering eyes to meet hers, his mouth poised just above the
taut, swollen bud of her nipple. Laurel tightened her every muscle against the desire to just let go. She brought a
chilling dose of shame down on her own head to cool the
fire.

What the hell was the matter with her, succumbing
to the charms of a rake like Jack Boudreaux? On a stone
bench in her aunt's courtyard, no less. She barely knew
him, didn't trust him, wasn't even sure she liked him.

Jack watched her, watched the flash of panic, the
wash of guilt. "You want me, angel. I want you." He
shifted his weight, pressing his erection against her hip
as proof of his statement.

"I . . . I don't." Laurel bit down hard on the urge to
panic. She kept her eyes locked on his, as if that contact
somehow gave her a measure of control. Foolish. He outweighed her by eighty pounds. He could take what he
wanted, as men had been doing since the dawn of time.

"Tu menti, mon ange," he murmured, shaking his
head. "You lie to yourself, not me."

His eyes held fast on hers as he touched the warm,
dewy cleft of her womanhood.

"I think you proved your point," she said bitterly.

"You're a bastard, and I want you anyway. You've made that fact very clear."

That age-old weariness crept into his expression again, seeped outward from some deep, dark well inside him. "*Oui*," he said. He slid his hand back up over her belly and pulled her T-shirt down, covering her. He smoothed the fabric gently, regretfully, his mouth twisting. "And now I have the whole long night to wonder why I made it at all."

Chapter Thirteen

Laurel checked her reflection in the hall mirror, frowning. She hadn't brought a suit home with her. The best she could do was a loose-fitting navy linen blazer over a white silk tank and a pair of taupe trousers. The outfit was more formal than she had ever planned to look during her stay here, less formal than she would ever have allowed herself on the job. No win.

It seemed she was stuck in a groove of no-win situations. She didn't want to tackle anything more mentally and emotionally taxing than gardening, but had given her pledge to T-Grace and Ovide. She had no intention of getting involved with a man, but had tossed and turned until dawn thinking about Jack, dreaming about Jack. Jack, with his devil's grin. Jack, with his brooding intensity. Jack, with weary dark eyes that had seen too much.

What if she hadn't said no?

"You look very lawyerlike."

Laurel glanced around to find Caroline on her way out for the day. "I don't want to do this," she admitted glumly.

Caroline put her arm around Laurel's waist to give her a reassuring squeeze. "You don't feel ready?"

"No."

She reached up to tuck an errant strand of ash brown hair behind Laurel's ear, her heart aching a little. Beneath the discreet makeup, behind the lenses of her oversize spectacles, Laurel had the look of a child braced for the first day of school—trying to be brave, wanting to stay safe at home.

"I think maybe you're more ready than you know, darlin'," Caroline said gently. "More time isn't going to change what happened. You'll never be able to get justice for those children. I think the best thing you can do is go and get justice for somebody else, then."

Laurel heaved a sigh and nibbled her lower lip, chewing off the soft coral lipstick she had just applied. She couldn't think of a thing to say. The feelings were too jumbled. She wanted to stand there forever with Caroline's arm around her, with her aunt's love supporting her. This was what she had come home for, not to jump into trouble with a religious charlatan, not to fend off Vivian's machinations, not to be tempted by Jack Boudreaux. For love, for someone who would judge her far less harshly than she judged herself. For the first time in a long while she felt an acute stab of longing for her father, who had solved all her childish problems with a hug and a kiss and a stick of Juicy Fruit gum. But all she had left of him were a few old snapshots, his crawfish tie pin, and his sister—Caroline.

She drew in a slow, deep breath, tamping down the emotions, drawing up some strength, focusing on the few items scattered on the Chippendale hall table, and cataloging them to give her mind something to do besides wallow in sad memories—an ivory French-style telephone, a blue willow vase holding a spray of fresh-cut flowers, a pewter dish holding an assortment of car keys and a lone earring.

"I'll be all right," she said, her gaze fastening on the earring. It was heart-shaped, large, tarnished silver studded with rhinestones and bits of colored glass. She fished

it out of the dish as an excuse to change the topic. "Is
this yours?"

Caroline frowned at the gaudy bauble. "Lord, no. It
must be Savannah's." She took a step back and gave her
niece one last, long look in the eye, not in the least bit
fooled by the diversion. "You come down to the store and
see me later if you need to talk, you hear?"

Laurel nodded. Caroline reached up and stroked her
niece's cheek gently, her thumb just grazing one of the
dark shadows of fatigue that arched beneath her eyes. "I
know how strong you really are, sweetheart," she said
softly, "and I know you'll be all right. You're a Chandler,
after all, and we're made of stern stuff. But don't expect
to climb back all in one day, and don't forget that I'm
here if you need me."

"Thanks, Aunt Caroline," Laurel murmured.

Caroline straightened her dainty shoulders, a gleam
in her dark eyes and a wry smile curling her mouth.
"Thanks, nothing. You go kick the figurative shit out of
that television preacher."

A chuckle bubbled up inside Laurel, and she smiled.
"I'll do my best."

As Caroline went out, Savannah came down the
stairs, wearing a plum silk kimono trimmed with a band
of ivory satin and wide ivory satin cuffs that fell past her
wrists. Laurel watched her descent by way of the mirror
as she repaired her lipstick, trying to assess her sister's
mood. It had been near dawn before Savannah had come
in, and she was obviously trying to fight off the afteref-
fects of her late night. She wore a blue gel eye mask to
combat puffiness and took the stairs one careful step at a
time. Her lips were swollen and red, and her hair was as
wild as a witch's mane around her shoulders.

Their eyes met in the mirror, and Laurel bit down on
the questions that sprang instantly to mind and the recriminations that came hard on their heels.

"Is this your earring?" She held up the heart-shaped
bob as she turned away from the mirror.

Savannah said nothing as she padded barefoot down
the hall. She stared blankly at the earring for a moment,

flicked at it with a finger to set it swinging. "It was in your car," she said flatly. "Where are you going?"

"Down to the courthouse to see about stopping Baldwin from harassing the Delahoussayes."

"Christ, Baby, you barely know them."

"I know all I need to know."

"You're not supposed to be upsetting yourself with other people's problems." *You're supposed to be letting me take care of you.*

Laurel opened her pocketbook and dropped in her lipstick and car keys. "So," she said with a shrug, "I'll solve this one and go back to laying low. How's that sound?"

"Like a load of bullshit," Savannah snapped. "Let the Delahoussayes take care of themselves. They can damn well fight their own fights." Her mouth bent into something like a smile. "You saw that for yourself yesterday. That bitch Annie damn near gave me a bald spot."

She lifted a hand to rub at her scalp, the sleeve of her kimono falling to her elbow. Laurel's eyes went round at the sight of her wrist. The delicate, porcelain skin was bruised and raw in spots.

"My God, Sister! What happened to you?" she demanded, snatching at Savannah's arm so she could get a better look.

Savannah bared her teeth, an expression made eerier by the blue mask she wore across her eyes like something left over from Mardi Gras. "You don't want to know."

"Yes, I do! What the hell—"

"No," she said coolly. "I distinctly remember you telling me you didn't want to hear about my sex life. You didn't want to hear that Ronnie Peltier has a cock like a jackhammer or that the Revver likes to play whip-me, whip-me games or that I like to do it with—"

"Stop it!" Laurel yelled. Flinging her sister's arm away, she stepped back, as if Savannah's admission was so repulsive, she couldn't stand the idea of touching her or breathing the same air. "Dammit, Savannah, why do

you have to do that? Why do you have to degrade yourself that way?"

"Because I'm a *slut.*" Savannah threw the word like a
dagger, her temper tearing through what little self-control she had left. She stalked toward Laurel, eyes narrowed behind her mask, lips pulled back. "I'm not a
shining little bright-eyed heroine. I'm what Ross Leighton turned me into."

"You're what you want to be," Laurel fired back.
"Ross hasn't laid a hand on you in fifteen years—"

"How do you know?" Savannah sneered, backing her
into the hall table. "Maybe I still fuck him twice a week
for old time's sake."

"Shut up!"

"What's the matter, Baby? Don't you want to hear
about how I spread my legs for our dear old stepdaddy
so you wouldn't have to?"

The words stung like nettles in Laurel's heart. "I
didn't have any control over what Ross did to you," she
said, her voice choked with emotion. "You can't blame
me, and you can't blame yourself. It's stupid to spend the
rest of your life punishing yourself for something that
was beyond your control."

Savannah stepped back, her expression beneath her
mask a combination of cynicism and incredulity. "My
God, aren't you the little hypocrite?" she said softly.
"What the hell have you been doing with your whole
damn life?"

Laurel stared at her, stunned, weak. Her knees felt
like water, and her stomach tightened like a fist.

Mama Pearl rumbled into the hall, wringing her
plump hands in a red checked dish towel, a scowl folding
her forehead into burls of flesh. "What the world goin'
on out here?" she demanded. "All I hear is yellin' an'
cursin' like to burn the Almighty's ears! What goin' on?"

Savannah pulled her temper in and wrapped it tight
around her as she adjusted the sash on her kimono.
"Nothing, Mama Pearl," she said calmly. She picked a
piece of dead leaf out of her hair and crumbled it between her fingers. "I just came down to get a pot of tea."

Mama Pearl looked to Laurel for corroboration. Laurel straightened her glasses and picked up her purse, her hand trembling visibly. "I have to go," she mumbled, refusing to meet anyone's eyes, focusing on maintaining some semblance of control.

She walked out of the house and into the sauna heat of midmorning on wobbly legs, thinking that after what she had just been through, a trip to the courthouse was going to be a piece of cake.

The air-conditioning in the sheriff's office was fighting a losing battle against the afternoon sun that came glaring in through the window. Sheriff Duwayne Kenner stood behind his desk with his hands on his slim hips, overseeing the futile attempts of two maintenance men who were trying to install a new venetian blind.

"Get the goddamn bracket straight," he growled. "And the left one's half an inch higher than the right. What the hell you boys thinkin'—that y'all can tip the whole goddamn courthouse so the shade'll hang straight?"

The maintenance man on the right shot a glance over his meaty shoulder, blinking at the sweat that dribbled down his shining dark forehead and into his eyes. His blue shirt was soaked down the back and sides, the tails crawling up out of the low-riding waistband of his pants, giving glimpses of a generous tube of fat around his middle. He gulped a breath and mumbled the expected, "No, sir."

The other man—younger, thinner, harder, darker—set his jaw at the word "boy" and dropped his end of the blind so that the blazing sun struck Kenner full in the face.

"Jesus Christ!" The sheriff took a quick step back, snapping his head to the side and squeezing his eyes shut. The badge pinned to the chest of his sweat-stained khaki uniform shirt glinted like gold.

The younger man's mouth flicked up on the corners.

"I's sorry, Sheriff Kenner," he said in an exaggerated drawl.

"Your sorry black ass," Kenner grumbled under his breath. He jerked around, muttering about the squandering of tax dollars on equal opportunity programs, and faced the young woman who had come into his office a full five minutes ago to speak with him.

Laurel Chandler. Ross Leighton's stepdaughter. While Kenner curried favor with Leighton, he was in no particular hurry to listen to the girl. Everyone in town had heard about her—making wild accusations up in Georgia, blowing the case, losing her marbles over it. She was trouble. He could smell trouble a mile off— even when it was wearing perfume.

Laurel sat in the visitor's chair, sweat trickling down her sides and between her shoulder blades. Her linen jacket was wilted, her temper frayed down to the nub. While her morning's efforts had gone smoothly, she had a feeling Kenner was going to be a whole different story. He had the unmistakable aura of a redneck about him. He looked fifty, tough and sinewy, with the lean build of a cowboy. His steel gray hair was thinning fast on top, but she doubted anyone ribbed him about it. If Kenner had a sense of humor, the Klan backed the NAACP.

He regarded her with hard, dark eyes, his impatience charging the air around him, his mouth set in a grim line that would have done Clint Eastwood proud. "What can I do for you, Miz Chandler?" he asked in a flat tone that indicated both his level of interest and his lack of willingness to do anything at all for her.

Laurel took a deep breath of stifling, sweat-tinged air and shifted on her seat. "I wanted to make you aware of the situation between the Delahoussayes of Frenchie's Landing and Reverend Jimmy Lee Baldwin. He's been harassing them and disrupting their business. I've spoken with Judge Monahan on their behalf."

Kenner perched a skinny buttock on one corner of his desk, picked up a pack of unfiltered Camels, and shook one out just long enough to hook his lip over.

"Seems a might drastic," he said, cigarette bobbing as he
tore a match from a book and struck it.

"Baldwin is not only making a nuisance of himself,
he's defaming the Delahoussayes and inhibiting their
right to free trade."

He took a deep pull on the cigarette, pretending to
consider the facts as she had presented them. "He hadn't
hurt anybody, has he?"

"Is that your criterion for action?" Laurel asked
coolly. "You wait until someone has resorted to physical
violence?"

Eyes narrowing to slits, Kenner blew twin streams of
smoke out his slim nose and pointed a finger at her,
shaking ash down on the cheap linoleum floor. "I do a
damn good job in this parish, Missy. Everywhere around
us they got dead girls stacked up like cordwood and drug
dealers crawling around thick as copperheads in
canebreaks. You don't see that here, and I'll tell you
why—'cause I know damn well whose ass to kick."

"I'm sure you do."

"You're goddamn right I do." He took a quick drag
on his smoke and shot a glare over his shoulder at the
maintenance men, who were making an unholy racket
with the blind. "And I'll tell you this—I got better things
to do with my time than chase around after that television preacher, tellin' him where he can piss and where
he can't."

Laurel rose gracefully, smoothing the wrinkles from
her trousers, schooling her temper. Kenner was hardly
the first jerk she'd ever come up against. "I don't care
where he pisses, Sheriff," she said smoothly. "I don't
care where he does anything, as long as he doesn't do it
at Frenchie's Landing. Judge Monahan has granted a
temporary injunction until the formalities can be taken
care of. Diligent as you are, I expect you'll do everything
in your power to see that Reverend Baldwin respects it."

Kenner gave her a flat look, the muscles in his lean
jaw working. His cigarette smoldered between his fingers, ribbons of blue smoke curling up into the stagnant
air. "I know who you are, Miz Chandler," he said softly.

"I don't need some female with an overactive imagination running around my parish crying wolf every time she turns around and dud'n like the look of somebody."

The jibe hit and stuck. Laurel tensed against it, steeled herself and her pride, and dug down for some of the grit she had been known for back in Scott County. Lifting her chin, she met Kenner's stare, unflinching. "I don't make empty accusations, Sheriff. If I cry wolf, there'll be one coming to chew your skinny ass."

He gave a snort of derision and stubbed out his cigarette, shooting another glare at the maintenance men, who had stopped working altogether to watch the confrontation.

"Get your lazy asses in gear and get that goddamn blind up before I get a heat stroke!"

Laurel turned and walked out, gritting her teeth as her stomach knotted and her nerves gave a belated tremor. The hall was cooler and darker. The courthouse had been built before the Civil War, and for a town the size of Bayou Breaux, it was an impressive structure, three stories of brick with Doric columns and a broad set of steps out front. Inside, the hallways were wide with soaring ceilings where old fans turned lazily to stir the humid air. The dark green plaster walls were decorated with a framed gallery of prominent citizens from the past.

For a moment Laurel leaned back against the cool, nubby plaster and rested her eyes, willing herself to relax. It didn't matter what Kenner thought of her. His opinion was no great surprise. She imagined a great many people held it. *The Prosecutor Who Cried Wolf.* The headline still made her angry, still made her want to lash out, to rail at those who had doubted her.

I wasn't wrong. They were guilty.

She wasn't wrong, she was a failure. That was the worst of it. Knowing that those children had been committed to terrible fates because she hadn't been able to prove it.

"No one will believe you, Laurel. . . . Don't tell Mama."

For an instant she was twelve again, standing in the door to the parlor, watching Vivian fuss with an arrangement of calla lilies and delphinium. The secret was there inside her, a big gooey ball of words that clogged her throat. Savannah's warning rang in her ears—*"No one will believe you, Laurel. Don't tell Mama. She'll only get cross with you. . . ."* Helplessness and fear gripped her like icy hands, grappling with her sense of justice. She wanted to tell, thought she ought to, but she just stood there, watching Vivian frown and fuss, her temper slipping visibly as the flowers failed to please her. . . .

Sucking in air like a diver just breaking the surface, Laurel shoved herself away from the wall and turned into a shallow alcove, where a water fountain gurgled. She bent over and swallowed a mouthful of cool, over-chlorinated water, dampened her fingers, and patted her cheeks. Dismissing the memories, she dug through her pocketbook for a roll of Maalox tablets.

She would have to go to Frenchie's and explain things to T-Grace and Ovide. Maybe she would stop by the antiques shop and tell Aunt Caroline everything had gone well enough.

"Back in harness, so to speak, Laurel?"

She jumped at the sound of Stephen Danjermond's voice. She hadn't heard his approach, had been too focused on herself, she supposed. Closing her purse, she casually took a step back. "Just doing a favor for some friends."

"The Delahoussayes?" he asked, his smile telling her he already knew the answer. He stood half in shadow, his face half light and half dark, like a figure in a dream. Laurel found the effect unsettling. "News travels fast in a town this size," he said, sliding his hands in the pockets of his tailored charcoal trousers. "I had a chat with Judge Monahan over lunch. He was very taken with you."

"He was taken with the idea of making Reverend Baldwin's life unpleasant," Laurel said. "Some years ago his mother gave a sizable fortune to a man of Baldwin's ilk, and it was later discovered he spent the contributions of his flock on such things as air-conditioned dog houses and spiritual retreats to nude beaches on the French Riviera."

"You sell yourself short, Laurel. I was discussing with him the possibility of your coming to work for me. The idea pleased him."

She frowned a little. "I wish you wouldn't have said anything. I told you, Mr. Danjermond, I'm not thinking about going back to work at this point."

"But you're thinking about seeing justice done, aren't you, Laurel? A job title has little to do with it. You are who you are."

The way he said it had a ring of inevitability, as if mankind's little play of the busy, bustling world was all superfluous to the core of life. The trappings could all be stripped away and everyone reduced to their very essence. She was the champion for justice.

"It's what matters most to you, isn't it?"

Laurel kept her answer to herself, feeling it would somehow give him an advantage in their chess game. She resettled her purse strap on her shoulder and shifted her weight toward the door. "I ought to be on my way. I have to go tell T-Grace and Ovide what's going on and make sure Baldwin gets the message. I don't have a lot of faith that Kenner will do the job."

Amusement lit the district attorney's eyes and widened his smile. He turned and started toward the door with her, checking his long, fluid strides to stay beside her. "I assume it wasn't love at first sight between you and Duwayne."

"He's a racist, a sexist, and a jerk," Laurel said flatly.

"And he's very good at his job."

"Because he knows whose ass to kick. Yes, he told me."

They stepped out onto the broad portico. A capricious breeze slithered between the columns, riffling Danjermond's raven hair and playing with the end of his burgundy tie. He cut a handsome figure, Laurel admitted, athletic and elegant, perfectly at home in his tailored suit standing at the portal to the halls of justice. He would go far on looks alone, farther with a mind as sharp and clever as his. She really couldn't blame her mother for seeing him as a potential son-in-law. Vivian had been raised to believe in matches made for family allegiance and social prominence. Stephen Danjermond had to fit her requirements to a T.

"There's a trick to dealing with Kenner, you know," he pointed out.

Laurel frowned. "Yes, well, I don't think I'm going to grow a penis any time soon."

Danjermond laughed, delighted with her plain talk. People never expected her to speak her mind, assuming that because she was petite and pretty, she was automatically shy and retiring. She had used that erroneous assumption to her advantage more than once.

"Heaven forbid!" He lifted a hand and cupped her chin, his thumb stroking along her jaw, sending a jolt of awareness through her. Sexuality, sensuality, hummed in the air around him as if he had suddenly turned up the power on his magnetism. "You're delicate, lovely, exquisite just as you are, Laurel. Bright, forthright, brimming with integrity."

"Kenner thinks I'm a troublemaker." She backed away from him and turned to look out at the street.

"I'll speak with him."

"No. I fight my own battles, thank you."

"Yes, you do, Laurel. That's a matter of record." His gaze turned speculative. The breeze died. "The battle you fought in Scott County—should you have won?"

Laurel had to brace herself against the barrage of feelings his blunt question brought on. Yes, she should have won—for the children, for the name of right. But she hadn't been strong enough, and in the end evil had won out.

"They were guilty," she said, and without another glance at Stephen Danjermond, she headed down the steps.

Chapter Fourteen

Laurel wheeled her Acura into Meyette's Garage, dreading the thought of getting out of the car's air-conditioned comfort. She had shed her jacket, but the day had simply turned too hot to move. It was a day to be spent in a cool room with quiet music and a good book. That image would remain in her imagination, however, shimmering like a mirage for another hour or so.

Savannah had brought the car home with a near-empty tank and a coat of mud splatters from God knew where. Laurel had decided she would fill up on her way to Frenchie's Landing and wash the car herself after the heat of afternoon had subsided. The prospect of doing something physical, simple, and gratifying held enormous appeal. Just herself and her car in the shade of the driveway, a bucket and a sponge, Mozart playing softly in the background . . .

She pulled up along pumps of a type most stations had traded in for newer models ten years ago and got out, sending a smile to the mechanic who stuck his head out from under the hood of a putty-color Ford.

"Hey, Miz Chandler."

"Hey, Nipper."

"I'll be right with you."

"That's fine."

He beamed a smile at her, strong white teeth flashing in a lean face that was covered with grime and running with sweat. He was twenty-five, with a flat-topped hedge of brilliant red hair. Laurel thought he was probably something of a local heartthrob when he was clean, but she had only ever seen him tinkering under the hood of a car, looking like Pigpen grown up.

Meyette's was the kind of station that didn't exist anywhere but small, out-of-the-way towns. City folk would have shied away from the shabby buildings, the dark, dirty, cavernous garage. They might have found the old chest-type Coca-Cola cooler that squatted on the gallery by the front door quaint and might have tried to wheedle the antique away from the old rube who ran the place, but they would have let their bladders burst before asking for the restroom key and would have starved before trying a stick of the homemade *boudin* sausage Mrs. Meyette sold over the counter in the office.

The thought offered a margin of security. While Cajun country had become a trendy tourist draw, there were still parts of home that would never be violated.

Laurel's gaze hit on Jimmy Lee Baldwin, who stood on the gallery of the garage, a bottle of Orange Crush in hand, and the word "violated" reverberated in her head. Her enjoyment of her surroundings dimmed. She couldn't look at him without thinking of the things Savannah had said about him. The man was slime. His mere existence was a violation against decent people. Preaching salvation and performing lewd sex acts on the side was a kind of hypocrisy that touched off an almost uncontrollable fury in her.

Straightening away from the side of the building as she marched toward him, he smoothed a hand over his slicked-back tawny hair, at the same time pasting on his too-white smile, making the two actions seem like cause and effect. He had sweated through his white dress shirt and rolled up the sleeves in a futile attempt to battle the heat. His skinny black necktie hung limply around his neck, pulled loose at the collar, and the button beneath it was undone. The crease in his black trousers had melted out, the total effect leaving him looking like a rumpled and disreputable traveling salesman.

"Miz Chandler, what a pleasant surprise," he said. He discreetly wiped the condensation from the soda bottle off on the side of his pants leg and offered his hand to her. He had given the subject of Laurel Chandler considerable thought as he had lain in bed this morning, the fan blowing across his naked body as he recuperated from his night's play. He wanted her if not as an ally, then at least out of the Delahoussaye camp. He was ready to pluck the rose of his future, but every time he reached for it, he was pricked by this lovely little thorn.

Laurel scowled at him as if he were holding out a dead rat for her inspection. "I don't see much of anything pleasant about it, Mr. Baldwin."

Jimmy Lee tightened his jaw against the urge to call her a snotty little bitch. He pulled his hand back and planted it at his waist. "There's no need to be hostile. We're not enemies, Miz Chandler. In fact, we could be allies. We fight on the same side, you and I. Against evil, against sin."

Laurel almost laughed. "Save the sermons for the poor fools who believe in you. We're not on the same side, Baldwin. I have my doubts that we belong to the same species. From what I've heard about you and seen of you, I'd have to say you're more closely related to things that crawl out from under dead tree stumps. Don't waste your time trying to charm me. I've dealt with too many snakes not to know one when I see one."

Fury burned hot in Jimmy Lee's belly. If there was one thing in this world he couldn't tolerate, it was a mouthy broad. He would have given just about anything for a chance to cuff her one, but he wouldn't have given up his shot at stardom, and Nipper Calhoun was too handy a witness.

He lifted his shoulders in a stiff shrug and stared

down at her, his tawny eyes as cold and flat as gold coins. "That's not what I've heard about you," he said tightly. "The way I hear it, you point fingers at random."

The blow to her pride landed, but Laurel didn't bat an eyelash. She wouldn't give him the satisfaction. "It doesn't matter what you've heard about me. All you need to hear is what Judge Monahan has to say. As of today you are hereby ordered to cease and desist your harassment of the Delahoussayes and are forbidden from setting foot on their property. I'm pleased to give you the news in person," she said, flashing him a nasty smile. "The paperwork will be delivered. You have yourself a real nice day, Mr. Baldwin."

She turned and pranced away toward Meyette's office, prim little nose in the air. Jimmy Lee watched her go and felt all his carefully stacked plans for his big campaign tumble around him like a house of cards. Before he could stop himself, he had lunged after her and clamped a hand down on her shoulder, meaning to spin her around and tell her a thing or two about playing hard ball.

Jack stepped out of the shadows of the garage and hooked the toe of his boot in front of the preacher's ankle. As Laurel twisted away from the man's touch, Jack pulled back, and the Revver went sprawling, facedown in the dirt. Baldwin's breath left him in a painful grunt.

"Oh, hey, I'm sorry, Jimmy Lee," Jack said without a drop of sincerity. "I guess I wasn' lookin' where I was goin'."

Baldwin shoved himself up onto his hands and knees, coughing and spitting dirt in between curses. He shot a vicious look at Jack over his shoulder, his face burgundy beneath the layer of gritty dirt.

"*Bon Dieu!*" Jack exclaimed with exaggerated shock. "There's some words comin' out your mouth I never seen in the Bible!"

"I doubt you ever cracked the spine of a Bible, Boudreaux," Jimmy Lee snarled. He hauled himself to his feet, trying in vain to dust his clothes off. His eyes locked on Jack in a stare as hard and cold as a billiard ball.

"Well," Jack drawled, "mebbe I never have read it, but I looked at the pictures." He put on a quizzical look and scratched his head. "Do you think Jesus got his tan at Suds 'n' Sun too?"

Jimmy Lee glared at him for a second, his jaw working to chew back his rage.

"What do you think, Miz Chandler?" Jack arched a brow at Laurel.

Laurel stared at him for several seconds, caught completely off guard by his appearance, to say nothing of his question. She hadn't expected to see him here, hadn't finished preparing herself for speaking to him after what had happened in the courtyard. She had strategies filed away in her brain for every kind of courtroom situation, but she had no strategies for near-miss sexual encounters. She had no string of lovers in her past to draw experience from. Her ex-husband was the only man she had ever been seriously involved with, and while Wesley was a good man, an intelligent man, a kind man, he wasn't the kind of man Jack was.

He was shirtless and tan. He held a cherry Popsicle in his left hand, his elegant musician's fingers deftly holding the stick so the thing wouldn't drip on him. He brought it to his mouth and nipped off a corner.

"This is quite a day for me," he said, his dark eyes glittering with mischief. "I get to see a lawyer speechless and a television preacher wearing his dirt on the *outside* for once."

"I don't have to take this from you, Boudreaux," Jimmy Lee said, his voice low and thrumming with anger. He raised an accusatory finger and shook it in Jack's face. "Mr. Big-Shot Best-Selling Author. You're nothing but a no-account, alcoholic piece of trash. All the money in the world can't change that."

"Naw," Jack said, his pose deceptively casual, one leg cocked, his right hand propped at his waist. He heaved an exaggerated sigh and hung his head. "A man is what he is."

In the blink of an eye, he had Baldwin by the shirt front and slammed up against the side of the building.

That quickly the mask of humor was gone, and in its place was a fury that burned like hot coals in the depths of his eyes.

"A man is what he is, Jimmy Lee." He ground the words out between his teeth, his face inches from Baldwin's. "You, you're a piece-of-shit con man. Me, I'm the guy who's gonna kick your balls up to your throat and knock your teeth down to meet 'em if you *ever* lay a hand on Miz Chandler again." He let the fire shimmer in his eyes for a moment longer, then flashed an unholy smile. "Have I made myself perfectly clear, Jimmy Lee?"

Slowly he loosened his hold on Baldwin's shirt front. Smiling affably, he made a token attempt to smooth out the fabric and brush off some of the dirt, then stepped back and dropped his hands to the waist of his jeans.

"Mebbe you just better go on home and change, Jimmy Lee. You don' want people lookin' at you and thinkin' you had a run-in with the devil and lost."

He walked away a few paces and poked his toe at the Popsicle he had dropped, frowning. Dismissing Baldwin entirely, he dug some change out of his pocket and headed for the little white freezer that hummed laboriously beside the Coca-Cola cooler. He could feel Baldwin's eyes boring into his back, but didn't give a damn. There was nothing any two-bit cable TV preacher could do to him. He didn't run a business, and he already had a bad reputation. He shot an inquiring look at Laurel.

"You want a Popsicle, *'tite chatte*?"

"You're messing with the wrong man, Boudreaux," Baldwin said, his voice trembling with rage and humiliation. "You don't want to tangle with me."

Jack flicked a glance at him, looking supremely bored with the whole scene. "That's right, preacher. I don' want to tangle with you. I got better things to do with my time than scrape you off the bottom of my shoe, so mebbe you oughta just stay the hell outta my sight."

Jimmy Lee shook his head, a strange look of amazement dawning on his face. "You don't know who you're dealing with," he muttered, then turned on the heel of his wingtip and stalked off toward his car.

Laurel watched him walk away, then turned toward Jack, stepping up onto the gallery. He stared down into the freezer as cold billowed up out of it in a cloud.

"For someone who claims not to be anybody's hero, you seem to spend an awful lot of time coming to my rescue," she said.

"Mais non," Jack mumbled, reaching in for a Fudg- sicle. "Me, I was just having a little fun with Jimmy Lee while my carburetor gets looked at."

He didn't want her reading anything into his actions, he told himself. But the truth was that he didn't want to look at those actions too closely himself. He didn't want to dig too deep for the reason behind the rush of anger he'd felt when Baldwin had put his hand on her. He didn't own her, would never have any claim on her, and therefore had no business feeling jealous or overprotec- tive.

Conditioned response. That was what it was. How many times had he rushed at Blackie when the old man reached out and put a hand on Maman or Marie? Count- less times. They had called him their hero, too. But he hadn't been anything but a kid full of rage and hate. Small and weak and worthless, and Blackie had shaken him off more times than not. He wasn't small or weak anymore. The feeling of slamming Baldwin up against the building had sent a rush of adrenaline and power through him that was still buzzing in his veins.

He glanced at Laurel as he unwrapped his treat, try- ing to defuse her concentration with a teasing smile. "Besides, I didn't want you to pull your gun out and shoot him. Day's too hot to have a corpse laying around out in the sun." She made a disgusted face, and he chuckled to himself. "Popsicle or Fudgsicle, angel? What do you think?"

Laurel narrowed her eyes as he blatantly dismissed her line of questioning. "I think you ought to make up your mind, Jack," she said. "Are you a good guy or a bad guy?"

"That all depends on what you want me for, darlin',"

he murmured, his voice rough and smooth at once, beckoning a woman to reach out and touch him.

Laurel's heart beat a little harder; nerve endings he had awakened and tantalized the night before stirred restlessly. She frowned at him. "I don't want you for anything."

Jack leaned across the open freezer, "It's a good thing you're not under oath, counselor," he whispered.

"Close the freezer, Boudreaux," she said sarcastically, "before your hot air melts all the Popsicles."

She went into the station and paid for her gas, spending a few moments chatting with Mrs. Meyette, who asked after Aunt Caroline and Mama Pearl, told her she was too thin, and made her take half a dozen sticks of *boudin* with her. When she came out, Jack was nowhere in sight.

She staunchly refused to acknowledge the disappointment that slid down through her. She had better things to do with her time than spar with him, and she had to assume he had better things to do, as well. He was supposed to be some hot-shot best-selling author, but he never seemed to work. It seemed to her he was always at Frenchie's or giving her a hard time. And it took no imagination at all to picture him spending the rest of his time sprawled in a hammock asleep with that awful hound sacked out right beneath him.

Trying like a demon *not* to picture him at all, she drove home and changed out of her slacks into a cool gauzy blue skirt and a loose-fitting pale blue cotton tank. The house was silent, the shades drawn. Mama Pearl had left a note on the hall table: *Gone to card club. Red beans and rice in the pot. Eat, you!* Monday. Wash day. Red beans and rice for supper. Laurel smiled at the comfort of tradition.

There was no sign of Savannah. Laurel wasn't sure whether to be disappointed or relieved. She didn't like the memories from their morning's argument lingering in her mind like acrid smoke, but she didn't know how they would clear the air, either. They had both said things that would have been better left unsaid. They couldn't go back and change their childhoods. Laurel wanted to leave it all in the past, to start fresh, but Savannah dragged her past around with her like an enormous, overloaded suitcase.

And so do you, Baby. She could almost hear her sister's voice, angry, accusatory.

"What the hell have you been doing with your whole damn life?"

Looking for justice.

There was a difference, she insisted. She was an attorney; that was her job. She wasn't trying to change the past. She wasn't trying to atone for anything.

The word "liar" drifted through her mind, and she slammed down on it before it had the chance to do more than rattle her nerves. She had to go out and take care of some business. No doubt by the time she got home, Savannah would be here, begging forgiveness for the nasty things she'd said, promising she hadn't meant any of them. That was the way their fights usually ran. That was the way Savannah's temper ran—hot and cold, from emotional conflagration to contrition in a flash. She was probably off somewhere right now thinking about coming home to red beans and rice and a side order of apologies.

Savannah stared out at the heat. It seemed so thick, so oppressive, she thought she could see it hanging in the air above the bayou, pressing down on everything. It permeated the cabin, seeping in through the screens, soaking into everything, bringing with it the wild, feral scent of the swamp.

She brushed at the stray tendrils of hair that had escaped her topknot and shifted restlessly from one bare foot to the other. Sweat coated her skin like a fine mist, despite the fact that she wore nothing but a pair of ragged cut off jeans and a black bandeau bikini top with a sheer white blouse hanging open over it.

The quiet was getting to her. She had promised Coop she wouldn't disturb him, but the day had come to a complete standstill. Even the birds had fallen silent beneath the blanket of heat. The sense of expectation that was so much a part of the swamp had thickened until everything waited, breath held, for something unknown, unseen.

The two-room cabin squatted on stilts above the murky green water. From Savannah's vantage point, no solid land was visible, only bald cypress, their thick hard trunks thrusting up from the water, scruffy, stubby branches sticking out like deformities, knobby knees jutting out at the bases. They looked like tortured creatures that had been cast under an enchantment and petrified so that they resembled death. Floating on the surface around their trunks were sheets of delicate green duckweed and rafts of water hyacinth, shimmering violet and looking deceptively fragile beneath the brutal sun. Lily pads lay scattered like an array of deep green Frisbees tossed randomly across the bayou.

She could see a partially submerged log lying at the edge of a thicket of cattails and knew it could well be an alligator. Not far to the south, the jagged stump of a dead cypress had become home to a nest of herons, and the pair posed there, motionless, looking like a woodcarver's exquisite craftings, their long necks arched and tucked, black beaks as straight and slender as fencing foils.

The birds' stillness irritated Savannah. She wanted them to squawk and fly away, huge wings beating the air. She wanted the gator to lunge for one of the fish that dimpled the surface of the water as they rose unseen to catch insects. She wanted the air to stir, wanted to see the reeds sway. Most of all she wanted Coop to move.

He sat at a rough plank table that was pushed up against one screened wall, staring out, making notes from time to time, nearly as motionless as the surroundings. He had bought the cabin as a fish camp, but he never fished when he met her here. He mostly stared. "Absorbing the profound intensity of life in the swamp," he'd explained once. He would sit there for hours, seemingly doing nothing, then he would come to her and they would make love on the old moss-stuffed mattress.

This was their secret hideaway; an idea that usually appealed to Savannah. She liked going out on the bayou in her old flat-bottomed aluminum boat, not saying anything to anybody, winding her way into the dense, lush wilderness to meet her lover. But today something about the arrangement grated on her. She blamed it on the fight she'd had with Laurel.

"Why do you have to do that? Why do you have to degrade yourself that way?"

She jerked around and burned a hole in Cooper's broad back with her glare. "Haven't you stared out that screen long enough?"

Coop sat back, wincing a little at the stiffness that had settled in his joints. He scratched a hand back through his blond hair like a man just waking from a long, deep sleep, and looked at Savannah over his shoulder. He was struck as always by her raw sexuality and by the soft, stunning natural beauty she had seen fit to make slightly grotesque with collagen and silicone. She was so alluring, so flawed, she never failed to captivate him utterly.

He longed to turn and jot those thoughts down in his notebook, but he refrained. Savannah's mood seemed as volatile as the weather—a tense stillness that hid a building storm. Instead, he put down his pen, rose and stretched.

"I don't mean to ignore you, love," he mumbled in his low, smooth voice. "But I have to get my notes made. I'm doing an APR broadcast from N'Awlins next weekend."

Savannah's eyes lit up like a child's. "You'll take me with you?"

It was more a statement than a question. Coop doubted she even heard him when he said, "We'll see." She was already racing ahead, making plans for them to meet in one of the cottages of the Maison de Ville, chattering about dinner in her favorite restaurants, the shopping she would do, the clubs they might visit.

Of course, he wouldn't take her. While he loved her, he knew that love must be contained within very definite boundaries. If he allowed it to escape the small pen of Bayou Breaux, it would run wild and in its delirium destroy itself and them. Like a fine wine, it was something to be sipped and savored. Savannah would drink it all in greedy, sloppy gulps, spilling it down her, splashing it all over, laughing madly.

He stroked a hand over the back of her head down to her neck and smiled with pleasure as she arched into his touch like a cat.

"Let's get you out of these clothes," he murmured, stepping away from her, reaching for one cuff of the gossamer blouse she wore.

"No." Savannah pulled her hand back, smiling shyly to cover her shame. Laurel's words were too fresh in her mind. Coop would think the same when he saw the marks on her wrists—that she degraded herself. She didn't want to hear that from him, not today. Today she wanted to pretend they had a normal life. She sent him a coy look. "I want to wear it for you."

He said nothing, but stood and watched as she shed the bikini top and the cutoffs, leaving only the sheer white blouse to cover her. The picture she presented was more tantalizing than if she had been completely naked. She knew because she had stood in front of the mirror in her room and studied the look. Provocative. Dressed but not decent. The sheer fabric was a misty barrier that invited a man to reach past it to the treasures of her lush feminine body.

Time lost its meaning for her. They could have been in bed a week. She wanted it to last forever. With his slow, gentle lovemaking, Cooper made her think it *could* last forever, that they had all the time in the world instead of just a few stolen hours.

And time meant nothing as they lay together afterward, skin sticky with their mingled sweat, the air redolent with the exotic musk of sex and perfume, the dusty scent of the moss-stuffed mattress. They lay touching, despite the heat, limbs tangled, hearts thudding slowly, their breathing shallow, as if to keep from disturbing the peace that had settled around them.

This was happiness, Savannah thought, being here with Coop. She loved him so much it frightened her. Too good to be true. Too good to be hers. Sex with him was so different from what she sought out with others. With others she felt wild, wicked. With Coop there was nothing depraved, debauched, dissipated, dissolute. She felt all the things she had spent her life yearning for but never finding. She shivered a little at the thought. Too good to be true.

"Will you marry me, Coop?" The words seemed to spill directly out of her overflowing heart, and instantly a part of her wished them back, because she knew deep down what his answer would be.

The air hummed with silence for a few moments, then with the electric whine of cicadas, then with the tension of an answer unspoken. Tears stung Savannah's eyes and seared her heart like acid, and all the gold wore off the afterglow, leaving her feeling like what everyone said she was—a slut, a whore, not deserving of anything like the love of a good man.

"Why do you have to degrade yourself that way?"
Because that's what whores, do, Baby.

Coop sighed and sat up with his back against the headboard as Savannah got out of bed. "I can't give you that commitment, Savannah," he said sadly. "You know that. I have a wife."

She stepped into her shorts and jerked them up, her fingers fumbling with the fastenings as she shot him a burning look from under her lashes. "You have a vegetable."

"I can't abandon her, Savannah. Don't ask me to."

Frustration swelled and burst inside her like a festered wound, its hot, caustic poison shooting through her, penetrating every muscle, every fiber. Unable to stand it, she clamped her hands on her head and doubled over, a wild animal scream tearing from her throat.

"She doesn't even know who you are!" she sobbed.

He just sat there, looking handsome and sad, his blue eyes locked on her as if he were gazing at her for the very last time, memorizing her every feature.

"But *I* know who I am," he whispered, that low, smooth voice capturing futility and fatalism and a sense of inevitability she recognized but didn't want to hear.

He would never leave Astor as long as she was alive. And Savannah knew he would never marry her because wife was not the role he had cast her in in his real-life drama of the South. Unless she could purge herself somehow, cut out and dispose of what she had been all these years, and that seemed as impossible a task as cutting out a piece of the ocean.

She stared at him through tear-washed eyes for several silent moments, thinking she could feel her heart shatter like a glass ornament. Then she turned and left the cabin without a word, hating him, hating herself for what she was . . . and for what she would never be.

Chapter
Fifteen

Frenchie's was a madhouse. Annie had failed to show up for work, and one of the other waitresses was out sick, leaving T-Grace to wait tables herself. She stormed around the bar at a lightning pace, slinging plates of red beans and rice, serving beer, taking orders and barking out her own as she went. The heat and humidity had combined with her short temper to leave her looking frazzled and dangerous. Her red hair was a cloud of frizz around her head. Her eyes looked ready to pop out of her heat-polished face. She stopped in a clearing between tables and brushed her bangs off her forehead with the back of a hand, blowing a cooling breath upward as Laurel approached her.

"You get dat Jimmy Lee thrown in jail or what, *chère*?" she asked without preamble.

"He's been officially warned off," Laurel said, raising her voice to be heard above the racket of pool games, loud talk, and jukebox Zydeco.

T-Grace gave a derisive snort and propped a hand on

her skinny hip. "Ovide, he warn dat bastard's ass off with some buckshot next time he come 'round.'"

"I wouldn't advise that," Laurel said patiently, silently thankful the Delahoussayes hadn't already resorted to such measures. The Cajuns had their own code of folk justice, a tradition that predated organized law enforcement in these parts. "If he bothers you again, call the sheriff and press charges."

"If he bothers us again," T-Grace said, a sly smile pulling at one corner of her thin mouth, "we're gonna need to hire more help. All dat rantin' and ravin' what he done on television was like free advertisin' for Frenchie's. My Ovide, he's in a panic tryin' to serve ever'body."

Laurel turned to see Ovide, stoic as ever, planted behind the bar, filling mugs and popping the tops off long-neck bottles, sweat beading on his bald spot like dew on a pumpkin. Leonce was playing backup bartender, his Panama hat tipped back on his head. As he slid a bottle across the bar to a customer, a grin slashed white across his close-cropped beard in counterpoint to the scar that ran red across his cheek.

"So what's the difference between a dead lawyer and a dead skunk in the middle of the road?" the customer asked. "There's skid marks in front of the skunk."

Leonce howled at the old joke and moved to dig another beer out of the cooler. Jack swiveled around on his bar stool, grinning like the Cheshire cat as his gaze landed smack on Laurel. He had made a token concession to the "No Shirt, No Shoes, Get the Hell Out" sign that hung on the wall behind the bar, but the red team shirt from the Cypress Lanes Bowling Alley hung open down the front, framing a wedge of muscular chest and flat belly.

T-Grace reached out and patted Laurel's cheek, her eyes glowing as they darted between *une belle femme* and Jack. "*Merci, ma petite.* You done a fine job, you. Now come sit you pretty self down and have some supper before the wind comes up and blows you away, you so little!"

She took hold of Laurel's arm with a grip that could have cracked walnuts and ushered her to the bar, where she ordered Taureau Hebert to go in search of some other place to sit his lazy behind, thereby vacating the seat next to Jack.

"Hey, Ovide!" Jack called, his devilish gaze on Laurel. "How 'bout a champagne cocktail for our heroine here?"

Laurel gave him a look and busied her hands arranging her skirt. Ovide slid a foaming mug of beer in front of her. Jack leaned over conspiratorially and murmured, "What he lacks in sophistication, he makes up for in sensitivity."

A chuckle bubbled up, and Laurel shook her head. She couldn't seem to stay mad at him, no matter what he did or said or made her feel.

"Don't you ever work, Boudreaux?" she asked, frowning at him.

His grin stretched, dimples biting deep in his lean cheeks. "Oh, yeah. Absolutely. All the time." He leaned closer, bracing one hand on the back of her stool, resting the other on her knee. His voice dropped a husky notch, and his breath tickled the side of her neck. "I'm workin' on you now, *'tite chatte.*"

Laurel arched a brow. "Is that right? Well," she drawled, poking him hard in the ribs with her thumb, "you've been laid off, hot shot."

Jack rubbed his side and pouted. "You're mean." His scowl, however, was ruined by the gleam in his eyes as he added, "I like that in a woman."

"You mind your manners, Jack," T-Grace said with a wry smile as she set a steaming plate of food down in front of Laurel. "This one, she's gonna show you what's what, just like what she did wit' dat damn preacher."

Jack grinned and winked at Laurel, and she felt a wave of warmth sweep through her that had nothing to do with the heat of the day. It had to do with laughter, with friends, with a sense of belonging. The realization flashed like a light bulb going on above her head. She couldn't remember the last time she had felt welcome anywhere besides Aunt Caroline's house.

In Scott County she had always been an outsider, and then a pariah as she had leveled accusations at people no one wanted to believe capable of evil. She had told herself it didn't matter, that the only thing that mattered was justice, but it *had* mattered. She would have given anything back then to have someone in the community believe in her, support her, smile at her, joke with her.

She thought back to the first night she had come in here and remembered the sense of isolation that had enveloped her and the loneliness that had accompanied it. In just a matter of days the people here had accepted her, and acceptance was something she had ached for. She had called that need a weakness, but maybe it wasn't so much weak as it was human.

Dr. Pritchard's voice came back to her, soft and steady. *"You're not perfect, Laurel, you're human."*

"So, you managed to save the day again, did you, Baby?"

Savannah's voice cut sharply into her thoughts. Laurel turned toward her sister, a fist of anxiety tightening in her belly. Savannah stood with a tall drink in one hand, the other propped on her hip. Her breasts were threatening to spill over the edge of her black bikini top, the sheer blouse she wore over it offering no backup modesty. Her hair was a mess, falling out of its topknot in curling dark ribbons.

"It was nothing so dramatic as that," Laurel said, automatically downplaying her accomplishment, as she had done all her life.

"Come on, Baby," Savannah said with a tight, unpleasant smile, her pale blue eyes shining too bright. "Don't be modest. We're a helluva team, you and me. You knock 'em on their butts, and I screw their brains out."

Laurel clenched her jaw and squeezed her eyes shut for an instant, trying to gather strength and patience.

Jack caught the action and turned to Savannah with a frown.

"Hey, sugar, why you don' give it a rest for one night, huh?"

"Ooooh!" Savannah drew back with an exaggerated expression of mock fear, pressing her free hand to her throat. "What's this? Jack Boudreaux rising to an occasion that doesn't have its legs spread for him?"

"*Bon Dieu,*" he muttered, shaking his head.

"What?" Savannah demanded, two vodka tonics beyond reason, too upset with the turns her life was taking to give a damn. "I'm too crude for you, Jack? That's hard to imagine, considering the way you butcher people in your books. I can't imagine anything offending you."

She wedged herself between his stool and Laurel's, deliberately brushing his arm with her breast, sending him her most sultry expression. "We ought to go a couple rounds, Jack," she purred, raking a hot gaze from his crotch to his belly to his bare chest, finally landing on his face. "Just to find out."

He met her look evenly, his dark eyes intense, his mouth set in a grim line.

Laurel slipped down off her stool, doing her best to control the fine trembling in her limbs. "Sister, come on," she said, trying to take the glass from Savannah's fingers. "Let's go home."

Savannah turned on her, angry that Laurel was always the one with the cooler head, always in control, always respectable and bright and perfect.

"What's the matter, Baby? Am I being an embarrassment?" she asked, as angry with herself as she was with Laurel. "You'll never say so in here, will you? Don't make a public scene. Don't call attention to yourself. Never air the dirty laundry in plain sight. Christ," she sneered, "you're just as bad as Vivian."

She jerked her hand free of Laurel's grasp, sloshing vodka and tonic over the rim of her glass, her expression something that bordered so closely on hate that it took Laurel's breath away.

"You go on and be little Miss Prim and Proper," she

sneered, her voice laced with venom. "Always do the right thing, Laurel. Me, I've got better ways to spend my time."

She whirled around, almost losing her balance, the vodka numbing her equilibrium, as well as her inhibitions. Willing the floor to stop pitching, she walked away, her sights set on the pool players, her hips swinging, a hard laugh ringing out of her as she caught sight of Ronnie Peltier.

Laurel pressed a hand to her mouth and tensed against the emotions that were buffeting her like hurricane winds. She couldn't seem to get ahead. Every time she thought she was getting her feet under her, she got knocked back a step. She pulled in on herself, not hearing the noise of the bar, not seeing the look of concern Jack was giving her. All she heard was her pulse roaring in her ears. All she saw was the mistake she had made in coming home.

Without a word she turned and walked out of the bar. She didn't allow herself to think of anything at all as she crossed the parking lot. She just put one foot in front of the other until she had reached the levee, then she stood on the bank and stared out at the bayou, working furiously to tamp down the feelings Savannah had torn loose. It didn't do any good to get upset. Savannah was who she was. Her problems were rooted in a past she refused to let go of, was perhaps incapable of letting go of. She had her moments when she would say anything, do anything, and damn the consequences. It was pointless to let any of that get to her.

But it hurts, a small voice inside her said. The voice of a little girl who had only her big sister to rely on for love and comfort. The big sister who looked out for her, who protected her, who sacrificed for her.

But who looked out for Savannah?

Laurel bit her lip against the pain, squeezed her eyes shut against it. She pressed her hands over her face and stood there trembling, afraid if she even breathed, the dam would burst and she would dissolve into a quivering mass of weakness and guilt and pain.

Jack stood behind her on the levee, his feet rooted to the spot as he watched her struggle. He should have left her alone. There was no way in hell he wanted to get caught in the middle of what had gone on in the bar. But he couldn't seem to make himself turn around. He damned Savannah for being such a bitch, damned Laurel for being so brave, damned himself for caring. No good could come of it for any of them. But even as he was convincing himself of that fact, his feet were moving forward.

"She's drunk," he said.

Laurel hugged herself, her eyes fixed on the far bank of the bayou. "I know. She's got problems that go back a long way. I've been gone a long time. I didn't realize she was this . . . troubled," she murmured, searching desperately for a word that seemed safe, a word that skirted way around the one that came strongest to mind. "If I'd known, I don't think I would have come back now."

She braced herself against the wave of guilt that admission brought. *Selfish, weak, coward.* She should have been willing to help Savannah, regardless of her own fragile state. She owed her sister that much and more. Much, much more.

Jack stepped closer. His hands settled on her shoulders, so slim, so delicate, so strong, and still he told himself he should just go on back into Frenchie's and order himself another beer. "I can't see you running from trouble, *'tite chatte.'*"

Laurel stood still for his touch, while she told herself not to. His hands were big and warm, his long, musician's fingers gentle and soothing. Comforts she didn't deserve. Despair rose on a tide inside her. "Why do you think I came home in the first place?" she asked, her voice choked with the shame of it.

Because she needed a place to hide, a place to heal, Jack thought, but he said nothing of the sort. It didn't seem wise to let her know he'd been reading up on her, thinking about her. She didn't need a mercenary right now. She needed a shoulder. Cursing himself for a fool, he turned her around and offered his.

"Come here," he growled as he pulled her glasses off and folded his arms around her.

Laurel squeezed her eyes shut against the tears, refusing to let them fall. She told herself not to succumb to the temptation of leaning on him, but her arms slipped around Jack's lean waist just the same. It felt too good to be held, to let someone else be strong for a minute or two. Ironic that that someone was Jack, the self-professed antihero. She might have pointed that out to him if she hadn't felt so damn weak.

Trembling with the effort of holding it all at bay, she pressed her cheek to his chest, to the soft washed cotton of his bowling shirt. She concentrated on the sound of his heartbeat, the feel of the taut muscles in the small of his back, the scent of Ivory soap underlying the subtle tang of male sweat.

"You've had a hard day, huh, *mon coeur*?" Jack murmured, his lips brushing her temple, her faint perfume filling his head. She was so delicate in his arms, he couldn't believe she was strong enough to take on the burdens she had. It killed him to think of her trying. "You oughta be more like me," he muttered. "Don't give a damn about anyone but yourself. Let people do what they will. Take what you want and leave the rest."

"Oh, yeah?" Laurel scoffed, leaning back to look up at him. "If you're so tough, what are you doing standing here holding me?"

He grinned and swooped down to nip at the side of her neck, surprising a little squeal out of her. "I like the way you smell," he whispered, nuzzling her cheek, skimming his hands up and down her back.

Laurel squirmed and wriggled, laughing, finally breaking free of his hold. Snatching her glasses out of his hand, she danced a couple of steps back from him, her gaze suddenly catching on his. While her heart beat a little harder, her laughter faded away, and something warm and seductive and invisible pulled at her, like the allure of the moon on the tides.

"I told you, sugar," he said, lifting his shoulders in a lazy shrug. "Me, I just like to have a good time. And you strike me as a lady in serious need of a good time." He shuffled a step closer, held a hand out to her. "Come on, angel. Let's you and me go and have us some fun."

She eyed him warily. "Fun? What's that?"

She couldn't remember the last time she'd done anything just for fun. Her work had consumed her life for so long, then had come the struggle just to keep herself from falling into a million tiny broken bits. And since she had come home, her focus had been on doing constructive things. She had enjoyed her time in the garden, but the goal had been to accomplish something tangible, a success she could see.

Jack ducked around behind her and got her by the shoulders, steering her down the levee toward the dock. "You need a lesson from the master, sweetheart. I'll teach you all about havin' fun."

Reluctantly letting him herd her along, Laurel shot him a skeptical look over her shoulder. "Would this 'fun' you're alluding to be of a sexual nature?"

His dimples flashed. "I sincerely hope so."

"I'm out of here." She changed directions deftly, ducking under his arm and marching back up the levee toward the parking lot.

"Aw, come on, *'tite ange,*" Jack begged, jogging around to cut her off. He gave her his most sincere look, pressing his hands to his heart. "I'll behave myself. Promise."

Laurel gave a sniff of disbelief. "Are you going to try to sell me swampland, too?"

"No, but I'll show you some. I thought we could take a nice relaxing sunset boat ride."

"Go into the swamp at sunset? Are you crazy? The mosquitoes will cart us off and carve us up for dinner!"

"Not in the boat I have in mind."

She gave him a long, considering look, amazed that she could even be considering his offer. She didn't trust him an inch. But the idea of a leisurely cruise on the bayou, of escaping to the wilderness that had been her refuge as a child, held a strong appeal. And Jack himself was temptation personified.

"Come on, sugar," he cajoled, his head tipped boy-ishly, an irresistible smile canting his lips. He held his hand out to her. "We'll pass a good time."

Three minutes later they were climbing aboard a boat that was essentially a small screened porch on pontoons. The roof was waterproof canvas in a jaunty red-and-white stripe. A pair of redwood planters filled with geraniums and vinca vines sat as decoration flanking the door to the screened area.

"This is *your* boat?" Laurel asked, not bothering to hide her skepticism.

Jack reached under the velvety leaves of a geranium, plucked out the starter key, and blew the dirt off it. "No."

"No?" she followed him into the cabin. "What do you mean, no? You're *stealing* this boat?"

He frowned at her as he started the engine and gunned the throttle. "I'm not *stealing* it. I'm *borrowing* it." Laurel rolled her eyes. "Lawyers," he grumbled, scowling as he concentrated on piloting the pontoon away from the dock. "Relax, will you, angel? The boat belongs to Leonce."

With the issue of ownership out of the way, Laurel sank down on one of the deep cushioned benches that faced each other in front of the console. She tried to concentrate on the passing scenery—the businesses that backed onto the bayou and the ramshackle boat houses that were tucked along the bank behind them; the houses that lined the bank farther down, many with people in the yard gardening or talking with neighbors or watching children play. Normal scenes of people with normal lives. People who had ordinary backgrounds and boring jobs.

The thought struck a pang of envy inside her that hummed and vibrated like a tuning fork. If she had had a boring job, an ordinary background, maybe she and Wesley would still be together. Maybe they would have a child by now.

Sighing, she toed her shoes off, pulled her feet up on the bench, and tucked them under her, settling in, unconsciously letting go of the tension and easing into melancholy. Slowly, the fierce grip she held on her mind eased, and her thoughts drifted. They passed L'Amour, the brick house looking vacant and lonely standing amid the moss-draped live oak and magnolia trees. Huey watched them pass from the bank, a woebegone expression on his face. Then civilization grew scarce—the occasional plantation house visible in the distance, the odd tarpaper shack teetering above the black water on age-grayed pilings.

The scenery grew lusher, wilder. Trees crowded what land there was, shoulder to shoulder, their crowns entangling into a dense canopy of green that blotted out the evening sun, leaving the ground below them veiled in darkness. Sweet gum and persimmon and water locust, ironwood and redbud and a dozen other species with buttonbush and thorny dewberry and greenbriar skirting their bases. The banks were thick with patches of yellow spiked cane and coffee weed, fan-fronded palmetto trees and verdant ferns. Vines and flame-flowered trumpet creeper braided together along the edge like embroidery, and the shallows grew thick with spider lilies and water lettuce.

The bayou branched off again and again, each arm reaching into another pocket of wilderness. Some of the channels were as wide as rivers, others narrow trickles of streams, all of them part of a vast labyrinth of no-man's-land. The Atchafalaya was a place where it seemed the world was still forming, ever-changing, metamorphosing, and yet always primitive. Laurel could never come out here without feeling transported back in time. That had always been the appeal for her, to escape to a time when none of her problems existed. The swamp worked its magic on her again, pulling her into another dimension, leaving all her troubles in the distance as the pontoon chugged along.

They passed through a shadowy corridor of trees where no land was visible at all, giving testimony to the constant battle here between water and earth. A cat squirrel vaulted from one gray trunk to the next, skitter-

ing around behind it to peek its head around and stare at
the passing boat. Birds darted everywhere, warblers and
wildly painted buntings and orioles; flashes of color in
the gloom, flitting among the lacework of branches.

Finally, they emerged from the natural bower into an
area where the bayou grew wide, looking more like a
lake than a stream. Jack maneuvered the pontoon into a
spot near the south bank, positioning them so they had
a panoramic view of the swamp as the sun slid down in
the west. He cut the grumbling motor and stepped out of
the cabin to cast the anchor over the side. When he returned, he sank down beside Laurel, stretching his legs
out in front of him, laying his arms along the back of the
bench.

"It's beautiful, no?" he said softly.

"Mmmm . . ."

The sky was an artist's palette of color. The eastern
horizon was a deep, luxurious purple that gave way to
azure that faded into a smoky white that grew deeper
and deeper orange to the west, where the sun was a
huge ball of flame. Before them lay the swamp, desolate,
beautiful, full of secrets. Laurel soaked it all in, absorbed
the quiet of it, let the peace of it seep into her. The
pontoon swayed gently on the current and the tension
leeched out of her, leaving her limbs feeling heavy and
relaxed.

In the absence of motor noise, the bayou chorus began. Crickets trilled in the reeds, an unseen string section. Then came the bass *chug-a-rum* of the bullfrog,
then the rattling banjo twang of the green frog. From a
distance came the occasional accompaniment of bird
calls, and nearer the boat the low hum of mosquito
squadrons lifting off the surface of the dark water to fly
their sunset sorties.

"Savannah and I used to come out here when we
were kids," Laurel said softly. "Never too far from home.
Just far enough so we thought we were in another
world."

To escape. Jack heard the words. They hung in the
air, there for anyone who knew the secret desires of un-

happy children. "Me too," he said. "I grew up over on Bayou Noir. I spent more time in the swamp than I did in the house."

To escape, Laurel thought. They had that in common.

"I had a secret hideout," he admitted, staring out past the swamp to another time. "Built it out of peach crates and planks I robbed from a neighbor's pasture fence. I used to go out there and read my stolen comic books and make up stories of my own."

"Did you write them down?"

"Sometimes."

All the time. He had scribbled them down in notebooks and read them aloud to himself with a kind of shy pride he had never experienced in anything else. He'd never had anything to be proud of. His daddy was a piss-mean, drunken, good-for-nothing son of a bitch who had told him time and again he would never be anything but a good-for-nothing son of a son of a bitch. But his stories were good. That realization had been a surprise as wonderful as the Christmas his *maman* had given him a real cap gun—which he also kept at his hideout. More wonderful, really, because the stories came from him and proved he was worth something.

Then had come the day Blackie had followed him out to his secret hideaway. Drunk, as usual. Mean, as always. And the hideout was smashed, and the comic books and his stories and the dreams that were attached to them plunged into the bayou.

As worthless and useless as you are, T-Jack . . .

Laurel watched his face, saw the way his jaw hardened against some unpleasant memory, saw the anger in his dark eyes and the vulnerability that lay beneath it, and her heart ached for him. The few words he had spoken about his childhood had sketched a bleak picture. She could only guess that what was passing before his mind's eye now was a chapter from that time.

"Daddy had an old *bâteau* with a little trolling motor on it," she murmured to break his tension. "He taught Savannah how to work it. It was our secret, because Vivian would never have approved of her daughters doing such a thing. After he died, we used to sneak away and go out in it all the time. It made us feel closer to him somehow."

And far away from Beauvoir.

Jack turned toward her, shifting his weight on the bench, searching her face with his gaze. She looked a little embarrassed, as if she had never told anyone this particular secret before. The idea pleased him in a way he shouldn't have allowed, but he didn't try to stop it.

"When I was a kid, I used to think my family would be great if only we had money," he said. "I thought every problem we had was because we were poor. That wasn't true at all, was it?"

"No," she whispered, bleakly.

She stared down at her hands, fingering a thumbnail that had been bitten to the quick. She looked small and tired and vulnerable, not strong enough to fight off all the feelings coming home had churned up. She had gone off to create a life for herself, never suspecting that life would chase her right back to the problems she had been escaping from.

"*Dieu,*" Jack muttered, letting his arm slip off the bench and around Laurel's shoulders. "I'm not doin' my job very well, am I?" he asked in a teasing voice while he massaged her shoulder. He leaned down close and nuzzled her ear. "I brought you out here to have fun, to make you happy."

Warmth bloomed inside Laurel. She told herself she didn't want it, but the voice wasn't stern enough to make her move away from him. She shot him a wry look. "I think you brought me out here with ideas of raiding my panties."

He grinned an unholy grin, his eyes shining like polished onyx in the fading light. "*Mais oui, mon coeur,*" he murmured, his smoky voice purring deep in his throat as he slipped his other arm around her. "That's how I plan to make you happy."

Had any other man made such a statement to her, she would have cut him off at the knees with her rapier tongue and sent him crawling home. Jack's arrogance, tempered with his sense of humor, only made her want to go along on whatever wild adventure he suggested. That wasn't the smart thing or the safe thing, but it was the most tempting thing. As his lips found her throat and he began to kiss her with teasing little taste-testing kisses, the temptation grew stronger.

"I thought—" She broke off at the breathless sound of her voice, cleared her throat, and tried again. "I thought you were going to be on your best behavior."

He chuckled wickedly against her neck, sliding a hand up and down her upper arm, his thumb brushing seductively against the side of her breast. "Sugar, this *is* my best behavior."

A shudder of pure longing went through her. She had ignored her physical needs for so long, she had forgotten what it was to want a man.

No, her mind insisted, the correction cutting through the haze of desire, she had *never* known what it was to want a man. Not the way she wanted Jack. She had grown up subduing herself sexually, avoiding something she had seen only the ugly side of. Her marriage to Wesley had been a marriage of friends, passionless on her part because she didn't think herself capable of passion.

She'd been wrong. As Jack trailed kisses down the column of her throat to the sensitive curve of her shoulder, passion came to life inside her like a fire that had been smoldering beneath cold ash. It startled her, frightened her. She didn't want to want him. She had never wanted to think of herself as being vulnerable to the lure of sex.

"You told me not to trust you," she said, trying to stiffen muscles that had begun to melt with the warmth of desire. "You said yourself, you're bad for me."

"Well, you can't listen to me, darlin'," he murmured, kissing his way back up her neck to her ear. He traced the tip of his tongue around the rim of the delicate shell, drew the lobe between his lips and sucked gently. "I'm a writer; I tell lies for a livin'."

"Then I should know better than to get within an arm's length of you."

"Why? We don't need to talk at all for making love. Bodies don't tell lies, sweetheart." To prove his point he caught her hand and drew it to the front of his jeans, pressing her palm against his erection, holding her there while he feathered kisses along her jaw to the corner of her mouth and probed delicately with the tip of his tongue. "I want you, angel," he whispered seductively. "That's no lie."

She snatched a breath and forced herself to stand instead of succumb. Her legs wobbled beneath her, and she was glad her flowing, gauzy skirt hid her quaking knees. She folded her arms across her middle, holding herself together, keeping her hands from reaching out to him.

"I don't have casual sex with men who are admittedly liars and bastards," she said, struggling for and not quite managing the calm, cutting voice that had won her more than one court case.

Jack looked up at her from the bench, eyes wide with false innocence. He splayed his hands against his chest and rose with careless grace, stalking her across the narrow confines of the pontoon.

"Did I say I was a liar?" he asked with disbelief. "Oh, no, *chère*," he purred, backing her into the console. "I meant to say I was a *lover*. Come here and let me show you."

Laurel shook her head, sidestepping him as he reached for her, amazed at his ability to change personas—teasing, then sober, then seductive, then teasing again. It was almost more unnerving than his ability to make her want him. "Last night you warned me away from you. Today you act as if it never happened. Who are you this time, Jack?"

His expression grew serious, intense, as he stared down at her, and a tremor went through her. This Jack looked like a dominant male, a predator, capable of anything. "I'm the man whose gonna make love to you until you forget every stupid thing I ever said," he muttered.

If he had tried to snatch her against him, she would have bolted. If he had stepped too close, she would have kneed him. If he had tried to force her, she would have done her best to get her hands on the gun in her purse and shoot him. But he did none of those things. Instead, he lifted his hand and cupped her cheek, the fire in his eyes softening to tenderness.

"Let yourself live a little bit, angel," he whispered. "Live. Not for work, not for somebody else's cause. For the moment. For yourself. Reach out and take something you want for once."

Then he lowered his head and kissed her, softly, gently, experimentally. His lips, firm and smooth and oh-so-clever, moved against hers, rubbed over hers, seduced hers into softening and responding. He inched a step closer, raising his other hand and sliding his fingers back into her silky hair.

"Kiss me back, *mon coeur*," he commanded on a phantom breath. "There's no reason you shouldn't."

Just that she didn't trust him or respect him or want the complication of an affair in her life, she thought dimly. But she gave voice to none of those reasons, thinking that they didn't really have much to do with the here and now. *Let yourself live a little bit, angel. . . .*

She'd been so careful for so long, she couldn't believe she was being seduced by a rogue like Jack. But then that was his allure, wasn't it? He was bad for her. He was wicked. And she had always followed the rules, made the correct choices, done the right thing.

Reach out and take something you want for once.

Jack's mouth moved insistently over hers, coaxing, luring, tempting, offering pleasure, promising bliss, guaranteeing an hour or two of blessed oblivion of the problems in her life. And God knew she wanted him.

Hesitantly, she obeyed his command, rising on tiptoe, relaxing her lips beneath his. Her fingers curled into fists, gathering the fabric of his shirt in bunches. Then he slid his arms around her, anchoring her against him, holding her safe and secure as she opened to him.

Jack groaned at her surrender and deepened the kiss. With a slow, sensuous stroke, he eased his tongue into her mouth, probing deeply, suggestively. She answered him with a tentative foray of her own, her tongue tracing his lower lip, dipping inside his mouth.

He wanted her, had wanted her from the first, this angel with her alluring combination of fire and fragility. He wanted her in a way he hadn't wanted a woman in a long time—possessively, obsessively. He wanted her to be his in a way she had never been any other man's. He would have seen it as dangerous thinking if he had been able to think at all.

Without breaking the kiss, he took her glasses off and set them aside on the steering console, then guided her hands down to his waist and abandoned them there as he shrugged his shirt off and tossed it aside. He gasped a little at the feel of her hands, so cool and soft, gliding back up his chest.

Laurel explored the smooth, hard planes and ridges of his body, marveling at the strength there, marveling at her own response to his fever-hot skin. She couldn't get enough of touching him, wanted to press into him and feel that strength and heat against the length of her and absorb it through her skin. When he lifted the hem of her top, the sound she made in her throat wasn't protest, but the eager anticipation of pleasure. Naked from the waist up, she moved into him, what was left of her breath vaporizing in her lungs as her breasts flattened against him.

Jack growled low in his throat as he kissed her. Like a sculptor admiring a work of art, he traced his hands down her back, caressing, exploring, interpreting every graceful curve, every plane and hollow. Lifting her into him, he pressed her hips to his, pressed her into his arousal, letting her know how badly, how urgently, he wanted her. He felt her tongue dip into the hollow at the base of his throat, and the flames of desire licked at his sanity.

Need making his fingers clumsy, he fumbled with the button and zipper at the back of her skirt and pushed the garment out of his way. At last she was naked in his arms. He stood back for a moment and drank in the sight of her with greedy eyes.

She was slender and sleek, but there was no mistaking her feminine curves—or her uncertainty about showing them to him. A delicate blush rose up her neck into her cheeks as he studied her, as if she were afraid he would somehow find her lacking.

"*Viens ici, chérie,*" he whispered, holding out his hand to her. "Come here before your beauty undoes me."

He pulled her tight against him, kissing her greedily, hungrily, letting her know his words were more than just the clever prattle of an experienced Lothario. They were truth.

Slowly he lowered her to the red flowered cushions of the bench that was directly behind her, following her down, sprawling over her. She arched her back off the cushion as he found her breast with his mouth, capturing her nipple between his lips and sucking hard on the turgid tip, then sucking gently, massaging her with his tongue.

Laurel tangled her hands in his dark hair and moved restlessly beneath him, soft, wild sounds of yearning keening in her throat. She wrapped her legs around him, lifting her hips against his belly, seeking contact, seeking to assuage the urgent ache that burned at the core of her desire.

He stroked the swollen petals of her woman's flesh tenderly, seductively, opening her to his touch like a precious, fragile flower. She gasped with pleasure as he eased two fingers into the hot, tight silken pocket between her thighs. Then he found the sensitive bud of her desire with his thumb, tapping against it with the slightest of touches, then rubbing gently until she was breathless.

"You like this, sugar?" he whispered, stroking deep, then easing slowly out of her, opening her, stretching her.

"Yes—no—" she gasped, lifting her hips.

"Enjoy it, darlin'. Let yourself go," he coaxed. "Let me make you happy," he murmured. He kissed her quivering stomach, mouth open, hot, wet, tongue dipping into her navel. "Are you ready for me, angel?"

"Yes. Jack, please . . ."

She gulped a breath and strained against the fist of desire that tightened and tightened within her. She'd never wanted like this. When Jack sat up, reaching for the button on his jeans, Laurel reached out to help him. Sitting up, she pressed fervent kisses to his chest as she closed her fingers around his thick, pulsing shaft.

Jack's control broke at the feel of her small hand stroking him. He tumbled her back on the cushion, pushed her hand aside and guided himself, squeezing his eyes shut as he eased into her.

"*Mon Dieu,* you're tight!"

Laurel moaned. "I'm a little tense," she said breathlessly. "It's been a long time for me."

Her admission caught Jack by the heart and squeezed. "No," he said, bending down to kiss her. "It's the first time. Our first time. Just relax and enjoy, darlin'."

Laurel closed her eyes and wrapped her arms around him as he began to move against her and within her. He kissed her deeply, then playfully. He nipped the side of her neck, murmured hot, sexy words to her as they moved together. The pleasure built and intensified, swelling inside her until she could barely breathe for the pressure of it.

Jack's kisses grew more urgent, more carnal, his thrusts deeper, driving, straining, filling her to bursting. The time for play faded, paled in the face of something hot and intense that enveloped them and threatened to consume them. Something like fear gripped Laurel by the throat, and she tightened her hold on him, not sure where this was taking her or what would happen after.

"Don't fight it, sweetheart," he whispered urgently. He rubbed his cheek against hers, swept her hair back from her face, kissed her temple. "Don't fight it. Let it happen. Take us to heaven, angel."

Not giving her a choice, he slipped a hand between them and touched the tender nerve center of her desire, taking her over the edge. Taking them both over the edge.

"*Mon Dieu,* angel."

Even in the dim light of dusk he could see the color rise into her cheeks as she turned her face away from him. "Oh, no, sweetheart," he said softly, skimming his fingertips along her jaw. "Don' be shy with me now. Don' be embarrassed. That was beautiful. That was perfect."

"I'm not very good at this," she mumbled, still not looking at him, despite the gentle pressure he applied to her chin.

"At what? Sex?"

That, too, Laurel thought, chagrined. "Talking afterward."

"Your ex-husband, he was a mute, or what?"

She laughed at that because she was still feeling embarrassed and because laughter was what Jack had been aiming for with his teasing. He tickled the side of her neck, and she cringed, turning toward him at last. "No. He just never had much to say afterward."

Jack looked down into her face, reading vulnerability there in her wide dark eyes, and it tugged at his heart. So fiery, so sure of herself in other ways, she was uncertain about this most natural and basic aspect of her femininity. How different she was from Savannah, whose expertise in the bedroom was the stuff of legends. He wanted to know what forces had shaped their lives to make them so different from one another, but this wasn't the time to ask. This was the time to reassure.

"What was he—paralyzed from the neck down?" he queried dryly.

No, Laurel thought, he was sweet and kind and honest, and he'd tried his best to make their marriage work, but she had failed him in so many ways. What she had felt with Wes was friendship and a sense of emotional security, not all-consuming passion. She had used him to anchor her life and had given him little in return, had in fact turned on him when The Case had been at its most stressful, all but pushing him out of her life.

"Hey, sugar . . ." Jack murmured. "Don' look sad, angel. I didn' mean to drag up bad memories."

If it weren't for bad memories, I'd have no memories at all. She looked away from him and tensed herself against the ridiculous urge to cry at his concern.

"We've all of us got bad memories," he said. "But they don' belong here, between us. We came out here to have fun, remember?" His fingers found another ticklish spot along her ribs and tortured a little smile out of her. "We were doin' pretty damn good there for a while, no?"

"Yes," she whispered, the corners of her mouth turning up in pleasure, in embarrassment.

"That's it," he praised her in a warm, seductive voice. Settling himself on top of her, he lowered his head until they were nose to nose, lips to lips. "Smile for me." He smiled as she did. "Kiss me," he whispered, groaning with pleasure as she complied.

Her breath caught as he shifted his hips and eased into her again. Need took precedence over old memories. *Reach out and take something you want for once.* She wanted this. She wanted Jack—for now, for the pleasure he could give her and the bliss that transported her mind away from the problems that plagued her. Heaven, he called it. She arched her hips against his, closed her eyes, and held on to him for the return trip.

Midnight was nearing when they finally dressed. The process was complicated with much touching and teasing and long pauses for kisses and hot, whispered words. Laurel felt like a teenager—not the quiet, serious teenager she had been, but an ordinary, hormone-crazed teenager out for a night of forbidden fooling around with the class bad boy. Jack played his role to the hilt, trying to take off every article of clothing she put on, trying to talk her into spending the night on the bayou with him.

"Come on, sweetheart, stay with me," he coaxed, murmuring the words against her throat as he dragged the hem of her blouse upward, stroking his fingers up her sides toward her breasts. "We're just gettin' started. . . ."

Laurel's sense of responsibility was too ingrained, and she wriggled out of his grasp and reached for her glasses on the steering console, settling them on her nose and settling the issue.

"If I don't get back soon, Aunt Caroline and Mama Pearl will worry," she said, brushing futilely at the wrinkles in her clothes. "You don't want them sending the sheriff out looking for us, do you?"

Jack jammed his hands at his waist, the picture of a disgruntled male who was too sexy for his own good. He wore nothing but his jeans, and they weren't quite zipped. "Kenner couldn't find his own ass in the dark, let alone us."

"He could get lucky."

"But I'm not gonna," he grumbled.

"You already have."

Instantly he grinned his wicked grin and backed her against the console. "*Mais yeah*, angel." He chuckled, dipping his head to nibble her neck again. "And I like my odds for another go."

Laurel ducked away before he could get his arms around her. "Go weigh anchor, sailor, before I pull my gun on you."

Purring low in his throat, he sprang toward her and stole a kiss, dancing deftly away when she would have slugged him. "I love it when you boss me around."

She snatched up a pillow from the bench and hurled it at his head. Jack darted outside and used the door for a shield, chuckling the whole time.

Giving up on the idea of seducing her again, he went about the business of pulling up the anchor, cursing under his breath as it caught on something tangled in the reeds. He hauled back on the nylon rope, damning people who used the swamp for a garbage dump. The anchor finally pulled free, and he hauled it aboard. Minutes later the motor was puttering and the pontoon eased away from the bank and headed west . . .

. . . and the body of a naked woman, brutally tortured, cruelly slain, buoyed by the dense growth beneath her, floated out of the reeds and bobbed in the wake of the boat, her sightless eyes staring after them, her arm outstretched toward them in a plea for help that was much too silent and far too late.

Chapter
Sixteen

The sun shone, butter yellow, a soft, indistinct ball on the far side of the morning haze. Laurel sat at the table on the gallery, staring out across the courtyard, through the back gate, and toward the bayou, where the mist hung in gauzy strips above the water and wound like ribbons of smoke through the trees. She stared toward the bayou . . . and L'Amour.

The old brick house stood stately and alone, half hidden by trees and shrubbery that had been allowed to encroach during generations of neglect. From the branches of one gnarled live oak hung two dozen or more neckties, their tails fluttering in the slight breeze—a testimony to Jack's abdication from the world of corporate law, she supposed. She certainly couldn't imagine him putting on a tie, much less a suit, in his current phase—the rebel, the rogue. But she thought of him younger, intense, hungry to prove himself, and the image came quite easily. Jack, elegant in double-breasted gray silk. Handsome, yet rough around the edges. Educated, but with some aura of that boy who had grown up wild on the edge of the swamp. Like a panther that had been domesticated, always with a shadow of his former self nearby, the air of danger lingering around him.

She wondered what had driven him from that world he had worked so hard to conquer. She wondered if it was wise to care.

She shifted on her cushioned chair, curling her feet beneath her, and lifted her tea cup with both hands to take a sip of Earl Grey. The rest of the household would be stirring soon. Caroline would be subjecting her body to the contortions of her daily yoga regimen. Mama Pearl would be shuffling around her kitchen in a cotton shift and terrycloth slippers, starting the coffee, setting out a bowl of chilled fruit, grumbling to herself about the state of the world while the morning news came over the radio. But for now, the gallery and the morning belonged to Laurel, and she relished the peace. Unable to sleep past four o'clock, she had showered and dressed.

She had expected to feel a certain amount of turmoil concerning her night of lovemaking with Jack. After all, she had never been one to indulge in reckless passion—had, in fact, disdained and avoided it. But sitting in the dewy-soft quiet of the courtyard, she could find no regrets, no recriminations. He had offered something she wanted, needed—not just sex, but a release from other tensions—and she had accepted. And it had been wonderful. . . .

"People who get up this early shouldn't look so happy."

Savannah stood in the open French doors to the hall, looking sleep-rumpled and groggy in her champagne silk robe. Her hair tumbled around her shoulders in wild disarray, and mascara smudges ringed her eyes. She looked tough, dissipated by dissolute living, like a hooker the morning after. The glow of excitement had diffused, the allure had vanished with the moon.

She pushed herself away from the door and stepped out onto the gallery, barefoot, one hand tucked into the deep pocket of her robe, the other toying with the heart on her necklace.

Laurel tried to think of an innocuous comeback line, but she couldn't get past the hurt that still lingered from the night before. "Would you like some tea?" she asked quietly.

Savannah shook her head, her lips tightening against a bittersweet smile. That was Baby, falling back on good manners to hide her feelings. If all else failed her, she would at least be a gracious hostess. Such a little belle. Vivian would have been proud of her.

"I want to apologize for yesterday. I said a lot of things I shouldn't have." The words came out in a rush of embarrassment and contrition. She busied her fingers twisting the sash of her robe. "And I never should have been such a bitch to you last night, but I was just feeling so hurt and so damn angry—"

Laurel set her cup down and rose, concern knitting her brows. "I didn't mean to hurt you, Sister—"

"No, not you, Baby. Cooper." She stared down at the table through a bright sheen of tears, feeling as fragile as Laurel's china teacup. "I don't know what I'm going to do," she said, trying to smile, shaking her head at the futility of it all. "I love that man something awful."

She turned and walked away a few steps, breathing deep of the sweet, dew-damp scents of the garden—flowers and sweet olive and boxwood—green, vibrant scents of life. As if she could scrub away the feeling of despair that clung to her, she rubbed her hands over her face. But a dozen other feelings gurgled up inside her like tainted water from an underground spring—guilt and anger, remorse and jealousy. She didn't want any of it.

Trying to tamp it all down, she turned back toward Laurel, who stood watching her with wide eyes and a serious face. For just an instant she was that same little waif who had looked to Savannah for love and support when they had no one else to turn to, and Savannah felt a welcome rush of strength.

"It doesn't matter," she said, finding a smile for her baby sister. "It doesn't have anything to do with us. I won't let anything come between us."

Laurel went into her sister's arms, vowing to say nothing about Conroy Cooper or any other man Savannah involved herself with. She couldn't change Savannah, couldn't change the way Savannah thought about her past, and those were not the reasons she had come home in the first place. This was what she had come for, she thought as she hugged her sister—unconditional love and support. That had to work both ways. And so she said nothing about the scent of stale perfume and stale sex that clung to Savannah.

"I won't let anything come between us," Savannah said again, vehemently, her embrace tightening around Laurel's slender frame.

"You might let some air come between us," Laurel teased. "You're squeezing the life out of me."

A nervous laugh rattled out of her, and she loosened her hold, stepping back, settling her hands on Laurel's shoulders. "Maybe I will have a cup of that tea, after all. We can sit out here and chat. You've made the garden so pretty again. We'll make some plans."

She rushed back into the house, hurrying as if she were afraid the moment would pass and the wall of tension would rise up between them again. Laurel settled into her chair, reaching for the matchbook she had found on the seat of her car the night before. Savannah's, she supposed. She turned it around and around in her fingers, absently, just something to busy her hands. Not five minutes passed before Savannah returned with a tray bearing the teapot, a cup for herself, and a plate heaped with powdery *beignets*.

"These are left over from yesterday," she chattered, arranging everything to her satisfaction on the table. "I just popped them into the microwave to warm them up and sprinkled fresh sugar on them. Have one," she ordered, suddenly full of life and hope. "Have half a dozen. If anyone ever needed to load up on Mama Pearl's cooking, it's you, Baby. You don't have an ounce to spare."

Laurel tossed the matchbook down on the tabletop between them and reached for a *beignet*. "You left that in the car."

Savannah picked it up and sat back, studying it idly as she nibbled on the corner of her breakfast. She said nothing for a long moment, staring at the blood red square blankly, then dropped it. "I use a lighter."

A vague sense of unease shifted through Laurel. She set her *beignet* aside on her napkin, her gaze moving from her sister's expressionless face to the matchbook. An elaborate Mardi Gras mask was stamped in black above the words "Le Mascarade" and a French Quarter address in New Orleans. "If it's not yours, then how did it get in my car?"

A careless shrug was her only answer. Savannah pushed her chair back from the table and rose. "I forgot the sugar for my tea."

As she padded back into the house, Laurel fingered the matchbook, a strange chill pebbling the flesh of her arms with goose bumps.

"Bonjour, mon ange. For you."

Laurel gasped as a perfect red rose appeared before her. She hadn't heard Jack's approach, hadn't even caught a glimpse of him from the corner of her eye. His ability to appear and disappear seemingly from and into thin air rattled her, and she narrowed her eyes to compensate with annoyance.

"You damn near gave me a heart attack."

Jack frowned, leaning over her, breathing in the clean scent of her hair. "Is that any way to thank a man for bringing you flowers?"

She gave a little sniff of disdain but accepted the rose. "You probably stole it from one of Aunt Caroline's bushes."

"It's no less a gift," he said, leaning closer, his gaze fastening on her lips.

Anticipation fluttered in her throat. "How can it be a gift if it's something I already possessed?"

He lowered his head another fraction of an inch, closing the space between them to little more than a deep breath. His lashes drifted down, thick and black. "Isn't that just like a lawyer?" he whispered. "If I offered you the moon, you'd probably want to see my deed to it."

Any retort she might have made was lost. Any thought she might have had in her head vanished as Jack settled his mouth against hers. He kissed her deeply, intimately, leisurely, reminding her graphically and frankly of the intimacy they had shared the night before.

When he lifted his mouth from hers at last, he made a low, purring sound of satisfaction in his throat, then chuckled wickedly. "Why you blushin', *ma jolie fille*?" he asked, his voice dark and smoky. "You gave me a helluva lot more than a kiss last night."

"But you probably didn't have an audience, did you, Jack?" Savannah asked sharply. She stepped out from behind a pillar and set a silver sugar bowl on the table, never taking her eyes off him. She picked up the red matchbook and tapped it against her cheek. "Or have you led my baby sister that far astray?"

He straightened, his eyes cold, his face set in a stony mask. "That's none of your damn business, Savannah."

"Yes, it is," she argued. "I won't have you fucking my baby sister, Jack."

"Why is that? Because I didn't do you first?"

She threw the matchbook down, color rising high into her cheeks. "You son of a bitch."

"Stop it!" Laurel snapped, shoving her chair back and rising to her feet. She turned toward her sister, a part of her shocked by the pure hatred she saw burning like pale blue flame in Savannah's eyes as she stared at Jack, a part of her too annoyed to pay attention to it. "Sister, I appreciate your concern, but I'm a big girl. I can take care of myself."

Savannah blinked at her, looking stunned. "No, you can't. You need me."

"I need your support," Laurel qualified. "I don't need you screening my dates."

Savannah picked out four words from the rest and drove them through her own heart like a stake. "*I don't need you.*" Baby didn't need her, didn't want her, preferred the company of Jack Boudreaux. Panic clawed through her, and fury poured out of the wounds as hot and red as blood. Her one chance to do something im-

portant was being snatched away from her. Everything
she wanted was always beyond her reach. Coop. Laurel.
Baby was turning away from her for a man. And she was
left with nothing, just another slut like every other slut in
south Louisiana.

"After all I've done for you," she muttered, her lush
mouth twisting at the bitterness, at the irony. "After all
I've done for you, you don't need me."

Laurel's jaw dropped. "That's not what I said!"

"Well, fine," Savannah went on. "You go on and have
a high old time with him and just forget about me. I
don't need you, either. You're nothing but an ungrateful
little hypocrite, and I can't think why I ever would have
saved you from anything."

Tears shone like diamonds in her eyes. She caught at
her artificially plump lower lip with her teeth, raking
color into it. "I never will again," she vowed, her voice
choked and petulant. "You can count on that. I *never* will
again."

"Savannah!" Laurel started after her as she whirled
and ran into the house, but Jack caught her by the shoulder.

"Let her go, angel. She's in no mood to listen. Let
her cool off."

Seconds later the Acura roared to life at the side of
the house, and then came the angry screech of tires on
asphalt.

Laurel turned and slammed her fist into Jack's shoulder, not to punish him, but because she needed to hit
something, anything. "I don't understand what's going
on with her!"

"She's jealous."

"No," she murmured, leaning into him as the anger
seeped out of her muscles, leaving her trembling. "It's
not as simple as that."

"Yeah, well . . ." He heaved a sigh and slipped his
arms around her, resting his chin atop her head. *"C'est
vrai,* life's a bitch. Nothin's ever simple. . . ."

Certainly not in Laurel's life. She seemed intermina-
bly tangled in a web of obligations. He wanted to cut her

loose, if only for a little while, give her a break . . . have her all to himself so he might pretend she could be his.

"Except fishin'," he said, going with the impulse that had brought him here at this ungodly hour in the first place. "You ready to come fishin' with me, *ma petite?*"

"I never said I'd go fishing with you," Laurel said, frowning.

"Sure you did. Last night." He tucked a knuckle under her chin and tipped her face up. "You whispered it in my ear while we were makin' love. You said I could take you anywhere. I'm taking you fishin'."

They went out in a *pirogue* Laurel had more than a few reservations about. Slender and shallow as a pea pod, it was made of weathered cypress planking and bobbed like a cork on the inky, oily surface of the bayou. Laurel stood on the dock for a long moment, looking dubious, as Jack loaded fishing gear into the bow.

"Are you sure this thing is safe?"

"Oh, absolutely," he drawled, adding a cooler to the cargo in the nose of the boat. The *pirogue* dipped and swayed on the water as if protesting even that slight load. Unconcerned, Jack climbed in, braced his feet, and reached a hand up to help her aboard. "An old friend of mine made this *pirogue* for me. As he would say, 'This boat, she rides the dew.'"

Laurel swallowed hard as she stepped down into the craft and felt it bob beneath her. She grabbed hold of Jack's biceps for an instant to steady herself and to pull him with her if she went overboard. "Was he sober at the time?"

"Hard to say," Jack mused, easing her down on the boat's plank seat. He jammed a red USL Ragin' Cajuns baseball cap down on her head and stepped deftly over the seat to take up the push-pole at the stern. "Ol' Lucky Doucet, he used to be some kind of wild."

He pushed off, and they moved away from the dock, the *pirogue* seeming to skate across the water, as graceful as a blade on ice. Laurel took a deep breath and willed herself to relax.

"Used to be?" Tipping the oversize cap back on her head, she twisted around to look at him. "Is he dead?"

"Naw, he's married. Got himself a beautiful wife, a little daughter, another baby on the way."

"Busy man," Laurel said dryly.

Happy man, Jack thought, sinking the fork of the push-pole into the muddy bottom and sending the *pirogue* gliding forward. A hard, hollow ball of longing lodged in his chest, taking up valuable air space, and he scowled and did his best to smash it with a mental mallet of self-punishment. He'd had his chance, and he'd blown it in the worst possible way. He didn't deserve another.

Pushing the dark thoughts from his mind, he turned his attention on Laurel and all the little puzzle pieces he had yet to find to complete his picture of her. She sat on the hard plank seat of the *pirogue* with the posture of a debutante, her gaze scanning the far bank of the bayou, where an alligator was sunning itself. Even in her baggy clothes and the too-big cap she looked feminine and graceful. He shook his head at that, a wry smile tugging at one corner of his mouth.

She wasn't his type. Not at all. These days he usually went for curvy, carefree girls with big breasts and uncomplicated brains, women who wanted nothing more from him than a good tussle between the sheets. He didn't know what Laurel Chandler would want. She claimed she wanted nothing from him, and yet he felt something about her drawing on him like a magnet. Instinct told him his curiosity could be dangerous, but the warning wasn't strong enough to overpower the attraction. Besides, he told himself smugly, he couldn't get in any deeper than he wanted to.

He piloted the *pirogue* to a favorite fishing hole, a place where willows shaded the banks, and bass, bream, and crappie cruised among the cypress stands and wallowed in the sluggish water edging the thickets of reeds and cattails. Laurel passed on the offer of a pole and instead pulled *Evil Illusions* out of the canvas tote bag she had brought with her. The morning passed to the trill of cicadas, the whine of a fishing reel, the splash of fish fighting against a future in a frying pan. Conversation became as sporadic and desultory as the breeze.

Laurel found the quiet soothing in the wake of Savannah's blow-up. With an effort she pushed the questions about her sister's behavior to the back of her mind and tried to lose herself in the pages of Jack's book. Not a difficult thing to do. Despite his show as a simple Cajun boy, he was an excellent writer, talented, clever. He had the ability to pull the reader into the story as if through a portal into another dimension. The visual images were sharp, dark; the emotions so thick and electric, they left her skin tingling. The fear that built from paragraph to paragraph was almost unbearably intense. The sense of evil that overshadowed it all was at once subtle, insidious, and overwhelming.

Strong impressions from a man who claimed he didn't care much about anything that went on in the world around him except having a good time. No, she thought, watching as he cast gracefully toward the edge of a tangle of water hyacinth, these impressions, these dark fantasies didn't come from Jack the Party Animal. They came from the other Jack. The man with the burning gaze and the aura of danger. The man who stood silent and watchful behind the facade of the rogue.

"Where does it come from?" she asked as they spread a blanket on shore, preparing to have lunch.

"What?"

"What you write."

Everything about him went utterly still for a split second, as if her question had literally stopped him cold. But he recovered so quickly, Laurel almost convinced herself she had imagined the response.

"It's just made up," he said, smoothing a corner of the blue plaid blanket. "That's why they call it fiction, sugar."

"I don't believe you just sit down, put your hands on a keyboard, and come up with that stuff."

"Why not?"

"Because it's too good."

He gave a dismissive shake of his head. "It's a talent, a trick, that's all." Some trick, he thought bitterly. Just sit down at the typewriter and open a vein. Bleed out all the poison that simmered inside him.

Laurel knelt on the blanket, studying him with her head tilted on one side. "Some writers say it's like method acting. That they mentally live through every action and emotion."

"And others will tell you it's like doing paint-by-numbers."

"What do *you* say?"

"I say, I'm too damn hungry to play twenty questions," he growled, stalking her across the blanket on his knees. A wicked smile played at the corners of his mouth and carved his dimples into his lean cheeks.

Nerve endings on red alert, Laurel held her ground as he approached. It seemed amazing to her, the way her body came alive and aware of him. Her heart picked up a beat, her breasts grew heavy and tingled with electricity.

"What's for lunch?" she asked breathlessly as he stopped before her, a scant inch of charged air separating them.

"You."

He knocked the baseball cap from her head with a flick of his wrist. Then she was in his arms, immersed in his embrace, lost in his kiss. It occurred to her vaguely that he was trying to distract her from her line of questioning, but she couldn't bring herself to object to his method. His touch unleashed a host of needs that had lain dormant inside her until last night. Now they leaped and twisted, wild with the prospect of freedom.

Afterward they dozed exhausted, replete. Jack settled on his side with one leg thrown across Laurel's. She turned toward him and curled one small hand against his chest, too hot to cuddle, but needing to maintain contact with him. And they lay there in the quiet, in the heat, listening to the cicadas and the songbirds and the pounding of their own hearts.

A belated tremor of fear rumbled through Laurel. Fear of the control she had lost so completely. Fear of the incredible pleasure Jack had given her. An old fear that had its roots in a time of her life when she had seen sex as only a negative experience. She knew better now, but old fears never quite died—they just hid in dark corners of the mind and waited for the chance to slip out. Deliberately, she dismissed it and blinked her eyes open to look at Jack.

He lifted a hand and touched her cheek, idly brushing back a strand of hair. "Where'd you go, *'tite chatte*?" he whispered, his brows drawing together.

"Nowhere important," she said, dodging his gaze.

"Back to Georgia?"

"No."

"But you do go back there, in your mind, *oui*?"

She thought about that for a moment, debating the wisdom of revealing anything about that time in her life. A part of her wanted to guard the secrets, hide the past, protect herself. But it seemed ironic to try to hide anything from a man who had shared the most private parts of her body, who had taken her to dizzying heights of pleasure and held her safe in his arms as they floated together to earth. She had opened her body to him, now she opened another part of her, tentatively, hesitantly, feeling more vulnerable than a virgin.

"It comes to me sometimes," she said at last. She sat up and began dressing, not wanting to feel any more naked than was necessary.

Jack hitched his jeans up and zipped them, leaving the button undone. "Can you talk about it?"

She shrugged, as if it were unimportant or easy, when it was far from being either. "I guess you read about it in the papers."

"I read some of what the papers had to say, but I've been around the block a time or two, sugar. I know there's a helluva lot more to any story than sound bites and photo ops."

Dressed, Laurel sat on the blanket with her arms wrapped around her knees and stared at the bayou. A squadron of wood ducks banked around in tight formation and came down with wings cupped and feet outstretched. They hit the water in unison and skied several feet, finally settling down to paddle away, chuckling among themselves.

"It started with three children and a story about a 'club' that met once a week," she began, bracing herself inwardly against what was to come. Even now, months after the case had been taken away from her, the details had the power to sicken her, the images came back as bright and ugly as ever. Her hands tightened against her shins until her knuckles turned white.

"The allegations were incredible. Child pornography. Sexual abuse. The children had been sworn to secrecy. Small animals had been slaughtered in front of them, killed and torn apart, as a demonstration of what might happen if they talked. But eventually they became more frightened of what might happen if they *didn't* talk.

"They came to me because I had been to their school during career week. I had talked about justice, about doing the right thing and fighting for the truth." Her mouth twisted at the irony. "The poor little things believed me. I believed myself."

She could still see them, all those little faces staring up at her from the floor of the gymnasium, their eyes round as they absorbed her sermon on the pride and nobility of working to see justice served. She could still feel that sense of pride and self-righteousness and naivete. She had still believed then that right would always win out if one worked hard enough, believed strongly enough, fought with a pure heart.

"Nobody wanted me to touch their story. The adults they were accusing were above reproach. A teacher, a dentist, a member of the Methodist church council. Fine, upstanding citizens—who just happened to be pedophiles," she said bitterly.

"What made you believe them?"

How could she explain? How could she describe the

sense of empathy? She knew what it was to hold a terrible secret inside, because she had held one of her own. She knew what courage it took to let the secret out, because she had never been able to muster it.

The guilt twisted like a knife inside her, and she squeezed her eyes shut against the pain. She had never found the strength to brave her mother's unpredictable temperament or risk her mother's love.

"Don't tell Mama, Laurel. She won't believe you. She'll hate you for telling. She'll have one of her spells, and it will be all your fault."

If she hadn't been such a coward, if she had done the right thing, the brave thing . . .

A picture of Savannah swam before her eyes, rumpled, seductive, playing the harlot with a tragic sense of reckless desperation underlying her sexuality.

She pushed to her feet and walked down to the edge of the water, wanting to escape not only Jack and his questions, but her past, herself. He followed her. She could sense him behind her, feel his dark gaze on her back.

"Why did you believe them, Laurel?"

"Because they needed me. They needed justice. It was my job."

The denial of her own feelings built a sense of pressure in her chest that grew and grew, like an inflating balloon. It crowded against her lungs, squeezed her heart, closed off her throat, pushed hard on the backs of her eyes. She had crushed it out before, time and again. She had railed at Dr. Pritchard for trying to make her let it out.

"I wasn't atoning for anything. I had a job to do, and I did it. My childhood had nothing to do with it."

He just gave her that long, patient look that held both pity and disappointment. And she wanted to pick up one of the fat psychology books from his desk and hit him in the face with it.

"I didn't come here to talk about ancient history. I want help for what's happening now."

"Don't you see, Laurel? The past is what this is all

*about. You wouldn't be where you are today if not for
where you started and what went on there."*

"*I'm not trying to atone for anything!*"

She tried to suck in a breath, but her lungs couldn't
expand to accommodate the humid air. The pressure was
so great, she wondered wildly if she would simply explode.

Control. She needed control.

Ruthlessly, she tried to push aside the other thoughts
and concentrate on simply relating the facts in a way that
would satisfy Jack and keep her emotional involvement
to a minimum.

"We worked day and night to build a case. There was
evidence, but none of it could be tied directly to the
accused. And the whole time, they were soliciting sympathy in the community, claiming to be the victims of a
witch hunt, claiming that I was trying to climb on their
backs to the state attorney general's office." Her hands
balled into tight fists at her sides as she tried to leash the
fury building inside her. Her whole body trembled with
the power of it. "God, they were so slick, so clever, so
smug!"

So evil.

You believe in evil, don't you, Laurel?

She clenched her teeth against the need to scream.

. . . and good must triumph over evil . . .

"All we really had was the testimony of the children."

She snatched half a breath, feeling as if her lungs
would burst.

"Children aren't considered reliable witnesses."

Don't bother telling, Laurel. No one will believe you.

"Parker—the state AG—" She was gasping now, as if
she had run too far too fast. A fine sheen of sweat coated
her skin, sticky and cold. "He took the case away from
me—It—was politically explosive—He said I—I—
couldn't handle it—"

Jack stepped closer, his heart pounding with hers, *for*
her. He could feel the tension, brittle in the air around
her, snapping with electricity. He reached out to lay a

hand on her shoulder, and she jolted as if he had given her a shock.

"You did the best you could," he said softly.

"I lost," she whispered, the words lashing out of her like the crack of a whip, the anguish almost palpable. Shaking violently, she raised her fists and pressed them hard against her temples. "They were guilty."

"You did your best."

"It wasn't good enough!" she screamed.

The ducks departed in a flurry of wings and splashing water. Egrets and herons that had been wading in the shallows for fish took flight and wheeled over the bayou, squawking angrily at the disturbance. Laurel twisted away from Jack's touch and ran along the bank, stumbling, sobbing, frantic to escape but with nowhere to run. She fell to her knees in the sandy dirt and curled over into a tight ball of misery, dry, wrenching sobs tearing at her throat.

For a moment Jack stood there, stunned by the depth of her pain, frightened by it. Instinct warned him off, like an animal scenting fire. He didn't want to get too close to it, didn't want to risk touching it, but an instant after that thought had passed through his head, he was kneeling beside her, stroking a hand over the back of her head.

"Darlin', don't cry so," he murmured, his voice a hoarse rasp. "You did your job. You did what you could. Some cases you win, some you don't. That's just the way the game goes. We both know that."

"It isn't a game!" Laurel snapped, batting his hand away. She glared at him through her tears. "Dammit, Jack, this isn't Beat the System, it's justice. Don't you see that? Justice. I can't just shrug and walk away when the bet doesn't pan out. Those children were counting on me to save them, and I failed!"

It was a burden with the weight of the world, and she crumpled beneath the pressure of it.

Gently, Jack drew her into his arms and rocked her. He kissed the top of her head and stroked her hair and shushed her softly, and time passed by them, unnoticed, unmarked.

Justice, he thought cynically. What justice was there in a world where children were used and abused by the people who were supposed to protect and nurture them? What justice was there when a woman as noble, as brave, as truehearted as the one in his arms suffered so for the sins of others? What justice allowed a man the like of himself to be the only one here to offer her comfort?

There was no justice in his experience. He had never seen any evidence of it growing up. As an attorney, he had been trained to play the court system like an elaborate chess game, maneuvering, manipulating, using strategy and cunning to win for his client. There had been no justice, only victory at any cost.

If there was such a creature as justice, he thought, then it had an exceedingly sadistic sense of humor.

Chapter Seventeen

They saw the commotion all the way from the dock at Frenchie's Landing. Cars were parked up and down the road. A crowd of considerable size had gathered. From that distance only the indistinct crackle of a voice could be heard through a bad speaker system; not individual words, just the rise and fall of pitch and tempo, but there was no mistaking the fact that something exciting was going on at the former Texaco station that had only yesterday stood empty across the road from Frenchie's.

Laurel glanced at Jack—something she had been avoiding doing all afternoon, since the humiliation of breaking down in front of him. His shoulders rose and fell in a lazy shrug. He was the picture of indifference with his khaki shirt hanging open, baseball cap tipped back on his head, stringer of glossy fish hanging from his fist.

He had no interest in what was going on across the road. His focus was on Laurel and the curious shyness that had come over her. He had never known a woman who didn't shed tears with gusto and impunity. Yet Laurel had shrunk from her emotional outburst—and from him—clearly embarrassed that she had shown such vulnerability in front of him.

He wondered if she ever cut herself an inch of slack. She demanded perfection of herself, a goal that was simply unattainable for any mortal human being. A trait he should have steered well clear of. *Le bon Dieu* knew he was the farthest thing from perfect. But he caught himself admiring her for it. She seemed so small and fragile, but she had a deep well of strength, and she went to it again and again, and accepted no excuses.

That's more than you can say for yourself, mon ami.

They crunched across the crushed shell of the parking lot another few yards, aiming for the bar, but Laurel's gaze held fast on the goings-on across the road. Spectators milled around, craning their necks for a better look at something. An auction, perhaps, she thought, though she couldn't recall seeing anything at the old gas station worth buying. The place had been stripped bare and abandoned back in the seventies, during the oil embargo. Then one word crackled across the distance, and stopped her dead.

". . . damnation!"

She sucked in an indignant breath and let it out in a furious gust. "That son of a bitch!"

Before Jack could say a word, she wheeled and made a beeline toward the station, her shoulders braced squarely, her stride quick and purposeful. He should have just let her go. He stood there for a second, intending to do just that. He wanted to drop off the fish for T-Grace and have himself a tall, cold beer. He didn't want to stick his nose into some damned hornet's nest. But as he watched Laurel stomp away, he couldn't put from his mind the image of her in his arms, weeping against his chest because she hadn't been able to give Lady Justice the miracle of sight.

Swearing under his breath, he tightened his grip on the stringer of dripping fish and jogged to catch up with her.

"He's not on the Delahoussayes' property," he pointed out.

Laurel scowled. "He'd damn well better have a lease on that place and a permit to hold a public demonstration," she snarled, secretly hoping he had neither so she could sic Kenner on him.

"You've done your part, angel," Jack argued. "You got him out of Ovide's hair—such as it is. Why you don' just leave him be and we can go have us a drink?"

"Why?" she asked sharply. "Because I'm here. I'm an officer of the court and have an obligation to the Delahoussayes." She shot him a glare. "Go have your drink. I didn't say you had to come with me."

"*Espèces de tête dure,*" he grumbled, rolling his eyes.

"Yes, I am," she said, never slowing her stride. "Hardheadedness is one of my better qualities."

Baldwin and his followers hadn't wasted any time. The tall "For Sale or Lease" sign that had stood propped in the front window of the station had been replaced with one that read "End Sin. Find the True Path." The door to the garage was open, and a stage had been hastily built across its mouth, giving Jimmy Lee a dark, dramatic background for his ranting and pacing routine.

His followers had gathered on the cracked concrete outside, crowding together despite the heat. Many of the women pressed toward the stage for a closer look at him, their faces glowing with sunburn and adulation. And Jimmy Lee stood above them all, drenched in sweat and glory, his hair slicked back and his caps gleaming white in the late afternoon sun. He stalked across the stage, his white shirt soaked through, his tie jerked loose, pleading with his followers to march valiantly on beneath the weight of their respective crosses, urging them to lighten his load by donating to keep the ministry going.

"I will fight on, brothers and sisters! No matter how Satan may try to smite me down, no matter the obstacles in my path, no matter if I have nothing with which to fight my battle except my faith!" He let his declaration ring in the air for a few seconds, then sighed dramatically and stood with shoulders drooping. "But I don't want to

fight this battle alone. I need your help, the help of the
faithful, of the brave, of the devout. Sad as I am to admit
it, we live in a world ruled by the almighty dollar. The
ministry of the True Path cannot continue to bring the
good news to untold thousands of believers each week
without money. And without the ministry, I am powerless. Alone, I am only a man. With you behind me, I am
an army!"

While the faithful and the devout applauded Baldwin's acting skills, Laurel skirted around the edge of the
mob. She watched them with a mix of anger and pity—
anger because they were gullible enough to listen to a
charlatan like Baldwin, and pity for the very same reason. They needed something to believe in. She didn't
begrudge them that. But that they had chosen to believe
in a perverted con man made her want to knock their
heads together.

She didn't see the cameras until it was too late. Her
gaze caught first on the van parked alongside the garage.
It bore the call letters of the Lafayette cable television
station that was home to Baldwin's weekly show. Then
her eye caught one of the video cameras that was capturing the spectacle for the home audience. By then she was
nearly at the front of the throng, and Baldwin had already spotted her.

His gaze, luminous gold and glowing with the light of
fanaticism, flashed on her like a spotlight, and he broke
off in midsentence. The anticipation level of the crowd
rose with each passing second of his silence. The cheap
sound system underscored it all with a low, buzzing
hum.

Laurel froze, her heart picking up a beat as both the
cameraman and Jimmy Lee moved toward her. She
could feel the cyclops eye of the camera zooming in on
her, could feel the heat of Baldwin's gaze, could feel the
additional weight of a hundred pair of eyes as one by one
the crowd turned toward her. She braced herself and
drew in a slow, deep breath.

"Miz Laurel Chandler," he said softly. "A woman of

intelligence and deep convictions. A good woman drawn in by deception to battle on the side of Satan."

Gasps and murmurs ran through the crowd. The woman standing closest to Laurel stepped back with a protective hand to her bosom.

"I don't think Judge Monahan will be too pleased with the comparison," Laurel said archly, crossing her arms. "But you're probably amused, being an expert at drawing in good people by means of deception, yourself."

Those close enough to hear her began to grumble and boo. Baldwin cut them off with a motion of his hand. "Condemn not, believers!" he shouted. "Christ himself, in his infinite wisdom, preached forgiveness for those who would hurt you. He has counseled me in matters of forgiveness—"

"Has He counseled you in matters of the law?" Laurel queried. "Do you have any right to be on this property, holding this assembly?"

Something ugly flashed in Baldwin's eyes. He didn't like her interrupting his divinely inspired lines. *Tough shit, Jimmy Lee.*

"We have every right, lost sister," he said tightly. "We have legal rights, granted by man. We have moral rights, granted by God Himself, to gather in this humble setting and—"

"Appropriate setting," Jack drawled. He stepped around Laurel to lean indolently against the edge of Jimmy Lee's stage, the stringer of fish still swinging from his fist. "You always did give me gas, Jimmy Lee."

He was near enough that the mike picked up the last of his words, and people at the back of the crowd, who had come only out of curiosity, burst out laughing.

Jimmy Lee's face flushed a dark blood red beneath his artificial tan. His mouth quivered a little as he fought to keep from sneering at the man who was leaning lazily against his platform. Damn Jack Boudreaux. Damn Laurel Chandler. She was the troublemaker, the little bitch. Boudreaux only came along sniffing after her. But as much as he wanted to drag out all the dirt on Laurel

Chandler, Jimmy Lee kept himself in check. His followers wouldn't tolerate an attack on a woman of her standing. Boudreaux, on the other hand, was a whole different breed of cat.

He smiled inwardly, a feral, vicious smile. "Do I indeed, Mr. Boudreaux?" he asked. "Shall I tell you what your books do for me? They sicken and disgust me, as they do any good Christian. The content is vile, brutal, a celebration of evil and an instruction manual in the ways of Satan. Or are you here to tell us you've given up that path of wickedness?"

A slow grin spread across Jack's face. He plopped his fish down on Jimmy Lee's wing tips, sending him scooting backward, and hopped onto the stage to sit with his legs swinging over the edge. "Well, hell, Jimmy Lee, that's sort of like askin' you if you've quit stealin' people's money. The way the question is phrased, denial is an admission of guilt. Having been an attorney in a previous incarnation, I know better than to answer." He tipped his head and treated Baldwin to a merciless, wicked grin so hard and sharp, it could have cut glass. "Me, I'm just amazed to hear you know how to read."

Another volley of laughter sounded at the back of the crowd and rippled forward. Jimmy Lee clenched his jaw against a stream of profanity. His fist tightened around his microphone while he indulged himself in the fantasy that it was Boudreaux's windpipe he was crushing.

"Evil is no laughing matter," he said sternly. He turned his gaze back out across the small sea of faces that had gathered to hear him and pointed hard at Jack. "Do we want our children growing up on the kind of twisted and depraved tales this man tells? Tales of murder and mutilation and horrors that should surely be beyond the imaginings of decent people!"

"Hey, Jack!" Leonce called out from near the dusty old gas pumps. "What's the name o' dat book?"

"*Evil Illusions!*" Jack called, laughing. "On sale everywhere for five ninety-nine!"

"And he laughs and makes money off this filth!" Jimmy Lee shouted to the devout above the laughter of the others. "What other sins might a sick mind like that commit? We hear every day about crimes against women and children in this country. Our own Acadiana is being terrorized by an animal who stalks and murders our women. And where do creatures like that get their ideas for their crimes?"

The grin vanished from Jack's face. He met Baldwin's gaze evenly, never breaking the stare as he rose to his feet and closed the distance between them, booting the fish aside. Hostility rolled off him in hot waves.

"You better watch your mouth, preacher," he growled, gently pushing Baldwin's microphone aside. "You never know what kind of revenge a sick mind like mine might come up with."

Jimmy Lee savored the small victory of striking a nerve, meeting Jack's hard stare with a smugness that came from having the safety of a crowd around him. "I'm not afraid of you, Boudreaux."

"No?" Jack arched a brow. "Are you afraid of the words 'slander suit'? You'd better be, Jimmy Lee, because I could have my lawyers tie you up in court for the rest of your unnatural life. I wouldn't leave you a pot to piss in, and this preacher act of yours will have been for nothing."

Baldwin narrowed his eyes. A muscle twitched in his jaw. "It's a free country, Boudreaux. If I think reading trash pushes unstable minds to commit unspeakable acts, I can say so."

"Uh-huh. And if you utter my name in connection with those unspeakable acts, I'll have the right to beat the ever-lovin' shit out of you—figuratively speaking." He smiled like a crocodile and lifted Jimmy Lee's hand so that the mike picked up his next words. "Mebbe you oughta try to cast the demons outta me, Jimmy Lee. Run 'em into some pigs or somethin'. Give the folks their money's worth." Baldwin glared at him. "No? Well, that's okay, Jimmy Lee."

He bent and snatched up the stringer of fish and swung them hard at Jimmy Lee. Baldwin barely had time to react, catching the slimy mass against his belly with a grunt and a grimace.

"There you go," Jack said. "Now you get yourself a couple'a loaves of bread, and mebbe you can do *that* miracle."

Howls of laughter went up from the back of the crowd. Laurel pressed a hand over her mouth and tried to contain herself. Jack hopped down off the stage and sauntered toward her, slipping a cigarette out of his shirt pocket and dangling it from his lip.

"You are *so* bad!" she whispered as he turned her by one arm and escorted her away from the crowd.

His dark eyes sparked with mischief as he slanted a look at her. "That's what makes me *so* good, sugar," he drawled. "Now let's go get that drink you owe me."

They hadn't taken three strides toward the road when a terrible scream split the air—piercing, blood-curdling, a sound that cut straight to the bone. Laurel pulled herself up, chilled and shaken, her hand grasping Jack's forearm, her heart thundering in her breast. She could hear the crowd behind her murmuring, gasping, shuffling their feet on the concrete as they turned. Then the scream came again and again. It emanated from Frenchie's, a terrible, keening wail, that carried in it a note instinctively understood by all, and everyone stood, breath held, waiting.

Laurel's grip tightened on Jack's arm as she spotted the Partout Parish cruiser parked out front. Sheriff Kenner walked out of the bar and down the steps, his mirrored aviator sunglasses glinting in the sun. The side door on the building slammed, and a thin young man in surfer shorts and a neon green shirt jumped the rail and came barreling across the parking lot, running as if the devil were at his heels, his face chalk white, shirttails flying.

The front door swung open again, and T-Grace literally hurled herself out onto the gallery, screaming, "My *bébé*! My *bébé*!" She fell to her knees, smashing her fists against the floor over and over, wild, terrible sobs tearing up from her very soul. Then Ovide stumbled out onto the gallery, feeling his way like a blind man. Finding his wife with his hands, he sank down behind her, tilted his face heavenward and cried out, *"Bon Dieu avoir pitié!"*

"Oh, God, Jack," Laurel whispered, tears crowding her throat and pressing at her eyes. The feeling that swelled inside her as she turned toward him was unmistakably grief, and a small, disconnected part of her brain marveled at the body's ability to react so strongly to something as yet unannounced.

Seconds later the young man who had dashed out of the bar arrived with the news: Annie Delahoussaye-Gerrard, who had not been seen since Sunday night, had been found. Her nude, brutalized body had been discovered by a pair of hikers along the bank of the bayou.

The murder rocked the town of Bayou Breaux to its core. As the terror of the Bayou Strangler had gripped other parts of Acadiana, residents here had felt immune. Partout Parish had seemed a safe haven, a magical place where bad things didn't happen. In the time it took Annie Delahoussaye-Gerrard to gasp her last breath, the illusion of safety had vanished. The world tilted on its axis, and the residents of Bayou Breaux cast about frantically for something to hang on to.

That evening the streets were abandoned. Businesses closed early. People went home to be with their families. Doors that had never been locked before were bolted shut against the threat of evil that lurked along the dark, misty banks of the bayou.

T-Grace, inconsolable in her grief, had to be carried to her bed and sedated. As if the news had been carried to them on telepathic waves, the rest of the Delahoussaye children began arriving. The family banded together to mourn, to offer each other strength, to fill the tiny house where they had all been raised and try to banish the emptiness left by that one missing face.

The bar was not open, but a core of regulars gathered inside in much the same way as the Delahoussaye clan in their home. They were family of sorts—Leonce and

Taureau, Dede Wilson and half a dozen others. Annie had been one of them, and now she had been torn from the fabric of all their lives, leaving a ragged, ugly hole.

Leonce took charge of the bar, dispensing drinks without a trace of his usual carefree grin. His Panama hat hung on the rack by the front door, removed out of respect, and he had traded his trademark aloha shirt for a somber black T-shirt. The rest of the group sat at or near the bar, everyone avoiding the dance floor and stage, except Jack. He sat on the piano bench, drinking Wild Turkey and playing soft sad songs on his small Evangeline accordion.

Laurel watched him from her perch on the corner barstool. He sat with his head bent, his graceful hands working the instrument, squeezing out notes so poignant, it seemed to be weeping. He hadn't said ten words since the announcement—to her or to anyone. Despite the fact that he remained physically present, she couldn't get away from the feeling that he had gone into retreat. He had pulled in on himself and closed all doors and shutters, the same as the residents of Bayou Breaux had locked up their homes. His face was a stark, blank mask, offering nothing, giving nothing away. There was no sign of the man who had teased her or the man who had held her while she cried. She nibbled on a thumbnail and wondered where he'd gone . . . and wished he hadn't gone there without her.

She felt like an outsider again. The others all had their memories of Annie to bind them together, common tales and common experiences. She hadn't known Annie. Until recently, her life had never crossed paths with any of the people who thought of a place like Frenchie's as a second home.

An old feeling came back to her from childhood, a memory of herself and Savannah dressed in their matching Sunday best, standing on the sidewalk out front of the church, watching with longing while other children ran and played in the park adjacent to the church grounds.

"Can't we play, too, Mama?"

*"No, darling, you don't want to get your pretty dress
all dirty, do you?"* Vivian, in a red-on-white dot dress
that matched her daughters', an elegant wide-brimmed
white hat perched just so on her head, bent and smoothed
a sausage curl behind Laurel's ear. *"Besides, sweetheart,
those aren't the kind of children you should play with."*

"Why not?"

"Don't be silly, Laurel." She smiled that brittle smile
that always made Laurel's tummy knot. *"They're common. You're a Chandler."*

A stupid memory, she thought, trying to crush the
residual vulnerability. This was a time of tragedy for the
Delahoussayes; she had no business feeling sorry for herself. Besides, no one in their right mind would *want* to
be included among the mourners.

"Here you go."

Laurel looked up and blinked at the tumbler of milk
Leonce had set on the bar before her.

"My grandpapa, he had an ulcer," he said softly. He
put his elbows on the bar and leaned toward her, a
knowing look raising one dark eyebrow and the knot of
scar tissue that interrupted it. "He used to rub his belly
same as what you're doin'. When he ran out of the cabbage juice the local *traiteur* used to give him, he drank
milk."

Laurel shot a guilty glance at the hand she had absently pressed to her middle. "I'm fine," she said, wrapping both hands around the cold glass. "But thank you,
anyway, Leonce."

He took a deep drag on his cigarette and sighed out a
cloud of pale smoke, staring across the room at nothing.
"I can't believe she's gone, snatched away from us just
like dat," he said, snapping his fingers.

"Were you close?"

He smiled sadly. "Ever'body loved Annie."

Laurel sipped her milk and looked at Jack out of the
corner of her eye, wondering if he had loved Annie. "She
was married, wasn't she?"

"Oh, yeah, but Tony, he didn' treat her good, so all
bets were off, if you get my drift."

He took another pull on his smoke and crushed the butt out in a Jax Beer ashtray. Lost in memories for a moment, he lifted a hand to rub absently at the scar on his cheek. "Annie, she liked to pass a good time," he murmured. "She wasn' a bad girl. She just liked to pass a good time, is all."

Meaning she cheated on her abusive husband. Automatically, Laurel's mind sorted and filed the facts, formulated theories. Old habit. Comforting in its way. There was solace, consolation to be found in making sense of tragedy. Murders could be solved. Justice could be served.

But nothing would ever bring Annie back.

The side door near the kitchen opened, and Ovide stumbled in like a zombie. He looked twenty years older and frail, despite his bulk. The hair that fringed his head stood out in an aura of silver. The ruddy color had leeched out of his face, leaving his skin a ghostly shade of gray.

Talk stopped, and everyone looked to him expectantly. Everyone except Jack, who hunched over his accordion, playing "Valse de Grand Meche." Ovide just stood there looking lost and confused, as if he had no idea where he was or what he was doing there. Leonce went to him and took hold of his arm, speaking to him softly in French. He didn't appear to listen, but looked around the bar at the people who had gathered to talk, at Jack, who had set himself apart. Finally, his gaze settled on Laurel.

"*Viens ici, chérie,*" he murmured, holding a hand out toward her. "T-Grace, she wants to see you."

Laurel just barely kept from looking over her shoulder to see if there was a more likely person standing behind her. "Me?" she murmured, touching her chest.

"*Oui,* come. Please."

With a heavy, black feeling of foreboding pressing down on her, and with the ironic thought that she was going to be included after all, she slid down off her stool.

They entered the Delahoussaye home through the kitchen, which proved to be the largest room of the house. Inappropriately cheerful and bright, the rich aroma of coffee and the spicy bite of *etouffée* lingered in the air. The walls sported yellow-and-white checked paper and a boggling array of knickknacks that ranged from plastic praying hands to thimbles from Las Vegas to salt-and-pepper sets in the guise of squirrels and chickens—all of it striking Laurel as being painfully sweet and too revealing about the woman who had raised her children in this house.

Delahoussaye children and grandchildren filled the benches at the long harvest table in the center of the room. Sleepy-eyed children sat on the laps of parents or elder siblings. The glare of the fluorescent light washed the color from all their faces, emphasizing eyes that had been cried raw and red. Laurel envied them their family, but not the grief that hung like a pall around them.

"I'm so sorry," she whispered, apologizing for both their loss and her intrusion on this private time.

Her words triggered a flood of tears from a woman who might have been Annie's twin—apple cheeks and corkscrew curls, a tank top two sizes too small. A brawny husband folded his arms around her and the dark-haired baby who sat on her lap and rocked them both. At the other end of the table, a younger version of T-Grace stood abruptly and looked straight at Laurel.

"Thank you for coming," she said automatically. "I'll make us a fresh pot of coffee."

She set about the task with the frenetic energy of someone trying to keep a step ahead of inner demons. Laurel recognized the signs from experience, and she felt empathy drawing on her, pulling at her limited reserve of strength.

She followed Ovide through the cramped living room, where two boys of about ten sat on the floor watching an age-old rerun of *Star Trek* on a television that had the sound turned so low, the actors seemed to be whispering. A toddler had been settled to sleep on the green plaid sofa with a nubby orange afghan covering all but her face and the fist pressed against her mouth as she sucked her thumb.

T-Grace lay in bed in a room that would have been considered a closet at Beauvoir. Meager light from a red glass Spanish-look lamp on the nightstand glowed off the imitation walnut paneling that displayed gold plastic candle sconces and gaudy metal butterflies. The smell of mothballs and cheap perfume permeated the air. Clothes were folded and stacked in precariously tipping piles on every available surface, giving the cramped little room the feel of a storage cupboard at the Salvation Army store.

When Laurel stepped through the door, her breath caught hard in her throat. Her first thought was that T-Grace had died of shock and heartbreak, and she could only wonder why Ovide had dragged her over here to view the body. The woman lay propped against half a dozen pillows, her bulging eyes staring into nothingness, her thin mouth hanging slack, as if she had been stricken down midsentence. Her orange hair stood up in thin, ratty tufts around her head. Then she stirred, lifting a hand from the green chenille bedspread, and Laurel forced herself to move farther into the room.

"I'm so sorry, T-Grace," she said softly as she took the woman's hand and settled a hip on the edge of the bed.

T-Grace rolled her head from side to side on the pillow, too sedated to do much more. "My poor, poor *bébé*. She's gone from us. Gone from dis world," she mumbled. "I can't bear it."

"You should try to rest," Laurel whispered, unable to find adequate words that could soothe a mother's suffering.

"There is no pain like to lose a child," T-Grace said, her eyes filling. She made no move to brush the tears away. They spilled down her sunken cheeks and trickled back along her jaw. What little energy she had left she concentrated into speech. "I would give myself a hundred times in her place."

Laurel bit her lip and held tight to the hand that seemed so frail in hers.

"Someone gotta pay for dis."

"They'll catch the man," Laurel said thickly, to placate T-Grace and to reassure herself. Someone would pay. Justice would triumph in the end. It had to.

But not soon enough for Annie.

T-Grace looked her square in the face, a glimmer of her old fire flickering in her eyes. "You gonna help us wit' dat, *chère*, or what?"

Panic booted Laurel in the stomach. "What can I do, T-Grace? I'm not a deputy. You don't need a lawyer." *You don't need me. Please, please, don't ask me to get involved in this.*

"My Ovide and me, we don' trust dat jackass Kenner," T-Grace said. "You go, you make sure he's doin' right by our poor *bébé* Annick."

Laurel shook her head. "Oh, T-Grace—"

T-Grace gathered the last of her strength and lunged ahead, grasping at Laurel with hands as cold and bony as death. "Please, Laurel, help us!" she exclaimed, desperation ragged in her voice. "Please, *chère, s'il vous plait!*"

The words rang in Laurel's head, clashing with the pleas she heard every night in her sleep. She pushed herself to her feet as T-Grace fell back on the pillows, and backed away from the bed, fighting to keep herself from running out. Tears crowded her eyes and throat, and she tried to fight them back with reason. This wasn't the same as Scott County. She wouldn't be taking on the investigation or trying to shoulder the burden of proof. All they were asking was that she keep an eye on things for them.

Still, her first, her strongest instinct was to say no, to protect herself.

Selfish. Coward. Weak.

"Please, help us, Laurel. . . ."

"You'll never be able to get justice for those children . . . go and get justice for somebody else. . . ."

She looked at T-Grace, lying on the bed like a corpse, her incredible energy sapped from her by grief. Then she turned to Ovide, who stood in the doorway, looking old and lost and helpless. She had the power to help

them in some small way—if she could get past her own
weakness.

"I'll do what I can."

Jack had forsaken the accordion for the piano by the time
Laurel came back to the bar. His fingers moved slowly,
restlessly, caressing the keys. His head was tipped back,
his eyes closed. The old upright piano that was more
accustomed to belting out boogie-woogie whispered the
opening movement of Beethoven's Moonlight Sonata,
dark, brooding, quiet, sad.

The last of the people who had gathered to talk were
on their way out the front door as Laurel walked in the
side. Only Jack remained, and Leonce, who was turning
out lights and putting the chairs up, sweeping as he
went.

He glanced up at her, leaning against his broom, his
scarred face in the shadows, a Dixie sign glowing red
neon behind him. "Hey, *chère*, you want a ride home?"
he asked softly. "Me, I don' think ol' Jack oughta get
behind a wheel, you know?"

"That's okay, Leonce," she murmured. "We didn't
drive. A long walk will do us both good."

He dropped his gaze to the broom bristles and
started sweeping again before she could read anything in
his expression. "Suit yourself."

Laurel tucked her hands in the pockets of her shorts
and wandered to the stage. Jack made no move to acknowledge her presence, even when she sat down beside
him on the piano bench. He went on playing like a man
in a trance, his long fingers stroking the yellowed keys
with the care of a lover. The song rose and fell, melodies
twining around one another, wrapping around Laurel
and drawing her into another world, a world of stark poignancy and bittersweet emotion. Every note swelled
with longing. A crushing pain filled the silences in between.

This was what hid behind the other Jack, the man
with the haunted eyes and the aura of danger—loneli-

ness, anguish, artistry. The realization struck a chord deep within her, and she closed her eyes against the pain. How many other layers were there? How many Jacks? Which one was at the core of the man? Which one held his heart?

She closed her mind to the questions and lay her head against his shoulder, too overwhelmed by feelings to think. She had held herself in tight check all evening, not allowing herself to react to Annie's murder or any of the emotions that had tried to surface since. But now, with no witnesses except a man who had already seen her cry, she stopped fighting. The feelings rushed up through her chest to her throat and clogged there in a hard lump. The tears came, not in a torrent, but in a painful, stingy trickle, spiking her lashes and dampening her cheeks.

Jack's hands slowed on the keyboard as the piece softened to its close. His fingers crept down to touch the final note, a low minor chord that vibrated and hung in the air like the echo of a voice from the dark past.

"Did you care about her?" Laurel asked, the question slipping out without her permission. Her breath held fast in anticipation of his answer.

"You mean, did I sleep with her?" Jack corrected her. He stared at the black upper panel of the piano, willing himself to see nothing, not the wood, not the ghost of Annie's sunny smile, nothing. "Yeah, sure," he said, his voice flat, emotionless. "A couple times."

His answer stung, though she told herself it shouldn't have. He was a rake, a womanizer. He'd probably slept with half the women in the parish. It shouldn't have meant anything to her. She pushed the reaction aside and tried to decipher what he might be feeling in the aftermath of the death of a woman he had known—intimately—whose parents were friends of his.

"I'm sorry," she whispered.

"Be sorry for Annie, not for me. I'm alive." For all the good he did anybody. His mouth twisted at the irony, and he reached for his whiskey to numb the ache. The liquor went down, as smooth as silk, to pool in his belly and send a familiar warmth radiating outward.

"I'm sorry for T-Grace and Ovide," Laurel said, recalling too vividly the scene that had been played out on the gallery, remembering too clearly the desperation in T-Grace as she begged for help. "They asked me to be their liaison with the sheriff."

"And you agreed."

"Yes."

"Naturally."

Even though he settled his fingers on the piano keys once again and started to play something slow and bluesy, she caught the caustic note in his voice. Slowly she straightened away from him, her gaze hard and direct. "What's that supposed to mean?"

Jack didn't bother looking at her. He could feel the defensiveness going up like a wall around her, just as he had intended. "It means you're a good little girl, doin' the right thing."

"They're friends," she said shortly. "They asked me for a favor. It seemed a small enough thing to give them in light of the fact that their daughter has just been murdered. They don't understand police procedure. They don't trust the system to work for them."

"Imagine that," he drawled sardonically.

Laurel bristled. "You know, I'm sick of your smartass remarks, Jack. It may not be perfect, but it's the only system we've got. It's up to people like you and me to make it work."

He went on playing, wishing it would release some of the tension that was coiling inside him like a copperhead about to strike. He was feeling mean. He was feeling too sensitive, as if all his nerve endings had been exposed and rubbed raw. His strongest instinct was not to let anyone near. He wanted to draw himself into that small, dark room inside himself, as he had when he'd been a boy waiting for the thundering hand of Blackie Boudreaux to come down on him. He wanted to go to that place where no one could touch him, no one could hurt him, where he couldn't feel and didn't care.

But Laurel Chandler sat beside him, prim and properly affronted by his lack of faith in her precious system of jurisprudence. Damn her.

"It didn't work very well for you, did it, *'tite chatte*?"

The slyness in his tone cut Laurel to the quick, and pain flowed through her at the thought that she had shared that experience with him—had trusted him with that fragile, damaged part of her heart—only to have him use it against her.

"Fine," she said. She hit the keyboard with her fists, pounding out a discordant tangle of notes as she rose from the bench. "The system sucks. So we should just throw our hands up and let crime run rampant?" She paced behind him, trying to channel the hurt into anger. An argument was something she could grasp and wield with skill. More productive than grief or fear. "That would be great, Jack. Then we could all do what you do—sit around and do nothing while our society comes apart at the seams."

He arched a brow as he swung around on the bench to face her. Stretching out with deceptive laziness, he leaned his elbows back against the piano and crossed his ankles in front of him. "What?" he demanded belligerently. "You think I should do somethin'? What would you have me do? Wave a wand and bring Annie back to life? I can't. Shall I look into a crystal ball and see who killed her? I can't do that, either. See, sugar? It's like my old man always told me—I'm just fuckin' good for nothin'."

"How convenient for you," Laurel snapped, ignoring the softer part of her heart that ached for Jack the abused child. She was too angry with him to feel sympathy. He reminded her too much of Savannah, wallowing in the polluted waters of her past instead of picking herself up and doing something positive with her life. "You don't have to take responsibility for anything. You don't have to aspire to anything. If the going gets tough, you can always turn around and blame your past. You don't have time to care about anyone else because you're so damn busy feeling sorry for yourself!"

He was on his feet and towering over her so quickly, she barely had time to suck in a breath of surprise. Common sense demanded she back away from him, the way she might back away from a panther encountered in the wild. But a deeper instinct made her hold her ground, and a tense, itchy silence descended between them.

He stared at her long and hard, his chest heaving with temper, his jaw set so rigid that the scar on his chin glinted like silver in the faint light. But the fire that had flared in his dark eyes died slowly, leaving that age-old abject weariness. The corners of his mouth cut upward in a bitter imitation of a smile.

"You don' want me to care about you, sugar," he murmured. "Everybody I ever cared about is dead." He raised a hand to caress her cheek, and she started at his touch. "See? I told you I'd be bad for you. You should have listened."

She batted his hand away and took a step back. He was trying to frighten her. The same man who had only hours ago wooed her with his wicked smile—No. Not the same man.

Angry with his chameleon act, angry that he would try to scare her, angry with herself for giving a damn what he did, she gave him one last look of defiance. "Play your games with someone else, Jack. I'm going home."

He watched her hop down off the stage and head for the front door, telling himself to let her go, telling himself he was better off not caring that she would walk out into the night alone. But he couldn't quite pull the door shut on that little room. He couldn't quite get the images out of his mind—Annie . . . Evie . . . Lost forever. The need to protect Laurel pulled against the need to protect himself, stretching his nerves as taut as violin strings, and he trembled with the tension of it, waiting for the thread to simply snap.

Laurel kept on walking, her head up, her slim shoulders squared, her tiny feet barely making a sound as her sneakers struck the floor. So small, so fragile, so fiercely determined to take on every rotten thing the world tossed her way.

Swearing under his breath, Jack jumped off the stage. He caught up with her in half a dozen strides and grabbed hold of her arm, halting her progress toward the door.

"I'll walk you."

"Why?" she demanded, glaring up at him. "What are you going to do, Jack? Protect me? You just finished telling me how dangerous you are. Why would I go with you, anyway? You're drunk."

His hand tightened on her arm. His temper boiled hotter, harder as the warring factions within him fought between the urge to throttle her or crush her against him.

"I'm not that drunk," he growled. "I said, I'll walk you home."

"And I asked you why," Laurel said, too angry to be cautious. A small, rational corner of her brain told her she was taunting a tiger, but she didn't listen. Something inside her was pushing her to recklessness. She didn't understand it, wasn't sure she *wanted* to understand it, but she couldn't seem to stop it. "Why?"

His nostrils flared. His brows pulled ominously low over his eyes. He looked like the devil glaring down at her, the hard planes and angles of his lean face cast in sharp relief. "Don't be stupid. Women are gettin' killed. Do you wanna be one of them?"

"What's it to you one way or the other, Jack?" she returned. "You don't care about anyone but yourself. After they find my body, you can drink a quart of Wild Turkey in my honor and tell people you slept with me a couple of times."

The leash on his control stretched to the breaking point. Rage rumbled through him like thunder, shaking him, swelling in his chest, roaring in his ears. He gripped her shoulders with both hands, trembling with the need to shake her like a rag doll and hurl her aside, out of his life.

"Damn you," he snarled, not even sure whether he

was cursing Laurel or himself. "If you wanted an idealist, you shoulda gone shoppin' in a better neighborhood, sugar. I'm a bastard and a user and a cynic—"

"Why do you want to walk me home, Jack?" she demanded, matching him glare for glare.

"Because I've got enough corpses on my conscience to last me!"

A thick, heavy silence hung in the air around them as their gazes held. Jack's expression was fierce, wild. His fingers bit into the tender flesh of Laurel's upper arms. She had the feeling that he could have snapped her in half like a twig. She had never been quite so aware of the differences in their sizes, had never felt quite so physically fragile.

I've got enough corpses on my conscience to last me . . . The words sank into her brain one by one to be scrutinized, and a chill ran through her.

She stared at him for a long moment, watching him struggle to rein back the beast that was his temper. As his breathing slowed, she forced herself to relax by degrees, and breathed easier herself as his grip loosened.

"Would you care to elaborate on that statement?" she asked softly.

Very deliberately he lifted his hands from her shoulders and turned away from her. "No, I wouldn't," he said, and he headed for the door.

They walked the dark, deserted streets to Belle Rivière in silence, not speaking, not touching. Jack had closed himself off entirely. Laurel watched him surreptitiously, wondering, the wheels of her lawyer's mind whirling as she scrambled for a logical explanation, her heart swearing there had to be one.

He walked her to the courtyard and held the gate open for her. She stepped into the garden, trying desperately to think of something to say that would somehow ease the tension between them, but when she turned to say it, he was gone. Without a word he had slipped into

the black shadows of the trees that stood between Belle
Rivière and L'Amour.

Time slipped by unnoticed as she stood with her
hands wrapped around the iron bars of the gate, staring
toward the brick house that stood on the bank of the
bayou. No lights came on in the windows.

Everyone I ever cared about is dead.

*I've got enough corpses on my conscience to last
me . . .*

Who had he lost? Who had he cared about? Why
were their deaths on his conscience?

The only thing she knew for certain was that it wasn't
wise of her to want that knowledge. She had all she
could handle just getting herself from one day to the
next. She didn't need the kind of trouble that was brewing between herself and Savannah. She didn't want to
get involved with the Delahoussayes or a murder investigation. She wasn't strong enough to endure a relationship with a man like Jack. He had too many facets, too
many secrets, too many shadows in his past, too much
darkness in his soul.

And still she felt attraction to him pulling on her like
a magnetic force.

"Oh, God," she whispered, closing her eyes and
pressing her forehead against the cool iron bars of the
gate. "I never should have come back here."

A scrap of cloud scudded across the sliver of moon. A
sultry breeze whispered through the branches of the
trees. A chill raced over Laurel's flesh, and she looked up
abruptly, sensing . . . something. She strained her eyes,
staring into the darkness, seeing nothing, but sensing
. . . a presence. The sensation lingered like a dark, intent gaze, and the hair rose on the back of her neck.

"Jack?" she called, a faint quiver of doubt vibrating in
her voice.

Silence.

"Jack? Huey?"

Nothing but the heavy feeling of eyes.

Somewhere in the woods beyond L'Amour a screech
owl called, its voice like a woman's scream. Laurel swal-

lowed hard as her heart climbed into her throat. Slowly, she backed toward the house, sliding her feet on the uneven brick pathway to keep from tripping. As she scanned the shadows of the courtyard for unfamiliar shapes, she chided herself for spooking so easily, trying not to think about the fact that Annie's body had been discovered not so very far from here.

It seemed to take forever to reach the gallery, but when she did, she felt like a child reaching the safe place in a game of tag. Relief swirled through her in a dizzying wave as she slipped into the house and locked the French doors behind her.

The predator is cloaked in shadows. A creature of the night. A creature of darkness. Watching. Waiting. Contemptuous. Smug.

The adversary has been chosen. Good, golden, champion of justice. But goodness and justice have nothing to do with this game. In this game, only the strong and the clever survive.

Chapter
Eighteen

Tony Gerrard sat hunched over the small table in the interrogation room like a sullen sixteen-year-old hood in detention. His curly black hair was renegade length, his wide jaw shadowed blue by his beard. The sleeves of his faded denim work shirt had been cut off to reveal bulging biceps adorned with the artistic handiwork of Big Mamou of Mamou's Tattoos fame. His right arm proudly proclaimed him to be 100% Coonass. An alligator lounged on his left, seeming to come to life as he reached for an ashtray to tap off his cigarette. The gator stretched and twisted, all but bellowing before shrinking back into complacency.

In truth Tony hadn't changed a bit in the ten years since he'd dropped out of high school. Physically, he had matured early, reaching his full height of five feet eight and bulking out with muscle the instant his hormones had sprung to life. Psychologically, he hadn't matured at all. His temper was still the volatile and unpredictable creature of an adolescent. He used his penis like a homing device, and his idea of a good time invariably included sports, crude humor, and mass quantities of beer.

He'd been in trouble off and on since junior high, but his trouble had never amounted to much, to his way of thinking—a few smashed cars, the occasional fist fight. Twice he had been hauled in for pushing Annie around, but he had never hurt her badly. The court never wanted to hear it, but she'd always given as good as she got, the little hellcat.

He smiled a little at the memory of her hurling beer cans at him, swearing at him a mile a minute. But the smile twisted into a knot of pain as he reminded himself that Annie wouldn't be around to throw anything at his head anymore.

He stared down at the plain gold wedding band on his left hand, unable to look away from it, unable to stop from twisting it around and around on his finger.

"You can take that off and hock it, Tony," Sheriff Kenner drawled, planting a boot on the seat of the only other chair at the table. He rested his forearms on his lean thigh and looked at Tony sideways, feeling exhausted and mean. He'd gotten two hours' sleep since the discovery of the body. "You're not married anymore."

Tony just sniffed and looked away.

"Divorce would have been cheaper," Kenner said, watching his man with narrowed eyes. "You don't have jack shit to sue for. Might have lost your truck, is all. You're gonna pay now, boy. They'll throw your pretty ass in Angola Pen, and you'll pay for the rest of your miserable life."

Tony blinked at the itchy pressure in his eyes, never glancing Kenner's way, and mumbled, "I didn't kill her."

"Sure you did. You just spent six weeks in our little parish hotel 'cause of the missus. You had six weeks to get up a good head of steam. You got out, went to pay her back, got a little carried away . . ."

"I didn't kill her."

"Tell me, Tony, what's it like to wrap a scarf around a woman's throat and choke the life out of her? Did you watch her face? Did you watch her turn color, watch her eyes bug out as she realized the man she married was gonna kill her?"

"Shut up."

"Did you like the sounds she made, Tony?"

"Shut up."

"Or did you like it better when she was begging you to stop using that knife on her?"

"Shut up!" Tony exploded to his feet, sending his chair skittering backward on the linoleum. His face contorted with rage, and spittle flew as he shouted, "Shut the fuck up!"

Kenner pounced like a wolf, grabbing him by the back of his thick neck and digging his fingertips in. As Tony gasped at the pain shooting down his spine, Kenner leaned in close, invading the man's personal space in every way he could. "No, you shut up, dickhead!" he bellowed in Gerrard's ear. "Shut up and sit down." He let go of Tony's neck and shoved the old wooden straight chair back under him just in time to catch him.

Tony hit the seat of the chair so hard, it felt like a baseball bat hitting his balls. Another swarm of red and blue dots swirled before his eyes. He swallowed hard and propped his elbows on the scarred table, hanging his head and rubbing weakly at the back of his neck. What was left of his cigarette smoldered in the ashtray, the smoke nauseating him.

Kenner walked away to an old army green metal desk that squatted along one wall of the barren room and picked up a manila file folder. He took his time about it, believing firmly in fucking with a perp's mind. Tony Gerrard wanted out of this room. Let him think that wasn't going to happen any time soon. Let him think that the reason was the cops figured they had all the time in the world to question him was that they were damn certain he did the deed.

"You're a sad sack of shit, Tony," he muttered, thumbing through the file. "Getting off on this kind of sick torture stuff."

"I didn't do it," Tony whispered, pinching the bridge of his nose. He wanted to cry, and he hated Kenner for that. He wanted out of this crackerbox of a room. He wanted to stop thinking about Annie and words like "torture" and "murder."

"Hell, everybody knows you knocked her around."

"But I never would'a done—" He broke off and swallowed hard as the gossip came back to him in an ugly rush. Everyone in town was talking about what those hikers had found. "I never would'a done that. Never."

"You mean, this?" Kenner pulled the crime scene Polaroids out of the file and tossed them on the table.

For one long, terrible second Tony stared at the body of his wife, his brain cataloging the gruesome atrocities—the scarf knotted around her throat, the cuts the knife had made in her breasts and belly and thighs. In that one second the images were forever branded into his memory. The skin, unnaturally pale, mottled with bruises, sliced open in places, torn and ragged in others. And her eyes. Those beautiful big brown eyes, frozen in a stare of pure horror.

"She probably looks worse than when you dumped her body," Kenner said coldly. "She was in the bayou a couple days. Lucky there was anything left, what with the fish and the gators and—"

Tony swept the pictures off the table with a cry of anguish, then turned and vomited on the floor, his guts wrenching at the images flashing through his head.

"Annie! Oh, God, Annie!" he cried, the sobs tearing up from his heart. He rose in a half crouch, doubled over by the terrible pain of loss, and stumbled away from the table to sink down on his knees in the corner.

Kenner frowned and sighed. He picked up the snapshots, careful not to look at them, and slipped them back in the folder. The hot, acidic scent of Tony's stomach contents burned his nostrils, but that wasn't what left the bad taste in his mouth.

He had wanted Gerrard to be guilty, had honestly believed he could have committed the crime. A confession would have justified what he had just put Tony Gerrard through. It was a hell of a lot more gratifying to torment a guilty man than a grieving husband.

"You're free to go," he said in a low voice, then let himself out of the room.

The next door down the hall opened, and Danjermond walked out looking cool and composed, unaffected by what he had seen through the two-way glass.

"My God, you're a ruthless bastard," he drawled mildly.

Kenner watched him straighten a shirt cuff and align his onyx cuff link with the top stitching. "No," he said. "Whoever killed Annie Delahoussaye-Gerrard is a ruthless bastard. I just mean to catch him."

Danjermond glanced at him from under his brows. "You don't think Gerrard is guilty?"

He shook his head as he dug a cigarette out of his shirt pocket and hung it from his lip. "You saw him."

"He could be acting. Or perhaps what we witnessed was abject remorse."

"If he's acting, then he deserves the goddamn Academy Award." He struck a match and cupped his hands around his cigarette as if he were standing outside in a stiff wind. To banish the sour taste and smell that lingered in his senses, he drew the smoke deep into his lungs and exhaled through his nostrils. "I got a call in to the sheriff in St. Martin Parish, where they found that last dead girl. A hundred says the same piece of shit did this one."

He tossed his match down on the floor and ground it to shreds with the toe of his boot. "I'll catch the son of a bitch," he swore. "Nobody does this in my parish and gets away with it."

The very corners of Danjermond's mouth curled in a sardonic, unamused smile. "I appreciate your attitude. Killers running around loose don't do my career any good, either."

Kenner shot him a hard look, his eyes mere slits in his lean, leathery face. "Fuck your career, Danjermond. I got a wife and two daughters. This maniac comes sniffing around my turf, I'll tear his goddamn throat out."

He turned and headed for his office. Danjermond fell in step beside him, his stride fluid and graceful beside the sheriff's cowboy swagger. "Our constituents can be grateful you have the sensibilities of a pit bull, Sheriff."

"Yeah, and I'm mean enough to take that as a compliment." He glanced through the window into his office and pulled up short of the door, a headache instantly piercing his temples as he caught a glimpse of Laurel Chandler's profile through the venetian blind. "Shit. This is all I need. She's probably here to tell me Jimmy Lee Baldwin did it."

Danjermond gazed between the slats of the blinds, taking in the feminine lines of Laurel Chandler's face and the determined set of her chin. She sat in the chair beside Kenner's desk with her legs crossed, and bent as he watched to scratch a spot on her stockinged calf. "She does have a reputation for being . . . dogged."

Kenner snorted and stubbed his cigarette out in the dirt of a potted orange tree that sat beside his secretary's desk. "She has a reputation for causing trouble, and I don't want any more than I've already got."

Laurel emerged from her interview with Kenner feeling like she'd just gone three rounds with Dirty Harry. How the man had ever won an election was beyond her. He certainly hadn't gone the route of charming the voters. More likely they had been afraid not to vote for him. A territorial sort, he'd torn into her first for invading his office. Then had come the "I have better things to do" speech. He calmed down only marginally when she explained herself, explained that the Delahoussayes didn't understand procedure and only wanted someone to act as go-between on their behalf.

Grudgingly he gave her the barest of details concerning the investigation. Because of the priority nature of the case, the autopsy was already being performed. He couldn't say when the body would be released. He wouldn't say if they had any solid physical evidence. No arrests had been made.

"You brought Tony Gerrard in for questioning."

He narrowed his eyes at her. She couldn't even see the pupils. A muscle ticked in his cheek.

"It's common knowledge, Sheriff. This is a small town."

He lit a cigarette and slowly went through with the ritual of shaking out the match and taking his first deep drag. "We brought him in. Had a little chat."

"I suppose you're aware that his wife had had relationships with a number of other men."

"You gonna tell me they all did it? It was a goddamn conspiracy, right? You're big on that kind of bullshit."

"I'm not telling you anything."

She wanted to tell him to do the anatomically impossible, she thought as she marched down the hall. He had her pegged as a head case, and everything she said he twisted into the ineffectual babblings of a hysterical woman. He wouldn't have believed her if she had told him the earth was round. Of course, Neanderthal that he was, he probably had doubts about that anyway. A nasty insinuation concerning the species residing in Kenner's family tree ran through her head, and she smiled a little at the mental image of orangutans with slitted eyes and cigarettes dangling from their nonexistent lips.

"I've seen people convicted on the basis of a smile like that one."

Danjermond stepped out of the water fountain alcove, seeming to materialize out of nothing. Laurel's heart jolted, but she managed to keep from shying sideways. She looked up at the district attorney, finding the quiet amusement in his clear green eyes both irritating and inappropriate—just as her smile must have looked.

"I should probably be fined at the very least," she said with a rueful look. "Psychic defamation of character."

He tipped his head. "Not on the books in the state of Louisiana."

"Then I'm off the hook as long as Kenner can't read minds."

"I believe his talents lie in other areas."

Laurel sniffed and crossed her arms, allowing a little

of her anger to sizzle up. "Yes, I'm sure he's a whiz with a rubber truncheon and thumbscrews, but that's not my idea of a good time."

"No?" Danjermond chuckled, then the sound faded away and a heavy silence fell between them like a blanket of humidity. His gaze turned speculative and held fast on her face, searching, probing. "What is, Laurel?" he asked softly.

Something about his question froze her tongue to the roof of her mouth. She had the feeling, as she looked up into that calm, stunningly handsome face that he was running possible scenarios through his head. Hot, dark, erotic. The air around them seemed suddenly charged with his powerful sexuality. She felt it envelope her, felt it penetrate the skirt and blouse she wore and stroke over the silk beneath. A delicate shiver of arousal rippled through her, followed closely by something like revulsion. She wasn't sure she understood either.

"We might discuss it over lunch," he said quietly, his gaze lingering on her mouth, as if he were imagining watching her lips close over a red, ripe strawberry. He stroked the fingertips of one hand along the stylish silk necktie he wore, smoothing it with a lover's caress. His voice softened to the texture of velvet. "Or after."

"That seems a highly improper suggestion, Mr. Danjermond," Laurel said coolly, wishing fervently that someone else would happen out into the hall and break the sexual tension or at least witness it. But then she had the eerie feeling that no one else would see it or sense it. The signals he was sending out were for her alone.

Sliding his hands into the pockets of his coffee brown trousers, he smiled that all-knowing feline smile that made her feel as if he were a superior life-form who had taken the guise of a mere mortal for amusement. "I don't believe I've broken any rules by asking you to lunch."

Once again he had neatly maneuvered her into a corner. The realization annoyed her. If she wanted to make an argument against his statement, she would have to be the one to bring up the topic of sexual tension and implied propositions.

Or maybe she was just imagining the whole thing. Perhaps she had taken such an aversion to Vivian's notions of him as a son-in-law, she was reading into everything he said. Whatever the case, she didn't want to deal with him; she didn't have the energy.

"Thank you for the invitation," she said smoothly. "But I'm afraid I already have plans."

One straight brow lifted. His gaze seemed to intensify, his pale green eyes glowing like precious stones held up to the sun. "Another man?"

"My aunt. Not that it's any of your business."

He treated her to a full-fledged smile that was perfectly even, perfectly symmetrical, bright, white, handsome as she imagined all the Danjermonds had been since the days of the Renaissance. "I like to know if I have competition."

"I told you before," Laurel said, edging toward impatience. "I'm not looking to get involved with anyone at the moment."

The word "liar" rang in her head, and she had the distinct feeling Stephen Danjermond heard it, too. But he would have to call her on it. She wasn't bringing up the subject of Jack Boudreaux. Today she honestly wished she'd never heard the name.

"Sometimes we get things we are not necessarily expecting, though, don't we, Laurel?" he said.

He didn't like her rebuff. She could hear the faintest edge in his smooth, cultured voice, and behind the affable smile his eyes had a coldness about them that hinted at temper. Too bad. She had no intention of becoming entangled with him—emotionally or otherwise.

"Annie Delahoussaye certainly got something she wasn't expecting," she said, neatly shifting gears to business. God, how appalling that murder seemed safer territory than personal relationships.

"You're here on her behalf, Laurel? For someone who claims not to be interested in going back to work you certainly are spending a great deal of time in the courthouse."

"Her parents asked me to act as their liaison with the

sheriff's department," she said. "They're devastated, naturally, and Kenner is less than forthcoming, to say nothing of the fact that sympathy is a completely foreign concept to him."

Danjermond nodded thoughtfully. "He's a hard man. He would tell you there's no place for sympathy in his work."

"Yes, well, he'd be wrong."

"Would he?" he asked, looking doubtful. "Sympathy can sometimes be equated with weakness, vulnerability. It can draw a person into situations where perspective becomes warped and emotion takes over where logic should rule. We're taught in law school not to allow ourselves to become emotionally involved, aren't we, Laurel? As you well know, the results can be disastrous."

He couldn't have cut her more cleanly if he had used a scalpel. And he'd done it so subtly, seemingly without effort. And once again, Laurel could say nothing without incriminating herself. She had the distinct feeling he was punishing her for turning down his invitation, but she could hardly accuse him. The best thing she could do was concede to an opponent she was no match for and get the hell out.

She took a very rude, very deliberate look at her watch and said flatly, "Oh, my, look at the time. I have to be going."

Danjermond gave her a mocking little half bow. "Until we meet again, Laurel."

She left the courthouse feeling battered. Kenner had been bad enough, but she couldn't encounter Stephen Danjermond without feeling she had walked into a tiger's cage. He was beautiful, charismatic, but there was a strength, an ego, a temper there beneath the handsome stripes. This time he had reached out and swiped at her with his elegant paw, and she felt as if his claws had sliced into her as sure and sharp as razor blades. She thanked God she would never have to face him in a courtroom.

The Acura was parked beneath the heavy shade of a live oak at the edge of the courthouse lot. Laurel slid behind the wheel, and the tension that had gripped her in its fist all morning finally let go, leaving her feeling like a puddle of melted Jell-O. She stared across the street for a moment, watching the weathered old men who sat on their bench in front of the hardware store.

They gathered there every morning in their summer hats and short-sleeved shirts, suspenders holding up baggy dark pants. Laurel knew the faces had changed over the years, but she could remember old men sitting there when she had been a small child. They took their places on the bench to watch the day go by, to swap stories and gossip. Today they looked grim, unsmiling, wary of every car that drove past, watchful of strangers. A woman emerged from the store, holding the hand of a daughter who had probably considered herself too old for it just yesterday.

Annie Delahoussaye was on a lot of minds today.

Was she on Jack's mind?

"Shit," Laurel whispered, her lashes drifting down as weariness weighed like lead on her every muscle—most especially her heart. His image drifted into her mind without her permission, that haunted, brooding look in his eyes, his face hard. She'd seen that look all night, heard his harsh, smoky voice. *I've got enough corpses on my conscience. . . .*

He might have been referring to his work, but he had played the cynical mercenary hack every time she brought the subject up. He wrote horror for the money. He would claim he had no trouble distinguishing fact from fiction. Her thoughts turned back to what little mention he'd made of his life as corporate attorney for Tristar Chemical. Hardly a violent occupation. Still, every time she started to dismiss it, something pulled her back. He had crashed and burned, he'd said, and taken the company down with him. Why?

Intuition told her she would find some of the answers she was looking for in Houston, where Tristar had its headquarters. She had acquaintances there, could make a phone call. . . . Practicality told her not to look. She was far better off leaving Jack and his moods alone. He obviously had problems he needed to work out—or wallow in, as seemed to be his choice. They would be disastrous together, both of them wounded, looking to each other for strength that simply wasn't there. He didn't want her anyway. Not in any permanent sense. They had had some fun together, "passed a good time" as the Cajuns said. That was all Jack wanted.

She ignored the way that knowledge stung, and reached for the ignition, firing the car's engine and air-conditioning to life. How many times had she said she wasn't looking for a relationship? She was in no emotional condition to enter into one. That she had taken him as a lover was a whole other matter, a matter of letting herself live, of taking something for her own pleasure. She told herself she wanted nothing more than that from him, and did her damnedest to forget the way his arms had felt around her while she cried.

Lunch consisted of stuffed tomatoes and garden-fresh salad that no one seemed to have an appetite for. They sat at the glass-topped table on the back gallery, looking out at the courtyard where old growth was flourishing, now that it was free of choking weeds, and new flowers were growing fuller and more vibrant by the day.

Whether deliberately or subconsciously, Laurel thought Caroline had chosen to eat out here so they would be surrounded by positive affirmations of life and beauty when talk around town all morning had been of death and ugliness. They could sit and feel the breeze sweep under the shade trees and along the gallery, bringing with it the heavy perfume of sweet olive and gardenia. They could listen to the songs of the warblers and buntings and look out on the abundance of life in the garden and try to counterbalance thoughts of death.

"Me, I dunno what dis world comin' to," Mama Pearl grumbled, wagging her head. She dug a good-size chunk of chicken out of her tomato with a ferocious stab of her fork, but she didn't bring it to her mouth. Setting the fork aside, she heaved a sigh and rubbed a plump hand across her lips, as if to push back the words that might have spilled out. As tears rose, her eyes darted to the courtyard and she stared hard at the old stone fountain with its grubby-faced cherubs cavorting around the base.

Caroline toyed with her salad, turning a ring of black olive over and over with the tines of her fork. Her usual air of command seemed dimmed, subdued by the weight of events, but she was still the head of Belle Rivière, their leader, their rock, and she rose to the occasion as best she could. Drawing in a deep breath to fortify herself, she squared her dainty shoulders beneath the soft white chiffon blouse she wore.

"The world has been a violent place since the days of Cain," she said quietly. "It's no worse today. It only seems so because the violence has hit so close to home."

Mama Pearl gave her a sharp look of disapproval and hefted her bulk up from the table, scraping her chair back. "You tell dat to T-Grace Delahoussaye. I gots to check my cake."

Grumbling under her breath, she waddled into the house, her red print cotton shift swishing around her with every step. Caroline watched her go, feeling helpless to do anything to alleviate the grief and worry and anger that had tempers running short and fears running close to the surface of everyone she knew. She turned her gaze to Laurel, who was picking at her chicken salad.

"How are you doing, darlin'?"

"Fine." The answer was automatic. Caroline ignored it and waited patiently for something closer to the truth.

Resigning herself to the inevitable, Laurel set her fork aside and rested her forearms on the cool glass of the tabletop. "I feel stronger than I did," she said, a little amazed by the admission. "But with all the things that have happened . . . everything I feel myself getting dragged into . . . A part of me would like very much to run away to a resort someplace where I wouldn't know a soul."

In a gesture of love and an offer of support, Caroline reached across the table and twined her fingers with her niece's. "But you won't."

To leave now, with her word given to the Delahoussayes, with tension between her and Savannah, would be the coward's way out. She couldn't walk away and live with herself. "No, I won't."

Caroline squeezed her hand, her heart brimming with love, with sympathy. "Your father would have been so very proud of you," she said, her voice suddenly husky with emotion. "I'm proud of you."

Laurel couldn't think of a single thing she had done to be proud of, but she didn't say so. She didn't say anything for a minute for fear she would burst into tears. For a long moment she stared off at a particularly beautiful cluster of purple clematis that was twining around one of the gallery pillars, and just hung on to her aunt's hand, savoring the contact and the strength that passed to her from someone who loved her unconditionally.

She suspected a great many people in Bayou Breaux were paying special attention to family today, having been struck aware that loved ones could be snatched away in a heartbeat with feelings left unspoken and dreams never realized. Today, life would seem more precious, more urgent, something to be clung to and relished.

Bringing her emotions back in line, she gently extricated her fingers from Caroline's and reached for the stack of mail she had picked up at the post office on her way to the courthouse. "You've got some interesting-looking letters today," she said, sorting through the stack. She plucked out several fine-quality envelopes, each with a different postmark—Biloxi, New Orleans, Natchez—all of them addressed in flowing, feminine script, one smelling faintly of jasmine.

Caroline accepted them, a soft smile turning her lips as she perched her reading glasses on her slim, upturned nose and scanned the addresses. "How lovely to hear from friends on such a terrible day."

"Old friends from school?" Laurel asked carefully, watching closely as her aunt used a table knife to open the pink one. "Or business?"

"Mmm . . . just friends."

Laurel chided herself for her curiosity. Caroline's privacy was her own. Of course, Savannah might have just asked her outright.

"I can't believe Savannah is sleeping in so late," she murmured, wondering if today might not be the perfect time to start mending the tears in their relationship. Arguments seemed petty and pointless in the face of death, and life seemed so finite. They could take the rest of the day and drive down to Cypremort Point for bluepoint crabs and a view of the gulf at sunset. They would sit together with the salty breeze on their faces and in their hair, and talk and watch the saw grass sway in the shallows while gulls wheeled overhead. "Do you think I dare wake her up on the pretense of delivering her Visa bill?"

"Hmm? Oh, a—" Caroline glanced up from her letter. "Savannah isn't here, darlin'."

"Where did she go?" Laurel asked, annoyed that the perfect day that had painted itself in her mind was going to be put off. "More to the point, *how* did she go? I had the car all morning."

"I'm not sure. Perhaps she had a friend pick her up. I couldn't say; I was at the store. Did you have plans?"

"No. It's just that we've been talking about spending some time together. She wanted to do something yesterday, and then Jack showed up."

"She left here in a state yesterday, I do know that," Caroline said, folding back a sheet of pink stationery. "I take it she doesn't approve of your seeing Mr. Boudreaux."

"I don't think Jack is her problem." Concern tugged at the corners of Laurel's mouth and furrowed her brow. She wrestled for a moment with the thoughts that had been troubling her since Savannah's blowup, finally deciding they were best shared. "I'm worried about her. She seems so . . . volatile. Up one minute and down the next. She got into a fight with Annie Gerrard Sunday. A *fist fight*! Aunt Caroline, I'm frightened for her."

And for myself, she thought, in a small way. The child in Laurel had always depended on Savannah. That child felt lost at the prospect of Savannah's not being dependable any more.

Caroline set her letters aside and slipped her reading glasses off, her expression somber. "She was seeing a psychiatrist in Lafayette for a while. I think she might have gotten help there, but she wouldn't stay with it."

Naturally. Just as she never stayed with a job or anything else that might have given her help or a sense of purpose that didn't involve sex. Laurel's hands fisted on the tabletop, and she wished for something she could hit to let off some of the impotent anger that was building inside her. "She's determined to let the past rule her life, dictate who she is, what she is. We had an awful fight about it the other day. I lost my temper, but it makes me angry to see her throw her life away for something that ended fifteen years ago."

For a moment Caroline said nothing. She sat quietly toying with one of the heavy gold hoops that hung from her ears and let Laurel's statement hang in the air, let it sink in not for her own benefit, but for her niece's.

"Tell me," she said at last. "Do you not still see those children from Scott County in your sleep?"

The abrupt change of subject jolted Laurel for a second. The question brought the faces up in her memory, and she had to force them back into the little compartment she tried to stow them in during the day. "Yes," she murmured.

"But that's over and done with," Caroline said. "Why can't you let them go?"

"Because *I* failed them," Laurel said, tensing against the guilt. "It was *my* fault. I deserve to be haunted by that—"

"No," Caroline cut her off sharply, her dark eyes bright with the strength of her feelings. "No," she said again, softening her tone. "You did all you could. The outcome was not in your hands. You had no control over the attorney general or the lack of evidence or what other members of the community did, and yet you blame yourself and let that part of your past torment you."

Laurel didn't try to argue her culpability; she knew

what the truth was. The point her aunt was making had little to do with her, anyway.

"Are you saying Savannah blames herself for the abuse?" she asked, incredulous at the thought. "But what happened was Ross's fault! He forced himself on her. She couldn't possibly believe that was her fault."

Caroline stroked a fingertip thoughtfully along her cheekbone and raised a delicately arched brow. "You think not? Savannah is a beautiful, sensual, sexual creature. She always has been. Even as a child she had a certain power over men, and she knew it. You think she hasn't blamed herself for being attractive to Ross or that Ross hasn't taken every opportunity to blame her himself? He is and always has been a weak man, taking credit that isn't his due and shedding blame like water off a duck's back."

A fresh spring of hate for Ross Leighton welled up inside Laurel, and she recognized that a large part of her anger was for the fact that Ross had never been made to pay for his crime. Justice had never been served. Some of the blame for that was hers, she knew, and the guilt for that was terrible.

If only she had found the courage to tell their mother or go to Aunt Caroline. But she hadn't. Vivian was still in ignorance of her husband's atrocities. Caroline had found out the truth years after the fact. There had been no justice for Savannah . . . so Laurel had spent her life seeking justice for others.

I'm not trying to atone for anything!

God, what a lie. What a hypocrite she was.

Caroline rose gracefully from her chair, tucking her letters into a patch pocket on the full yellow skirt that hugged her tiny waist and swirled around her calves. She came around the table and slipped her arms around Laurel's shoulders, hugging her tight from behind. "The past is always with us, Laurel," she said gently. "It's a part of us we can't ignore or abandon. And it's not always easy to keep it behind us, where it belongs. You'd do well to remember that for yourself, as well as for your sister."

She pressed a kiss to her temple and went inside,

leaving Laurel alone on the gallery to listen to the bird-
song and to think.

When her thoughts had chased each other around
her brain sufficiently to give her a headache, Laurel
turned her attention back to the mail, thumbing through
the bills and pleas from missions. At the back of the stack
was a plain white envelope with no address, return or
otherwise.

Puzzled, she opened the flap and extracted not a letter, but a cheap gold necklace with a small golden butterfly dangling from it. She lifted the chain and watched
the butterfly turn and sway, and a strange shiver passed
over her, like a chill wind that had slipped out of another
dimension to crawl over her skin.

The wheels of her mind turned automatically, searching for the most logical explanation for the necklace. It
was Savannah's—though Savannah's tastes were much
more expensive. She had forgotten it on the seat of the
car—but why was it sealed in an envelope?

No answer satisfied all the questions, and none explained the knot of nerves tingling at the base of her
neck.

In his office in the Partout Parish courthouse, Duwayne
Kenner leaned over his desk, hammers pounding inside
his temples, acid churning in his gut. He leaned over the
fax copies of crime reports from four other parishes. His
eyes scanned the photographs the sheriff from St. Martin
had brought along with him of Jennifer Verret, who had
been found dead Saturday morning, strangled with a silk
scarf and mutilated. On the other side of the desk,
Danjermond stood looking pensive, twisting his signet
ring around on his finger.

"There's no doubt in my mind," Kenner growled, his
voice turned to gravel by two packs of Camels. "We're
dealing with the same killer."

"Everything matches?"

"So far. We'll have more details when the lab reports
on Annie Gerrard come in, but it's all there—the silk

scarf, the same pattern of knife wounds. Most importantly, details that were kept away from the press match, eliminating the possibility of a copycat."

"Such as?"

"Such as the markings on the wrists and ankles, and the fact that each woman had items of jewelry taken off her body. Sick bastard likely keeps them as souvenirs," he mumbled, his eyes narrowing to slits as he took in the savagery one human being could commit against another. "Well, by God, I'll find out when I catch him. I swear I will."

Chapter Nineteen

One of Vivian's more annoying traits was her sporadic attempts at spontaneity. Laurel recalled the times during her childhood when her mother would snap out of her day-in-day-out routine of clubs and civic responsibilities and life as mistress of Beauvoir, and scramble frantically to do something spontaneous, something she thought terribly clever or fun, which the events seldom proved to be. There was always an air of desperation about them and a set of expectations that were never achieved. Not at all like the spur-of-the-moment notions of Laurel's father, which had always been unfailingly wonderful in one way or another, never planned, never entered into with a set of criteria or goals.

"Seize the moment and take what it gives you," Daddy had always said with a simple joy for life glowing in his handsome face.

Vivian had always seized her moments with grasping, greedy hands and tried to wring out of them the things she wanted. Laurel had always felt sorry for her mother because of it. It wasn't in Vivian's makeup to be spontaneous. That she felt compelled to try, and tried too hard, had always left Laurel feeling sad, particularly when one of Vivian's failed attempts led her into yet another spell of depression.

Perhaps that was why, when Vivian had called to invite her to have dinner out with her—dinner and "girl talk," God forbid—Laurel hadn't managed to find an excuse during that slim five-second window of opportunity when lies can go undetected over the phone lines. Or perhaps her reasons had more to do with the day and the thoughts she had had of family and the fickleness of life.

Savannah would have no doubt had a scathing commentary on the subject. But as Savannah had yet to return from wherever she had spent the day, Laurel didn't have to listen to it. She accepted the invitation with an air of resignation and did her best to turn off the internal mechanism of self-examination.

They sat in one of the small, elegant dining rooms of the Wisteria Golf and Country Club, chatting over equally elegant meals of stuffed quail and fresh sea bass. The club was housed in a Greek revival mansion on what had once been the largest indigo plantation in the parish. The house and grounds had been meticulously restored and maintained, right down to the slave cabins that sat some two hundred yards behind the mansion and now served as storage sheds for garden equipment and between-round hangouts for the caddies—who were quite often black youths. No one at Wisteria worried about offending them with the comparison between caddies and slaves, and there were no other people of color to be offended other than hired help, because Wisteria was, always had been, and always would be an all-white establishment.

Laurel poked at her sea bass and thought longingly of bluepoint crabs and the colors of the Gulf sky at sunset, the sound of the sea and gulls, the tang of salt air. Instead, she had a grouper glaring up at her from a Limoges plate, green velvet portieres at tall French doors, a Vivaldi concerto piping discreetly over cleverly hidden speakers, and the artificial cleanliness of central air-conditioning. Her mother sat across from her, completely in her element, ash blond hair sleekly coiffed, a vibrant blue linen blazer bringing out the color of her eyes. Beneath the jacket she wore a chic white sheath splashed with the same shade of blue. Sapphire teardrops dripped from her earlobes.

"The world has gone stark raving mad," Vivian declared, spearing a fresh green bean. She chewed delicately, as a lady should, breaking her train of thought absolutely to savor the taste of her food. After washing it down with a sip of chardonnay, she picked up the thread of the conversation and went on. "Women being murdered in our backyards, practically. Lunatics running loose through town in the dead of night.

"Tell me why on earth anyone would want to vandalize St. Joseph's Rest Home, scaring those poor elderly people witless."

Laurel went on point like a bird dog, straightening in her chair, her fork hovering over her mutilated fish. "St. Joseph's?"

"Yes." Vivian went on with appropriate disgust as she took a knife after her quail and dismembered it. "Spray-painted obscenities outside one of the rooms, left a terrible mess on the lawn that I simply won't even speak of in public or anywhere else, banged on the windows, shouting and carrying on. It was an absolute disgrace, the things that were done."

"Did they catch this person?" Laurel asked carefully.

"No. She ran screaming into the night."

Foreboding quivered down Laurel's spine. "She?"

"Oh, yes. A woman. Can you imagine that? I mean, one might expect a certain kind of hooliganism from a young man, but a woman?" Vivian shuddered at the thought of the natural order of things being so badly twisted. "I volunteer at the library, as you know. This was my day to take books to the rest home. Ridilia Montrose assists the activities coordinator there on Wednesdays. You remember Ridilia, don't you, Laurel dear? Her daughter Faith Anne was the one who had such extensive orthodontia and then wound up being elected homecoming queen at Old Miss? Married a financier from Birmingham? Ridilia says it was most definitely a female, according to the night staff."

She pressed her lips into a thin line of disapproval and shook her head, setting her sapphires swinging. "Terrible goings-on. I swear, some people just breed indiscriminately and let their children grow up running like wild dogs. Blood will tell, you know," she said, as she always said. And, as always, it made Laurel grit her teeth on a contradiction she had been trained not to voice. "Anyway, the person I feel most sorry for is that poor Astor Cooper. All this went on right outside her window. Can you imagine?"

What little Laurel had eaten of her meal turned into a lump of grease in her stomach. "Astor Cooper?" she managed weakly as her mind pieced together facts without her consent.

"Yes. Her husband is Conroy Cooper, the Pulitzer Prize–winning author? Such a charming man. So generous to the local charities. It's just a tragedy that his wife has to be so afflicted. Alzheimer's, you know. And I'm told her people up in Memphis are just lovely. It's such a shame. Ridilia said Mr. Cooper was absolutely beside himself over the vandalism. He's so very loyal to his wife, you know. . . ."

Laurel placed her hands in her lap, fighting the urge to grip the table to steady herself. While her mother sat across from her, going on about Conroy Cooper's sterling character, that same voice drifted out of the back of her mind, admonishing her for her manners. *Young ladies do not lay their hands on the table, Laurel.* . . . Then Savannah's face came to mind, her expression sly. *His wife has Alzheimer's. He put her in St. Joseph's. . . . I hear she doesn't know her head from a hole in the ground.*

Sick dread ran down her throat like icy fingers. It couldn't be, she told herself. It simply couldn't be. Savannah had her problems, but she wouldn't resort to—As if to mock her defense, her memory hurled up a picture of her sister locked in combat with Annie Delahoussaye, screaming like a banshee and whirling like a dervish around Frenchie's.

"Laurel? Laurel?" Her mother's sharp tone prodded her back to reality. Vivian was frowning at her. "André would like to know if you've finished with your fish."

"I'm sorry." Laurel scrambled to compose herself, ducking her head and smoothing her napkin on her lap. She glanced up at the patient André, who watched her with soulful brown eyes set in a bloodhound's face. "Yes, thank you. It was excellent. My apologies to the chef that I was unable to finish it."

As the dinner plates were whisked away and the tablecloth dusted for crumbs, Vivian studied her daughter and sipped her wine. "I hear you've been to the courthouse twice this week. They're seeing more of you than I am."

An untrained ear may not have picked up the note of censure. Laurel received it loud and clear. "I'm sorry, Mama. I got caught up helping the Delahoussayes."

"Hardly the sort of people—"

Laurel brought a hand up to stop her like a crossing guard. "Can we please skip this conversation? We're not going to agree. We'll both end up angry. Could we just not have it?"

Vivian straightened into her queen's posture on her chair, her chin lifting, her eyes taking on the same cold gleam as the sapphires she wore. "Certainly," she said stiffly. "Never mind that I have only your best interests at heart."

That Vivian had never had any interests at heart but her own was a truth Laurel chose to keep to herself. If she provoked her mother into an argument in public, she would never be forgiven. A part of her thought she shouldn't care, but the plain truth was Vivian was the only mother she had, and after a lifetime of walking on eggshells to gain approval, to garner what Vivian would consider love, she was probably not going to change. Just as Vivian would never change.

The pendulum of Vivian's moods swung yet again as she turned toward the entrance to the dining room. Like the sun coming out from behind a thunderhead, a smile brightened her face. Laurel turned to get a look at whoever had managed to perform such a miracle and caught another unpleasant surprise square on the chin.

"Stephen!" Vivian said, offering her beringed hands to Danjermond as he strode to their table. He took them both and bent over one to bestow a courtly kiss. Vivian beamed. All but purring, she turned toward Laurel. "Look, Laurel dear, Stephen is here! Isn't this a lovely surprise?"

In a pig's eye. Laurel forced a smile that looked as if she had a lip full of novocaine. "Mr. Danjermond."

"Stephen, you're just in time for dessert. Do say you'll join us."

He treated her to a dazzling square smile. "How could I decline an offer to spend time with two of the most beautiful belles in the parish?"

Vivian blushed on cue and batted her lashes, impeccably schooled in the feminine art of flirtation. "Well, this belle needs to powder her nose. Do keep Laurel company, won't you?"

"Of course."

As she walked away from the table, Danjermond slid into the empty chair to Laurel's right. He was, as she was, dressed in the same clothes he had worn to the courthouse that morning—the coffee brown suit, the ivory shirt and stylish tie—but he had somehow managed to come through the day without a wrinkle, while Laurel felt wilted and rumpled. Something about his elegance made her want to comb her hair and take her glasses off, but she refrained from doing either.

"You're angry with me, Laurel," he said, simply.

Laurel crossed her legs and smoothed her skirt, taking her time in replying. Outside, a squall line had tumbled up from the Gulf and was threatening rain. Wind pulled at the fingers of the palmetto trees that lined the putting green. She stared out at them through the French doors, debating the wisdom of what she wanted to say.

"I don't like the games you play, Mr. Danjermond," she said at last, meeting his cool green gaze evenly.

He arched a brow. "You think my being here is part of a conspiracy, Laurel? As it happens, I dine here often. You do concede that I have to eat, don't you? I am, after all, merely human."

The light in the peridot eyes danced as if at some secret amusement. Whether it was her he was laughing at or the line about his being a mere mortal, she couldn't tell. Either way, she had no intention of joining in the joke.

"Anything new on the murder?" she asked, toying with the stem of her water glass.

He plucked a slice of French bread from the basket on the table, tore off a chunk, and settled back in his chair with the lazy arrogance of a prince. Chewing thoughtfully, he studied her. "Kenner released Tony Gerrard. He feels the murder is the work of the Bayou Strangler."

"And what do you think? You don't think Tony Gerrard might have pulled a copycat?"

"No, because if he had, he would have screwed up. Our killer is very clever. Tony, regrettably," he picked a white fleck of bread off his tie and flicked it away, "is not."

"You sound almost as if you admire him—the killer."

He regarded her with a look of mild reproach. "Certainly not. He intrigues me, I admit. Serial killers have fascinated students of criminal science for years." He tore another chunk off the fresh, warm bread, closed his eyes, and savored the rich, yeasty aroma of it before slipping it into his mouth. As he swallowed, his lashes raised like lacy black veils. "I'm as horrified by these crimes as anyone, but at the same time, I have a certain"—he searched for the word, picking it cleanly and carefully—"*clinical* appreciation for a keen mind."

As he said it, Laurel had the distinct impression that he was probing hers. She could feel the power of his personality arching between them, reaching into her head to explore and examine.

"What do you think of sharks, Laurel?"

The change of direction was so abrupt, she thought it was a wonder she didn't get a whiplash. "What should I think of them?" she said, annoyed and puzzled. "Why should I think of them at all?"

"You would think of them if you found yourself overboard in the ocean," Danjermond pointed out. He leaned forward in his chair, warming to his subject, his expression serious. "In all of nature, they are the perfect predator. They fear nothing. They kill with frightening efficiency.

"Serial killers are the sharks of our society. Without souls, without fear of recrimination. Predators. Clever, ruthless." He tore off another chunk of bread and chewed thoughtfully. "A fascinating comparison, don't you think, Laurel?"

"Frankly, I think it's stupid and dangerously romantic," she said bluntly as her temper began to snap inside her like a live wire. Ignoring the dictates of her upbringing, she planted her fists on the table and glared at the district attorney. "Sharks kill to survive. This man is killing for the pure, sick enjoyment of seeing women suffer. He needs to be stopped, and he needs to be punished."

Danjermond scrutinized her pose, her expression, the passion in her voice, and nodded slightly, like a critic approving of an actor's skills. "You were born for the prosecutor's office, Laurel," he declared, then his gaze intensified, sharpened, as if he had sensed something in her. Slowly, gracefully, he leaned forward across the table until he was just a little too close. "Or were you *made* for it?" he murmured.

Laurel met his gaze without flinching, though she was trembling inside. The air between them vibrated with Danjermond's potent sexuality. He was close enough that she could pick up the hint of a dark, exotic cologne. Somewhere outside the cube of tension that boxed them in, thunder rumbled and fat raindrops spat down out of the clouds. The wind hurled handfuls under the veranda, pelting the panes in the French doors.

"You do fascinate me, Laurel," he whispered. "You have an astonishing sense of chivalry for a woman."

Vivian chose that moment to return to the table, and Laurel thought that if she was never grateful to her mother for anything else, she was grateful for this interruption. Stephen Danjermond made the short hairs stand up on the back of her neck. The less she had to be alone with him, the better.

He sat with them for coffee. Vivian ordered bread pudding and enjoyed it with a side order of political talk and chatter about the upcoming League of Women Voters dinner. Laurel sat studying the stubs of her fingernails, wishing she were anywhere else. Her thoughts turned unbidden to Jack, and she wondered, as she stared out at the rain, where he was tonight, what he was feeling.

Judge Monahan and his wife were shown into the dining room, capturing Danjermond's attention, and the district attorney abandoned them for more influential company. While Vivian took care of the bill, Laurel took her first deep breath in thirty minutes.

They walked out onto the veranda together and stood watching as the valets dashed out into the rain to retrieve their cars.

"This was lovely, darling," Vivian said, smiling benevolently. "I'm glad we could have this evening together after that unpleasantness with your sister Sunday. I swear, I don't know at times how she could even be mine, the way she behaves."

"Mama, don't," Laurel snapped, then softened the order with a request. "Please."

Instead of pique, Vivian chose to move on as if Savannah had never been mentioned at all. "I'm so glad Stephen was able to join us for a little while. He's very highly thought of in these parts and in Baton Rogue, as well. With his family connections and his talent, there's no telling how far he might go." Her white Mercedes arrived under the portico, but she made no move toward it, turning instead to give her daughter a shrewd look. "As I walked across the dining room tonight, I couldn't help thinking what a handsome couple the two of you would make."

"I appreciate the thought, Mama," Laurel lied, "but I'm not interested in Stephen Danjermond."

Disapproval flickered in Vivian's light eyes. She reached up impatiently and brushed at a wayward strand of Laurel's hair, succeeding in making her feel ten years old. "Don't tell me you're interested in Jack Boudreaux," she said tightly.

Laurel stepped back from her mother's hand. "Would it matter if I were? I'm a grown woman, Mama. I can chose my own men."

"Yes, but you do such a poor job of it," Vivian said cuttingly. "I asked Stephen about Jack Boudreaux—"

"Mama!"

"He told me the man was disbarred from practicing law because he was at the heart of the Sweetwater chemical waste scandal in Houston." Laurel's eyes widened automatically at the name "Sweetwater." Gratified, Vivian went on with relish. "Not only that, but it isn't any wonder he writes those gruesome books. Everyone in Houston says he killed his wife."

If her mother said anything after that, Laurel didn't hear it. She didn't hear the murmured words of parting, didn't feel the compulsory kiss on her cheek, noticed only in the most abstract of ways that Vivian was being ushered into her car and the gleaming white Mercedes was sliding out into the darkening night.

She stood on the veranda in a puddle of amber light from the carriage lanterns that flanked the elegant carved doors to the Wisteria. Beyond the pillars that supported the roof, rain pounded down out of the swollen clouds and splattered against the glossy black pavement of the drive. And it was Jack's voice she heard. *"I've got enough corpses on my conscience. . . ."*

He wanted to kill somebody.

Jimmy Lee stalked the confines of his steamy, shabby bungalow in his underwear, frustration bubbling inside

him, gurgling in a low growl at the back of his throat as
he recounted all the shit mucking up his road to fame
and fortune.

The cheap secondhand television he had picked up at
Earlene's Used-a-Bit sat on an old crate in the corner.
Instead of his own regularly scheduled hour of glory, the
screen was filled with the flickering image of Billy Graham on a crusade to save the heathen communist souls of
Croatia. A rerun hastily dug up to take the place of the
fiasco that had been taped the day before at the old Texaco station.

The horizontal hold was slipping like fingers on a
greased pig, the picture jumping up, catching, jumping
up, catching. Passing the set on his circuit around the
room, Jimmy Lee gave it a smack along the side that
served only to send the volume blaring.

Swearing, he fumbled with the knob, managing to
break it off in his hand. The control on his temper
snapped just as readily, and he grabbed a lamp off an
imitation wood end table and hurled it at the wall, the
horrific crash drowning out Billy Graham right in the
middle of his rage against the excesses of modern life.

Fuck Billy Graham. Jimmy Lee turned from the set,
ignoring it even though it was rattling with the wrath of
the master televangelist. The guy had one foot in the
grave. He was old hat, passé, not in touch with what
needy fanatics of the nineties wanted. In another few
years, Jimmy Lee would be the one crusading around
the world, begging the faithful of all races to stand up
and be counted—and, most importantly, to stand up and
have their money counted.

He'd be there, at the top, at the pinnacle, worshiped.
And he wouldn't wear anything but tailor-made white
silk suits. Hell, he'd even have tailor-made white silk underwear. He did love the feel of cool white silk. He'd
have sheets of silk and curtains and white silk socks and
white silk ties. Silk, the feel of money and sex. White, the
color of purity and angels. The dichotomy appealed to
him.

He'd get there, he promised himself, no matter what he had to do, no matter who got in his way.

Immediately several faces came to mind. Annie Dela-houssaye-Gerrard, whose corpse had upstaged him in the local news. Savannah Chandler, whose taste for adventure dragged his thoughts away from his mission. Her sister, Laurel Goody Two Shoes, who plagued him like a curse. Bitches. His life was infested with bitches. Good for nothing but slaking a man's baser needs. On the television, a fat white broad who looked like Jonathan Winters in drag was belting out a chorus of "How Great Thou Art." Inside Jimmy Lee, the restless hunger burned. The night beckoned like a harlot, hot, stormy, tempestuous, and he cursed women in his best televangelist voice for leading him into temptation.

Jack prowled the grounds of L'Amour, too restless to be hemmed in by walls. He hadn't slept in . . . what? Two days? He'd lost track of time, lost track of everything but thoughts of death and worthiness . . . and Laurel. He couldn't get her out of his mind. Such indomitable honor, so much courage. He couldn't help caring about her. She was too pure, too brave, too good.

Too good for the like of you, T-Jack . . .

Dieu, what irony, as twisted as a lover's knot, that the most caring thing he could do for her would be to not care about her at all. Everything he touched died. Everything he wanted withered just within his grasp. He had no right to take her as part of his penance for other sins.

He walked down to the bank of the bayou and stood in the deep moon shadows of the live oak, staring out at the glassy water, the *pirogue* that bobbed at the end of the dock. The night sang around him, a chorus of frog song and insects in between thundershowers. A breeze teased the ends of the moss that hung down from the branches, and they swayed heavily, like ropes on the gallows.

He could see Evie's face hanging there in front of him, pale and pretty even in death, her beautiful dark eyes full of accusation and anger and disappointment. Evie, so trusting, so loving. He had loved her so carelessly, had taken so casually the precious gift she had made of her heart. Shallow, selfish bastard that he was, he had taken all she offered as if it were his due, part of the spoils of his success.

The guilt that weighed on him was heavier than anything in this world. It pressed down on him from above, in on him from all sides. He jerked around in a circle, looking for an escape route and finding none. He tried to back away, but came up against the rough trunk of the live oak, the bark biting into his back through the thin fabric of his T-shirt as the guilt pressed in on him.

Tipping his head back, he closed his eyes tight against the pain, and scalding tears trickled in a stream across his temples and into his hair. There were no adjectives in his writer's mind to describe the anguish, no words for the way it raked through his heart.

"Bon Dieu, Evangeline, sa me fait de le pain. Sa me fait de le pain."

He whispered the words over and over, a hoarse, broken chant for forgiveness, a mantra for relief from the terrible weight of his remorse. But he was granted no pardon. He knew he deserved none, because no matter how sorry he was, Evie would always be dead. And all the dreams she had dreamed would be dead. And all the babies she had planned to love would never be at all.

Because of him.

"Sa me fait de le pain," he mumbled, his face contorting against the pain. He turned into the trunk of the tree and pressed his cheek against the corrugated surface, clinging to the tree as regret wrung tears from him with merciless hands.

Sweet, sweet Evie, his wife.

Sweet, sweet Annie, like family.

Sweet, sweet Laurel . . .

Bad Jack Boudreaux. Never good enough. Not worthy of love, never meant for a family. Never anything a decent woman should want. A bastard, a cad, a killer.

What a cruel lie to think he could have anything.

Better not to care at all than watch something so precious, something so deeply desired, slip through his grasp like smoke, like a magician's trick—there and gone in a heartbeat.

As fragile as life—there and gone in a heartbeat.

Whining softly with concern, Huey padded up to him and nosed the hand that hung limp at his side, sniffing for trouble or a treat. The dog's rough pink tongue slid along his palm hesitantly, offering comfort and sympathy, and Jack pulled away.

"Get outta here," he growled, swinging an arm at the dog.

The hound scuttled back clumsily, ears cocked, his head tilted in a quizzical expression. He woofed softly, falling into a play-bow and wagging his slender wand of a tail.

"Get outta here!" Jack roared.

All the anger and hurt that had gathered into a hard ball inside him burst like a nova and sent a hot, white rage through him. It tore out of him in a wild cry, and he lashed out at the dog, the toe of his boot just grazing Huey's rib cage. The dog let out a yelp of betrayal and fright, and ran ten feet away to stand cowering, looking at Jack with his mismatched eyes as hurt and innocent as a child's.

"Get the hell away from me!" Jack snapped. "I don' have a dog! I don' have a dog," he repeated, the adrenaline spent, his voice a ragged whisper. "I don' have nothin'."

And he turned and walked away from the hound, from L'Amour, and disappeared into the shadows of the night.

Chapter Twenty

Thunder rolls like distant cannon fire. Clouds scud across the night sky like tattered wisps of smoke. The battlefield runs red.

The captive taunts and screams in the night in the swamp. Agony like a wild euphoria fills the air with electricity and the sweet, cloying scent of blood. Desperation and hate. Need and desire. Emotions twist and tear apart, overwhelming both captive and captor. The walls of the shack tremble with the terrible power of dark needs unleashed in the predator and in the prey lashed to the bed.

More than the hunter had bargained for. Madness strips away control, pulls even the soulless over its edge and into the maelstrom.

Outside, the wind rips through the trees, lays flat the slender stalks that grow in the shallows. The creatures of the night bolt and shy, heads turning, eyes wide, nostrils scenting the air as they turn toward the eye of a vortex of violence. The moon punches a hole in the blackness, but the thunder rolls nearer, and lightning fractures the sky like cracks in glass.

*The storm comes. Without. Within. Savage and wild.
Screaming. Slashing. Rain pelts the bayou and tears at
tender growth. Blood spatters walls, prey, and predator.
The silk tightens. The end rushes up from the black
depths of hell. The moment explodes with power
unimagined. With triumph, with defeat, with release from
torment—torment from within and without.*

*The wind dies. The storm wanes. The need ebbs. Con-
trol settles in place like dust. Calm returns, and logic with
it.*

*Another dead whore for the unsuspecting to find. An-
other crime committed to go unsolved. The predator
smiles in the blood-drenched night. An adversary might
suspect, but none will believe her.*

Laurel didn't awaken, she was torn from sleep. In the
middle of a dark, disturbing dream, cold, frantic hands
reached into her psyche and pulled her out of one realm
of existence and into another. She emerged gasping for
air, like a swimmer breaking the surface after a long dive
in frigid waters. The air around her was warm and moist,
a pocket of heat and humidity that had sucked in through
the French doors to escape the storm. The room was
dark and still, a stillness that held something other than
simple quiet. Loss. She felt alone in a way she had never
felt before in her life, and her thoughts turned automatically toward Savannah. She had never been alone; she
had always had Savannah.

Heart bumping hard against her breastbone, she
fought to untangle her legs from the sheet and raced out
onto the balcony in nothing but the camisole and slip she
had fallen asleep wearing. Down the corridor she ran to
the set of doors that opened into her sister's room. She
fumbled with the latch and threw them back, stumbling
as she pitched herself into the bedroom.

The stillness lingered here, too, hanging like a
shroud. An unseen hand closed around Laurel's throat as
she looked around the room. The bed was unmade,
empty, the covers left in a drift, pillows strewn every-

where. It looked the same as the last time she had seen it. She tried to swallow the fear that crowded her tonsils and turned slowly, taking in the jumble of jars and pots and bottles on the dressing table, the discarded clothes draped over chairs and abandoned on the floor. There was no way of telling when last Savannah had occupied the room.

A chill raced over her and seeped bone-deep into her. Tears pooled in her eyes. She twisted her hands together, pacing beside the bed. "Don't be stupid, Laurel," she muttered, her voice cutting and harsh. "Savannah has slept elsewhere more times than you can count. Just because she isn't here tonight—that doesn't mean anything. She's with a lover, that's all."

To distract herself, she tried to think of which one it might be. Ronnie Peltier with his jackhammer penis. Taureau Hebert—the man Savannah had fought over with Annie. Jimmy Lee Baldwin—who preached morals and played bondage games. Conroy Cooper—whose invalid wife had been terrorized only the night before.

The tag lines that accompanied each name swarmed in Laurel's mind like gnats. She was trained to add up facts as an accountant does a row of figures. She was trained to put puzzle pieces together in her sleep. Tonight she wanted to do neither. The subtotal of the column, the picture that began to take shape—both gave an answer she didn't want to know.

Standing beside the bed, she leaned over and gathered up Savannah's champagne silk robe, bringing the elegant fabric to her cheek. Cool, soft as a whisper, smelling of Obsession. She didn't want to think that Savannah was ill. She didn't want to face the truth that the sister who had mothered her and shielded her had declined to this point without her doing anything but judging. How many times had she wished Savannah would block out the past, rise above it, get beyond what Ross Leighton had done to her? While Laurel herself had lived to atone for that same past, ignoring her martyrdom, calling it a career.

Tears spilled across the silk, and she wished with all

her heart her sister would walk through the door so she could go into Savannah's arms and beg her forgiveness. But no one came through the door. Only the empty room heard her cry.

Drained, she tossed the robe back on the rumpled bed and wandered back out onto the balcony. The latest fit of rain had passed, leaving everything dripping. Moonlight caught on droplets, turning them to diamonds. The wind rustled restlessly in the trees. Laurel curled an arm around the pillar outside her own room and leaned against it, her gaze traveling the distance to L'Amour.

Some people said it was haunted. She wondered if the ghosts that haunted Jack had anything to do with the history of the house, or if they were his own, brought here with him from Texas.

He'd been at the heart of the Sweetwater incident, Vivian had said. Sweetwater was a Houston subdivision built by developers that touted the good life, a place to raise families. A little piece of heaven that backed onto a little piece of hell. Illegally buried in the field beyond, drums of chemical waste poisoned the ground. Laurel hadn't followed the case except in snatches caught on the nightly news. She had been wrapped up in legal battles of her own. She remembered the barrels had been almost impossible to trace. The trail had led from dummy company to dummy company.

Jack had unraveled the snare for the feds. He was the best man for the job, she supposed, because, if Vivian's information was correct, he had been the one to lay the paper trail away from Tristar. If she hadn't known him, she would have called him a dozen names. Ruthless, godless, greedy bastard would have been one of the nicer ones. But she did know him. She knew he had clawed his way up through the ranks because he thought he needed to prove himself. What must it have done to him to reach the peak only to find out he was on the wrong mountain? He said he had crashed and burned and taken the company down with him.

And his wife?

The word lay bitter on Laurel's tongue. She might have said she didn't want him, didn't want any kind of a lasting relationship, but the bald truth was she didn't want to think of his loving someone else.

But had he loved her, or had he killed her?

A light winked on in one of the second-story windows of L'Amour, faint, as if it came from a room within the depths of the house. Faint, yet it pulled at her like a beacon. She needed to know who he really was. Which Jack stood behind the final facade? The shark, the rogue, the man who claimed he didn't care about anyone but himself, or the man who had held her and offered her comfort, who had come to her rescue, who had distracted her from problems and fears?

She couldn't see him as a killer. Killers didn't warn potential victims away or walk them home to keep them safe. No, "homicidal" wasn't a word she could apply to Jack. Troubled. Angry. Wounded.

Wounded. The word struck a chord inside her. The light in the old house beckoned.

Jack climbed the stairs to the second floor, bone tired, his body aching, begging for sleep. But he knew his mind would never grant the wish. Not tonight. Ignoring the rustlings of mice in a pile of fallen wallpaper down the hall, he shuffled into his bedroom and flicked on the lamp that perched on his desk a level above the old black Underwood typewriter. A white page glared up at him, reminding him not of deadlines or plot twists, but of Jimmy Lee Baldwin. Jimmy Lee standing above his devoted followers, asking them where demented minds get the inspiration to kill.

Their eyes meet in the dim light of the woods. Predator and prey. Recognition sparks. Realization dawns. Awareness arcs between them. Strange needs commingle. Dark desires intertwine. It is understood that the game will end in death. She opens her arms to welcome it, to end the torment that has haunted her life.

A slim silver blade gleams in the dark. . . .

What followed was death, presented in a way that was disturbingly seductive, poetically artistic, gruesome and graphic, and frightening as hell.

That was his job—to frighten people, to keep them awake nights and tighten their nerves until every sound heard in a lonely house held the potential for unspeakable terror. People called it entertainment, not inspiration. He wouldn't think otherwise. To believe it inspired meant to take responsibility, and everybody knew Jack Boudreaux didn't take responsibility for anyone or anything.

"They say she never met him here."

Jack's head came up, and he looked toward the door, not entirely certain what he was seeing was real. Laurel stood just outside the chipped white door frame, against a background of black. A pale portrait of a woman in a flowing skirt painted with old cabbage roses, a blue cotton blouse with the tails hanging down. She was a vision, an angel, something he should never have touched. Better to have longed from a distance and had her only in his imagination. No one could take that away.

"Madame Deveraux," she said and took a step nearer. "Her wealthy, married lover, August Chapin, built this place for her. Everyone in the parish knew. He flaunted his obsession for her, much to the shame of his poor wife."

Jack found his voice with an effort. "She never met him here?"

"Mr. Chapin, yes. The man she truly loved, no." She walked into the room slowly, lingering by the tall French doors, out of the glow of the desk light. "She loved a man named Antoine Gallant. A no-account Cajun trapper. He refused to set foot in the house Chapin built to house her as a whore. They met in secret in a cabin in the swamp.

"Of course, they were found out. His pride smarting sorely, Chapin challenged Gallant to a duel, which he meant to win by tampering with the pistols. Madame Deveraux learned of the plot just minutes before the duel was to take place. She rushed to warn her love, but the men had already stepped off the distance and had turned to take aim. In order to save Antoine, she hurled herself in front of him and took Chapin's shot herself. She died in Antoine's arms."

She wandered to the old rolltop desk and stood behind it with her hands resting on the high back. Her expression was somber, searching as she slowly scanned the room with her eyes. "I grew up hearing her spirit still haunted this house."

Jack shrugged, avoiding the penetrating stare she turned on him. "I haven't seen her."

"Well," she murmured, "you have ghosts of your own."

Oui. More than you know, angel.

"Someone mentioned Sweetwater today," Laurel said, treading carefully. "You were Tristar's man, weren't you?"

He smiled bitterly and took a bow, backing away from the desk. "*C'est vrai*, you got it in one, sugar. Jack Boudreaux, star shyster. Wanna bury some poison and get away with it? I'm your man. I can tie the trail in a Gordian knot that loops around and around, and twists and doubles back and dead-ends. Holding companies, dummy corporations, the works." He jammed his hands at the waist of his jeans and stared up at the intricate plasterwork medallion on the ceiling, marveling not at it but at his own past life. "I was so clever, so bright. Working my way up and up, never caring who I stepped on as I climbed that ladder. The end always justified the means, you know."

"In the end, you brought them down."

One dark brow curving, he pinned her with a look. "And you think that makes me a hero? If I set houses on fire, then put the fires out after the people inside had all burned, would I be a hero?"

"That would depend on your motives and intent."

"My motives were selfish," he said harshly, pacing back and forth along the worn ruby rug. "I wanted to be punished. I wanted everyone associated with me to be punished. For what *I* did."

"To the people in Sweetwater?" she asked cautiously, studying him from beneath the shield of her lashes.

He halted, watching her intently out of the corner of his eye, old instincts scenting a trap. "Where are you trying to lead me, counselor?" he asked, his voice a low, dangerous purr. Slowly, he moved toward her, his gait deceptively lazy, his gaze as hard as granite behind a devil's smile, one hand raised to wag a finger in warning. "What kind of game are you playin', *'tite chatte*?"

Laurel curled her fingers into the fabric of her skirt and faced him squarely, her face carefully blank. "I don't play games."

Jack barked a laugh. "You're a lawyer. You're trained to play games. Don't try to fool me, sugar. You're swimmin' with a big shark now. I know every trick there is."

He stopped within inches of her, leaning down, meeting her at her level, his nose almost touching hers. In the soft lamplight his eyes sparkled like onyx, hard and fathomless.

"Why don' you just ask me?" he whispered, his whiskey-hoarse voice cutting across her nerve endings like a rasp. "Did you kill her, Jack? Did you kill your wife?"

She swallowed hard and called his bluff, betting her heart on his answer. "Did you?"

"Yes."

He watched her blink quickly, as if she were afraid to take her eyes off him for even a fraction of a second. But she held her ground, brave and foolhardy to the last. And his heart squeezed painfully at the thought. She was waiting for a qualification, something that would dilute the truth into a more palatable mix.

"I told you I was bad, angel," he said, stepping back from her. "You know what they say, blood will tell. Ol' Blackie, he always told me I'd be no good. I shoulda listened. I coulda saved a whole lotta people a whole lotta grief."

He drifted away from her in body and mind, losing himself in a past that was as murky as the bayou. Wandering across the room, past the heavy four-poster with its sensuous drape of white netting and its tangle of bed-

clothes, he found his way to another set of French doors
and stood looking out into the dark. The wind had come
up again and chattered in the branches of the trees, a
natural teletype of the next storm boiling up from the
Gulf. Lightning flashed in the distance, casting his hard,
hawkish profile in silver.

Laurel moved toward him, skirting the foot of the
bed. She should have left him. Regardless of the details
she was waiting to hear, he was trouble. She may even
have had cause to be frightened of him—Jack, with his
dual personality and his dark secrets, a temper as volatile
as the weather in the Atchafalaya. But she took another
step and another, her heart drumming behind her breastbone. And the question slipped past her defenses and out
of her mouth.

"What was her name?"

"Evangeline," he whispered. Thunder rattled the
glass in the windows, and rain began to fall, the scent of
it cool and green and sweet. "Evie. As pretty as a lily, as
fragile as spun glass," he said softly. "She was another of
my trophies. Like the house, like the Porsche, like crocodile shoes and suits from Italy. It never penetrated the
fog that she loved me." He ducked his head, as if he still
couldn't believe it.

"She was the perfect corporate wife for a while. Dinner parties and cocktail hours. Iron my shirts and brew
my coffee."

Amazed by the sting of his words, Laurel wrapped an
arm around an elegantly carved bedpost and anchored
herself to it. This woman had shared his life, his bed, had
known all his habits and quirks. But she was gone now,
forever. "What happened?"

"She wanted a life with me. I loved my work. I loved
the game, the challenge, the rush. I was in the office by
seven-thirty. Didn't go home most nights until eleven, or
one, or two. The job was everything.

"Evie started telling me she wasn't happy, that she
couldn't live that way. I thought she was temperamental,
cloying, selfish, punishing me for working hard so I
could give her fine things."

Regret burned like acid in his throat, behind his eyes. He clenched his jaw against it, whipped himself mentally to get past it. "The first Sweetwater story had broken, and I was working like mad to cover the company's ass in triplicate. I barely took time to shave or eat."

Tension rattled through him like the thunder shaking the windowpanes as the scenes played out in his memory. His emotions rushed ahead frantically, knowing the ending, torn between the need to protect himself and the need to punish. He drew in a sharp breath through his nostrils and curled a fist into the fragile old lace of the curtain.

"One night I came home in a bitch of a mood. Two o'clock. Hadn't had a meal all day. There wasn't anything in the kitchen. I went looking for Evie, spoiling for a fight. Found her in the bathroom. In the tub. She'd slit her wrists."

"Oh, God, Jack." Laurel's arm tightened around the pillar. She brought a hand to her mouth to hold back the cry that tore through her, but the tears still flooded and fell. Through them she watched Jack struggle with the burden of his guilt. His broad shoulders were braced against it, trembling visibly. In the lightning glow she could see his face, his mouth twisting as he fought, chin quivering.

"The note she left was full of apologies," he said, his voice thickening, cracking. He cleared his throat and managed a bitter smile. " 'I'm sorry I couldn't make you need me, Jack. I'm sorry I couldn't make you love me, Jack.' Sorry for the inconvenience. I think she did it in the bathtub so she wouldn't leave a mess."

This time when the urge came, Laurel let go of the post and let herself go to him. "She made her own choice, Jack," she murmured. "It wasn't your fault."

When she started to lay her hand against the taut muscles of his back, he twisted away and swung around to face her. His eyes were burning with anger and shame, swimming with tears he refused to let fall.

"The hell it wasn't!" he roared. "She was *my* responsibility! *I* was supposed to take care of her. *I* was supposed to look out for her. *I* was supposed to be there when she needed me. *Bon Dieu*, I might as well have taken the blade to her myself!"

He whirled and cleared a marble-topped table with a violent sweep of his arm, sending antique porcelain figurines crashing to their doom on the cypress floor. Laurel flinched at the sound of shattering china, but didn't back away.

"You couldn't have known—"

"That's right, I couldn't have," he snapped. "I was never there. I was too busy manipulating the illegal disposal of toxic waste." He threw back his head and laughed in sardonic amazement. "Jesus, I'm a helluva guy, aren't I? Huh? A helluva match for you, Lady Justice."

She pressed her lips together and said nothing. She couldn't condone what he'd done at Tristar—it was both illegal and immoral—but neither could she find it in her to condemn him. She knew what it was to get caught up in the job, to be driven to it by demons from the past. And she knew what guilt could do to a person, the changes it could wreak, the pain of it eating inside.

"You didn't kill her, Jack. She had other choices."

"Yeah?" he asked, his voice thin and trembling, his face a mask of torment. "And what about the baby she was carrying? Did he have a choice?"

The pain was as sharp as ever. As sharp as the razor blade that had ended his dream of a wife and a family. It sliced at his heart, severed what was left of his strength. He turned back to the French doors and leaned into the one that stood closed, pressing his face against the cool glass, crying silently while rain washed across the other side, soft and cleansing, never touching him. He could still see the pathologist's face, could still hear the disbelief in his voice. *"You mean she hadn't told you? She was nearly three months along. . . ."*

His child. His chance to atone for all his father's sins. There and gone before he even had the joy of knowing. Gone because of him, just as Evie was gone because of him.

Not for the first time he thought he was the one who should have sliced open a vein and drained his life away.

Laurel slipped her arms around his waist and pressed her cheek against his back, her tears dampening the soft cotton of his T-shirt. She could see it all so clearly. Jack, so eager to prove himself, scrambling up that sheer granite face of the odds that were stacked against his making anything of himself. Then all of it crumbling beneath him, sucking him down and crushing him with the weight of the debris. He must have thought he'd had everything he ever wanted right in the palm of his hand, and then it was swept away, and every line of degradation his father had ever hammered into him must have come rushing back.

He shoved her away so suddenly, so unexpectedly, Laurel nearly fell. She stumbled back against the table, her shoes crunching over a fortune in shattered porcelain. Jack wheeled on her, his face dark with rage.

"Get out! Get outta here! Get outta my life!" he shouted in her face. "Get out before I kill you too!"

Laurel just stared at him, at the wild gleam of pain in his eyes, the muscles and tendons that stood out in his neck, the heavy rise and fall of his chest as he breathed. She should have run like hell. Inside he was as fractured as any of the statuettes grinding to dust beneath her feet. She wasn't in much better shape herself. She certainly wasn't strong enough to take on his healing too.

She should have run like hell. She didn't.

She fell in love.

He was trying to push her away, not because he didn't care, but because he cared too much; not because he didn't feel, but because his heart was so badly battered. Losing her heart to him wasn't the smart thing or the timely thing. It wasn't the choice she would have made with her logical, practical attorney's mind, but logic had nothing to do with it.

She met his pain and fury with her chin up and her eyes clear. "Why should I go?"

Jack stared at her, dumbfounded. He thought he could actually feel the gears in his mind slipping.

"Why?" he repeated, incredulous. He swept his hands back over his hair, turned around in a circle, stared at her some more. "How can you ask that? After all I've just told you, how can you stand there and ask that?"

"You didn't kill your wife, Jack," she said gently. "You didn't kill your child. You're not going to kill me, either. Why should I leave?"

"I can't have you," he whispered, more to himself than to Laurel.

She stepped up to him, calm and fearless, and whispered, "Yes, you can."

He wanted to tell her she didn't understand. He couldn't have her, couldn't care, because he didn't deserve her and because everything he ever wanted was ripped away from him in the end anyway. He didn't need the pain, didn't think he could stand it. But he said none of those things. The words simply wouldn't come.

All he could think as he stared down into that earnest, angelic face was that he wanted to hold her. Just for a little while. Just for what was left of the night. He wanted to hold her, and kiss her, and find some comfort in her body.

Use her.

He'd be a bastard to the very end, he thought. No use fighting his true nature. It wasn't as if he hadn't warned her.

It wasn't as if he didn't need her. . . .

Longing welled inside him, and he reached out to touch her, to ease the ache, to fill the hole in his heart if only temporarily. She sank against him, so small, so fragile. His . . . for the moment . . . for the night . . . for a memory he could hold forever.

Outside, the storm shook the night with sound and fury, but in this room all was stillness except the beating of hearts, the caress of flesh against flesh. Mist blew in through the open door and settled like silver dew, shimmering on the cypress floor when the lightning flashed, but all that touched them was a warmth that glowed from needs within.

Every sense was heightened. Every sense was filled.

The fragrance of her skin. The hardness of his muscle. The taste of tears, of gentleness, of desire. The sound of breath catching. The growl of passion. The contrast of light skin on dark. The delicate lacework of her lashes as they swept against her cheek. The planes and angles of his beard-shadowed jaw. Laurel immersed herself in it all. Jack soaked it up greedily.

He touched her like a blind man trying to see with his fingertips, tracing the lines and gentle curves. Fingers fanned wide, he skimmed her jaw, her throat, the slope of her shoulders. He cradled her breasts then let his touch flow downward, over her ribs to her tiny waist, along the subtle flare of her hips.

As he mouthed phantom kisses across her eyelids, along her jawline, his fingers explored her most tender flesh. Laurel whispered his name, and need shuddered through them both.

He wouldn't be an easy man to love. He had branded himself unworthy, thought of himself only in terms of his flaws. He would push her away in the name of caring, break her heart and call it fate. But she went to him. She went to him and offered him everything she was, everything her heart could hold. Without words. Without strings.

He took her in his arms, and they fell across the bed. Springs creaked, linens rustled. The storm rolled on toward Lafayette, thunder sounding like the faint echo of hoofbeats, rain hissing like the sound of steam.

One arm hooked behind her gracefully arching back, Jack bent himself over her and took her breast in his mouth. Her nipple budded beneath the coaxing of his tongue, beneath the wet silk of her camisole, and he drew on it hotly, greedily.

His fingers caught in the hem of the garment and pulled it up. She lay back and stretched her arms above her head. He pushed the camisole to her wrists and held it there, held her there, pinned to the mattress. His eyes locked on hers as he kneed her legs apart and settled his hips against hers.

Laurel's breath fluttered in her throat, not with fear

but with anticipation. He would never hurt her physically. He would break her heart—of that she had little doubt—but she trusted him implicitly with her body. She offered herself totally, opened herself, wound her legs around his hips.

And he filled her. Slowly. Inch by inch. His eyes on hers. Giving her the essence of his maleness, being welcomed and embraced by the warm, tight glove of her woman's body. Pressing deeper, deeper, until she gasped his name. When the joining was complete, he cast the silk aside and gathered her to him in a crushing embrace.

It went on forever. It could never have lasted long enough. They moved together, body to body, need to need, heart to heart. Scaling peaks of pleasure, soaring from height to dizzying height.

Jack lost himself in the heat, in the bliss, in the comfort she offered him without words. He gave himself over to desire, thought nothing of right or wrong, only of Laurel. So sweet, so strong. He wanted to give her everything, be everything for her. He wanted to press her to his heart and never let her go. She filled up the hole inside him, flooded all the pain away, made him believe for a moment he could start over . . . with her . . . have a family . . . have peace . . . find forgiveness.

Foolish thoughts. Foolish heart. But for this night he would cling to them as he clung to the woman in his arms, and soothe his aching soul with visions of love.

Chapter Twenty-One

Laurel slipped from the bed at dawn and dressed silently in the soft light that filtered through the French doors and lace curtains. For a long while she stood by the balcony door and just studied him, as an artist might study a subject before putting brush to canvas, taking in everything about the man, the mood. The light seemed the color and consistency of fine sand, golden and grainy, and it didn't quite penetrate the shadows of the graceful four-poster. Jack lay sprawled on his belly taking up most of the bed, his face buried in the crook of his arm. His bronzed back was a sculpture of lean, rippling muscle. The sheet, a drift of white, covered only a section of thigh and hips. One leg was bent at the knee, thigh and calf strong, masculine, dusted with rough, dark hair.

Laurel memorized the way he looked in that moment, this first morning after she'd fallen in love with him. It didn't seem any wiser today than it had in the night. She had no idea where these feelings would lead, but she wouldn't deny to herself that she felt them. She'd lied to herself enough in her lifetime. She had, however, refrained from telling Jack, knowing without being told that he wouldn't want to hear it.

Her heart squeezed painfully at the thought, but she pushed the pain away. She would let things take their natural course. The feelings were too new, too sensitive to be trod upon by something as heavy as practicality or an awkward morning-after scene.

She touched two fingers to her kiss-swollen lips and wondered how she had gotten in so deep so fast with a man like Jack Boudreaux. They were opposites in many ways, too alike in others. An unlikely match drawn together by pain, bound by something neither of them would speak of—love.

It had to have been love in his touch during the long, sultry night. The tenderness, the poignancy, the sweetness, the desperation—in her logical, analytical mind, those components added up to more than mere lust, she was sure. Just as she was sure Jack would never acknowledge it and she would never speak the word. Not now. Not when he was so certain he didn't deserve anything good. She wouldn't try to bind him to her with words and guilt. He had enough guilt of his own.

Unbidden, thoughts came of the wife and child he had lost, and she ached for him so, she nearly cried out. She knew about loss, and she knew about blame. She thought of the unloved, battered boy he had been, and the frightened, emotionally neglected little girl in her wanted to reach out and gather him close. And she knew if Jack had suspected any of what she was thinking, he would have done his damnedest to chase her away. He hoarded his pain like a miser, stored it deep inside, and shared it with no one. It stayed stronger that way, more potent, more punishing. She knew.

God, why him? Why did she have to go and fall in love with a man like Jack at a time like this, when all she really wanted to do was get her feet back under her and get her life back on track—any track?

No answer came to her as dawn broke over the bayou in ribbons of soft color. No answer but her heartbeat.

In the frame of the open French door a small dark

spider was carefully spinning a web of hair-fine silk that glistened in the new light with crystal beads of morning dew. Laurel watched for a moment, thinking of her own attempt to build a new life. She had come home to heal, to start over, and she felt as if she were as fragile, as vulnerable as that newly spun web. She looked for toe-holds and tried to weave back together all that had been torn asunder inside her, but the slightest outside force would tear it all apart again, and once again she would be left with nothing.

Her gaze shifted to Jack, who was still asleep—or pretending to be—and she felt that tenuous foundation tremble beneath her. With a heavy, tender heart, she tiptoed out of the room and left the house.

As he heard the hollow echo of the front door closing, Jack turned over slowly and stared up at the morning shadows on the ceiling. He wanted to love her. His heart ached for it so, it nearly took his breath. It surprised him after all this time, after all the hard lessons, that he could still be vulnerable. He should have been able to steel himself against it. He should have known enough to turn her away last night. But he had wanted so badly just to hold her, just to take some comfort in her sweetness.

He had wanted her from the first. Desire he under-stood. It was simple, basic, elemental. But this . . . this was something he could never be trusted with again. And because he knew that, he had somehow believed he would never be tempted. Now he felt like a fool, be-trayed by his own heart, and he kicked himself merci-lessly for it. *Stupid, selfish bastard* . . . He couldn't allow himself to fall in love with Laurel Chandler. She deserved far better than him.

And maybe, a lost, lonely part of him thought as the pain of those self-inflicted blows burst through him, maybe after all the penance he had done, he deserved to be left in peace.

. . .

Laurel went up to her room via the courtyard and balcony, not wanting to alert anyone else in the house that she was only just returning. Preoccupied with turbulent thoughts of Jack and the night they had spent together, she took a long, warm shower, then dressed for the day in a pair of black walking shorts and a loose white polo shirt. She assessed her looks in the mirror above the walnut commode, seeing a woman with troubled eyes and damp, dark hair combed loosely back.

There should have been some external sign of the changes made inside her during the last few days—the strength she had regained fighting for her new friends, the humility that remained after her pompous ideas concerning Savannah's life had been shattered, the uncertainty in her heart about her own future.

With a sigh she dropped her gaze to the small china tray on the commode where she had left the little pile of oddities she'd come across recently. The gaudy earring no one would lay claim to, the matchbook from Le Mascarade she had found in her car, the necklace that had come in the plain white envelope. At a glance they seemed unrelated, harmless, but something about the way they had simply appeared made her uneasy. Looks could be deceiving. An earring with no mate. A matchbook with a name that conjured images of people in disguise. A necklace. There was no thread to tie the items to one another other than the mystery of their origin.

She lifted the necklace, draping the flimsy chain over her index finger. The little butterfly wobbled and danced in a bar of light that slanted through the door. It was probably Savannah's, she told herself again. She'd left it somewhere with a lover. She was notoriously careless with her things. The man had sent it . . . in an envelope with no address. No. It had to have been left in the car. Unless the Bayou Breaux post office was employing psychics, blank envelopes didn't get delivered.

The obvious solution was to simply ask Savannah herself. Forgetting the hour, Laurel marched down the balcony to her sister's room and let herself in.

The bed was empty. The sheets were tangled. The

same abandoned clothes littered the chairs and floor. The
same sense of stillness as had been there the night before
hung, damp and musty in the air.

The memory of that stillness hit Laurel like a wall. It
had seemed so surreal, she had almost convinced herself
it had been a dream, but here it was again with panic
hard on its heels. Savannah hadn't slept in this bed.
When was the last time anyone in the house had seen
her? She had returned the Acura sometime Tuesday
night or Wednesday morning—How did anyone know
that? The car had been in the drive Wednesday morning,
but no one had actually seen Savannah that day.

*"Murders?" ". . . four now in the past eighteen
months . . . women of questionable reputation . . .
found strangled out in the swamp . . ."*

"Oh, God," Laurel whispered as tears swam in her
eyes and crowded her throat till it ached.

She clutched the little necklace in her fist and bit
down hard on a knuckle as wild, terrible, conflicting images roared around in her head like debris caught up in a
tornado wind. Savannah lying dead someplace. Savannah
locked in combat with Annie Gerrard, her eyes glazed
with blood lust. T-Grace screaming on the gallery at
Frenchie's. Vivian relating the tale of the vandal at St.
Joseph's rest home. *"Blood will tell."* Blood. Blood from
wounds. Blood red—the color of the matchbook from Le
Mascarade. Savannah's face blank as she tossed it on the
table. *"I use a lighter. . . ."* Savannah, finally pushed
over that mental edge after all these years because of that
son of a bitch Ross Leighton. Savannah, used by men, by
Conroy Cooper, by Jimmy Lee Baldwin, who liked his
women bound. . . .

All of it whirled around and around in Laurel's mind
like fractured bits of glass in a kaleidoscope, every picture uglier than the one before it, every possibility too
terrible to be true. And over it all came the harsh voice
of logic, scolding her for her foolishness, for her lack of
faith, for her lack of evidence. All she really knew was
that her sister wasn't home, and no one in the family had

seen her since Tuesday. The only logical thing was to go looking for her.

She seized on the notion with a rush of relief and resolve. Don't fall apart, *do something.* Get results. Solve the mystery.

Focused, all the tension drawn into a tight ball of energy that lodged in her chest, she left the room and went to her own to get shoes and her purse. She would leave the back way, she thought as she trotted down the steps to the courtyard. No use alarming Aunt Caroline or Mama Pearl. She would find Savannah, and everything would be all right.

Mama Pearl was up already, shuffling out onto the gallery with a cup of coffee and the latest *Redbook.* She caught sight of Laurel the instant her sneaker touched ground at the foot of the stairs.

"Chile, what you doin' up dis hour?" she demanded, her brow furrowing under the weight of her worry.

Laurel pasted on a smile and stepped toward the back gate. "Lots to do, Mama Pearl."

The old woman snorted her disgust for modern femininity and tossed her magazine down on the table. "You come eat breakfast, you. You so little, the crows gonna carry you 'way."

"Maybe later!" Laurel called, waving, picking up the pace as she turned for the back gate.

She thought she could still hear Mama Pearl grumbling when she was halfway to L'Amour. It might have been her stomach, but she doubted it; it had gotten too used to being empty. Out of habit, she dug an antacid tablet out of her pocketbook and chewed it like candy.

She had left Jack to avoid the awkwardness of morning-after talk. What had passed between them during the night had gone far beyond words and into a realm of unfamiliar territory. But this was safe ground. She wanted to ask his opinion, tap his knowledge. It was like business, really. And friendship. She wanted his support, she admitted as Huey bounded between a pair of crepe myrtle trees and bore down on her with his tongue loll-

ing out the side of his mouth and a gleam in his mismatched eyes.

The hound crashed into her, knocking her into the
front door with a thud. As she called him a dozen names
that defamed his character and his lineage, he pounced
at her feet, yipping playfully, snapping at her shoelaces.
He whirled around and leaped off the front step, running
in crazy circles with his tail tucked, clearly overjoyed to
see her. Laurel scowled at him as he dropped to the
ground at the foot of the step and rolled over on his back,
inviting her to scratch his blue-speckled belly.

"Goofy dog," she muttered, giving in and bending
over to pat him. "Don't you know when you're being
snubbed?"

"Love is blind," Jack said sardonically, swinging the
door open behind her.

He was in the same rumpled jeans. No shirt. He
hadn't shaved. A mug of coffee steamed in his hand. As
Laurel stood, she could see that the brew was as black as
night. She breathed in its rich aroma and tried to will her
heartbeat to steady. He didn't look pleased to see her.
The man who had held her and loved her through the
night was gone, replaced by the Jack she would rather
not have known, the brooding, angry man.

"If you've got some milk to cut that motor oil you're
drinking, I could use a cup myself."

He studied her for a minute, as if trying to decipher
her motives, then shrugged and walked into the house,
leaving her to follow as she would. Laurel trailed after
him down a long hall, catching glimpses of rooms that
had stood unused for decades. Water-stained wallpaper.
Moth-eaten draperies. Furnishings covered with dustcloths, and dustcloths thick with their namesake.

It was as if no one lived here, and the thought gave
her an odd feeling of unease. Certainly Jack, *The New
York Times* best-selling author, could afford to have the
place renovated. But she didn't ask why he hadn't, because she had a feeling she knew. Penance. Punishment.
L'Amour was his own personal purgatory. The idea
tugged at her heart, but she didn't go to him as she

longed to. His indifference to her presence set the ground rules for the morning—no clinging, no pledges.

He led her into a kitchen that, unlike the rest of the house, was immaculate. The red of the walls had faded to the color of tomato soup, but they were clean and free of cobwebs. The refrigerator was new. Cupboards and gray tile countertops had been cleaned and polished. The only sign of food was a rope of entwined garlic bulbs and one of red peppers that hung on either side of the window above the sink, but it was a place where food could be prepared without threat of ptomaine.

He pulled a mug down from the cupboard and filled it for her from the old enamel pot on the stove. Laurel helped herself to the milk—a perfect excuse to snoop. Eleven bottles of Jax, a quart of milk, a jar of bread-and-butter pickles, and three casseroles, each bearing a different name penned on a strip of masking tape like offerings for a church pot luck supper. Lady friends taking care of him, no doubt. The thought brought a mix of jealousy and amusement.

She leaned back against the counter, stirring her coffee. "Have you seen Savannah since the other morning when she left in such a huff?"

"No. Why?"

"I haven't, either. Nor has Aunt Caroline or Mama Pearl." She fiddled with her spoon as the nerves in her stomach quivered. She fixed her gaze on Jack's belly button and the dark hair that curled around it. "I'm a little concerned."

He shrugged. "She's with a lover."

"Maybe. Probably. It's just that . . ." She trailed off as the suspicions and theories tried to surface. She wished she could share it all with him, but he wasn't in a sharing mood, and faced with the stony expression he was wearing, she couldn't bring herself to tell him any of it. She felt alone; the one thing she had come to him to avoid. ". . . with all that's been going on, I'd feel better knowing for certain."

"So what do you want from me, sugar?" he asked bluntly. "You know for a fact she's not in my bed."

"Why are you doing this?" she demanded, setting her cup aside on the counter. She halved the distance between them, hands jammed on her hips.

"What?"

"Being such a bastard."

Jack arched a brow and grinned sharply. "It's what I do best, angel."

"Oh, stop it!" she snapped. "It's too early in the morning for this kind of bullshit." She dared another step toward him, peering up at him in narrow-eyed speculation. "What did you think, Jack? That I was coming over here to ask you to marry me?" she said sarcastically. "Well, I'm not. You can relax. Your martyrdom is safe. All I want is a little help. A straight answer or two would be nice."

He scowled at her as the martyrdom barb hit and stuck dead center. Giving in to the need to escape her scrutiny, he abandoned his coffee and sauntered across the room to pull a beer from the fridge.

"What do you want me to say?" he asked, twisting off the top with a quick motion of his wrist. "That I know who was screwing your sister last night? I don't. If I were to hazard a guess as to the possible candidates, I could just as well hand you a phone book."

"Oh, fine," Laurel bit back. She stalked him across the room like a tiger. Fury bubbled up inside her, and she wished to God she were big enough and strong enough to pound the snot out of Jack Boudreaux. He deserved it, and it would have gone a long way to appease her own wounded pride. "You're a big help, Jack."

"I told you, sugar, I don' get involved."

"What a crock," she challenged, toe to toe with him now, leaning up toward him with her chin out and fire in her eyes. She might have been uncertain treading the uneven ground of their suddenly formed relationship, but she knew what to do in an argument. "You're dabbling around the edges everywhere, Jack—with Frenchie's, with the Delahoussayes, with Baldwin, with me. You're just too big a coward to do more than get your feet wet."

"Coward?" He gaped at her, at the sound of the word. He described himself in many ways, few of them flattering, but "coward" was not on the list.

Laurel pressed on, shooting blind, fighting on instinct. Her skills were rusty, and she had never been good at keeping her heart out of a fight, anyway. It tumbled into the fray now, tender and brimming with new emotion. The words were out of her mouth before she could even try to rope them back. "Every time it starts looking like you might have a chance at something good, you turn tail and run behind that I-don't-give-a-damn facade."

"A chance at something good?" Jack said, his gaze sharp on hers, his heart clenching in his chest. "Like what? Like us?"

She bit her tongue on the answer, but it flashed in her eyes just the same. Jack swore under his breath and turned away from her. Struggling for casual indifference, he shook a cigarette out from a pack lying on the counter and dangled it from his lip. "*Mon Dieu*, a couple'a good rolls in the sack and suddenly—"

"Don't!" Laurel snapped. She held a finger up in warning and pressed her lips together hard to keep them from trembling. "Don't you dare." She gulped down a knot of tears and struggled to snatch a breath that didn't rattle and catch in her throat. "I didn't come here to have this fight," she said tightly. "I came here because I thought you might be able to help me, because I thought we were friends."

Jack blew out a huff of air and shook his head. "I can't help anybody."

Laurel tugged her composure tight around herself. Damned if she'd let him make her cry. "Yeah? Well, forgive me for asking you to breach the asshole code of conduct," she sneered. "I'll just go ask Jimmy Lee Baldwin flat out if he had my sister tied to his bed the past two nights. I'll just go knock on every goddamn door in the parish until I find her!" She held up a hand as if to ward off an offer that was not forthcoming. "Thanks anyway, Jack," she said bitterly, "but I don't need you after all."

He watched her storm out of the kitchen and down the hall, a frown tugging at his mouth, a lead weight sinking in his chest. "That's what I've been tellin' you all along, angel," he muttered, then he turned and went in search of matches.

Coop stared into his underwear drawer, frowning at the array of serviceable cotton Jockey shorts and boxers and the little silk things Savannah had bought him. He lifted out a white silk G-string, dangling it from his finger, shaking his head. He'd felt stupid as hell wearing it, too big and too old and too set in his ways. But as he dropped it in the wastebasket beside the dresser, he felt a little twinge of regret, just the same.

She wouldn't be back this time. The fight to end all fights had been fought. It was over, once and for all.

Too bad, he thought as he stared out the window. He had loved her. If only she had been able to take that love for what it was worth and find happiness. Of course, that restless, insatiable quality had been one of the things to draw him to her in the first place. So needy, so desperate to assuage that need, so utterly, pitiably incapable of filling that gaping hole within her heart.

He sighed as his mind idly drew character sketches of Savannah, and his gaze fell through the window, taking in the details of the setting. The bayou was a strip of bottle green beyond the yard, and beyond the banks lay the tangled wilderness of the Atchafalaya. Wild and sultry, like Savannah, unpredictable and deceivingly delicate, fragility in the guise of unforgiving toughness.

He thought he ought to write the image down, but he couldn't work up the ambition to go and get his notebook. Instead, he let the lines fade away and tended to his packing. Five pair of shorts, five pair of socks, the tie bar Astor had given him the Christmas before she forgot his name.

Astor. God, how different she had been from Savannah. She had always worn her fragility like a beautiful orchid corsage, as if it were the badge of a true lady, a sign of breeding. Her toughness had been inside, a stoic strength that had borne her through the stages of her decline with dignity. She would have disapproved of Savannah—silently, politely, with a tip of her head and a cluck of her tongue. But he imagined Astor would have forgiven Savannah her sins. He wasn't so sure the same could be said for his case. He had made his wife a pledge, after all.

The doorbell intruded on his musings, and Coop abandoned the closet and his shirt selections to answer it, never expecting to find Laurel Chandler standing on the stoop.

"Mr. Cooper, I'm Laurel Chandler," she said, all business, no seductive smile, no gleam of carnal fire in the eyes behind the oversize, mannish spectacles.

"Yes, of course," he said. Remembering his manners, he stepped back from the door. "Would you care to come in?"

"I'll be blunt, Mr. Cooper," Laurel said, making no move to enter the house. "I'm looking for my sister."

Coop sighed heavily, wearily, feeling his age and the weight of his infidelity bearing down on his broad shoulders. "Yes. Do come in, Miz Chandler, please. I'm afraid I'm in a bit of a hurry, but we can talk as I pack."

Determined to dislike him, Laurel stepped past him and into the entry hall of a lovely old home that held family heirlooms and an ageless sense of loneliness with equal grace. Everything was in its place and polished to a shine, with no one here to see it. A grandfather clock ticked the seconds away at the foot of the stairs, marking time to the end of a family. Cooper and his wife had no children. When they were gone, so would be the memories they had made in this house over the generations.

She cast a hard glance at Conroy Cooper. Behind the lenses of his gold-rimmed glasses, he met her gaze with the bluest, warmest, saddest eyes she had ever seen, and he smiled, wistfully, regretfully. It wasn't difficult to see what had attracted her sister. He was a big, strong, athletic man, even at an age that had to be near sixty. His face had probably taken young ladies' breath in his heyday. A strong jaw and a boyish grin. Now it was a map etched with lines of stress and living. No less handsome; more interesting. He stood there in rumpled chinos with one leg cocked, his head tipped on one side. A gray T-shirt with a faded Tulane logo spanned his shoulders and hung free of his pants.

"I am certain you are well aware of my relationship with your sister," he drawled, that smooth, wonderful voice rolling out of him, rolling over Laurel like sun-warmed caramel. She steeled herself against its effects. "And you think less of me for it."

"You're an adulterer, Mr. Cooper. What am I supposed to think of you?"

"That perhaps I loved Savannah as best I could while trying to keep a promise to a woman who no longer remembers me or anything of the life we once had together."

Laurel pressed her lips together and looked down at her shoes, dodging the steady blue gaze.

"Savannah once told me you thought in absolutes," he said. "Right or wrong. Guilty or not guilty. Life isn't quite so black and white as you would like for it to be, Laurel. Nothing is as absolute in reality as it is in our minds in our youth."

"Loved," Laurel repeated, seizing on the thought to fend off any pangs of contrition his words may have inspired. She raised her head and looked at him sharply again. "You said *loved*. Past tense."

"Yes. It's over." He ran a hand back through his blond hair, glancing at the clock as it ticked away another few seconds. "I don't mean to be rude, but I have to be in N'Awlins this afternoon. If you'll excuse my back, I'll lead the way."

As she followed him into his bedroom, a feeling of something like déjà vu stole over her. The furnishings were big and masculine. The smell of leather and shoe polish underscored the faint woodsy tang of aftershave.

Like Daddy's room back home before Vivian had dismantled it and given it over to Ross.

A duffel bag sat open on the white counterpane on the bed, giving her a peek of white cotton and polished wingtips. Cooper went to the closet and selected three shirts, which he hung neatly in a black garment bag on the closet door.

"She wanted to go with me on this trip," he said. "Of course, I had to tell her no. She knew very well the boundaries of our relationship. If you think she took the news well, I should point out to you that I used to have a collection of fine antique shaving mugs left to me by my grandfather. I kept them in that cabinet next to the bathroom door."

The curio cabinet stood, an empty frame with no glass in its sides and no antique shaving mugs within. All signs of the destruction had been vacuumed away, but Laurel could very easily picture her sister hurling mugs at Cooper's head. She had that kind of rage in her, that kind of violence.

Fingers of tension curled around her stomach and squeezed.

"When did this argument take place?" she asked, turning to face Cooper once again.

He hung a pearl gray suit in the garment bag and smoothed the sleeves. "Tuesday. Why?"

"Because I haven't seen her since Tuesday morning."

He pulled another suit from the closet and added it to the bag, frowning as his mind rushed to plot out scenarios. "Then she's probably gone on to N'Awlins. I wouldn't put it past her to think she could disrupt my stay."

"She didn't have a car."

"She may have caught a ride with a friend." His mouth compressed into a tight line as he zipped the bag shut. "Or another man. You might check with the Maison de Ville. She likes to stay in the cottages there."

"Yes," Laurel murmured. "I know."

They had stayed there the spring before their father died. A family outing, one of the few she remembered happily. She could still hear Vivian going on about how movie stars sometimes stayed there. She could still see the thick-walled cottages and the courtyard, could still hear the noise and smell the ripe smells of New Orleans as she had perceived them then, through the senses of a child.

Cooper pulled the garment bag down from the closet door, folded and latched it securely. Laurel watched his hands. They were thick and strong with square-cut nails. The hands of a farmer or a carpenter, not a writer. A gold band, burnished with age, circled the third finger of his left hand.

"How is your wife?"

His head came up sharply, eyes shining with interest and surprise as he studied her. He swung the bag onto the bed beside the duffel.

Laurel picked at her ravaged thumbnail absently, uncomfortable with the topic and his scrutiny. "I heard about the incident at St. Joseph's. I'm sorry."

Coop nodded slowly, finding it interesting that Laurel would apologize for the actions of her sister. They were two sides of the same coin—one light, one dark; one driven by angst to acts of justice, one to strange fits of passion. Laurel subdued everything feminine about herself; Savannah flaunted and magnified. Laurel held everything within; Savannah knew no boundaries and no control.

"She's doing well enough," he said. "One of the few saving graces of her illness is that she forgets unpleasantness almost as quickly as it happens. It's the rest of us who have to go on with bad memories lingering like the smell of smoke."

The past was gone, but its taint was stubborn and pervasive. An apt analogy, Laurel thought as she left the house.

She slid behind the wheel of her car and just sat there for a moment, her mind trying to go in eight directions at once. Cooper thought Savannah had gone to New Orleans. It didn't feel right. Savannah had always treated a trip to New Orleans as an event, something to fuss over and pack and repack for. She would have told Aunt Caroline, promised to bring back something outrageous for Mama Pearl just to hear the old woman huff and puff. She wouldn't have slipped away like a thief in the night, regardless of who she had gone with.

She would call the Maison de Ville, just to be sure, but there were other possibilities, and one of them was Jimmy Lee Baldwin.

Jimmy Lee stretched out across his rumpled bed and groaned. He felt near death with exhaustion. He smelled of rank, ripe sweat with an undertone of liquor and an overtone of sex. Without question, he needed a long shower before his lunch meeting with his deacons. Deacons. Christ, the saps would go nuts over that title.

"You're fucking brilliant, Jimmy Lee," he snickered, staring up at the creaking old ceiling fan as it strained to stir the stale air. "You're a Grade A-mazing, God damn-tastic genius."

It was the sign of a man who would go far. When things turned sour, he found a way to sweeten the deal. The taping at the Texaco station hadn't turned out the way he had planned, but ultimately it was going to be to his advantage. He would make sure of it.

The brainstorm had come in the middle of a wild, hard fuck. In a way, he had a whore to thank, ironic as that seemed. The answer to his troubles was what she had begged from him—mercy, sympathy. He would play on the sympathies of his followers. He didn't believe in giving sympathy himself. Go for the throat. Look out for Number One. Those were his mottoes. But the American people had traditionally loved an underdog. He would get a few key puppets whipped into a frenzy for his flagging cause, they would rally the troops, and he'd be back on track in nothing flat.

He smiled a wicked smile as he pictured it. The looks on their gullible, stupid faces as he poured his heart out to them about the plight of his ministry and his campaign to end sin. His cause was being sabotaged by Satan in

the guise of Jack Boudreaux. He was being thwarted and
made to look a fool at every turn, and he just didn't know
if he had the heart to go on alone. Perhaps if one or two
good men would be willing to shoulder some of his burden by filling the role of deacon . . . Their eyes would
go wide, and their faces would shine with imagined
grace.

The timing was perfect. Discovery of a mutilated female in their own backyards tended to turn people's
thoughts to God and to vengeance. They would want a
leader and a scapegoat, and Jimmy Lee intended to give
them both.

He sat up just enough to snag the paperback off his
nightstand and fell back across the lumpy mattress,
thumbing through the pages.

*Blood ran in rivulets, pearling and tumbling in the
knife's wake. She tried to scream, but the sound vibrated
only in her mind. Her throat was raw. Silk filled her
mouth, like a stopper in a bottle, and the tie of the gag
pulled her lips back in a macabre smile. . . .*

"Twisted stuff, Jack my man." He chuckled as he
folded down the corner on the page.

This was all playing right into his hands. He fanta-
sized about all the possibilities as he stripped and showered in the grungy, mildew-coated shower stall. Jack
Boudreaux would get pinned for the murders. Jimmy
Lee would be a hero. Free publicity. Fan mail. The faithful would come out of the woodwork and follow him anywhere, do anything for him. What a perfectly wonderful
dream.

He was a happy and satisfied man as he dressed. He
even hummed a few bars of an old gospel tune as he
polished off the knot in his tie and stood back to critique
his look in the mirror above the bathroom sink.

His tawny hair was slicked back, his cheeks perfectly
tan and clean-shaven. He flashed a smile, euphoric as
always with the dental wonders he had invested in. He
looked, quite simply, perfect. The shirt and tie were
neat, but the knot was just slightly loose and askew. The
suit was sufficiently limp with just enough wrinkles to

make him look a little downtrodden. He took a deep breath and let it out slowly, letting his shoulders sag and the muscles of his face droop into a worried frown. For a crowning touch, he mussed his hair a little in front, flicking a few strands loose to tumble across his forehead.

The deacons wouldn't know what hit them.

Someone banged on the screen door, and Jimmy Lee let whoever it was wait a few seconds, setting the mood. It was probably one of his chosen come to check on him. He had sounded despondent when he'd called them this morning. He shambled out of the bathroom, head hanging low, hands dangling by his sides.

Laurel Chandler stared in at him through the screen. She didn't look the least bit sympathetic. She looked like trouble.

"Miz Chandler," he said, pushing the door open. "What a surprise to see you here."

"Yes, I suppose you'd be less surprised to see my sister," Laurel said. She stepped across the threshold, staying as far away from Baldwin as she could, never turning her back to him for a second. From the corners of her eyes, she did a quick reconnaissance of the shabby bungalow, her gaze lingering a second on the old bed with its scrollwork iron headboard and footboard.

Jimmy Lee let the door bang shut. His face carefully blank, his gaze steady on the woman who looked up at him with undisguised contempt, he pushed back the sides of his suit coat and planted his hands at his waist. "Just what is that supposed to mean?"

"Exactly what you think it means."

"You're suggesting I have a relationship with your sister?"

"No. I'm saying you have sex and play bondage games with my sister."

His reaction was something that artlessly combined incredulous laughter and choking astonishment. Jaw hanging slack, head wagging, he staggered back a step, as if her words had struck him physically and dazed him. "Miz Chandler, that's simply outrageous! I am a man of God—"

"I know exactly what you are, Mr. Baldwin."

"I think not."

"Are you calling my sister a liar?" she challenged, planting her hands on her slim hips.

Jimmy Lee bit his tongue and assessed the situation. Back in his youth, when he'd hustled small-time for pocket money, he had prided himself on being able to read a mark in nothing flat. What he saw behind the glasses, in the depths of Laurel Chandler's deep blue eyes, behind the temper and the intelligence, was a hint of vulnerability. Maybe she didn't approve of Savannah's freewheeling sex life. Maybe she was every bit as prim as she appeared to be. Maybe she didn't quite trust Savannah's sanity.

He sighed dramatically and slipped his hands into his trouser pockets, forcing his shoulders down. Letting her hang for a minute, he turned away from her—not so far that she couldn't see him furrow his brow and frown, as if in contemplation.

" 'Liar' is a harsh word. I think your sister is a very troubled woman. I don't deny she's come to me. I've tried to counsel her."

"I'll bet you have."

Her whole body vibrating with temper, Laurel took a slow turn around the room. When she came to the foot of the unmade bed, she stopped and curled her fingers over the curving bow of the foot rail. It was bumpy with layers of old paint, rough in spots where the rust was coming through. She gave it a yank, testing for sturdiness, and shot a look at Baldwin over her shoulder.

"Psychiatrists still favor using a couch for their sessions. I guess you decided to take it a few steps further."

She gave the bed another shake, but turned her back to it the instant her imagination began to picture Savannah there with her wrists bound.

Annie Gerrard had been bound by her wrists too.

She settled her right hand on her pocketbook and pressed the pocketbook against her hip, imagining that she could feel the outline of her Lady Smith through the glove-soft leather.

"Do you know what I think of men who have to tie women up in order to feel superior to them?" she asked, giving Baldwin the same look that had cracked more than one defendant's story. "I think they're spineless, twisted, despicable scum."

A muscle ticked in Jimmy Lee's cheek. In his pockets he balled his hands into fists. His temper strained with the need to use them. "I told you, I've never had anything to do with your sister sexually. Only the Lord can decipher what might go on in a mind like Savannah's. I don't doubt but that she's capable of saying—of doing—anything at all. But I'm telling you, as God is my witness, I have never laid a hand on her."

"God is a very convenient witness," Laurel said dryly. "Difficult to cross-examine."

Baldwin's tawny brows scaled his forehead. He all but raised a finger and declared her a blasphemer. "You would doubt the Lord?" he gasped, incredulous.

The act was lost on Laurel. "I would doubt you," she said. "I came here to ask if you've seen Savannah in the last couple of days, but I can see I'm wasting my time waiting for a straight answer. Perhaps Sheriff Kenner will have better luck."

She hadn't taken three steps past him when his hand snaked out and caught her by the shoulder. Laurel twisted around, chopping at his arm as she had been taught in self-defense class, breaking his hold. He glared at her, but made no move to touch her again.

"I haven't seen your sister," he said, struggling to maintain a facade of calm. "That's God's honest truth. No need to drag the sheriff out here."

Laurel took another step back toward the door and inched her hand into her purse. Her heart was thumping. Her palms were sweating. She hoped to hell she would be able to hang on to the gun if the need arose.

"Why don't you want him out here? Skeletons in your closet, Reverend?"

"Scandal is deadly in my position," he said, following her retreat toward the door. "Even though I've done nothing wrong, people tend to believe where there's smoke, there's fire."

"They're usually right."

"Not in this case."

"Save your breath, Baldwin," she sneered. "You couldn't win me over if you turned water into wine right before my very eyes. You're a charlatan and a fraud, and if I didn't have better things to do with my time, I'd make certain the whole damn world found out about it."

She could ruin him. The thought hit Jimmy Lee like a brick in the belly. His stomach twisted into a knot. His shot at wealth and glory could be dead in the water. No one would believe her sister, but people would at least pause to listen to Laurel Chandler. They might dismiss what she said after, since she had a reputation for crying wolf, but the damage would be done.

The press would focus on him. Despite the pains he had always taken to disguise himself, some whore would recognize him on the news and sell a juicy story to the *Enquirer*. Christ, he wished he'd never set eyes on a Chandler woman in his life. Bitches and whores, both of them. He wanted to choke the life out of this one, the pompous little do-gooder.

As the picture flashed like a strobe in his brain, his hold on his temper broke with a snap. He opened his jaws in a snarl that was made only more eerie by the white of his too-perfect caps. A red haze filmed across his eyes, and he lunged toward her, growling, "You little bitch."

Heart catapulting into her throat, Laurel stumbled backward to give herself room. Staying just out of Baldwin's reach, she jerked the Lady Smith from her purse and held it chest-high, with both hands wrapped around the grip.

Jimmy Lee's eyes bugged out at the sight of the gun. "Jesus Fucking Christ!"

"Amen, Revver," Jack drawled.

Adrenaline was searing his veins. He wanted nothing more than to throw the door open, tackle Baldwin, and pound the life out of him for whatever he had done to

spook Laurel, but he held the machismo in firm check.
Laurel and her purse pistol had the situation under control. Sort of. Her hands were trembling badly.

With deliberately, deceptively lazy movements, Jack
drew open the screen door and propped himself up
against the jamb.

"And if you think she can't use it, you better think
again, Jimmy Lee," he said. "She'll shoot your balls off
and feed 'em to stray dogs."

Jimmy Lee glared at him with a look of pure, unadul-
terated hate. "I didn't ask you in, Boudreaux."

Jack arched a brow in amusement. "Oh, yeah? Well,
you gonna do somethin' 'bout that, Jimmy Lee? Ms.
Smith & Wesson might have somethin' to say 'bout that."

"Isn't that just like you—hiding behind a woman,"
Baldwin sneered. He raised an impotent finger in warning. "You take my word for it, Boudreaux. You won't be
able to hide much longer."

He had a card up the sleeve of that cheap suit. Jack
could tell by the gleam in his eyes. He couldn't imagine
what it was, but he couldn't imagine that he'd give a
damn, either. He blinked wide in mock fear and splayed
a hand across his heart.

"Did you hear that, Miz Chandler? Why I do believe
the good reverend just threatened me." With the same
casual grace, Jack reached out and gently pushed her
hands and the gun down so the barrel pointed at the
floor. "Sugar, mebbe you could wait outside for me. I
think Reverend Baldwin and I need to clear up this little
misunderstanding."

Laurel looked up at him, more curious as to why he
had shown up than what he was going to do to Jimmy
Lee Baldwin. She probably should have stood her
ground or made him leave with her. After all, assault was
against the law, and she was sworn to uphold the law.
But she glanced over at Baldwin and felt a surge of
something primal and angry, and for once turned her
back on rules and regulations. She didn't like the things
Baldwin had intimated about Savannah—even if she
knew deep down they may well have been true.

She slipped the Lady Smith back into her pocketbook and without a word turned and left the bungalow.

Jack settled his hands at the waist of his jeans and waited for the echo of the screen door slamming to fade away before he turned fully toward Jimmy Lee. Jimmy Lee, who believed the best defense was a good offense, snatched up the mostly empty bottle of E&J brandy off the three-legged coffee table and brandished it like a big glass club.

"Get the hell out of my house, Boudreaux."

"Not before we have us a little chat." Jack circled Baldwin slowly, moving in on him by imperceptible degrees. He didn't appear threatening. He scuffed his boots along on the gritty linoleum, his head down, as if he had nothing better to do than count the cigarette burns in the floor. "Now, Jimmy Lee, I don' know what you did to make Miz Chandler pull her little peashooter on you, but it had to be somethin' bad—her being such a law-abiding sort and all."

"I didn't do shit to her," Jimmy Lee snapped, turning, turning, to keep Boudreaux in front of him. His fingers flexed on the neck of the brandy bottle. "She's unbalanced. She was in an asylum, you know. She's nuts, just like her sister."

Jack shook his head in grave disappointment, still shuffling along, still turning, still moving in a little at a time. "You're impugning the character of a fine, upstanding woman, Jimmy Lee. Even I have to take exception to that."

Jimmy Lee made another quarter turn, wondering dimly at the way the floor seemed to dip beneath his feet. "I don't give a rat's ass what you take exception to, you coonass piece of shit."

Jack suddenly moved toward him, and Jimmy Lee swung the heavy, unwieldy brandy bottle. He did so with gusto, imagining the mess it would make of the Cajun's head, but he missed badly, throwing himself off balance in the process.

Jack ducked the blow easily. Quick and graceful as a cat, he stepped around Baldwin, caught hold of the preacher's free arm, twisted it up high behind him, and ran him face-first into the rough plaster wall. The bottle shattered and fell to the floor in tinkling shards, the last of the brandy soaking into Baldwin's wingtips.

"I told you once to leave Laurel Chandler alone," Jack growled, his mouth a scant inch from Baldwin's ear. "You shouldn't make me tell you twice, Jimmy Lee. Me, I don' have that kind of patience."

Jimmy Lee tried to suck in a watery breath. His face was mashed against the nubby plaster, and he was sure he'd chipped at least three of his precious caps. While the blood pounded in his head and spittle bubbled between his ruined teeth and down his quivering chin, he damned Jack Boudreaux to hell and plotted a hundred ways to torment him once they were both there.

"I mean it, Jimmy Lee," Jack snarled, jerking his arm up a little higher and wringing a whimper out of him. "If you give her another moment's trouble, I'll rip your dick off and use it for crawfish bait."

He gave one last little push, then stepped back and dusted his palms off on his thighs as Baldwin stood, still facing the wall, doubled over, clutching his arm.

"Hope I don' see you 'round, Jimmy Lee."

Jimmy Lee spat on the floor, a big gob of blood and saliva flecked with fragments of porcelain. "God damn you to hell, Boudreaux!" he yelled around the thumb that was feeling gingerly for the sorry condition of his caps.

Jack waved him off and walked out and away from the bungalow.

"I don't want to know one thing about it," Laurel said as she came toward him from the base of a huge old magnolia tree. "If I don't know anything, I can't be called to testify."

"He'll live," Jack said sardonically. They walked toward the vehicles they had left on the scrubby lawn beside Baldwin's beat-up Ford. Huey sat behind the wheel of Jack's Jeep, ears up like a pair of black triangles, mismatched eyes bright. Jack shot Laurel a sideways glance. "You okay?"

Laurel gave him a look. "What are you doing here, Jack? Two hours ago you weren't even willing to give me a straight answer, let alone ride to my rescue."

He scowled blackly, caught in a trap of his own making. He should have stayed the hell out of it, but as he sat at his desk, smoking the first pack of Marlboros he had allowed himself in two years, trying to conjure up a violent muse, he hadn't been able to get the image out of his head—Laurel charging at Baldwin with the courage of a lion and the stature of a kitten. Baldwin was a con man, but that didn't mean he wasn't capable of worse, and try as he might to convince himself otherwise, Jack couldn't just stand back and let her take a chance like that alone.

"I followed you," he admitted grudgingly. "I don' want to get involved, but I don' want to see you get hurt, either. I've got enough on my conscience."

Too late for that, Laurel thought, biting her lip. He had hurt her in little ways already. He would break her heart if she gave him the chance, and damn her for a fool, some part of her wanted to give him that chance. Knowing everything she knew about him. Even after everything they had said in his kitchen. She couldn't think of his tenderness in the night, of the vulnerability that lay inside that tough, alley-cat facade, and not want to give him that chance.

"Why, Mr. Boudreaux," she said sardonically, gazing up at him with phony, wide-eyed amazement, "you'd better watch yourself. One might deduce from a statement such as that one that you actually feel concern for my well-being. That could be hazardous to your image as a bastard."

"Quit bein' such a smartass," he growled, his expression thunderous. "I didn't like the idea of you comin' out here alone. Ol' Jimmy Lee, he might not be as harmless as he seems, you know."

"He might not be harmless at all," Laurel muttered, turning her gaze back toward the shabby little bungalow. Reverend Baldwin was into kinky sex and bondage, and he had an ugly temper. He also had a near-perfect cover. Who would ever suspect a preacher of murder?

"Murder." The word made her shudder inside. She had come here looking for her sister, and now she was thinking of murder. She wouldn't begin to allow the two subjects near one another in her mind. In any regard.

"Well, whatever your reasons, thank you for coming."

They seemed beyond the formality of thanks, and it hung awkwardly between them. Laurel pushed her glasses up on her nose and shuffled toward her car. Jack shrugged it off and curled his fingers around the door handle of the Jeep.

"Where you goin' lookin' for trouble next, angel?" he asked, calling himself a fool for caring.

"To the sheriff," she said, already steeling herself for the experience. "I think he and I need to have a little chat. Want to come?"

It was a silly offer. She had no business feeling disappointed when he turned her down, but she didn't want to break the fragile thread of communication between them. *Foolish.* Even as she chastised herself, her fingers snuck into her purse and came out with the red matchbook. She offered it to him, simply to feel his fingertips brush against hers.

"Would you happen to know anything about this place?"

Jack's expression froze as he stared down at the elaborate black mask and the neat script title. "Where'd you get this?"

Laurel shrugged, her mouth going dry as his tension was telegraphed to her. "I found it. I think Savannah left it in my car, but she wouldn't admit it was hers. Why? What kind of place is it?"

"It's the kind of place you don' wanna go, sugar," he said grimly, handing it back to her. "Unless you like leather and you're into S&M."

Chapter
Twenty-Two

Kenner lit his fifth cigarette of the day and sucked in a lungful of tar and nicotine. His eyeballs felt as if they'd been gone over with sandpaper, his vocal cords as if they'd grown bark. He had ice picks stabbing his brain and a stomach full of battery acid disguised as coffee. In comparison, a rabid dog had a pleasant attitude. He was getting nowhere with the Gerrard murder, and it pissed him off like nothing else—except maybe Laurel Chandler.

He stared at her through the haze of smoke that hovered over his cluttered desk, his eyes narrowed to slits, his mouth twisting at the need to snarl.

"So you think Baldwin killed your sister and all them other dead girls?"

Laurel bit back a curse. Her fingers tightened on the arms of the visitor's chair. "That isn't what I said."

"Hell, no," Kenner barked, shoving to his feet. "But that's what you meant."

"It is not—"

"Jesus, I've been just waiting to hear this—"

"Then why don't you listen?"

"—haven't I, Steve?"

Danjermond, lounging against a row of putty-color file cabinets, tightened his jaw at the shortening of his name. Kenner didn't notice. He'd been looking for an excuse to blow off some steam. First someone had the balls to kill a woman in his jurisdiction. Then he'd had to let Tony Gerrard walk. Then every hoped-for lead had piddled into nothing. Now this. He let his temper have free rein, not giving a damn that Laurel Chandler was connected. Ross Leighton himself said the girl was a troublemaker, said she always had been.

"I've just been waiting for you to come charging in here, pointing fingers and naming names."

"I'm only trying to give you information. It's my civic duty—"

"Fuck that, lady." He cut her off, leaning over the desk to tap his cigarette off in the ashtray. "You're trying to make trouble, same as you did up in Georgia. Point your finger, shoot your mouth off, get your name in the paper. You get off on that or something?"

Laurel ground her teeth and cut a look Danjermond's way, wondering why the hell he didn't do something. "I never said Baldwin killed anyone. I just thought you might like to know—"

"That he's some kind of pervert. A preacher." Kenner snorted his derision and shook his head as he pulled hard on his smoke. "What was it up in Georgia? A dentist? A banker? Is there anyone you *don't* suspect of being a pervert?"

"Well, I doubt you are," Laurel snapped, coming up out of her chair. She planted her hands on Kenner's littered desktop and met him glare for glare. "Why should you resort to perversity when you obviously have a license to fuck over anyone you want!"

While Kenner snarled and foamed at the mouth, her gaze cut again to Danjermond, who had the gall to be amused with her. She could see it in the translucent green depths of his eyes, in the way the corners of his mouth flicked upward ever so slightly. He roused himself from his stance against the file cabinets and came forward, turning his attention on Kenner.

"Now, Duwayne," he said calmly. "Miz Chandler came in here with the best of intentions. If she believes she has information pertinent to the case, you ought to listen."

"Pertinent to the case!" Kenner made a contemptuous sound in his throat and smashed out his cigarette in the overflowing plastic ashtray. "Savannah Chandler says the preacher gets off on tying women up. Savannah Chandler. Jesus, everyone in town knows she's got screws as loose as her morals!"

Fury misting her vision red, Laurel all but dove for his throat. "You son of a bitch!"

Kenner shrugged. "Hey, I'm not saying anything that idn't common knowledge."

"But you're not saying it very tactfully," Danjermond pointed out, frowning.

"Shit, I don't have time to be David Fucking Niven. I've got a murder to solve." He snagged another Camel from the pack and lit it with a match, his gaze hard on Laurel. "Leave the investigating to me, *Ms.* Chandler."

"Fine," Laurel said through her teeth. "But it would probably be helpful if you would take your head out of your ass so you could see to do it."

Kenner's color deepened to burgundy. He snatched his cigarette from his lip and shook it at her, raining ash down on his desktop and the drift of papers strewn across it. "You want a little advice on where you might find your sister? I wouldn't look any farther than a few dozen bedrooms."

"And that's what you would have said about Annie Gerrard, too, isn't it?" Laurel felt a little surge of triumph as the hit scored. A muscle flexed in Kenner's jaw, and he glanced away. "Yeah, Annie liked to sleep around a little. Look where they found her."

Kenner turned his back on her and stared out through the slats in the crooked venetian blind. Danjermond came around the end of the desk and caught her gently by the arm. "Perhaps it would be better if you and I discussed this in my office, Laurel."

Gracefully, he turned her toward the door and ushered her into the outer office, where Kenner's secretary, Louella Pierce, sat with nail file in hand, absorbing every detail of the melee so she would be able to relate it blow by blow to everyone in the break room. A couple of uniformed officers looked up from the paperwork on their desks with smirks on their faces.

Adrenaline still pumping, Laurel glared at them. "What the hell are you looking at?"

Eyebrows shot up as heads ducked down. Danjermond continued into the hall without pause, herding her along. His grip on her arm seemed deceptively light, but when she tried to discreetly pull away, she couldn't.

"I'll thank you to let me go, Mr. Danjermond," Laurel said softly, angrily, her eyes flashing fiercely as she looked up at him. "I didn't appreciate your little Good Cop–Bad Cop routine back there. I'm not some wide-eyed civilian walking in here with a head full of gossip."

"No," he said calmly, never altering his stride or his expression, but there was something hard in his gaze as he glanced down at her. "You're a former prosecutor with a reputation for making allegations you can't back up. How did you expect him to react?"

There was considerable activity in the hall. Court was in session, but in addition to the usual cadre of attorneys and clerks and stenographers, there were reporters hovering like vultures, waiting for some meat on the latest of the Bayou Strangler's cases. Laurel sensed their presence. Her stomach tightened, and the hair on the back of her neck rose as she felt eyes turn her way—eyes that brightened with feral anticipation at the sight of her walking arm in arm with the parish's golden boy district attorney. Just as in old times, they homed in, scrambling to switch on tape recorders, fumbling for pencils and notebooks. They came forward in a rush, sound bursting out of them like a television that had suddenly been turned on high volume.

"Mr. Danjermond!"

"Ms. Chandler!"

"—is there any connection—?"

"—are you aiding in the investigation—?"

"—have there been any new leads—?"

Danjermond walked on, calm as Moses strolling through the Red Sea. "No comment. We have no comment to make at this time. Ms. Chandler has no comment."

Hating herself for it, Laurel leaned into him and let him take the brunt of the media storm. He guided her into his outer office, and while he dealt the press a final, frustrating "No comment" at the door, she made a bee-line past the curious gaze of his secretary and went into the quiet of his inner sanctum.

The details of the office penetrated only peripher-ally—hunter green walls, heavy brass lamps, dark leather chairs, the smell of furniture polish and cherry tobacco, a place for everything and everything in its place. The shades were drawn, giving the room the feeling of twi-light. The mood of the room may have soothed her, but she was too caught up in the churning memories and emotions and self-recriminations. The way she had lost her temper with Kenner was too reminiscent of scenes from Scott County—fights with the sheriff, tirades un-leashed on her assistants and colleagues.

She gulped a breath and stopped her pacing, bring-ing up both hands to press them against her temples. As in a dream, she could see herself tearing her office apart, wild, ranting, throwing things, smashing things, scream-ing until her assistant, Michael Hellerman, had called in Bubba Vandross from security to come and subdue her.

After months of riding that mental edge, she had gone over. She wasn't on the brink now, but she was damn close. The frustration of trying to deal with Kenner pushed a button. She had no control over him, and con-trol was the one thing she had needed most since her father had died.

And then the press. God, would she never escape the loop of recurrences? If she had gone to Bermuda instead

of Bayou Breaux, would she now be standing in the mag-
istrate's office, embroiled in some island intrigue?

She let out a shuddering breath and tried to let go
some of the tension in her shoulders. She needed to regroup, to think things through. She needed to find Savannah and dispel the dark shadows lurking in the back
of her mind.

She ran a hand over the soft leather of her pocketbook, thinking of the odd trinkets she had dropped into
it—the earring, the necklace, the matchbook. She had
shown none of them to Kenner, knowing he would only
have taken them as further proof of her mental instabil-
ity. They might have come from anywhere. They might
all have been Savannah's.

The matchbook lingered in her mind. Jack turning it
over with his nimble musician's fingers. His expression
going carefully blank at the sight of the name. A leather
bar in the Quarter. Secretive, seclusive, exclusive. A
place where masks were commonplace and anything
might be had for a price or a thrill. He had been there
doing research for a book.

He had pinned her arms above her head, held her
down as he joined their bodies. . . .

Jimmy Lee Baldwin was into bondage, Savannah
said.

Savannah had allowed herself to be tied up. . . .

Nausea swirled around Laurel's stomach, and she
leaned against an antique credenza and closed her eyes.

"Would you care for a brandy?"

She jerked her head up as Danjermond closed the
door softly behind him.

"For medicinal purposes, of course," he added with a
ghost of a smile.

"No," she said, stiffening her knees, squaring her
shoulders. "No, thank you."

He slid his hands into the pockets of his trousers and
wandered along a wall of leather-bound tomes. "Forgive
me for being less than supportive in Kenner's office. I've
learned the best way to handle him is not to handle him
at all." He shot her a sideways look, taking her measure.

"And I admit I wanted to see you in action. You're quite ferocious, Laurel. One would never suspect that looking at you—so delicate, so feminine. I like a paradox. You must have taken many an opponent by surprise."

"I'm good at what I do. If the opposition is taken by surprise by that, then they're simply stupid."

"Yes, but the plain fact is that people draw certain conclusions based on a person's looks and social background. I've been on the receiving end of such impressions myself, being from a prominent family."

Laurel arched a brow. "Are you trying to tell me you may be a son of the Garden District Danjermonds, the shipping Danjermonds, but at heart you're just a good ol' boy? I have a hard time believing that."

"I'm saying one can't judge a book by its cover— pretty or otherwise. One never really knows what might hide behind ugliness or lurk in the heart of beauty."

She thought again of Savannah, her beautiful sister, spinning around Frenchie's with Annie Gerrard in a headlock, smearing excrement on the wall of St. Joseph's rest home outside Astor Cooper's window, screaming obscenities in the moonlight. Sighing, she closed her eyes and rubbed at her forehead as if she could scrub her brain clean of doubt.

"I'll do what I can to influence Kenner," Danjermond said softly.

He was behind her now, close enough that she could sense his nearness. He settled his elegant hands on her shoulders and began to rub methodically at the tension. Laurel wanted to bolt, but she held her ground, unsure of whether his gesture was compassion or dominance, unsure of whether her response was courage or acquiescence.

"I can't make any promises, though," he said evenly. "I'm afraid he has a valid point concerning the information on Baldwin. Your sister has something of a credibility problem. Particularly as she's gone missing. You know all about credibility problems, don't you, Laurel?"

She jerked away from his touch and turned to face him, her anger blazing back full force. "I can do without the reminder, thank you, and all the other little snide remarks you so enjoy slipping into our conversations like knives. Just whose side are you on, anyway?"

"Justice takes the side of right. Nature, however, chooses strength," he pointed out. "Right and strength don't always coincide."

He let that cryptic assertion hang in the air as he opened a beautiful cherrywood humidor on his desk top and selected a slim, expensive cigar. "The courtroom often more resembles a jungle than civilization," he said as he went about the ritual of clipping the end of the cigar. "Strength is essential. I need to know how strong you are if we're going to work together."

"We're not," Laurel said flatly, moving toward the door.

He slid into his high-backed chair, rolling his cigar between his fingers. "We'll see."

"I have other things to see to," she snapped, infuriated by his smug confidence that she wouldn't be able to resist the lure of his offer or the lure of him personally. "Finding my sister for one, since the sheriff's department is obviously going to be of little help."

A lighter flared in his hands, and he drew on the cigar, filling the air with a rich aroma. "I wouldn't worry overmuch, Laurel," he said, his handsome head wreathed in fragrant, cherry-tinted smoke. "She may well have gone to N'Awlins, as her lover suggested. Or perhaps she's enjoying the charms of another man. She'll turn up."

But what condition would she be in when she did? The question lodged like a knot in Laurel's chest. If Savannah had gone off some inner precipice, what would be left to find? The possibilities sickened her. One thing was certain—Savannah wouldn't be the sister Laurel had always leaned on. The child within her wept at the thought.

Prejean's Funeral Home was typical in Acadiana. Built in the sixties, it was a low brick building with a profusion of flower beds outside and a strange mix of sterility, tranquillity, and grief within. The floors were carpeted in flat, industrial-grade, dirt brown nylon, made to last and to deaden the sounds of dress shoes pounding across it. The ceilings were low-hung acoustical panels that had absorbed countless cries and murmured condolences.

Prejean's had two parlors for times that were regrettably busy, and a large kitchen that, if people had known how closely it resembled the embalming room, may well have gone unused. But, as with every social situation in South Louisiana, food was served for comfort and for affirmation of life. Women friends of T-Grace's, neighbors, fellow parishioners from Our Lady of the Seven Sorrows Catholic church would be in the kitchen brewing strong coffee and making sandwiches. Laurel knew Mama Pearl had brought a coconut cake.

Those who had come to pay respects to the Delahoussayes gathered in the Serenity room. The casket was positioned at the front of the room beneath a polished oak cross. Closed, the lid was piled high with white mums and gardenias, as if to discourage anyone from trying to lift it. Candles flickered at either end in tall brass candelabras.

People stood in knots of three and four at the back of the room, distancing themselves from death as much as they could while still supporting the family with their presence. Up front, more serious mourners sat in rows of chrome-and-plastic chairs that interlocked like Lego toys. Enola Meyette led the chanting of the rosary, a low murmur of French that underscored whispered conversations and muffled sobs.

T-Grace sat front and center in an ill-fitting black dress, her face swollen, her red hair standing out from her head as if she had been given an electric shock, her eyes huge and bloodshot. She was supported on one side by a burly son. To her right, Ovide sat in a catatonic state, his mouth slack, shoulders drooping beneath the weight of his grief.

Laurel's heart ached for them as she made her way through the throng to pay her respects. She knelt before

T-Grace and took hold of a bony hand that had to be as
least as cold as that of the daughter lying dead in the
casket.

"I'm so sorry, T-Grace, Ovide," she whispered, tears
rising automatically. She had been schooled from childhood to keep her emotions politely concealed. Even at
her father's funeral, Vivian had admonished her and Savannah to cry softly into their handkerchiefs so as not to
make spectacles of themselves. But the day had been too
long, and she was too tired and keyed-up for anything
but a modicum of restraint.

T-Grace looked down on her, valiantly trying to
smile, her thin mouth twisting and trembling with the
effort. "*Merci*, Laurel. You're all the time so good to us."

Laurel squeezed the hand in hers and pressed back
the emotions crowding her throat. "I wish I could do
more," she whispered, feeling impotent.

She turned to Ovide, trying to think of something to
say to him, but his eyes were on his daughter's casket,
glazed with a kind of numb shock, as if he had only just
realized how permanent Annie's absence would be.

As Mrs. Meyette began another decade of the rosary,
Laurel rose and moved off toward the back of the room,
restless and uncomfortable as she always had been with
the rituals of death. She scanned the crowd, looking for
Jack, but not finding him. She didn't know if she was
more disappointed for T-Grace and Ovide or for herself.
Stupid. How many times had he told her she couldn't
count on him?

How many times had he made a lie of his own
words?

He was a con man in his own right, playing a shell
game with his personality. Distract the mark with the
appearance of a rogue, while under one shell hid a heart
filled with compassion and under another one compressed with grief and guilt. The shells swept and
danced beneath his clever hands. Now you see it, now
you don't. Which one held the real Jack? Would he ever
let her close enough to find out?

She felt a little guilty, thinking about him during a

wake, but in that moment she would have given just about anything to feel his arms slip around her, to hear his smoky voice murmur something irreverent in her ear. She was tired and worried, and she wanted very badly to share those fears with someone.

A call to Maison de Ville in New Orleans had assured her Savannah wasn't staying there. A call to Le Mascarade had gotten her nothing but a derisive laugh. Patrons names were confidential. She had tracked down Ronnie Peltier, who was hefting sacks at Collins Feed and Seed. He hadn't seen Savannah since Tuesday night. She had come to his trailer in a temper and left an hour or two later. He claimed he hadn't seen her since.

Laurel spotted him standing with a group of cronies across the room—Taureau Hebert and several other regulars from the bar. They looked young and uncomfortable in neckties. Their eyes avoided the casket at the front of the room.

"It's fascinating, isn't it?"

She jumped as Danjermond's voice sounded low and soft in her ear. He stood beside her, looking as perfectly pressed as he had that morning, his suit immaculate, tie neat. Laurel felt wilted and rumpled beside him even though she had showered and changed into a skirt and fresh blouse before coming. That effect alone was enough reason to avoid him, as far as she was concerned.

"All the different defense mechanisms people develop to deal with death," he said, frowning slightly as his gaze moved over the gathering of the faithful and the bereaved. "A dose of religion, gossip, and jokes served up with coffee and a slice of pie afterward."

"People take comfort in ritual," Laurel said, trying to sidle away from him, but he had her neatly trapped between himself and a potted palm.

"Yes, that's true," he murmured, his sharp green gaze taking in the tableau of grief at the front of the room. T-Grace had begun to sob again, and her children gathered around her. Mrs. Meyette raised her voice, but never broke cadence in the recitation of the Hail Marys.

"Are you here in an official capacity or just out of morbid curiosity?"

He arched a brow at her sarcasm. "Would you rather Kenner had come to represent Partout Parish?"

"Not even he would be that callous."

T-Grace let out a series of soul-raking, ear-piercing wails, and one of her sons and Leonce Comeau half dragged her from the room. They were followed by old Doc Broussard, toting his black bag, and Father Antaya, each of them ready to dispense his own brand of medicine.

"Any sign of your sister, yet?" Danjermond asked.

"No, but if you'll excuse me, I see someone who may be able to help me."

Calling on skills honed at countless cocktail parties, Laurel slipped away from him before he could voice a protest and worked her way through the crowd to the front of the room. The final amen was uttered, and those who had been praying rose stiffly, beads clacking as they stored their rosaries in purses, pouches, pockets.

Leonce came back into the room, his marred face grim, his bald spot shining with sweat. He pulled a red handkerchief out of his hip pocket and dabbed at the moisture. He had thrown a black jacket on over his black T-shirt and jeans, and shoved the sleeves to his elbows, making him look more like an artist or a rock star than a mourner.

"Hey, *chère,* where y'at?" he said, managing a weary smile as he settled a hand on Laurel's arm. "Jack here?"

"No."

His gaze cut away so she couldn't see the hope that sparked in his eyes. He looked to the coffin, gleaming polished oak beneath its drape of waxy gardenias and frayed mums. "I shoulda guessed not. Jack, he don' do funerals. Been to one too many, I guess."

Laurel made a noncommittal sound. "How's T-Grace?"

"She's laying down in old man Prejean's office." He shook his head, still amazed. "Dat's some kinda scream she got, no?"

"I imagine losing a child tears loose a lot of things inside."

"Yeah, I guess." His dark gaze settled on the casket again because he was a little superstitious about turning his back on it. "Poor Annie," he murmured. "Teased one dick too many. All she wanted was to pass a good time. Look what it got her."

The implication made Laurel frown. No one asked to be tortured and killed. No woman deserved the kind of end Annie had met, regardless of what kind of life she had led. That thought bled into thoughts of Savannah, and Laurel's heart thumped at the base of her throat.

"Leonce, have you seen Savannah lately?"

He jerked around toward her, his brows slashing down over his eyes in a way that made his scar seem longer and more prominent. "Hey, yeah, I gotta talk to you 'bout dat one," he said ominously.

Taking her by the arm again, he led her out the door and into the shadows of the hall that led to the room where Prejean practiced his craft of readying people for the great beyond. The skin prickled at the base of Laurel's neck, and she cast a nervous glance back toward the Serenity room.

Leonce let go of her and stepped back, one hand propped at his waist, the other unconsciously touching his cheek, fingertips rubbing at the scar as if it might be erased. "Tuesday night I'm comin' back from Loreauville—me, I sing with a band down there sometimes, you know?—and I'm drivin' down Tchoupitoulas 'bout a block from St. Joe's home. Here comes Savannah runnin' 'cross the grass, 'cross the street right in front of me. I damn near hit her. I lean out the window and I yell, 'Hey, what's a matter wit' you, *chère*? You gone crazy or somethin'?'"

Laurel felt as if an anvil had dropped on her from a great height. This wasn't the story she had wanted to hear. She wanted him to tell her he'd seen her sister driving off to Lafayette to visit friends or leaving with a lover for a tryst in New Orleans. She didn't want confirmation of a suspicion that made her weak with dread.

Leonce was watching her, waiting for some kind of response. She somehow managed to open her mouth and make words come out. "Did she answer you?"

"Oh, yeah," he snorted. "She comes around the side window and tells me why don't I go fuck myself. How you like dat?"

"I don't," Laurel murmured. She blew out a breath and combed her fingers back through her hair, walking in a slow circle around Leonce, her mind working automatically to assimilate the story into the other facts and pieces she'd stored away. Tears rose in her eyes as the nerves in her stomach twisted tight around a hot lump of fear.

"Hey," Leonce drawled, spreading his hands wide. "I didn' mean to upset you, *chère*. I just thought you oughta know." He reached out to her, offering comfort and concern. Curling his fingers over her shoulder, he let his thumb brush against the pulse point in her throat. "You wanna go get a drink or somethin' and talk about it? Me, I'm a pretty good listener."

While the idea of escape appealed to her enormously, the idea of escaping with Leonce did not. There was just enough male interest in his big dark eyes to override the sympathy he was offering. And truth to tell, as ashamed as it made her feel, she didn't like looking at him. The scar continually drew her eye—the smooth, shiny quality of it, the grotesque burls of scar tissue that left brow and nose and lip slightly misshapen.

"We can go someplace dark," he said, the musical quality of his voice flattened and hard. His fingers tightened briefly on her shoulder, then he jerked them away.

Laurel felt an immediate kick of guilt. "No, Leonce, I didn't mean—"

"Is everything all right, Laurel?"

Danjermond stood at the end of the hall, half in light, half in shadow, his steady gaze shifting slowly from her to Leonce and back. Leonce swore under his breath in French and pushed past her, heading for a side exit.

Laurel heaved a sigh and pushed her glasses up on her nose. "Yes, everything is just peachy."

"I was just leaving," he said, producing the keys to his Jag and dangling them from his hand. "Would you care to join me for a nightcap or a cup of coffee?"

She shook her head, amazed at his inability to grasp the concept of the word "no." "Your persistence is astounding, Mr. Danjermond."

He smiled that feline smile. She could almost imagine him purring low in his throat. "As I've said, nature rewards strength and tenacity."

"Not tonight she doesn't." Laurel slipped her hand into her pocketbook and brushed the chain of the butterfly necklace away from her tangle of keys. "I'm going home."

Danjermond inclined his handsome head, conceding. "Some other time."

When hell freezes over, Laurel thought as she walked out. The sky was purple and orange in the west. The light above the parking lot was winking on with a series of clicks and buzzes. She unlocked the door of the Acura and slid behind the wheel, thinking she would rather have gum surgery than go out with Stephen Danjermond. A date with him would have to be like consenting to have her brain poked with needles. She wondered if he had ever had a conversation that didn't run on three levels simultaneously. Perhaps as a child—if he had ever been a child. The Garden District Danjermonds probably frowned on childhood the same way her own mother had.

Odd, she thought, that they would have that in common and turn out so very different from one another. But then she'd already seen firsthand that shared experiences didn't guarantee shared responses. She and Savannah could scarcely have been less alike. Thousands of teenage girls were molested by stepfathers or other men in their lives; not all of them responded the way Savannah had. Statistics showed that abused boys grew into abusive men, but she couldn't picture Jack beating a child— he had wept over the one he had lost without knowing.

Jack. She wondered where he was, if he was privately mourning the loss of a friend or if he was tipping back a

bottle of Wild Turkey and telling himself he didn't have
any friends. He drank too much. She cared too much.
She had read once somewhere that love wasn't always
convenient, but she had never wanted to believe it could
be hopeless. Jack swore he didn't want emotional entanglements. With tensions pulling her in all directions, she
didn't feel strong enough to convince him otherwise.

She didn't feel strong enough to face Aunt Caroline
tonight, either, but circumstances weren't offering any
options. She had put it off as long as she could. Now she
was going to have to sit down with her aunt and give
voice to all the facts and fears about her sister.

Dread lying like a lead weight in her stomach, she
put the car in gear and headed toward Belle Rivière,
never aware of the eyes that watched her with vicious
intent from cover of darkness.

The house was dark. Laurel let herself in the front door,
feeling a guilty sense of relief. As necessary as it was to
talk to Caroline about Savannah, she couldn't help being
glad for a reprieve. The day had been long enough, trying enough.

The note on the hall table said Caroline had gone to
New Iberia to spend the evening with friends. Mama
Pearl would still be down at Prejean's, on kitchen duty
until the last of the wake crowd had drunk the last of the
coffee.

Laurel leaned against the hall table for a moment,
trying to absorb the quiet. The old house stood around
her, solid, substantial, safe, giving the odd creak and
groan, sounds that were familiar and usually comforting.
But tonight they only magnified the hollow feeling of
loneliness that yawned inside her.

She felt alone. Abandoned. Guilty for having let her
sister slip away toward madness.

Struggling with the feelings, she let herself out the
hall door and went into the courtyard. Restlessly she
walked the brick paths, staying near the gallery. After a

few moments she settled on a bench and curled herself into the corner, tossing her purse onto the seat beside her.

The garden was mysterious by moonlight. Dark shapes that crouched and huddled, long shadows and hushed rustlings. By day it was growing lush and beautiful and in need of a weeding. That was what she had come to Belle Rivière for—quiet days of gardening, Mama Pearl's gruff fussing and fattening meals, Aunt Caroline's unflagging strength and pragmatism, Savannah's support.

Don't cry, Baby. Daddy's gone, but we'll always have each other.

How selfish she had been. Always taking Savannah's comfort, Savannah's protection. Too afraid of losing her mother's love to fight on Savannah's behalf. Burying herself in school, college, law school, work, while Savannah was left with bitter memories and her self-esteem in tatters.

Rise above your past. Put it behind you. Forget. She claimed she had, and it had always angered her that Savannah couldn't, *wouldn't.* Maybe all her sister had needed was someone to lean on, to help her, to support instead of ridicule, but Laurel had been off fighting other people's battles.

"I'm sorry, Sister," she whispered, tears slipping down her cheeks. "I'm so sorry. Please come home so I can tell you that in person."

Her only answer was the call of a barred owl from the woods beyond L'Amour. Then stillness. Absolute stillness. The back of her neck tingled, and she sat up straighter, straining her eyes to see into the night, holding her breath and trying to hear beyond the rushing of her pulse in her ears. She imagined she could feel eyes on her, staring in through the back gate, but she could see nothing beyond the iron bars. She thought of her sister running through the night, wild with anger, full of pain.

"Savannah?"

Crickets sang, frogs answered back from the bayou, where a heavy mist crept over the bank.

Malevolence crawled over her skin like worms.

Eyes on the gate, she bent over her purse and fumbled for her gun.

"If you wanna shoot me, you're gonna have to turn around, *'tite chatte.*"

Laurel shrieked and whirled around to find Jack standing not three feet from her. Her heart went into warp drive. "How the hell did you get in here?"

"The front door was open," he said with a shrug. "You really oughta be more careful, sugar. There's all kinds of lunatics running around these days."

"Yes," Laurel said, ignoring his wry tone. She was too damned spooked for banter. "I thought I heard one on the other side of the gate."

Frowning, Jack stepped past her and went to look. He came back, shaking his head. "Nothing. What did you think it was? Someone in the bushes?"

Savannah, she thought, sick that it might have been, relieved that it hadn't been. "What are you doing here?"

Good question. Jack stuffed his hands in the pockets of his jeans and wandered along the edge of the gallery and back. He had spent the evening walking along the bayou, trying to put as much distance as he could between himself and Prejean's Funeral Home. He couldn't bear the thought of a wake, and yet his thoughts had been filled with all of it—the coffin, the choking perfume of flowers, the intoning of the rosary. He could as well have been there for as raw as he felt now.

"I don' know," he whispered, turning back toward Laurel. Lie. He knew too well. He needed her, wanted the feel of her in his arms because she was real and alive and he loved her. *Dieu,* how stupid, how cruel that he should fall in love with someone so good. He couldn't even tell her, because he knew it couldn't last. Nothing good ever did once he touched it.

"I saw your car," he said, his voice strained and hoarse. "Saw the light . . ."

His broad shoulders rose and fell. He turned to pace, but her small hand settled on his arm, holding him in place as effectively as an anchor. He looked down into her angel's face, and the air fisted in his lungs. She had left her glasses on the hall table, and she looked up at him with night blue eyes that mirrored the need that ached in his soul.

"I don't really care," she said softly.

It didn't matter they had fought or that she had no hope for their future. This was just one night, and she felt so alone and so afraid. She looked up into his shadowed face, taking in the hard angles, the scarred chin, the eyes that had seen too much pain. It wasn't the face of the kind, safe lover she always envisioned for herself, but love him she did, and as they both stood there hurting, she needed him so badly, she thought she might die of it.

"Just tell me you'll stay," she whispered. "Just tonight."

He should have said no. He should have walked away. He should never have come to her in the first place, but then he'd never been very good at doing what was right. And he couldn't look into her eyes and say no.

"You shouldn't want me," he murmured, amazed that she did.

Laurel raised a hand and pressed her fingers to his lips. "Don't tell me how bad you are, Jack. Show me how good you can be."

He closed his eyes against a wave of pain, leaned down and brushed his lips against her cheek. It was as much of an answer as Laurel needed. Taking him by the hand, she led him up the back stairs and into her moonlit room.

They undressed each other quietly, patiently. They made love the same way, immersing themselves in the desire, steeping themselves in the experience, savoring the tenderness. Gentle touches. Soft, deep kisses. Caresses as sensuous as silk. A joining of bodies and two scarred souls. Straining to reach together for a kind of ecstasy that would banish shadows. A brilliant golden burst of pleasure. Trying desperately to hold on as it slipped away like stardust through their fingers.

And when it was over and Laurel lay asleep in his arms, Jack stared into the dark and wished with all that was left of his heart that he wouldn't have to let her go.

Chapter
Twenty-Three

Chad Garrett tipped his battered Saints cap back on his head and let the sunrise hit him flush in the face. Above the Atchafalaya the sky was aglow with soft stripes of color. Orange the shade of a ripe peach, warm and estival. Pink as vibrant and silken as the underside of a conch shell. Deep, velvet blue, the last of the night, set with a diamond that was the morning star.

He grinned to himself at the image he had painted with his thoughts. He had a natural gift for words. He figured he would write down the description as part of his makeup work for playing hooky from school. Mrs. Cromwell would give him a thundering lecture for missing English class again, but she would melt like butter when he handed in his short story about dawn in the swamp and the peace a man could find on the water. She'd do handsprings over his new word—"estival"— and that was an image that nearly made him chuckle. Mrs. Cromwell was fifty-eight and wore support hose and dresses that had enough fabric in them to clothe a family of four.

She was a good old girl, though, and Chad liked her as well as he liked any of his teachers. He was a good student, bright, capable. Hardly knew what a B was. But he didn't really care much for school, and, to the dismay of his teachers and the heartbreak of his mother, had no immediate plans to further his education once he graduated in June. This was where he wanted to be. In the swamp, observing nature, absorbing the beauty, the peace. He supposed he would relent after a year or two, go up to USL and study to become a naturalist or an environmental scientist of some kind or another. But for a while all he wanted to do was just be. He figured he would only be eighteen once. Might as well enjoy it.

He was his father's son in more respects than his big, raw-boned frame and square, good-looking face. Hap Garrett knew the value of contentment. He usually just smiled and turned a blind eye on those mornings when Chad didn't quite make it out of the boat shed without getting caught. As his dad liked to remind him, he'd been young once, too, and hadn't had much use for advanced algebra himself.

Chad steered his bass boat toward the shallows along a shaded bank, where a bit of yellow plastic ribbon marked one of his nets. The catch was good. He would make a couple hundred dollars today if his luck held down the line. The economics would appeal to Mr. Dinkle, whose class at ten he would miss.

He dumped the crawfish into an onion sack, sorting out the contorted body of a drowned water snake, which he tossed onto the bank. Some hungry scavenger would make a meal of it. Nothing went to waste in the swamp. Chad figured, if he was real lucky, he would witness nature's recycling, and that would appease Mr. Loop, fourth-period biology. He didn't figure he would have much of a wait. There was something up on the bank creating a powerful stink, the gagging, curiously sweet stench of death. The scent would act as a beacon.

Curious, he waded ashore and tied off his boat on a hackberry sapling. While he might not have given a fig how the balance of world power worked or how to find the square root of a negative, Chad wanted to know every detail about the life of the swamp.

It looked to him as if something had been dragged up on the bank. The weeds were bent and stained with blood. Might have been a deer that had gotten itself in trouble with a gator while drinking from the stream. It could have pulled itself back up onto the shore only to die of blood loss and shock. Or it could have been that a bobcat had caught himself a coon or a possum or a nutria, ate his fill, and left the rest. There were a dozen possibilities he could think of.

He pushed aside a tangle of branches and stopped cold in his tracks. Of the dozen possibilities he had considered, he hadn't included this. For the rest of his life he would see that face in his nightmares—beauty distorted grotesquely by death and the plain, hard realities of nature, blue eyes forever frozen in a shocked stare that made him think she had witnessed her own terrible fate and had seen beyond it to a terrible afterlife.

A woman lay dead at his feet. Horribly dead. Hideously dead. Naked and mutilated, with a white silk scarf knotted around her throat and a scrap of paper clutched in her stiff, lifeless hand.

Laurel woke alone. She wasn't surprised, so she told herself she couldn't be disappointed. But she was. Her brain told her she was foolish, that it wasn't practical or smart to want a future with Jack Boudreaux. He had too many ghosts, too much emotional baggage. But her brain couldn't do anything to banish her memories of the night—Jack's tenderness, the longing in his eyes, the pounding of his heart beneath her hand. Her heart was determined to hold on to those memories and the slim hope that went with them. Foolish, foolish heart.

He had gone at first light, she knew. Just as she had done before. She swept her arm across the vacant space beside her, finding nothing but a tangled sheet and a twisted spread. Not even his warmth lingered, just the scent of man and loving.

What would she do about him? What *could* she do? She couldn't change his image of himself. She had enough on her hands as it was.

That reminder brought thoughts of Savannah, and Laurel's stomach tensed like a fist at the thought of the conversation she would have with Aunt Caroline this morning. Restless, anxious, she climbed out of bed, pulled on a T-shirt and panties, and went in search of her pocketbook and the roll of Maalox tablets therein. It lay on the bench in the courtyard, where she had left it, the fine calfskin coated with thick, velvety dew. She wiped it off with the tail of her oversize T-shirt and went back upstairs to sit on the bed.

Careless, Laurel thought, reaching into the bag in search of her antacid tablets. She knew better than to leave a purse lying around, especially one with a semiautomatic handgun in it. Instead of the roll of tablets, she came up with the gaudy heart-shaped earring that had no mate and no explanation. The earwire had caught the chain of the little gold necklace, and she fished that out as well to untangle the mess and to work at untangling the mystery. It would give her mind something to do besides worry about her sister for a few moments. It would delay her conversation with Caroline.

The chain was twisted and knotted, and there seemed to be too many dangling ends. Strange, she thought, noting dimly that her heart was beating a little faster and her fingers fumbled at their task. She plucked at the gold butterfly and tugged a little harder at the chain, her breath coming in shorter bursts. Tears brimmed up in her eyes, not from frustration, not for any discernible reason. Silly, she thought, scratching at the tangle with the stub of a fingernail.

The butterfly and its necklace came free of the snag and fluttered to Laurel's lap, forgotten as cold, hard fingers of terror gripped her throat and squeezed. Hanging down from her trembling fist was a fine gold chain, and from the chain, swaying gently, a diamond chip winking as it caught the morning light, hung a small gold heart.

Savannah's.

"Oh, God. Oh, my God."

The words barely broke the silence of the room. She sat there, shaking, icy rivulets of sweat running down her spine. Her lungs seemed to have turned to concrete, crushing her heart, incapable of expanding to draw breath. She stared at the pendant until her eyes were burning, fragmented thoughts shooting across her mind like shrapnel—Daddy standing behind Savannah at twelve, fastening the chain, smiling, kissing her cheek; Savannah at twenty, at thirty, still wearing it. She never took it off. Never.

It swung from Laurel's fist, the tiny diamond bright and mocking, and dread crept through her like disease, weakening her, breaking her down. Tears blurred the image of the heart as she thought back to the night she had gone into Savannah's room. The feeling of stillness, of loss, of an absence that would never be filled.

"Oh, God," she said, choking on the fear, doubling over. She pressed her fist and the necklace against her cheek as scalding tears squeezed out from between her lashes.

She couldn't deal with this, couldn't face what she knew in her heart must be true. God, she couldn't go to Aunt Caroline and Mama Pearl—She couldn't go to Vivian—She didn't want to be here—should never have come back. She wanted Jack, wanted his arms around her, wanted him to be the kind of man she could lean on—

Selfish, weak, coward.

The recriminations came hard, as sharp as the crack of a whip. She had to do something. She couldn't just huddle here on her bed, half naked and sobbing, wishing someone else would be strong for her. There had to be something she could do. It couldn't be too late.

"No. No. No," she chanted, stumbling away from the bed.

She repeated the word over and over like a mantra as she tore open her wardrobe and drawers and grabbed a wrinkled pair of jeans, never letting go of the necklace. It wasn't too late. It couldn't be too late. She would go to

Kenner and make him see. She would call in the damn FBI. They would find Savannah. It couldn't be too late.

Wild urgency drove her as she tugged on the jeans. At the heart of the feeling was futility, but she refused to recognize it or accept it. The situation couldn't be futile. She couldn't lose her sister. She wouldn't let it happen. There had to be something she could do. Dammit, she would *not* let it happen!

Frantic, she flung the bedroom door back and ran down the hall and down the stairs, the railing skimming through one hand, Savannah's necklace gripped tight in the other. Her sneakers pounded on the treads, her pulse pounded in her ears. She didn't register the pounding at the front door.

Caroline came into the hall from the dining room, already dressed for the day in stark black and white. She glanced up at Laurel, concern knitting her brows, her hand reaching out automatically for the brass knob.

As if in a dream, time became strangely elastic, stretching, slowing. Laurel's perceptions became almost painfully sharp. The blocks of white in Caroline's dress hurt her eyes, the smell of Chanel filled her head, the creak of door hinges shrieked in her ears. She tightened her fist, and the golden heart burned into her palm.

Kenner stepped into the hall, lean and grim, eyes shaded. The shadow of death. His hat in his hands. His lips moved, but Laurel couldn't hear his words above the suddenly amplified roaring of her pulse. She saw the color drain from Caroline's face, the stricken look in her eyes. Together Kenner and Caroline turned and looked up at Laurel, and the knowledge pierced her heart like a knife.

"NO!!!" The denial tore from her throat like a scream. "NO!!!" she screamed, stumbling down the last few stairs.

She hurled herself at Kenner, striking his chest with her fists.

Surreal, she thought dimly, a part of her feeling strangely detached from the turmoil of the moment. This couldn't be happening. She couldn't be yelling or lashing out at Kenner. This couldn't be the real world, because everything in her field of vision had become suddenly magnified, as if she were shrinking and shrinking. And the sound of Caroline's voice came to her as if through a fog.

"Laurel, no! She's gone. She's gone. Oh, dear God! She's dead!"

Another cry of anguish and shock reverberated against the high ceiling of the hall. In her peripheral vision, Laurel could see Mama Pearl, her face contorted, reaching for Caroline with one hand, the other groping along the wall as if she had gone blind.

"God have mercy, I love dat chil'. I love dat chil' like my own!"

"Mama doesn't love me," Savannah said, her voice hollow and sad, breaking the stillness of the cool fall night.

They lay in bed together, wide awake, way past Laurel's bedtime. She cuddled against her sister, knowing she was supposed to be too old for it but afraid to move away. Not a week had passed since Daddy's funeral, and she was too aware of the precious, precarious state of life.

It was a knowledge no child should ever have to grasp. The weight of it was terrible. The fear it inspired had been with her day and night—that the world could be tipped upside down in a heartbeat. Everything she knew, everything she loved could be snatched away from her without warning.

Knowing that made her want to hang on with both hands to everything that was dear to her—her dolls, the kittens old mama cat had hidden in the boat house, Daddy's tie pin, Savannah. Most especially she wanted to hang on to Savannah—the person who loved her most after Daddy, the person who kept her from being alone.

"I love you, Sister," she said, quivering inside at the desperation in her voice. "I'll always love you."

"I know, Baby," Savannah murmured, kissing the top of her head. "We'll always have each other. That's all that matters."

Laurel sat down on the bottom step, dazed and weak,

her stunned gaze locked on the small pendant that dangled from her fist. And the feeling she had feared so badly all those years ago crept over her and into her, spreading through her like ink, opening her heart like a chasm that grew wider by the second.

The sister who had loved her, protected her, defined her world, was gone. And it didn't matter that she was thirty, or that there were other people in her life now who mattered. In that moment, as she sat there on the step, she was ten years old all over again, and she was alone. Her world had turned upside down, and the most precious thing in it had been snatched away, leaving nothing behind but a small heart of gold.

"I want to see her."

They sat in the parlor at Belle Rivière, Kenner, Danjermond, Laurel, and Caroline. An incongruous scene. The parlor with its soft pink walls and quietly elegant furnishings, a place of serenity and comfort, filled with brittle tension and people who had gathered to talk of a brutal, heinous crime. Men for whom this death was a part of their business, and family who couldn't reconcile the idea of one of their own being torn from their lives.

The sound of Mama Pearl weeping drifted in from the kitchen, breaking the silence that hung as Kenner and Danjermond exchanged a look. Laurel set her jaw and rose from the camelback sofa to pace.

Caroline sat at the other end of the sofa. Her aura of power and control had been snuffed out, doused by a tidal wave of shock and grief, leaving her powerless. A queen who had suddenly been stripped of her potency. For the first time since her brother had died she seemed completely at a loss, so stunned by the news that she wasn't even sure this was really happening. But of course it was. Savannah had been found murdered. That was the terrible reality.

Lifting a crumpled tissue to her eyes, Caroline looked up at Laurel, who paced the width of the Brussels carpet like a soldier, shoulders back, chin up. She had been this way when her daddy had died, as well, full of stubborn denial and anger. Ten years old, demanding she be taken to him, insisting that he wasn't dead.

She could remember too clearly the rage, the fear, the heartbreak, Vivian telling the girls to cry softly into their hankies like little ladies. Caroline had gone up to Savannah's room with them, and they had all lain on the bed and sobbed their hearts out together.

"I want to see her," Laurel said again.

Caroline caught her eye and shook her head sadly, reproachfully. "Laurel, darlin', don't . . ."

Laurel jerked away, clinging to her stubbornness like a life preserver. After her initial reaction to the news Kenner had brought, she had slammed the door on her grief, bottling it up, saving it for later. For now, she had to hang tough, she had to keep her head . . . or lose her mind altogether.

Kenner rose from the armchair, restless, unnerved by what he'd seen this morning out on Pony Bayou. If he lived to be a hundred, his sleep would forever be plagued by Annie Gerrard and Savannah Chandler, their bodies carved up like biology experiments, rotted and bloated by the effects of death and the merciless southern sun.

"I don't think that would be a very good idea," he murmured.

Laurel wheeled on him, ears pinned, eyes flashing fire. "You didn't think she was in any danger, either. You didn't think she would be anyplace but in bed with one of a hundred men," she said bitterly, stalking him across the carpet. Toe to toe with him, she glared up into his lean, hard face and narrow eyes. "Pardon me if I don't have a whole helluva lot of faith in what you think, Sheriff."

He glanced away from her, unable to meet the accusation in her eyes. His gaze landed on a graceful side table that held framed photographs of the Chandler girls, Savannah's senior year high school picture catching his eye. He had a daughter nearly that age.

"Next of kin has to make a positive ID," Laurel said, grasping hold of practicality for an excuse. She wasn't feeling practical. Desperation was like a wild thing inside her. She had to see her sister now, sooner than now. Maybe someone had made a mistake. Maybe it wasn't really her. Maybe Savannah wasn't really dead. God, she couldn't be dead. They had parted so angrily, left so many things unsaid. It just couldn't be true—

"We already have an ID, Laurel," Danjermond said, his smooth, low voice penetrating her thoughts. He sat in Caroline's throne, his masculine grace perfectly at home draped over rose damask. He met her gaze evenly. "Your stepfather came down to the funeral parlor."

He could just as well have slapped her. The idea of Ross Leighton's being the first of them to see Savannah appalled her. The bastard had dealt Savannah enough degradation in her life. He shouldn't have been allowed anywhere near her in her death. Fresh hot tears welled in Laurel's eyes, and she turned her back on the district attorney.

"Sheriff Kenner and I realize the grief you've been dealt, Laurel," he said, "but time is of the essence here if we're to catch your sister's murderer. We need to talk about this necklace you found. You were a prosecutor. You understand, don't you, Laurel?"

Yes, she understood. Business. Danjermond and Kenner would take her sister's death and boil it down to facts and figures. It was their job. It had been her job once too.

"The necklace was Savannah's," she said flatly. "She never took it off. This morning it was in my pocketbook."

"Do you have any idea how it might have gotten there?"

"I expect someone put it in there, but I didn't see it happen."

"You think the killer put it there?"

Killer. Her stomach churned at the word, sending sour bile up the back of her throat. She choked it down and snatched a quick, hard breath, rubbing a hand at the base of her throat. "No one else would have gotten it off

Savannah. It meant the world to her. She would never have willingly taken it off."

Danjermond rose and came around to face her, his hands in the pockets of his gray trousers. His expression was one she had seen in the courtroom a hundred times, a look she had honed to perfection herself—subtle disbelief, designed to rattle a witness. "You think the murderer took it off her and somehow slipped it into your handbag without your knowledge—for what purpose?"

The rush of anger was welcome. It distracted her, focused her attention on something she could affect the outcome of—an argument. She went to the Sheraton table and with jerky, angry movements, dug through the purse she had left there, tossing out Kleenex, Life Savers, a tampon. In one handful she scooped out the heart-shaped earring and the butterfly necklace and dumped them on a silver tray, then swung around to face Danjermond again. "For the same reason he made certain I found these."

The idea shook her to the core. A murderer, a psychopath had singled her out to send his trophies to. Why? To taunt, to challenge? She didn't want the challenge. She hadn't come here to be sucked into something twisted and sinister. The thought that someone was trying to do that made her want to cut and run as far as she could go, as fast as she could get there.

Danjermond pulled a slim gold pen out of his jacket pocket and poked at the items like a scientist, frowning. Kenner's eyes caught on the butterfly necklace, and he swore long and colorfully.

He shouldered Danjermond aside and bent to stare at the evidence Laurel Chandler had been carrying around in her handbag. "That was Annie Gerrard's. Tony gave it to her. He asked about it when he picked up her personal effects." Hard and sharp, his gaze cut to Laurel. "Goddammit, why didn't you bring this to me?"

"Why would I?" Laurel snapped back. "I found it in an envelope on the seat of my car. Why would I have assumed a serial killer had sent it to me? Why would I think you would do anything about it but laugh in my face?"

"Where'd you find the earring?" he demanded, knowing in his gut it belonged to another victim. The killer had kept a souvenir from each.

"I found it on the hall table. Savannah told me she brought it in from my car." She felt violated as she thought of it. The animal who had killed her sister, who had killed at least half a dozen women, had let himself into her car, touched things she touched, left behind mementos of his crimes. A shudder passed through her at the idea, chilling her to the marrow.

Kenner straightened, still swearing half under his breath. He couldn't believe this was happening in his parish. He ruled with an iron fist and an eagle eye. How could this have happened? He felt like a cleanliness fanatic who had turned a light on only to find roaches in his kitchen.

"I'm impounding the car," he declared, stalking across the room in search of a telephone. "We'll dust it for prints, have the lab boys from New Iberia go over it for trace evidence. And I'll take the handbag too."

Laurel nodded.

He snarled and turned to Caroline. "I need to use a phone, and I need to bag this jewelry as evidence. Have you got any Ziploc bags?"

"I don't know," she murmured, rising, shaken anew by this bizarre turn of events. She fussed with the black beads she wore, trying without success to think clearly. "They would be in the kitchen, I suppose," she mumbled, her gaze darting nervously to Laurel, to Kenner, to Danjermond, and back, as if one of them might have the answer. "Pearl would know. We'll ask Pearl."

They went out and down the hall. As the parlor door swung open then shut, the sound of Mama Pearl's wailing rose and fell. Laurel stood staring down at the cheap, gaudy earring with its chips of colored glass. Some woman had thought it was pretty, had worn it to feel special, had died wearing it. Had she died a brutal death, as Savannah had, suffering horribly, alone with her tormentor, begging for death? Tears rose in her eyes, in her throat. She held them at bay with sheer willpower.

"Why you, Laurel?" Danjermond's voice flowed over her like silk, the question burned like acid.

"I don't know," she whispered.

"Why would he single you out? Is he someone you know? Are you someone he wants?"

She flinched at the thought, struggled to hang on to her logic. "I—I d-don't fit the pattern."

"No, you don't." He hooked a finger beneath her chin and lifted her face, as if he thought he might see the answers in her eyes. "Does he want you to catch him, Laurel? Or does he want to show you he can't be caught?"

She met his steady green gaze, felt it probing, felt its power. She backed away from it, from him, shaking her head, feeling too raw for this kind of cross examination. "I don't know. I don't want to know."

He arched a brow. "You don't want to see him caught?"

"Of course I do," she said vehemently. She paced away from him again, raking a hand back through the hair she hadn't even combed yet today. "I want him caught," she said, her voice trembling with the need for it. "I want him tried and convicted and sentenced to a death worse than anything the courts would allow." She stopped and glared up at him, hating him for his calm control. "If I could, I'd be the one to drive the stake through his heart with my own two hands."

"You have to catch him first."

"That's Kenner's job, your job," Laurel said, backing down again mentally and physically. "Not mine."

Danjermond lifted the earring on the end of his fine gold pen, watching as it twisted in the air and caught the light like a Christmas ornament. "I don't think he would agree, Laurel."

Chapter
Twenty-Four

News of the murder cut through Bayou Breaux like a hurricane that left emotional devastation and uprooted fears in its wake. By noon there wasn't anyone in town who hadn't heard a telling and a retelling of Chad Garrett's story. It was the hot topic over comb-outs and manicures at Yvette's House of Style, where Savannah had had her nails done by Suzette Fourcade only days before. Suzette was near to inconsolable with hysterical grief over the loss of a friend and the idea of having touched someone who had since been killed. Yvette waited for the call to come from Prejean's asking her to do the grim honors of fixing Savannah's hair and makeup for her final public appearance before being laid to rest.

The story was served up with coffee and *beignets* at Madame Collette's, where Ruby Jeffcoat pontificated on the evils that awaited girls who wore skirts cut up to their fannies and no underwear, and Marvella Whatley refilled cups absently as her mind wandered back over the years she had served the Chandler girls rhubarb pie and Coca-Cola.

The old men on their bench in front of the hardware store shook their heads over the state of the world and watched the street with rheumy eyes that held anger and fear, and frustration that they were too old to protect their loved ones or to avenge them. And down at Collins Feed and Seed the boys all patted a dazed Ronnie Peltier on the shoulder and gathered in the break room without him to retell the tales of his and others' sexual exploits with Savannah. She was a legend among the male population of Partout Parish. If it hadn't been so gruesome, her sensational death would have seemed almost fitting.

All over town the details of the crime were broken down, scrutinized, analyzed, compared to the details of Annie Gerrard's death. Both women had been strangled. Both had been raped—or so everyone figured; the sheriff was keeping mum on that particular topic. Both had been subjected to the kind of horrors folks in Bayou Breaux had never dreamed one human being could put another through. But someone had dreamed it. Someone had done it. And rumor had it Savannah Chandler had been found with a page from a book clutched in her hand. A book called *Evil Illusions* by Jack Boudreaux.

"No one ever did know what to make of him," Clem Haskell said, stirring a third packet of sugar into his coffee. Doc Broussard was after him to cut calories and reduce the size of the spare tire around his middle, but he was a cane grower and hell would freeze over before anyone got him to put chemical sweetener in his coffee or anyplace else. The stuff caused cancer and who knew what all, he was certain. His spoon rattled against his saucer, and he took hold of the cup and raised it to his lips, wishing he had something stronger to fortify his nerves. Too bad Reverend Baldwin frowned on strong drink.

March Branford forked up a chunk of cherry pie and stared down at it, his appetite in revolt as images of dead women flashed behind his sunken eyes like scenes from a movie. "What kind of twisted mind writes trash the like of that? No normal God-fearing man," he ventured, putting the fork down to tug on one long earlobe. "The Lord never intended for man to profit from evil. That's the work of the devil, that's what that is."

"That it is, Deacon Branford."

Jimmy Lee nodded sagely, sadly, looking out on the audience of eavesdroppers in Madame Collette's as he ran his tongue along the jagged edges of two chipped caps. There wasn't a soul in the place who didn't look edgy. They'd had two murders in a matter of days. Annie Gerrard wasn't even in her tomb, and now poor Savannah Chandler was dead. People wanted an explanation. They wanted someone to be guilty. They wanted to be able to point a finger and say, "He did it," so they would be able to sleep nights. Jack Boudreaux seemed a prime candidate.

"Didn't I say the very same to y'all when last we met to pray?" he said, struggling to keep from lisping through the cracks in his dental work. "Those books are the product of an evil mind. The poisonous spewings of Satan."

Ken Powers knew all about poisonous spewings. His stepson Rick listened to rock groups with names like Megadeth and Slayer. Bunch of long-haired drug freaks who screamed out nothing but Satanic messages. And the kid was rotten to the core because of it. No respect for God or man. Sneaking pornographic magazines into the house and doing who-knew-what with that crowd of hoodlums he hung out with. They probably all read Jack Boudreaux's books and acted out the sex and violence with rock music blasting in the background.

"I knew the minute he bought that whore's house there was something strange about him," Ken said, planting his elbows on the table and leaning toward the reverend, his round, pink face shining with conviction. He was himself a good Christian man, and wanted everyone to know it. By God, him and Nan and the rest of their kids would show the whole town what upstanding people they were. Never mind the bad seed son Nan had spawned from her first husband.

"He bought the house of a harlot who died a violent death. He writes of evil and vileness and sin. Now one of our own fallen daughters is found dead with a page from one of his books. It's a sign, as sure as the sign of Lucifer himself."

Jimmy Lee bowed his head and folded his hands on the Formica tabletop. "Amen, Deacon Powers. If only our good Sheriff Kenner could be made to see the light."

While his deacons grumbled among themselves over who would have the honor of representing them with the sheriff, Jimmy Lee rubbed his tongue over his ruined teeth and wished Jack Boudreaux a nice trip to hell via Angola Penitentiary.

At that same moment Jack stood on the balcony at L'Amour, staring out at the bayou, suffering through a kind of hell Jimmy Lee Baldwin had never known—the hell of conscience. He had wandered the empty streets of town after leaving Laurel, trying to clear his head, and had ended up at Madame Collette's for a cup of coffee just as the breakfast crowd was coming in. Ruby Jeffcoat had wasted no time telling him the news, her eyes gleaming with malicious relish. Her sister Louise was a dispatcher in the sheriff's office and had it all firsthand. Some maniac had up and killed Savannah Chandler and left a page from one of Jack's books in her hand—stuck right under her thumb, so as not to blow away.

The rest of her juicy details had glanced off Jack. He didn't hear a word about how Chad Garrett had gotten sick and started a chain reaction with the deputies at the scene. He didn't hear Ruby's first sermon of the day on how women who behaved as whores were just asking for the kind of end Savannah Chandler had met. He didn't hear the clatter of coffee cups or the ring of flatware on china. He sat there at the counter, feeling as if he were having an out-of-body experience, and fragments of something Jimmy Lee Baldwin had said flashed in his head like lightning. ". . . *unstable minds . . . commit unspeakable acts . . .*"

Savannah was dead. All that wild, tormented spirit gone, wrung out and discarded like a rag. She had been so vibrant, so full of need and hate. He could hardly imagine all of that energy simply ceasing to exist.

No, not simply. There had been nothing simple about her death. It had been prolonged and hideous. ". . . *unstable minds . . . unspeakable acts . . .*" And she'd been found with a scrap of one of his books in her hand.

Stupidly, he wondered which book, which page, calling to mind a hundred scenes of death that had been telegraphed from his imagination down through his fingers and onto the pages of a book. Which one had Savannah been forced to endure?

Furious with himself, he stalked back into his bedroom and went to his desk. He didn't write to inspire; he wrote to entertain. He wrote to exorcise his own inner demons, not to lure others' out of hiding. He couldn't be held responsible because someone had used him as an excuse to commit murder. If it hadn't been his book, it would have been a song on the radio or a voice on television or a telepathic message from God. Blame could always be placed elsewhere.

Christ, he knew that, didn't he? He wasn't responsible; it was someone else's fault.

His writer's mind too easily conjured up an image of Savannah lying dead along the bayou, sightless eyes staring up at an unmerciful heaven. Swearing viciously, he swept an arm across his desk, sending debris flying— manuscript pages, scribbled notes, a royalty statement, pens, paper clips. He snatched up a stack of copies of *Evil Illusions* and hurled them one by one across the room as hard as he could throw them, knocking a water glass off his dresser and sending an etched glass lamp crashing to the cypress floor.

He didn't want Savannah Chandler in his head. He didn't want Laurel Chandler in his heart. He didn't want responsibility, couldn't handle it. He'd proven himself time and again. He was his father's son, the product of his mother's weakness and his old man's hate.

And he had another corpse on his conscience.

Clutching his hands over his head, he howled his

rage and his pain up at the plaster medallion on the ceiling.

Why? When he wanted nothing from anyone, when he had given up all hope of having the kind of life he had always dreamed of—why did he still get pulled in? He'd done his best to avoid emotional entanglements. He'd made it clear to everyone that he shouldn't be relied upon. Yet here he was, in it up to his ears. The frustration of it hardened and trembled inside him. Eyes wild, chest heaving, he swung around in search of something else to vent it on.

Laurel stood in the doorway.

Everything inside Jack went instantly still and soft at the sight of her. The anger that had cloaked him vaporized, leaving him feeling naked and vulnerable, his heart pumping too hard in his chest. She looked like a waif in her baggy jeans and rumpled T-shirt. Her eyes, so warm and blue, dominated her small, pale face.

"Savannah is dead," she whispered.

"I heard."

She crossed her arms and kicked herself for wishing he would come to her and wrap her up in his embrace. That was what she had come here for: comfort and to escape the sound of sobbing and the incessant ringing of the telephone. Reporters calling in search of a story, friends calling to express genuine sympathy, townspeople calling on the pretense of compassion to appease their morbid curiosity. She had come to escape the ghoulish bustle of cops searching her sister's room and hauling her car away and asking redundant questions until she wanted to scream. She had come in search of a moment's peace, but as her gaze scanned over the wreckage from Jack's rage, she had the sinking feeling she wasn't going to find any.

"I'm going down to Prejean's to see her."

"Jesus, Laurel . . ."

"I have to. She's—" She blinked hard and swallowed back the present tense, grimacing at the bitter taste. "She was my sister. I can't just let her go . . . alone . . ."

Tears glossed across her vision, blurring her image of Jack. She didn't want to let them fall, not yet. Not in front of anyone. Later, when night had come and she'd seen to all the duties she needed to, when she was alone. All alone . . . She had to be strong now, just like when Daddy had died. Only when Daddy had died, she had had Savannah to lean on.

Don't cry, Baby. Daddy's gone, but we'll always have each other.

She gulped a breath of air and tried to distract herself from the memory by making a mental list of the things she needed to do. See Savannah, see that the arrangements were being made, and that Mr. Prejean had the right clothes to put her in, and that pink roses were ordered. Pink roses were Savannah's favorite. She would want lots of them, with baby's breath and white satin ribbons.

The grief hit her broadside, like a battering ram, and staggered her, shattering the strength that had somehow managed to hold her up during the endless interview with Kenner and Danjermond. She fell to her knees amid the debris from Jack's desk and put her face in her hands, sobbing as it tore through her with talons like daggers.

"Oh, God, she's dead!"

Jack didn't give himself time to think about his own pain, his own needs, the distance he had meant to put between himself and Laurel. He couldn't stand by and watch her fall apart. He didn't have it in him to walk away. The love he never should have allowed to take root bound him there, drew him to her.

He knelt beside her and gathered her close, squeezing his eyes shut at the sound of her weeping. The sobs racked her body, making him acutely aware of how small she was, how fragile. He cradled her against him as if she were made of crystal, and stroked her hair and kissed her temple, and rocked her, crooning to her softly in a language he wasn't even sure she understood.

"I miss her so much!" Laurel choked the words out, a fist of regret and remorse lodged in her throat.

The feelings filled her, ached in her bones, in her muscles, like a virus. Loss. Such a terrible sense of loss, an emptiness as hard as steel inside her. It had been only a matter of hours, and yet the sense of loneliness was crushing.

Why? That one question arose again and again. Savannah's death seemed so senseless, so sadistic. What kind of God could allow such cruelty? *Why?* It was the same question she had asked twenty years ago, when her father had been taken away from her. No one had had an answer for it then, either.

That was perhaps the worst of it. She was a person with a logical, practical mind. If a thing made sense, had a reason behind it, she could understand at least. But things that struck from out of the blue defied logic. There was no reason, no explanation she might find some comfort in. That left her with nothing, nothing to cling to, not even hope, because in a world where anything might happen at any time, unpredictability shoved hope aside and left fear in its place.

"I hate this!" she whispered, her face pressed into Jack's shoulder. "I hate these feelings. God, I wish I'd never come back here!"

Jack rocked her, tightening his arms around her. "It wouldn't have mattered, angel. It wouldn't have changed anything."

Laurel thought of the trinkets the killer had left for her and wondered. Would he have sent them to someone else? Would he have killed some other woman's only sister?

Regardless of the answer, she was caught with the burden of guilt; someone died either way. Responsibility pressed down on her, just as it had in Scott County. She thought she would have given anything for the chance to get out, but she knew she wouldn't take the chance if it were offered. She was trapped by her own sense of duty and honor, stuck here in yet another nightmare.

"I'd undo it for you if I could," Jack said softly.

Jack, who claimed to be nobody's hero, would have gone back and changed history for her. Laurel slipped her arms around him and held on, knowing he wasn't the man to anchor her life to. But the need and the knowledge clashed inside her, and need won out for the moment.

"We can go away for a few days," he whispered. "Get away from it. I know a cabin over on Bayou Noir—"

"I can't." Laurel sat back a little, blinking up at him through her tears. She swiped a hand under her eyes and combed her hair back with her fingers. "I—I can't go anywhere. There are things to do—arrangements—" She swallowed hard and let the real reason come to the fore. "I have to find out who did this. Someone has to pay."

"And you have to be the one to catch him?" Jack said sharply, her sense of responsibility rubbing against the grain of his selfishness. He wanted her safe and all to himself, if not forever, then for a little while. "We've got a sheriff for that."

"The killer isn't sending the sheriff trophies from his conquests," she said bleakly. "He's sent me three."

The news hit Jack with the force of a baseball bat, leaving him incredulous, a little dizzy, a little sick. A murderer had singled her out. He sat back on his heels, his jaw slack, his fingers tight as he held her at arm's length. "He's sent you what?"

"An earring. I don't know whose. And Annie Gerrard's necklace. This morning I found a necklace of Savannah's in my pocketbook."

"Jesus Christ, Laurel! That's all the more reason to get the hell out!"

"That's what you'd do, Jack?" She arched a brow, studying him hard enough that he dropped his hands and glanced away. "Cut and run? I don't think so. For all you like to play it that way, I don't think you would. I know I can't."

"You'd rather end up with a silk scarf knotted around your throat?" he said brutally, his hands shaking at the idea of anyone's hurting her. The concern set everything inside him shaking. He never should have gotten involved with her. Of all the women he could have had, he'd fallen for the one who carried the weight of the world on her shoulders.

"I don't fit the pattern," she said. "I'm not promiscuous."

"You been sleeping with me, haven't you, *'tite chatte*?"

Laurel scowled at the sardonic edge in his voice. "That's different."

He gave an exaggerated shrug. "How is that different? You hardly know me, we go to bed together, we have sex. How is that different? You think this killer is gonna split hairs?"

"Stop it!" she snapped, hating him for belittling what they had had together. Even if he didn't want to call it love, it was more than sex. It certainly wasn't in the same category as what Savannah had shared with the likes of Ronnie Peltier and Jimmy Lee Baldwin. Her fingers curled over some of the papers he had swept off his desk in his rage, and she snatched them up and threw them at him, a gesture that was more symbolic of futility than fury.

"You amaze me," Jack said, grabbing hold of his anger with both hands. Better to be angry than afraid. Better to push her away than to cling to her when he knew he'd lose her in the end anyway. "You think you're Wonder Woman or something. Every bad thing that happens, you think you could have stopped it, you think you have to solve it, win the day for justice."

"Oh, excuse me for being a responsible person!"

"That's not responsibility, that's arrogance."

Laurel gasped as the jab stuck deep. "How dare you say that to me!" she said, her voice a trembling whisper that rose in pitch and volume with each word. "You sit up here in this private prison you bought yourself, drinking your liver into a knot, taking the blame for someone else ending their own life! Everything that happened was *your* fault—but, no, it's not really *your* fault because your father was a son of a bitch. Let's get him up here and we can have us a real finger-pointing session."

"We can't," he shouted, leaning over her.

"Why not?" she yelled, meeting his glare.

"Because I killed him!"

Like a marionette whose strings had been cut, Laurel plopped down on the floor amid the drift of manuscript pages and scribbled notes, stunned speechless.

"With my own two hands," Jack whispered, lifting his hands for examination, the long, elegant fingers spread wide as he turned them this way and that.

He rose slowly to his feet, a strange calm settling inside him. He had wanted to be rid of her. Wasn't that what he had told himself as he walked the deserted streets of town in the gray mist before dawn? Loving her hurt too much, and the end, which was inevitable, would be excruciating. This was his chance to make the break, his chance to show her once and for all just what he was. Then *she* could walk away from him.

"He hit Maman one time too many. He knocked me aside too many times without ever thinking one day I wouldn't be puny and weak."

He stared right through her, into his past, seeing it all once more—the shabby kitchen that smelled of grease, his mother cowering by the stained sink, Blackie going after her with his arm raised.

"I grabbed an iron skillet off the stove—it was the first thing that came to hand—and I hit him, smashed his skull in like an eggshell," he said flatly, as if he needed to unplug all emotion to be able to tell the story. "I don't think I meant to kill him," he said, though after all these years he still wasn't sure. Christ knew he had wished Blackie dead often enough, to put an end to the fear and the shame. "I just wanted him to stop hitting Maman. I was finally big enough to make him stop. That's all I wanted—for him to stop, for him to leave us alone."

He sniffed and held his breath a moment, fighting the rise of childhood feelings and gathering the old bitterness as fuel to go on. "And while my mother sat on the floor with blood running out of her broken nose, crying over this man who had abused her and her children for seventeen years, I dragged his body out to our *bâteau*. I took ol' Blackie for a ride into the swamp, tied an anchor around his middle, and dumped him in the deepest, darkest water I could find. No need for a decent burial when he was going straight to hell anyway. No need to drag the sheriff into it. We all just pretended he went out on a bender and never came back.

"That's the kind of man you think you fell in love with, sugar," he said, his voice low and rough. "You think you know me? You think you've got me pegged? You think mebbe there's something worth loving under all the scars? Think again. I killed my own father, drove my wife to suicide. I went from a profession where I got paid to lie and cheat to one that inspires twisted minds to commit murder." A bitter smile twisted his mouth. "Yeah, I'm a helluva guy, *chère*. You oughta fall in love with the like of me."

She didn't say a word, just sat there staring up at him with those wide eyes, and he knew he would have given anything to be the kind of man she needed. A bitter thought. A foolish thought. He was the last man she needed. Laurel deserved a champion, a knight in shining armor, not a jaded mercenary, not a man with ghosts. He was nothing but the worst kind of bastard. What he was doing to her now was absolute proof of that. *Dieu*, she'd just lost her sister, and here he was breaking her heart just to save what was left of his own.

One of the papers on the floor caught his eye, and he bent and grabbed it up, a sad parody of a smile pulling at his lips as he read his own handwriting. He had forgotten all about his ulterior motive for getting to know her. Such a poor ruse, he hadn't made more than a token effort to convince himself. But here it was in black and white, just in time to finish the job of cutting his own throat.

"Here," he murmured, handing it to her. "Here's the kind of man you come to in your hour of grief, angel. I'm sorry you didn' believe me the first time I told you."

Laurel didn't look at the piece of notebook paper she held in her hand. She stood up slowly on rubbery legs and watched Jack walk away from her. He went out onto the balcony without looking back, and she felt as though he had taken her heart out there with him. When she finally dropped her gaze to the carelessly scrawled notes, she knew he had pitched it off the balcony and into the murky waters of the bayou.

Laurel—obsessed with justice. A burden of guilt from past sins, real or imagined. Subdues femininity (unsuccessfully) with baggy clothes, etc. Represses sexuality (perfect conflict with prospective hero). A fascinating dichotomy of strength and fragility. Strong ties to dead father.

Need to get details on case that sent her over the edge. Were the accused guilty? Did she just want them to be? Why? Could write abuse into background.

A character profile. He'd been studying her, making notes for future reference. Her gaze fell to the floor, picking out the odd newspaper clippings among the sheets of typing paper and lined paper. The headlines jumped up at her as if they were three-dimensional: *Scott County Prosecutor Cries Wolf. Charges Dismissed, Chandler Resigns.*

She wouldn't have believed it was possible to hurt more than she already did. She would have been wrong. A new spring of pain bubbled up inside her. It was on a different level than the pain of losing Savannah, but it was no less sharp, no less acidic.

It wasn't as if he hadn't warned her, she thought, lashes beating back a fresh sheen of tears. It wasn't as if she hadn't warned herself. He wasn't the man for her. This wasn't the time. Too bad she had never gotten her heart to listen.

"Was it all grist for the mill, Jack?" she asked, going slowly, shakily to the open French doors. "The way we made love? The way you cried when you told me about Evie? The way Annie died, and Savannah—is that all plot for the next best-seller?" The thought sickened her. "Everything we did together, everything we—I— felt . . ." The words trailed off, the prospects too cruel to consider aloud.

"You missed your calling, Jack," she said bitterly. "You should have been an actor."

He said nothing in his own defense. He just stood
with his hands braced on the balcony railing, broad
shoulders hunched, gaze fixed on the bayou. His expression was hard, closed, remote, as if he had taken himself
to some dark place of solitude—or torment—within himself. Laurel wanted to hit him. She wanted to pound a
confession out of him, a confession that refuted the
damning evidence he had handed her himself. But she
didn't hit him, and he didn't recant a word of his testimony. There wasn't a judge in the country who wouldn't
have convicted him—for crimes of the heart, at the very
least.

"I guess you proved your point," she whispered.
"You're a bastard and a user. Bad for me."

She stepped out onto the balcony, appalled that the
day could be so beautiful, that the birds could be singing.
Below them, the bayou moved, a sluggish stream of
chocolate. Huey lay sleeping on the bank.

"I know that you can't help the things that shaped
you," she said, looking up at him through a watery haze
that made him seem more dream than real. "None of us
can. Savannah couldn't change the fact that our stepfather used her as his private whore. I can't change the
fact that I knew and never did anything about it," she
admitted, her voice choked with pain. "But you know
something, Jack? I'll be damned if I'll believe we don't
have the power within us to get past all that and be
something better.

"You put that in your book, Jack." Chin up, tears
streaming down her cheeks, she slipped the folded note-
paper in his hip pocket. "And at least be decent enough
to write me a happy ending."

Standing on pride alone, she turned and left him
. . . left L'Amour . . . left her heart in pieces.

Chapter
Twenty-Five

The summons to Beauvoir came before Laurel could leave the house for Prejean's. Vivian was on the brink of one of her spells, distraught over the news of Savannah's death. Dr. Broussard and Reverend Stipple had been sent for, but what she *really* needed was the comfort of having her only remaining child nearby.

Laurel's strongest urge was to say no. Vivian had disowned Savannah in life, had long ago ceased to love her. She couldn't keep from thinking that this was a ploy to gain attention, not a plea for sympathy or support. Vivian and Savannah had been rivals since the day of Savannah's birth. Why would that change after her death?

But the burden of guilt and family duty won out in the end. Laurel found herself in Caroline's burgundy BMW, turning up the tree-lined drive of her childhood home, cursing herself for being weak. She could almost envision Savannah looking down on her with disapproval. *Still scrambling for Mama's love, Baby? Aren't you pathetic.*

She cut the engine and lay her forehead against the

steering wheel for a moment, shutting her eyes against the exhaustion that pulled at her. She couldn't have felt more battered if someone had taken a club to her. Every part of her felt bruised, every cell of her body ached— her skin, her hair, her teeth, her muscles, her heart. Most especially her heart.

Images of Jack kept rising before her mind's eye, and her besieged brain struggled to rationalize in the name of self-preservation. He had pushed her away because he was afraid of hurting her. He had pushed her away because he was afraid of being hurt. But nothing she came up with could refute the evidence she had held in her hands.

God, he'd been studying her, jotting down notes, formulating theories as if she were nothing more than a fictitious character. The pain of that was incredible.

And still she wanted him to love her. The shame of that was absolute. She wanted him to come to her and tell her it was all a mistake, that he loved her, that he would be there for her as she struggled with the grief of loss. What a fool she was. She'd known from the start he wasn't the kind of man to depend on.

She sucked in a jerky breath, fighting the tears. She would get through this. She would get over it. She would get over him. She would find some way to be strong for Savannah.

Olive answered the door, looking appropriately dolorous, her skin as gray as her uniform, her eyes bleak. The maid led the way up the grand staircase and down the hall, and Laurel followed automatically, her mind on other times spent here.

Like ghosts, she heard the voices of her childhood— Savannah's wild laugh, her own shy giggle, Daddy promising he would come find them and tickle them silly. The memories bombarded her—good and bad. She remembered walking down this same hall to her mother's room the day of Daddy's funeral, and watching while Vivian applied her makeup artfully around her puffy red eyes.

You must endeavor to be a little lady, Laurel. You're a Chandler, and that's what's expected.

Then Vivian had loaded up on Valium and sat through the funeral in a daze, while her daughters struggled to weep gracefully into their handkerchiefs.

Vivian's spell of depression after Jefferson's death had lasted two months. Then Ross Leighton had begun worming his way into their lives.

Vivian's rooms comprised a spacious suite that saw a decorator from Lafayette once a year. The latest incarnation was a festival of floral chintz in shades of teal and peach. Olive escorted Laurel through the sitting room with its clutter of English antiques, knocked on the door to the bedroom, and opened it an inch when the muffled invitation came from within. Eyes downcast like a whipped dog, the maid slunk away as Laurel went in.

Her mother stood by the French doors, wrapped in teal silk, one arm banded across her middle, the other hand rubbing absently at the base of her throat. Opals glowed warmly on her earlobes. A ring with a stone the size of a sparrow's egg drew the eye to the hand pressed against her chest. She turned as Laurel entered the room, her features drawn tight, eyes looking dramatically sunken beneath the camouflage of dark eye shadow.

"Oh, Laurel, thank God you've come," she said, her voice reedy and strained. "I had to see you for myself."

"I'm here, Mama."

Vivian shook her head in disbelief and paced listlessly. "Savannah. I just can't accept what the sheriff had to say. That she was murdered. Like those other women, she was murdered. Strangled." She whispered the word as if it were profane, her right hand still rubbing at her throat. "Right here in our own backyard, practically. I swear, I can't bear the thought of it. The instant he told us, I nearly fainted. My throat constricted so, I could barely breathe. Ross had to bring my medication to the parlor, and I could hardly swallow it. He brought me straight to bed, but I couldn't rest until I'd seen you."

"I was on my way to the funeral home," Laurel said, toying with an arrangement of tiger lilies that filled a Dresden pitcher. "Would you like to come?"

Vivian gasped and sank down on the edge of the bed,

careful to keep her knees together and tilted properly, one hand expertly seeing that her robe was tucked just so. "Heavens, no! I just couldn't bear it. Not now. I'm simply not up to it. I—I'm just weak with shock from it all, and filled with such emotions—"

She broke off as her beautiful aquamarine eyes filled, plucked a lace-edged hankie out of her breast pocket, and blotted at the moisture.

Anger built inside Laurel as she watched from beneath her lashes. Her sister was dead, and their mother sat here doing a one-woman show for sympathy. Poor Vivian lost the daughter she never loved. Poor Vivian, so fragile, so sensitive, like something out of Tennessee Williams.

"I haven't had a spell in so long," she went on, twisting her handkerchief in her fingers. "But I can feel it coming on, stealing over me like a shadow of doom. You can't know how I dread it. It's a terrible thing."

"So is your daughter's murder," Laurel said tightly.

Her mother's eyes went wide. Her hands stilled in her lap. "Well, of course it is. It's horrible!"

Laurel turned and gave her a hard look of accusation. "But the most important thing is how it affects you. Right?"

"Laurel! How can you say such a thing to me?"

She shouldn't have. She knew she shouldn't have. Good girls didn't sass back. Ladies kept their opinions to themselves. But all the dictates from her upbringing couldn't hold back the rage she had stored inside her all these years. In her mind she could see Savannah lying dead, could hardly allow herself to imagine the way her sister had suffered. And here was Vivian, playing Blanche DuBois. Always the center of attention. Never mind who else might be in pain.

"It was just the same when Daddy was killed," she said, her voice trembling with the power of her emotions. "It wasn't a matter of all of us losing him. You had to turn it around so the focus was on *you,* so people flocked out here to check on *you,* so they all went around town saying 'Poor Vivian. She's in such a state.'"

"I *was* in such a state!" Vivian exclaimed, pushing to her feet. "I had lost my husband!"

"Well, it didn't take you long to find another one, did it?" Laurel snapped, the pains of childhood flowing through her like fresh, hot blood.

Her mother's eyes narrowed. "You still resent my marrying Ross. All the sacrifices I made for you and your sister, and all I get in return is bitterness and criticism."

"Daddy was barely cold in the ground!"

"He was dead," she said harshly. "He was gone and never coming back. I had to do something."

"You didn't have to bring *him* into this house, into Daddy's room, into our lives."

Into Savannah's bed. God, if it hadn't been for Ross Leighton, Savannah might still be alive. She might have grown up to fulfill all the potential he had crushed out from inside her.

"Ross was a fine catch," Vivian said defensively, fussing with the lace at the throat of her nightgown. "From a good family. Respected. Handsome. Wealthy in his own right. And willing to take on the children of another man. Not every man is willing to do that, you know. I can tell you, I was very grateful to have him come calling. I couldn't manage the plantation by myself. I was in such a weakened state after Jefferson died, I just didn't know if I'd ever function again."

And along came Ross Leighton. Like a vulture. Like a wolf scenting lambs. Willing to take on another man's children? Willing to take their innocence. Vivian had no idea just how willing Ross had been.

Because Laurel had never told her.

"Don't tell Mama. . . . No one will ever believe you. . . ."

She wheeled toward her mother to let the terrible secret loose at long last, but the words turned to concrete in her mouth. What good would it do now? Would it bring Savannah back? Would it give them back their childhood? Or would it only prolong the pain and mire them all more deeply in the muck of the past?

"I did what was best for all of us," Vivian said imperiously. "Not that you or your sister ever showed a moment's appreciation. Your father spoiled you both so.

"And Savannah was always jealous of any attention I might have garnered for myself from Jefferson. She was no different with Ross. I swear, I don't know where that girl got her wildness, her stubbornness. I'd say from Jefferson's side; Caroline is just that way, you know. But Caroline never had an interest in men—"

"Stop it!" Laurel shouted, her voice ripping across the quiet, elegant room. Her mother gaped at her, mouth working soundlessly, like a bass out of water. "It's none of your business who Aunt Caroline sleeps with. At least she's happy. At least she's not deluding herself into believing she needs to have a relationship with a man no matter what kind of slime he is."

"No, she's not like Savannah that way, is she?" Vivian said archly.

Her own anger simmering, she resumed her pacing along the length of the half-tester bed. "I don't know how many times I told her to be a lady. All the hours of training, of showing by example how a lady should comport herself, and none of it doing any good at all. She lived like a tramp—dressing like a slut, going off to bed with any man who crooked his finger. God, the shame of it was almost too much to bear!" she said bitterly. "And now she's killed because of it."

She shook her head, wrapping her arms around herself as if trying to physically hold herself together. A fresh sheen of tears glistened in her eyes as she resumed her pacing. "I don't know how I'll be able to hold my head up in town."

"That's all you care about?" Laurel demanded, stunned. "You think Savannah embarrassed you by falling prey to a psychopath?"

Vivian wheeled on her, eyes flashing. "That's not what I said!"

"Yes, it is! That's exactly what you said. Christ, she was your daughter!"

"Yes, she was my daughter," Vivian snapped, her face turning a mottled red as long-held feelings surfaced inside her. "And I will *never* understand how that could be, how God could give me a child like her—so beautiful on the outside and rotten to the core. I will never understand—"

"Because we kept it from you!" Laurel cried.

She clamped her hands on top of her head and turned around, everything within her in turmoil. She had tried to tamp the truth down inside her again, to bury it for all time, but it ripped loose and clawed its way free. Savannah was dead indirectly because of what Ross had made her into. *And because I kept the silence.*

The guilt was like a vise, twisting and twisting, crushing her. She couldn't change the past, but someone had to pay. Vivian couldn't go on living in her watercolor fantasies. Ross couldn't be allowed to escape the consequences of his actions. Justice had to be served somehow, some way.

Vivian watched her with wary eyes. She swiped a strand of ash blond hair back behind her ear in an impatient gesture. "What do you mean, 'kept it from me'? Kept what from me?"

"That Ross, the wonderful, well-bred, charitable knight in shining armor who swept in and rescued you, molested your daughter." She met her mother's shocked stare evenly, unblinking. "He used her, in the carnal sense, night after night, week after week, year after year."

"You're lying!" Vivian said on a gasp. She clutched a hand to her throat and swallowed twice, as if the words Laurel had spoken were gagging her. "That's a horrid lie! Why would you say such a thing?"

"Because it's the truth and because I'm sick to death of keeping it a secret!" Laurel advanced on her mother, her hands balled into tight, white-knuckled fists at her side. "Everything Savannah became is because of Ross Leighton. Now she's dead, and the one person who should be inconsolable is more concerned about her own image than her daughter's murder. I can't stand it!"

The slap connected solidly with her cheek and snapped her head to the side. She didn't try to block it or the second blow Vivian glanced off her shoulder. She deserved worse—not for what she had said to her mother, but for what she hadn't said all those years ago. Vivian shoved her, then backed away, her eyes wild, her lips twitching and trembling.

"You ungrateful little bitch!" she spat, her silky hair falling across her forehead and into her eyes. "Lies. That's all you have in you is lies! You lied to those people in Georgia, now you're lying to me! You hated Ross from day one. You'd do anything to hurt him!"

"Yes, I hate him. I hate him for taking my father's place, but I hate him more for taking my sister." The incredulity she had known during those years came back in a violent rush. How could their mother not have realized? How could that have gone on in her house without her suspecting? "Didn't you ever wonder where he was all those nights, Mama? Or were you just thankful he wasn't coming to your bed?"

Vivian's face washed white, and she brought a trembling hand up to press against her mouth, to press back the cry, to hold back the bile that rose in her throat. She'd never cared for sex. It was messy and revolting, all that grunting and sweating. She'd never questioned Ross's calm acceptance of her disinclination to share her bed. She'd never thought once of where he might be relieving his manly urges—as long as he was discreet, she didn't care. But with her own daughter?

No. It couldn't be. Things like that didn't happen in good families.

"No," she said softly, rejecting the possibility with her mind, with her body. She flung her hands out as if to push the idea away.

"Yes," Laurel insisted. "He came to her room two or three nights a week and had his way with her, whatever way he happened to be in a mood for—intercourse, oral sex—"

"Shut up! Shut up! I won't listen to this!" Vivian planted her hands over her ears to try to block out the ugly accusations. Laurel grabbed her wrists and jerked them down, shouting in her face.

"You *will* listen! You should have listened twenty years ago! If you had given a damn about anyone but yourself, you would have seen, you would have known," she said, the realization bringing tears of bitterness to cloud her vision. "I wouldn't have been afraid to tell you. I wouldn't have been afraid of losing your love. I was too young to know you weren't capable of giving any."

Her mother pulled back from her, reeling as if she had been struck full in the face. "I *always* loved you!"

"When it was convenient. When we were good little girls and no trouble. That's not love, Mama," Laurel murmured, despair choking her. "If you had loved us, you would have seen that Savannah needed help, that something was wrong, that Ross was a child molester."

"He wasn't!" He couldn't be. She couldn't bear the thought of it.

"Ross Leighton treated your daughter like a whore until she believed that was all she could ever be."

The red had crept back into Vivian's face, and her eyes bulged out like T-Grace Delahoussaye's. "I don't believe you. You're a vicious little liar. Get out. Get out of my house!" she screamed. "You're not my daughter! I don't have any daughters!"

Laurel gave her a long, hard stare. The hurt was sharp and deep, the disillusionment absolute. "You know something," she said quietly, the fury spent. "I wish to God that were true."

She left the room without looking back, without acknowledging the maid who had been eavesdropping in the hall. The more people who knew the truth, the better. Now that it was out of that terrible little black box of secrets inside her, Laurel had every intention of making Ross Leighton's perversity common knowledge in Partout Parish. He would never face the charges in court, but he could damn well face them every time he walked down a street or walked into a store or a restaurant. He would never do time inside the walls of a penitentiary; a sentence of public disgrace would have to suffice.

The front door swung open as Laurel came down the

grand staircase, and her stepfather ushered in Reverend Stipple.

"Laurel," Ross said, beaming one of his bland smiles up at her. "I'm so glad you could come for your mother's sake."

"You won't be." Laurel stepped down onto the polished tile and cut a glance at the minister, whose small eyes widened as he scented trouble like a mouse scenting the approach of cats. He took an instinctive step back, his bony hands fumbling to straighten his limp seersucker jacket. Laurel wondered what he would think of Ross Leighton now; if he would condemn, or in his weak and ineffectual way find some excuse to make it all right.

"I told her," she said, turning back to her stepfather.

Understanding dawned like shock in his eyes, but he pretended not to know, as he had pretended innocence all these years. "Told her what, darlin'?"

"The truth about the way you used my sister when she was too young to stop you. The truth about the way you turned her into a whore for your own personal enjoyment."

Reverend Stipple gasped at the words and their implications. Color crept up Ross's thick neck and into his face. He opened his mouth to protest, but Laurel cut him off with a sharp motion of her hand.

"Don't bother denying it while I'm standing here, you son of a bitch. I know what happened. I knew all along. I know what you turned her into. I know that she's dead because of it. I kept the silence all this time, kept that terrible secret inside me, let you get off scotfree. Not anymore," she promised, her voice trembling as badly as the rest of her.

"I told Vivian," she said, glaring up at him—hale and hearty with his suntan and his swept-back hair, the man of wealth and leisure in his green country club shirt and khaki slacks. He should have been the one cut up and left for dead. "I told Vivian, and I sincerely hope that she kills you."

Ross caught her arm as she started toward the door. "Laurel, wait—"

She jerked away from him with a violent move, her eyes burning hate into his. "No. I waited long enough."

Hatred boiling inside her like a poison, she left the house and left the grounds, the tires of the car flinging crushed shell up in its wake.

And Ross Leighton stood at the door of the mansion he had taken from another man, and watched her go, panic writhing like a snake in his gut.

"Jesus Christ, I hate religious fanatics." Kenner stretched back in his chair, trying to work out the kink between his shoulder blades. His gaze trailed the followers of The True Path out of the outer office and into the hall. He especially hated that they were men who lived around Bayou Breaux and were of an age to vote. That meant he had to give at least some token credence to what they had to say.

He turned his narrowed eyes on their ringleader, who still sat in the visitor's chair on the other side of the desk. Slick. That was the way he would describe Jimmy Lee Baldwin. He hated slick. Slick was damn near always trouble.

"So you think Jack Boudreaux strangled all them girls and cut 'em up for kicks?"

Jimmy Lee steepled his fingers and looked concerned, his tawny brows drawing into a little tent above his eyes, his tongue worrying over his chipped teeth. "You've heard the testimony of my deacons, Sheriff. I'm not alone in my suspicions."

"No. Well, other people have other suspicions." Kenner shook a cigarette out of the crumpled pack on his desk and searched in vain for his matches. Danjermond, who was standing against the row of file cabinets, came forward and offered him a light from a slim wand of twenty-four karat gold. The sheriff inhaled deeply and blew a stream of blue at the grimy ceiling, never taking his eyes off Baldwin. "What would you say if I told you someone came to me with a little story about you and Savannah Chandler?"

The preacher closed his eyes and shook his head as if he were in deep emotional pain. "Laurel," he murmured, privately cursing her to hell and gone. "She came to me with the same story. Apparently the workings of Savannah's sadly twisted mind. Heaven only knows where she might have come up with such tales of depravity. I fear she walked a dark path," he said with a dramatic sigh.

Kenner sniffed in derision and cleared his throat nosily. "I don't give a rat's ass what path she walked. Why would she have it in for you?"

Jimmy Lee cut the theatrics in half. The sheriff was not a patient man. "She was a regular at Frenchie's Landing. I would see that den of iniquity shut down."

"You ever tie a woman up to have sex with her?" Kenner asked bluntly.

"Sheriff! I am a man of God!"

"Plenty of shit gets done in the name of God. Did you ever?"

Jimmy Lee looked him square in the eye, as innocent as an altar boy. "I wouldn't dream of it."

But he was dreaming of it when he left the sheriff's office five minutes later. And the face of the woman bound beneath him was Laurel Chandler's.

Kenner stubbed his cigarette out in the overflowing ashtray and swung his chair around to face Danjermond, privately wondering how the district attorney could manage to stay looking like some cover boy from *GQ* while he looked and felt and smelled like a survivor of a jungle campaign. They had all been putting in hellish hours since the discovery of Annie Gerrard's body. The stress, the fatigue rolled off Danjermond like oil off Teflon.

"What do you think, Steve?" Kenner asked. "Is the preacher a pervert, or is Jack Boudreaux our man?"

Danjermond tightened his jaw at the nickname, but made no comment. Twisting his signet ring on his finger, he wandered to the window, noticing with irritation that the blind had been hung crooked. "I can't think that Annie Gerrard would have had anything to do with Bald-

win, considering he was trying to shut down her parents'
bar. He denies involvement with Savannah Chandler. No
one has actually seen them together. As to Savannah's
accusations—well, we know she was a woman who might
say or do anything. She may well have had a grudge
against him. We'll never know."

"And Boudreaux?"

"Certainly has the kind of imagination it would take.
If his books are anything to go by, he has a taste for
violence. He knew both women. He has a reputation as a
ladies' man."

"But no stories floating around about him tying them
up or getting rough."

Danjermond turned from the window, pinning the
sheriff with a penetrating stare. "He may have killed his
wife back in Houston, Sheriff Kenner," he said darkly.
"Is that rough enough for you?"

Frowning hard in thought, Kenner reached for the
pack of Camels on his desk, shook out the last one, and
dangled it from his lip. "Maybe we'd better have us a
little chat with Mr. Jack Boudreaux."

It was late afternoon by the time Laurel made it to
Prejean's Funeral Home. Aunt Caroline had tried to talk
her out of it. Hadn't the day been terrible enough?
Wouldn't it be better to wait until after the autopsy and
after Mr. Prejean had done his part? Wouldn't she rather
remember her sister as something other than the victim
of a brutal crime?

Yes, but she *was* the victim of a brutal crime, a crime
she had suffered through alone. Laurel couldn't bear the
thought of it. They had always had each other. Even
when Ross was making his secret visits to Savannah's
room, they had still shared the pain afterward. The idea
that her sister had faced her killer all alone, in the
swamp, where there was no one to hear her cries for
help, where there was no such thing as forgiveness, no
mercy . . .

Blinking back the tears, she pulled open the front

door and stepped into the hall, then gagged at the heavy perfume of carnations and Lemon Pledge. A vacuum cleaner was droning in the Serenity room. Mantovani seeped out of the speaker system—syrupy violins and twittering flutes.

Lawrence Prejean stepped out of his office and walked right to her, as if he had sensed her presence. He was a small man, not much taller than Laurel, spare and wiry with an elegance that had long made her think of him as a Cajun Fred Astaire. He had a thin layer of neatly combed dark hair and big, liquid brown eyes that were perpetually sympathetic.

"*Chérie,* I'm so sorry for your loss," he said softly, sliding an arm around her shoulders.

Laurel wondered dimly how, after so many losses, so many tragedies, he could still dispense such genuine feeling to the bereaved.

"Your Tante Caroline called to tell me you were coming down," he said, taking her by the hand. "Are you sure you want to do this, *chère?*"

"Yes."

"You know we are transporting her to Lafayette tonight?"

"Yes, I know. I just want to sit with her for a while. I need to see her."

She almost choked on the words, and shook her head, annoyed with herself. She had gone back to Belle Rivière from Beauvoir, taken a long shower, followed the dictates of Mama Pearl and lay down for a time, thinking all the while that she was composing herself, that she would be able to do this without breaking down. "*Comport yourself as a lady, Laurel. You're a Chandler; it's expected.*"

Prejean paused at the door to the embalming room and patted her hand consolingly, his big dark eyes as warm and deep as an ancient soul's. "She was your sister," he murmured. "Of course you need to see her. Of course you will cry. You need to grieve. Grieve deeply, *chérie.* There is no shame in that you loved your sister."

Her eyes glossed over, and she dug a hand into the

pocketbook she'd borrowed from Caroline to pull out a crumpled pink tissue.

He ushered her into the room with a gentle hand on her shoulder. The aromas of flowers and dust spray were replaced by medicinal and strongly antiseptic scents, reminiscent of a high school biology lab. And beneath the overpowering smell of formaldehyde and ammonia, the fetid stench of death lingered. The room was as neat as any operating room, as cold and sterile. The linoleum shone under the glare of fluorescent lights. In the center of the floor stood the table.

Laurel stood beside the draped figure, still managing to find some fragment of hope that it wouldn't be her sister. Prejean pulled a chrome-and-plastic chair over and situated it in a way that suggested he thought she might pass out.

"You're ready, *chère*?" he whispered. After all his years in this business, he seldom tried to contradict the wishes of those who were left behind. Death stirred up many needs, both bright and dark. Only the one experiencing the loss could know what those needs were and how they had to be met.

At Laurel's nod he slowly folded down the drape, uncovering only the dead woman's face and carefully arranging the sheet so that it covered the horrible discoloration on her throat.

Laurel took one long, painful look at her sister's face, swollen and distorted, and that small, irrational part of her mind tried to tell her that her most desperate hope was a reality. This wasn't Savannah. It couldn't be. Savannah was beautiful. Savannah had always been the pretty one, and she had always been the little mouse. This couldn't be Savannah's wild, silken mane, this dull, matted tangle of hair. This couldn't be Savannah's elegant, patrician face, this flat-featured, gray mask.

But another part of her brain, the logical, practical part, overruled with a harsh voice. *That's your sister. Your sister is dead. Dead. Dead. Dead* . . . Her gaze seemed to zoom in on the grotesquely distorted features, on the single gold earring still pinned to the right ear—a loop of brightly polished, hammered gold that hung from a smaller loop of braided gold wire. Savannah had had a pair made in New Orleans. A present to herself for her last birthday. *This is your sister, this ugly corpse. She's dead.* The truth filled her mind, the putrid smell of it filled her nostrils and throat.

With a weak, piteous sound mewing in her throat, she sank down into the plastic chair and bent over her knees, torn between the need to cry and the need to vomit. Prejean had anticipated the possibility and sat a stainless steel bucket beside the chair. He squatted down beside her and brushed cool, soft fingers against her cheek.

"Are you all right, *chérie*? Should I call someone to take you home?"

"No," she whispered, swallowing hard and willing her stomach to settle. "No, I just want to sit here for a while, if that's all right."

He patted the hand that gripped the arm of the chair. She was a brave little thing. "Stay as long as you need, *petite*. The sheriff will be coming later. If you need anything, there's a buzzer near the door."

Laurel nodded, knowing the procedure. She had always stood on the other side of it, where it looked logical and necessary. From where she sat now, her perceptions distorted by emotion, it seemed unbelievably cruel. Her sister had been taken from her, killed, and now the authorities would put her through the indignity of dissecting her body. The ME might find some crucial evidence that could solve the case and condemn the killer, she knew. But in that moment when grief threatened to swamp all else, she had a hard time accepting.

Questions from childhood drifted up through the layers of memory. Questions she had asked Savannah about death. *"Where did Daddy go, Sister? Do you think he's with the angels?"* They had been raised to believe in heaven and hell. But doubts had edged in on those beliefs from time to time, as they did for every child, for everyone. What if it wasn't true? What if life was all we had? Where would Savannah go? Savannah, so lost, so tormented. *Oh, please, God, let her find peace.*

Time slipped away as she sat there wondering, remembering, hurting, grieving. She let go of all the tears she had tried to hold on to, of all the pain she had been so afraid to feel. It all came pouring out in a torrent, in a storm that shook her and drained her. She knew Prejean checked on her once, but he left her alone, wise enough to realize she had to weather the onslaught of her grief alone. Alone, the way her sister had died.

She thought of that when the tears had all been cried. The way Savannah had died, the way Annie had died, the way their killer had chosen her to play games with.

"Does he want you to catch him, Laurel? Or does he want to show you he can't be caught?"

"I'll catch you, you bastard," she whispered, staring hard at the shrouded body on the table. "I'll catch you before you can put anyone else through this hell."

The "how" of that question eluded her for the moment. She had no jurisdiction here. Kenner wouldn't let her interfere. But the "how" was unimportant just now. The vow was important. She had come home to hide from the shame and the failure of Scott County, where justice had not prevailed. She had wanted to turn away from the challenge here. She had watched Danjermond poke through the pieces of jewelry with his slim gold pen and listened to him ask her questions in his smooth, calm voice, and she had wanted nothing more than to turn and run. But she couldn't.

Justice would win this time. It had to. If there was no justice, then all the suffering was for nothing. Senseless. Meaningless. There had to be justice. Even now, even too late, she wanted justice for Savannah.

"What are you trying to atone for, Laurel?" Dr. *Pritchard asked, tapping his pencil against his lips.*

For my silence. For my cowardice. For the past.

Justice was the way.

She couldn't just put the past behind her. It would never be forgotten. But there could be justice, and she would do everything in her power to get it, she vowed as old fears and old guilts settled inside her and melded and solidified into a new strength. She would fight for justice, and she would win it . . . or die trying.

They came for the body at seven-thirty. Kenner and a deputy. They would escort the hearse to Lafayette and witness the autopsy, which would be performed by a team of pathologists. Partout Parish had neither the budget nor the need for the kind of equipment necessary for detailed forensic work. Laurel went out into the hall and stood there, not able to watch them zip her sister into a body bag. But she stayed until she heard the cars drive away and Prejean came back out of the room.

"I'll bring some clothes for her tomorrow," she said, her heart like a weight in her chest. "And there's a necklace—something our father gave her. I'll have to get it back from the sheriff. She wouldn't want to go anywhere without it."

"I understand."

But would Kenner? she wondered as she walked out into an evening that smelled of fresh-mowed grass and approaching rain. The necklace was evidence.

How had it gotten into her pocketbook? When? These were questions she had gone over with the sheriff half the morning. She turned them over and over again as she leaned on the roof of the BMW and watched the thin stream of traffic pass on Huey Long Boulevard. She either had to have been separated from the bag when it happened or had to have been in a crowd. Someone could have come into the house, into her room, but that seemed far too risky for a killer as smart as this one.

If not for the fact that she was now on her way to an appointment with a coroner, Laurel knew she once might have suspected Savannah, and the shame of that curled inside her. She hadn't wanted to think about it, but her mind had sorted all the information into logical rows and columns, and, God help her, the theory had begun to take shape. Savannah—unstable, jealous, filled with hate for the image she had of herself as a whore, a violent temper simmering just beneath the surface. Savannah—her big sister, her protector, the one person in the world she loved above all.

"I'm sorry, Sister," she whispered, squeezing her raw, burning eyes shut against a fresh wave of guilt.

Think. She had to think. Savannah was gone; it wouldn't do any good to be sorry now.

The necklace could easily have been planted while she was in a crowded room. It would have been a simple matter of stepping close, making the drop, walking away. Easier than picking a pocket.

A crowd. Annie's wake. The thought that the killer might have come to his victim's wake was almost too ghoulish to contemplate. He might have stood in that room, as a hundred people had stood in that room, witnessed the kind of pain he had caused T-Grace and Ovide and their family, and felt what? Triumph? Amusement? It turned her stomach to think of it.

Half the town had crowded into the Serenity room to pay their respects to the Delahoussayes. She had wound her way through them, taking little notice of whom she passed or brushed up against. It literally could have been anyone.

A gleaming black, late-seventies Monte Carlo wheeled into Prejean's drive and pulled in behind the BMW. The tinted window on the driver's side slid down to reveal Leonce and a red leather interior. Beausoleil was playing on the tape deck, Michael Doucet's frenzied fiddle unmistakable. Leonce turned it down to a whine, then leaned out the window.

"Hey, *chère*, I heard about Savannah," he said, frowning beneath the brim of his Panama hat. "I'm really sorry."

"Thank you, Leonce."

"She was kinda wild, dat one, but me, I always liked her." He shrugged. On the leather-wrapped steering wheel his fingers absently drummed time to the music. "She just liked to pass a good time."

Laurel couldn't find a suitable comment. Savannah

had been far too complex to be described in one light sentence.

"Look," he said. "Why you don' come with me out to Frenchie's, *chère*? The bar's still closed, but there's a few of us gettin' together to talk and lift a few in Savannah's name. It might make you feel better. You can ride out with me."

She was standing beside a perfectly good car with the keys in her hand. Why would she want to ride with him?

Her mind was working like a prosecutor's. She started to chide herself for it, but stopped short. She had every reason to be cautious and suspicious. Six women were dead. A killer had singled her out. Leonce had known both Annie and Savannah. . . .

She looked at him, at the scar that slashed across his face, at the tilt of his dark eyebrows and the neatly trimmed Vandyke, scrambling to say something before the silence became strained. "Oh, I don't think so, Leonce. . . ."

"Come on," he cajoled, motioning her closer with a flick of his wrist. "It's good to talk through grief with friends."

"I appreciate the thought, but I'm really not up to it. It's been a very long, very trying day." That was the truth. She couldn't remember ever feeling as drained in quite the same way.

Leonce frowned and gunned the engine of the Monte Carlo. "Suit yourself."

"I should get home to Aunt Caroline. Thanks anyway."

Without another word, he pulled back into the car, buzzed the window up, and wheeled out of Prejean's circular drive. The Monte Carlo hit the street and pulled away with an impressive show of horsepower and what Laurel imagined was a small show of temper.

The wheels of her mind began to turn again. Leonce. Jack's friend. Ovide and T-Grace treated him like a son. He took care of the bar in their absence and dispensed beer, shots, taproom wisdom . . . and milk. He had guessed at her stomach problems and given her a glass of milk the night they found Annie. Not the attitude of a homicidal misogynist.

Yes, he had known Annie and Savannah, but did she have any reason to suspect he killed them? Or was it only his appearance that made her see him in a sinister light? The scar that cut across his face both fascinated and repulsed her, but it wasn't proof of guilt. And she knew only too well that looks could be deceiving.

She was too exhausted to think straight; her beleaguered brain kept dropping the ball. Shaking loose the key to the car's door, she blew out a breath and tried to think of only one thing instead of ten—Belle Rivière. She would be in bed within the hour. If she was very, very lucky, she wouldn't dream.

Chapter Twenty-Six

Laurel almost cried when she saw the Jaguar parked in Caroline's drive. Danjermond. He was the last thing she needed to cap off the evening.

No, she amended, as Vivian's white Mercedes pulled in behind her at a drunken angle to the curb. *This* was the last thing she needed.

Ross bolted from the car, leaving the door wide open, and hurried toward her as she climbed out of the BMW. He looked a mess for the first time in the twenty years she had known him. His steel gray pompadour had been dismantled by numerous finger-combings. His expression, usually bland and smugly satisfied, was taut, thinned by stress, and his eyes seemed wider and darker—desperate.

"Laurel, for God's sake, you've got to talk to Vivian," he said, grabbing for her arm.

She twisted away and took a step back. "I don't have anything more to say to my mother, and I certainly don't have anything to say to you."

"Jesus Christ," he mumbled, rubbing a hand across

his mouth. He glanced away from her, toward the sunset that bled over the western horizon. In that light, with a stubble of evening beard shadowing his cheeks and that haunted look in his eyes, he appeared like a drunk in dire need of a bottle. In fact, the aroma of whiskey clung to him like cologne, and he was weaving a little on his feet. "You don't know what you've done."

"No," she said, taking another step back. "This is about what *you* did, Ross. All I did was tell the truth. I should have told it twenty years ago."

"I can handle Stipple," he muttered, still not looking at her. "The man is spineless. Besides, why should anyone believe you?" He turned his head and glared at her, hatred flaring bright in his eyes for one frightening moment. Laurel wished to hell Kenner hadn't confiscated her pocketbook with the handgun in it.

"Everyone knows you've got a screw loose," he said. "Look what happened up in Georgia. It's Vivian I'm not sure about. She won't let me in her room."

"What difference should that make to you?" Laurel jeered, her temper overtaking her common sense. "Pervert that you are, you've probably got some little fifteen-year-old on the side."

He scowled at her, the thin, weak line of his mouth twisting. "It's not the sex, you stupid little bitch. I haven't slept with Vivian in years. Why would I? She's colder than a witch's tit. She never wanted it."

"And why would you care, when you could rape her daughter instead?"

His fleshy face turned scarlet, the color creeping up from his neck like a tide that pooled in his narrowed bloodshot eyes. "I never raped anybody. Savannah was a little prick-teaser—"

"She was thirteen!" Laurel shouted, not caring if her voice carried through every screen in the neighborhood.

Ross waved it off, making an impatient face. "It's in the past—"

"I'll say. Savannah is dead. You don't get more past tense than that."

"Well, I didn't kill her!"

"You as good as did, you snake! If you think for a minute I'm going to make this easy on you—"

"Just talk to your mother, for chrissake!" he bellowed, weaving toward her.

"Why?" Laurel demanded. "What do you need her for? She's all fresh out of teenage daughters for you to molest!"

"It's the money," he snapped, admitting in his drunken rage what had been a secret all these years. He stalked her up the walk toward the house. "It was always the money. Jefferson left everything in trust, that bastard. I can't touch a goddamn nickel without Vivian knowing."

Laurel wanted to laugh. She doubted Vivian would end up believing her in the end. Her mother had an amazing capacity for rationalization and denial. But in the meantime, at least, Ross was suffering. And he would suffer every time he wondered who else she might have told and whether or not they had believed her even a little bit. Cowards died a thousand deaths. Not one too many for Ross Leighton, as far as she was concerned.

He shook his head, his face contorting in disgust. "You're all the same. Whores and bitches to the end. That's what your sister was, you know," he said tauntingly, poking a finger at her, his upper body listing heavily to the right. "Hot-tailed little whore. She used to beg me for it."

If she had had her gun, she would have killed him. Without hesitation. Without remorse. Screw "a thousand deaths"—one bloody, agonizing death would have suited her fine. But she didn't have her gun. She could only stand on the walk in front of Belle Rivière, shaking with rage and hate.

"You son of a bitch!" she spat. "She was a child!"

Ross sneered at her. "Not when she was in bed with me."

Laurel didn't know what she might do. The idea of clawing his eyes out was dawning in her brain when the front door opened and Danjermond's voice cut through the tension.

"Is there a problem here, Laurel? Ross?"

"The problem *is* Ross," Laurel said tightly. She turned and brushed past the district attorney and went into the hall.

Caroline came out of the parlor wearing copper silk lounging pajamas, no jewelry, no makeup. She looked tiny and fragile—a word Laurel had never associated with her aunt.

"Is everything all right, darlin'?" she murmured. "I thought I heard you drive up."

Laurel heaved a sigh and snagged a hand back through her hair. "I'm as all right as I'm going to be."

"Did I hear Ross's voice?" she asked, puzzled.

"Yes, but don't worry about it, Aunt Caroline. He won't be staying."

Shades of her usual spunk glowed in Caroline's cheeks as she lifted her chin. "He certainly won't be. I haven't let that man in this house in twenty years. I'm not about to start tonight."

"What's Danjermond doing here?"

"He wanted to speak with you about—" She broke off, pressing a small hand to her mouth as she struggled to search her brain for a word that seemed less threatening than "murder." "The situation. He thought perhaps you'd be more relaxed without Sheriff Kenner present."

"Mmmm."

Needing something mundane to focus on, Laurel set her purse aside and shuffled through the mail that had been left for her on the hall table. It seemed wrong that she should have gotten mail on a day like this, but the post office didn't close down for personal tragedies. There was a letter from her attorney in Atlanta. A bill from the Ashland Heights Clinic. An ivory vellum envelope addressed in her mother's precise, elegant cursive. She tore it open carelessly and extracted an invitation.

The Partout Parish League of Women Voters
cordially invites you to a dinner with guest of honor
District Attorney Stephen Danjermond
Saturday evening, May the twenty-third

The Wisteria Golf and Country Club
Cocktails from 7 until 8
RSVP

The man himself came in from the lawn, looking mildly bemused. "I can't say that I've ever seen Ross in such a state," he said, his gaze falling squarely on Laurel. "Were he and Savannah close?"

"In a manner of speaking," Laurel grumbled, tossing the invitation back onto the table.

"Deputy Lawson is seeing him home. A stroke of luck that he was driving by."

"You wanted to speak to me, Mr. Danjermond?" she asked, too exhausted to suffer small talk. "I don't mean to be rude, but can we get on with it? I'd really like to see an end to this day."

He tipped his head like a prince granting her an audience and motioned for her to precede him into Caroline's office. He assumed the throne of command behind the feminine French desk. Somehow, it only made him look more masculine. In the amber light from the desk lamp his sexuality glowed around him like a holy aura.

Laurel wandered from bookshelf to bookshelf, too exhausted to be on her feet, too restless to sit. She felt his gaze follow her, but didn't turn to meet it.

"You had questions?" she prompted.

"How are you, Laurel?"

That one stopped her cold. She looked at him sideways. "How am I supposed to be? My sister is dead. Her killer is playing cat-and-mouse games with me. That's not my idea of a good time."

He studied her more intently than she would have cared for in the best of circumstances. As always, he made her feel underdressed and underfed, and she resisted the urge to reach up and check her hair, pushing her glasses up on her nose instead. Sitting behind the desk, he looked like the handsome, trustworthy anchor of a nightly news program, straight and tall, jacket cut to emphasize his shoulders, lighting set to show off his perfectly even features.

"You appear to be bearing up well, all things considered."

She gave a short, cynical laugh and walked from behind one green velvet wing chair to the other, wishing she smoked so she could at least have the comfort of something to do with her hands. "Don't be afraid to sound incredulous," she said dryly. "I am."

"I think you're stronger than you give yourself credit for," he murmured.

Laurel thought the strength was an illusion, that she was being held together by pressure and fear, but she didn't tell Danjermond that.

"What does this have to do with the case?" she asked.

"Strength is essential if you're going to help catch your sister's killer."

"I'll do whatever I have to do."

He hummed a note of approval as he toyed with his signet ring. "Have you come up with any theories as to how or when your sister's necklace was deposited in your pocketbook?"

Tugging methodically on her earlobe, she called up what possibilities she had come up with earlier and sorted through them to pick and choose which she would give to Danjermond. "I think it may have happened at Annie Gerrard's wake. Could have been anyone in the room."

Leonce came vividly to mind, but she wasn't ready to say his name. No evidence. She couldn't get a conviction without evidence. Danjermond wouldn't like to hear about hunches.

"What about earlier that day?" he said, rising. Sliding his hands into the pockets of his trousers, he rounded the desk and squared off with her across the cherrywood butler's table. "Who did you see that day?"

"Caroline, Mama Pearl, you, Kenner, Conroy Cooper. Jimmy Lee Baldwin—has Kenner spoken with him?"

"Yes, and he denies he's into kinky sex."

She gave a sniff. "What did you expect him to do—show you snapshots?"

"He denied the charges."

"He's lying," she said flatly.

Danjermond's broad shoulders lifted in an almost imperceptible shrug. "Perhaps Savannah was lying."

"No," Laurel insisted stubbornly.

"You can be that certain?"

"I saw the marks on her wrists." She dropped her gaze from his and did her best to concentrate on the polished surface of the table instead of the memory. "She told me the Revver liked to play whip-me, whip-me games."

"Did you see anyone else that day, that evening?" He let a pause hang in the air, then struck with precision, his gaze on her like radar. "Jack Boudreaux, for instance?"

Laurel held herself steady, called on old skills, played her cards close to her vest. "Why?"

He pursed his lips and contemplated word choices for a moment, almost seeming to relish the hint of the game in their conversation. "He was . . . well acquainted . . . with Annie Gerrard," he said carefully. "Who knows how well he knew your sister? He's a man with a dark mind and a violent past."

"Jack's no killer," Laurel stated unequivocally.

One dark brow sketched upward. "How can you be so sure of that, Laurel? You've known him how long? A week?" His logic was as cold as ice. When she didn't answer, his gaze narrowed, his voice softened. "Or is it that you think you know him so well? Intimately, perhaps?"

Laurel backed away from him, away from the heat of his body and the chill of his peridot eyes. "That's none of your damn business."

She retreated, he pursued—physically, verbally, psychologically. "Your sister was found with a page from one of his books in her hand."

"A plant," she said, putting a wing chair between them. "Only a fool would incriminate himself that way."

Danjermond ignored her supposition and pressed on. "He had a wife, you know—"

With one sharp slash of her hand, Laurel tried to end

the discussion. "That's it," she snapped, pushing past him and striding toward the door. She let him see the anger, but not the hurt. She didn't want to think of his knowing about Jack's tragedy. It was a violation, somehow. It was playing out of bounds. He fought slick and dirty. She would remember that if she ever had to face him in a courtroom. "I've had all I can stand for one day. This conversation is over. You know your way out."

She started out of the room, but his voice pulled on her like the strings of a puppet master as she neared the door. "Kenner wants to talk to him, but he didn't seem to be anywhere around today," he said softly. "I wonder why that is."

There could have been a hundred reasons for Jack's absence, Laurel thought as she stood with one hand gripping the door frame. He had certainly been around this morning—long enough to break her heart.

"Not everyone is what they seem, Laurel," Danjermond murmured. "You should know that. You should think about that."

"I do know," she said, staring straight ahead as his gaze bore into her back. "I also know that I lost my only sister today. I'd like to mourn in private, thank you."

She walked out on him and down the hall, but she had the feeling that his eyes followed her all the way upstairs.

Sleep came in fits and starts. The dreams were dark and relentless. Faces floated through her mind—Savannah's, Jack's, Jimmy Lee Baldwin's, and Leonce Comeau's. Danjermond's voice and visions of jewelry. The sick dread that came with thoughts of Ross and her mother and childhood nightmares.

At one-thirty Laurel gave up and switched on the bedside lamp, remembering the night Savannah had come in to check on her and had teased her about her poor taste in nightwear. She got up and changed from one baggy T-shirt to another, and came back to bed with a notepad and pen. Methodically she began making lists and notes, considering suspects and possibilities.

She was exhausted, body and soul, but she forced her mind to work. Like an athlete who had been away from the game with an injury, she felt every move was an effort, but the skills were still there. If she could hang on to the emotion, control her feelings, think clearly, the thoughts would flow easier and answers would come.

Baldwin. His name was a slash of capital letters at the top of the page. He was a liar and a con man. He had a temper. It wasn't difficult to imagine him getting rough with a woman. He had known Savannah, but what about Annie? Why would she have had anything to do with him? She might have gone to him on her parents' behalf. Might even have thought to discredit him with sex.

What about the other women? What about the jewelry? Could Baldwin have gotten Savannah's necklace into her purse without her knowledge? She would never have allowed him near enough when she had the bag with her, but Laurel remembered too clearly the feeling of being watched the night of Annie's wake, when she had come home and gone into the courtyard. The pocketbook had lain on a bench all night. Anyone might have crept into the garden . . .

. . . like Jack.

No. She wouldn't even consider it. Jack was no killer.

Did she think that because it was a fact, or because she loved him?

Loved. Past tense.

The thought triggered another memory. Conroy Cooper packing his bags. ". . . *I loved Savannah as best I could . . .*" *Loved.* Past tense. She scribbled the words down and lifted the pen to chew thoughtfully on the end of it. It was difficult to picture Cooper as a killer with his warm blue eyes and his warm molasses voice.

"Not everyone is what they seem, Laurel. . . ."

She sketched a question mark beside Cooper's name and went on.

Leonce made her uncomfortable, but not through any effort to do so. She felt vaguely guilty suspecting him.

He had helped out the Delahoussayes all he could. He'd done his best to be a friend to her. Did she have any real reason to question him?

He had known Annie and Savannah. The others? He traveled some to sing with bands in other towns. That gave him opportunity, but short of questioning him herself, she had no way of knowing the when or where of his schedule. He liked to flirt, but the scar had to turn more women off than on. What kind of resentment would build inside a man from that constant rejection? Enough to make him hate women? Enough to make him kill?

The thought of resentment brought thoughts of Ross, and she added his name to the list, but knew that had less to do with fact than feeling. Still, look what he'd gotten away with for twenty years with no one suspecting.

Laurel blew a breath of frustration up into her bangs as she contemplated the list. Six women were dead. There had to be something that linked someone to all the murders.

Then why hadn't anyone caught him?

A chill crept over her flesh as she stared out the French doors into the dark of the night.

Eyes shine in the night along the bayou. The creatures of the night stalk and prowl. In the shadows the predator waits, watches, savors thoughts of victory. Above, an adversary sits in the glow of a lamp and wonders. An answer may come, but none will believe the truth. Too clever, too cunning, instincts too sharp to make a mistake. Mistakes are made by the weak, by the desperate, by the victim. The predator's mind is clear and sharp. No clouds of grief. No distractions of conscience. Only thoughts of ultimate victory and the taste of blood.

Jack rose from his desk to wander through the halls and rooms of L'Amour, trying not to think, trying not to feel, not at all surprised when he found himself on the balcony, staring across at the light in Laurel's room. She wasn't sleeping. Again.

He couldn't blame her. He knew what it was to lose someone. He knew the automatic questions and recriminations. *Could I have done anything to stop it? How could I have let it happen?* He still asked himself those questions of Evie's death. Laurel would ask them in regard to Savannah. She would take the burden on her small shoulders. He had accused her of arrogance, but that wasn't it. Responsibility. In a world that seemed increasingly out of anyone's control, Laurel chose to take responsibility—not only for herself, but for everyone around her.

And he wanted responsibility for no one.

But he wanted her love.

Selfish through and through, Jack.

He wasn't meant for love. Had never been. The comforts and warmth of it were for other men, better men.

Even as he thought it, he heard Laurel's voice, trembling with pain and pride. "*. . . I'll be damned if we don't have the power to get past all that and be something better.*"

He had thought so, too, once. He'd been wrong. He wouldn't risk being wrong again. The pain was too much, too cruel, for a heart that had been broken too many times.

For another long moment he stood on the balcony and listened to thunder rumble in the distance and watched the light across the way. The air was heavy with the scent of rain and the feel of something dark and restless, like eyes in the night. For a second he thought he was being watched, but the restlessness was within him. A need for something he could never have, regret for things he couldn't change. Slowly, he turned and went back in to his bottle and his work with the idea of immersing himself in both.

And in the dark shadows along the bayou, a predator's eyes shine.

Chapter Twenty-Seven

Laurel woke with a start and headache. Her breath came in pants as the residual uneasiness of a dream hung around her. Eyes. She'd felt eyes on her, staring from the dark. But she hadn't been able to see the face, had only known somehow that it was familiar.

It was only a dream, but the uneasiness lingered as she sat up slowly and took stock of herself and the room around her. It had rained. The glass of the French doors was spattered with windblown droplets. The weather system had moved on, but gray still clung to the sky where dawn should have been.

She rubbed a hand over her face, groaning a bit as the headache kicked the backs of her eyeballs. She didn't know how long she had slept. An hour, maybe two. The state of the bedclothes was a testimony to how badly she had slept. The sheets were torn loose from the foot of the bed, the spread was rumpled. The notes she had made were scattered.

Grimacing at the taste of bitter dreams in her mouth, she forced herself to get up and gather the papers and the pen. She snatched them up, one by one, following a trail of them across the floor. She dug her glasses out of the folds of the bedspread, slipped them on, and combed her bangs back with her fingers. The gears of her brain strained into motion with much creaking and grinding, slipping and catching.

Baldwin, Cooper, Leonce, Ross. Names and question marks filled the pages. Notes, hunches, feelings. Hunches and feelings weren't admissible in a court of law. She knew that better than most people.

She walked to the French doors, shuffling the pages, brow furrowed as she retraced the ramblings of her mind. *Not Jack.* The bold declaration caught her eye, and her heart gave a traitorous thump. Bits of evidence tried to surface in her mind—his duality, the way he could seemingly appear and disappear at will, his past, his profession. And she beat every one of them back down.

Through the windowpanes she could see a bit of L'Amour—mysterious, shabby, standing alone on the bank of the bayou—and she let herself wonder for just a second what he was doing, whether he regretted the things he'd said to her, whether he wished as strongly as she did for the feel of familiar arms around him.

"You've known him how long? A week?"

God, was it only that? It seemed so much longer. The minutes and hours of the past week had somehow been elongated, magnified, and packed densely with experience and needs and fears. It seemed like forever, and at the same time, it could never be enough.

Not productive thinking. He didn't want her, didn't want any chance at a relationship. He wanted his solitude and his self-inflicted pain. He wanted to play the party animal, then go home to his empty prison. And when she was thinking straight, she knew it was just as well that she leave him to it. She needed time to heal— the old wounds and the new. She needed to get her world back on its axis and find her own place in it. A fresh start was what she needed, not a man with a past haunting him.

Craving a breath of fresh, rain-washed morning air to

clear her muzzy head, Laurel set the notes aside on a table, unlocked and swung open the doors, as she had done hundreds of times in her life.

A scream tore from her throat and she shot back across the room before her conscious mind could even register what she had seen. Hand clutched to a heart that was racing out of control, she forced her eyes to focus, forced her brain to accept the information sent to it.

Wound around the outside door handle was the limp, dead body of a cottonmouth snake.

"Goddamn it, I thought you were watching her, Deputy Pruitt!" Kenner bellowed.

The thin, pasty-faced young man stood on the balcony outside Laurel's room looking as if he were contemplating the advantages of jumping off.

"Yessir, I was, sir," he said, trying unsuccessfully to swallow the knot in his throat. His Adam's apple bobbed as his eyes darted to the body of the snake. Christ Almighty, he hated snakes. Everyone knew he hated snakes. Dollars to doughnuts, Kenner would make him unwrap this one from that handle and bag it as evidence. It looked to be a good four feet long. "I came on at four A.M., sir, and I swear I didn't see nothin'. I watched this house like a hawk."

Kenner swaggered to the door, reached down, and flicked a finger under the head of the snake. It flipped up, exposing the patches of cream color on the underside of the throat, and flopped back down, hitting the wood with a dull thud. Deputy Pruitt turned a little grayer. Kenner scowled. Goddamn prissy kid.

"You came on at four. Myers left. How long did the two of you stand around chewing the fat out by the cars?"

Despite his pallor, a hint of red managed to creep into the deputy's cheeks. "Just a while, sir. There wasn't nothin' goin' on. We'da heard."

Snarling, Kenner stepped up to his underling and jabbed the kid's sternum hard with a forefinger. "There sure as hell was *somethin'* going on, and the hell if you heard it," he growled.

Pruitt clenched his jaw against the need to wince. "Yessir," he mumbled, miserable.

"Bag that snake as evidence, and don't touch one other goddamn thing. If you so much as smudge a fingerprint, I'll cram that cottonmouth down your throat. Do you understand me, Deputy Pruitt?"

"Yessir." Too well. The image had him on the brink of gagging.

Kenner jerked away and turned back toward Laurel.

She sat on the bed in jeans and the T-shirt she had slept in. Caroline stood beside her, wrapped in a white silk robe, her expression the fierce look of a tiger whose cub had been threatened. Mama Pearl, a vision in red chenille, had planted her enormous bulk on a vanity stool that all but disappeared beneath her.

"Y'all didn't hear anything, didn't see anything?" Kenner asked.

Laurel answered, pushing herself to her feet. "For the fourth time, no."

She hadn't seen anything, hadn't heard anything. She had awakened haunted by the feeling of eyes on her. Her skin crawled.

Caroline crossed her arms and started pacing beside the bed, her lips pressed into a thin line of disapproval. She cut a dark, sharp look at Kenner. "This is intolerable, Sheriff. My niece is being tormented by a psychopath, and your office can't manage to do so much as to keep her safe inside a locked house?"

"The house was under surveillance, Miz Chandler."

"It would seem it was under better surveillance by the killer than by your deputies."

Kenner shot a look at Pruitt, who was damn near green as he fumbled with the long, rubbery body of the dead snake, then his gaze moved beyond. Beyond the balcony, beyond the courtyard, to the house Jack Boudreaux had taken. The house of a dead whore. It would have been a simple matter to watch for the change of shifts, slip into the garden, and climb the stairs. Wrap a dead cottonmouth around the door handle—just as the killer had done in *Blood Will Tell.*

He'd been scanning the collective works of Jack Boudreaux last night. After seeing the kind of stuff that rotted in the man's imagination, the sheriff had no difficulty picturing him as a killer.

"It won't happen again, ma'am," he growled. He dismissed Caroline and swung around to Deputy Wilson, a kid who had been built for the NFL but not blessed with speed. "Go see if Boudreaux is home. I want to have me a little talk with him downtown."

"Why?"

Laurel's question drew a narrow stare from the sheriff. "Why not?"

Because I know him. Because I've slept with him. The answers weren't going to dissuade Kenner.

He strode from the room with his linebacker at his heels, leaving the unhappy Pruitt to wrestle with the snake and the contents of his own stomach.

Mama Pearl rocked herself up from the little vanity chair and reached out to pat Laurel's arm. "You come on down to my kitchen, *chère.* I fix you tea and biscuits with honey."

"I'm sorry, Mama Pearl," she said, moving to the wardrobe to hunt for clothes. "I have to get down to the courthouse."

Caroline's brows snapped down over her dark eyes. "Laurel, you can't mean it! You've had no rest and one terrible shock after another! Stay here," she insisted, wrapping an arm around her niece's shoulders, keeping her from reaching for a blouse. She hugged Laurel hard, emotion suddenly clogging her throat. "Stay here with me, sweetheart," she whispered. "Please. I don't want you getting involved in this. I don't want to lose you, too."

Laurel looked from her aunt to the door, where the snake hung in a single loop and Deputy Pruitt leaned over the balcony disgracing himself all over the clematis vine. "I'm already in it, Aunt Caroline," she said softly. "And there's only one way out."

. . .

Jack woke with a pounding in his head and pounding on the front door of the house. He wished he could manage to ignore both. The banging in his head was the farewell gong of a substantial amount of Wild Turkey. The banging on the door turned out to be a very large deputy named Wilson, a man without sympathy or humor, who hauled him downtown to "have a little talk" with Sheriff Kenner.

Now he was sitting in a straight chair that had to be an antique from the Inquisition, staring across a scarred table at Kenner's ugly mug.

"Do you want a lawyer?"

"Do I need one?" Jack returned, arching a brow. "Am I being charged with something?"

"No. Should I be charging you?"

Depends, he thought. Heaven knew he was guilty of plenty. He dug a cigarette out of the breast pocket of his chambray shirt and dangled it from his lip. "You catch a lot of idiots with that question?"

"A few."

He struck a match and sucked crud deep into his lungs with the kind of greed known only to an ex-smoker fallen off the wagon.

"What do you call two thousand lawyers at the bottom of Lake Pontchartrain?" He left the appropriate pause for an answer, even though Kenner just sat there glaring at him. Jack flashed him a wry grin and blew twin streams of smoke out his nose. "A good start."

Kenner didn't so much as blink. "Where were you this morning about four o'clock?"

"In my bed, dead sound asleep."

"Interesting choice of words."

Jack shrugged expansively. "*C'est vrai.* Words are my life."

"Yeah," Kenner sniffed. "I've been reading some of your best-sellers, Jack. *Blood Will Tell. Evil Illusions.* You've got a sick mind."

"I'm just doing my job," Jack said glibly. He rubbed

the ruby stud in his earlobe between thumb and forefinger and gave Kenner a wry look. "You're the one plunked down six bucks for the pleasure of reading it."

"I got them from the library."

"Ouch." He winced. "No royalties from you."

Again Kenner ignored him, sticking to his own agenda. "Pretty reckless of you to steal ideas from your own work."

Dread hit Jack in the belly like a boot. *Mon Dieu*, not again, not another dead girl. He sat up straighter and abandoned his cigarette in the tin ashtray on the table. "What are you talkin' about?"

Kenner planted his elbows on the table and leaned forward, as well, jaw set, eyes narrowed. "I'm talking about slipping over to Belle Rivière while the deputies were changing shifts and wrapping a dead cottonmouth around the handle to Laurel Chandler's bedroom door."

A potent combination of rage and fear swirled through Jack, and he surged to his feet, sending the chair screeching back on the linoleum. A killer had been playing games with her. Apparently the game was not over. And on the heels of those feelings came the guilt that a truly twisted mind had borrowed from his imagination.

He stalked the cheerless box of the interrogation room with his shoulders braced and his hands jammed at the waist of his jeans, doing his best to fight it all off. What he really needed, he told himself, was to get the hell out of town for a while. Until the killer was behind bars. Until Laurel had packed up and moved on with her life.

He stopped his pacing in front of what had to be a two-way glass and stared hard at the reflection of himself, wondering who might be on the other side.

Kenner watched him with hard, cold eyes, trying to read every nuance of expression and movement. "You didn't happen to have anybody in bed with you can vouch for your whereabouts?"

Jack swung around to face him, brows pulling low over his eyes. "I wouldn't do anything to hurt Laurel."

The word "liar" rang like a gong in his head, but he

ignored it. He had pushed her out of his life for her own good, not to hurt her. And damn but he missed her already. The thought of her finding that snake, especially after everything else she had gone through, made him want to go to her to protect her. But he couldn't do that. Wouldn't. He was nobody's white knight.

Something thumped against the door, breaking his train of thought, then came the sound of an argument loud enough to be heard quite clearly.

"I don't give a damn what Sheriff Kenner had to say. Mr. Boudreaux has a right to counsel."

"But, ma'am—"

"Don't you 'But, ma'am' me, Deputy. I know my way around a police station, and I know my way around the law. Now open that door."

The door cracked open, and the massive Wilson stuck his head in, looking browbeaten and sheepish. "Excuse me, Sheriff Kenner?"

Kenner was out of his seat and fuming. He went to the door, grumbling under his breath, and grabbed the knob, just barely resisting the urge to slam it shut on Wilson's head.

"What's the problem here, Deputy?" He ground the whisper between his teeth like dust. "You can't keep one goddamn little slip of a woman out of my hair for five minutes?"

Laurel's voice sliced through the crack in the door like a knife. "Denying people their rights is serious business, Sheriff. I suggest you open that door at the risk of having me really tear through your hair—what's left of it."

Jack rubbed a hand across his mouth to hide his smile. She was a spitfire—no two ways about it. Most women in her situation would have been home, hiding. They certainly wouldn't have come to his rescue after the things he'd said and the way he'd behaved, he thought, the smile dying abruptly.

"I don't need a lawyer, angel," he said as Kenner stepped back and let her into the room.

She shot him a look that had turned better men to

ashes. "A man who represents himself has a fool for a client."

"Miz Chandler," Kenner began on a long, bone-weary sigh, "I'm speaking with Mr. Boudreaux about the case you're involved in. This is a conflict of interest."

"Not if I don't believe he did it," Laurel said. "Besides, this is a noncustodial interview, is it not?" She arched a brow above the rim of her oversize glasses, waiting for Kenner to refute the statement. "No charges are being filed. In the event it becomes a conflict of interest, I will recommend Mr. Boudreaux seek other representation."

Not giving a damn if either man wanted her there, Laurel marched across the room to the table and took the only seat that looked remotely comfortable—Kenner's. In her heart, she knew she wanted to be here for Jack, but she told herself she was really doing it for Savannah. The more she could find out about what was going on, the better her chance of helping crack the case, and the sooner it could all be laid to rest inside her.

Kenner scowled at her, then at Boudreaux, wishing fleetingly that he had listened to his old man way back when and gone into insurance. He pulled another straight chair out from the wall, set it at the end of the table, and planted one booted foot on the seat.

Jack slid lazily back down on the chair he had vacated and took up the smoldering butt of his cigarette between thumb and forefinger. He met Laurel's gaze for an instant and tried to read what she was thinking. She didn't flinch, didn't blink, didn't smile. There were delicate purple shadows beneath her eyes and a vulnerability around her mouth he was certain she didn't realize was there, but she didn't give him anything—except the impression that he'd hurt her badly and she was too damn proud to bend beneath the weight of it.

Kenner sniffed and cleared his throat rudely, digging a finger into the breast pocket of his uniform to pull a cigarette out from behind his badge. "So, you don't have an alibi for this morning."

Crushing out the stub of his smoke, Jack shot the sheriff a look. "Innocent people don't need alibis."

"You got an alibi for Wednesday night, ten 'til two A.M.?"

The question struck Laurel harder than it did Jack. Wednesday night. That had to be Savannah's time of death. Sometime between the hours of ten and two. Midnight. The dead of night. She felt chilled.

Wednesday night between ten and two. She had come home from dinner with Vivian around nine and gone to bed early because Aunt Caroline had been out with friends and Mama Pearl had been engrossed in a television movie. And something had jerked her from sleep in the middle of the night.

Oh, God, had she somehow known? Had she somehow sensed the moment her sister had passed from this world?

The thought left her feeling dizzy and weak.

Kenner deliberately ignored the sudden pallor of Laurel Chandler's skin. If she couldn't stand heat, she shouldn't have come into the kitchen. He kept his eyes on Jack and repeated the question.

Howling at the moon, Jack thought. Wandering the banks of the bayou, as he had done most of the day yesterday. Thinking, remembering, punishing himself. Alone.

"Where were you?" Kenner asked again.

"He was with me," Laurel said softly, her heart pounding in her breast. She'd seen the light come on in his window. It had to have been two or after, but he wasn't answering, and she wasn't going to let Kenner pin Savannah's murder on him. Jack couldn't have killed Savannah. He couldn't have brutally murdered a woman and then been moved to tears at the thought of the wife and child he had lost. He couldn't have killed Savannah and then come home and made love with her sister until dawn.

She glanced up at him. His face was a blank, unreadable mask, the scar on his chin looking almost silver under the harsh fluorescent light. "He was with me. We were together. All night."

Swell. Kenner ground his teeth as he ground out his cigarette. The lady lawyer was the alibi. Wasn't that neat? He regarded her for long, silent moments, trying to read a lie in the delicate pink tint of her cheeks. She had loved her sister. He couldn't imagine her lying to cover the murderer's ass. He turned back to Boudreaux. "Is that a fact?"

"Ah, me," Jack drawled, forcing the corners of his mouth up into a smug, cat-in-the-cream smile as he splayed his hands across his chest. "I'm not the kind of man to kiss and tell."

"You're a smartass, that's what you are," Kenner barked, his temper snapping. He leaned down in Boudreaux's face, his forefinger pointed like a pistol. "There's nothing I hate like a smartass. Poor little Cajun kid got himself a scholarship and went off to college. You think that makes you a big shot now? You think 'cause some bunch of New York dickheads pay you money to write trash, that makes you better than ever'body? I say you're still a smartass little swamp rat."

Laurel watched Jack's jaw tighten at the insult and knew Kenner had managed to strike a nerve more sensitive than most. "Does this character assassination have anything to do with the case, Sheriff?" she asked sharply. "Or are you just getting your jollies for the day?"

Kenner didn't take his eyes off Jack. "I'll tell you what it has to do with the case. I've got me a dead woman found with a page from one of ol' Jack's books in her stiff little hand. I've got a dead snake wrapped around a door handle—just like in one of Jack's books. What does that add up to, counselor?"

"It adds up to shit," Laurel declared. "He'd be a fool to implicate himself that way."

"Or a genius. What do you say, Jack? You think you're a genius?"

Jack lit another Marlboro and rolled his eyes, slouching back in his chair. "Jesus, Kenner, you've been watching too many Clint Eastwood movies."

"You ever tie a woman up to have sex with her?"

He held his gaze on Kenner's, avoiding even a glance at Laurel. "I don't have to force women to go to bed with me."

"No, but maybe you like it that way. Some men do."

"Speak for yourself," Jack said, tapping the ashtray. "You're the one wearing handcuffs on your belt. I'm only into violence on paper. Ask anyone who knows me."

Kenner's eyes glittered. "I'd ask your wife, but it so happens she's dead too."

"You son of a bitch."

In one move, Jack came up out of the chair and flung his cigarette down on the floor to singe a hole in the linoleum. Fury built and burned inside him like steam, searing his skin from the inside out. He would have given anything for the chance to tear Kenner's head off without running the risk of prosecution. His hands balled into tight, white-knuckled fists at his sides.

Kenner smiled coldly, careful to move back a step or two, just in case. "That's a nasty temper you have there, Jack," he drawled.

Jack's mouth twisted into a sneer. "Fuck you, Kenner. I'm outta here." Without a backward glance, he stormed from the interrogation room.

"You have a real way with people, Sheriff," Laurel said, brushing past Kenner on her way to the door.

"So does the killer," he growled as she walked out.

Laurel followed Jack through a side door that got them out of the building without being seen by any of the reporters hanging around inside the courthouse. She caught up with him on the sidewalk that cut through the park north of the courthouse, where the moss-draped canopy of live oak offered token protection from the choking heat. The sun had finally emerged to boil the humidity left over from the rain. As a result, the park was empty, air-conditioning being favored way above perspiration. As she hurried down the sidewalk, sweat pearled between her breasts and shoulder blades.

Jack stopped and wheeled on her suddenly, and she

brought herself up short, eyes wide at the fierce expression on his face.

"What the hell did you do that for?" he demanded.

Laurel brought her chin up defiantly. "I knew Kenner was questioning you. I couldn't envision you calling an attorney for anything other than to ask him if he had Prince Albert in a can," she said sarcastically.

"That's not what I'm talkin' about, sugar," he said, wagging a finger under her nose. "But while we're on the subject, I can damn well take care of myself."

"Yeah, that's what I like," Laurel drawled, rolling her eyes. "A show of gratitude."

"I'd be grateful if you'd keep that pretty little nose out of my business."

"Oh, never mind that you follow me all over creation, butting in whenever you damn well feel like it! Besides, this is my business, too, Jack," she said, jabbing her chest with a forefinger. "It's my sister who's dead. Her killer is going to pay if I have to catch him with my own two hands!"

"And what if *I* killed her? You just gave me an alibi!"

"You didn't," she declared stubbornly, blinking back the tears of frustration and fury that swam in her eyes.

"How do you know that?" Jack demanded. "You don' know shit about where I was that night!"

"I know where *I* was half that night, and I wasn't with a killer!"

"Because we had sex—"

She hauled back a fist and slugged him on the arm as hard as she could. "We made love, and don't you dare call it anything else. We made love, and you know it."

He *did* know it. She had given herself to him without reserve, and he had taken and cherished every minute of it. He had known that night she was everything he'd ever wanted, and the knowledge scared him bone-deep.

"Why'd you lie to Kenner?" he demanded.

"Because you weren't giving an answer—"

"Why?"

"—and Kenner and Danjermond are more than willing to pin this whole Strangler case on you if they can—"

"Why'd you lie, Laurel?" he taunted, driven by a need that terrified him, knowing damn well he shouldn't want to hear the answer. "Miss Law and Order," he sneered. "Miss Justice For All. Why'd you lie?"

"Because I love you!" she shouted, toe to toe with him.

"Oh, shit!" He jammed his hands on his waist, then planted them on top of his head and turned around in a circle. Panic snapped inside. Love. *Dieu*, the one thing he secretly always wanted, never deserved. The thing that held the most potential for pain. And Laurel was offering it to him—No. She was throwing it in his face, like a challenge, daring him to take it.

"Yeah, well I'm real happy about it, too, Jack," Laurel shot back, his reaction stinging like a slap in the face. She sniffed and wiped a hand under her nose. "I really need to fall in love right now. I really need to be in love with a man who's dedicated his life to self-torment."

"Then just drop it," Jack said cruelly. "I never meant to give you more than a good time."

"Oh, yeah, it's been a riot," Laurel sneered, fighting the tears so hard, her head was pounding like a triphammer. "It's been a regular Dr. Jekyll–Mr. Hyde laugh a minute!"

"Fair exchange for a little research," he said, driving the knife a little deeper and hating himself for it.

"I don't believe you," Laurel declared, grabbing onto that disbelief and clinging to it desperately, swinging it at him like a club. "I don't believe that's the only reason you've been with me."

"You can't dismiss evidence just because it doesn't suit you, counselor," he said coldly.

"Tell me there's a book," she demanded, glaring at him through her tears. She grabbed his arm and tried in vain to turn him toward her. "You look me in the eye, Jack Boudreaux, and tell me there's a book with me in it. You couldn't be that cruel and be so tender with me at the same time."

Jack had thought once that she would be a lousy poker player because he could see everything she felt in her eyes, but she was calling his bluff now with more guts than any man he'd ever faced across a table. And damned if he could do it. He couldn't look down into that earnest, beautiful face and tell her he'd never done anything but use her.

"I don't need this," he grumbled, waving her off.

"No, you don't, do you, Jack?" Laurel said, advancing as he backed away across the thin grass. "You'll be happy to sit in that dump of a house, beating on yourself for the next fifty years or until your liver gives out, whichever comes first. That's a helluva lot easier than taking a chance on finding something better."

"I don't deserve anything better."

"And what do I deserve?" she demanded. "You called me arrogant. How dare you presume to know what's best for me? And what a fool you are to take the blame for someone else's weakness. Evie needed help. She could have gotten it for herself. Other people could have tried to help her. It wasn't all on your shoulders, Jack. You're not the keeper of the world."

"Oh, Christ, that's rich! The pot calls the kettle black! You take everything on as if God Himself appointed you! You take the responsibility, you take the blame. Well, I've got news for you, sugar: I don' wanna be one of your great causes. Butt outta my life!"

Laurel stood there and watched him stalk away, so filled with pain and impotent fury that she couldn't seem to do anything but clench her muscles until she was trembling with it. "Damn," she muttered as a pair of tears slipped over her lashes and rolled down her cheeks. The wall of restraint cracked a little, and another drop of anger leaked out.

"Damn, damn, damn you, Jack Boudreaux!" she snarled under her breath.

Without a thought to the consequences, she turned and slammed her fist against the rough bark of a persimmon tree, scraping the thin skin on her knuckles and sending pain singing up her arm. Good. It was at least a better kind of pain than the one burning in her chest.

She loved him.

"Damn you, Jack," she whispered.

Blinking against the tears, she lifted her hand and sucked on her knuckles, trying to think of what to do next. She had more important things to think of than her broken heart. She would go home and regroup. Spend some time with Aunt Caroline while her brain turned over clues and theories, trying to come up with a picture of a killer. Not because she didn't believe anyone else could do it, but because she was bound by duty and love for a sister who had sheltered and cared for her.

Danjermond was waiting for her beside Caroline's BMW. His coffee brown jacket hung open, the sides pushed back. His hands were in his trouser pockets. But if his stance was casual, his mood was not. Laurel sensed a tension about him, humming around him like electricity in the air.

"I'm surprised at you, Laurel," he murmured, his gaze as sharp and steady as the beam of a laser.

The word "surprised" translated to "disappointed," but Laurel wasn't particularly interested in what Stephen Danjermond thought of her, one way or the other. He was Vivian's choice for her, not her own, and she was through trying to please her mother. Without a word of comment, she dug a hand into her bag to fish out the keys.

"You lied," he said flatly.

She didn't bother asking him how he knew any of what had happened in the interrogation room; she had been a prosecutor, had stood on the other side of two-way mirrors herself. Poker-faced, she looked up at him. "I was with Jack the night Savannah died."

"But not all night," he insisted. "I could hear the hesitation in your voice. Slight, but there. And Boudreaux's reaction—good, but guarded. He was surprised you would lie for him. So am I. I thought you were a purist. Justice by the book."

"Jack didn't kill Savannah," she said, sorting out the proper key and resisting the urge to back away from him.

"How do you know?" he queried softly. "Instinct? Would you know the killer if you looked him in the eye, Laurel?"

She stared up at him, remembering the feel of a gaze in her dreams. Eyes without a face. Memory stirred uneasily. "Perhaps."

"The way you knew the defendants in Scott County were guilty? Instinct, but no evidence. You need evidence, Laurel," he persisted. "No one will believe you without evidence."

The charges are being dismissed, Ms. Chandler . . . lack of sufficient evidence . . . You didn't do your job, Ms. Chandler. . . . You blew it. . . ." The voices echoed in her head, bringing with them shadows of the stress, the desperation. The combination threatened to shake her, but she held firm against them.

"You're the one who'll try this case if Kenner can make an arrest, Mr. Danjermond," she said evenly. "Maybe you should be more concerned about finding some evidence yourself instead of worrying about what I'm doing or not doing."

He said nothing while she unlocked the door to the BMW and pulled it open. She stepped around it on the pretense of tossing her handbag on the seat, but was just as glad to put the distance and the steel between them.

"Isn't that right?" she said, turning toward him once again.

He smiled slightly, a smile that for its strange perfection made the nerves tingle along the back of her neck.

"Oh, I am working on it, Laurel," he said softly, his green eyes shining as if he had sole possession of a wonderful secret. "Rest assured, I will have enough evidence to get a conviction. More than enough."

He let that promise ring in the air for a moment, then changed directions so smoothly and quickly, Laurel thought it was a wonder she didn't lose her balance. "Are you coming to the dinner tonight?"

"No," she said, appalled that he might think she would even consider it. "After all that's happened recently, I'm sure you understand that I'm not feeling up to it."

"Of course," he murmured, reaching into an inside jacket pocket to extract a long, slim cigar. He trimmed the end with a pocket-size device, snipping it cleanly and efficiently. "I understand completely. You've lost your sister. The best suspect we have is your lover—"

"What about Baldwin?" Laurel snapped, an odd, niggling feeling of panic fluttering in her stomach. "What about—"

"He isn't intelligent enough," Danjermond said sharply, cutting her off with his look as much as his words. His eyes were as bright and fervid as gemstones beneath the dark slash of his brows. "He's a petty con man with delusions of grandeur. Do you really believe he could have committed crime after crime without implicating himself?"

"I think there's enough evidence to suspect him—"

"Then you haven't been paying attention, Laurel." He shook his head almost imperceptibly, his eyes never letting go of hers. "You disappoint me," he whispered.

Slowly, almost sensuously, he slipped the tip of the cigar between his lips. Laurel watched, feeling oddly mesmerized, vaguely nervous. He dipped a hand into his pants pocket and came out not with the wafer-thin gold lighter, but with a book of matches.

A blood red book of matches.

Laurel caught only glimpses of black lacework script beneath his meticulously manicured fingers as he went about the ritual of lighting the cigar, but somehow, she didn't really need to see the name of the bar. Her heart pounded in her throat, in her head. Nausea swirled through her, and she curled her fingers tighter over the edge of the car door.

"This killer is brilliant, Laurel," he said softly, smoothly. "Brilliant, careful, strong. Strength is essential for success in his avocation. Strength of mind, strength of will."

Laurel said nothing. Her eyes were glued to the matchbook. Already her brain had hit the denial stage. It couldn't be. There was an explanation. He'd taken it from the purse Kenner had confiscated.

Or he was a killer and he wanted her to know it.

Danjermond puffed absently on his cigar, turning the folder of matches over in his fingers like a magician warming up for a sleight of hand routine.

"Le Mascarade," he murmured. "Where no one is quite what they seem. We all wear masks, don't we, Laurel?" he asked, lifting a brow. "The trick is finding out what lies behind them."

He slipped the matchbook back into his pocket and strolled away, cherry-scented smoke curling in his wake like mystical ribbons.

Chapter
Twenty-Eight

Laurel sank down sideways on the seat of the BMW, her feet still on the concrete of the parking lot. All the questions, all the fears, swirled in her brain like a dirty, foaming whirlpool. Fragments of conversations, of feelings, of thoughts, bobbed and floated on the rest, one rising above the others—*"You believe in evil, don't you, Laurel?"*

"Oh, God. Oh, God," she murmured as she sat there shaking, remembering the flash of lightning, the rumble of thunder, those clear green eyes on hers across the dinner table at Beauvoir. Tears flooded her eyes, and she raised her trembling hands to press them over her face.

It couldn't be. Stephen Danjermond was the district attorney. The League of Women Voters was giving him a dinner. He was sworn to uphold the law.

"Not everyone is what they seem, Laurel. You should know that. You should think about that."

"Oh, Jesus."

He was a man above suspicion. Above reproach. From one of the finest families in New Orleans. She had to be wrong. She had to be. The matchbook was a coincidence.

"Le Mascarade . . . We all wear masks, don't we, Laurel? The trick is finding out what lies behind them."

"Le Mascarade . . . It's the kind of place you don' wanna go, sugar. Unless you like leather and you're into S&M."

S&M. Bondage. Annie had been tied up. Savannah had been—

She clamped a hand over her mouth as her stomach heaved. She bent over, putting her head between her knees, and gagged as terrible images flashed behind her eyes. Blood. Pain. Screams. Delicate wrists straining against their bonds. Blood, so much blood. There was nothing in her stomach to come up, leaving her choking, coughing, as her body did its best to reject the possibilities that continued to bombard her.

Stephen Danjermond. District Attorney Danjermond. The golden boy. The favorite son. Destined for great things. What if he really was the killer?

And she was the only person who knew.

Laurel Chandler. The prosecutor who cried wolf.

No one would believe her. Not in a million years.

And he damn well knew it.

Cold sweat slicked over her face and her body, sour with the scent of fear. She dragged a hand across her forehead and into the damp tendrils of her bangs as she sat up and leaned heavily against the back of the seat. Funny, she thought, without the least trace of humor, she had actually been holding up pretty well in spite of everything. Savannah's death had devastated her heart, but mentally she had hung tough. Dr. Pritchard would have been proud. Until now. Stephen Danjermond had stood back and watched her fight, watched her hang on to her strength, then with no more effort than he would use to swat a fly, he stepped out of the shadows and knocked her legs completely out from under her.

"Right and strength don't always coincide."

Was that what this was all about? A contest between justice and the laws of nature? A game? *"Does he want*

*you to catch him, Laurel? Or does he want to show you
he can't be caught?"* Was this what he had been alluding
to when he had spoken of the two of them working together?

Or was she imagining things?

He had made her uncomfortable from the moment
they had first met, but that wasn't a crime. She'd been
under a terrible strain lately, hadn't eaten, hadn't slept.
As she sat there panting for breath in the stagnant heat,
the sounds of traffic rumbled in the background like the
murmur of a distant ocean, someone stepped out of
Bentley's Small Engine Shop across the street and hol-
lered for Sonny. An indigo bunting fluttered down from
the branches of a magnolia tree to poke its tiny head in
an abandoned McDonald's bag in hopeful search of
crumbs.

Beautiful little bird, she mused, her thoughts breaking into desultory chunks. It was decorated with gaudy,
bright colors—yellow-green, violet-blue, red—that made
it look as if an artist had flung paint at it with verve and
abandon. How could anything that pretty just happen
along for her to see if she had just been confronted by a
murderer?

"You haven't been paying attention, Laurel. . . ."

"This killer is brilliant. . . ."

"What do you think of sharks, Laurel?"

Sharks moved silently, swiftly, cutting through the
deep water, disturbing nothing until they struck. When
they killed, they killed brutally, efficiently, completely
without mercy or remorse.

"Serial killers are the sharks of our society. . . ."

Nerves trilled at the base of her neck. Memory
stirred. The feel of a gaze in the dark. Eyes without a
face. As her skin crawled and pebbled with goose bumps,
she turned and looked out through the windshield at the
courthouse. From a second-story window he looked
down at her, knowing she saw him, knowing she could
do nothing to stop him. She had no evidence he was a
killer.

"You need evidence to get a conviction, Laurel. . . ."

The matchbook was all she had that could link him in any way. There was no law against having a red book of matches. At any rate, he could throw them away, say he'd never had them. It would be her word against his. No question who would win that contest. Besides, she couldn't prove who had left the matches in her car. There was no doubt there would be many prints—her own, Savannah's, Jack's.

Jack's.

"The best suspect we have is your lover. . . . Rest assured, I will have enough evidence to get a conviction. More than enough."

"Oh, God," she whispered, her throat nearly closing on the words. "He's building a case against Jack."

The notion hit her like a sledgehammer, literally knocking her back in her seat. No one would have better access to hard evidence than the real killer. No one would be more adept at building a case than Stephen Danjermond. The politically ambitious Stephen Danjermond.

The sense of dread and disgust seeped deep into her bones as she considered the implications. What better feather in his cap than successfully convicting a man for crimes that had terrorized South Louisiana for a year and a half? A sensational crime. A sensational trial. A defendant whose name was known across America as the Master of the Macabre.

The press would have a field day. Danjermond would be hailed as a hero. Lifted up on the shoulders of the people of Acadiana without their ever suspecting there was blood on his hands. The case could take him anywhere he wanted to go.

Unless someone stopped him.

He'd thrown the gauntlet at her feet. He had chosen her as his adversary, then turned his back on her and sauntered away as if he didn't have a care in the world, as if he knew she didn't have a chance in hell of besting him. He was bigger, stronger, his mental skills honed to a razor's edge. He was admired and adored. And she was the woman who cried wolf, small and weak, her credibility in tatters, her battle skills rusted and atrophied. The only line of defense between Stephen Danjermond and his future.

If it would have done any good, she would have broken down and cried.

There was enough food in the house to feed an army platoon for a week. The rich, spicy aromas of gumbo and *etouffée* blended with the milder scents of sundry casseroles with a cream of mushroom soup base and the sweet perfumes of fresh fruit pies and spice cakes. Offerings from neighbors and friends who knew it wouldn't assuage the grief, but brought it anyway to show that they cared.

As she set her purse aside on the hall table, Laurel wondered absently if anyone had taken gumbo or spice cake out to Beauvoir. She supposed someone had. Not these same, salt-of-the-earth folk who had come to comfort Mama Pearl or Caroline's eclectic group of friends, but the women from the Junior League and the Hospital Auxiliary. They would have gone out to deliver their deviled eggs and chicken salad with a thin dose of sympathy. Pained smiles and sugarcoated apologies. Poor Vivian, how terrible to lose a daughter (but at least it was the tacky one). Poor Vivian, you must be beside yourself (it was such a scandalous death). And Vivian would nod and dab at her tears while casting glances askance to see if Ridilia Montrose had put dark meat in her chicken salad.

"Laurel?"

It was all Laurel could do to keep from jumping out of her skin, her nerves were strung so tight. She had hoped to slip upstairs unnoticed. Irrational as the thought was, she was sure her suspicions were written all over her face, that anyone who glanced at her would know what she was thinking and shake their heads sadly over her mental state.

Trying to compose herself, she bent her head and fussed with her glasses as Caroline stepped out of the parlor and came toward her with hands outstretched.

Laurel caught her aunt's fingertips and squeezed, but her gaze moved past Caroline to the tall, striking redhead in the dark yellow dress, who came only as far as the doorway.

"Laurel, this is Margaret Ascott," Caroline said, glancing between them. "Margaret is a friend of mine from Lafayette."

Margaret sent her a look of genuine sympathy from big dark eyes. "I'm so sorry about your sister, Laurel," she said in a low voice.

"Thank you," Laurel murmured, too distracted to care just what kind of friend Margaret could be. All she could think was that she envied Caroline her friend. She would have dearly loved to have someone she could spill her heart out to.

Caroline's brow furrowed in concern. "Darlin', you're as pale as milk. You must be exhausted. Come sit down."

She couldn't. There was no way she could sit down and pretend she didn't have knowledge of her sister's killer, nor could she tell them—or anyone—yet. No one would believe her, she thought, her heart thudding wildly. Caroline would say she was under too much stress. Others would point to Scott County and say this was just another wild conclusion of an unbalanced mind.

She needed a plan. She needed to make her brain work until all the rust had flaked off and the gears turned swiftly and smoothly.

"Actually, I was thinking I might just go upstairs and lie down," she said, amazed that she could sound so calm. It was as if her voice and her brain had detached from one another. Her gaze turned to the statuesque Ms. Ascott. "I don't mean to be rude—"

"Not at all," the woman assured her. "I came to offer support and a shoulder, not to be entertained."

"Do try to get some rest, sweetheart," Caroline said, stroking a hand down Laurel's cheek. "And have Pearl fix you a plate to take up with you. You need the nourishment, and she needs to fuss."

"I'll do that."

. . .

The afternoon passed like a year in prison. Laurel lay on the bed, her body begging for rest, her mind too overloaded and too exhausted to handle all the information it was trying to process. She forced herself to eat and struggled to keep the meal down as her thoughts dwelled on murder and broken trust. Every time she closed her eyes, she saw Danjermond. Too handsome, his features too perfect, his smile too symmetrical. Green eyes glowing into hers in a way that seemed not quite human.

But then, if he was what she thought he was, the word "human" didn't really apply. If he had done the things she suspected he had done, then he had no soul, no conscience, and that made him an animal. The most cunning, the most dangerous predator in nature's chain.

Needing facts, she paged through back issues of the Lafayette *Daily Advertiser* she had dug out of the recycling stacks in the garage, and read and reread everything she could find on the Bayou Strangler case. But the stories were thin compared with the police reports she was accustomed to poring over, and she knew that critical information would have been withheld for official reasons—to weed out real suspects from the poor crazies who confessed to every crime that came down the pike, to allow genuine perps the opportunity to trip themselves up by revealing information that wasn't known to the general public. While the accounts of the killings were gruesome enough, Laurel knew that details had been toned down and left out. The reality of a murder scene, the horror of a corpse that had been abandoned—

God, an abandoned corpse. She closed her eyes against the sting of fresh tears. That was what her vibrant, beautiful, complex sister had been reduced to by Stephen Danjermond.

He had to be stopped, and she had to be the one to do it.

She thought longingly of her Lady Smith languishing in the evidence room of the sheriff's office, thought fleetingly of simply planting it between Danjermond's eyes and pulling the trigger. But she knew it couldn't happen that way.

Proof. Evidence. Her brain hammered on the words, and she got up from the bed to pace and chew the ragged edge of her thumbnail. He would know better than to keep things around that might implicate him. But might his arrogance outstrip his common sense?

He thought he was invincible. She had seen it in his eyes and had read it in profiles of other serial killers. He had run unchecked long enough to make him believe no one could catch him. That kind of power, that feeling of omnipotence, could ultimately be his downfall.

Keeping souvenirs from victims was a common practice among serial killers. She knew he had kept pieces of jewelry because he had given them to her, drawing her into his web without her even knowing it. Did that mean there were more pieces hidden somewhere?

No one knew where the women had been killed, only that their bodies had been transported and dumped. The bodies had been found in five parishes. Most of the victims had been from a parish other than the one where their bodies were found. Clever. He would know that involving multiple jurisdictions would complicate the investigations.

But the most important question was where had the murders taken place. All in one spot, a lair where he felt safe to practice his depravity? If that was the case, she didn't have a prayer of finding it. The area involved encompassed thousands of acres, much of it the wildest, most remote swampland in the United States. It would be easier to find the proverbial needle.

He would never have risked killing in his own home. He would never have risked being seen entertaining any of the women he had killed. They weren't the kind of women a man of Stephen Danjermond's position and breeding would associate with. But he was the sort of man women would trust—handsome, well dressed, well educated. Everyone expected homicide to come wild-eyed and ugly, poor and desperate and ill bred.

"One never really knows what might hide behind ugliness or lurk in the heart of beauty."

His words rang in Laurel's head as she paced the confines of the room. To distract herself from the emotion that threatened to intrude on her thought processes, she did a mental inventory of the furniture and appointments. Then her gaze homed in on the invitation she had carried up with her from the hall table.

"The Partout Parish League of Women Voters cordially invites you to a dinner . . ."

With special guest the honorable Stephen Danjermond.

He probably hadn't killed anyone in his home, but he may well have brought his trophies there. And he would be out all evening, charming the people who would pave his way to greatness.

"What you're suggesting is against the law," she murmured, pulling methodically on her earlobe.

She had never broken a law in her life.

She had never lost a sister, either.

She stood there for a long while, chewing contemplatively on her thumbnail, waiting for some solid reason to dissuade her. Some overriding sense of right and wrong. None came, only the memory of Danjermond slipping that matchbook into his pocket and strolling away as if he hadn't a care in the world. He thought he was invincible. He believed he could literally get away with murder. If he succeeded, then there was no justice. No law could overrule that simple truth.

"You believe in evil, don't you, Laurel. . . . And good must triumph over evil. . . ."

"Yes, Mr. Danjermond," she whispered. "It must."

The sun was just setting when she finally slipped from the house. The dinner had begun at eight, but Laurel had been to enough functions of the same ilk to know that, while the baked Alaska would be served by nine, no one would get out of the Wisteria Club before ten-thirty. Then whoever would be usurping Vivian's role for the evening would whisk Danjermond off for drinks and inane small talk with the power elite of the group.

She calculated she would have a solid ninety minutes to search the house and get out safely. Provided she could escape from Belle Rivière without being caught.

Kenner had a deputy watching the house. The massive Wilson, who strolled the grounds like an overprotective Rottweiler. Laurel changed into dark jeans and a navy blue T-shirt, and prowled the balcony, waiting. In the end, Mama Pearl unwittingly came to her aid, coaxing the deputy into her kitchen for coffee and a piece of chocolate stack cake.

With Wilson out of the way, it was a simple matter of creeping down the outer staircase and slipping out a side gate.

Simple . . . except for the pair of eyes that followed her out of the courtyard and away from Belle Rivière.

Chapter Twenty-Nine

Danjermond lived in a gracious old brick house three doors down from Conroy Cooper. Once part of a row of town houses, the building was three stories high and very narrow. The rest of the town houses had long ago fallen to the wrecking ball, leaving this one tall, elegant reminder of more genteel times. The front yard was graced with a pair of live oak heavily festooned with Spanish moss. The interlaced branches of the trees created a bower above the walk to a front entrance that boasted a black lacquered front door with a fanlight above. The only light that glowed in the gathering darkness came from the brass carriage lamp beside the door.

Laurel cut through Cooper's lawn and approached Danjermond's house from the rear, where the properties gradually backed down to the bayou. The neighborhood was quiet, populated primarily by older couples whose families had long since grown up and moved on. There were a few lights in windows up and down the block, but no one was outside to see her slip through a break in the tall hedge that surrounded Danjermond's backyard.

As at Belle Rivière, the small backyard had been paved with bricks more than a century ago and turned into a private courtyard where a small stone fountain gurgled and bougainvillea climbed what was left of the original brick wall. But there the similarities ended. There was no jungle of plant life here, no clutter of tables and chairs. The area had a very spare, austere, almost vacant feel to it. A single black wrought-iron bench sat dead center, directly behind the house, facing the fountain.

Laurel envisioned Danjermond sitting there, staring, contemplating, saying nothing, and a chill crawled over her despite the heat of the night. She had the strangest feeling she could sense his presence here, even though she knew he was away, and the idea of going into his home brought a sense of dread that lay in her stomach like a stone. Her skin was clammy with sweat, making her T-shirt stick to her in spots, drawing mosquitoes that she waved away impatiently as she forced herself to take one step and then another toward the house. She didn't have a choice and didn't have much time. There was no sense in dawdling just because she was spooked.

Even as she thought it, something rustled in the shrubbery at the back of the courtyard, and she whirled, wide-eyed to find—Nothing. A bird. A squirrel. Her imagination. Heart thumping at the base of her throat, she turned back to the house.

The last of the day had faded to black. Stars were winking on in the sky above, but their pinpoints of light did nothing to illuminate the courtyard. The hedge, a thicket well over six feet high, blocked out the surrounding world so completely that Laurel had to remind herself there were people in their living rooms watching television on either side.

The back door was locked. There had been a time when no one in Bayou Breaux would have dreamed of locking a door. Then crime had seeped out from the cities. Then Stephen Danjermond had come.

Nibbling on her thumbnail, she descended the stairs, trying to think of an alternate way in. The front would be locked, as well, not that she could risk going in that way. He might have a spare key hidden somewhere, but she didn't want to take time to search for it. The first-floor windows were way out of her reach—but the ground-floor windows weren't.

Like many old homes in south Louisiana, this one had been built with a ground floor used for storage; the living areas were above, high enough to thwart the inevitable floodwaters from the bayou. Laurel checked the nearest window, finding it jammed shut and stuck with age and old paint. Quickly she moved around the other side of the stairs and found a door that led beneath the stoop and presumably into the storage space.

She closed her fingers around the knob and tried to turn it, her hand slipping, slick with sweat, and her fingers weak with nerves. She wiped her palm on the leg of her jeans and tried again, holding her breath as the hardware caught, stuck, then, with an extra twist, released, and the door creaked open, revealing a space that was thick with cobwebs and dust. And who knew what else, Laurel thought as she pulled a flashlight from the hip pocket of her jeans. Shaded, undisturbed space close to the bayou. There wouldn't be anything unusual in finding a copperhead or two . . . or more. The famous scene from *Raiders of the Lost Ark* slithered up from the depths of her memory and crawled over her skin.

Shuddering, she steeled herself, drew a deep breath, pushed the door open—and a hand clamped over her mouth from behind. An arm banded around her middle, as strong as steel, and hauled her back against a body that was lean, rock-solid, and indisputably male.

Panic exploded in Laurel, shooting adrenaline through her veins, pumping strength into her arms and legs. She tried to bolt, tried to kick, tried to jab back with her elbows all at once, twisting violently in her captor's grasp. He grunted as her heel connected with his shin, but her satisfaction was small and short-lived as he tightened his hold around her middle.

"Dammit, *'tite chatte*, be still!"

As quick as a heartbeat, all the fight in her froze into

paralyzing disbelief. Jack. She went limp with relief, and he loosened his hold in response. Jack had come. Jack had followed her. Jack had scared the living hell out of her.

She twisted around in his embrace and smacked his arm as hard as she could with the barrel of the flashlight. "You jackass!" she hissed under her breath. "You scared me near to death!"

Jack jumped back to avoid a second thumping. He scowled at her while he rubbed at the rising welt on his arm. "What the hell are you doin' here?" he demanded in a low, graveled voice.

Laurel gaped at him. "What the hell are *you* doing here?"

"I followed you," he admitted grudgingly, still cursing himself for it. If he hadn't been standing on the balcony when she had crept down the back steps of Belle Rivière . . . If he hadn't wondered why and let his imagination loose on the possibilities . . . If he had a lick of sense and the brains God gave a goat, he would have gone back in and sat down to work.

"Why?" she demanded, glaring up at him with fire in her eyes and a smudge of dirt on the tip of her upturned nose.

"'Cause even money said you were gettin' into trouble."

"So what do you care if I am?" Laurel snapped. "You looked me in face this morning and told me in no uncertain terms you didn't want me in your life. Make up your mind, Jack. You want me or you don't. You're in this or you're out."

He set his jaw and looked past her into the dark of the storage space beneath the house. He wanted her. That wasn't the question, had never been the question. The question was whether he deserved her, whether he dared take the chance to find out. The answers eluded him still, lay inside him beneath a dark cloak he hadn't worked up the courage to look beneath. It was easier not to, simpler to let her walk out of his life.

"Why are you here?" he asked again, bringing his gaze back to her.

"Because I think I know who killed my sister." Fingers tightening around the flashlight, eyes locked hard on his face, she took the plunge. "Stephen Danjermond."

Laurel held her breath, waiting for his reaction, praying he would believe her, certain he would not. Needing him to believe her.

Jack blew out a breath, tunneled his fingers back through his hair, feeling as if she had knocked him upside the head with a lead pipe. "Danjermond!" he murmured, incredulous. "He's the goddamn district attorney!"

Laurel's jaw tightened against the first wave of hurt. "I know what he is. I know exactly what he is."

He swore long and fluently. "Why? Why do you think he's the one?"

"Because he all but told me he was," she said, turning her back to him to shine her light under the stairs and to hide the disappointment. "I don't have time to explain. You either believe me or you don't. Either way, I'm going into this house to look for some kind of proof."

Jack took in the rigid set of her shoulders—so slim, so delicate, too often carrying a burden that would have crushed a lesser person. He thought of the burden that had broken her. She had lost everything—her career, her credibility, her husband—because she had believed justice had to win at all cost. And she would fight this fight, too, alone if she had to, because she believed.

Dieu, he couldn't remember if he had ever believed in anything except looking out for his own hide.

Laurel suffered through the silence, refusing to let her heart break. She didn't have the time for it now. Later, after she had figured out a way to nail Danjermond, then she would let herself deal with this. Now she had a job to do, and if she had to do it alone, so be it.

She choked down the knot in her throat and took a step into the space beneath the house. Jack clamped a hand over her shoulder and held her back.

"Hey, gimme that light, sugar. There might be snakes under here."

They emerged on the first floor of the house, through a door tucked under the main staircase. Laurel toed her sneakers off to avoid tracking in sand and dirt. Jack, in boots, opted to dust them off on the legs of his jeans.

The house was dark, all looming shapes and sinister shadows. The smells of lemon polish and cherry-tinted tobacco hung in the air. A grandfather clock marked time in the hall, ticking the seconds away, chiming the half hour. Nine-thirty.

"What are we looking for?" Jack whispered, keeping a hand on Laurel's shoulder in deference to the protective instincts rising up in him.

"Trophies," she answered, shining the narrow beam of the flashlight on the floor. Her breath hitched in her throat as something tall caught her eye near the front door, then seeped back out as she recognized the lines of a coat tree. "We know the killer kept jewelry as souvenirs because he sent some to me. I'm betting he kept some for himself, as well, as keepsakes."

"Jesus."

She shone the light into the front room—a parlor—backed out of the doorway, and continued down the hall, past a small, elegant dining room, past a bathroom. A blocky ginger cat bolted out of the next room and streaked past them, growling, making a beeline for the stairs. Laurel paused to get her heartbeat down from warp speed, then ducked into the room the cat had dashed out of.

Bookcases covered the walls from the twelve-foot-high ceiling to the polished pine floor. Here the scent of Danjermond's expensive tobacco was strongest, the furniture polish an undertone to leather chairs and the faintly musty-sweet aroma of old books. A handsome cherrywood partners desk dominated the floor space. Behind it, an entertainment center held shelves of sophisticated stereo equipment.

Laurel skirted around a wing chair and took a look at the desktop. She was afraid they would have to go upstairs to find what they were looking for. Her instincts told her a killer would keep items that secret, that meaningful, in his most private lair—his bedroom. But a study was a close second, and Danjermond obviously spent a good deal of time in his.

Slipping around behind the desk, she cast the light over a humidor, a tray of correspondence, an immaculate blotter. She slipped two fingers into a brass pull and tried the slim center drawer.

"Damn, it's locked."

Jack scanned the bookshelves by the thin, silvery light from the window, looking for a title that might strike a spark. People often hid things in books. Hollowed them out and filled them with treasures and secrets. He assumed there wasn't time to look through all of them, and searched for a likely candidate instead, but there were no titles like *The Naked and the Damned*, or *The Quick and the Dead*, or anything else that might appeal to a twisted sense of humor, just tomes on law and order, classics, poetry.

"Where's Danjermond?" he asked, pulling out a Conan Doyle first edition.

Laurel tried the drawers on the file cabinet with no luck. "Being toasted by the royal order of pearls and girdles as a man they can all look up to and entrust with the chastity of their debutante daughters."

She checked her watch and swore. They needed to find something soon, before the window of opportunity slid closed and locked them inside.

"What happens if we find something?" Jack asked as they climbed to the next floor. "We don' exactly have a warrant, angel. No judge in the country would allow evidence obtained this illegally."

"All I need is one piece," Laurel said as she crept past a small guest room and a linen closet. "Just one damning piece I can take to Kenner and hit him over the head with. He's probably turning your place upside down as we speak. Danjermond is trying to build a case against you."

The news stopped Jack in his tracks. He had thought Kenner was grasping at straws, not that anyone in the courthouse had a plan. "He really thinks he can pin Savannah's murder on me? And Annie's?"

"And four others. And don't think he won't figure out a way to do it. The man has a mind a Celtic knot would envy."

And she was going to stop him, Jack thought, watching as she shone the beam of the flashlight into another bedroom. She was risking what was left of her reputation in part to protect him.

"Bingo," she muttered, and pushed open the door.

The bed gave the room away as Danjermond's—a massive mahogany tester with ornately carved posts and a black velvet spread trimmed in gold. The underside of the canopy was decorated with shirred white silk. Jack reached up and pushed a section of fabric aside to reveal a mirror. Laurel said nothing to his arched brow. She didn't allow her mind to form any kind of scenario. She didn't want to imagine where Danjermond's sexual tastes ran, because one thought would lead to the next and on to delicate wrists bound and screams for mercy and—

"You okay, sugar?" Jack whispered. He didn't even try to stop himself from slipping his arms around her and pulling her back against him. She had gone pale too suddenly, her eyes were too wide. He bent his head and pressed a kiss to her temple. "Come on. We'll take a look and get the hell outta here."

Like every other room they had seen, this one was immaculate, impeccably decorated, strangely cold-feeling, as if no one lived here—or the one who did was not human. Not a thing was out of place. Every piece of furniture looked to be worth a fortune. Nothing appeared to have sentimental value. There were no photos of family, no small mementos of his youth. A barrister's bookcase between the windows held another collection of antique books—first editions of erotica that dated back to

Renaissance Europe. But there was nothing else, no jewelry, no weapons, no photographs.

Disappointment pressed down on Laurel. She should have known better than to think Danjermond would make it easy on her, but she had hoped just the same. Now that hope slipped through her grasp like sand. If the evidence she needed wasn't here, then it could be anywhere in the Atchafalaya.

And with the disappointment came self-doubt. What if she was wrong? What if the killer was Baldwin or Leonce? Or Cooper. Or some nameless, faceless stranger.

No. She closed the last drawer on the dresser and straightened, rubbing her fingers against her temples. She wasn't wrong. She hadn't been wrong in Scott County; she wasn't wrong now. Stephen Danjermond was a killer. She knew it, could feel it, had always felt something like wariness around him. He was a killer, and he thought he was going to get away with murder.

If she couldn't find one way to implicate him, Laurel knew she would have to find another. And the longer it took her, the more women would die, and the more time Danjermond would have to build a case to frame Jack. The longer he would play his game with her, destroying her credibility, her confidence, her belief in a higher law than survival of the fittest.

"Let's go," she whispered, hooking a finger through a belt loop on Jack's Levi's and pulling him away from the bookcase. "I doubt he'll be back from the dinner for another hour, but we can't take chances."

"Wait."

It hit Jack like an epiphany as the flashlight beam swept across the collection of books. A trio bound in faded red leather sitting side by side by side on the upper lefthand shelf. *Le Petite Mort*, volumes one, two, and three. *The Little Death.* His eyes had scanned past them when he'd first realized that this collection was erotica. Erotica—the little death—orgasm. The title hadn't seemed out of place, but as he guided the beam of the light across the bindings, a sixth sense tensed in his gut like a fist.

Gently, he lifted the glass panel on the front of the case and slid it back out of the way. The three volumes came off the shelf as one.

Emotion lodged like a rock in Laurel's throat as she shone the light across a tangle of earrings and necklaces. More than six pieces. Many more. Tears swimming in her eyes, she reached in with a tweezers she'd pulled from her pocket and lifted out a heavy gold earring. A large circle of hammered gold hanging from a smaller loop of finely braided strands of antiqued gold.

"This is—" The present tense stuck to the roof of her mouth. She swallowed it back and tried again. "This was Savannah's. She had a pair made in New Orleans. A present to herself for her birthday. She was wearing the other one when they found her."

Jack kept his silence as they watched the gold hoop turn and catch the light. There were no words adequate to assuage the kind of pain he heard in Laurel's voice. Gently he closed the box and returned it to its spot in the bookcase. Laurel just stood there, her gaze locked on the earring, her eyes bleak. Jack slid an arm around her shoulders and bent his head down close to hers.

"You got him, sugar," he whispered. "That's the best you can do."

"I wish it were enough," Laurel murmured. She handed him the flashlight and dropped the earring into a Ziploc bag.

They took a final, quick glance around the room to make certain they had left everything as they had found it, then Laurel led the way into the hall, flashlight scanning the floor ahead of them—until the beam fell on a pair of polished black dress shoes.

Her first instinct was to run, but there was nowhere to run to. He stood between them and the head of the stairs. Behind her, Jack swore under his breath.

Slowly, she raised the flashlight, up the sharp, flawless crease of his black tuxedo trousers and higher, until the beam spotlighted the barrel of a silencer on the nine-millimeter gun he held in one hand and the pair of small canvas sneakers he held in the other.

"I believe these are yours, Laurel," he said in that same even tone of voice he used for all occasions. "How considerate of you to take them off."

"What happened with the League of Women Voters?" she asked, a small, detached part of her mind wondering how she could be so calm. Her pulse rate had gone off the chart. Her blood pounded so in her ears, it was a wonder she could hear herself think. And she asked him about his dinner as if this were the most normal of circumstances.

Danjermond frowned in the pale wash of light that reached his face. "In view of all the recent tragedies, I thought it inappropriate to allow the festivities to go on as they would have ordinarily."

"A selfless gesture."

A small, feline smile tucked up the corners of his mouth. "I can be a very generous man, when I so choose."

"Did you 'so choose' with my sister?" Laurel asked bitterly, her voice trembling with rage, her left hand trembling badly enough to rattle the small plastic bag holding Savannah's earring.

He tipped his head in reproach, but his gaze went directly to the evidence, and anger rolled off him like steam. "Now, Laurel, you don't really expect me to answer that, do you?"

"You might as well," Jack said, easing out from behind Laurel. He took a step and then another to Danjermond's left, forcing him to split his attention between them. "You're gonna kill us now, too—right?"

Danjermond contemplated the question for a moment, finally deciding to be magnanimous and gift them with an answer. "*C'est vrai*, Jack, as you might say yourself. It isn't quite according to my plan, but adjustments must sometimes be made."

"Sorry to inconvenience you," Jack drawled sarcastically, moving a little forward, enough to draw Danjermond's full concern. The barrel of the gun swung even with his chest.

"That's near enough, Jack. Don't come any closer."

"Or what?" Jack taunted. "You'll shoot? You're gonna shoot anyway. Dead is dead."

"No, no, *mon ami*," Danjermond purred. "There is most definitely a difference between instant death and being made to beg for death. Your cooperation could make all the difference for Miss Chandler."

Jack weighed the odds, not liking them. Danjermond was going to kill them. Heaven only knew what kind of hell he planned to put them through. He had murdered at least six women, brutally, horribly. Jack had long ago ceased to care what happened to himself, but the idea of anything like that happening to Laurel was intolerable. He couldn't just stand helpless and let it happen. Damned if he was going to play into the hands of a madman.

Never looking away from Danjermond, he grabbed Laurel's arm and jerked it up, shining the beam of the flashlight in Danjermond's face, at the same time, twisting his body to shield Laurel and push her off to the side.

Danjermond swore and flung an arm up to block the blinding light. The gun bucked once in his hand, the explosion reduced to a soft thump by the silencer. A fat Chinese vase on a stand along the wall shattered, sending shards of porcelain flying in all directions. Water cascaded to the floor, and delphinium stems fell like pickup sticks.

Propelled by Jack's weight, Laurel stumbled sideways and fell to her knees. The flashlight sailed out of her grip and crashed to the floor, rolling out of her reach, sending bands of bright amber light tumbling across the wall. She tried to scramble after it, but Jack was in front of her and Danjermond beyond him, and it was clear the battle between them was far from over.

Head down, Jack lunged for Danjermond, planting a shoulder hard in the man's chest. The two of them landed on the polished wood floor, inches from the head of the stairs, and began wrestling for control of the gun. Jack grabbed hold of Danjermond's arm and slammed it hard against the floor, but before he could shake the pistol loose, a white-hot pain sliced into his right side, momentarily shorting out all thought and all strength.

Howling in pain and rage, he twisted around to find the source. A jagged shard of white porcelain protruded from his side with Danjermond's hand closed around it, as if around the hilt of a knife, blood oozing from between his fingers. As Jack reached to dislodge the impromptu knife, Danjermond swung the gun up and slammed it into his temple.

In the blink of an eye, the balance of power shifted. Jack struggled to stay on top as his consciousness dimmed, but the world dipped and tilted beneath him. Then suddenly they were rolling, through the water, over the broken vase, pain biting, muscles burning, heart pumping.

He managed to get a hand on Danjermond's throat and started to squeeze, but the district attorney was on top of him and pulling back, pulling away. Bringing the gun up. Laurel might have screamed, but all Jack was certain of was the sharp *thunk!* of a bullet splintering the floor millimeters from his head as he let go of Danjermond's windpipe and knocked his gun hand to the side.

Jack surged up, twisting to reverse their positions. Pain sliced through his side, pounded in his head. He blocked it out and fought on adrenaline, groping, pushing, turning. Danjermond's back slammed into the delicately turned white balusters that guarded the second-story landing, cracking one and shaking the whole balustrade, and the gun came out of his hand and skidded across the floor, toward the stairs.

Laurel jumped back as they wrestled, wanting to do something, but the gun was on the other side of the hall and the flashlight was somewhere on the floor beneath the tangle of grunting, straining male bodies. She glanced around for something, anything, she might use as a weapon, finding nothing, but she wasn't about to settle for prayer.

Do something, do something, she chanted mentally, turning and running back into Danjermond's bedroom.

She had to find a weapon, something she could hit him with, stab him with, anything.

Jack slammed a left into Danjermond's face, then lunged up and forward, scrambling for the gun that was just out of his reach. His fingertips hit the silencer, and it spun away, sliding through the pool of water and broken glass. Focused, intent, he grabbed for it again and closed his fingers around the rubber grip on the handle.

At the same time, Danjermond found the flashlight. As Jack came up and started to swing around with the gun, Danjermond came to his knees and swung the flashlight like a club. It caught Jack a vicious blow on the side of his head, snapping his head around and clouding his vision to a gray blur. Brain synapses shorted out. The gun fell from his hand and tumbled down the steps, firing a useless shot into the wall.

He tried to stand, tried to block the second strike, but the messages never connected with the appropriate muscles. The blow landed, and everything faded to black.

Laurel burst out of the bedroom with a heavy ginger jar lamp in her hands, brandishing it like a club to swing at Danjermond's head. But he grabbed her arm as she stepped into the hall and her gaze went to Jack, and the lamp crashed to the floor.

"Jack!" Laurel screamed as he lay limp at the top of the stairs, the side of his face running with blood. Thoughts flashed fast-forward through her mind in that one elongated moment she stood there staring at his still body in the dark hall—he was dead, she'd lost him, she was alone with a killer.

She started to move forward, but Danjermond held her.

"Careful, Laurel," he said quietly, his breath whistling in and out of his lungs. She could smell his sweat and his expensive cologne. She could smell blood and could only hope it was his. "You don't want to step on glass," he murmured.

"You're insane," she charged, her voice a sharp, trembling whisper. She twisted around to glare up at him, her breath catching at the sinister cast his features took on in the orange-shadowed glow of the flashlight.

"No," he said in return, smiling ever so faintly, his cool green eyes on hers, unblinking. "I'm not."

Chapter Thirty

"I dislike compromise as a rule," Danjermond said as he worked at binding Jack's hands and feet. "But one has to be flexible in times of emergency."

Laurel sat on an elegant Hepplewhite shield-back chair in the front hall, her wrists bound to the arms with straps of white silk, her ankles bound to the front legs. She wanted to scream, but silk clogged her mouth, leeching away the moisture and literally making her gag.

She watched Danjermond with a sick sense of dread pushing at the base of her throat and a strange, lethargic numbness dragging down on her. Dreamlike. No, nightmarish. If she could believe this was a nightmare, then it wouldn't be real. A trick of the mind. She couldn't decide what would be better—to be alert and terrified with the reality of the situation, or to be stunned senseless and believe it was all a bad dream.

Danjermond looked up at her, as if he had expected some response to his statement. He had taken the time to change out of his tuxedo and neatly bandage the hand he had cut during the fight. He was now in black jeans, boots, and a loose-fitting black shirt, an outfit that made him look like a modern-day warlock.

He had spread a blanket out on the floor so as not to get Jack's blood on the Oriental hall runner, and he checked and double-checked the bindings on his unconscious prisoner to make certain they were tight enough to hold but not so tight as to make impressions beneath the padding he had used first. The Bayou Strangler's victims were the ones who were to have bruises on their wrists, not the Strangler himself.

Laurel's gaze kept slipping down to Jack. She wasn't certain he was breathing. He had been unconscious nearly half an hour. Utterly motionless. Blood, sticky and brilliant red, matted his hair and glazed his temple and cheek like candy on an apple, but she couldn't tell whether or not he was still bleeding. *Dead men don't bleed.* She stared at his chest, willed it to move.

"I would rather have brought him to trial," Danjermond went on. He rose gracefully and picked up a glass of burgundy from the hall table, sipping at it thoughtfully, savoring the wine. "That was my intent all along. A murderer on a spree in Acadiana, running unchecked, no one able to stop him—until he reached Partout Parish. That was why I left the bodies where they could be found. There are, of course, many ways of disposing of bodies so as not to leave a trace. A man can get away with murder again and again if he is intelligent, careful, coolheaded."

He finished his drink. The grandfather clock chimed the hour. Eleven. Jack still didn't move.

With a sigh, Danjermond hauled him up off the blanket and maneuvered him into a fireman's lift. Without a word to Laurel, he went down the hall, toward the kitchen. She heard the back door open and close, then silence.

Oh, God, Jack, please be alive, please come around. I don't want to die alone.

Alone. As Savannah had been, as Annie had been, as all those other women had been. God knew how many. He had left six bodies to be found because that suited his plans. There could have been dozens more, all of them gone without a trace, swallowed up by the Atchafalaya, never to be seen again, the victims' cries for pity heard only by the swamp.

The numbness began to fade, and fear took its place. Tears rose to burn the backs of her eyes.

A vision of Savannah's face floated through her mind. The scents of formaldehyde and ammonia with death lingering, cloyingly sweet, beneath it all. The stainless steel table. The draped figure. Prejean murmuring something apologetic. Savannah's face—not as it had been in life, but as death and its aftermath had distorted it.

The back door opened and closed again. Footsteps sounded in the kitchen, in the hall. She bit down hard on the gag and tried to beat back the tears with her lashes. *Don't show fear. He feeds on fear. It gives him power.*

"All right, Laurel," Danjermond said, kneeling down to untie her feet. "We're going to go for a little drive." He looked up at her and smiled like a snake. "To my little place in the country."

Laurel knew the action was both futile and foolish, but she kicked him anyway, as hard as she could with her bare foot, catching him square in the diaphragm. He fell back, wheezing as the air punched out of his lungs, the look on his face worth whatever price he would make her pay.

Coughing, he rolled onto his knees and forced himself to his feet with one arm banded across his belly. He leaned against the hall table, sending her a sideways glare of pure, cold hate.

"You'll pay for that, Laurel," he ground out between short, painful gasps.

She met his glare evenly. *Don't show fear. It gives him power.*

"Defiant little bitch," he said, straightening slowly. A fire lit in his clear green eyes, glowing bright as he came toward her. "Just as your sister was," he said, smiling. "Right up to the end. She defied me. Dared me. I think she quite liked being tortured. There was a certain . . . exultant quality to her screams.

"And she laughed," he said softly, bending over her, careful to stay to the side. He brought his face down even with hers so she could see the wicked pleasure on his features as he spoke. "She laughed as I took my blade and cut her breasts."

Slowly, he reached out and cupped her breast with his long, elegant hand, testing its weight, molding its shape. He rubbed his thumb over the hard nub of her nipple, around and around, his gaze locked on hers, then began to tighten his fingers, squeezing and squeezing until she could no longer hold back the whimper of pain.

"She was completely insane by the end," he whispered.

Laurel shuddered, trembling with revulsion as much as fear. She had expected him to strike back at her physically, but this was much worse. Psychological torment, giving her the intimate details of her sister's murder. She would rather have been beaten. And he knew it.

"She wanted the sex," he said, untying her wrists from the arm of the chair. "Even when she knew I was going to kill her, she had an orgasm. Even as I tightened the scarf around her throat, she had an orgasm as powerful as any I've ever experienced." He met her eyes once again, that slight smile curling the corners of his wide, sensual mouth. "But then they say death is the ultimate aphrodisiac. Perhaps you'll experience that kind of ecstasy, as well, Laurel."

She was shaking uncontrollably as he hauled her up out of the chair and tied her hands behind her back. Thoughts of Savannah flashed through her mind. Thoughts of the two of them as children, before Ross had entered their lives and twisted the paths they would take. In that moment she hated him as much as she hated Stephen Danjermond. More. But it wasn't going to do any good to dwell on the past. The present held a clear and imminent danger. She was going to need all her energy, all her strength—physical and mental—directed to getting out of this alive.

Danjermond guided her out of the house the back way and took her around the side to an old carriage house that now served as a garage. They bypassed the Jaguar in favor of an old brown Chevy Blazer. He stuffed Laurel in the passenger's side and closed the door.

While he walked around the hood, she twisted around awkwardly to see Jack facedown on the seat behind her. He lay motionless, body bent at an awkward angle, feet on the floor behind the driver's seat. The dark blanket had been tossed carelessly over him and covered him from chin to boots.

In minutes they were driving out of town without having passed a car or a pedestrian who might have taken notice of them. When they were well beyond the town limits, alone on the bayou road, Danjermond pulled over and untied the gag.

Laurel spat the wad of cloth out of her mouth, glaring at him in the gloom of the cab. "You won't get away with this," she charged hoarsely, her throat and mouth parched.

Danjermond flicked a brow upward as he slid the Blazer into gear and started them on their journey once again. "What a trite line, Laurel. And ridiculous. Of course I'll get away with it. I've been getting away with it since I was nineteen."

He chuckled at her involuntary gasp of horror, like an indulgent adult amused at the naivete of a child. "I was a college student," he began, leaning over to push a cassette into the tape player. Mozart whispered out of the speakers, orderly and serene. "I was an excellent student, naturally, with a great future ahead of me. But I had certain sexual appetites that required discretion.

"My father introduced me to the pleasures of the darker side of sex—indirectly. As a boy I once followed him on a visit to his mistress, and watched them through a window, fascinated and aroused by the games they played. I followed him many times after that before I realized he knew. When I was fourteen, he allowed me to visit her myself. To be properly initiated.

"I learned the privileges of wealth and the wisdom of discretion early on. So I knew better than to appease myself with a coed. Whores are much better at pleasing a man, anyway, and so much more expendable. I got carried away with one. Strangled her while we were in the throes of passion.

"No one ever suspected me. Why would they? I was the handsome, talented son of a prominent family, and she was just another whore who fell victim to a professional hazard."

Laurel listened, shocked and repulsed at the lack of feeling in his voice. He was completely without remorse, completely devoid of conscience. Emotionless, soulless; he had said so himself that day at Beauvoir. There would be no appealing to his sense of mercy or humanity, because he didn't have any. Escape was their only hope, and that hope was so slim as to be nearly nonexistent. She couldn't leave Jack, couldn't take him with her even if she could somehow get away. And what chance did she have out here, barefoot with her hands tied behind her back? None. If Danjermond didn't get her, something else would.

They turned off the bayou road and onto a narrow dirt track that led deeper into the swamp. Branches slapped at the sides of the truck as it crept down the path. The growth was so thick, the headlights barely penetrated. Laurel felt cocooned within the dark confines of the Blazer, cocooned in a bizarre world where Mozart played while a murderer calmly told her his life story.

She tried to memorize the turns they took, tried to gauge how far they had gone, but everything seemed distorted—time, distance, reality. Her arms ached abominably from being held in such an unnatural position. Every lurch of the truck sent pain shooting between her shoulder blades.

She glanced into the backseat at Jack, and her heart flipped over as his left eye blinked open for a moment. He was alive. Though not much, it was something to hang on to.

"You surprised me, Laurel," Danjermond said. He slowed the Blazer to a crawl as he piloted it through a shallow stream. As they climbed back onto what passed for solid ground out here, he stared at her across the cab, his lean face lit by the glow of the dashboard instruments. "I really didn't think you would break into my home. Even after you lied to Kenner, I believed you were too 'by the book' for that."

"I don't give a damn about the book," she said. "I believe in justice. I'll take it whatever way I can get it."

He smiled at that, truly pleased, and faced forward again as the path turned and ran along a bank. "I was right. You're much stronger than you thought, Laurel. It's really too bad I had to catch you with evidence that could incriminate me. I would have enjoyed a longer game."

He would have put her through Scott County all over again—the accusations, the disbelief, the desperation, all of it—for his own amusement. Laurel wanted to berate him for calling life and death a game. She wanted to rail at him for playing with the system he had sworn to uphold, but there seemed no point in it. He believed he was above it all—the law, the rules of society. And to date he had no reason to think otherwise. He had fooled everyone, had gotten away with the ultimate crime again and again.

"What will you do with us?" she asked flatly, deciding it was better to know than to imagine.

"I will lead the sheriff out to the site of a grisly murder-suicide I heard about through an anonymous tip. Poor Jack went over the edge at last. Couldn't deal with what he'd done to you. Took a gun and shot himself in the head."

Thereby obliterating the head wound Danjermond had already dealt him. And she would die exactly as the others had died, tying Jack firmly to the series of murders. Danjermond would see to every detail. No one would question the outcome.

"Not quite the glamour of a trial," she muttered.

"No. I do regret that. But still, there will be a good deal of regional and national news coverage, and as district attorney I will, naturally, act as spokesman for the parish."

"Naturally."

"Don't take it too hard, Laurel," he said, as he piloted the Blazer into a ramshackle shed that was tucked between trees and nearly obscured by vines. He cut the engine and turned to face her. "You couldn't have won. You couldn't have stopped me."

Laurel said nothing. She stared at him across the narrow space of the cab, remembering clearly the way he had looked over the dinner table in the house she had grown up in. *"You believe in evil, don't you, Laurel?"*

Yes, she did believe in evil, and she knew without a doubt that she was looking into the face of it.

He hauled Jack out of the truck first, carrying him out of the shed and out of her sight. Laurel struggled against the cloth that bound her hands, while her gaze scanned the cab for some kind of weapon—both acts useless. Danjermond was back for her quickly, and guided her ahead of him by her bound hands, down the muddy bank to an old *bâteau* that bobbed among the reeds.

At his prodding, she climbed in and sat on a black tarp at the flat bottom of the boat, with Jack lying in a heap behind her. Laurel leaned back and brushed her fingertips along the scuffed leather of his boots, trying to take some comfort in his nearness, and then her fingers stumbled over the lump of a knot.

Danjermond's attention was on the outboard motor. With a snap of his wrist, it roared to life and the boat eased away from the shore.

The black water gleamed like glass under the light of a partial moon. Bald cypress and tupelo trees jutted up from the smooth surface, straight and dark, looming above the swamp. In the near distance, thunder rolled and lightning flashed pink behind a bank of clouds. South, Laurel thought automatically, fingers picking awkwardly at the knot behind her. A storm moving up from the Gulf.

A storm, Jack thought dimly. Or was the rumbling in his head? *Dieu,* his head felt like an overripe melon that had met abruptly with the business end of a hammer. He forced his eyelids open—a monumental effort—and tried

to take stock of his surroundings. A boat. He could hear
the weak whine of a small outboard, feel the buoyancy of
water beneath him, smell the rank aromas of damp and
decomposing vegetation that was the bayou.

Fighting against the urge to cry out, he turned his
head a scant inch and tried to make out the image above
him. Women. Two. One. The shape blurred and multi-
plied, came together, then divided. Trying to clear his
vision drained his strength, and he slipped back toward
oblivion.

"I find the swamp a fascinating place, don't you, Laurel?"

Laurel. He struggled into full consciousness again,
the strain making him dizzy. Laurel. Danger.
Danjermond. The fight came back to him in broken
snatches, just the memory intensifying the pain in his
head. Danjermond had clubbed him. He had a concussion at the very least. At worst, what he was lapsing in
and out of was not consciousness but existence. He
forced a message down from his battered brain to his
fingers, flexing them slowly, slightly. They moved—he
thought.

He rested then, and conversation came to him in bits,
fading in and out like a radio with poor reception.

". . . a perfect world in many ways," Danjermond
said, his voice hollow and distant, as if it were coming
down a long tunnel.

". . . for predators . . . senseless killing . . ."

". . . thrill of the hunt . . ."

". . . sadistic son of a bitch . . ."

He almost smiled at that. Laurel. She would stand up
to a tiger and spit in its eye before it had her for lunch.
Her courage never ceased to amaze him. She wouldn't
back down from Danjermond. But Danjermond would
kill her just the same.

While I lie here and let it happen.

Blackie's face loomed up behind his eyelids, snarling,
taunting. *"Good for nothin', T-Jack. Always were, always
will be."*

The boat seemed to spin beneath him, and nausea

crawled up the back of his throat. An old hand at hang-
overs, he fought off the sensations, opened his eyes, and
focused them hard on Laurel's back until the pounding
in his head was so loud and relentless, he thought it a
wonder no one else heard it. Gathering his strength, he
made one effort to push himself up, but at that moment
the motor cut and the *bâteau* bumped gently against a
dock. Knocked off balance, he slumped back down,
groaning as his head hit the bottom of the boat.

Laurel fought against the overwhelming urge to turn
toward the faint moan. It was best not to react. If Jack
was coming around, she didn't want Danjermond to
know. They needed whatever slight edge they could get.
She groaned, twisting her head to the side, as if trying to
alleviate a cramp in her neck. Danjermond flicked a
glance at her as he tied the boat off.

They had moved toward the storm as the storm had
been moving toward them. It was overhead now. The sky
was rumbling and crackling. The first flurry of fat raindrops hurled down on them, as Danjermond grabbed her
by the arm and hauled her up on the rickety dock beside
him. The boards groaned and dipped, elastic with rot,
but they held as he turned and herded her onto shore
and toward a tarpaper shack that teetered on stilts a few
yards back from the dock.

The rain came harder. Lightning shattered the black
of the sky, and the clouds ripped open, drenching them.
Gasping, Laurel ducked her head as the water sluiced
down her face. Danjermond hustled her up the steps and
produced a key to the padlock that held the door shut.

The cabin was pitch-black inside, but the scent of
blood assaulted her nostrils and balled in her throat. Human blood. Her sister's blood. Laurel squeezed her eyes
closed as fear surged through her in a flood tide and bile
rose up the back of her throat. Beneath the noise of rain
on the tin roof, she could hear Danjermond shuffling
around, striking a match.

"It isn't much, but it's dry," he said, playing the humble host. Amusement tinted his voice as he reached out a
hand and cupped her chin. "Now, Laurel, you're not the

sort to hide. Open your eyes and face your destiny head-on."

He had lit candles, half a dozen or more. Tall tapers with flames that flickered and danced, their light waving sinuously over the meager contents of the ten-by-twelve room. A small dresser stood along the wall to her left with a cluster of candle stands on its scarred surface. A straight chair sat directly in front of her. Beyond it stood two more small, spindle-legged stands, one on either side of the bed, both of them crowned with a flickering candle.

All this Laurel took in through her peripheral vision, the facts filing themselves away in her brain while her attention was riveted on the bed. It was iron. Black iron. Slender pieces curved into graceful shapes to form the headboard and footboard. The four posts were low, entwined with pencil-slim iron vines and topped with polished brass finials in the shape of a spade. It was beautiful. Sinister. White silk ties hung from the headboard. A drape of sheer, pristine white silk covered the mattress, but dark stains showed through like shadows. Bloodstains.

Savannah had lain on that bed and had the life bled out of her, choked out of her. And Annie. And women whose names she would never know. Their screams filled her head like the echoes of ghosts. Their pain clawed at her. Their panic rose in her throat.

The thunder rolled. Lightning flashed through the window as bright as a spotlight. The rain poured down, pounding like nails on the roof.

Beyond the cabin stretched miles of wilderness. No one to help her. No one to hear her cries. No mercy. No justice. She thought of Jack and what might have been if fate had taken a kinder path for them both. Wondered dimly if any of it had ever been within their power.

Then Danjermond's hand closed on her arm and he led her toward the bed.

.   .   .

The rain came down as hard as hailstones, pelting exposed skin, slicing and pounding. A real frog strangler. Frogs, hell, Jack thought, coughing as the water pooled in the bottom of the boat and drifted into his mouth.

Strangler.

The word slapped him into consciousness, and he jerked his head up, grunting hard at the pain, the dizziness. *Laurel.* She was gone. Danjermond was gone. Danjermond would kill her. *And you're lying in a goddamn boat in the rain. Worthless, good for nothing, son of a son of a bitch.*

Gritting his teeth against the agony, he tried to right himself, confused at first that he couldn't seem to move his arms. Pain came in staccato bursts as he rolled partway onto his back and took the pounding rain full in the face. His hands were tied behind him. His feet were tied.

But he had moved his feet. He thought. He tried now with some success. They were bound but not tightly. Loose enough to struggle against. Loose enough that he could work his boots off, and the binding with them.

The task sapped his energy, left him gasping for breath and choking on the rain, but he managed to get his feet free. Slowly he rolled over onto his knees and tried to bring his head up an inch at a time. The pain beat relentlessly, like a mallet inside his skull, the rhythm syncopated with a driving urgency.

Laurel. He had to get to Laurel. He would die in the process or in the aftermath, of that he had no doubt, but he had to try. For her . . . to make her proud . . . to show her he loved her . . . he hadn't told her . . . should have told her . . . wished he could have made it work . . .

The thoughts swirled around his brain as he struggled to stand in the boat, and the blackness swirled with them. Flecked with stars . . . promising relief . . . beckoning . . . sweeping in . . .

· · ·

Fighting him was futile, but she fought him just the same. There was a principle involved. Honor. She would not go meekly to her death like a sheep to the proverbial slaughter. She wouldn't make it easy for him, would do her utmost to spoil his enjoyment.

The instant Danjermond's hand settled on her arm, Laurel jerked away from him and bolted for the door. He lunged after her, catching hold of her ponytail and jerking her back hard enough to make her teeth snap together. Laurel shrieked, in anger and pain, and twisted toward him, lashing out with her feet, kicking at his knees, his shins, any part of him she could hit.

His lips pulled back against his teeth in a feral snarl, and the back of his hand exploded against the side of her face, snapping her head to the side, bringing a burst of stars behind her eyes and the taste of blood to her mouth. The room seemed to swirl once around her, and unable to use her arms for balance, she staggered sideways and fell. On her knees, she tried to scramble for the door, never taking her eyes off it, willing herself to stand, to run, to get away. Adrenaline pumped through her like a drug, driving her forward even when Danjermond caught hold of her bound wrists and hauled her up and back, wrenching her arms in the sockets.

But her struggles stilled automatically as the blade of a dagger glinted in the candlelight.

Laurel's heart drummed, impossibly hard, impossibly loud, as the blade came nearer and nearer her face. It was slim and elegant, like the hand that curled around its golden hilt. The blade was polished steel that had been ornately engraved from the guard to the tip. Beautiful, deadly, like the man who held it.

"I would prefer if you would cooperate, Laurel," he said, stepping in close behind her, his left hand sliding along her jaw, fingers pressing into her flesh. The knife inched nearer.

The pitch of his voice was the same even tone that had always somehow managed to strike a nerve in her, but no longer was it devoid of emotion. Anger strummed through every carefully enunciated word as he brought the dagger closer and closer. Her breath caught hard in her lungs as he touched the point of it to the very tip of her nose.

"Be a good girl, Laurel," he murmured, sliding the dagger lightly downward. Over her upper lip to her lower lip. He let it linger in the valley between as if he were contemplating sliding it into her mouth. "I know Vivian raised you to be a good girl."

"Be a good girl, Laurel. Don't make trouble, Laurel. Keep your mouth closed and your legs crossed, Laurel." Somehow, she didn't think this was a situation that had come to her mother's mind during those lectures on comportment.

Laurel said nothing, afraid to speak, afraid to breathe as the blade point traced down her chin, down the center of her throat to the vulnerable hollow at its base. If she struggled now, would he slice her throat and be done with her? That seemed preferable, but there were no guarantees. If she waited, bought time—even a minute or two—might she find another chance to break away?

Outside, the storm had rolled past and gone on its way toward Lafayette, but the rain continued, pelting the roof, tapping at the single, small window like bony fingertips. What kind of chance at survival would she have in the swamp? What kind of chance would she have here?

The dagger rested in the V of her collarbone, the point tickling the delicate flesh above. The sensation made her want to gag. She swallowed back the need, felt the tip bite into her skin. Every cell of her body was quivering. She felt as fragile as a twig, poised to snap in Danjermond's grasp. Her eyes filled, but she held back the tears, held back the hysteria, grabbed her sanity with both mental hands, and hung on as Danjermond's words about Savannah echoed in her head—*"She was completely insane by the end."*

She wouldn't give him the satisfaction. He had killed her sister for sport, meant to climb on the bodies of his victims to fame in a profession he mocked with every breath he took.

"Damn you," she whispered, seizing her anger and hate and using them as shields to beat back the terror. "Damn you to hell."

Danjermond leaned close, bringing his face down next to hers, rubbing his cheek against hers. "I don't believe in an afterlife, Laurel," he murmured, dragging the dagger down between her breasts, where her heart pounded beneath the thin fabric of her T-shirt. With a slight motion of his wrist the point nipped into the cotton and nudged her breast. "I'd say, if there's a hell, it's here and now, and you're in it with me."

A scream tore from her throat as Danjermond sliced violently downward with the blade, opening her T-shirt from neck band to hem. Instinctively, she bolted back, colliding with his long, lean body, her hands pressing against his engorged sex. His left arm snaked around her middle and held her there as he eased his pelvis forward and raised the dagger slowly to her left breast.

Razor-sharp, the blade kissed along the plump swell beneath her nipple, and her blood beaded, bright red, along the knife edge, rolling across it like pearls to splash down on the floor. The pain came seconds later, throbbing with her heartbeat. And finally the tears spilled over her lashes and rolled down her cheeks, pale counterpoints to the drops of blood sliding down her rib cage.

"Be a good girl, Laurel," he purred, rubbing himself rhythmically against her. She shuddered in disgust as he traced his tongue up the line of her throat to her ear and caught the lobe between his teeth. "There's no justice out here for you to find, Laurel," he whispered. "The only law is my law."

He dragged her back to the bed, ignoring her resistance. With the dagger, he sliced the ties that bound her hands and quickly shoved her down on the bed, planting a knee in the middle of her chest to pin her down with his weight. Using the ties that had tethered other victims to this deathbed, he lashed her to the headboard.

"Too bad it's raining so," he said conversationally as he sat on the bed beside her, admiring the sight of her glaring up at him. Taking up the dagger, he dipped it in her navel and drew it lightly up the quivering flesh of her belly, between her breasts. "I would have brought Jack in and tried to rouse him for the performance. He should witness what his imagination only hints at, see for himself the power of it, the seduction. He has the darkness within him. Before he dies, he should witness the glory of it unleashed."

The blade hooked under the neck band of her T-shirt and, with a practiced move, he sliced it open. With the tip of the dagger he peeled back the ruined garment on either side, baring her to his gaze.

"Dainty," he whispered, rubbing the flat of the knife against her uninjured breast. "Exquisitely feminine."

"What happened to make you hate women so?" she asked, choking with revulsion as he dipped a thumb in the blood from the wound he had inflicted and painted it across first one nipple then the other.

Danjermond raised a brow. "I don't hate women," he said, sounding amused. "This is my hobby. It's nothing personal."

"I consider being murdered highly personal."

He rose with a sigh and rounded the foot of the bed to sit on the straight chair. He dropped the dagger on the floor at his feet and casually began to unbutton his shirt. "Well, yes, I suppose you would, all things considered. But then, that's been a longtime problem of yours, hasn't it, Laurel? You tend to personalize everything. That's what got you into such trouble in Georgia. You were too personally involved. You couldn't see the forest for the trees. We both know how important perspective is in building a case. A prosecuting attorney must be cold, thorough, detached. Emotionalism only leaves the door open for surprises from the opposition. As you've discovered for yourself, Laurel, I am a very thorough man. I don't tolerate surprises."

Without warning, the cabin door exploded inward, the rotted frame splintering, rain and wind sweeping in, and Jack with it. His momentum carried him forward, and he bowled into a stunned Danjermond before the district attorney could do more than turn and gape at him. The wooden chair disintegrated into kindling beneath their combined weight and the two men crashed to the floor.

Laurel screamed Jack's name and struggled to sit up, trying to see. She could hear the struggle—the scuff of boots on the floor, the grunts and curses. She knew in her heart what the outcome would be. Jack was fighting literally with both hands tied behind his back, and he had to be barely conscious. Danjermond would kill him, just as surely as he would kill her—unless she could somehow manage to get herself free.

She wriggled up toward the headboard, inches at a time, trying not to strain against the ties that held her by her wrists, trying to move into a position that would give her some slack. Gritting her teeth, she concentrated on shutting out the sounds of the fight and tried to focus her mind on her bonds. Silk. Smooth, strong, slick, slippery. Her hands were small, fine-boned, her wrists delicate. If she concentrated, moved just right, didn't tighten them by struggling . . .

Jack struggled to keep Danjermond pinned beneath him, but his strength ebbed and flowed in erratic bursts, and his faulty sense of balance made it difficult to determine which way was up. He fought as best he could with his knees and his feet, jabbing, kicking when he could, ignoring the pain that screamed through his head and bit into his side.

Danjermond writhed beneath him, twisting, heaving upward. He reached for the dagger that had skittered across the floor, and Jack threw his weight hard against him, sending them both crashing into a table along the wall, and sending the table crashing to the floor.

Candles rolled like tenpins, their flames licking at anything in their path, catching hungrily at the old tarpaper that lined the walls of the shack.

The men rolled away from the fire, still struggling for supremacy. Jack managed to catch his adversary in the belly with his knee, but Danjermond struck back viciously, slamming his fist into the side of Jack's head. The pain sent Jack rolling, plummeting toward unconsciousness like a diver shooting toward the bottom of a black, black ocean.

He fought against it, held his breath, and fought to claw his way back up through the dark, up through the fireflies that swarmed in his brain. His vision cleared enough for him to make out flames licking greedily up the wall and three wavering versions of Danjermond silhouetted in front of the glow. Three devils from hell. Three Danjermonds raising an arm, three daggers gleaming, slashing toward him.

He dove for the man in the center, his shoulder hitting solid mass at the same instant the dagger plunged into his back. He felt a rib break, then a strange vacuum sensation in his chest. What little strength he had left sucked out of him, and he fell heavily to the floor, mouthing Laurel's name.

"Jack! Jack!" Laurel shouted his name to be heard above the roar of the fire that was devouring the wall of the shack. She shouted a third time, frantic to hear him answer, knowing that he wouldn't.

She had seen Danjermond rise, had seen the dagger slash down. Jack was dead. She was alone. It wouldn't matter that she had managed to work one hand free. She wouldn't have time to untie the other. Danjermond was on his feet already. Coming toward her. The dagger dripping blood. Jack's blood. Danjermond smiled like Lucifer himself against the backdrop of flame.

Don't look at him, work the knot, work the knot. Crying, coughing against the black smoke that was beginning to press down from the ceiling, she scrambled across the bed, fumbling to free her left hand.

Jack raised his head a fraction of an inch. All he could see were Danjermond's feet. Moving toward Laurel. From some deep inner well he drew the last drops of will and courage he had and swung his legs. He hit Danjermond in the backs of the knees, and the district attorney's legs buckled beneath him, sending him sprawling headlong into the flames.

The screams were terrible. Inhuman. Engulfed in flame, he managed to stand and tried frantically to run, stumbling and falling across the bed. Laurel screamed and flung herself off the other side as the silk spread ignited in a flash.

She staggered back from the ghoulish scene, choking on the smoke, eyes stinging so badly, she could barely hold them open. There was nothing to be done for Danjermond. And in that terrible, fire-bright moment, she didn't know whether she would have tried. All she knew with any certainty was that the cabin was going up like a tinderbox, and if they didn't get out quickly, she and Jack would share Danjermond's fate.

Crouching low to escape the worst of the smoke, she ran around the foot of the bed and dropped to her knees beside Jack's sprawled form.

"Jack!" she screamed, the sound almost consumed by the roar of the fire. "Damn you Jack, don't die on me now!"

She pulled at him, gritted her teeth, and threw all her strength into dragging him toward the door, shouting every inch of the way. Her curses and pleas penetrated the fog of Jack's consciousness. Her determination made him move his legs when he wasn't sure he could remember how. He latched onto the sound of her voice and the feel of her hand and the incredible power of her will, and used it all to propel himself forward. At the door, he caught hold of the splintered frame and got his feet under himself.

"Hurry!" Laurel shouted, wrapping an arm around his waist and trying to take his weight against her as they stumbled down the steps and started toward the bayou.

The rain was still falling, but it was no match for the old dried wood of the shack. The cabin lit up the night sky like a torch. The fire devoured it as if hell had opened up to consume all evidence of the atrocities that had been practiced there, devouring the perpetrator, as well, condemning him to a justice that was absolute.

Weak, choking from the smoke, staggering under Jack's weight, Laurel fell to her knees on the muddy bank, and Jack went down like a ton of bricks beside her.

"Oh, God, Jack! Don't die!" she demanded, bending over him. "Don't be dead! Please don't be dead!"

She bent over him, bawling, her tears combining with the rain to splash down onto his face. With hands shaking violently, she touched his soot-covered cheek, his lips—trying to feel his breath, fumbled to find a pulse in his throat. Was it weak and thready, or was that her own?

His lashes fluttered upward, and he looked at her. Tried to smile. Tried to catch more than a teaspoon of air. "Hey, angel," he whispered, then had to try to breathe again. "Mebbe I'm one of the good guys after all."

Then darkness swept over him like a velvet blanket, and he surrendered to the pain.

Chapter
Thirty-One

He remembered in dreamlike bits and pieces. A force of will pushing, prodding, begging, swearing, goading him to move his feet. Take a step and another. The pain was blocked out, but not the weakness or the sense of disconnection between his mind and his body. He remembered feeling as if the essence of him were floating free, connected to his physical shell by the finest of threads. He remembered the powerful temptation to sever that tie and just drift away, but Laurel kept yanking him back. He remembered wondering vaguely how she could be so little and be so strong.

There was a boat in the fragments of memory. And rain. Rain and tears. Laurel crying over him. He wanted to tell her not to. He couldn't stand the thought of making her cry, even though he knew he had done it more than once, bastard that he was. There were many things he wanted to tell her, but he couldn't gather more than the urgency. The words bounced around in his head like bubbles. He had forgotten how to use his voice. The frustration exhausted him.

Darkness, light. The murmured voices of men and women in white clothes. Couldn't be heaven; he never would have gotten in the gate. Had to be a hospital.

Cool hands touching his arm, his cheek. Soft lips and whispers of love. Laurel.

Laurel had stayed with him, Nurse Washington had told him as she shuffled around his room, fussing and checking things. She was a short, squat, cube of a woman with mahogany skin and little sausage fingers that read his pulse with the feather-light touch of expertise. Miz Chandler had visited during the days he had spent in deep, drugged sleep. But didn't she have a lot on her plate, the poor little thing, what with her sister being killed and the sheriff's investigation and all? And weren't they lucky to have escaped with their lives? Mr. Danjermond a killer—Lord have mercy!

Jack tuned out the memory of her chatter now as he stood on his front step and watched Leonce drive away. As the Monte Carlo rolled out of sight, his gaze was drawn inexorably to Belle Rivière. At the core of his pounding head were thoughts of Laurel. She had sat with him, kissed his cheek, whispered that she loved him. He didn't deserve her love, but he knew without a doubt it was what had made him hang on to life when he could have easily let go. Laurel's voice coming to him through the mists, begging him to live, bribing him with her love.

Huey crawled out from under a tangle of long-neglected azalea bushes and climbed up in the step to give Jack's hand a sniff and a lick of welcome. Jack stared down at the hound, meeting the pair of weirdly mismatched eyes, and grudgingly scratched the dog's ear. Huey groaned and thumped his tail against the bricks.

"You're all the welcome I get, eh, Huey? That's what I get for breaking out."

He pushed the door open and wandered into the house, letting the dog trail after him. Huey abandoned him to nose around the old draped furniture in search of mice. Jack took as deep a breath as he could manage and climbed the stairs one excruciating step at a time.

Somehow, he had expected to feel at home once he made it to his bedroom, but as he looked around, he realized this wasn't his home at all. It was still Madame Deveraux's boudoir. He was just marking time here. He hadn't done much more than change the sheets on the bed. He hadn't made this house his home, he admitted as he sank down on the mattress, wincing at the bite of his broken rib and the stab wound that sliced the tissue around it. It was his prison, the place where he turned on himself and endlessly cracked the whips of self-flagellation. The one thing he had done to make the place his own was hanging all his neckties in the live oak out front, and that had been more a sign of shame than of freedom. Like a flag on the door of a plague victim, it was a warning to those who would venture near that he couldn't handle a life that required ties of any kind.

That life had blown up in his face, and he had had to live with the fact that he'd been the one to lay the powder and light the fuse. What he had rebuilt for himself in the aftermath of the debacle was simple and safe for all concerned, he reminded himself as he stared up at the intricate plaster medallion on the ceiling. He had his writing, his pals at Frenchie's, enough willing lady friends to warm his bed when he wanted.

He had an empty house and an empty heart and no one to share them with save the ghosts of his past and a dog that wasn't his.

Jack shoved the thought away with an effort that had him squinting against the pain. His life swung on a pendulum between penance and parties, and it suited him fine. He was accountable to no one, responsible for nothing.

And still Laurel Chandler had managed to fall in love with him. The irony of it was too much—Laurel, the champion for justice, upholder of the law, in love with a man who had broken so many so carelessly, a man for whom justice was a sentence to emotional exile. She offered him everything he had ever wanted, everything he'd told himself he could never have.

If he had a shred of honor, he would walk away and

leave her to fall in love with a better man than he could ever be.

The service was private. A blessing and a curse, Laurel thought. The pain went too deep for her to share it with people she hardly knew, but some of the deepest wounds had been inflicted by the only people present.

She sat with Caroline and Mama Pearl on one side of the chapel. Vivian and Ross sat on the other side, in the same pew but not together. Separated by an invisible wall of hate, together only out of Vivian's automatic attempt to put a "normal" face on ugly family secrets. She would never confirm or deny the rumors once they began to spread—a lady didn't lower herself to airing the dirty laundry in public. She would most likely divorce Ross quietly and go on with her life as if he had never been a part of it, leaving him hanging alone on the gallows of public opinion.

Ross stared dully at the casket with its blanket of pink tea roses and baby's breath. Laurel wondered if he felt remorse or just regret for being exposed after all this time. She wouldn't have allowed him to come, regardless, but the choice hadn't been hers to make.

She wondered how he would weather the storm of accusation and condemnation once the story of the abuse became common knowledge—and she would damn well make certain it became common knowledge. Caroline had told her once that Ross was a weak man. If there was a God in heaven, the shame of the truth would crush him.

Reverend Stipple had pitifully little to say in the way of a eulogy. Laurel would have preferred he say nothing, but it was his church, this church where she and Savannah had been christened, where their father had pledged to love their mother until death. Where death had brought them all and half the parish to see Jefferson Chandler off to the next world.

She looked down at the lace-edged handkerchief she held and remembered too well how Savannah had sat

beside her and taken her hand and whispered to her. *"Daddy's gone, but we'll always have each other, Baby."*
Always.

Now death had brought them here again, these people whose lives were tied together in a painful knot of common experience.

Toward the end of the ceremony, Conroy Cooper slipped in the back and took a seat by himself. Laurel met his somber, soul-deep blue gaze as she walked out of the church, and saw the regret there, and the love, and she ached at the irony that of all the men her sister had known, she would love the one whose nobility put him out of her reach.

When everyone else had gone out, Laurel lingered in the shadows of the vestibule and watched Cooper lay a single white rose on the casket. For a long while he just stood there, head bent, one hand on the polished wood, saying good-bye in his low, smooth voice.

Laurel had labeled him an adulterer and condemned him for not being able to give Savannah the kind of commitment she wanted. But he had loved her as best he could, he said, while trying to keep a vow to a wife who no longer knew him. He had given Savannah all he could. It wasn't his fault she had needed so much more.

There was no coffee served after the burial. No time for normalcy to dilute the grief with talk of crops and babies and everyday things. Caroline drove them home to Belle Rivière in silence.

Mama Pearl went into her kitchen to take solace in the familiar ritual of brewing a pot of *café noir*. Caroline laid her keys on the hall table, turned and took Laurel's hands in hers. "I'm going upstairs to lie down for a while," she said, her strong voice softened by strain to a whisper. "You should do the same, darlin'. It's been a terrible few days."

Laurel struggled for a game smile and shook her head. "I'm too restless to sleep. I was thinking I'd go into the courtyard for a while."

Dark eyes shining with the kind of love and wisdom a mother should possess, Caroline nodded and squeezed

Laurel's fingers. "You've got it so pretty out there. It's a good place to look for a little peace."

Laurel didn't expect to find any, but it was true she was going to look, to hope.

She strolled the pathways slowly, with her hands tucked deep in the pockets of her flowered skirt. A fitful breeze swirled the hem around her calves and brushed the ends of her hair across her shoulders. The day was warm and muggy with a sky that couldn't decide whether it should be a clear blue bowl or a tumble of angry gray clouds.

Despite the moods of the weather and the aura of sadness that hung on Laurel like a shroud, the garden offered what it always did. The rich scents of green growth, the soft, sweet perfumes of flowers bathed her senses, trying to soothe, offering comfort. Even the weeds tried to distract her, reminding her they needed pulling. Tomorrow, she promised, moving on down the path, searching for something she couldn't hope to find today.

She felt as if a crucial, turbulent chapter of her life had been abruptly closed. Savannah was gone. The secret they had shared all these years had been unlocked. Danjermond was dead, and while the investigation continued into the dark shadows of his past, and the headlines were still selling papers, the bottom line had been drawn. Between her testimony and the evidence in his home, and at the scene, Stephen Danjermond, Partout Parish district attorney, son of the Garden District Danjermonds of New Orleans, had been established as a serial killer.

She should have felt a sense of closure, she thought as she took a seat on the corner bench. But she felt more as if something had started to unravel and had been discarded with loose threads trailing all around. Savannah was gone. They would never have the chance to repair the cracks in their relationship; it would remain forever broken. The secret had been revealed, but she would go on being Vivian's daughter; Ross Leighton would forever be a part of her past, if not her future. Danjermond was dead, but every life he had touched would be indelibly marked by his betrayal.

And then there was Jack. The man who was bent on paying with his life for the sins of his past.

If she had a brain in her head, she would walk away, make a clean break, start over somewhere new. What had happened between her and Jack had happened too quickly, too intensely. A relationship had been the last thing she'd come home looking for, and Jack was far from the kind of man she had pictured herself with. He had used, abused, and derided the profession they once had in common. She didn't respect him because of it— but she respected the way he had turned himself around in the end, even if he claimed his motives were selfish. He lived a life built on shirking responsibility, another trait that irritated her strong sense of duty, but she had seen him defy that role time and again.

She kept seeing him in her mind's eye—not the rogue male with the wicked grin and the ruby in his earlobe, but the lonely, haunted man whose hidden needs reached deep into a loveless boyhood. She kept feeling the ache inside him that had touched her own heart, the ache of longing for things he thought he shouldn't have.

Jack painted himself as a user and a cad, good for nothing but a good time, but the fact of the matter was he had saved her life and shown a heroism that was exceedingly rare in this world.

He was so distinctly two different people. The trouble was convincing the "bad" Jack that the "good" Jack existed and deserved to have a chance at something better than a half life filled with pain.

Laurel closed her eyes and let her head fall back, turning her face up to the sky as the sun played hide-and-seek with the clouds. For a moment she let herself picture a life where they could truly start over, where people really did rise above their pasts and lived beyond the shadows, where she and Jack could simply have happiness without all the baggage attached.

"Dreamin' about me, sugar?"

It took a moment for Laurel to realize the voice had not come from inside her mind. Her eyes flew open, and she swung around on the bench to see him standing there leaning against one of Aunt Caroline's armless goddess statues in faded jeans and a chambray shirt hanging open down the front. He was pale beneath his tan, and there were lines of strain etched deep beside his dark eyes that combined with the shadow of his beard to make him look tough and dangerous. He smiled his pirate's grin, but there was too much pain in his eyes for him to quite pull it off.

"What the devil are you doing here?" Laurel exclaimed, shooting up off the bench. "Don't you even try to tell me Dr. Broussard released you!"

He winced a little as the volume of her voice set off hammers in his head. "*Mais non,*" he drawled. "Me, I sorta escaped."

"Why does that not surprise me?"

"It's no big deal, '*tite chatte,*'" he grumbled, rubbing a thumb against the goddess's forehead. "All's I got is a boomer of a headache and a busted rib."

Laurel scowled at him, jamming her hands on her hips. "Your lung collapsed! You've got a concussion and stab wounds and—"

"*Bon Dieu!*" he gasped in mock surprise, black hair tumbling across his forehead as he looked up at her with wide eyes. "Then mebbe I oughta sit down."

He caught an arm around her waist and pulled her down with him, his actions stiff and slightly awkward, but effective enough to land her on his lap as he took her seat on the bench. She immediately scooted off him, but swung her legs around and remained on the bench beside him.

Jack frowned, shooting her a sideways look. "I must be losin' my touch."

Laurel sniffed. "Losing your mind is more like it. You belong in a hospital. My God, you weren't even conscious the last time I saw you!"

"I'll live."

Dismissing the topic, he looked down at her, taking

in the deep shadows beneath her eyes. She couldn't have looked more exquisitely feminine or fragile, like a priceless piece of porcelain. That fragility had frightened him once, before he had discovered the strength that ran through it like threads of steel. But he had a feeling the strength was flagging today.

"How about you, sugar? How you doin'?"

"Savannah's funeral was today," she said quietly.

Jack slipped an arm around her shoulders and eased her against him, pressing a kiss to the top of her head. It was all he needed to do. Laurel splayed her hand against his warm bare chest, above the pristine white bandage that bound his ribs, and simply cherished the way his heartbeat felt beneath her hand.

"I would have been there for you if I could have."

She looked up at him, her face carefully blank as she tried to assess the shift of feelings in him and between them. "You don't do funerals."

"Yeah, well . . ." He sighed, fixing his gaze on the roses that climbed the brick wall beside them. "That doesn't stop me from losin' friends, does it? It only stops me from being one."

"Is that what we are?" Laurel asked quietly. "Friends?"

"You saved my life."

"And you saved mine," she returned, rising to pace in front of the bench with her arms crossed tight against her. "What does that make us? Even?"

"What do you want it to make us?" Jack asked, hearing the edge in his voice and cursing himself for it. He hadn't come here to fight with her. He had come for— what? And why? Because he couldn't stay away? Because he thought he had to end what had taken root and twined around his heart like the ivy that curled around the foot of the bench? *You can't have it both ways, Jack.*

"I want more," Laurel admitted. If that made her a fool, then she was a fool. If it made her weak, then she was weak. It was the truth. Too much of her life had been tied up in lies. She stopped her pacing and looked him in the eye, as sober as a judge. "I love you, Jack. I keep telling myself I shouldn't, but I do."

"You're right, angel." Gritting his teeth against the pain, he rose slowly. "You shouldn't," he murmured and moved toward the gate, avoiding looking at her. If he looked at her, he would never be able to walk away.

"Not because you don't deserve it, Jack," Laurel said, catching hold of his arm. "Because it would be easier not to. But I had an easy relationship once, and it might have been safe, but it wasn't fair to either of us.

"I can't take the easy way out, Jack," she murmured, already trembling inside in anticipation of his answer. "Will you?"

"Sure," he said, his voice little more than rough smoke, his eyes trained on some indistinguishable point in the middle distance. "Haven't you figured it out by now, sugar? I'm a coward and a cad—"

"You're neither," Laurel said strongly. "If you were a coward, they would have buried me beside my sister today. If you were a cad, you wouldn't be trying so damn hard to do the noble thing and walk away from this."

Tears rose effortlessly in her eyes, riding on the crest of her emotions. She tightened her grip on the solid muscle of his biceps, her small fingers barely making a dent. "In a lot of ways you're as good a man as I've ever known, Jack Boudreaux," she said hoarsely. "I'd like a chance to make you believe that."

And he wanted to believe it. God in heaven, how he wanted to believe it. The need was an ache within him he had spent a lifetime trying to bury. The need to be worth something, the need to be important to somebody.

He closed his eyes against it now, terrified the need would swallow him whole, terrified this moment was just a dream, a cruel joke, as every small hope of his childhood had been a cruel joke. It didn't make sense that she should love him. It didn't follow the plot line of his life that he should have this chance at happiness. There had to be a catch. The other shoe would drop on his head any minute now.

He just stood there, waiting, staring past her. His

chin was quivering as he pressed his lips into a thin line. He blinked to clear his vision.

"Haven't you paid enough, Jack?" Laurel whispered. "Haven't we both?"

"I dunno." He tried to shrug, winced at the pain. "You want a husband? You want babies?"

More than anything, she thought. The idea of giving him a second chance at those dreams, the idea of giving him a child, of the two of them creating a brand new life that would begin with no mistakes and no regrets was a wish she had scarcely let herself imagine.

"I want a future," she said simply, the wish too precious, too fragile to voice. "I want to go beyond the past. I want you to go with me."

A life beyond the past. A life he had told himself he could have only in his dreams. He stepped back from her, slicking a hand back through his hair to rub the back of his neck.

Laurel watched him, holding her breath while her heart raced.

Jack turned and faced her, seeing all her hope, her fear, her pure, sweet beauty.

"I told myself if I had a drop of honor in me, I'd walk away from you," he said softly. His lips twisted at the corners into a crooked, ironic smile. "Lucky me, I never had much to start with."

Laurel went into his arms, her heart overflowing. She pressed her cheek against his chest. "You've got more than you know," she whispered.

"I've got all I need if I've got you," he said, and he lowered his mouth to hers for a kiss that was both bonding and beginning, promise and fulfillment . . . and love.

Epilogue

The pirogue *slices through the bayou, as silent as a blade. The sun melts down in the west, as rich and warm as molten gold. All around, the swamp is dim and hushed. Waiting, peaceful. The frogs sing among the lilies. An egret glides down to join its mate in their nest of sticks on the trunk of a fallen cypress.*

I look down at the woman in the boat. She smiles as if I own the moon. The courage of a tiger. The gentleness of a dove. My wife. I was nothing without her.

I pole the boat forward, toward home, and know contentment for the first time in my life.

Glossary of Cajun French Words and Phrases Used in This Book

allée   avenue, path

allons danser   let's dance

allons jouer la music, pas les femmes   let's go play music, not women

arrête sa   stop it

baire   mosquito netting

bâteau   boat

beau-père   stepfather

bébé   baby

bon à rien, tu, 'tit souris   good for nothing, you, little mouse

bon Dieu   good God

bon Dieu avoir pitié   good God have mercy

bonjour   good day

c'est assez   that is enough

c'est la vie   that is life

c'est vrai   that is true

c'est la guerre   that is war

catin   doll

cher/chère/chérie   term of endearment

coonass   slang term for Cajun, often derogatory

dépêche-toi   hurry up

espèces de tête dure   you hardheaded thing

etalon   stud, stallion

grand rond   literally

"big circle," tradition-
ally called at the start
of a fight

grand-mère   grand-
mother

gris-gris   spell, charm
(as with voodoo)

joie de vie   joy of life

jolie fille   pretty lady

laissez le bon temps rouler
let the good times roll

Le Mascarade   The
Masquerade

ma belle   my beautiful

ma douce amie   my
sweet love

ma bon pichouette   my
good little girl

mais oui/mais yeah   but
yes

mais sa c'est fou   that's
crazy

ma jolie fille   my pretty
girl

"Ma Petite Fille Est
Gone"   My Little
Girl Is Gone

merci/merci boucoup
thanks/many thanks

mon ami   my friend

mon coeur   my heart

oui   yes

pas de bétises   no jok-
ing

pas du tout   not at all

petite fleur   little
flower

pirogue   canoelike craft

*restaurant et salle de
danse*   restaurant
and dance hall

roux   flour browned in
fat, used for thicken-
ing gravy etc.

s'il vous plait   please

sa c'est de la couyonade
that is foolishness

sa me fait de le pain
I'm sorry

sa c'est honteu   that's a
shame

son pine   his penis

tcheue poule   chicken
ass

'tit boule   little balls

'tite ange   little angel

'tite chatte   little cat

traiteur   folk healer

tu menti   you lie

une belle femme   the
pretty woman

va-te'n   go away

"Valse de Grand Mèche"
The Big Marsh Waltz

viens ici   come here

About the Author

Tami Hoag's first novel was published in 1988, and since then she has won numerous awards for her writing. She lives with her husband and her menagerie of pets in rural Minnesota.

Look for Tami Hoag's

GUILTY AS SIN

available in paperback
in January 1997
from Bantam Books

Here is an exciting preview of this *New York Times* best-
selling thriller.

$\mathcal{H}$e said it was a game," she murmured, her voice whisper-soft, and tight with pain.

She lay in a hospital bed, the deep purple bruises on her face a stark contrast to the bleached white of the sheets and the ash white of her skin. Her right eye was nearly swollen shut, the flesh the color of an overripe plum. Bruises circled her throat like a purple satin band where she had been choked. A fine line of stitches mended a split in her lip.

The pain triggered flashes of memory—sudden, violent, blaring. A memory of pain so sharp, so intense, it took on qualities of sound and taste, the smell of fear, the presence of evil.

"Clever girl. You think we're going to kill you? Perhaps."

Her throat being closed by hands she couldn't see. The instinct to survive surging. Fear of death riding the crest of the wave.

"We could kill you." The voice a silky murmur. "You wouldn't be the first. . . ."

The air caught like a pair of fists in her lungs, then slowly seeped out between her teeth.

Assistant County Attorney Ellen North waited for the moment to pass. She sat on a high stool beside the bed, a legal pad and small cassette recorder on the bedside tray to her right. She had met Megan O'Malley only days before. Her impression of the field agent for the Minnesota Bureau of Criminal Apprehension had consisted of a handful of adjectives: tough, gutsy, capable, determined, a small woman with fierce green eyes and a big chip on her shoulder. The first woman to break the male ranks of BCA field agents. Her first day on the job in the Deer Lake regional office had been day one of the Kirkwood kidnapping. Twelve days ago. Twelve days that had taken the previously innocent, quiet, rural college town into the depths of a nightmare.

In her efforts to crack the case, the chip had been effectively knocked off Megan's shoulder and smashed, and Megan along with it. She had come too close to unraveling the puzzle. Beneath the covers, her damaged right knee was elevated. Her right hand was encased in a cast. According to her doctor, the hand was badly smashed, and he despaired of the "poor darling little bones" recovering, even with the meticulous attention of a specialist.

Megan's transfer from Deer Lake Community Hospital to the Hennepin County Medical Center in Minneapolis was scheduled for Tuesday, weather permitting. She would have been transported the night of her ordeal, but Minnesota had been clutched in the grip of a January storm. Two days later Deer Lake was just beginning to dig out from under ten inches of new snow.

"He said it was a game," Megan started again. "Taking Josh. Taking me. Fooling everyone. We fooled you all along, he said . . . We, always we . . ."

"Did you at any time hear another person in the room?"

"No." She tried to swallow and her face tightened against a new wave of pain.

"We've calculated all the moves, all the options, all the possibilities. . . . We can't lose. Do you understand me? You can't defeat us. We're very good at this game. . . . brilliant and invincible."

Eight-year-old Josh Kirkwood had disappeared from outside the Gordie Knutson Memorial Ice Arena after hockey practice on an otherwise normal Wednesday night. No useful physical evidence left behind. The only witness a woman casually glancing out her window half a block away and seeing nothing to cause alarm: a little boy being picked up from hockey practice; no sign of fear or force. The only trace of him left behind had been his duffel bag with a note tucked inside.

A game. And she had been used as a pawn. The idea brought Megan a rush of useless emotions—anger, outrage, a hated sense of vulnerability. The only satisfaction was in the fact that they had spoiled his little coup de grâce and now Garrett Wright was sitting in a cell in the Deer Lake city jail.

Garrett Wright. Professor of psychology at Harris College. The man the media had pulled in as an "expert witness" to attempt to explain the twisted workings of the mind that had perpetrated this crime. The Kirkwoods' neighbor. A respected member of the community. A volunteer counselor of juvenile offenders. A man above reproach.

But though Wright had been apprehended, there was still no sign or word of Josh.

"You were blindfolded?"

"Yes."

"You didn't actually see Garrett Wright."

"I saw his feet. He has this habit of rocking back on his heels. I noticed it the first time I met him. He was doing it that night. I could see his boots when he stood close enough."

"That's not exactly a fingerprint."

Megan scowled at the assistant county attorney, her temper cutting through the haze of drugs and pain. Goddamn lawyers. Garrett Wright had drugged her, terrorized her, abused her, humiliated her. He may well have ended the career that was everything to her. A decade in law enforcement, a degree in criminology, a certificate from the FBI academy—she was a damn good cop, yet Ellen North could sit here, every blond hair in place, and calmly question her as if she were just another civilian as blind as Lady Justice herself.

"It was him, the son of a bitch. He knew where I was going. He knew I was that close to finding him out. He caught me, beat the shit out of me, wrapped me in a sheet of evidence proving he stole Josh—"

"We don't know yet what the bedsheet will prove,"

Ellen interjected. "We don't know whose blood is on it. The lab has a rush on it, but DNA tests take weeks. The blood could be Josh's or not. We have the blood samples from his parents. If the DNA analysis shows the blood on the sheet could be from a child of Paul Kirkwood and Dr. Hannah Garrison, we've got something we can use. We might just as easily have a red herring. It would make more sense for the kidnapper to try to throw us *off* his trail—"

"It makes *his* kind of sense," Megan argued. "He believes he can get away with anything, but he underestimated us. We got him dead to fucking rights. Whose side are you on?"

"You know what side I'm on, Megan. I want to see Wright punished as much as you—"

"You can't even come close."

She couldn't argue the point. The bitter hate that laced Megan's tone was indisputable. The emotion Wright had forged and hammered within her with every blow was something deeper than Ellen could even imagine. It was a victim's private rage compounded by the humiliation of a proud cop. Ellen knew that her own personal, moral hunger for justice was a pale appetite in comparison.

"I want him convicted." she clarified. "But the case against him has to be airtight. I don't want his attorney to see even a hairline crack. The stronger our case, the better our chances of squeezing the truth out of him. It could mean getting Josh back."

Or finding out the whereabouts of his body.

She left that line unspoken. Everyone involved in the case knew the chances of finding Josh Kirkwood alive. Wright and his accomplice, whoever that accomplice might be, could not afford to let go the one person who could identify them absolutely as the kidnappers.

"If we can present Wright and his attorney with a strong enough case. If we can threaten them with a murder charge and make them believe we can make it stick even though we have no body, then Wright might give us Josh. We can force his hand if we're careful and clever enough."

"We thought you were a clever girl, but you're just another stupid bitch!" A disembodied voice. Never rising above a whisper, but taut and humming with fury.

She trembled. Blind. Powerless. Vulnerable. Waiting. Then the pain struck from one direction, then another, then another.

A cry of pain, of weakness, of fear started in the heart of her, and Megan struggled to choke it off in her throat.

"Are you all right?" Ellen asked with quiet concern. "Should I call for a nurse?"

"No."

"Maybe we should quit for now. I could come back in half an hour—"

"No."

Ellen said nothing, giving her a chance to change her mind, though she didn't expect that to happen. Megan O'Malley hadn't got where she was in the bureau by backing off. The BCA was the top law-enforcement agency in the upper Midwest. One of the best in the country. And Megan was one of the best of the best. A good cop with the tenacity and fire of a pit bull.

Ellen was counting on that fire. She had a meeting with the county attorney in an hour. She needed Megan's statement and time to fit it into the game plan she was formulating in her head.

She wanted her ducks in a row when she sat down across the table from her boss. Rudy Stovich could be unpredictable, but he could also be herded. In her two years in Park County, Ellen had honed her shepherding skills to the point that they had become instinctive, reflexive. She didn't know that she even *wanted* the Wright case, and still she was aligning her strategy.

"Will you be handling the prosecution?" Megan asked, working hard to even out her breathing. A fine sheen of sweat glazed her forehead.

"I'll certainly be a part of it. The county attorney hasn't made his final decision yet."

"Well, hell, why rush? It's only been two days since we made the collar. Initial appearance is what—all of hours away?"

"The bond hearing is tomorrow morning."

"Will he charge it out or wimp out and go for a grand jury?"

"That remains to be seen."

The media loved to make much of grand jury proceedings. As if the word "grand" somehow implied "better" or "more important." A grand jury hearing was a prosecutor's showcase—they got to present their evidence with no interference from the defense, no cross-examination of their witnesses. There was no need to prove anything beyond a reasonable doubt; all they had to show was probable cause that the defendant committed the crime. The grand jury had its uses. In the state of Minnesota only a grand jury could hand down first-degree-murder indictments. But, as yet, they weren't dealing with murder, and the thought of handing the fate of this indictment into the hands of two dozen citizens made Ellen's palms sweat.

The members of a grand jury could do whatever they wanted. They didn't have to listen to the prosecutor's argument. If they didn't want to believe Garrett Wright was capable of evil, he would walk. She could only hope that the ego appeal of doing a solo act in front of a grand jury didn't override Rudy's common sense.

Stovich had survived more than a decade as Park County attorney not so much by his legal wits as by his political wiles. More comfortable with civil law than with criminal law, he handpicked the few felony trials he prosecuted, choosing them for their political value. His courtroom style was dated and clumsy, with all the finesse of a vaudeville player. But Rudy's constituents seldom saw him in a courtroom, and as a glad-handing, ass-kissing backwoods politician he was without peer.

"Is Wright talking?" Megan asked quietly.

"He isn't saying anything we want to hear. He insists his arrest was a mistake."

"Yeah, right. *His* mistake. Who's his lawyer?"

"Dennis Enberg, a local attorney."

"Is he just a lawyer or is he an asshole lawyer?"

"Denny's okay," Ellen said, flicking off the tape recorder. She'd been in the system too long to take affront. The distinction was one she had made herself from time to time. And, having come from a family of attorneys, she was long since immune to lawyer jokes and slurs.

She slid down off the stool and reached for her briefcase. Megan was slipping away from consciousness. Exhaustion and medication were going to end the interview whether Ellen was finished asking questions or not.

"He's your basic ham-and-egger," Ellen continued. "He does the misdemeanor prosecutions for the city of Tatonka, gets pressed into service as a public defender here from time to time, has a decent practice of his own. You know how the system works in these rural counties."

"Yeah. *Mayberry RFD.* So what're you doing here, counselor?"

She struggled into her heavy wool coat and worked the thick leather buttons into their moorings. "Me? I'm just here to do justice."

"Amen to that."

And don't miss Tami Hoag's newest thriller

A THIN DARK LINE

coming in hardcover
in March 1997
from Bantam Books

Following is a sneak peek. . . .

Her body lay on the floor. Her slender arms outflung, palms up.

The people rose in unison as the judge emerged from his chambers. The Honorable Franklin Monahan settled himself behind the bench and looked out on the court-room. The decision would be his.

Black pools of blood in the silver moonlight.

Richard Kudrow, the defense attorney. A man thin and gray, as if the fervor for justice had burned away all ex-cess within him and had begun to consume muscle mass.

Her life drained from her to puddle on the hard cypress floor.

Smith Pritchett, the district attorney. Smartly turned out in pearl gray from Brooks Brothers, the gold of his cuff-links catching the light as he raised his hands.

Her naked body carved with the point of a knife.

Chaos and outrage rolled through the crowd in a wave of sound as Monahan pronounced his ruling. The victim's desk keys had not been listed on the search warrant of the defendant's home and were, therefore, beyond the scope of the warrant and not legally subject to seizure.

Pamela Bichon, thirty-seven, separated, mother of a nine-year-old girl. Sexually assaulted. Brutally murdered. Her naked body found in an abandoned house on Pony Bayou, spikes driven through the palms of her hands into the wood floor; her sightless eyes starting up at nothing through the slits of an elaborate silk and feather Mardi Gras mask.

Case dismissed.

The crowd spilled from the Partout Parish courthouse, past the thick Doric columns and down the broad steps, a buzzing swarm of humanity centering on the key figures of the drama that had played out in Judge Monahan's courtroom.

Smith Pritchett focused his narrow gaze on the dark blue Lincoln that awaited him at the curb and snapped off a staccato line of "no comments" to the frenzied press. The taste of defeat sour in his mouth, he wanted nothing more than to escape the scrutiny of second-guessers and hole up in the private dining room at the Wisteria Country Club where he could begin to regroup, strategize, and satisfy his vengeful bloodlust with a rare steak.

Richard Kudrow, however, stopped his descent dead center on the steps.

Trouble was the word that came immediately to Annie Broussard as the press began to ring themselves around the defense attorney and his client. Like every other deputy in the sheriff's department, she had hoped against hope that Kudrow would fail in his attempt to get the keys thrown out as evidence. They had all hoped Smith Pritchett would be the one crowing on the courthouse steps, and they had hoped this for more reasons than one.

The cops weren't the only ones who wanted the suspect, Marcus Renard, drawn and quartered.

Sergeant Hooker's voice crackled over the portable radio. "Savoy, Mullen, Prejean, Broussard, move in front of those goddamn reporters. Establish some distance between the crowd and Kudrow and Renard before this turns into a goddamn cluster fuck."

Annie edged her way between bodies, her hand resting on the butt of her baton, her eyes on Renard as Kudrow began to speak.

He stood beside his attorney looking uncomfortable with the attention being focused on him. He wasn't a man to draw notice. Quiet, unassuming, an architect in the firm of Bowen & Briggs. Not ugly, not handsome. Thinning brown hair neatly combed and hazel eyes that seemed a little too big for their sockets. He stood with his shoulders stooped and his chest sunken, a younger shadow of his attorney.

"Some people will call this ruling a travesty of justice," Richard Kudrow said loudly. "The only travesty of justice here has been perpetrated by the Partout Parish sheriff's department. Their *investigation* of my client has been nothing short of harassment. Two prior searches of Mr. Renard's home produced nothing that might tie him to the murder of Pamela Bichon."

"Are you suggesting the sheriff's department manipulated evidence?" a reporter from KJUN News Radio called out.

"Mr. Renard has been the victim of a narrow and fanatical investigation led by Detective Nick Fourcade. Y'all are aware of Mr. Fourcade's record with the New Orleans police department, of the reputation he brought with him to this parish. Detective Fourcade *allegedly* found those keys in my client's home. Draw your own conclusions."

Situation escalates from bad to worse, Annie thought, elbowing past a television cameraman. As she broke into the inner circle, she could see Fourcade turning around, half a dozen steps down from Kudrow, the people around him backing away with caution. Beyond him.

Smith Pritchett had turned, his lips pressed into a thin white line.

The cameras focused hastily on Fourcade, his expression a stone mask, his eyes hidden by a pair of mirrored sunglasses. He had made sartorial concessions to the court, his standard uniform of old jeans and an older leather bomber jacket exchanged for a shirt and tie and dark trousers. A cigarette smoldered between his lips. Even a dozen feet away Annie thought she could feel the tension crackling in the air around him. His temper was a thing of legend. Rumors abounded through the department that he was not quite sane. In the best of circumstances he gave the impression of being barely socialized.

These were not the best of circumstances.

The Bichon homicide was Fourcade's case. Fourcade's obsession. He had worked the case day and night for the last three months. It was Fourcade who had zeroed in on Marcus Renard. It was Fourcade who had pulled Pamela Bichon's car keys from a drawer in Marcus Renard's drafting table at his home just seven miles from the scene of the crime.

He said nothing in answer to Kudrow's insinuation, and yet the air between them seemed to thicken. Anticipation held the crowd's breath. Fourcade pulled the cigarette from his mouth and flung it down, exhaling smoke through his nostrils. Annie took a half step toward Kudrow, her fingers curling around the grip of her baton. In the next heartbeat Fourcade was bounding up the steps—straight at Marcus Renard, shouting, "NO!"

"He'll kill him!" someone shrieked.

"Fourcade!" Hooker's voice boomed as the big sergeant lunged after him, grabbing at and missing the back of his jacket.

"You killed her! You killed my baby girl!"

The anguished shouts tore from the throat of Hunter Davidson, Pamela Bichon's father, as he hurled himself down the steps at Renard, his eyes rolling, one arm swinging wildly, the other hand clutching a .45. The KJUN reporter was shoved sideways into Deputy Savoy, sending him stumbling back when he would have grabbed Fourcade.

Fourcade knocked Renard aside with a beefy shoulder, grabbed Davidson's wrist and shoved it skyward as the .45 barked out a shot. Annie hit Davidson from the right side just as Fourcade threw his weight against the man from the left. Davidson's knees buckled and they all went down in a tangle of arms and legs, grunting and shouting, bouncing hard down the steps, Annie on the bottom of the heap. Her breath was pounded out of her as she hit the concrete steps with four-hundred pounds of man on top of her.

"He killed her!" Hunter Davidson sobbed, his big body going limp as the emotions swamped him. "He butchered my girl!"

Annie wriggled out from under him and sat up, grimacing. All she could think was that no physical pain could compare with what this man must have been enduring.

Swiping back the strands of dark hair that had pulled loose from her short ponytail, she gingerly brushed over the throbbing knot on the back of her head. Her fingertips came away sticky with blood. Wiping them on the torn leg of her slate-colored uniform pants, she blinked the blur from her vision and assessed the situation.

The cameras were still rolling, though Renard and his attorney had been hustled off the steps. The focus was the Hunter Davidson now.

"Take this," Fourcade ordered in a low voice, thrusting Davidson's gun at Annie buttfirst. Frowning, he leaned down over Davidson and put a hand on the man's shoulder even as Prejean snapped the cuffs on him. "I'm sorry," he murmured. "I wish I could'a let you kill him."

Annie pushed to her feet and tried to straighten the bulletproof vest she wore beneath her shirt. Hunter Davidson was a good man. An honest, hardworking planter who had put his daughter through college and walked her down the aisle the day she married Donnie Bichon. Her death had shattered him and the subsequent lack of justice had driven him to this desperate edge. And tonight Hunter Davidson would be the man sitting in jail while Marcus Renard slept in his own bed.

"Broussard," Sergeant Hooker snapped irritably, suddenly looming over her. "Gimme that gun. Don't just stand there gawking. Get down to that cruiser and open the goddamn doors."

"Yes, sir," Annie mumbled. Not quite steady on her feet, she started around the backside of the crowd.

With the danger past, the press was in full cry again, more frenzied than before. Cameramen jostled each other for shots of the despondent father. Microphones were thrust at Smith Pritchett.

"Will you file charges, Mr. Pritchett?"

"Will charges be filed, Mr. Pritchett?"

"Mr. Pritchett, what kind of charges will you file?"

Smith Pritchett glared at them. "That remains to be seen. Please back away and let the officers do their job."

"Davidson couldn't get justice in court, so he sought to take it himself. Do you feel responsible, Mr. Pritchett?"

"We did the best we could with the evidence we had," he said.

"Tainted evidence?"

"I didn't gather it," he snapped, starting back up the steps toward the courthouse, his face as pink as a new sunburn.

Annie descended the last of the steps and opened the back door of the blue-and-white cruiser sitting at the curb. Fourcade escorted the sobbing Hunter Davidson to the car, with Savoy and Hooker just behind them, and Mullen and Prejean flanking them. The crowd rushed along behind them and beside them like guests at a wedding seeing off the happy couple.

"You gonna book him in, Fourcade?" Hooker asked as Davidson disappeared into the backseat.

"The hell," Fourcade growled, slamming the door. "He didn't commit the worst crime here today. Not even if he'd'a killed the son of a bitch. Book him yourself."

The belligerence brought a rise of color to Hooker's bulldog face, but he said nothing as Fourcade crossed the street to a battered black Ford 4X4, climbed in and drove off in the opposite direction of the parish jail.

The sheriff would chew his ass later, Annie thought as she headed for her own squad car. But then a breach in procedure was the least of Fourcade's worries, and, if anything Richard Kudrow had said was true, the least of his sins.